A
G. K. CHESTERTON OMNIBUS

A
G. K. CHESTERTON
OMNIBUS

containing

THE NAPOLEON OF NOTTING HILL
THE MAN WHO WAS THURSDAY
THE FLYING INN

METHUEN & CO. LTD. LONDON
36 Essex Street W.C.2

First Published	.	.	.	.	October 28th	1932
Second Edition	.	.	.	.	April	1943
Third Edition	.	.	.	.	April	1947
Fourth Edition	.	.	.	.	May	1949
Fifth Edition	.	.	.	.	1950	

CATALOGUE NO. 3102/U

PRINTED IN GREAT BRITAIN

CONTENTS

THE NAPOLEON OF NOTTING HILL

BOOK I

THE MAN WHO WAS THURSDAY

THE FLYING INN

ACKNOWLEDGMENTS

FOR permission to include *The Napoleon of Notting Hill* and *The Man Who was Thursday* in this volume, the publishers' thanks are due to Messrs. John Lane, The Bodley Head, Ltd., and Messrs. J. W. Arrowsmith (London) Ltd., respectively.

THE NAPOLEON OF NOTTING HILL

TO HILAIRE BELLOC

For every tiny town or place
God made the stars especially;
Babies look up with owlish face
And see them tangled in a tree:
You saw a moon from Sussex Downs.
A Sussex moon, untravelled still,
I saw a moon that was the town's,
The largest lamp on Campden Hill.

Yea; Heaven is everywhere at home
The big blue cap that always fits,
And so it is (be calm; they come
To goal at last, my wandering wits),
So is it with the heroic thing;
This shall not end for the world's end
And though the sullen engines swing,
Be you not much afraid, my friend.

This did not end by Nelson's urn
Where an immortal England sits—
Nor where your tall young men in turn
Drank death like wine at Austerlitz.
And when the pedants bade us mark
What cold mechanic happenings
Must come; our souls said in the dark,
'Belike; but there are likelier things.'

Likelier across these flats afar
These sulky levels smooth and free
The drums shall crash a waltz of war
And Death shall dance with Liberty;
Likelier the barricades shall blare
Slaughter below and smoke above,
And death and hate and hell declare
That men have found a thing to love.

3

Far from your sunny uplands set
I saw the dream; the streets I trod
The lit straight streets shot out and met
The starry streets that point to God.
This legend of an epic hour
A child I dreamed, and dream it still,
Under the great grey water-tower
That strikes the stars on Campden Hill.

G. K. C.

BOOK I

CHAPTER I

INTRODUCTORY REMARKS ON THE ART OF PROPHECY

THE human race, to which so many of my readers belong, has been playing at children's games from the beginning, and will probably do it till the end, which is a nuisance for the few people who grow up. And one of the games to which it is most attached is called, 'Keep to-morrow dark', and which is also named (by the rustics in Shropshire, I have no doubt) 'Cheat the Prophet'. The players listen very carefully and respectfully to all that the clever men have to say about what is to happen in the next generation. The players then wait until all the clever men are dead, and bury them nicely. They then go and do something else. That is all. For a race of simple tastes, however, it is great fun.

For human beings, being children, have the childish wilfulness and the childish secrecy. And they never have from the beginning of the world done what the wise men have seen to be inevitable. They stoned the false prophets, it is said; but they could have stoned true prophets with a greater and juster enjoyment. Individually, men may present a more or less rational appearance, eating, sleeping, and scheming. But humanity as a whole is changeful, mystical, fickle, delightful. Men are men, but Man is a woman.

But in the beginning of the twentieth century the game of Cheat the Prophet was made far more difficult than it had ever been before. The reason was, that there were so many prophets and so many prophecies, that it was difficult to elude all their ingenuities. When a man did something free and frantic and entirely his own, a horrible thought struck him afterwards; it might have been predicted. Whenever a duke climbed a lamp-post, when a dean got drunk, he could not be really happy, he could not be certain that he was not fulfilling some prophecy. In the beginning of the twentieth century you could not see the ground for clever men. They were so common that a stupid man was quite exceptional, and when they found him, they followed him in crowds down the street and treasured him up and gave him some high post in the State. And all these clever men were at work giving accounts of what would happen in the next age, all quite clear, all quite keen-sighted and ruthless, and all quite different. And it seemed that the good old game of hoodwinking your ancestors could not really be managed this time, because the ancestors neglected meat and sleep and practical politics, so that they might meditate day and night on what their descendants would be likely to do.

But the way the prophets of the twentieth century went to work was this. They took something or other that was certainly going on in their time, and then said that it would go on more and more until something extraordinary happened. And very often they added that in some odd place that extraordinary thing had happened, and that it showed the signs of the times.

Thus, for instance, there were Mr. H. G. Wells and others, who thought that science would take charge of the future; and just as the motor-car was quicker than the coach, so some lovely thing would be quicker than the motor-car; and so on for ever. And there arose from their ashes Dr. Quilp, who said that a man could be sent on his machine so fast round the world that he could keep up a long chatty conversation in some old-world village by saying a word of a sentence each time he came round. And it was said that the experiment had been tried on an apoplectic old major, who was sent round the world so fast that there seemed to be (to the inhabitants of some other star) a continuous band round the earth of white whiskers, red complexion and tweeds—a thing like the ring of Saturn.

Then there was the opposite school. There was Mr. Edward Carpenter, who thought we should in a very short time return to Nature, and live simply and slowly as the animals do. And Edward Carpenter was followed by James Pickie, D.D. (of Pocahontas College), who said that men were immensely improved by grazing, or taking their food slowly and continuously, after the manner of cows. And he said that he had, with the most encouraging results, turned city men out on all fours in a field covered with veal cutlets. Then Tolstoy and the Humanitarians said that the world was growing more merciful, and therefore no one would ever desire to kill. And Mr. Mick not only became a vegetarian, but at length declared vegetarianism doomed ('shedding', as he called it finely, 'the green blood of the silent animals'), and predicted that men in a better age would live on nothing but salt. And then came the pamphlet from Oregon (where the thing was tried), the pamphlet called *Why should Salt Suffer?* and there was more trouble.

And on the other hand, some people were predicting that the lines of kinship would become narrower and sterner. There was Mr. Cecil Rhodes, who thought that the one thing of the future was the British Empire, and that there would be a gulf between those who were of the Empire and those who were not, between the Chinaman in Hong Kong and the Chinaman outside, between the Spaniard on the Rock of Gibraltar and the Spaniard off it, similar to the gulf between man and the lower animals. And in the same way his impetuous friend, Dr. Zoppi ('the Paul of Anglo-Saxonism'), carried it yet further, and held that, as a result of this view, cannibalism should be held to mean eating a member of the Empire, not eating one of the subject peoples, who should, he said, be killed without needless pain. His horror at the idea of eating a man in British Guiana showed how they misunderstood his stoicism who thought him devoid of feeling. He was, however, in a hard position; as it was said that he had attempted the experiment, and, living in London, had to subsist entirely on Italian organ-grinders. And his end was terrible, for just when he had begun, Sir Paul Swiller read his great paper at the Royal Society, proving that the savages were not only quite right in eating their enemies, but right on moral and hygienic grounds, since it was true that the qualities of the enemy, when eaten, passed into the eater. The notion that the nature of an Italian organ-man was irrevocably growing and burgeoning inside him was almost more than the kindly old professor could bear.

There was Mr. Benjamin Kidd, who said that the growing note of our race would be the care for and knowledge of the future. His idea was developed more powerfully by William Borker, who wrote that passage which every schoolboy knows by heart, about men in future ages weeping by the graves of their descendants, and tourists being shown over the scene of the historic battle which was to take place some centuries afterwards.

And Mr. Stead, too, was prominent, who thought that England would in the twentieth century be united to America; and his young lieutenant, Graham Podge, who included the states of France, Germany, and Russia in the American Union, the State of Russia being abbreviated to Ra.

There was Mr. Sidney Webb, also, who said that the future would see a continuously increasing order and neatness in the life of the people, and his poor friend Fipps, who went mad and ran about the country with an axe, hacking branches off the trees whenever there were not the same number on both sides.

All these clever men were prophesying with every variety of ingenuity what would happen soon, and they all did it in the same way, by taking something they saw 'going strong', as the saying is, and carrying it as far as ever their imagination could stretch. This, they said, was the true and simple way of anticipating the future. 'Just as,' said Dr. Pellkins, in a fine passage, —'just as when we see a pig in a litter larger than the other pigs, we know that by an unalterable law of the Inscrutable it will some day be larger than an elephant, —just as we know, when we see weeds and dandelions growing more and more thickly in a garden, that they must, in spite of all our efforts, grow taller than the chimney-pots and swallow the house from sight, so we know and reverently acknowledge, that when any power in human politics has shown for any period of time any considerable activity, it will go on until it reaches to the sky.'

And it did certainly appear that the prophets had put the people (engaged in the old game of Cheat the Prophet), in a quite unprecedented difficulty. It seemed really hard to do anything without fulfilling some of their prophecies.

But there was, nevertheless, in the eyes of labourers in the streets, of peasants in the fields, of sailors and children, and especially women, a strange look that kept the wise men in a perfect fever of doubt. They could not fathom the motionless mirth in their eyes. They still had something up their sleeve; they were still playing the game of Cheat the Prophet.

Then the wise men grew like wild things and swayed hither and thither, crying, 'What can it be? What can it be? What will London be like a century hence? Is there anything we have not thought of? Houses upside down—more hygienic, perhaps? Men walking on hands—make feet flexible, don't you know? Moon . . . motor-cars . . . no heads . . .' And so they swayed and wondered until they died and were buried nicely.

Then the people went and did what they liked. Let me no longer conceal the painful truth. The people had cheated the prophets of the twentieth century. When the curtain goes up on this story, eighty years after the present date, London is almost exactly like what it is now.

THE MAN IN GREEN

VERY few words are needed to explain why London, a hundred years hence, will be very like it is now, or rather, since I must slip into a prophetic past, why London, when my story opens, was very like it was in those enviable days when I was still alive.

The reason can be stated in one sentence. The people had absolutely lost faith in revolutions. All revolutions are doctrinal—such as the French one, or the one that introduced Christianity. For it stands to common sense that you cannot upset all existing things, customs, and compromises, unless you believe in something outside them, something positive and divine. Now, England, during this century, lost all belief in this. It believed in a thing called Evolution. And it said, 'All theoretic changes have ended in blood and ennui. If we change, we must change slowly and safely, as the animals do. Nature's revolutions are the only successful ones. There has been no conservative reaction in favour of tails.'

And some things did change. Things that were not much thought of dropped out of sight. Things that had not often happened did not happen at all. Thus, for instance, the actual physical force ruling the country, the soldiers and police, grew smaller and smaller, and at last vanished almost to a point. The people combined could have swept the few policemen away in ten minutes; they did not, because they did not believe it would do them the least good. They had lost faith in revolutions.

Democracy was dead; for no one minded the governing class governing. England was now practically a despotism, but not an hereditary one. Some one in the official class was made King. No one cared how: no one cared who. He was merely a universal secretary.

In this manner it happened that everything in London was very quiet. That vague and somewhat depressed reliance upon things happening as they have always happened, which is with all Londoners a mood, had become an assumed condition. There was really no reason for any man doing anything but the thing he had done the day before.

There was therefore no reason whatever why the three young men who had always walked up to their Government office together should not walk up to it together on this particular wintry and cloudy morning. Everything in that age had become mechanical, and Government clerks especially. All those clerks assembled regularly at their posts. Three of those clerks always walked into town together. All the neighbourhood knew them: two of them were tall and one short. And on this particular morning the short clerk was only a few seconds late to join the other two as they passed his gate: he could have overtaken them in three strides; he could have called after them easily. But he did not.

For some reason that will never be understood until all souls are judged (if they are ever judged; the idea was at this time classed with fetish worship) he did not join his two companions, but walked steadily behind them. The day was dull, their dress was dull, everything was dull; but in some odd impulse he walked through street after street, through district after district, looking at the backs of the two men, who would have swung round at the sound of his voice. Now, there is a law written in the darkest of the Books of Life, and it is this: If you look at a thing nine hundred and ninety-nine times, you are perfectly safe; if you look at it the thousandth time, you are in frightful danger of seeing it for the first time.

So the short Government official looked at the coat-tails of the tall Government officials, and through street after street, and round corner after corner, saw only coat-tails, coat-tails, and again coat-tails—when, he did not in the least know why, something happened to his eyes.

Two black dragons were walking backwards in front of him. Two black dragons were looking at him with evil eyes. The dragons were walking backwards it was true, but they kept their eyes fixed on him none the less. The eyes which he saw were, in truth, only the two buttons at the back of a frock-coat: perhaps some traditional memory of their meaningless character gave this half-witted prominence to their gaze. The slit between the tails was the nose-line of the monster: whenever the tails flapped in the winter wind the dragons licked their lips. It was only a momentary fancy, but the small clerk found it imbedded in his soul ever afterwards. He never could again think of men in frock-coats except as dragons walking backwards. He explained afterwards, quite tactfully and nicely, to his two official friends, that while feeling an inexpressible regard for each of them he could not seriously regard the face of either of them as anything but a kind of tail. It was, he admitted, a handsome tail—a tail elevated in the air. But if, he said, any true friend of theirs wished to see their faces, to look

into the eyes of their soul, that friend must be allowed
to walk reverently round behind them, so as to see
them from the rear. There he would see the two black
dragons with the blind eyes.

But when first the two black dragons sprang out of
the fog upon the small clerk, they had merely the effect
of all miracles—they changed the universe. He discovered the fact that all romantics know—that adventures happen on dull days, and not on sunny ones.
When the chord of monotony is stretched most tight,
then it breaks with a sound like song. He had scarcely
noticed the weather before, but with the four dead
eyes glaring at him he looked round and realized the
strange dead day.

The morning was wintry and dim, not misty, but
darkened with that shadow of cloud or snow which
steeps everything in a green or copper twilight. The
light there is on such a day seems not so much to come
from the clear heavens as to be a phosphorescence
clinging to the shapes themselves. The load of heaven
and the clouds is like a load of waters, and the men
move like fishes, feeling that they are on the floor of
a sea. Everything in a London street completes the
fantasy; the carriages and cabs themselves resemble
deep-sea creatures with eyes of flame. He had been
startled at first to meet two dragons. Now he found
he was among deep-sea dragons possessing the deep
sea.

The two young men in front were like the small
young man himself, well-dressed. The lines of their frock-
coats and silk hats had that luxuriant severity which
makes the modern fop, hideous as he is, a favourite
exercise of the modern draughtsman; that element
which Mr. Max Beerbohm has admirably expressed

in speaking of 'certain congruities of dark cloth and the rigid perfection of linen'.

They walked with the gait of an affected snail, and they spoke at the longest intervals, dropping a sentence at about every sixth lamp-post.

They crawled on past the lamp-posts; their mien was so immovable that a fanciful description might almost say, that the lamp-posts crawled past the men, as in a dream. Then the small man suddenly ran after them and said:

'I want to get my hair cut. I say, do you know a little shop anywhere where they cut your hair properly? I keep on having my hair cut, but it keeps on growing again.'

One of the tall men looked at him with the air of a pained naturalist.

'Why, here is a little place,' cried the small man, with a sort of imbecile cheerfulness, as the bright bulging window of a fashionable toilet-saloon glowed abruptly out of the foggy twilight. 'Do you know, I often find hairdressers when I walk about London. I'll lunch with you at Cicconani's. You know, I'm awfully fond of hairdressers' shops. They're miles better than those nasty butchers'.' And he disappeared into the doorway.

The man called James continued to gaze after him, a monocle screwed into his eye.

'What the devil do you make of that fellow?' he asked his companion, a pale young man with a high nose.

The pale young man reflected conscientiously for some minutes, and then said:

'Had a knock on his head when he was a kid, I should think.'

'No, I don't think it's that,' replied the Honourable James Barker. 'I've sometimes fancied he was a sort of artist, Lambert.'

'Bosh!' cried Mr. Lambert, briefly.

'I admit I can't make him out,' resumed Barker, abstractedly; 'he never opens his mouth without saying something so indescribably half-witted that to call him a fool seems the very feeblest attempt at characterization. But there's another thing about him that's rather funny. Do you know that he has the one collection of Japanese lacquer in Europe? Have you ever seen his books? All Greek poets and medieval French and that sort of thing. Have you ever been in his rooms? It's like being inside an amethyst. And he moves about in all that and talks like—like a turnip.'

'Well, damn all books. Your blue books as well,' said the ingenuous Mr. Lambert, with a friendly simplicity. 'You ought to understand such things. What do you make of him?'

'He's beyond me,' returned Barker. 'But if you asked me for my opinion, I should say he was a man with a taste for nonsense, as they call it—artistic fooling, and all that kind of thing. And I seriously believe that he has talked nonsense so much that he has half bewildered his own mind and doesn't know the difference between sanity and insanity. He has gone round the mental world, so to speak, and found the place where the East and the West are one, and extreme idiocy is as good as sense. But I can't explain these psychological games.'

'You can't explain them to me,' replied Mr. Wilfrid Lambert, with candour.

As they passed up the long streets towards their restaurant the copper twilight cleared slowly to a pale yellow, and by the time they reached it they stood discernible in a tolerable winter daylight. The Honourable James Barker, one of the most powerful officials in the English Government (by this time a rigidly official one), was a lean and elegant young man, with a blank handsome face and bleak blue eyes. He had a great amount of intellectual capacity, of that peculiar kind which raises a man from throne to throne and lets him die loaded with honours without having either amused or enlightened the mind of a single man. Wilfrid Lambert, the youth with the nose which appeared to impoverish the rest of his face, had also contributed little to the enlargement of the human spirit, but he had the honourable excuse of being a fool.

Lambert would have been called a silly man; Barker, with all his cleverness, might have been called a stupid man. But mere silliness and stupidity sank into insignificance in the presence of the awful and mysterious treasures of foolishness apparently stored up in the small figure that stood waiting for them outside Cicconani's. The little man, whose name was Auberon Quin, had an appearance compounded of a baby and an owl. His round head, round eyes, seemed to have been designed by nature playfully with a pair of compasses. His flat dark hair and preposterously long frock-coat gave him something of the look of a child's 'Noah'. When he entered a room of strangers, they mistook him for a small boy, and wanted to take him on their knees, until he spoke, when they perceived that a boy would have been more intelligent.

'I have been waiting quite a long time,' said Quin, mildly. 'It's awfully funny I should see you coming up the street at last.'

'Why?' asked Lambert, staring. 'You told us to come here yourself.'

'My mother used to tell people to come to places,' said the sage.

They were about to turn into the restaurant with a resigned air, when their eyes were caught by something in the street. The weather, though cold and blank, was now quite clear and across the dull brown of the wood pavement and between the dull grey terraces was moving something not to be seen for miles around—not to be seen perhaps at that time in England —a man dressed in bright colours. A small crowd hung on the man's heels.

He was a tall stately man, clad in a military uniform of brilliant green, splashed with great silver facings. From the shoulder swung a short green furred cloak, somewhat like that of a Hussar, the lining of which gleamed every now and then with a kind of tawny crimson. His breast glittered with medals; round his neck was the red ribbon and star of some foreign order; and a long straight sword, with a blazing hilt, trailed and clattered along the pavement. At this time the pacific and utilitarian development of Europe had relegated all such customs to the Museums. The only remaining force, the small but well-organized police, were attired in a sombre and hygienic manner. But even those who remembered the last Life Guards and Lancers who disappeared in 1912 must have known at a glance that this was not, and never had been, an English uniform; and this conviction would have been heightened by the yellow aquiline face, like Dante carved in bronze, which rose, crowned with white hair, out of the green military collar, a keen and distinguished, but not an English face.

The magnificence with which the green-clad gentleman walked down the centre of the road would be something difficult to express in human language. For it was an ingrained simplicity and arrogance, something in the mere carriage of the head and body, which made ordinary moderns in the street stare after him; but it had comparatively little to do with actual conscious gestures or expression. In the matter of these merely temporary movements, the man appeared to be rather worried and inquisitive, but he was inquisitive with the inquisitiveness of a despot and worried as with the responsibilities of a god. The men who lounged and wondered behind him followed partly with an astonishment at his brilliant uniform, that is to say, partly because of that instinct which makes us all follow one who looks like a madman, but far more because of that instinct which makes all men follow (and worship) any one who chooses to behave like a king. He had to so sublime an extent that great quality of royalty —an almost imbecile unconsciousness of everybody, that people went after him as they do after kings—to see what would be the first thing or person he would take notice of. And all the time, as we have said, in spite of his quiet splendour, there was an air about him as if he were looking for somebody; an expression of inquiry.

Suddenly that expression of inquiry vanished, none could tell why, and was replaced by an expression of contentment. Amid the rapt attention of the mob of idlers, the magnificent green gentleman deflected himself from his direct course down the centre of the road and walked to one side of it. He came to a halt opposite to a large poster of Colman's Mustard erected on a wooden hoarding. His spectators almost held their breath.

He took from a small pocket in his uniform a little penknife; with this he made a slash at the stretched paper. Completing the rest of the operation with his fingers, he tore off a strip or rag of paper, yellow in colour and wholly irregular in outline. Then for the first time the great being addressed his adoring onlookers:

'Can any one,' he said, with a pleasing foreign accent, 'lend me a pin?'

Mr. Lambert, who happened to be nearest, and who carried innumerable pins for the purpose of attaching innumerable buttonholes, lent him one, which was received with extravagant but dignified bows, and hyperboles of thanks.

The gentleman in green, then, with every appearance of being gratified, and even puffed up, pinned the piece of yellow paper to the green silk and silver-lace adornments of his breast. Then he turned his eyes round again, searching and unsatisfied.

'Anything else I can do, sir?' asked Lambert, with the absurd politeness of the Englishman when once embarrassed.

'Red,' said the stranger, vaguely, 'red.'

'I beg your pardon?'

'I beg yours also, Señor,' said the stranger, bowing. 'I was wondering whether any of you had any red about you.'

'Any red about us?—well really—no, I don't think I have—I used to carry a red bandanna once, but——'

'Barker,' asked Auberon Quin, suddenly, 'where's your red cockatoo? Where's your red cockatoo?'

'What do you mean?' asked Barker, desperately. 'What cockatoo? You've never seen me with any cockatoo.'

'I know,' said Auberon, vaguely mollified. 'Where's it been all the time?'

Barker swung round, not without resentment.

'I am sorry, sir,' he said, shortly but civilly, 'none of us seem to have anything red to lend you. But why, if one may ask——'

'I thank you, Señor, it is nothing. I can, since there is nothing else, fulfil my own requirements.'

And standing for a second of thought with the penknife in his hand, he stabbed his left palm. The blood fell with so full a stream that it struck the stones without dripping. The foreigner pulled out his handkerchief and tore a piece from it with his teeth. The rag was immediately soaked in scarlet.

'Since you are so generous, Señor,' he said, 'another pin, perhaps.'

Lambert held one out, with eyes protruding like a frog's.

The red linen was pinned beside the yellow paper, and the foreigner took off his hat.

'I have to thank you all, gentlemen,' he said; and wrapping the remainder of the handkerchief round his bleeding hand, he resumed his walk with an overwhelming stateliness.

While all the rest paused, in some disorder, little Mr. Auberon Quin ran after the stranger and stopped him, with hat in hand. Considerably to everybody's astonishment, he addressed him in the purest Spanish.

'Señor,' he said in that language, 'pardon a hospitality, perhaps indiscreet, towards one who appears to be a distinguished, but a solitary guest in London. Will you do me and my friends, with whom you have held some conversation, the honour of lunching with us at the adjoining restaurant?'

The man in the green uniform had turned a fiery colour of pleasure at the mere sound of his own language, and he accepted the invitation with that profusion of bows which so often shows, in the case of the Southern races, the falsehood of the notion that ceremony has nothing to do with feeling.

'Señor,' he said, 'your language is my own; but all my love for my people shall not lead me to deny to yours the possession of so chivalrous an entertainer. Let me say that the tongue is Spanish but the heart English.' And he passed with the rest into Cicconani's.

'Now, perhaps,' said Barker, over the fish and sherry, intensely polite, but burning with curiosity, 'perhaps it would be rude of me to ask why you did that?'

'Did what, Señor?' asked the guest, who spoke English quite well, though in a manner indefinably American.

'Well,' said the Englishman, in some confusion, 'I mean tore a strip off a hoarding and . . . er . . . cut yourself . . . and . . .'

'To tell you that, Señor,' answered the other, with a certain sad pride, 'involves merely telling you who I am. I am Juan del Fuego, President of Nicaragua.'

The manner with which the President of Nicaragua leant back and drank his sherry showed that to him this explanation covered all the facts observed and a great deal more. Barker's brow, however, was still a little clouded.

'And the yellow paper,' he began, with anxious friendliness, 'and the red rag . . .'

'The yellow paper and the red rag,' said Fuego, with indescribable grandeur, 'are the colours of Nicaragua.'

'But Nicaragua . . .' began Barker, with great hesitation, 'Nicaragua is no longer a . . .'

'Nicaragua has been conquered like Athens. Nicaragua has been annexed like Jerusalem,' cried the old man, with amazing fire. 'The Yankee and the German and the brute powers of modernity have trampled it with the hoofs of oxen. But Nicaragua is not dead. Nicaragua is an idea.'

Auberon Quin suggested timidly, 'A brilliant idea.'

'Yes,' said the foreigner, snatching at the word. 'You are right, generous Englishman. An idea *brilliant*, a burning thought. Señor, you asked me why, in my desire to see the colours of my country, I snatched at paper and blood. Can you not understand the ancient sanctity of colours? The Church has her symbolic colours. And think of what colours mean to us—think of the position of one like myself, who can see nothing but those two colours, nothing but the red and the yellow. To me all shapes are equal, all common and noble things are in a democracy of combination. Wherever there is a field of marigolds and the red cloak of an old woman, there is Nicaragua. Wherever there is a field of poppies and a yellow patch of sand, there is Nicaragua. Wherever there is a lemon and a red sunset, there is my country. Wherever I see a red pillar-box and a yellow sunset, there my heart beats. Blood and a splash of mustard can be my heraldry. If there be yellow mud and red mud in the same ditch, it is better to me than white stars.'

'And if,' said Quin, with equal enthusiasm, 'there should happen to be yellow wine and red wine at the same lunch, you could not confine yourself to sherry. Let me order some Burgundy, and complete, as it were, a sort of Nicaraguan heraldry in your inside.'

Barker was fiddling with his knife, and was evidently making up his mind to say something, with the intense nervousness of the amiable Englishman.

'I am to understand, then,' he said at last, with a cough, 'that you, ahem, were the President of Nicaragua when it made its—er—one must, of course, agree—its quite heroic resistance to—er——'

The ex-President of Nicaragua waved his hand.

'You need not hesitate in speaking to me,' he said. 'I am quite fully aware that the whole tendency of the world of to-day is against Nicaragua and against me. I shall not consider it any diminution of your evident courtesy if you say what you think of the misfortunes that have laid my republic in ruins.'

Barker looked immeasurably relieved and gratified.

'You are most generous, President,' he said, with some hesitation over the title, 'and I will take advantage of your generosity to express the doubts which, I must confess, we moderns have about such things as—er— the Nicaraguan independence.'

'So your sympathies are,' said Del Fuego, quite calmly, 'with the big nation which——'

'Pardon me, pardon me, President,' said Barker, warmly; 'my sympathies are with no nation. You misunderstand, I think, the modern intellect. We do not disapprove of the fire and extravagance of such commonwealths as yours only to become more extravagant on a larger scale. We do not condemn Nicaragua because we think Britain ought to be more Nicaraguan. We do not discourage small nationalities because we wish large nationalities to have all their smallness, all their uniformity of outlook, all their exaggeration of spirit. If I differ with the greatest respect from your Nicaraguan enthusiasm, it is not because a nation or

ten nations were against you; it is because civilization
was against you. We moderns believe in a great
cosmopolitan civilization, one which shall include all
the talents of all the absorbed peoples——'

'The Señor will forgive me,' said the President.
'May I ask the Señor how, under ordinary circumstances, he catches a wild horse?'

'I never catch a wild horse,' replied Barker, with
dignity.

'Precisely,' said the other; 'and there ends your
absorption of the talents. That is what I complain
of your cosmopolitanism. When you say you want all
peoples to unite, you really mean that you want all
peoples to unite to learn the tricks of your people. If
the Bedouin Arab does not know how to read, some
English missionary or schoolmaster must be sent to
teach him to read, but no one ever says, "This schoolmaster does not know how to ride on a camel; let us
pay a Bedouin to teach him." You say your civilization
will include all talents. Will it? Do you really mean
to say that at the moment when the Eskimo has
learnt to vote for a County Council, you will have
learnt to spear a walrus? I recur to the example I
gave. In Nicaragua we had a way of catching wild
horses—by lassoing the fore feet—which was supposed
to be the best in South America. If you are going to
include all the talents, go and do it. If not, permit
me to say, what I have always said, that something
went from the world when Nicaragua was civilized.'

'Something, perhaps,' replied Barker, 'but that
something a mere barbarian dexterity. I do not know
that I could chip flints as well as a primeval man, but
I know that civilization can make these knives, which
are better, and I trust to civilization.'

2

'You have good authority,' answered the Nicaraguan. 'Many clever men like you have trusted to civilization. Many clever Babylonians, many clever Egyptians, many clever men at the end of Rome. Can you tell me, in a world that is flagrant with the failures of civilization, what there is particularly immortal about yours?'

'I think you do not quite understand, President, what ours is,' answered Barker. 'You judge it rather as if England was still a poor and pugnacious island; you have been long out of Europe. Many things have happened.'

'And what,' asked the other, 'would you call the summary of those things?'

'The summary of those things,' answered Barker, with great animation, 'is that we are rid of the superstitions, and in becoming so we have not merely become rid of the superstitions which have been most frequently and most enthusiastically so described. The superstition of big nationalities is bad, but the superstition of small nationalities is worse. The superstition of reverencing our own country is bad, but the superstition of reverencing other people's countries is worse. It is so everywhere, and in a hundred ways. The superstition of monarchy is bad, and the superstition of aristocracy is bad, but the superstition of democracy is the worst of all.'

The old gentleman opened his eyes with some surprise.

'Are you, then,' he said, 'no longer a democracy in England?'

Barker laughed.

'The situation invites paradox,' he said. 'We are, in a sense, the purest democracy. We have become a despotism. Have you not noticed how continually in history democracy becomes despotism? People call it the decay of democracy. It is simply its fulfilment. Why take the trouble to number and register and enfranchise all the innumerable John Robinsons, when you can take one John Robinson with the same intellect or lack of intellect as all the rest, and have done with it? The old idealistic republicans used to found democracy on the idea that all men were equally intelligent. Believe me, the sane and enduring democracy is founded on the fact that all men are equally idiotic. Why should we not choose out of them one as much as another? All that we want for Government is a man not criminal and insane, who can rapidly look over some petitions and sign some proclamations. To think what time was wasted in arguing about the House of Lords, Tories saying it ought to be preserved because it was clever, and Radicals saying it ought to be destroyed because it was stupid, and all the time no one saw that it was right because it was stupid, because that chance mob of ordinary men thrown there by accident of blood, were a great democratic protest against the Lower House, against the eternal insolence of the aristocracy of talents. We have established now in England, the thing towards which all systems have dimly groped, the dull popular despotism without illusions. We want one man at the head of our State, not because he is brilliant or virtuous, but because he is one man and not a chattering crowd. To avoid the possible chance of hereditary diseases or such things, we have abandoned hereditary monarchy. The King of England is chosen like a juryman upon an official rotation list. Beyond that the whole system is quietly despotic, and we have not found it raise a murmur.'

'Do you really mean,' asked the President, incredulously, 'that you choose any ordinary man that comes to hand and make him despot—that you trust to the chance of some alphabetical list. . . .'

'And why not?' cried Barker. 'Did not half the historical nations trust to the chance of the eldest sons of eldest sons, and did not half of them get on tolerably well? To have a perfect system is impossible; to have a system is indispensable. All hereditary monarchies were a matter of luck: so are alphabetical monarchies. Can you find a deep philosophical meaning in the difference between the Stuarts and the Hanoverians? Believe me, I will undertake to find a deep philosophical meaning in the contrast between the dark tragedy of the A's, and the solid success of the B's.'

'And you risk it?' asked the other. 'Though the man may be a tyrant or a cynic or a criminal?'

'We risk it,' answered Barker, with a perfect placidity. 'Suppose he is a tyrant—he is still a check on a hundred tyrants. Suppose he is a cynic, it is to his interest to govern well. Suppose he is a criminal—by removing poverty and substituting power, we put a check on his criminality. In short, by substituting despotism we have put a total check on one criminal and a partial check on all the rest.'

The Nicaraguan old gentleman leaned over with a queer expression in his eyes.

'My Church, sir,' he said, 'has taught me to respect faith. I do not wish to speak with any disrespect of yours, however fantastic. But do you really mean that you will trust to the ordinary man, the man who may happen to come next, as a good despot?'

'I do,' said Barker, simply. 'He may not be a good man. But he will be a good despot. For when he comes to a mere business routine of government he will endeavour to do ordinary justice. Do we not assume the same thing in a jury?'

The old President smiled.

'I don't know,' he said, 'that I have any particular objection in detail to your excellent scheme of government. My only objection is a quite personal one. It is, that if I were asked whether I would belong to it, I should ask first of all, if I was not permitted, as an alternative, to be a toad in a ditch. That is all. You cannot argue with the choice of the soul.'

'Of the soul,' said Barker, knitting his brows, 'I cannot pretend to say anything, but speaking in the interests of the public——'

Mr. Auberon Quin rose suddenly to his feet.

'If you'll excuse me, gentlemen,' he said, 'I will step out for a moment into the air.'

'I'm so sorry, Auberon,' said Lambert, good-naturedly; 'do you feel bad?'

'Not bad exactly,' said Auberon, with self-restraint; 'rather good, if anything. Strangely and richly good. The fact is I want to reflect a little on those beautiful words that have just been uttered. "Speaking," yes, that was the phrase, "speaking in the interests of the public." One cannot get the honey from such things without being alone for a little.'

'Is he really off his chump, do you think?' asked Lambert.

The old President looked after him with queerly vigilant eyes.

'He is a man, I think,' he said, 'who cares for nothing but a joke. He is a dangerous man.'

Lambert laughed in the act of lifting some macaroni to his mouth.

'Dangerous!' he said. 'You don't know little Quin, sir!'

'Every man is dangerous,' said the old man without moving, 'who cares only for one thing. I was once dangerous myself.'

And with a pleasant smile he finished his coffee and rose, bowing profoundly, passed out into the fog, which had again grown dense and sombre. Three days afterwards they heard that he had died quietly in lodgings in Soho.

.   .   .   .   .

Drowned somewhere else in the dark sea of fog was a little figure shaking and quaking, with what might at first sight have seemed terror or ague: but which was really that strange malady, a lonely laughter. He was repeating over and over to himself with a rich accent: 'But speaking in the interests of the public. . . .'

CHAPTER III

THE HILL OF HUMOUR

'In a little square garden of yellow roses, beside the sea,' said Auberon Quin, 'there was a Nonconformist minister who had never been to Wimbledon. His family did not understand his sorrow or the strange look in his eyes. But one day they repented their neglect, for they heard that a body had been found on the shore, battered, but wearing patent leather boots. As it happened, it turned out not to be the minister at all. But in the dead man's pocket there was a return ticket to Maidstone.'

There was a short pause as Quin and his friends Barker and Lambert went swinging on through the slushy grass of Kensington Gardens. Then Auberon resumed.

'That story,' he said reverently, 'is the test of humour.'

They walked on farther and faster, wading through higher grass as they began to climb a slope.

'I perceive,' continued Auberon, 'that you have passed the test, and consider the anecdote excruciatingly funny; since you say nothing. Only coarse humour is received with pot-house applause. The great anecdote is received in silence, like a benediction. You felt pretty benedicted, didn't you, Barker?'

'I saw the point,' said Barker, somewhat loftily.

'Do you know,' said Quin, with a sort of idiot gaiety, 'I have lots of stories as good as that. Listen to this one.'

And he slightly cleared his throat.

31

'Dr. Polycarp was, as you all know, an unusually sallow bimetallist. "There," people of wide experience would say, "there goes the sallowest bimetallist in Cheshire." Once this was said so that he overheard it: it was said by an actuary, under a sunset of mauve and grey. Polycarp turned upon him. "Sallow!" he cried fiercely, "sallow! *Quis tulerit Gracchos de seditione querentes*." It was said that no actuary ever made game of Dr. Polycarp again.'

Barker nodded with a simple sagacity. Lambert only grunted.

'Here is another,' continued the insatiable Quin.

'In a hollow of the grey-green hills of rainy Ireland, lived an old, old woman, whose uncle was always Cambridge at the Boat Race. But in her grey-green hollows, she knew nothing of this: she didn't know that there was a Boat Race. Also she did not know that she had an uncle. She had heard of nobody at all, except of George the First, of whom she had heard (I know not why), and in whose historical memory she put her simple trust. And by and by, in God's good time, it was discovered that this uncle of hers was not really her uncle, and they came and told her so. She smiled through her tears, and said only, "Virtue is its own reward."'

Again there was a silence, and then Lambert said:

'It seems a bit mysterious.'

'Mysterious!' cried the other. 'The true humour is mysterious. Do you not realize the chief incident of the nineteenth and twentieth centuries?'

'And what's that?' asked Lambert, shortly.

'It is very simple,' replied the other. 'Hitherto it was the ruin of a joke that people did not see it. Now it is the sublime victory of a joke that people do not see it. Humour, my friends, is the one sanctity remaining to mankind. It is the one thing you are thoroughly afraid of. Look at that tree.'

His interlocutors looked vaguely towards a beech that leant out towards them from the ridge of the hill.

'If,' said Mr. Quin, 'I were to say that you did not see the great truths of science exhibited by that tree, though they stared any man of intellect in the face, what would you think or say? You would merely regard me as a pedant with some unimportant theory about vegetable cells. If I were to say that you did not see in that tree the vile mismanagement of local politics, you would dismiss me as a Socialist crank with some particular fad about public parks. If I were to say that you were guilty of the supreme blasphemy of looking at that tree and not seeing in it a new religion, a special revelation of God, you would simply say I was a mystic, and think no more about me. But if'— and he lifted a pontifical hand—'if I say that you cannot see the humour of that tree, and that I see the humour of it—my God! you will roll about at my feet.'

He paused a moment, and then resumed.

'Yes; a sense of humour, a weird and delicate sense of humour, is the new religion of mankind! It is towards that men will strain themselves with the ascetism of saints. Exercises, spiritual exercises, will be set in it. It will be asked, "Can you see the humour of this iron railing?" or "Can you see the humour of this field of corn? Can you see the humour of the stars? Can you see the humour of the sunsets?" How often I have laughed myself to sleep over a violet sunset.'

'Quite so,' said Mr. Barker, with an intelligent embarrassment.

'Let me tell you another story. How often it happens that the M.P.s for Essex are less punctual than one would suppose. The least punctual Essex M.P., perhaps, was James Wilson, who said, in the very act of plucking a poppy——'

Lambert suddenly faced round and struck his stick into the ground in a defiant attitude.

'Auberon,' he said, 'chuck it. I won't stand it. It's all bosh.'

Both men stared at him, for there was something very explosive about the words, as if they had been corked up painfully for a long time.

'You have,' began Quin, 'no——'

'I don't care a curse,' said Lambert, violently, 'whether I have "a delicate sense of humour" or not. I won't stand it. It's all a confounded fraud. There's no joke in those infernal tales at all. You know there isn't as well as I do.'

'Well,' replied Quin, slowly, 'it is true that I, with my rather gradual mental processes, did not see any joke in them. But the finer sense of Barker perceived it.'

Barker turned a fierce red, but continued to stare at the horizon.

'You ass,' said Lambert; 'why can't you be like other people? Why can't you say something really funny, or hold your tongue? The man who sits on his hat in a pantomime is a long sight funnier than you are.'

Quin regarded him steadily. They had reached the top of the ridge and the wind struck their faces.

'Lambert,' said Auberon, 'you are a great and good man, though I'm hanged if you look it. You are more. You are a great revolutionist or deliverer of the world, and I look forward to seeing you carved in marble between Luther and Danton, if possible in your present

attitude, the hat slightly on one side. I said as I came
up the hill that the new humour was the last of the
religions. You have made it the last of the superstitions. But let me give you a very serious warning.
Be careful how you ask me to do anything *outré*, to
imitate the man in the pantomime, and to sit on my
hat. Because I am a man whose soul has been emptied
of all pleasures but folly. And for twopence I'd
do it.'

'Do it then,' said Lambert, swinging his stick impatiently. 'It would be funnier than the bosh you and
Barker talk.'

Quin, standing on the top of the hill, stretched his
hand out towards the main avenue of Kensington
Gardens.

'Two hundred yards away,' he said, 'are all your
fashionable acquaintances with nothing on earth to
do but to stare at each other and at us. We are standing upon an elevation under the open sky, a peak as
it were of fantasy, a Sinai of humour. We are in a
great pulpit or platform, lit up with sunlight, and half
London can see us. Be careful how you suggest things
to me. For there is in me a madness which goes beyond
martyrdom, the madness of an utterly idle man.'

'I don't know what you are talking about,' said
Lambert, contemptuously. 'I only know I'd rather
you stood on your silly head, than talked so much.'

'Auberon! for goodness' sake . . .' cried Barker,
springing forward; but he was too late. Faces from
all the benches and avenues were turned in their
direction. Groups stopped and small crowds collected;
and the sharp sunlight picked out the whole scene in
blue, green, and black, like a picture in a child's toy-
book. And on the top of the small hill Mr. Auberon

Quin stood with considerable athletic neatness upon his head, and waved his patent-leather boots in the air.

'For God's sake, Quin, get up, and don't be an idiot,' cried Barker, wringing his hands; 'we shall have the whole town here.'

'Yes, get up, get up, man,' said Lambert, amused and annoyed. 'I was only fooling; get up.'

Auberon did so with a bound, and flinging his hat higher than the trees, proceeded to hop about on one leg with a serious expression. Barker stamped wildly.

'Oh, let's get home, Barker, and leave him,' said Lambert; 'some of your proper and correct police will look after him. Here they come!'

Two grave-looking men in quiet uniforms came up the hill towards them. One held a paper in his hand.

'There he is, officer,' said Lambert, cheerfully; 'we ain't responsible for him.'

The officer looked at the capering Mr. Quin with a quiet eye.

'We have not come, gentlemen,' he said, 'about what I think you are alluding to. We have come from headquarters to announce the selection of His Majesty the King. It is the rule, inherited from the old régime, that the news should be brought to the new Sovereign immediately, wherever he is; so we have followed you across Kensington Gardens.'

Barker's eyes were blazing in his pale face. He was consumed with ambition throughout his life. With a certain dull magnanimity of the intellect he had really believed in the chance method of selecting despots. But this sudden suggestion, that the selection might have fallen upon him, unnerved him with pleasure.

'Which of us,' he began, and the respectful official interrupted him.

'Not you, sir, I am sorry to say. If I may be permitted to say so, we know your services to the Government, and should be very thankful if it were. The choice has fallen . . .'

'God bless my soul!' said Lambert, jumping back two paces. 'Not me. Don't say I'm autocrat of All the Russias.'

'No, sir,' said the officer, with a slight cough and a glance towards Auberon, who was at that moment putting his head between his legs and making a noise like a cow; 'the gentleman whom we have to congratulate seems at the moment—er—er—occupied.'

'Not Quin!' shrieked Barker, rushing up to him; 'it can't be. Auberon, for God's sake pull yourself together. You've been made King!'

With his head still upside down between his legs, Mr. Quin answered modestly:

'I am not worthy. I cannot reasonably claim to equal the great men who have previously swayed the sceptre of Britain. Perhaps the only peculiarity that I can claim is that I am probably the first monarch that ever spoke out his soul to the people of England with his head and body in this position. This may in some sense give me, to quote a poem that I wrote in my youth:

> A nobler office on the earth
> Than valour, power of brain, or birth
> Could give the warrior kings of old.

The intellect clarified by this posture——'

Lambert and Barker made a kind of rush at him.

'Don't you understand?' cried Lambert. 'It's not a joke. They've really made you King. By gosh! they must have rum taste.'

'The great Bishops of the Middle Ages,' said Quin, kicking his legs in the air, as he was dragged up more or less upside down, 'were in the habit of refusing the honour of election three times and then accepting it. A mere matter of detail separates me from those great men. I will accept the post three times and refuse it afterwards. Oh! I will toil for you, my faithful people! You shall have a banquet of humour.'

By this time he had been landed the right way up, and the two men were still trying in vain to impress him with the gravity of the situation.

'Did you not tell me, Wilfrid Lambert,' he said, 'that I should be of more public value if I adopted a more popular form of humour? And when should a popular form of humour be more firmly riveted upon me than now, when I have become the darling of a whole people? Officer,' he continued, addressing the startled messenger, 'are there no ceremonies to celebrate my entry into the city?'

'Ceremonies,' began the official, with embarrassment, 'have been more or less neglected for some little time, and——'

Auberon Quin began gradually to take off his coat.

'All ceremony,' he said, 'consists in the reversal of the obvious. Thus men, when they wish to be priests or judges, dress up like women. Kindly help me on with this coat.' And he held it out.

'But, your Majesty,' said the officer, after a moment's bewilderment and manipulation, 'you're putting it on with the tails in front.'

'The reversal of the obvious,' said the King, calmly, 'is as near as we can come to ritual with our imperfect apparatus. Lead on.'

The rest of that afternoon and evening was to Barker

and Lambert a nightmare, which they could not properly realize or recall. The King, with his coat on the wrong way, went towards the streets that were awaiting him, and the old Kensington Palace which was the Royal residence. As he passed small groups of men, the groups turned into crowds, and gave forth sounds which seemed strange in welcoming an autocrat. Barker walked behind, his brain reeling, and, as the crowds grew thicker and thicker, the sounds became more and more unusual. And when he had reached the great market-place opposite the church, Barker knew that he had reached it, though he was rods behind, because a cry went up such as had never before greeted any of the kings of the earth.

BOOK II

CHAPTER I

THE CHARTER OF THE CITIES

LAMBERT was standing bewildered outside the door of the King's apartments amid the scurry of astonishment and ridicule. He was just passing out into the street, in a dazed manner, when James Barker dashed by him.

'Where are you going?' he asked.

'To stop all this foolery, of course,' replied Barker; and he disappeared into the room.

He entered it headlong, slamming the door, and slapping his incomparable silk hat on the table. His mouth opened, but before he could speak, the King said:

'Your hat, if you please.'

Fidgeting with his fingers, and scarcely knowing what he was doing, the young politician held it out.

The King placed it on his own chair, and sat on it.

'A quaint old custom,' he explained, smiling above the ruins. 'When the King receives the representatives of the House of Barker, the hat of the latter is immediately destroyed in this manner. It represents the absolute finality of the act of homage expressed in the removal of it. It declares that never until that hat shall once more appear upon your head (a contingency which I firmly believe to be remote) shall the House of Barker rebel against the Crown of England.'

Barker stood with clenched fist, and shaking lip.

'Your jokes,' he began, 'and my property——' and then exploded with an oath, and stopped again.

'Continue, continue,' said the King, waving his hands.

'What does it all mean?' cried the other, with a gesture of passionate rationality. 'Are you mad?'

'Not in the least,' replied the King, pleasantly. 'Madmen are always serious; they go mad from lack of humour. You are looking serious yourself, James.'

'Why can't you keep it to your own private life?' expostulated the other. 'You've got plenty of money, and plenty of houses now to play the fool in, but in the interests of the public——'

'Epigrammatic,' said the King, shaking his finger sadly at him. 'None of your daring scintillations here. As to why I don't do it in private, I rather fail to understand your question. The answer is of comparative limpidity. I don't do it in private, because it is funnier to do it in public. You appear to think that it would be amusing to be dignified in the banquet-hall and in the street, and at my own fireside (I could procure a fireside) to keep the company in a roar. But that is what every one does. Every one is grave in public, and funny in private. My sense of humour suggests the reversal of this; it suggests that one should be funny in public, and solemn in private. I desire to make the State functions, parliaments, coronations, and so on, one roaring old-fashioned pantomime. But, on the other hand, I shut myself up alone in a small store-room for two hours a day, where I am so dignified that I come out quite ill.'

By this time Barker was walking up and down the room, his frock-coat flapping like the black wings of a bird.

'Well, you will ruin the country, that's all,' he said shortly.

'It seems to me,' said Auberon, 'that the tradition of ten centuries is being broken, and the House of

Barker is rebelling against the Crown of England. It would be with regret (for I admire your appearance) that I should be obliged forcibly to decorate your head with the remains of this hat, but——'

'What I can't understand,' said Barker, flinging up his fingers with a feverish American movement, 'is why you don't care about anything else but your games.'

The King stopped sharply in the act of lifting the silken remnants, dropped them, and walked up to Barker, looking at him steadily.

'I made a kind of vow,' he said, 'that I would not talk seriously, which always means answering silly questions. But the strong man will always be gentle with politicians.

'The shape my scornful looks deride
Required a God to form';

if I may so theologically express myself. And for some reason I cannot in the least understand, I feel impelled to answer that question of yours, and to answer it as if there were really such a thing in the world as a serious subject. You ask me why I don't care for anything else. Can you tell me, in the name of all the gods you don't believe in, why I should care for anything else?'

'Don't you realize common public necessities?' cried Barker. 'Is it possible that a man of your intelligence does not know that it is every one's interest——'

'Don't you believe in Zoroaster? Is it possible that you neglect Mumbo-Jumbo?' returned the King, with startling animation. 'Does a man of your intelligence come to me with these damned early Victorian ethics? If, on studying my features and manner, you detect any particular resemblance to the Prince Consort, I assure you you are mistaken. Did Herbert Spencer ever convince you—did he ever convince anybody—did he ever for one mad moment convince himself —that it must be to the interest of the individual to feel a public spirit? Do you believe that, if you rule your department badly, you stand any more chance, or one-half of the chance, of being guillotined, that an angler stands, of being pulled into the river by a strong pike? Herbert Spencer refrained from theft for the same reason that he refrained from wearing feathers in his hair, because he was an English gentleman with different tastes. I am an English gentleman with different tastes. He likes philosophy. I like art. He liked writing ten books on the nature of human society. I like to see the Lord Chamberlain walking in front of me with a piece of paper pinned to his coat-tails. It is my humour. Are you answered? At any rate, I have said my last serious word to-day, and my last serious word I trust for the remainder of my life in this Paradise of Fools. The remainder of my conversation with you to-day, which I trust will be long and stimulating, I propose to conduct in a new language of my own by means of rapid and symbolic movements of the left leg.' And he began to pirouette slowly round the room with a preoccupied expression.

Barker ran round the room after him, bombarding him with demands and entreaties. But he received no response except in the new language. He came out banging the door again, and sick like a man coming on shore. As he strode along the streets he found himself suddenly opposite Cicconani's restaurant, and for some reason there rose up before him the green, fantastic figure of the Spanish General, standing, as he had seen him last, at the door with the words on his lips, 'You cannot argue with the choice of the soul.'

The King came out from his dancing with the air of a man of business legitimately tired. He put on an overcoat, lit a cigar, and went out into the purple night.

'I will go,' he said, 'and mingle with the people.'

He passed swiftly up a street in the neighbourhood of Notting Hill, when suddenly he felt a hard object driven into his waistcoat. He paused, put up a single eye-glass, and beheld a boy with a wooden sword and a paper cocked hat, wearing that expression of awed satisfaction with which a child contemplates his work when he has hit some one very hard. The King gazed thoughtfully for some time at his assailant, and slowly took a note-book from his breast-pocket.

'I have a few notes,' he said, 'for my dying speech'; and he turned over the leaves. 'Dying speech for political assassination; ditto, if by former friend—h'm, h'm. Dying speech for death at hands of injured husband (repentant). Dying speech for same (cynical). I am not quite sure which meets the present. . . .'

'I'm the King of the Castle,' said the boy, truculently, and very pleased with nothing in particular.

The King was a kind-hearted man, and very fond of children, like all people who are fond of the ridiculous.

'Infant,' he said, 'I'm glad you are so stalwart a defender of your old inviolate Notting Hill. Look up nightly to that peak, my child, where it lifts itself among the stars so ancient, so lonely, so unutterably Notting. So long as you are ready to die for the sacred mountain, even if it were ringed with all the armies of Bayswater——'

The King stopped suddenly, and his eyes shone.

'Perhaps,' he said, 'perhaps the noblest of all my conceptions. A revival of the arrogance of the old medieval cities applied to our glorious suburbs. Clapham with a city guard. Wimbledon with a city wall. Surbiton tolling a bell to raise its citizens. West Hampstead going into battle with its own banner. It shall be done. I, the King, have said it.' And hastily presenting the boy with half a crown, remarking, 'For the war-chest of Notting Hill', he ran violently home at such a rate of speed that crowds followed him for miles. On reaching his study, he ordered a cup of coffee, and plunged into profound meditation upon the project. At length he called his favourite Equerry, Captain Bowler, for whom he had a deep affection, founded principally upon the shape of his whiskers.

'Bowler,' he said, 'isn't there some society of historical research, or something of which I am an honorary member?'

'Yes, sir,' said Captain Bowler, rubbing his nose, 'you are a member of "The Encouragers of Egyptian Renaissance", and "The Teutonic Tombs Club", and "The Society for the Recovery of London Antiquities", and——'

'That is admirable,' said the King. 'The London Antiquities does my trick. Go to the Society for the Recovery of London Antiquities and speak to their secretary, and their sub-secretary, and their president, and their vice-president, saying, "The King of England is proud, but the honorary member of the Society for the Recovery of London Antiquities is prouder than kings. I should like to tell you of certain discoveries I have made touching the neglected traditions of the London boroughs. The revelations may cause some excitement, stirring burning memories and touching old wounds in Shepherd's Bush and Bayswater, in Pimlico and South Kensington. The King hesitates, but the honorary member is firm. I approach you invoking the vows of my initiation, the Sacred Seven Cats, the Poker of Perfection, and the Ordeal of the Indescribable Instant (forgive me if I mix you up with the Clan-na-Gael or some other club I belong to), and ask you to permit me to read a paper at your next meeting on the 'Wars of the London Boroughs'. Say all this to the Society, Bowler. Remember it very carefully, for it is most important, and I have forgotten it altogether, and send me another cup of coffee and some of the cigars that we keep for vulgar and successful people. I am going to write my paper.'

The Society for the Recovery of London Antiquities met a month after in a corrugated iron hall on the outskirts of one of the southern suburbs of London. A large number of people had collected there under the coarse and flaring gas-jets when the King arrived, perspiring and genial. On taking off his great-coat, he was perceived to be in evening dress, wearing the Garter. His appearance at the small table, adorned only with a glass of water, was received with respectful cheering.

The chairman (Mr. Huggins) said that he was sure that they had all been pleased to listen to such distinguished lectures as they had heard for some time past (hear, hear). Mr. Burton (hear, hear), Mr. Cambridge, Professor King (loud and continued cheers), our old friend Peter Jessop, Sir William White (loud laughter), and other eminent men, had done honour to their little venture (cheers). But there were other circumstances which lend a certain unique quality to the present occasion (hear, hear). So far as his recollection went, and in connexion with the Society for the Recovery of London Antiquities it went very far (loud cheers), he did not remember that any of their lecturers had borne the title of King. He would therefore call upon King Auberon briefly to address the meeting.

The King began by saying that this speech might be regarded as the first declaration of his new policy for the nation. 'At this supreme hour of my life I feel that to no one but the members of the Society for the Recovery of London Antiquities can I open my heart (cheers). If the world turns upon my policy, and the storms of popular hostility begin to rise (no, no), I feel that it is here, with my brave Recoverers around me, that I can best meet them, sword in hand' (loud cheers).

His Majesty then went on to explain that, now old age was creeping upon him, he proposed to devote his remaining strength to bringing about a keener sense of local patriotism in the various municipalities of London. How few of them knew the legends of their own boroughs? How many there were who had never heard of the true origin of the Wink of Wandsworth! What a large proportion of the younger generation in Chelsea neglected to perform the old Chelsea Chuff! Pimlico no longer pumped the Pimlies. Battersea had forgotten the name of Blick.

There was a short silence, and then a voice said, 'Shame.'

The King continued: 'Being called, however unworthily, to this high estate, I have resolved that, so far as possible, this neglect shall cease. I desire no military glory. I lay claim to no constitutional equality with Justinian or Alfred. If I can go down to history

as the man who saved from extinction a few old
English customs, if our descendants can say it was
through this man, humble as he was, that the Ten
Turnips are still eaten in Fulham, and the Putney
parish councillor still shaves one half of his head, I
shall look my great fathers reverently but not fearfully
in the face when I go down to the last house of
Kings.'

The King paused, visibly affected, but collecting
himself, resumed once more.

'I trust that to very few of you, at least, I need dwell
on the sublime origins of these legends. The very
names of your boroughs bear witness to them. So long
as Hammersmith is called Hammersmith, its people
will live in the shadow of that primal hero, the Black-
smith, who led the democracy of the Broadway into
battle till he drove the chivalry of Kensington before
him and overthrew them at that place which in honour
of the best blood of the defeated aristocracy is still
called Kensington Gore. Men of Hammersmith will
not fail to remember that the very name of Kensington
originated from the lips of their hero. For at the great
banquet of reconciliation held after the war, when the
disdainful oligarchs declined to join in the songs of the
men of the Broadway (which are to this day of a rude
and popular character), the great Republican leader,
with his rough humour, said the words which are
written in gold upon his monument, "Little birds that
can sing and won't sing, must be made to sing." So
that the Eastern Knights were called Cansings or
Kensings ever afterwards. But you also have great
memories, O men of Kensington! You showed that
you could sing, and sing great war-songs. Even after
the dark day of Kensington Gore, history will not

forget those three Knights who guarded your dis-
ordered retreat from Hyde Park (so called from your
hiding there), those three Knights after whom Knightsbridge is named. Nor will it forget the day of your
re-emergence, purged in the fire of calamity, cleansed
of your oligarchic corruptions, when, sword in hand,
you drove the Empire of Hammersmith back mile
by mile, swept it past its own Broadway, and broke it
at last in a battle so long and bloody that the birds of
prey have left their name upon it. Men have called
it, with austere irony, the Ravenscourt. I shall not,
I trust, wound the patriotism of Bayswater, or the
lonelier pride of Brompton, or that of any other
historic township, by taking these two special examples.
I select them, not because they are more glorious than
the rest, but partly from personal association (I am
myself descended from one of the three heroes of
Knightsbridge), and partly from the consciousness
that I am an amateur antiquarian, and cannot presume to deal with times and places more remote and
more mysterious. It is not for me to settle the question
between two such men as Professor Hugg and Sir
William Whisky as to whether Notting Hill means
Nutting Hill (in allusion to the rich woods which no
longer cover it), or whether it is a corruption of
Nothing-ill, referring to its reputation among the
ancients as an Earthly Paradise. When a Podkins
and a Jossy confess themselves doubtful about the
boundaries of West Kensington (said to have been
traced in the blood of Oxen), I need not be ashamed
to confess a similar doubt. I will ask you to excuse me
from further history, and to assist me with your
encouragement in dealing with the problem which
faces us to-day. Is this ancient spirit of the London

townships to die out? Are our omnibus conductors and policemen to lose altogether that light which we see so often in their eyes, the dreamy light of

> 'Old unhappy far-off things
> And battles long ago'

—to quote the words of a little-known poet who was a friend of my youth? I have resolved, as I have said, so far as possible, to preserve the eyes of policemen and omnibus conductors in their present dreamy state. For what is a state without dreams? And the remedy I propose is as follows:

'To-morrow morning at twenty-five minutes past ten, if Heaven spares my life, I purpose to issue a Proclamation. It has been the work of my life, and is about half-finished. With the assistance of a whisky and soda, I shall conclude the other half to-night, and my people will receive it to-morrow. All these boroughs where you were born, and hope to lay your bones, shall be reinstated in their ancient magnificence—Hammersmith, Kensington, Bayswater, Chelsea, Battersea, Clapham, Balham, and a hundred others. Each shall immediately build a city wall with gates to be closed at sunset. Each shall have a city guard, armed to the teeth. Each shall have a banner, a coat of arms, and, if convenient, a gathering cry. I will not enter into the details now, my heart is too full. They will be found in the proclamation itself. You will all, however, be subject to enrolment in the local city guards, to be summoned together by a thing called the Tocsin, the meaning of which I am studying in my researches into history. Personally, I believe a tocsin to be some kind of highly paid official. If, therefore, any of you happen to have such a thing as a halberd in the house, I should advise you to practise with it in the garden.'

Here the King buried his face in his handkerchief and hurriedly left the platform, overcome by emotions.

The members of the Society for the Recovery of London Antiquities rose in an indescribable state of vagueness. Some were purple with indignation; an intellectual few were purple with laughter; the great majority found their minds a blank. There remains a tradition that one pale face with burning blue eyes remained fixed upon the lecturer, and after the lecture a red-haired boy ran out of the room.

THE COUNCIL OF THE PROVOSTS

THE King got up early next morning and came down three steps at a time like a schoolboy. Having eaten his breakfast hurriedly, but with an appetite, he summoned one of the highest officials of the Palace, and presented him with a shilling. 'Go and buy me,' he said, 'a shilling paint-box, which you will get, unless the mists of time mislead me, in a shop at the corner of the second and dirtier street that leads out of Rochester Row. I have already requested the Master of the Buckhounds to provide me with cardboard. It seemed to me (I know not why) that it fell within his department.'

The King was happy all that morning with his cardboard and his paint-box. He was engaged in designing the uniforms and coats of arms for the various municipalities of London. They gave him deep and no inconsiderable thought. He felt the responsibility.

'I cannot think,' he said, 'why people should think the names of places in the country more poetical than those in London. Shallow romanticists go away in trains and stop in places called Hugmy-in-the-Hole, or Bumps-on-the-Puddle. And all the time they could, if they liked, go and live at a place with the dim, divine name of St. John's Wood. I have never been to St. John's Wood. I dare not. I should be afraid of the innumerable night of fir-trees, afraid to come upon a blood-red cup and the beating of the wings of the Eagle. But all these things can be imagined by remaining reverently in the Harrow train.'

And he thoughtfully retouched his design for the head-dress of the halberdier of St. John's Wood, a design in black and red, compounded of a pine-tree and the plumage of an eagle. Then he turned to another card. 'Let us think of milder matters,' he said. 'Lavender Hill! Could any of your glebes and combes and all the rest of it produce so fragrant an idea? Think of a mountain of lavender lifting itself in purple poignancy into the silver skies and filling men's nostrils with a new breath of life—a purple hill of incense. It is true that upon my few excursions of discovery on a halfpenny tram I have failed to hit the precise spot. But it must be there; some poet called it by its name. There is at least warrant enough for the solemn purple plumes (following the botanical formation of lavender) which I have required people to wear in the neighbourhood of Clapham Junction. It is so everywhere, after all. I have never been actually to Southfields, but I suppose a scheme of lemons and olives represent their austral instincts. I have never visited Parson's Green, or seen either the Green or the Parson, but surely the pale-green shovel-hats I have designed must be more or less in the spirit. I must work in the dark and let my instincts guide me. The great love I bear to my people will certainly save me from distressing their noble spirit or violating their great traditions.'

As he was reflecting in this vein, the door was flung open, and an official announced Mr. Barker and Mr. Lambert.

Mr. Barker and Mr. Lambert were not particularly surprised to find the King sitting on the floor amid a litter of water-colour sketches. They were not particularly surprised because the last time they had called on him they had found him sitting on the floor, surrounded by a litter of children's bricks, and the time before surrounded by a litter of wholly unsuccessful attempts to make paper darts. But the trend of the royal infant's remarks, uttered from amid this infantile chaos, was not quite the same affair. For some time they let him babble on, conscious that his remarks meant nothing. And then a horrible thought began to steal over the mind of James Barker. He began to think that the King's remarks did not mean nothing.

'In God's name, Auberon,' he suddenly volleyed out, startling the quiet hall, 'you don't mean that you are really going to have these city guards and city walls and things?'

'I am, indeed,' said the infant, in a quiet voice. 'Why shouldn't I have them? I have modelled them precisely on your political principles. Do you know what I've done, Barker? I've behaved like a true Barkerian. I've . . . but perhaps it won't interest you, the account of my Barkerian conduct.'

'Oh, go on, go on,' cried Barker.

'The account of my Barkerian conduct,' said Auberon, calmly, 'seems not only to interest, but to alarm you. Yet it is very simple. It merely consists in choosing all the provosts under any new scheme by the same principle by which you have caused the central despot to be appointed. Each provost, of each city, under my charter, is to be appointed by rotation. Sleep, therefore, my Barker, a rosy sleep.'

Barker's wild eyes flared.

'But, in God's name, don't you see, Quin, that the thing is quite different? In the centre it doesn't matter so much, just because the whole object of despotism is to get some sort of unity. But if any damned parish can go to any damned man——'

'I see your difficulty,' said King Auberon, calmly. 'You feel that your talents may be neglected. Listen!' And he rose with immense magnificence. 'I solemnly give to my liege subject, James Barker, my special and splendid favour, the right to override the obvious text of the Charter of the Cities, and to be, in his own right, Lord High Provost of South Kensington. And now, my dear James, you are all right. Good day.'

'But——' began Barker.

'The audience is at an end, Provost,' said the King, smiling.

How far his confidence was justified, it would require a somewhat complicated description to explain. 'The Great Proclamation of the Charter of the Free Cities' appeared in due course that morning, and was posted by bill-stickers all over the front of the Palace, the King assisting them with animated directions, and standing in the middle of the road, with his head on one side, contemplating the result. It was also carried up and down the main thoroughfares by sandwichmen, and the King was, with difficulty, restrained from going out in that capacity himself, being, in fact, found by the Groom of the Stole and Captain Bowler, struggling between two boards. His excitement had positively to be quieted like that of a child.

The reception which the Charter of the Cities met at the hands of the public may mildly be described as mixed. In one sense it was popular enough. In many happy homes that remarkable legal document was read aloud on winter evenings amid uproarious appreciation, when everything had been learnt by heart from that quaint but immortal old classic, Mr. W. W. Jacobs. But when it was discovered that the King had every intention of seriously requiring the provisions to be carried out, of insisting that the grotesque cities, with their tocsins and city guards, should really come into existence, things were thrown into a far angrier confusion. Londoners had no particular objection to the King making a fool of himself, but they became indignant when it became evident that he wished to make fools of them; and protests began to come in.

The Lord High Provost of the Good and Valiant City of West Kensington wrote a respectful letter to the King, explaining that upon State occasions it would, of course, be his duty to observe what formalities the King thought proper, but that it was really awkward for a decent householder not to be allowed to go out and put a post card in a pillar-box without being escorted by five heralds, who announced, with formal cries and blasts of a trumpet, that the Lord High Provost desired to catch the post.

The Lord High Provost of North Kensington, who was a prosperous draper, wrote a curt business note, like a man complaining of a railway company, stating that definite inconvenience had been caused him by the presence of the halberdiers, whom he had to take with him everywhere. When attempting to catch an omnibus to the City, he had found that while room could have been found for himself, the halberdiers had a difficulty in getting into the vehicle—believe him, theirs faithfully.

The Lord High Provost of Shepherd's Bush said his wife did not like men hanging round the kitchen.

The King was always delighted to listen to these

grievances, delivering lenient and kingly answers, but as he always insisted, as the absolute *sine qua non*, that verbal complaints should be presented to him with the fullest pomp of trumpets, plumes, and halberds, only a few resolute spirits were prepared to run the gauntlet of the little boys in the street.

Among these, however, was prominent the abrupt and business-like gentleman who ruled North Kensington. And he had, before long, occasion to interview the King about a matter wider and even more urgent than the problem of the halberdiers and the omnibus. This was the greatest question which then and for long afterwards brought a stir to the blood and a flush to the cheek of all the speculative builders and house agents from Shepherd's Bush to the Marble Arch, and from Westbourne Grove to High Street, Kensington. I refer to the great affair of the improvements in Notting Hill. The scheme was conducted chiefly by Mr. Buck, the abrupt North Kensington magnate, and by Mr. Wilson, the Provost of Bayswater. A great thoroughfare was to be driven through three boroughs, through West Kensington, North Kensington, and Notting Hill, opening at one end into Hammersmith Broadway, and at the other into Westbourne Grove. The negotiations, buyings, sellings, bullying and bribing took ten years, and by the end of it Buck, who had conducted them almost single-handed, had proved himself a man of the strongest type of material energy and material diplomacy. And just as his splendid patience and more splendid impatience had finally brought him victory, when workmen were already demolishing houses and walls along the great line from Hammersmith, a sudden obstacle appeared that had neither been reckoned with nor dreamed of, a small and strange obstacle, which, like a speck of grit in a great machine, jarred the whole vast scheme and brought it to a standstill, and Mr. Buck, the draper, getting with great impatience into his robes of office and summoning with indescribable disgust his halberdiers, hurried over to speak to the King.

Ten years had not tired the King of his joke. There were still new faces to be seen looking out from the symbolic head-gears he had designed, gazing at him from amid the pastoral ribbons of Shepherd's Bush or from under the sombre hoods of the Blackfriars Road. And the interview which was promised him with the Provost of North Kensington he anticipated with a particular pleasure, for 'he never really enjoyed', he said, 'the full richness of the medieval garments unless the people compelled to wear them were very angry and business-like.'

Mr. Buck was both. At the King's command the door of the audience-chamber was thrown open and a herald appeared in the purple colours of Mr. Buck's commonwealth emblazoned with the Great Eagle which the King had attributed to North Kensington, in vague reminiscence of Russia, for he always insisted on regarding North Kensington as some kind of semi-arctic neighbourhood. The herald announced that the Provost of that city desired audience of the King.

'From North Kensington?' said the King, rising graciously. 'What news does he bring from that land of high hills and fair women? He is welcome.'

The herald advanced into the room, and was immediately followed by twelve guards clad in purple, who were followed by an attendant bearing the banner of the Eagle, who was followed by another attendant bearing the keys of the city upon a cushion, who was followed by Mr. Buck in a great hurry. When the King saw his strong animal face and steady eyes, he knew that he was in the presence of a great man of business, and consciously braced himself.

'Well, well,' he said, cheerily coming down two or three steps from a dais, and striking his hands lightly together, 'I am glad to see you. Never mind, never mind. Ceremony is not everything.'

'I don't understand your Majesty,' said the Provost, stolidly.

'Never mind, never mind,' said the King, gaily. 'A knowledge of Courts is by no means an unmixed merit; you will do it next time, no doubt.'

The man of business looked at him sulkily from under his black brows and said again without show of civility:

'I don't follow you.'

'Well, well,' replied the King, good-naturedly, 'if you ask me I don't mind telling you, not because I myself attach any importance to these forms in comparison with the Honest Heart. But it is usual—it is usual—that is all, for a man when entering the presence of Royalty to lie down on his back on the floor and elevating his feet towards heaven (as the source of Royal power) to say three times "Monarchical institutions improve the manners". But there, there—such pomp is far less truly dignified than your simple kindliness.'

The Provost's face was red with anger, and he maintained silence.

'And now,' said the King, lightly, and with the exasperating air of a man softening a snub; 'what delightful weather we are having! You must find your official robes warm, my Lord. I designed them for your own snow-bound land.'

'They're as hot as hell,' said Buck, briefly. 'I came here on business.'

'Right,' said the King, nodding a great number of times with quite unmeaning solemnity; 'right, right, right. Business, as the sad glad old Persian said, is business. Be punctual. Rise early. Point the pen to the shoulder. Point the pen to the shoulder, for you know not whence you come nor why. Point the pen to the shoulder, for you know not when you go nor where.'

The Provost pulled a number of papers from his pocket and savagely flapped them open.

'Your Majesty may have heard,' he began, sarcastically, 'of Hammersmith and a thing called a road. We have been at work ten years buying property and getting compulsory powers and fixing compensation and squaring vested interests, and now at the very end, the thing is stopped by a fool. Old Prout, who was Provost of Notting Hill, was a business man, and we dealt with him quite satisfactorily. But he's dead, and the cursed lot has fallen to a young man named Wayne, who's up to some game that's perfectly incomprehensible to me. We offer him a better price than any one ever dreamt of, but he won't let the road go through. And his Council seem to be backing him up. It's midsummer madness.'

The King, who was rather inattentively engaged in drawing the Provost's nose with his finger on the window-pane, heard the last two words.

'What a perfect phrase that is,' he said. '"Midsummer madness!"'

'The chief point is,' continued Buck, doggedly, 'that the only part that is really in question is one dirty little street—Pump Street—a street with nothing in it but a public-house and a penny toyshop, and that sort of thing. All the respectable people of Notting Hill have accepted our compensation. But the ineffable Wayne sticks out over Pump Street. Says he's Provost of Notting Hill. He's only Provost of Pump Street.'

'A good thought,' replied Auberon. 'I like the idea of a Provost of Pump Street. Why not let him alone?'

'And drop the whole scheme!' cried out Buck, with a burst of brutal spirit. 'I'll be damned if we do. No. I'm for sending in workmen to pull down without more ado.'

'Strike for the purple Eagle,' cried the King, hot with historical associations.

'I'll tell you what it is,' said Buck, losing his temper altogether. 'If your Majesty would spend less time in insulting respectable people with your silly coats of arms, and more time over the business of the nation——'

The King's brow wrinkled thoughtfully.

'The situation is not bad,' he said; 'the haughty burgher defying the King in his own Palace. The burgher's head should be thrown back and the right arm extended; the left may be lifted towards Heaven, but that I leave to your private religious sentiment. I have sunk back in this chair, stricken with baffled fury. Now again, please.'

Buck's mouth opened like a dog's, but before he could speak another herald appeared at the door.

'The Lord High Provost of Bayswater,' he said, 'desires an audience.'

'Admit him,' said Auberon. 'This *is* a jolly day.'

The halberdiers of Bayswater wore a prevailing uniform of green, and the banner which was borne after them was emblazoned with a green bay-wreath on a silver ground, which the King, in the course of his researches into a bottle of champagne, had discovered to be the quaint old punning cognizance of the city of Bayswater.

'It is a fit symbol,' said the King, 'your immortal bay-wreath. Fulham may seek for wealth, and Kensington for art, but when did the men of Bayswater care for anything but glory?'

Immediately behind the banner, and almost completely hidden by it, came the Provost of the city, clad in splendid robes of green and silver with white fur and crowned with bay. He was an anxious little man with red whiskers, originally the owner of a small sweetstuff shop.

'Our cousin of Bayswater,' said the King, with delight; 'what can we get for you?' The King was heard also distinctly to mutter, 'Cold beef, cold 'am, cold chicken', his voice dying into silence.

'I came to see your Majesty,' said the Provost of Bayswater, whose name was Wilson, 'about that Pump Street affair.'

'I have just been explaining the situation to his Majesty,' said Buck, curtly, but recovering his civility. 'I am not sure, however, whether his Majesty knows how much the matter affects you also.'

'It affects both of us, yer see, yer Majesty, as this scheme was started for the benefit of the 'ole neighbourhood. So Mr. Buck and me we put our 'eads together——'

The King clasped his hands.

'Perfect,' he cried in ecstasy. 'Your heads together! I can see it! Can't you do it now? Oh, do do it now.'

A smothered sound of amusement appeared to come

from the halberdiers, but Mr. Wilson looked merely bewildered, and Mr. Buck merely diabolical.

'I suppose,' he began, bitterly, but the King stopped him with a gesture of listening.

'Hush,' he said, 'I think I hear some one else coming. I seem to hear another herald, a herald whose boots creak.'

As he spoke another voice cried from the doorway:

'The Lord High Provost of South Kensington desires an audience.'

'The Lord High Provost of South Kensington!' cried the King. 'Why, that is my old friend James Barker! What does he want, I wonder? If the tender memories of friendship have not grown misty, I fancy he wants something for himself, probably money. How are you, James?'

Mr. James Barker, whose guard was attired in a splendid blue, and whose blue banner bore three gold birds singing, rushed, in his blue and gold robes, into the room. Despite the absurdity of all the dresses, it was worth noticing that he carried his better than the rest, though he loathed it as much as any of them. He was a gentleman, and a very handsome man, and could not help unconsciously wearing even his preposterous robe as it should be worn. He spoke quickly, but with the slight initial hesitation he always showed in addressing the King, due to suppressing an impulse to address his old acquaintance in the old way.

'Your Majesty—pray forgive my intrusion. It is about this man at Pump Street. I see you have Buck here, so you have probably heard what is necessary. I——'

The King swept his eyes anxiously round the room, which now blazed with the trappings of three cities.

'There is one thing necessary,' he said.

'Yes, your Majesty,' said Mr. Wilson of Bayswater, a little eagerly. 'What does yer Majesty think necessary?'

'A little yellow,' said the King, firmly. 'Send for the Provost of West Kensington.'

Amid some materialistic protests he was sent for and arrived with his yellow halberdiers in his saffron robes, wiping his forehead with a handkerchief. After all, placed as he was, he had a good deal to say on the matter.

'Welcome, West Kensington,' said the King. 'I have long wished to see you, touching that matter of the Hammersmith land to the south of the Rowton House. Will you hold it feudally from the Provost of Hammersmith? You have only to do him homage by putting his left arm in his overcoat and then marching home in state.'

'No, your Majesty; I'd rather not,' said the Provost of West Kensington, who was a pale young man with a fair moustache and whiskers, who kept a successful dairy.

The King struck him heartily on the shoulder.

'The fierce old West Kensington blood,' he said; 'they are not wise who ask it to do homage.'

Then he glanced again round the room. It was full of a roaring sunset of colour, and he enjoyed the sight, possible to so few artists—the sight of his own dreams moving and blazing before him. In the foreground the yellow of the West Kensington liveries outlined itself against the dark blue draperies of South Kensington. The crests of these again brightened suddenly into green as the almost woodland colours of Bayswater rose behind them. And over and behind all, the great purple plumes of North Kensington showed almost funereal and black.

'There is something lacking,' said the King, 'something lacking.   What can—ah, there it is!—there it is!'

In the doorway had appeared a new figure, a herald in flaming red.   He cried in a loud but unemotional voice:

'The Lord High Provost of Notting Hill desires an audience.'

CHAPTER III

ENTER A LUNATIC

The King of the Fairies, who was, it is to be presumed, the godfather of King Auberon, must have been very favourable on this particular day to his fantastic god-child, for with the entrance of the guard of the Provost of Notting Hill there was a certain more or less inexplicable addition to his delight. The wretched navvies and sandwich-men who carried the colours of Bayswater or South Kensington, engaged merely for the day to satisfy the Royal hobby, slouched into the room with a comparatively hang-dog air, and a great part of the King's intellectual pleasure consisted in the contrast between the arrogance of their swords and feathers and the meek misery of their faces. But these Notting Hill halberdiers in their red tunics belted with gold had the air rather of an absurd gravity. They seemed, so to speak, to be taking part in the joke. They marched and wheeled into position with an almost startling dignity and discipline.

They carried a yellow banner with a great red lion, named by the King as the Notting Hill emblem, after a small public-house in the neighbourhood, which he once frequented.

Between the two lines of his followers there advanced towards the King a tall, red-haired young man, with high features, and bold blue eyes. He would have been called handsome, but that a certain indefinable air of his nose being too big for his face, and his feet for his legs, gave him a look of awkwardness and extreme youth. His robes were red, according to the

King's heraldry, and alone among the Provosts, he was girt with a great sword. This was Adam Wayne, the intractable Provost of Notting Hill.

The King flung himself back in his chair, and rubbed his hands.

'What a day, what a day!' he said to himself. 'Now there'll be a row. I'd no idea it would be such fun as it is. These Provosts are so very indignant, so very reasonable, so very right. This fellow, by the look in his eyes, is even more indignant than the rest. No sign in those large blue eyes, at any rate, of ever having heard of a joke. He'll remonstrate with the others, and they'll remonstrate with him, and they'll all make themselves sumptuously happy remonstrating with me.'

'Welcome, my Lord,' he said aloud. 'What news from the Hill of a Hundred Legends? What have you for the ear of your King? I know that troubles have arisen between you and these others, our cousins, but these troubles it shall be our pride to compose. And I doubt not, and cannot doubt, that your love for me is not less tender, no less ardent than theirs.'

Mr. Buck made a bitter face, and James Barker's nostrils curled; Wilson began to giggle faintly, and the Provost of West Kensington followed in a smothered way. But the big blue eyes of Adam Wayne never changed, and he called out in an odd, boyish voice down the hall:

'I bring homage to my King. I bring him the only thing I have—my sword.'

And with a great gesture he flung it down on the ground, and knelt on one knee behind it.

There was a dead silence.

'I beg your pardon,' said the King, blankly.

'You speak well, sire,' said Adam Wayne, 'as you

ever speak, when you say that my love is not less than
the love of these. Small would it be if it were not
more. For I am the heir of your scheme—the child
of the great Charter. I stand here for the rights the
Charter gave me, and I swear, by your sacred crown,
that where I stand, I stand fast.'

The eyes of all five men stood out of their heads.

Then Buck said, in his jolly, jarring voice: 'Is the
whole world mad?'

The King sprang to his feet, and his eyes blazed.

'Yes,' he cried, in a voice of exultation, 'the whole
world is mad, but Adam Wayne and me. It is true
as death what I told you long ago, James Barker,
seriousness sends men mad. You are mad, because
you care for politics, as mad as a man who collects
tram tickets. Buck is mad, because he cares for money,
as mad as a man who lives on opium. Wilson is mad,
because he thinks himself right, as mad as a man who
thinks himself God Almighty. The Provost of West
Kensington is mad, because he thinks he is respectable,
as mad as a man who thinks he is a chicken. All men
are mad, but the humorist, who cares for nothing and
possesses everything. I thought that there was only
one humorist in England. Fools!—dolts!—open your
cows' eyes; there are two! In Notting Hill—in that
unpromising elevation—there has been born an artist!
You thought to spoil my joke, and bully me out of it,
by becoming more and more modern, more and more
practical, more and more bustling and rational. Oh,
what a feast it was to answer you by becoming more
and more august, more and more gracious, more and
more ancient and mellow! But this lad has seen how
to bowl me out. He has answered me back, vaunt for
vaunt, rhetoric for rhetoric. He has lifted the only

shield I cannot break, the shield of an impenetrable pomposity. Listen to him. You have come, my Lord, about Pump Street?'

'About the city of Notting Hill,' answered Wayne, proudly. 'Of which Pump Street is a living and rejoicing part.'

'Not a very large part,' said Barker, contemptuously.

'That which is large enough for the rich to covet,' said Wayne, drawing up his head, 'is large enough for the poor to defend.'

The King slapped both his legs, and waved his feet for a second in the air.

'Every respectable person in Notting Hill,' cut in Buck, with his cold, coarse voice, 'is for us and against you. I have plenty of friends in Notting Hill.'

'Your friends are those who have taken your gold for other men's hearthstones, my Lord Buck,' said Provost Wayne. 'I can well believe they are your friends.'

'They've never sold dirty toys, anyhow,' said Buck, laughing shortly.

'They've sold dirtier things,' said Wayne, calmly; 'they have sold themselves.'

'It's no good, my Buckling,' said the King, rolling about on his chair. 'You can't cope with this chivalrous eloquence. You can't cope with an artist. You can't cope with the humorist of Notting Hill. O, *Nunc dimittis*—that I have lived to see this day! Provost Wayne, you stand firm?'

'Let them wait and see,' said Wayne. 'If I stood firm before, do you think I shall weaken now that I have seen the face of the King? For I fight for something greater, if greater there can be, than the hearthstones of my people and the Lordship of the Lion.

I fight for your royal vision, for the great dream you dreamt of the League of the Free Cities. You have given me this liberty. If I had been a beggar and you had flung me a coin, if I had been a peasant in a dance and you had flung me a favour, do you think I would have let it be taken by any ruffians on the road? This leadership and liberty of Notting Hill is a gift from your Majesty. And if it is taken from me, by God! it shall be taken in battle, and the noise of that battle shall be heard in the flats of Chelsea and in the studios of St. John's Wood.'

'It is too much—it is too much,' said the King. 'Nature is weak. I must speak to you, brother artist, without further disguise. Let me ask you a solemn question. Adam Wayne, Lord High Provost of Notting Hill, don't you think it splendid?'

'Splendid!' cried Adam Wayne. 'It has the splendour of God.'

'Bowled out again,' said the King. 'You will keep up the pose. Funnily, of course, it is serious. But seriously, isn't it funny?'

'What?' asked Wayne, with the eyes of a baby.

'Hang it all, don't play any more. The whole business—the Charter of the Cities. Isn't it immense?'

'Immense is no unworthy word for that glorious design.'

'Oh, hang you—but, of course, I see. You want me to clear the room of these reasonable sows. You want the two humorists alone together. Leave us, gentlemen.'

Buck threw a sour look at Barker, and at a sullen signal the whole pageant of blue and green, of red, gold, and purple rolled out of the room, leaving only two in the great hall, the King sitting in his seat on the dais, and the red-clad figure still kneeling on the floor before his fallen sword.

The King bounded down the steps and smacked Provost Wayne on the back.

'Before the stars were made,' he cried, 'we were made for each other. It is too beautiful. Think of the valiant independence of Pump Street. That is the real thing. It is the deification of the ludicrous.'

The kneeling figure sprang to his feet with a fierce stagger.

'Ludicrous!' he cried, with a fiery face.

'Oh, come, come,' said the King, impatiently. 'You needn't keep it up with me. The augurs must wink sometimes from sheer fatigue of the eyelids. Let us enjoy this for half an hour, not as actors, but as dramatic critics. Isn't it a joke?'

Adam Wayne looked down like a boy, and answered in a constrained voice:

'I do not understand your Majesty. I cannot believe that while I fight for your royal charter your Majesty deserts me for these dogs of the gold hunt.'

'Oh, damn your—— But what's this? What the devil's this?'

The King stared into the young Provost's face, and in the twilight of the room began to see that his face was quite white and his lip shaking.

'What in God's name is the matter?' cried Auberon, holding his wrist.

Wayne flung back his face, and the tears were shining on it.

'I am only a boy,' he said, 'but it's true. I would paint the Red Lion on my shield if I had only my blood.'

King Auberon dropped the hand and stood without stirring, thunderstruck.

'My God in Heaven!' he said; 'is it possible that there is within the four seas of Britain a man who takes Notting Hill seriously?——'

'And my God in Heaven!' said Wayne passionately; 'is it possible that there is within the four seas of Britain a man who does not take it seriously?'

The King said nothing, but merely went back up the steps of the dais, like a man dazed. He fell back in his chair again and kicked his heels.

'If this sort of thing is to go on,' he said weakly, 'I shall begin to doubt the superiority of art to life. In Heaven's name, do not play with me. Do you really mean that you are——God help me!——a Notting Hill patriot——that you are——'

Wayne made a violent gesture, and the King soothed him wildly.

'All right——all right——I see you are; but let me take it in. You do really propose to fight these modern improvers with their boards and inspectors and surveyors and all the rest of it——'

'Are they so terrible?' asked Wayne, scornfully.

The King continued to stare at him as if he were a human curiosity.

'And I suppose,' he said, 'that you think that the dentists and small tradesmen and maiden ladies who inhabit Notting Hill, will rally with war-hymns to your standard?'

'If they have blood they will,' said the Provost.

'And I suppose,' said the King, with his head back among the cushions, 'that it never crossed your mind that'——his voice seemed to lose itself luxuriantly——'never crossed your mind that any one ever thought that the idea of a Notting Hill idealism was——er——slightly——slightly ridiculous.'

'Of course they think so,' said Wayne. 'What was the meaning of mocking the prophets?'

'Where?' asked the King, leaning forward. 'Where in Heaven's name did you get this miraculously inane idea?'

'You have been my tutor, sire,' said the Provost, 'in all that is high and honourable.'

'Eh?' said the King.

'It was your Majesty who first stirred my dim patriotism into flame. Ten years ago, when I was a boy (I am only nineteen), I was playing on the slope of Pump Street, with a wooden sword and a paper helmet, dreaming of great wars. In an angry trance I struck out with my sword and stood petrified, for I saw that I had struck you, sire, my King, as you wandered in a noble secrecy, watching over your people's welfare. But I need have had no fear. Then was I taught to understand Kingliness. You neither shrank nor frowned. You summoned no guards. You invoked no punishments. But in august and burning words, which are written in my soul, never to be erased, you told me ever to turn my sword against the enemies of my inviolate city. Like a priest pointing to the altar, you pointed to the hill of Notting. "So long," you said, "as you are ready to die for the sacred mountain, even if it were ringed with all the armies of Bayswater." I have not forgotten the words, and I have reason now to remember them, for the hour is come and the crown of your prophecy. The sacred hill is ringed with the armies of Bayswater, and I am ready to die.'

The King was lying back in his chair, a kind of wreck.

'O Lord, Lord, Lord,' he murmured, 'what a life! what a life! All my work! I seem to have done it all.

So you're the red-haired boy that hit me in the waist-coat. What have I done? God, what have I done? I thought I would have a joke, and I have created a passion. I tried to compose a burlesque, and it seems to be turning half-way through into an epic. What is to be done with such a world? In the Lord's name, wasn't the joke broad and bold enough? I abandoned my subtle humour to amuse you, and I seem to have brought tears to your eyes. What's to be done with people when you write a pantomime for them—call the sausages classic festoons, and the policeman cut in two a tragedy of public duty? But why am I talking? Why am I asking questions of a nice young gentleman who is totally mad? What is the good of it? What is the good of anything? O Lord, O Lord!'

Suddenly he pulled himself upright.

'Don't you really think the sacred Notting Hill at all absurd?'

'Absurd?' asked Wayne, blankly. 'Why should I?'

The King stared back equally blankly.

'I beg your pardon?' he said.

'Notting Hill,' said the Provost, simply, 'is a rise or high ground of the common earth, on which men have built houses to live, in which they are born, fall in love, pray, marry, and die. Why should I think it absurd?'

The King smiled.

'Because, my Leonidas——' he began, then suddenly, he knew not how, found his mind was a total blank. After all, why was it absurd? Why was it absurd? He felt as if the floor of his mind had given way. He felt as all men feel when their first principles are hit hard with a question. Barker always felt so when the King said, 'Why trouble about politics?'

The King's thoughts were in a kind of rout; he could not collect them.

'It is generally felt to be a little funny,' he said, vaguely.

'I suppose,' said Adam, turning on him with a fierce suddenness, 'I suppose you fancy crucifixion was a serious affair?'

'Well, I——' began Auberon, 'I admit I have generally thought it had its graver side.'

'Then you are wrong,' said Wayne, with incredible violence. 'Crucifixion is comic. It is exquisitely diverting. It was an absurd and obscene kind of impaling reserved for people who were made to be laughed at —for slaves and provincials—for dentists and small tradesmen, as you would say. I have seen the grotesque gallows-shape, which the little Roman gutter-boys scribbled on walls as a vulgar joke, blazing on the pinnacles of the temples of the world. And shall I turn back?'

The King made no answer.

Adam went on, his voice ringing in the roof.

'This laughter with which men tyrannize is not the great power you think it. Peter was crucified, and crucified head downwards. What could be funnier than the idea of a respectable old Apostle upside down? What could be more in the style of your modern humour? But what was the good of it? Upside down or right side up, Peter was Peter to mankind. Upside down he still hangs over Europe, and millions move and breathe only in the life of his church.'

King Auberon got up absently.

'There is something in what you say,' he said. 'You seem to have been thinking, young man.'

'Only feeling, sire,' answered the Provost. 'I was

born, like other men, in a spot of the earth which I loved because I had played boys' games there, and fallen in love, and talked with my friends through nights that were nights of the gods. And I feel the riddle. These little gardens where we told our loves. These streets where we brought out our dead. Why should they be commonplace? Why should they be absurd? Why should it be grotesque to say that a pillar-box is poetic when for a year I could not see a red pillar-box against the yellow evening in a certain street without being wracked with something of which God keeps the secret, but which is stronger than sorrow or joy? Why should any one be able to raise a laugh by saying "the Cause of Notting Hill"?—Notting Hill, where thousands of immortal spirits blaze with alternate hope and fear.'

Auberon was flicking dust off his sleeve with quite a new seriousness on his face, distinct from the owlish solemnity which was the pose of his humour.

'It is very difficult,' he said at last. 'It is a damned difficult thing. I see what you mean—I agree with you even up to a point—or I should like to agree with you, if I were young enough to be a prophet and poet. I feel a truth in everything you say until you come to the words "Notting Hill". And then I regret to say that the old Adam awakes roaring with laughter and makes short work of the new Adam, whose name is Wayne.'

For the first time Provost Wayne was silent, and stood gazing dreamily at the floor. Evening was closing in, and the room had grown darker.

'I know,' he said, in a strange, almost sleepy voice, 'there is truth in what you say, too. It is hard not to laugh at the common names—I only say we should

not. I have thought of a remedy; but such thoughts
are rather terrible.'

'What thoughts?' asked Auberon.

The Provost of Notting Hill seemed to have fallen
into a kind of trance; in his eyes was an elvish light.

'I know of a magic wand, but it is a wand that only
one or two may rightly use, and only seldom. It is a
fairy wand of great fear, stronger than those who use
it—often frightful, often wicked to use. But whatever
is touched with it is never again wholly common.
Whatever is touched with it takes a magic from outside
the world. If I touch, with this fairy wand, the rail-
ways and the roads of Notting Hill, men will love them,
and be afraid of them for ever.'

'What the devil are you talking about?' asked the
King.

'It has made mean landscapes magnificent, and
hovels outlast cathedrals,' went on the madman. 'Why
should it not make lamp-posts fairer than Greek lamps,
and an omnibus ride like a painted ship? The touch
of it is the finger of a strange perfection.'

'What is your wand?' cried the King, impatiently.

'There it is,' said Wayne; and pointed to the floor,
where his sword lay flat and shining.

'The sword!' cried the King; and sprang up straight
on the dais.

'Yes, yes,' cried Wayne, hoarsely. 'The things
touched by that are not vulgar. The things touched
by that——'

King Auberon made a gesture of horror.

'You will shed blood for that!' he cried. 'For a
cursed point of view——'

'Oh, you kings, you kings,' cried out Adam, in a
burst of scorn. 'How humane you are, how tender,

how considerate. You will make war for a frontier, or the imports of a foreign harbour; you will shed blood for the precise duty on lace, or the salute to an admiral. But for the things that make life itself worthy or miserable—how humane you are. I say here, and I know well what I speak of, there were never any necessary wars but the religious wars. There were never any just wars but the religious wars. There were never any humane wars but the religious wars. For these men were fighting for something that claimed, at least, to be the happiness of a man, the virtue of a man. A Crusader thought, at least, that Islam hurt the soul of every man, king or tinker, that it could really capture. I think Buck and Barker and these rich vultures hurt the soul of every man, hurt every inch of the ground, hurt every brick of the houses, that they can really capture. Do you think I have no right to fight for Notting Hill, you whose English Government has so often fought for tomfooleries? If, as your rich friends say, there are no gods, and the skies are dark above us, what should a man fight for, but the place where he had the Eden of childhood and the short heaven of first love? If no temples and no scriptures are sacred, what is sacred if a man's own youth is not sacred?'

The King walked a little restlessly up and down the dais.

'It is hard,' he said, biting his lips, 'to assent to a view so desperate—so responsible . . .'

As he spoke, the door of the audience chamber fell ajar, and through the aperture came, like the sudden chatter of a bird, the high, nasal, but well-bred voice of Barker.

'I said to him quite plainly—the public interests——

Auberon turned on Wayne with violence.

'What the devil is all this? What am I saying? What are you saying? Have you hypnotized me? Curse your uncanny blue eyes! Let me go. Give me back my sense of humour. Give it me back. Give it me back, I say!'

'I solemnly assure you,' said Wayne, uneasily, with a gesture, as if feeling all over himself, 'that I haven't got it.'

The King fell back in his chair, and went into a roar of Rabelaisian laughter.

'I don't think you have,' he cried.

BOOK III

CHAPTER I

THE MENTAL CONDITION OF ADAM WAYNE

A LITTLE while after the King's accession a small book of poems appeared, called *Hymns on the Hill*. They were not good poems, nor was the book successful, but it attracted a certain amount of attention from one particular school of critics. The King himself, who was a member of the school, reviewed it in his capacity of literary critic to *Straight from the Stables*, a sporting journal. They were known as the Hammock School, because it had been calculated malignantly by an enemy that no less than thirteen of their delicate criticisms had begun with the words, 'I read this book in a hammock: half asleep in the sleepy sunlight, I . . .'; after that there were important differences. Under these conditions they liked everything, but especially everything silly. 'Next to authentic goodness in a book,' they said—'next to authentic goodness in a book (and that, alas! we never find) we desire a rich badness.' Thus it happened that their praise (as indicating the presence of a rich badness) was not universally sought after, and authors became a little disquieted when they found the eye of the Hammock School fixed upon them with peculiar favour.

The peculiarity of *Hymns on the Hill* was the celebration of the poetry of London as distinct from the poetry of the country. This sentiment or affectation was, of course, not uncommon in the twentieth century, nor was it, although sometimes exaggerated, and sometimes artificial, by any means without a great truth at its root, for there is one respect in which a town must be more poetical than the country, since it is closer to the spirit of man; for London, if it be not one of the masterpieces of man, is at least one of his sins. A street is really more poetical than a meadow, because a street has a secret. A street is going some-where, and a meadow nowhere. But, in the case of the book called *Hymns on the Hill*, there was another peculiarity, which the King pointed out with great acumen in his review. He was naturally interested in the matter, for he had himself published a volume of lyrics about London under his pseudonym of 'Daisy Daydream'.

This difference, as the King pointed out, consisted in the fact that, while mere artificers like 'Daisy Daydream' (on whose elaborate style the King, over his signature of 'Thunderbolt', was perhaps somewhat too severe) thought to praise London by comparing it to the country—using nature, that is, as a background from which all poetical images had to be drawn—the more robust author of *Hymns on the Hill* praised the country, or nature, by comparing it to the town, and used the town itself as a background. 'Take', said the critic, 'the typically feminine lines, "To the Inventor of The Hansom Cab"':

'Poet, whose cunning carved this amorous shell,
        Where twain may dwell.'

'Surely,' wrote the King, 'no one but a woman could have written those lines. A woman has always a weakness for nature; with her, art is only beautiful as an echo or shadow of it. She is praising the hansom cab by theme and theory, but her soul is still a child by the sea, picking up shells. She can never be utterly

of the town, as a man can; indeed, do we not speak
(with sacred propriety) of "a man about town"?   Who
ever spoke of a woman about town?   However much,
physically, "about town" a woman may be, she still
models herself on nature; she tries to carry nature with
her; she bids grasses to grow on her head, and furry
beasts to bite her about the throat.   In the heart of a
dim city, she models her hat on a flaring cottage garden
of flowers.   We, with our nobler civic sentiment, model
ours on a chimney-pot; the ensign of civilization.   And
rather than be without birds, she will commit massacre,
that she may turn her head into a tree, with dead birds
to sing on it.'

This kind of thing went on for several pages, and
then the critic remembered his subject, and returned
to it.

> 'Poet, whose cunning carved this amorous shell,
>   Where twain may dwell.'

'The peculiarity of these fine though feminine lines',
continued 'Thunderbolt', 'is, as we have said, that they
praise the hansom cab by comparing it to the shell,
to a natural thing.   Now, hear the author of *Hymns
on the Hill*, and how he deals with the same subject.
In his fine nocturne, entitled "The Last Omnibus", he
relieves the rich and poignant melancholy of the theme
by a sudden sense of rushing at the end:

> 'The wind round the old street corner
>   Swung sudden and quick as a cab.'

'Here the distinction is obvious.   "Daisy Daydream"
thinks it a great compliment to a hansom cab to be
compared to one of the spiral chambers of the sea.
And the author of *Hymns on the Hill* thinks it a great

compliment to the immortal whirlwind to be compared
to a hackney coach. He surely is the real admirer of
London. We have no space to speak of all his perfect
applications of the idea; of the poem in which, for
instance, a lady's eyes are compared, not to stars, but
to two perfect street-lamps guiding the wanderer. We
have no space to speak of the fine lyric, recalling the
Elizabethan spirit, in which the poet, instead of saying
that the rose and the lily contend in her complexion,
says, with a purer modernism, that the red omnibus
of Hammersmith and the white omnibus of Fulham
fight there for the mastery. How perfect the image of
two contending omnibuses!'

Here, somewhat abruptly, the review concluded,
probably because the King had to send off his copy
at that moment, as he was in some want of money.
But the King was a very good critic, whatever he may
have been as King, and he had, to a considerable
extent, hit the right nail on the head. *Hymns on the
Hill* was not at all like the poems originally published
in praise of the poetry of London. And the reason
was that it was really written by a man who had seen
nothing else but London, and who regarded it, therefore, as the universe. It was written by a raw, red-
headed lad of seventeen, named Adam Wayne, who
had been born in Notting Hill. An accident in his
seventh year prevented his being taken away to the
seaside, and thus his whole life had been passed in his
own Pump Street, and in its neighbourhood. And the
consequence was, that he saw the street-lamps as things
quite as eternal as the stars; the two fires were mingled.
He saw the houses as things enduring, like the mountains, and so he wrote about them as one would write
about mountains. Nature puts on a disguise when she

speaks to every man; to this man she put on the disguise
of Notting Hill. Nature would mean to a poet born
in the Cumberland hills, a stormy skyline and sudden
rocks. Nature would mean to a poet born in the
Essex flats, a waste of splendid waters and splendid
sunsets. So nature meant to this man Wayne a line
of violet roofs and lemon lamps, the chiaroscuro of the
town. He did not think it clever or funny to praise
the shadows and colours of the town; he had seen no
other shadows or colours, and so he praised them—
because they were shadows and colours. He saw all
this because he was a poet, though in practice a bad
poet. It is too often forgotten that just as a bad man is
nevertheless a man, so a bad poet is nevertheless a poet.

Mr. Wayne's little volume of verse was a complete
failure; and he submitted to the decision of fate with
a quite rational humility, went back to his work, which
was that of a draper's assistant, and wrote no more.
He still retained his feeling about the town of Notting
Hill, because he could not possibly have any other
feeling, because it was the back and base of his brain.
But he does not seem to have made any particular
attempt to express it or insist upon it.

He was a genuine natural mystic, one of those who
live on the border of fairyland. But he was perhaps
the first to realize how often the boundary of fairyland
runs through a crowded city. Twenty feet from him
(for he was very short-sighted) the red and white and
yellow suns of the gas-lights thronged and melted into
each other like an orchard of fiery trees, the beginning
of the woods of elf-land.

But, oddly enough, it was because he was a small
poet that he came to his strange and isolated triumph.
It was because he was a failure in literature that he

became a portent in English history. He was one of
those to whom nature has given the desire without the
power of artistic expression. He had been a dumb
poet from his cradle. He might have been so to his
grave, and carried unuttered into the darkness a
treasure of new and sensational song. But he was born
under the lucky star of a single coincidence. He happened to be at the head of his dingy municipality at
the time of the King's jest, at the time when all municipalities were suddenly commanded to break out into
banners and flowers. Out of the long procession of
the silent poets who have been passing since the
beginning of the world, this one man found himself
in the midst of an heraldic vision, in which he could
act and speak and live lyrically. While the author and
the victims alike treated the whole matter as a silly
public charade, this one man, by taking it seriously,
sprang suddenly into a throne of artistic omnipotence.
Armour, music, standards, watch-fires, the noise of
drums, all the theatrical properties were thrown before
him. This one poor rhymster, having burnt his own
rhymes, began to live that life of open air and acted
poetry of which all the poets of the earth have dreamed
in vain; the life for which the Iliad is only a cheap
substitute.

Upwards from his abstracted childhood, Adam
Wayne had grown strongly and silently in a certain
quality or capacity which is in modern cities almost
entirely artificial, but which can be natural, and was
primarily almost brutally natural in him, the quality
or capacity of patriotism. It exists, like other virtues
and vices, in a certain undiluted reality. It is not
confused with all kinds of other things. A child speaking of his country or his village may make every

mistake in Mandeville or tell every lie in Munchausen, but in his statement there will be no psychological lies any more than there can be in a good song. Adam Wayne, as a boy, had for his dull streets in Notting Hill the ultimate and ancient sentiment that went out to Athens or Jerusalem. He knew the secret of the passion, those secrets which make real old national songs sound so strange to our civilization. He knew that real patriotism tends to sing about sorrows and forlorn hopes much more than about victory. He knew that in proper names themselves is half the poetry of all national poems. Above all, he knew the supreme psychological fact about patriotism, as certain in connexion with it as that a fine shame comes to all lovers, the fact that the patriot never under any circumstances boasts of the largeness of his country, but always, and of necessity, boasts of the smallness of it.

All this he knew, not because he was a philosopher or a genius, but because he was a child. Any one who cares to walk up a side slum like Pump Street, can see a little Adam claiming to be king of a paving-stone. And he will always be proudest if the stone is almost too narrow for him to keep his feet inside it.

It was while he was in such a dream of defensive battle, marking out some strip of street or fortress of steps as the limit of his haughty claim, that the King had met him, and, with a few words flung in mockery, ratified for ever the strange boundaries of his soul. Thenceforward the fanciful idea of the defence of Notting Hill in war became to him a thing as solid as eating or drinking or lighting a pipe. He disposed his meals for it, altered his plans for it, lay awake in the night and went over it again. Two or three shops were to him an arsenal; an area was to him a moat;

corners of balconies and turns of stone steps were points for the location of a culverin or an archer. It is almost impossible to convey to any ordinary imagination the degree to which he had transmitted the leaden London landscape to a romantic gold. The process began almost in babyhood, and became habitual like a literal madness. It was felt most keenly at night, when London is really herself, when her lights shine in the dark like the eyes of innumerable cats, and the outline of the dark houses has the bold simplicity of blue hills. But for him the night revealed instead of concealing, and he read all the blank hours of morning and afternoon, by a contradictory phrase, in the light of that darkness. To this man, at any rate, the inconceivable had happened. The artificial city had become to him nature, and he felt the kerbstones and gas-lamps as things as ancient as the sky.

One instance may suffice. Walking along Pump Street with a friend, he said, as he gazed dreamily at the iron fence of a little front garden, 'How those railings stir one's blood.'

His friend, who was also a great intellectual admirer, looked at them painfully, but without any particular emotion. He was so troubled about it that he went back quite a large number of times on quiet evenings and stared at the railings, waiting for something to happen to his blood, but without success. At last he took refuge in asking Wayne himself. He discovered that the ecstasy lay in the one point he had never noticed about the railings even after his six visits, the fact that they were like the great majority of others in London, shaped at the top after the manner of a spear. As a child, Wayne had half unconsciously compared them with the spears in pictures of Lancelot and St. George, and had grown up under the shadow of the graphic association. Now, whenever he looked at them, they were simply the serried weapons that made a hedge of steel round the sacred homes of Notting Hill. He could not have cleansed his mind of that meaning even if he tried. It was not a fanciful comparison, or anything like it. It would not have been true to say that the familiar railings reminded him of spears; it would have been far truer to say that the familiar spears occasionally reminded him of railings.

A couple of days after his interview with the King, Adam Wayne was pacing like a caged lion in front of five shops that occupied the upper end of the disputed street. They were a grocer's, a chemist's, a barber's, an old curiosity shop, and a toyshop that sold also newspapers. It was these five shops which his childish fastidiousness had first selected as the essentials of the Notting Hill campaign, the citadel of the city. If Notting Hill was the heart of the universe, and Pump Street was the heart of Notting Hill, this was the heart of Pump Street. The fact that they were all small and side by side realized that feeling for a formidable comfort and compactness which, as we have said, was the heart of his patriotism and of all patriotism. The grocer (who had a wine and spirit licence) was included because he could provision the garrison; the old curiosity shop because it contained enough swords, pistols, partisans, cross-bows, and blunderbusses to arm a whole irregular regiment; the toy-and-paper-shop because Wayne thought a free Press an essential centre for the soul of Pump Street; the chemist's to cope with outbreaks of disease among the besieged; and the barber's because it was in the middle of all the rest, and the barber's son was an intimate friend and spiritual affinity.

It was a cloudless October evening settling down through purple into pure silver around the roofs and chimneys of the steep little street, which looked black and sharp and dramatic. In the deep shadows the gas-lit shop-fronts gleamed like five fires in a row, and before them, darkly outlined like a ghost against some purgatorial furnaces, passed to and fro the tall bird-like figure and eagle nose of Adam Wayne.

He swung his stick restlessly, and seemed fitfully talking to himself.

'There are, after all, enigmas,' he said, 'even to the man who has faith. There are doubts that remain even after the true philosophy is completed in every rung and rivet. And here is one of them. Is the normal human need, the normal human condition, higher or lower than those special states of the soul which call out a doubtful and dangerous glory? those special powers of knowledge or sacrifice which are made possible only by the existence of evil? Which should come first to our affections, the enduring sanities of peace or the half-maniacal virtues of battle? Which should come first, the man great in the daily round or the man great in emergency? Which should come first, to return to the enigma before me, the grocer or the chemist? Which is more certainly the stay of the city, the swift chivalrous chemist or the benignant all-providing grocer? In such ultimate spiritual doubts it is only possible to choose a side by the higher instincts and to abide the issue. In any case, I have made my choice. May I be pardoned if I choose wrongly, but I choose the grocer.'

'Good morning, sir,' said the grocer, who was a

middle-aged man, partially bald, with harsh red whiskers and beard, and forehead lined with all the cares of the small tradesman. 'What can I do for you, sir?'

Wayne removed his hat on entering the shop, with a ceremonious gesture, which, slight as it was, made the tradesman eye him with the beginnings of wonder.

'I come, sir,' he said soberly, 'to appeal to your patriotism.'

'Why, sir,' said the grocer, 'that sounds like the times when I was a boy and we used to have elections.'

'You will have them again,' said Wayne, firmly, 'and far greater things. Listen, Mr. Mead. I know the temptations which a grocer has to a too cosmopolitan philosophy. I can imagine what it must be to sit all day as you do surrounded with wares from all the ends of the earth, from strange seas that we have never sailed and strange forests that we could not even picture. No Eastern king ever had such argosies or such cargoes coming from the sunrise and the sunset, and Solomon in all his glory was not enriched like one of you. India is at your elbow,' he cried, lifting his voice and pointing his stick at a drawer of rice, the grocer making a movement of some alarm, 'China is before you, Demerara is behind you, America is above your head, and at this very moment, like some old Spanish admiral, you hold Tunis in your hands.'

Mr. Mead dropped the box of dates which he was just lifting, and then picked it up again vaguely.

Wayne went on with a heightened colour, but in a lowered voice:

'I know, I say, the temptations of so international, so universal a vision of wealth. I know that it must be your danger not to fall like many tradesmen into too dusty and mechanical a narrowness, but rather to be too broad, to be too general, too liberal. If a narrow nationalism be the danger of the pastrycook, who makes his own wares under his own heavens, no less is cosmopolitanism the danger of the grocer. But I come to you in the name of that patriotism which no wanderings or enlightenments should ever wholly extinguish, and I ask you to remember Notting Hill. For, after all, in this cosmopolitan magnificence, she has played no small part. Your dates may come from the tall palms of Barbary, your sugar from the strange islands of the tropics, your tea from the secret villages of the Empire of the Dragon. That this room might be furnished, forests may have been spoiled under the Southern Cross, and leviathans speared under the Polar Star. But you yourself—surely no inconsiderable treasure—you yourself, the brain that wields these vast interests—you yourself, at least, have grown to strength and wisdom between these grey houses and under this rainy sky. This city which made you, and thus made your fortunes, is threatened with war. Come forth and tell to the ends of the earth this lesson. Oil is from the North and fruits from the South; rices are from India and spices from Ceylon; sheep are from New Zealand and men from Notting Hill.'

The grocer sat for some little while, with dim eyes and his mouth open, looking rather like a fish. Then he scratched the back of his head, and said nothing. Then he said:

'Anything out of the shop, sir?'

Wayne looked round in a dazed way. Seeing a pile of tins of pineapple chunks, he waved his stick generally towards them.

'Yes,' he said, 'I'll take those.'

'All those, sir?' said the grocer, with greatly increased interest.

'Yes, yes; all those,' replied Wayne, still a little bewildered, like a man splashed with cold water.

'Very good, sir; thank you, sir,' said the grocer with animation. 'You may count upon my patriotism, sir.'

'I count upon it already,' said Wayne, and passed out into the gathering night.

The grocer put the box of dates back in its place.

'What a nice fellow he is,' he said. 'It's odd how often they are nice. Much nicer than those as are all right.'

Meanwhile Adam Wayne stood outside the glowing chemist's shop, unmistakably wavering.

'What a weakness it is,' he muttered. 'I have never got rid of it from childhood. The fear of this magic shop. The grocer is rich, he is romantic, he is poetical in the truest sense, but he is not—no, he is not super-natural. But the chemist! All the other shops stand in Notting Hill, but this stands in Elf-land. Look at those great burning bowls of colour. It must be from them that God paints the sunsets. It is superhuman, and the superhuman is all the more uncanny when it is beneficent. That is the root of the fear of God. I am afraid. But I must be a man and enter.'

He was a man, and entered. A short, dark young man was behind the counter with spectacles, and greeted him with a bright but entirely business-like smile.

'A fine evening, sir,' he said.

'Fine, indeed, strange Father,' said Adam, stretching his hands somewhat forward. 'It is on such clear and mellow nights that your shop is most itself. Then they appear most perfect, those moons of green and gold and crimson, which from afar, oft guide the pilgrim of pain and sickness to this house of merciful witchcraft.'

'Can I get you anything?' asked the chemist.

'Let me see,' said Wayne, in a friendly but vague manner. 'Let me have some sal volatile.'

'Eightpence, tenpence, or one and sixpence a bottle?' said the young man genially.

'One and six—one and six,' replied Wayne, with a wild submissiveness. 'I come to ask you, Mr. Bowles, a terrible question.'

He paused and collected himself.

'It is necessary,' he muttered—'it is necessary to be tactful, and to suit the appeal to each profession in turn.

'I come,' he resumed aloud, 'to ask you a question which goes to the roots of your miraculous toils. Mr. Bowles, shall all this witchery cease?' And he waved his stick around the shop.

Meeting with no answer, he continued with animation:

'In Notting Hill we have felt to its core the elfish mystery of your profession. And now Notting Hill itself is threatened.'

'Anything more, sir?' asked the chemist.

'Oh,' said Wayne, somewhat disturbed—'oh, what is it chemists sell? Quinine, I think. Thank you. Shall it be destroyed? I have met these men of Bayswater and North Kensington—Mr. Bowles, they are materialists. They see no witchery in your work, even when it is brought within their own borders. They think the chemist is commonplace. They think him human.'

The chemist appeared to pause, only a moment, to take in the insult, and immediately said:

'And the next article, please?'

'Alum,' said the Provost, wildly. 'I resume. It is in this sacred town alone that your priesthood is reverenced. Therefore, when you fight for us you fight not only for yourself, but for everything you typify. You fight not only for Notting Hill, but for Fairyland, for as surely as Buck and Barker and such men hold sway, the sense of Fairyland in some strange manner diminishes.'

'Anything more, sir?' asked Mr. Bowles, with unbroken cheerfulness.

'Oh, yes, jujubes—Gregory powder—magnesia. The danger is imminent. In all this matter I have felt that I fought not merely for my own city (though to that I owe all my blood), but for all places in which these great ideas could prevail. I am fighting not merely for Notting Hill, but for Bayswater itself; for North Kensington itself. For if the gold-hunters prevail, these also will lose all their ancient sentiments and all the mystery of their national soul. I know I can count upon you.'

'Oh, yes, sir,' said the chemist, with great animation, 'we are always glad to oblige a good customer.'

Adam Wayne went out of the shop with a deep sense of fulfilment of soul.

'It is so fortunate,' he said, 'to have tact, to be able to play upon the peculiar talents and specialities, the cosmopolitanism of the grocer and the world-old necromancy of the chemist. Where should I be without tact?'

CHAPTER II

THE REMARKABLE MR. TURNBULL

AFTER two more interviews with shopmen, however, the patriot's confidence in his own psychological diplomacy began vaguely to wane. Despite the care with which he considered the peculiar rationale and the peculiar glory of each separate shop, there seemed to be something unresponsive about the shopmen. Whether it was a dark resentment against the uninitiate for peeping into their masonic magnificence, he could not quite conjecture.

His conversation with the man who kept the shop of curiosities had begun encouragingly. The man who kept the shop of curiosities had indeed enchanted him with a phrase. He was standing drearily at the door of his shop, a wrinkled man with a grey pointed beard, evidently a gentleman who had come down in the world.

'And how does your commerce go, you strange guardian of the past?' said Wayne, affably.

'Well, sir, not very well,' replied the man, with that patient voice of his class which is one of the most heart-breaking things in the world. 'Things are terribly quiet.'

Wayne's eyes shone suddenly.

'A great saying,' he said, 'worthy of a man whose merchandise is human history. Terribly quiet; that is in two words the spirit of this age, as I have felt it from my cradle. I sometimes wondered how many other people felt the oppression of this union between quietude and terror. I see blank well-ordered streets and men in black moving about inoffensively, sullenly.

It goes on day after day, day after day, and nothing happens; but to me it is like a dream from which I might wake screaming. To me the straightness of our life is the straightness of a thin cord stretched tight. Its stillness is terrible. It might snap with a noise like thunder. And you who sit, amid the *débris* of the great wars, you who sit, as it were, upon a battlefield, you know that war was less terrible than this evil peace; you know that the idle lads who carried those swords under Francis or Elizabeth, the rude Squire or Baron who swung that mace about in Picardy or Northumberland battles, may have been terribly noisy, but were not like us, terribly quiet.'

Whether it was a faint embarrassment of conscience as to the original source and date of the weapons referred to, or merely an engrained depression, the guardian of the past looked, if anything, a little more worried.

'But I do not think,' continued Wayne, 'that this horrible silence of modernity will last, thought I think for the present it will increase. What a farce is this modern liberality. Freedom of speech means practically in our modern civilization that we must only talk about unimportant things. We must not talk about religion, for that is illiberal; we must not talk about bread and cheese, for that is talking shop; we must not talk about death, for that is depressing; we must not talk about birth, for that is indelicate. It cannot last. Something must break this strange indifference, this strange dreamy egoism, this strange loneliness of millions in a crowd. Something must break it. Why should it not be you and I? Can you do nothing else but guard relics?'

The shopman wore a gradually clearing expression,

which would have led those unsympathetic with the
cause of the Red Lion to think that the last sentence was
the only one to which he had attached any meaning.

'I am rather old to go into a new business,' he said,
'and I don't quite know what to be either.'

'Why not, said Wayne, gently, having reached the
crisis of his delicate persuasion—'why not be a Colonel?'

It was at this point, in all probability, that the
interview began to yield more disappointing results.
The man appeared inclined at first to regard the
suggestion of becoming a Colonel as outside the sphere
of immediate and relevant discussion. A long exposition of the inevitable war of independence, coupled
with the purchase of a doubtful sixteenth-century sword
for an exaggerated price, seemed to resettle matters.
Wayne left the shop, however, somewhat infected with
the melancholy of its owner.

That melancholy was completed at the barber's.

'Shaving, sir?' inquired that artist from inside his
shop.

'War!' replied Wayne, standing on the threshold.

'I beg your pardon,' said the other, sharply.

'War!' said Wayne, warmly. 'But not for anything
inconsistent with the beautiful and the civilized arts.
War for beauty. War for society. War for peace.
A great chance is offered you of repelling that slander
which, in defiance of the lives of so many artists,
attributes poltroonery to those who beautify and polish
the surface of our lives. Why should not hairdressers
be heroes? Why should not——'

'Now, you get out,' said the barber, irascibly. 'We
don't want any of your sort here. You get out.'

And he came forward with the desperate annoyance
of a mild person when enraged.

Adam Wayne laid his hand for a moment on the sword, then dropped it.

'Notting Hill,' he said, 'will need her bolder sons'; and he turned gloomily to the toyshop.

It was one of those queer little shops so constantly seen in the side-streets of London, which must be called toyshops only because toys upon the whole predominate; for the remainder of goods seem to consist of almost everything else in the world—tobacco, exercise-books, sweetstuff, novelettes, halfpenny paper clips, halfpenny pencil sharpeners, bootlaces, and cheap fireworks. It also sold newspapers, and a row of dirty-looking posters hung along the front of it.

'I am afraid,' said Wayne, as he entered, 'that I am not getting on with these tradesmen as I should. Is it that I have neglected to rise to the full meaning of their work? Is there some secret buried in each of these shops which no mere poet can discover?'

He stepped to the counter with a depression which he rapidly conquered as he addressed the man on the other side of it—a man of short stature, and hair prematurely white, and the look of a large baby.

'Sir,' said Wayne, 'I am going from house to house in this street of ours, seeking to stir up some sense of the danger which now threatens our city. Nowhere have I felt my duty so difficult as here. For the toy-shop keeper has to do with all that remains to us of Eden before the first wars began. You sit here meditating continually upon the wants of that wonderful time when every staircase leads to the stars, and every garden-path to the other end of nowhere. Is it thoughtlessly, do you think, that I strike the dark old drum of peril in the paradise of children? But consider a moment; do not condemn me hastily. Even that paradise itself contains the rumour or beginning of that danger, just as the Eden that was made for perfection contained the terrible tree. For judge childhood, even by your own arsenal of its pleasures. You keep bricks; you make yourself thus, doubtless, the witness of the constructive instinct older than the destructive. You keep dolls; you make yourself the priest of that divine idolatry. You keep Noah's Arks; you perpetuate the memory of the salvation of all life as a precious, an irreplaceable thing. But do you keep only, sir, the symbols of this prehistoric sanity, this childish rationality of the earth? Do you not keep more terrible things? What are those boxes, seemingly of lead soldiers, that I see in that glass case? Are they not witnesses to that terror and beauty, that desire for a lovely death, which could not be excluded even from the immortality of Eden? Do not despise the lead soldiers, Mr. Turnbull.'

'I don't,' said Mr. Turnbull, of the toyshop, shortly, but with great emphasis.

'I am glad to hear it,' replied Wayne. 'I confess that I feared for my military schemes the awful innocence of your profession. How, I thought to myself, will this man, used only to the wooden swords that give pleasure, think of the steel swords that give pain? But I am at least partly reassured. Your tone suggests to me that I have at least the entry of a gate of your fairyland—the gate through which the soldiers enter, for it cannot be denied—I ought, sir, no longer to deny, that it is of soldiers that I come to speak. Let your gentle employment make you merciful towards the troubles of the world. Let your own silvery experience tone down our sanguine sorrows. For there is war in Notting Hill.'

The little toyshop keeper sprang up suddenly, slapping his fat hands like two fans on the counter.

'War?' he cried. 'Not really, sir? Is it true? Oh, what a joke! Oh, what a sight for sore eyes!'

Wayne was almost taken aback by this outburst.

'I am delighted,' he stammered. 'I had no notion——'

He sprang out of the way just in time to avoid Mr. Turnbull, who took a flying leap over the counter and dashed to the front of the shop.

'You look here, sir,' he said; 'you just look here.'

He came back with two of the torn posters in his hand which were flapping outside his shop.

'Look at those, sir,' he said, and flung them down on the counter.

Wayne bent over them, and read on one:

'LAST FIGHTING.

REDUCTION OF THE CENTRAL DERVISH CITY.

REMARKABLE, ETC.'

On the other he read:

'LAST SMALL REPUBLIC ANNEXED.

NICARAGUAN CAPITAL SURRENDERS AFTER A
MONTH'S FIGHTING.

GREAT SLAUGHTER.'

Wayne bent over them again, evidently puzzled; then he looked at the dates. They were both dated in August fifteen years before.

'Why do you keep these old things?' he said, startled entirely out of his absurd tact of mysticism. 'Why do you hang them outside your shop?'

'Because,' said the other, simply, 'they are the records

of the last war. You mentioned war just now. It happens to be my hobby.'

Wayne lifted his large blue eyes with an infantile wonder.

'Come with me,' said Turnbull, shortly, and led him into a parlour at the back of the shop.

In the centre of the parlour stood a large deal table. On it were set rows and rows of the tin and lead soldiers which were part of the shopkeeper's stock. The visitor would have thought nothing of it if it had not been for a certain odd grouping of them, which did not seem either entirely commercial or entirely haphazard.

'You are acquainted, no doubt,' said Turnbull, turning his big eyes upon Wayne—'you are acquainted, no doubt, with the arrangement of the American and Nicaraguan troops in the last battle.' And he waved his hand towards the table.

'I am afraid not,' said Wayne. 'I——'

'Ah, you were at that time occupied too much, perhaps, with the Dervish affair. You will find it in this corner.' And he pointed to a part of the floor where there was another arrangement of children's soldiers grouped here and there.

'You seem,' said Wayne, 'to be interested in military matters.'

'I am interested in nothing else,' answered the toy-shop keeper, simply.

Wayne appeared convulsed with a singular, suppressed excitement.

'In that case,' he said, 'I may approach you with an unusual degree of confidence. Touching the matter of the defence of Notting Hill, I——'

'Defence of Notting Hill? Yes, sir. This way, sir,

said Turnbull, with great perturbation. 'Just step into this side room'; and he led Wayne into another apartment, in which the table was entirely covered with an arrangement of children's bricks. A second glance at it told Wayne that the bricks were arranged in the form of a precise and perfect plan of Notting Hill. 'Sir,' said Turnbull, impressively, 'you have, by a kind of accident, hit upon the whole secret of my life. As a boy, I grew up among the last wars of the world, when Nicaragua was taken and the dervishes wiped out. And I adopted it as a hobby, sir, as you might adopt astronomy or bird-stuffing. I had no ill-will to any one, but I was interested in war as a science, as a game. And suddenly I was bowled out. The big Powers of the world, having swallowed up all the small ones, came to that confounded agreement, and there was no more war. There was nothing more for me to do but to do what I do now—to read the old campaigns in dirty old newspapers, and to work them out with tin soldiers. One other thing had occurred to me. I thought it an amusing fancy to make a plan of how this district of ours ought to be defended if it were ever attacked. It seems to interest you, too.'

'If it were ever attacked,' repeated Wayne, awed into an almost mechanical enunciation. 'Mr. Turnbull, it is attacked. Thank heaven, I am bringing to at least one human being the news that is at bottom the only good news to any son of Adam. Your life has not been useless. Your work has not been play. Now, when the hair is already grey on your head, Turnbull, you shall have your youth. God has not destroyed it, He has only deferred it. Let us sit down here, and you shall explain to me this military map of

Notting Hill. For you and I have to defend Notting Hill together.'

Mr. Turnbull looked at the other for a moment, then hesitated, and then sat down beside the bricks and the stranger. He did not rise again for seven hours, when the dawn broke.

ō   ○   ●   ●   ●

The headquarters of Provost Adam Wayne and his Commander-in-Chief consisted of a small and somewhat unsuccessful milk-shop at the corner of Pump Street. The blank white morning had only just begun to break over the blank London buildings when Wayne and Turnbull were to be found seated in the cheerless and unswept shop. Wayne had something feminine in his character; he belonged to that class of persons who forget their meals when anything interesting is in hand. He had had nothing for sixteen hours but hurried glasses of milk, and, with a glass standing empty beside him, he was writing and sketching and dotting and crossing out with inconceivable rapidity with a pencil and a piece of paper. Turnbull was of that more masculine type in which a sense of responsibility increases the appetite, and with his sketch-map beside him he was dealing strenuously with a pile of sandwiches in a paper packet, and a tankard of ale from the tavern opposite, whose shutters had just been taken down. Neither of them spoke, and there was no sound in the living stillness except the scratching of Wayne's pencil and the squealing of an aimless-looking cat. At length Wayne broke the silence by saying:

"Seventeen pounds, eight shillings and ninepence.'

Turnbull nodded and put his head in the tankard.

'That,' said Wayne, 'is not counting the five pounds you took yesterday. What did you do with it?'

'Ah, that is rather interesting!' replied Turnbull, with his mouth full. 'I used that five pounds in a kindly and philanthropic act.'

Wayne was gazing with mystification in his queer and innocent eyes.

'I used that five pounds,' continued the other, 'in giving no less than forty little London boys rides in hansom cabs.'

'Are you insane?' asked the Provost.

'It is only my light touch,' returned Turnbull. 'These hansom-cab rides will raise the tone—raise the tone, my dear fellow—of our London youths, widen their horizon, brace their nervous system, make them acquainted with the various public monuments of our great city. Education, Wayne, education. How many excellent thinkers have pointed out that political reform is useless until we produce a cultured populace. So that twenty years hence, when these boys are grown up——'

'Mad!' said Wayne, laying down his pencil; 'and five pounds gone!'

'You are in error,' explained Turnbull. 'You grave creatures can never be brought to understand how much quicker work really goes with the assistance of nonsense and good meals. Stripped of its decorative beauties, my statement was strictly accurate. Last night I gave forty half-crowns to forty little boys, and sent them all over London to take hansom cabs. I told them in every case to tell the cabman to bring them to this spot. In half an hour from now the declaration of war will be posted up. At the same time the cabs will have begun to come in, you will have ordered out the guard, the little boys will drive up in state, we shall commandeer the horses for cavalry, use the cabs for barricade, and give the men the choice between serving in our ranks and detention in our basements and cellars. The little boys we can use as scouts. The main thing is that we start the war with an advantage unknown in all the other armies— horses. And now,' he said, finishing his beer, 'I will go and drill the troops.'

And he walked out of the milk-shop, leaving the Provost staring.

A minute or two afterwards, the Provost laughed. He only laughed once or twice in his life, and then he did it in a queer way as if it were an art he had not mastered. Even he saw something funny in the preposterous coup of the half-crowns and the little boys. He did not see the monstrous absurdity of the whole policy and the whole war. He enjoyed it seriously as a crusade, that is, he enjoyed it far more than any joke can be enjoyed. Turnbull enjoyed it partly as a joke, even more perhaps as a reversion from the things he hated—modernity and monotony and civilization. To break up the vast machinery of modern life and use the fragments as engines of war, to make the barricade of omnibuses and points of vantage of chimney-pots, was to him a game worth infinite risk and trouble. He had that rational and deliberate preference which will always to the end trouble the peace of the world, the rational and deliberate preference for a short life and a merry one.

CHAPTER III

THE EXPERIMENT OF MR. BUCK

AN earnest and eloquent petition was sent up to the King signed with the names of Wilson, Barker, Buck, Swindon, and others. It urged that at the forth-coming conference to be held in his Majesty's presence touching the final disposition of the property in Pump Street, it might be held not inconsistent with political decorum and with the unutterable respect they enter-tained for his Majesty if they appeared in ordinary morning-dress, without the costume decreed for them as Provosts. So it happened that the company appeared at that council in frock-coats and that the King himself limited his love of ceremony to appearing (after his not unusual manner), in evening dress with one order—in this case not the Garter, but the button of the Club of Old Clipper's Best Pals, a decoration obtained (with difficulty) from a halfpenny boy's paper. Thus also it happened that the only spot of colour in the room was Adam Wayne, who entered in great dignity with the great red robes and the great sword.

'We have met,' said Auberon, 'to decide the most arduous of modern problems. May we be successful.' And he sat down gravely.

Buck turned his chair a little and flung one leg over the other.

'Your Majesty,' he said, quite good-humouredly, 'there is only one thing I can't understand, and that is why this affair is not settled in five minutes. Here's a small property which is worth a thousand to us and is not worth a hundred to any one else. We offer the thousand. It's not business-like, I know, for we ought to get it for less, and it's not reasonable and it's not fair on us, but I'm damned if I can see why it's difficult.'

'The difficulty may be very simply stated,' said Wayne. 'You may offer a million and it will be very difficult for you to get Pump Street.'

'But, look here, Mr. Wayne,' cried Barker, striking in with a kind of cold excitement. 'Just look here. You've no right to take up a position like that. You've a right to stand out for a bigger price, but you aren't doing that. You're refusing what you and every sane man knows to be a splendid offer simply from malice or spite—it must be malice or spite. And that kind of thing is really criminal; it's against the public good. The King's Government would be justified in forcing you.'

With his lean fingers spread on the table he stared anxiously at Wayne's face, which did not move.

'In forcing you . . . it would,' he repeated.

'It shall,' said Buck, shortly, turning to the table with a jerk. 'We have done our best to be decent.'

Wayne lifted his large eyes slowly.

'Was it my Lord Buck,' he inquired, 'who said that the King of England "shall" do something?'

Buck flushed and said testily:

'I mean it must—it ought to, as I say we've done our best to be generous. I defy any one to deny it. As it is Mr. Wayne, I don't want to say a word that's uncivil. I hope it's not uncivil to say that you can be, and ought to be, in jail. It is criminal to stop public works for a whim. A man might as well burn ten thousand onions in his front garden or bring up his children to run naked in the street, as do what you say you have a right to do. People have been compelled to sell before now. The King could compel you, and I hope he will.'

'Until he does,' said Wayne, calmly, 'the power and Government of this great nation is on my side and not yours, and I defy you to defy it.'

'In what sense,' cried Barker, with his feverish eyes and hands, 'is the Government on your side?'

With one ringing movement Wayne unrolled a great parchment on the table. It was decorated down the sides with wild water-colour sketches of vestrymen in crowns and wreaths.

'The Charter of the Cities,' he began.

Buck exploded in a brutal oath and laughed.

'That tomfool's joke. Haven't we had enough——'

'And there you sit,' cried Wayne, springing erect and with a voice like a trumpet, 'with no argument but to insult the King before his face.'

Buck rose also with blazing eyes.

'I am hard to bully,' he began—and the slow tones of the King struck in with incomparable gravity:

'My Lord Buck, I must ask you to remember that your King is present. It is not often that he needs to protect himself among his subjects.'

Barker turned to him with frantic gestures.

'For God's sake don't back up the madman now,' he implored. 'Have your joke another time. Oh, for Heaven's sake——'

'My Lord Provost of South Kensington,' said King Auberon, steadily. 'I do not follow your remarks which are uttered with a rapidity unusual at Court. Nor do your well-meant efforts to convey the rest with your fingers materially assist me. I say that my Lord Provost of North Kensington, to whom I spoke, ought

not in the presence of his Sovereign to speak disrespectfully of his Sovereign's ordinances. Do you
disagree?'

Barker turned restlessly in his chair, and Buck
cursed without speaking. The King went on in a
comfortable voice:

'My Lord Provost of Notting Hill, proceed.'

Wayne turned his blue eyes on the King, and to
every one's surprise there was a look in them not of
triumph, but of a certain childish distress.

'I am sorry, your Majesty,' he said; 'I fear I was
more than equally to blame with the Lord Provost of
North Kensington. We were debating somewhat
eagerly, and we both rose to our feet. I did so first,
I am ashamed to say. The Provost of North Kensington is, therefore, comparatively innocent. I beseech
your Majesty to address your rebuke chiefly, at least,
to me. Mr. Buck is not innocent, for he did no doubt,
in the heat of the moment, speak disrespectfully. But
the rest of the discussion he seems to me to have
conducted with great good temper.'

Buck looked genuinely pleased, for business men are
all simple-minded, and have therefore that degree
of communion with fanatics. The King, for some
reason, looked, for the first time in his life, ashamed.

'This very kind speech of the Provost of Notting
Hill,' began Buck, pleasantly, 'seems to me to show
that we have at last got on to a friendly footing. Now
come, Mr. Wayne. Five hundred pounds have been
offered to you for a property you admit not to be
worth a hundred. Well, I am a rich man and I won't
be outdone in generosity. Let us say fifteen hundred
pounds, and have done with it. And let us shake
hands.' And he rose, glowing and laughing.

'Fifteen hundred pounds,' whispered Mr. Wilson of Bayswater; 'can we do fifteen hundred pounds?'

'I'll stand the racket,' said Buck heartily. 'Mr. Wayne is a gentleman and has spoken up for me. So I suppose the negotiations are at an end.'

Wayne bowed.

'They are indeed at an end. I am sorry I cannot sell you the property.'

'What?' cried Mr. Barker, starting to his feet.

'Mr. Buck has spoken correctly,' said the King.

'I have, I have,' cried Buck, springing up also; 'I said——'

'Mr. Buck has spoken correctly,' said the King; 'the negotiations are at an end.'

All the men at the table rose to their feet; Wayne alone rose without excitement.

'Have I, then,' he said, 'your Majesty's permission to depart? I have given my last answer.'

'You have it,' said Auberon, smiling, but not lifting his eyes from the table. And amid a dead silence the Provost of Notting Hill passed out of the room.

'Well?' said Wilson, turning round to Barker, 'Well?'

Barker shook his head desperately.

'The man ought to be in an asylum,' he said. 'But one thing is clear, we need not bother further about him. The man can be treated as mad.'

'Of course,' said Buck, turning to him with sombre decisiveness. 'You're perfectly right, Barker. He is a good enough fellow, but he can be treated as mad. Let's put it in simple form. Go and tell any twelve men in any town, go and tell any doctor in any town, that there is a man offered fifteen hundred pounds for a thing he could sell commonly for four hundred, and that when asked for a reason for not accepting it he pleads the inviolate sanctity of Notting Hill and calls it the Holy Mountain. What would they say? What more can we have on our side than the common sense of everybody? On what else do all laws rest? I'll tell you, Barker, what's better than any further discussion. Let's send in workmen on the spot to pull down Pump Street. And if old Wayne says a word, arrest him as a lunatic. That's all."

Barker's eyes kindled.

'I always regarded you, Buck, if you don't mind my saying so, as a very strong man. I'll follow you.'

'So, of course, will I,' said Wilson.

Buck rose again impulsively.

'Your Majesty,' he said, glowing with popularity, 'I beseech your Majesty to consider favourably the proposal to which we have committed ourselves. Your Majesty's leniency, our own offers, have fallen in vain on that extraordinary man. He may be right. He may be God. He may be the devil. But we think it, for practical purposes, more probable that he is off his head. Unless that assumption were acted on, all human affairs would go to pieces. We act on it, and we propose to start operations in Notting Hill at once.'

The King leaned back in his chair.

'The Charter of the Cities . . .' he said with a rich intonation.

But Buck, being finally serious, was also cautious, and did not again make the mistake of disrespect.

'Your Majesty,' he said, bowing, 'I am not here to say a word against anything your Majesty has said or done. You are a far better educated man than I, and no doubt there were reasons, upon intellectual grounds, for those proceedings. But may I ask you and appeal to your common good-nature for a sincere answer? When you drew up the Charter of the Cities did you contemplate the rise of a man like Adam Wayne? Did you expect that the Charter—whether it was an experiment, or a scheme of decoration, or a joke—could ever really come to this—to stopping a vast scheme of ordinary business, to shutting up a road, to spoiling the chances of cabs, omnibuses, railway stations, to disorganizing half a city, to risking a kind of civil war? Whatever were your objects, were they that?'

Barker and Wilson looked at him admiringly; the King more admiringly still.

"Provost Buck," said Auberon, 'you speak in public uncommonly well. I give you your point with the magnanimity of an artist. My scheme did not include the appearance of Mr. Wayne. Alas! would that my poetic power had been great enough.'

'I thank your Majesty,' said Buck, courteously but quickly. 'Your Majesty's statements are always clear and studied: therefore I may draw a deduction. As the scheme, whatever it was, on which you set your heart did not include the appearance of Mr. Wayne, it will survive his removal. Why not let us clear away this particular Pump Street, which does interfere with our plans, and which does not, by your Majesty's own statement, interfere with yours.'

'Caught out!' said the King, enthusiastically and quite impersonally, as if he were watching a cricket match.

'This man Wayne,' continued Buck, 'would be shut up by any doctors in England. But we only ask to have it put before them. Meanwhile no one's interests, not even in all probability his own, can be really damaged by going on with the improvements in Notting Hill. Not our interests, of course, for it has been the hard and quiet work of ten years. Not the interests of Notting Hill, for nearly all its educated inhabitants desire the change. Not the interests of your Majesty, for you say, with characteristic sense, that you never contemplated the rise of the lunatic at all. Not, as I say, his own interests, for the man has a kind heart and many talents, and a couple of good doctors would probably put him righter than all the free cities and sacred mountains in creation. I therefore assume, if I may use so bold a word, that your Majesty will not offer any obstacle to our proceeding with the improvements.'

And Mr. Buck sat down amid subdued but excited applause among the allies.

'Mr. Buck,' said the King, 'I beg your pardon, for a number of beautiful and sacred thoughts, in which you were generally classified as a fool. But there is another thing to be considered. Suppose you send in your workmen, and Mr. Wayne does a thing regrettable indeed, but of which, I am sorry to say, I think him quite capable—knocks their teeth out.'

'I have thought of that, your Majesty,' said Mr. Buck, easily, 'and I think it can simply be guarded against. Let us send in a strong guard of say a hundred men—a hundred of the North Kensington Halberdiers' (he smiled grimly), 'of whom your Majesty is so fond. Or say—a hundred and fifty. The whole population of Pump Street, I fancy, is only about a hundred.

'Still they might stand together and lick you,' said the King, dubiously.

'Then say two hundred,' said Buck, gaily.

'It might happen,' said the King, restlessly, 'that one Notting Hiller fought better than two North Kensingtons.'

'It might,' said Buck, coolly; 'then say two hundred and fifty.'

The King bit his lip.

'And if they are beaten, too,' he said viciously.

'Your Majesty,' said Buck, and leaned back easily in his chair, 'suppose they are. If anything be clear, it is clear that all fighting matters are mere matters of arithmetic. Here we have a hundred and fifty say of Notting Hill soldiers. Or say two hundred. If one of them can fight two of us—we can send in, not four hundred, but six hundred, and smash him. That is all. It is out of all immediate probability that one of them could fight four of us. So what I say is this. Run no risks. Finish it at once. Send in eight hundred men and smash him—smash him almost without seeing him. And go on with the improvements.'

And Mr. Buck pulled out a bandanna and blew his nose.

'Do you know, Mr. Buck,' said the King, staring gloomily at the table, 'the admirable clearness of your reason produces in my mind a sentiment which I trust I shall not offend you by describing as an aspiration to punch your head. You irritate me sublimely. What can it be in me? Is it the relic of a moral sense?'

'But your Majesty,' said Barker, eagerly and suavely, 'does not refuse our proposals?'

'My dear Barker, your proposals are as damnable as your manners. I want to have nothing to do with them. Suppose I stopped them altogether. What would happen?'

Barker answered in a very low voice:

'Revolution.'

The King glanced quickly at the men around the table. They were all looking down silently: their brows were red.

He rose with a startling suddenness, and an unusual pallor.

'Gentlemen,' he said, 'you have overruled me. Therefore I can speak plainly. I think Adam Wayne, who is as mad as a hatter, worth more than a million of you. But you have the force, and, I admit, the common sense, and he is lost. Take your eight hundred halberdiers and smash him. It would be more sportsmanlike to take two hundred.'

'More sportsmanlike,' said Buck, grimly, 'but a great deal less humane. We are not artists, and streets purple with gore do not catch our eye in the right way.'

'It is pitiful,' said Auberon. 'With five or six times their number there will be no fight at all.'

'I hope not,' said Buck, rising and adjusting his gloves. 'We desire no fight, your Majesty. We are peaceable business men.'

'Well,' said the King, wearily, 'the conference is at an end at last.'

And he went out of the room before any one else could stir.

.   .   .   .   .

Forty workmen, a hundred Bayswater Halberdiers, two hundred from South, and three from North Kensington, assembled at the foot of Holland Walk and marched up it, under the general direction of Barker, who looked flushed and happy in full dress.

At the end of the procession a small and sulky figure lingered like an urchin. It was the King.

'Barker,' he said at length, appealingly, 'you are an old friend of mine—you understand my hobbies as I understand yours. Why can't you let it alone? I hoped that such fun might come out of this Wayne business. Why can't you let it alone? It doesn't really so much matter to you—what's a road or so? For me it's the one joke that may save me from pessimism. Take fewer men and give me an hour's fun. Really and truly, James, if you collected coins or humming-birds, and I could buy one with the price of your road, I would buy it. I collect incidents—those rare, those precious things. Let me have one. Pay a few pounds for it. Give these Notting Hillers a chance. Let them alone.'

'Auberon,' said Barker, kindly, forgetting all royal titles in a rare moment of sincerity, 'I do feel what you mean. I have had moments when these hobbies have hit me. I have had moments when I have sympathized with your humours. I have had moments, though you may not easily believe it, when I have sympathized with the madness of Adam Wayne. But the world, Auberon, the real world, is not run on these hobbies. It goes on great brutal wheels of facts— wheels on which you are the butterfly. And Wayne is the fly on the wheel.'

Auberon's eyes looked frankly at the other's.

'Thank you, James; what you say is true. It is only a parenthetical consolation to me to compare the intelligence of flies somewhat favourably with the intelligence of wheels. But it is the nature of flies to die soon, and the nature of wheels to go on for ever. Go on with the wheel. Good-bye, old man.'

And James Barker went on, laughing, with a high colour, slapping his bamboo on his leg.

The King watched the tail of the retreating regiment with a look of genuine depression, which made him seem more like a baby than ever. Then he swung round and struck his hands together.

'In a world without humour,' he said, 'the only thing to do is to eat. And how perfect an exception! How can these people strike dignified attitudes, and pretend that things matter, when the total ludicrousness of life is proved by the very method by which it is supported? A man strikes the lyre, and says, "Life is real, life is earnest", and then goes into a room and stuffs alien substances into a hole in his head. I think Nature was indeed a little broad in her humour in these matters. But we all fall back on the pantomime, as I have in this municipal affair. Nature has her farces, like the act of eating or the shape of the kangaroo, for the more brutal appetite. She keeps her stars and mountains for those who can appreciate something more subtly ridiculous.' He turned to his equerry. 'But as I said "eating", let us have a picnic like two nice little children. Just run and bring me a table and a dozen courses or so, and plenty of champagne, and under these swinging boughs, Bowler, we will return to Nature.'

It took about an hour to erect in Holland Lane the monarch's simple repast, during which time he walked up and down and whistled, but still with an unaffected air of gloom. He had really been done out of a pleasure he had promised himself, and had that empty and sickened feeling which a child has when disappointed of a pantomime. When he and the equerry had sat down, however, and consumed a fair amount of dry champagne, his spirits began mildly to revive.

'Things take too long in this world,' he said. 'I detest all this Barkerian business about evolution and the gradual modification of things. I wish the world had been made in six days, and knocked to pieces again in six more. And I wish I had done it. The joke's good enough in a broad way, sun and moon and the image of God, and all that, but they keep it up so damnably long. Did you ever long for a miracle, Bowler?'

'No, sir,' said Bowler, who was an evolutionist, and had been carefully brought up. .

'Then I have,' answered the King. 'I have walked along a street with the best cigar in the cosmos in my mouth, and more Burgundy inside me than you ever saw in your life, and longed that the lamp-post would turn into an elephant to save me from the hell of blank existence. Take my word for it, my evolutionary Bowler, don't you believe people when they tell you that people sought for a sign, and believed in miracles because they were ignorant. They did it because they were wise, filthily, vilely wise—too wise to eat or sleep or put on their boots with patience. This seems delightfully like a new theory of the origin of Christianity, which would itself be a thing of no mean absurdity. Take some more wine.'

The wind blew round them as they sat at their little table, with its white cloth and bright wine-cups, and flung the tree-tops of Holland Park against each other, but the sun was in that strong temper which turns green into gold. The King pushed away his plate, lit a cigar slowly, and went on:

'Yesterday I thought that something next door to a really entertaining miracle might happen to me before

I went to amuse the worms. To see that red-haired maniac waving a great sword, and making speeches to his incomparable followers, would have been a glimpse of that Land of Youth from which the Fates shut us out. I had planned some quite delightful things. A Congress of Knightsbridge with a treaty, and myself in the chair, and perhaps a Roman triumph, with jolly old Barker led in chains. And now these wretched prigs have gone and stamped out the exquisite Mr. Wayne altogether, and I suppose they will put him in a private asylum somewhere in their damned humane way. Think of the treasures daily poured out to his unappreciative keeper! I wonder whether they would let me be his keeper. But life is a vale. Never forget at any moment of your existence to regard it in the light of a vale. This graceful habit, if not acquired in youth——'

The King stopped, with his cigar lifted, for there had slid into his eyes the startled look of a man listening. He did not move for a few moments; then he turned his head sharply towards the high, thin, and lath-like paling which fenced certain long gardens and similar spaces from the lane. From behind it there was coming a curious scrambling and scraping noise, as of a desperate thing imprisoned in this box of thin wood. The King threw away his cigar, and jumped on to the table. From this position he saw a pair of hands hanging with a hungry clutch on the top of the fence. Then the hands quivered with a convulsive effort, and a head shot up between them— the head of one of the Bayswater Town Council, his eyes and whiskers wild with fear. He swung himself over, and fell on the other side on his face, and groaned openly and without ceasing. The next moment the thin, taut wood of the fence was struck as by a bullet, so that it reverberated like a drum, and over it came, tearing and cursing, with torn clothes and broken nails and bleeding faces, twenty men at one rush. The King sprang five feet clear off the table on to the ground. The moment after the table was flung over, sending bottles and glasses flying, and the *débris* was literally swept along the ground by that stream of men pouring past, and Bowler was borne along with them, as the King said in his famous newspaper article, 'like a captured bride'. The great fence swung and split under the load of climbers that still scaled and cleared it. Tremendous gaps were torn in it by this living artillery; and through them the King could see more and more frantic faces, as in a dream, and more and more men running. They were as miscellaneous as if some one had taken the lid off a human dustbin. Some were untouched, some were slashed and battered and bloody, some were splendidly dressed, some tattered and half-naked, some were in the fantastic garb of the burlesque cities, some in the dullest modern dress. The King stared at all of them, but none of them looked at the King. Suddenly he stepped forward.

'Barker,' he said, 'what is all this?'

'Beaten,' said the politician, 'beaten all to hell!' And he plunged past with nostrils shaking like a horse's, and more and more men plunged after him.

Almost as he spoke, the last standing strip of fence bowed and snapped, flinging, as from a catapult, a new figure upon the road. He wore the flaming red of the halberdiers of Notting Hill, and on his weapon there was blood, and in his face victory. In another moment masses of red glowed through the gaps of

4

the fence, and the pursuers, with their halberds, came pouring down the lane. Pursued and pursuers alike swept by the little figure with the owlish eyes, who had not taken his hands out of his pockets.

The King had still little beyond the confused sense of a man caught in a torrent—the feeling of men eddying by. Then something happened which he was never able afterwards to describe, and which we cannot describe for him. Suddenly in the dark entrance, between the broken gates of a garden, there appeared framed a flaming figure.

Adam Wayne, the conqueror, with his face flung back, and his mane like a lion's, stood with his great sword point upwards, the red raiment of his office flapping round him like the red wings of an arch-angel. And the King saw, he knew not how, something new and overwhelming. The great green trees and the great red robes swung together in the wind. The sword seemed made for the sunlight. The preposterous masquerade, born of his own mockery, towered over him and embraced the world. This was the normal, this was sanity, this was nature; and he himself, with his rationality and his detachment and his black frock-coat, he was the exception and the accident—a blot of black upon a word of crimson and gold.

BOOK IV

CHAPTER I

THE BATTLE OF THE LAMPS

MR. BUCK, who, though retired, frequently went down to his big drapery stores in Kensington High Street, was locking up those premises, being the last to leave. It was a wonderful evening of green and gold, but that did not trouble him very much. If you had pointed it out, he would have agreed seriously, for the rich always desire to be artistic.

He stepped out into the cool air, buttoning up his light coat, and blowing great clouds from his cigar, when a figure dashed up to him in another yellow overcoat, but unbuttoned and flying behind him.

'Hullo, Barker!' said the draper. 'Any of our summer articles? You're too late. Factory Acts, Barker. Humanity and progress, my boy.'

'Oh, don't chatter,' cried Barker, stamping. 'We've been beaten.'

'Beaten—by what?' asked Buck, mystified.

'By Wayne.'

Buck looked at Barker's fierce white face for the first time, as it gleamed in the lamplight.

'Come and have a drink,' he said.

They adjourned to a cushioned and glaring buffet, and Buck established himself slowly and lazily in a seat, and pulled out his cigar-case.

'Have a smoke,' he said.

Barker was still standing, and on the fret, but after a moment's hesitation, he sat down, as if he might spring up again the next minute. They ordered drinks in silence.

'How did it happen?' asked Buck, turning his big bold eyes on him.

'How the devil do I know?' cried Barker. 'It happened like—like a dream. How can two hundred men beat six hundred? How can they?'

'Well,' said Buck, coolly. 'How did they? You ought to know.'

'I don't know. I can't describe,' said the other, drumming on the table. 'It seemed like this. We were six hundred and marched with those damned poleaxes of Auberon's—the only weapons we've got. We marched two abreast. We went up to Holland Walk, between the high palings which seemed to me to go straight as an arrow for Pump Street. I was near the tail of the line and it was a long one. When the end of it was still between the high palings, the head of the line was already crossing Holland Park Avenue. Then the head plunged into the network of narrow streets on the other side, and the tail and myself came out on the great crossing. When we also had reached the northern side and turned up a small street that points, crookedly as it were, towards Pump Street, the whole thing felt different. The streets dodged and bent so much that the head of our line seemed lost altogether: it might as well have been in North America. And all this time we hadn't seen a soul.'

Buck, who was idly dabbing the ash of his cigar on the ash-tray, began to move it deliberately over the table, making feathery grey lines, a kind of map.

'But though the little streets were all deserted (which got a trifle on my nerves), as we got deeper and deeper into them, a thing began to happen that I couldn't understand. Sometimes a long way ahead—three turns or corners ahead, as it were—there broke suddenly a sort of noise, clattering, and confused cries, and then stopped. Then, when it happened, something, I can't describe it—a kind of shake or stagger went down the line, as if the line were a live thing, whose head had been struck, or had been an electric cord. None of us knew why we were moving, but we moved and jostled. Then we recovered, and went on through the little dirty streets, round corners, and up twisted ways. The little crooked streets began to give me a feeling I can't explain—as if it were a dream. I felt as if things had lost their reason, and we should never get out of the maze. Odd to hear me talk like that, isn't it? The streets were quite well-known streets, all down on the map. But the fact remains. I wasn't afraid of something happening. I was afraid of nothing ever happening—nothing ever happening for all God's eternity.'

He drained his glass and called for more whisky. He drank it and went on.

'And then something did happen. Buck, it's the solemn truth, that nothing has ever happened to you in your life. Nothing had ever happened to me in my life.'

'Nothing ever happened!' said Buck, staring. 'What do you mean?'

'Nothing has ever happened,' repeated Barker, with a morbid obstinacy. 'You don't know what a thing happening means? You sit in your office expecting customers, and customers come; you walk in the street expecting friends, and friends meet you; you want a drink and get it; you feel inclined for a bet and make it. You expect either to win or lose, and you

do either one or the other. But things happening!'
and he shuddered ungovernably.

'Go on,' said Buck, shortly. 'Get on.'

'As we walked wearily round the corners, something
happened. When something happens, it happens
first, and you see it afterwards. It happens of itself,
and you have nothing to do with it. It proves a
dreadful thing—that there are other things besides
one's self. I can only put it in this way. We went
round one turning, two turnings, three turnings,
four turnings, five. Then I lifted myself slowly up from
the gutter where I had been shot half senseless, and
was beaten down again by living men crashing on top
of me, and the world was full of roaring, and big men
rolling about like ninepins.'

Buck looked at his map with knitted brows.

'Was that Portobello Road?' he asked.

'Yes,' said Barker. 'Yes; Portobello Road—I saw
it afterwards; but, my God—what a place it was!
Buck, have you ever stood and let a six foot of a man
lash and lash at your head with six feet of pole with
six pounds of steel at the end? Because, when you
have had that experience, as Walt Whitman says,
"you re-examine philosophies and religions".'

'I have no doubt,' said Buck. 'If that was Portobello Road, don't you see what happened?'

'I know what happened exceedingly well. I was
knocked down four times; an experience which, as I
say, has an effect on the mental attitude. And
another thing happened, too. I knocked down two
men. After the fourth fall (there was not much blood-
shed—more brutal rushing and throwing—for nobody could use their weapons), after the fourth fall,
I say, I got up like a devil, and I tore a poleaxe out

of a man's hand and struck where I saw the scarlet
of Wayne's fellows, struck again and again. Two of
them went over, bleeding on the stones, thank God—
and I laughed and found myself sprawling in the gutter
again, and got up again, and struck again, and broke
my halberd to pieces. I hurt a man's head, though.'

Buck set down his glass with a bang, and spat out
curses through his thick moustache.

'What is the matter?' asked Barker, stopping, for
the man had been calm up to now, and now his
agitation was far more violent than his own.

'The matter?' said Buck, bitterly; 'don't you see how
these maniacs have got us? Why should two idiots,
one a clown and the other a screaming lunatic, make
sane men so different from themselves? Look here,
Barker; I will give you a picture. A very well-bred
young man of this century is dancing about in a frock-
coat. He has in his hands a nonsensical seventeenth-
century halberd, with which he is trying to kill men
in a street in Notting Hill. Damn it! don't you see
how they've got us? Never mind how you felt—that
is how you looked. The King would put his cursed
head on one side and call it exquisite. The Provost
of Notting Hill would put his cursed nose in the air and
call it heroic. But in Heaven's name what would you
have called it—two days before?'

Barker bit his lip.

'You haven't been through it, Buck,' he said. 'You
don't understand fighting—the atmosphere.'

'I don't deny the atmosphere,' said Buck, striking
the table. 'I only say it's their atmosphere. It's Adam
Wayne's atmosphere. It's the atmosphere which you
and I thought had vanished from an educated world
for ever.'

'Well, it hasn't,' said Barker; 'and if you have any lingering doubts, lend me a poleaxe and I'll show you.'

There was a long silence, and then Buck turned to his neighbour and spoke in that good-tempered tone that comes of a power of looking facts in the face; the tone in which he concluded great bargains.

'Barker,' he said, 'you are right. This old thing—this fighting, has come back. It has come back suddenly and taken us by surprise. So it is first blood to Adam Wayne. But, unless reason and arithmetic and everything else have gone crazy, it must be next and last blood to us. But when an issue has really arisen, there is only one thing to do—to study that issue as such and win in it. Barker, since it is fighting, we must understand fighting. I must understand fighting as coolly and completely as I understand drapery; you must understand fighting as coolly and completely as you understand politics. Now, look at the facts. I stick without hesitation to my original formula. Fighting, when we have the stronger force, is only a matter of arithmetic. It must be. You asked me just now how two hundred men could defeat six hundred. I can tell you. Two hundred men can defeat six hundred when the six hundred behave like fools. When they forget the very conditions they are fighting in; when they fight in a swamp as if it were a mountain; when they fight in a forest as if it were a plain; when they fight in streets without remembering the object of streets."

'What is the object of streets?' asked Barker.

'What is the object of supper?' cried Buck, furiously. 'Isn't it obvious? This military science is mere common sense. The object of a street is to lead from one

place to another; therefore all streets join; therefore
street fighting is quite a peculiar thing. You advanced
into that hive of streets as if you were advancing into
an open plain where you could see everything. Instead of that you were advancing into the bowels of a
fortress, with streets pointing at you, streets turning
on you, streets jumping out at you, and all in the
hands of the enemy. Do you know what Portobello
Road is? It is the only point on your journey where
two side-streets run up opposite each other. Wayne
massed his men on the two sides, and when he had let
enough of your line go past, cut it in two like a worm.
Don't you see what would have saved you?'

Barker shook his head.

'Can't your "atmosphere" help you?' asked Buck,
bitterly. 'Must I attempt explanations in the romantic
manner? Suppose that, as you were fighting blindly
with the red Notting Hillers who imprisoned you on
both sides, you had heard a shout from behind them.
Suppose, oh, romantic Barker! that behind the red
tunics you had seen the blue and gold of South Kensington taking them in the rear, surrounding them in
their turn and hurling them on to your halberds.'

'If the thing had been possible,' began Barker,
cursing.

'The thing would have been as possible,' said Buck,
simply; 'as simple as arithmetic. There are a certain
number of street entries that lead to Pump Street.
There are not nine hundred; there are not nine
million. They do not grow in the night. They do
not increase like mushrooms. It must be possible with
such an overwhelming force as we have to advance
by all of them at once. In every one of the arteries,
or approaches, we can put almost as many men as

Wayne can put into the field altogether. Once do that and we have him to demonstration. It is like a proposition in Euclid.'

'You think that is certain,' said Barker, anxious but dominated delightfully.

'I'll tell you what I think,' said Buck, getting up jovially. 'I think Adam Wayne made an uncommonly spirited little fight. And I think I am confoundedly sorry for him.'

'Buck, you are a great man,' cried Barker, rising also. 'You've knocked me sensible again. I am ashamed to say it, but I was getting romantic. Of course, what you say is adamantine sense. Fighting, being physical, must be mathematical. We were beaten because we were neither mathematical nor physical nor anything else—because we deserved to be beaten. Hold all the approaches, and with our force we must have him. When shall we open the next campaign?'

'Now,' said Buck, and walked out of the bar.

'Now!' cried Barker, following him eagerly. 'Do you mean now? It is so late.'

Buck turned on him, stamping.

'Do you think fighting is under the Factory Acts?' he said. And he called a cab. 'Notting Hill Gate Station,' he said, and the two drove off.

.   .   .   .   .

A genuine reputation can sometimes be made in an hour. Buck, in the next sixty or eighty minutes showed himself a really great man of action. His cab carried him like a thunderbolt from the King to Wilson, from Wilson to Swindon, from Swindon to Barker again; if his course was jagged, it had the jaggedness of the lightning. Only two things he carried with him, his inevitable cigar and the map of North Kensington and Notting Hill. There were, as he again and again pointed out, with every variety of persuasion and violence, only nine possible ways of approaching Pump Street within a quarter of a mile around it; three out of Westbourne Grove, two out of Ladbroke Grove, and four out of Notting Hill High Street. And he had detachments of two hundred each, stationed at every one of the entrances before the last green of that strange sunset had sunk out of the black sky.

The sky was particularly black, and on this alone was one false protest raised against the triumphant optimism of the Provost of North Kensington. He overruled it with his infectious common sense.

'There is no such thing,' he said, 'as night in London. You have only to follow the line of street lamps. Look, here is the map. Two hundred purple North Kensington soldiers under myself march up Ossington Street, two hundred more under Captain Bruce, of the North Kensington Guard, up Clanricarde Gardens.[1] Two hundred yellow West Kensingtons under Provost Swindon attack from Pembridge Road. Two hundred more of my men from the eastern streets, leading away from Queen's Road. Two detachments of yellows enter by two roads from Westbourne Grove. Lastly, two hundred green Bayswaters come down from the North through Chepstow Place, and two hundred more under Provost Wilson himself, through the upper part of Pembridge Road. Gentlemen, it is mate in two moves. The enemy must either mass in Pump Street and be cut to pieces—or they must retreat past the

[1] Clanricarde Gardens at this time was no longer a cul-de-sac, but was connected by Pump Street to Pembridge Square. See map.

Gaslight & Coke Co.—and rush on my four hundred —or they must retreat past St. Luke's Church, and rush on the six hundred from the West. Unless we are all mad, it's plain. Come on. To your quarters and await Captain Bruce's signal to advance. Then you have only to walk up a line of gas-lamps and smash this nonsense by pure mathematics. To-morrow we shall be all civilians again.'

His optimism glowed like a great fire in the night, and ran round the terrible ring in which Wayne was now held helpless. The fight was already over. One man's energy for one hour had saved the city from war.

For the next ten minutes Buck walked up and down silently beside the motionless clump of his two hundred. He had not changed his appearance in any way, except to sling across his yellow overcoat a case with a revolver in it. So that his light-clad modern figure showed up oddly beside the pompous purple uniform of his halberdiers which darkly but richly coloured the black night.

At length a shrill trumpet rang from some way up the street; it was the signal of advance. Buck briefly gave the word, and the whole purple line, with its dimly shining steel, moved up the side alley. Before it was a slope of street, long, straight, and shining in the dark. It was a sword pointed at Pump Street, the heart at which nine other swords were pointed that night.

A quarter of an hour's silent marching brought them almost within earshot of any tumult in the doomed citadel. But still there was no sound and no sign of the enemy. This time, at any rate, they knew that they were closing in on it mechanically, and they marched on under the lamplight and the dark without any of that eerie sense of ignorance which Barker had felt when entering the hostile country by one avenue alone.

'Halt—point arms!' cried Buck, suddenly, and as he spoke there came a clatter of feet tumbling along the stones. But the halberds were levelled in vain. The figure that rushed up was a messenger from the contingent of the North.

'Victory, Mr. Buck!' he cried, panting, 'they are ousted. Provost Wilson of Bayswater has taken Pump Street.'

Buck ran forward in his excitement.

'Then, which way are they retreating? It must be either by St. Luke's to meet Swindon, or by the Gas Company to meet us. Run like mad to Swindon and see that the yellows are holding the St. Luke's Road. We will hold this, never fear. We have them in an iron trap. Run!'

As the messenger dashed away into the darkness, the great guard of North Kensington swung on with the certainty of a machine. Yet scarcely a hundred yards farther their halberd points again fell in line gleaming in the gas-light. For again a clatter of feet was heard on the stones, and again it proved to be only the messenger.

'Mr. Provost,' he said, 'the yellow West Kensingtons have been holding the road by St. Luke's for twenty minutes since the capture of Pump Street. Pump Street is not two hundred yards away, they cannot be retreating down that road.'

'Then they are retreating down this!' said Provost Buck, with a final cheerfulness, 'and by good fortune down a well-lighted road, though it twists about. Forward!'

As they moved along the last three hundred yards of their journey, Buck fell, for the first time in his life, perhaps, into a kind of philosophical reverie, for men of his type are always made kindly, and as it were melancholy, by success.

'I am sorry for poor old Wayne, I really am,' he thought. 'He spoke up splendidly for me at that Council. And he blacked old Barker's eye with considerable spirit. But I don't see what a man can expect when he fights against arithmetic, to say nothing of civilization. And what a wonderful hoax all this military genius is. I suspect I've just discovered what Cromwell discovered, that a sensible tradesman is the best general, and that a man who can buy men and sell men can lead and kill them. The thing's simply like adding up a column in a ledger. If Wayne has two hundred men, he can't put two hundred men in nine places at once. If they're ousted from Pump Street they're flying somewhere. If they're not flying past the church they're flying past the Works. And so we have them. We business men should have no chance at all except that cleverer people than we get bees in their bonnets that prevent them from reasoning properly—so we reason alone. And so I, who am comparatively stupid, see things as God sees them, as a vast machine. My God, what's this?' And he clapped his hands to his eyes and staggered back.

Then through the darkness he cried in a dreadful voice:

'Did I blaspheme God?—I am struck blind.'

'What?' wailed another voice behind him, the voice of a certain Wilfred Jarvis of North Kensington.

'Blind!' cried Buck; 'blind!'

'I'm blind, too!' cried Jarvis, in an agony.

'Fools, all of you,' said a gross voice behind them; 'we're all blind. The lamps have gone out.'

'The lamps—but why? where?' cried Buck, turning furiously in the darkness. 'How are we to get on? How are we to chase the enemy? Where have they gone?'

'The enemy went——' said the rough voice behind, and then stopped, doubtfully.

'Where?' shouted Buck, stamping like a madman.

'They went,' said the gruff voice, 'past the Gas Works, and they've used their chance.'

'Great God!' thundered Buck, and snatched at his revolver; 'do you mean they've turned out——'

But almost before he had spoken the words, he was hurled like a stone from a catapult into the midst of his own men.

'Notting Hill! Notting Hill!' cried frightful voices out of the darkness, and they seemed to come from all sides, for the men of North Kensington, unacquainted with the road, had lost all their bearings in the black world of blindness.

'Notting Hill! Notting Hill!' cried the invisible people, and the invaders were hewn down horribly with black steel, with steel that gave no glint against any light.

.   .   .   .   .

Buck, though badly maimed with the blow of a halberd, kept an angry but splendid sanity. He groped madly for the wall and found it. Struggling with crawling fingers along it, he found a side opening and retreated into it with the remnants of his men. Their adventures during that prodigious night are not to be described. They did not know whether they were going towards or away from the enemy. Not knowing where they themselves were, or where their opponents were, it was mere irony to ask where was the rest of their army. For a thing had descended upon them which London does not know—darkness, which was before the stars were made, and they were as much lost in it as if they had been made before the stars. Every now and then, as those frightful hours wore on, they buffeted in the darkness against living men, who struck at them and at whom they struck, with an idiot fury. When at last the grey dawn came, they found they had wandered back to the edge of the Uxbridge Road. They found that in those horrible eyeless encounters, the North Kensingtons and the Bayswaters and the West Kensingtons had again and again met and butchered each other, and they heard that Adam Wayne was barricaded in Pump Street.

CHAPTER II

THE CORRESPONDENT OF THE
COURT JOURNAL

JOURNALISM had become like most other such things in England, under the cautious government and philosophy represented by James Barker, somewhat sleepy and much diminished in importance. This was partly due to the disappearance of party government and public speaking, partly to the compromise or dead-lock which had made foreign wars impossible, but mostly, of course, to the temper of the whole nation, which was that of a people in a kind of back-water. Perhaps the most well known of the remaining news-papers was the *Court Journal*, which was published in a dusty but genteel-looking office just out of Kensington High Street. For when all the papers of a people have been for years growing more and more dim and decorous and optimistic, the dimmest and most decorous and most optimistic is very likely to win. In the journalistic competition which was still going on at the beginning of the twentieth century, the final victor was the *Court Journal*.

For some mysterious reason the King had a great affection for hanging about in the *Court Journal* office, smoking a morning cigarette and looking over files. Like all ingrainedly idle men, he was very fond of lounging and chatting in places where other people were doing work. But one would have thought that, even in the prosaic England of his day, he might have found a more bustling centre.

On this particular morning, however, he came out

of Kensington Palace with a more alert step and a busier air than usual. He wore an extravagantly long frock-coat, a pale-green waistcoat, a very full and *dégagé* black tie, and curious yellow gloves. This was his uniform as Colonel of a regiment of his own creation, the 1st Decadents Green. It was a beautiful sight to see him drilling them. He walked quickly across the Park and the High Street, lighting his cigarette as he went, and flung open the door of the *Court Journal* office.

'You've heard the news, Pally—you've heard the news?' he said.

The Editor's name was Hoskins, but the King called him Pally, which was an abbreviation of Palladium of our Liberties.

'Well, your Majesty,' said Hoskins, slowly (he was a worried, gentlemanly-looking person, with a wandering brown beard)—'well, your Majesty, I have heard rather curious things, but I——'

'You'll hear more of them,' said the King, dancing a few steps of a kind of negro shuffle. 'You'll hear more of them, my blood-and-thunder tribune. Do you know what I am going to do for you?'

'No, your Majesty,' replied the Palladium, vaguely.

'I'm going to put your paper on strong, dashing, enterprising lines,' said the King. 'Now, where are your posters of last night's defeat?'

'I did not propose, your Majesty,' said the Editor, 'to have any posters exactly——'

'Paper, paper!' cried the King, wildly; 'bring me paper as big as a house. I'll do you posters. Stop, I must take my coat off.' He began removing that garment with an air of set intensity, flung it playfully at Mr. Hoskins' head, entirely enveloping him, and looked at himself in the glass. 'The coat off,' he said, 'and hat on. That looks like a sub-editor. It is indeed the very essence of sub-editing. Well,' he continued, turning round abruptly, 'come along with that paper.'

The Palladium had only just extricated himself reverently from the folds of the King's frock-coat, and said bewildered:

'I am afraid, your Majesty——'

'Oh, you've got no enterprise,' said Auberon. 'What's that roll in the corner? Wall-paper? Decorations for your private residence? Art in the home, Pally? Fling it over here, and I'll paint such posters on the back of it that when you put it up in your drawing-room you'll paste the original pattern against the wall.' And the King unrolled the wall-paper, spreading it over the whole floor. 'Now give me the scissors,' he cried, and took them himself before the other could stir.

He slit the paper into about five pieces, each nearly as big as a door. Then he took a big blue pencil and went down on his knees on the dusty oil-cloth, and began to write on them, in huge letters:

'FROM THE FRONT.

GENERAL BUCK DEFEATED.

DARKNESS, DANGER, AND DEATH.

WAYNE SAID TO BE IN PUMP STREET.

FEELING IN THE CITY.'

He contemplated it for some time, with his head on one side, and got up, with a sigh.

'Not quite intense enough,' he said—'not alarming. I want the *Court Journal* to be feared as well as loved.

Let's try something more hard-hitting.' And he went down on his knees again. After sucking the blue pencil for some time, he began writing again busily. 'How will this do?' he said:

'WAYNE'S WONDERFUL VICTORY.'

'I suppose,' he said, looking up appealingly, and sucking the pencil—'I suppose we couldn't say "wictory"—"Wayne's wonderful wictory"? No, no. Refinement, Pally, refinement. I have it':

'WAYNE WINS.
ASTOUNDING FIGHT IN THE DARK.

The gas-lamps in their courses fought against Buck.'

'(Nothing like our fine old English translation.) What else can we say? Well, anything to annoy old Buck'; and he added, thoughtfully, in smaller letters:

'Rumoured Court-martial on General Buck.'

'Those will do for the present,' he said, and turned them both face downwards. 'Paste, please.'

The Palladium, with an air of great terror, brought the paste out of an inner room.

The King slabbed it on with the enjoyment of a child messing with treacle. Then, taking one of his huge compositions fluttering in each hand, he ran outside, and began pasting them up in prominent positions over the front of the office.

'And now,' said Auberon, entering again with undiminished vivacity—'now for the leading article.'

He picked up another of the large strips of wall-paper, and, laying it across a desk, pulled out a fountain-pen and began writing with feverish intensity, reading clauses and fragments aloud to himself, and rolling them on his tongue like wine, to see if they had the pure journalistic flavour.

'The news of the disaster to our forces in Notting Hill, awful as it is, awful as it is—(no, distressing as it is), may do some good if it draws attention to the what's-his-name inefficiency (scandalous inefficiency, of course) of the Government's preparations. In our present state of information, it would be premature (what a jolly word!)—it would be premature to cast any reflections upon the conduct of General Buck, whose services upon so many stricken fields (ha, ha!), and whose honourable scars and laurels, give him a right to have judgment upon him at least suspended. But there is one matter on which we must speak plainly. We have been silent on it too long, from feelings, perhaps of mistaken caution, perhaps of mistaken loyalty. This situation would never have arisen but for what we can only call the indefensible conduct of the King. It pains us to say such things, but, speaking as we do in the public interests (I plagiarize from Barker's famous epigram), we shall not shrink because of the distress we may cause to any individual, even the most exalted. At this crucial moment of our country, the voice of the People demands with a single tongue, "Where is the King?" What is he doing while his subjects tear each other in pieces in the streets of a great city? Are his amusements and his dissipations (of which we cannot pretend to be ignorant) so engrossing that he can spare no thought for a perishing nation? It is with a deep sense of our responsibility that we warn that exalted person that neither his great position nor his incomparable talents will save him in the hour of delirium from the fate of all those who, in the madness of luxury or tyranny, have met the English people in the rare day of its wrath.'

'I am now,' said the King, 'going to write an account of the battle by an eye-witness.' And he picked up a fourth sheet of wall-paper. Almost at the same moment Buck strode quickly into the office. He had a bandage round his head.

'I was told,' he said with his usual gruff civility, 'that your Majesty was here.'

'And of all things on earth,' cried the King, with delight, 'here is an eye-witness! An eye-witness who, I regret to observe, has at present only one eye to witness with. Can you write us the special article, Buck? Have you a rich style?'

Buck, with a self-restraint which almost approached politeness, took no notice whatever of the King's maddening geniality.

'I took the liberty, your Majesty,' he said shortly, 'of asking Mr. Barker to come here also.'

As he spoke, indeed, Barker came swinging into the office, with his usual air of hurry.

'What is happening now?' asked Buck, turning to him with a kind of relief.

'Fighting still going on,' said Barker. 'The four hundred from West Kensington were hardly touched last night. They hardly got near the place. Poor Wilson's Bayswater men got cut about, though. They fought confoundedly well. They took Pump Street once. What mad things do happen in the world. To think that of all of us it should be little Wilson with the red whiskers who came out best.'

The King made a note on his paper:

'*Romantic conduct of Mr. Wilson.*'

'Yes,' said Buck, 'it makes one a bit less proud of one's *h*'s.'

The King suddenly folded or crumpled up the paper, and put it in his pocket.

'I have an idea,' he said. 'I will be an eye-witness. I will write you such letters from the Front as will be more gorgeous than the real things. Give me my coat, Palladium. I entered this room a mere King of England. I leave it, Special War Correspondent of the *Court Journal*. It is useless to stop me, Pally; it is vain to cling to my knees, Buck; it is hopeless, Barker, to weep upon my neck. "When duty calls"—the remainder of the sentiment escapes me. You will receive my first article this evening by the eight o'clock post.'

And, running out of the office, he jumped upon a blue Bayswater omnibus that went swinging by.

'Well,' said Barker, gloomily, 'well.'

'Barker,' said Buck, 'business may be lower than politics, but war is, as I discovered last night, a long sight more like business. You politicians are such ingrained demagogues that even when you have a despotism you think of nothing but public opinion. So you learn to tack and run, and are afraid of the first breeze. Now we stick to a thing and get it. And our mistakes help us. Look here! at this moment we've beaten Wayne.'

'Beaten Wayne,' repeated Barker.

'Why the dickens not?' cried the other, flinging out his hands. 'Look here. I said last night that we had them by holding the nine entrances. Well, I was wrong. We should have had them but for a singular event—the lamps went out. But for that it was certain. Has it occurred to you, my brilliant Barker, that another singular event has happened since that singular event of the lamps going out?'

'What event?' asked Barker.

'By an astounding coincidence, the sun has risen,' cried out Buck, with a savage air of patience. 'Why the hell aren't we holding all those approaches now, and pressing in on them again? It should have been done at sunrise. The confounded doctor wouldn't let me go out. You were in command.'

Barker smiled grimly.

'It is a gratification to me, my dear Buck, to be able to say that we anticipated your suggestions precisely. We went as early as possible to reconnoitre the nine entrances. Unfortunately, while we were fighting each other in the dark, like a lot of drunken navvies, Mr. Wayne's friends were working very hard indeed. Three hundred yards from Pump Street, at every one of those entrances, there is a barricade nearly as high as the houses. They were finishing the last, in Pembridge Road, when we arrived. Our mistakes,' he cried bitterly, and flung his cigarette on the ground. 'It is not we who learn from them.'

There was a silence for a few moments, and Barker lay back wearily in a chair. The office clock ticked exactly in the stillness.

At length Barker said suddenly:

'Buck, does it ever cross your mind what this is all about? The Hammersmith to Maida Vale thorough-fare was an uncommonly good speculation. You and I hoped a great deal from it. But is it worth it? It will cost us thousands to crush this ridiculous riot. Suppose we let it alone?'

'And be thrashed in public by a red-haired madman whom any two doctors would lock up?' cried out Buck, starting to his feet. 'What do you propose to do, Mr. Barker? To apologize to the admirable Mr. Wayne? To kneel to the Charter of the Cities? To clasp to your bosom the flag of the Red Lion? To kiss in succession every sacred lamp-post that saved Notting Hill? No, by God! My men fought jolly well—they were beaten by a trick. And they'll fight again.'

'Buck,' said Barker, 'I always admired you. And you were quite right in what you said the other day.'

'In what?'

'In saying,' said Barker, rising quietly, 'that we had all got into Adam Wayne's atmosphere and out of our own. My friend, the whole territorial kingdom of Adame Wayne extends to about nine streets, with barricades at the end of them. But the spiritual kingdom of Adam Wayne extends, God knows where—it extends to this office at any rate. The red-haired madman whom any two doctors would lock up is filling this room with his roaring, unreasonable soul. And it was the red-haired madman who said the last word you spoke.'

Buck walked to the window without replying.

'You understand, of course,' he said at last, 'I do not dream of giving in.'

.   .   .   .   .

The King, meanwhile, was rattling along on the top of his blue omnibus. The traffic of London as a whole had not, of course, been greatly disturbed by these events, for the affair was treated as a Notting Hill riot, and that area was marked off as if it had been in the hands of a gang of recognized rioters. The blue omnibuses simply went round as they would have done if a road were being mended, and the omnibus on which the correspondent of the *Court Journal* was sitting swept round the corner of Queen's Road, Bayswater.

The King was alone on the top of the vehicle, and was enjoying the speed at which it was going.

'Forward, my beauty, my Arab,' he said, patting the omnibus encouragingly, 'fleetest of all thy bounding tribe. Are thy relations with thy driver, I wonder, those of the Bedouin and his steed? Does he sleep side by side with thee——'

His meditations were broken by a sudden and jarring stoppage. Looking over the edge, he saw that the heads of the horses were being held by men in the uniform of Wayne's army, and heard the voice of an officer calling out orders.

King Auberon descended from the omnibus with dignity. The guard or picket of red halberdiers who had stopped the vehicle did not number more than twenty, and they were under the command of a short, dark, clever-looking young man, conspicuous among the rest as being clad in an ordinary frock-coat, but girt round the waist with a red sash and a long seventeenth-century sword. A shiny silk hat and spectacles completed the outfit in a pleasing manner.

'To whom have I the honour of speaking?' said the King, endeavouring to look like Charles I, in spite of personal difficulties.

The dark man in spectacles lifted his hat with equal gravity.

'My name is Bowles,' he said. 'I am a chemist. I am also a captain of O Company of the army of Notting Hill. I am distressed at having to incommode you by stopping the omnibus, but this area is covered by our proclamation, and we intercept all traffic. May I ask to whom I have the honour—— Why, good gracious, I beg your Majesty's pardon. I am quite overwhelmed at finding myself concerned with the King.'

Auberon put up his hands with indescribable grandeur.

'Not with the King,' he said; 'with the special war correspondent of the *Court Journal*.'

'I beg your Majesty's pardon,' began Mr. Bowles, doubtfully.

'Do you call me Majesty? I repeat,' said Auberon firmly, 'I am a representative of the Press. I have chosen, with a deep sense of responsibility, the name of Pinker. I should desire a veil to be drawn over the past.'

'Very well, sir,' said Mr. Bowles, with an air of submission, 'in our eyes the sanctity of the Press is at least as great as that of the throne. We desire nothing better than that our wrongs and our glories should be widely known. May I ask, Mr. Pinker, if you have any objection to being presented to the Provost and to General Turnbull?'

'The Provost I have had the honour of meeting,' said Auberon, easily. 'We old journalists, you know, meet everybody. I should be most delighted to have the same honour again. General Turnbull, also, it would be a gratification to know. The younger men are so interesting. We of the old Fleet Street gang lose touch with them.'

'Will you be so good as to step this way?' said the leader of O Company.

'I am always good,' said Mr. Pinker. 'Lead on.'

CHAPTER III

THE GREAT ARMY OF SOUTH KENSINGTON

THE article from the special correspondent of the *Court Journal* arrived in due course, written on very coarse copy-paper in the King's arabesque of handwriting, in which three words filled a page, and yet were illegible. Moreover, the contribution was the more perplexing at first as it opened with a succession of erased paragraphs. The writer appeared to have attempted the article once or twice in several journalistic styles. At the side of one experiment was written, 'Try American style', and the fragment began:

'The King must go. We want gritty men. Flap-doodle is all very . . .'; and then broke off, followed by the note, 'Good sound journalism safer. Try it.'

The experiment in good sound journalism appeared to begin:

'The greatest of English poets has said that a rose by any . . .'

This also stopped abruptly. The next annotation at the side was almost indecipherable, but seemed to be something like:

'How about old Steevens and the *mot juste*? E.g. . . .'

'Morning winked a little wearily at me over the curt edge of Campden Hill and its houses with their sharp shadows. Under the abrupt black cardboard of the outline, it took some little time to detect colours; but at length I saw a brownish yellow shifting in the obscurity, and I knew that it was the guard of Swindon's West Kensington army. They are being held as a reserve, and lining the whole ridge above the Bayswater

Road. Their camp and their main force is under the great waterworks tower on Campden Hill. I forgot to say that the waterworks tower looked swart.

'As I passed them and came over the curve of Silver Street, I saw the blue cloudy masses of Barker's men blocking the entrance to the high-road like a sapphire smoke (good). The disposition of the allied troops, under the general management of Mr. Wilson, appears to be as follows: The Yellow Army (if I may so describe the West Kensingtonians) lies, as I have said, in a strip along the ridge; its farthest point westward being the west side of Campden Hill Road, its farthest point eastward the beginning of Kensington Gardens. The Green Army of Wilson lines the Notting Hill High Road itself from Queen's Road to the corner of Pembridge Road, curving round the latter, and extending some three hundred yards up towards Westbourne Grove. Westbourne Grove itself is occupied by Barker of South Kensington. The fourth side of this rough square, the Queen's Road side, is held by some of Buck's Purple warriors.

'The whole resembles some ancient and dainty Dutch flower-bed. Along the crest of Campden Hill lie the golden crocuses of West Kensington. They are, as it were, the first fiery fringe of the whole. Northward lies our hyacinth Barker, with all his blue hyacinths. Round to the south-west run the green rushes of Wilson of Bayswater, and a line of violet irises (aptly symbolized by Mr. Buck) complete the whole. The argent exterior . . . (I am losing the style. I should have said "Curving with a whisk" instead of merely "Curving". Also I should have called the hyacinths "sudden". I cannot keep this up. War is too rapid for this style of writing. Please ask the office-boy to insert *mots justes*.)

'The truth is that there is nothing to report. That commonplace element which is always ready to devour all beautiful things (as the Black Pig in the Irish Mythology will finally devour the stars and gods); that commonplace element, as I say, has in its Black Piggish way devoured finally the chances of any romance in this affair; that which once consisted of absurd but thrilling combats in the streets, has degenerated into something which is the very prose of warfare—it has degenerated into a siege. A siege may be defined as a peace plus the inconvenience of war. Of course Wayne cannot hold out. There is no more chance of help from anywhere else than of ships from the moon. And if old Wayne had stocked his street with tinned meats till all his garrison had to sit on them, he couldn't hold out for more than a month or two. As a matter of melancholy fact he has done something rather like this. He has stocked his street with food until there must be uncommonly little room to turn round. But what is the good? To hold out for all that time and then to give in of necessity, what does it mean? It means waiting until your victories are forgotten and then taking the trouble to be defeated. I cannot understand how Wayne can be so inartistic.

'And how odd it is that one views a thing quite differently when one knows it is defeated. I always thought Wayne was rather fine. But now, when I know that he is done for, there seems to be nothing else but Wayne. All the streets seem to point at him, all the chimneys seem to lean towards him. I suppose it is a morbid feeling; but Pump Street seems to be the only part of London that I feel physically. I suppose, I say, that it is morbid. I suppose it is exactly how a man feels about his heart when his heart is weak. "Pump Street"—the heart is a pump. And I am drivelling.

'Our finest leader at the front is beyond all question General Wilson. He has adopted alone among the other Provosts the uniform of his own halberdiers, although that fine old sixteenth-century garb was not originally intended to go with red side-whiskers. It was he who, against a most admirable and desperate defence, broke last night into Pump Street and held it for at least half an hour. He was afterwards expelled from it by General Turnbull, of Notting Hill, but only after desperate fighting and the sudden descent of that terrible darkness which proved so much more fatal to the forces of General Buck and General Swindon.

'Provost Wayne himself, with whom I had, with great good fortune, a most interesting interview, bore the most eloquent testimony to the conduct of General Wilson and his men. His precise words are as follows: "I have bought sweets at his funny little shop when I was four years old, and ever since. I never noticed anything, I am ashamed to say, except that he talked through his nose, and didn't wash himself particularly. And he came over our barricade like a devil from hell." I repeated this speech to General Wilson himself, with some delicate improvements, and he seemed pleased with it. He does not, however, seem pleased with anything so much just now as he is with the wearing of a sword. I have it from the front on the best authority that General Wilson was not completely shaved yesterday. It is believed in military circles that he is growing a moustache. . . .

'As I have said, there is nothing to report. I walk wearily to the pillar-box at the corner of Pembridge

Road to post my copy. Nothing whatever has happened, except the preparations for a particularly long and feeble siege, during which I trust I shall not be required to be at the Front. As I glance up Pembridge Road in the growing dusk, the aspect of that road reminds me that there is one note worth adding. General Buck has suggested, with characteristic acumen, to General Wilson, that in order to obviate the possibility of such a catastrophe as overwhelmed the allied forces in the last advance on Notting Hill (the catastrophe, I mean, of the extinguished lamps), that each soldier should have a lighted lantern round his neck. This is one of the things which I really admire about General Buck. He possesses what people used to mean by "the humility of the man of science", that is, he learns steadily from his mistakes. Wayne may score off him in some other way, but not in that way. The lanterns look like fairy lights as they curve round the end of Pembridge Road.

'*Later.*—I write with some difficulty, because the blood will run down my face and make patterns on the paper. Blood is a very beautiful thing; that is why it is concealed. If you ask me why blood runs down my face, I can only reply that I was kicked by a horse. If you ask me what horse, I can reply with some pride that it was a war-horse. If you ask me how a war-horse came on the scene in our simple pedestrian warfare, I am reduced to the necessity, so painful to a special correspondent, of recounting my experiences.

'I was, as I have said, in the very act of posting my copy at the pillar-box, and of glancing as I did so up the glittering curve of Pembridge Road, studded with

the lights of Wilson's men. I don't know what made
me pause to examine the matter, but I had a fancy
that the line of lights, where it melted into the indistinct brown twilight, was more indistinct than usual.
I was almost certain that in a certain stretch of the
road where there had been five lights there were now
only four. I strained my eyes; I counted them again,
and there were only three. A moment after there were
only two; an instant after only one; and an instant
after that the lanterns near to me swung like jangled
bells, as if struck suddenly. They flared and fell; and
for the moment the fall of them was like the fall of
the sun and stars out of heaven. It left everything in
a primal blindness. As a matter of fact, the road was
not yet legitimately dark. There were still red rays
of a sunset in the sky, and the brown gloaming was
still warmed, as it were, with a feeling as of firelight.
Bur for three seconds after the lanterns swung and
sank, I saw in front of me a blackness blocking the
sky. And with the fourth second I knew that this
blackness which blocked the sky was a man on a great
horse; and I was trampled and tossed aside as a swirl
of horsemen swept round the corner. As they turned
I saw that they were not black but scarlet; they were
a sortie of the besieged, Wayne riding ahead.

'I lifted myself from the gutter, blinded with blood
from a very slight skin-wound, and, queerly enough,
not caring either for the blindness or for the slightness
of the wound. For one mortal minute after that
amazing cavalcade had spun past, there was dead
stillness on the empty road. And then came Barker
and all his halberdiers running like devils in the track
of them. It had been their business to guard the gate
by which the sortie had broken out; but they had not

5

reckoned, and small blame to them, on cavalry. As it was, Barker and his men made a perfectly splendid run after them, almost catching Wayne's horses by the tails.

'Nobody can understand the sortie. It consists only of a small number of Wayne's garrison. Turnbull himself, with the vast mass of it, is undoubtedly still barricaded in Pump Street. Sorties of this kind are natural enough in the majority of historical sieges, such as the siege of Paris in 1870, because in such cases the besieged are certain of some support outside. But what can be the object of it in this case? Wayne knows (or if he is too mad to know anything, at least Turnbull knows) that there is not, and never has been, the smallest chance of support for him outside; that the mass of the sane modern inhabitants of London regard his farcical patriotism with as much contempt as they do the original idiocy that gave it birth—the folly of our miserable King. What Wayne and his horsemen are doing nobody can even conjecture. The general theory round here is that he is simply a traitor, and has abandoned the besieged. But all such larger but yet more soluble riddles are as nothing compared to the one small but unanswerable riddle: Where did they get the horses?

'*Later.*—I have heard a most extraordinary account of the origin of the appearance of the horses. It appears that that amazing person, General Turnbull, who is now ruling Pump Street in the absence of Wayne, sent out, on the morning of the declaration of war, a vast number of little boys (or cherubs of the gutter, as we pressmen say), with half-crowns in their pockets, to take cabs all over London. No less than a hundred

and sixty cabs met at Pump Street; were comman-
deered by the garrison. The men were set free, the
cabs used to make barricades, and the horses kept in
Pump Street, where they were fed and exercised for
several days, until they were sufficiently rapid and
efficient to be used for this wild ride out of the town.
If this is so, and I have it on the best possible authority,
the method of the sortie is explained. But we have
no explanation of its object. Just as Barker's Blues
were swinging round the corner after them, they were
stopped, but not by an enemy; only by the voice of
one man, and he a friend. Red Wilson of Bayswater
ran alone along the main road like a madman, waving
them back with a halberd snatched from a sentinel.
He was in supreme command, and Barker stopped at
the corner, staring and bewildered. We could hear
Wilson's voice loud and distinct out of the dusk, so
that it seemed strange that the great voice should come
out of the little body. "Halt, South Kensington!
Guard this entry, and prevent them returning. I will
pursue. Forward, the Green Guards!"

'A wall of dark blue uniforms and a wood of poleaxes
were between me and Wilson, for Barker's men blocked
the mouth of the road in two rigid lines. But through
them and through the dusk I could hear the clear
orders and the clank of arms, and see the Green Army
of Wilson marching by towards the west. They were
our great fighting-men. Wilson had filled them with
his own fire; in a few days they had become veterans.
Each of them wore a silver medal of a pump, to boast
that they alone of all the allied armies had stood
victorious in Pump Street.

'I managed to slip past the detachment of Barker's
Blues, who are guarding the end of Pembridge Road,

and a sharp spell of running brought me to the tail of Wilson's Green Army as it swung down the road in pursuit of the flying Wayne. The dusk had deepened into almost total darkness; for some time I only heard the throb of the marching pace. Then suddenly there was a cry, and the tall fighting men were flung back on me, almost crushing me, and again the lanterns swung and jingled, and the cold nozzles of great horses pushed into the press of us. They had turned and charged us.

' "You fools!" came the voice of Wilson, cleaving our panic with a splendid cold anger. "Don't you see? The horses have no riders!"

'It was true. We were being plunged at by a stampede of horses with empty saddles. What could it mean? Had Wayne met some of our men and been defeated? Or had he flung these horses at us as some kind of ruse or mad new mode of warfare, such as he seemed bent on inventing? Or did he and his men want to get away in disguise? Or did they want to hide in houses somewhere?

'Never did I admire any man's intellect (even my own) so much as I did Wilson's at that moment. Without a word, he simply pointed the halberd (which he still grasped) to the southern side of the road. As you know, the streets running up to the ridge of Campden Hill from the main road are peculiarly steep, they are more like sudden flights of stairs. We were just opposite Aubrey Road, the steepest of all; up that it would have been far more difficult to urge half-trained horses than to run up on one's feet.

' "Left wheel!" hallooed Wilson. "They have gone up here," he added to me, who happened to be at his elbow.

' "Why?" I ventured to ask.

"Can't say for certain," replied the Bayswater General. "They've gone up here in a great hurry anyhow. They've simply turned their horses loose, because they couldn't take them up. I fancy I know. I fancy they're trying to get over the ridge to Kensington or Hammersmith, or somewhere, and are striking up here because it's just beyond the end of our line. Damned fools, not to have gone farther along the road, though. They've only just shaved our last outpost. Lambert is hardly four hundred yards from here. And I've sent him word."

' "Lambert!" I said. "Not young Wilfrid Lambert —my old friend."

' "Wilfrid Lambert's his name," said the General; "used to be a 'man about town'; silly fellow with a big nose. That kind of man always volunteers for some war or other. And what's funnier, he generally isn't half bad at it. Lambert is distinctly good. The yellow West Kensingtons I always reckoned the weakest part of the army; but he has pulled them together uncommonly well, though he's subordinate to Swindon, who's a donkey. In the attack from Pembridge Road the other night he showed great pluck."

' "He has shown greater pluck than that," I said. "He has criticized my sense of humour. That was his first engagement."

'This remark was, I am sorry to say, lost on the admirable commander of the allied forces. We were in the act of climbing the last half of Aubrey Road, which is so abrupt a slope that it looked like an old-fashioned map leaning up against the wall. There are lines of little trees, one above the other, as in the old-fashioned map.

'We reached the top of it, panting somewhat, and were just about to turn the corner by a place called (in chivalrous anticipation of our wars of sword and axe) Tower Crecy, when we were suddenly knocked in the stomach (I can use no other term) by a horde of men hurled back upon us. They wore the red uniform of Wayne; their halberds were broken; their foreheads bleeding; but the mere impetus of their retreat staggered us as we stood at the last ridge of the slope.

' "Good old Lambert!" yelled out, suddenly, the stolid Mr. Wilson of Bayswater, in an uncontrollable excitement. "Damned jolly old Lambert! He's got there already! He's driving them back on us! Hurrah! hurrah! Forward the Green Guards!"

'We swung round the corner eastwards, Wilson running first, brandishing the halberd.

'Will you pardon a little egotism? Every one likes a little egotism, when it takes the form, as mine does in this case, of a disgraceful confession. The thing is really a little interesting, because it shows how the merely artistic habit has bitten into men like me. It was the most intensely exciting occurrence that had ever come to me in my life; and I was really intensely excited about it. And yet, as we turned that corner, the first impression I had was of something that had nothing to do with the fight at all. I was stricken from the sky as by a thunderbolt, by the height of the Waterworks Tower on Campden Hill. I don't know whether Londoners generally realize how high it looks when one comes out, in this way, almost immediately under it. For the second it seemed to me that at the foot of it even human war was a triviality. For the second I felt as if I had been drunk with some trivial

orgy, and that I had been sobered by the shock of
that shadow. A moment afterwards, I realized that
under it was going on something more enduring than
stone, and something wilder than the dizziest height
—the agony of man. And I knew that compared to
that, this overwhelming tower was itself a triviality; it
was a mere stalk of stone which humanity could snap
like a stick.

'I don't know why I have talked so much about this
silly old Waterworks Tower, which at the very best
was only a tremendous background. It was that, certainly, a sombre and awful landscape, against which
our figures were relieved. But I think the real reason
was, that there was in my own mind so sharp a transi-
tion from the tower of stone to the man of flesh. For
what I saw first when I had shaken off, as it were, the
shadow of the tower, was a man, and a man I knew.

'Lambert stood at the farther corner of the street
that curved round the tower, his figure outlined in
some degree by the beginning of moonrise. He looked
magnificent, a hero; but he looked something much
more interesting than that. He was, as it happened,
in almost precisely the same swaggering attitude in
which he had stood nearly fifteen years ago, when he
swung his walking-stick and struck it into the ground,
and told me that all my subtlety was drivel. And,
upon my soul, I think he required more courage to
say that than to fight as he does now. For then he
was fighting against something that was in the ascen-
dant, fashionable, and victorious. And now he is
fighting (at the risk of his life, no doubt) merely against
something which is already dead, which is impossible,
futile; of which nothing has been more impossible and
futile than this very sortie which has brought him into

contact with it. People nowadays allow infinitely too little for the psychological sense of victory as a factor in affairs. Then he was attacking the degraded but undoubtedly victorious Quin; now he is attacking the interesting but totally extinguished Wayne.

'His name recalls me to the details of the scene. The facts were these. A line of red halberdiers, headed by Wayne, were marching up the street, close under the northern wall, which is, in fact, the bottom of a sort of dyke or fortification of the Waterworks. Lambert and his yellow West Kensingtons had that instant swept round the corner and had shaken the Waynites heavily, hurling back a few of the more timid, as I have just described, into our very arms. When our force struck the tail of Wayne's, every one knew that all was up with him. His favourite military barber was struck down. His grocer was stunned. He himself was hurt in the thigh, and reeled back against the wall. We had him in a trap with two jaws. "Is that you?" shouted Lambert, genially, to Wilson, across the hemmed-in host of Notting Hill. "That's about the ticket," replied General Wilson; "keep them under the wall."

'The men of Notting Hill were falling fast. Adam Wayne threw up his long arms to the wall above him, and with a spring stood upon it, a gigantic figure against the moon. He tore the banner out of the hands of the standard-bearer below him, and shook it out suddenly above our heads, so that it was like thunder in the heavens.

' "Round the Red Lion!" he cried. "Swords round the Red Lion! Halberds round the Red Lion! They are the thorns round the rose."

'His voice and the crack of the banner made a

momentary rally, and Lambert, whose idiotic face was almost beautiful with battle, felt it as by an instinct, and cried:

' "Drop your public-house flag, you footler! Drop it!"

' "The banner of the Red Lion seldom stoops," said Wayne, proudly, letting it out luxuriantly on the night wind.

'The next moment I knew that poor Adam's sentimental theatricality had cost him much. Lambert was on the wall at a bound, his sword in his teeth, and had slashed at Wayne's head before he had time to draw his sword, his hands being busy with the enormous flag. He stepped back only just in time to avoid the first cut, and let the flagstaff fall, so that the spear-blade at the end of it pointed to Lambert.

' "The banner stoops," cried Wayne, in a voice that must have startled streets. "The banner of Notting Hill stoops to a hero." And with the words he drove the spear-point and half the flagstaff through Lambert's body and dropped him dead upon the road below, a stone upon the stones of the street.

' "Notting Hill! Notting Hill!" cried Wayne, in a sort of divine rage. "Her banner is all the holier for the blood of a brave enemy! Up on the wall, patriots! Up on the wall! Notting Hill!"

'With his long strong arm he actually dragged a man up on to the wall to be silhouetted against the moon, and more and more men climbed up there, pulled themselves and were pulled, till clusters and crowds of the half-massacred men of Pump Street massed upon the wall above us.

' "Notting Hill! Notting Hill!" cried Wayne, unceasingly.

' "Well, what about Bayswater?" said a worthy working-man in Wilson's army, irritably. "Bayswater for ever!"

' "We have won!" cried Wayne, striking his flagstaff in the ground. "Bayswater for ever! We have taught our enemies patriotism!"

' "Oh, cut these fellows up and have done with it!" cried one of Lambert's lieutenants, who was reduced to something bordering on madness by the responsibility of succeeding to the command.

' "Let us by all means try," said Wilson, grimly; and the two armies closed round the third.

.   .   .   .   .

'I simply cannot describe what followed. I am sorry, but there is such a thing as physical fatigue, as physical nausea, and, I may add, as physical terror. Suffice it to say that the above paragraph was written about 11 p.m., and that it is now about 2 a.m., and that the battle is not finished, and is not likely to be. Suffice it further to say that down the steep streets which lead from the Waterworks Tower to the Notting Hill High Road, blood has been running, and is running, in great red serpents, that curl out into the main thoroughfare and shine in the moon.

'*Later*.—The final touch has been given to all this terrible futility. Hours have passed; morning has broken; men are still swaying and fighting at the foot of the tower and round the corner of Aubrey Road; the fight has not finished. But I know it is a farce.

'News has just come to show that Wayne's amazing sortie, followed by the amazing resistance through a whole night on the wall of the Waterworks, is as if it had not been. What was the object of that strange exodus we shall probably never know, for the simple reason that every one who knew will probably be cut to pieces in the course of the next two or three hours.

'I have heard, about three minutes ago, that Buck and Buck's methods have won after all. He was perfectly right, of course, when one comes to think of it, in holding that it was physically impossible for a street to defeat a city. While we thought he was patrolling the eastern gates with his Purple Army; while we were rushing about the streets and waving halberds and lanterns; while poor old Wilson was scheming like Moltke and fighting like Achilles to entrap the wild Provost of Notting Hill—Mr. Buck, retired draper, has simply driven down in a hansom cab and done something about as plain as butter and about as useful and nasty. He has gone down to South Kensington, Brompton, and Fulham, and by spending about four thousand pounds of his private means, has raised an army of nearly as many men; that is to say, an army big enough to beat, not only Wayne, but Wayne and all his present enemies put together. The army, I understand, is encamped along High Street, Kensington, and fills it from the Church to Addison Road Bridge. It is to advance by ten different roads uphill to the north.

'I cannot endure to remain here. Everything makes it worse than it need be. The dawn, for instance, has broken round Campden Hill; splendid spaces of silver, edged with gold, are torn out of the sky. Worse still, Wayne and his men feel the dawn; their faces, though bloody and pale, are strangely hopeful . . . insupportably pathetic. Worst of all, for the moment they are winning. If it were not for Buck and the new army they might just, and only just, win.

'I repeat, I cannot stand it. It is like watching that wonderful play of old Maeterlinck's (you know my partiality for the healthy, jolly old authors of the nineteenth century), in which one has to watch the quiet conduct of people inside a parlour, while knowing that the very men are outside the door whose word can blast it all with tragedy. And this is worse, for the men are not talking, but writhing and bleeding and dropping dead for a thing that is already settled —and settled against them. The great grey masses of men still toil and tug and sway hither and thither around the great grey tower; and the tower is still motionless, as it will always be motionless. These men will be crushed before the sun is set; and new men will arise and be crushed, and new wrongs done, and tyranny will always rise again like the sun, and injustice will always be as fresh as the flowers of spring. And the stone tower will always look down on it. Matter, in its brutal beauty, will always look down on those who are mad enough to consent to die, and yet more mad, since they consent to live.'

Thus ended abruptly the first and last contribution of the Special Correspondent of the *Court Journal* to that valued periodical.

The Correspondent himself, as has been said, was simply sick and gloomy at the last news of the triumph of Buck. He slouched sadly down the steep Aubrey Road, up which he had the night before run in so unusual an excitement, and strolled out into the empty dawn-lit main road, looking vaguely for a cab. He saw nothing in the vacant space except a blue-and-gold glittering thing, running very fast, which looked at first like a very tall beetle, but turned out, to his great astonishment, to be Barker.

'Have you heard the good news?' asked that gentleman.

'Yes,' said Quin, with a measured voice. 'I have heard the glad tidings of great joy. Shall we take a hansom down to Kensington? I see one over there.'

They took the cab, and, were, in four minutes, fronting the ranks of the multitudinous and invincible army. Quin had not spoken a word all the way, and something about him had prevented the essentially impressionable Barker from speaking either.

The great army, as it moved up Kensington High Street, calling many heads to the numberless windows, for it was long indeed—longer than the lives of most of the tolerably young—since such an army had been seen in London. Compared with the vast organization which was now swallowing up the miles, with Buck at its head as leader, and the King hanging at its tail as journalist, the whole story of our problem was insignificant. In the presence of that army the red Notting Hills and the green Bayswaters were alike tiny and straggling groups. In its presence the whole struggle round Pump Street was like an ant-hill under the hoof of an ox. Every man who felt or looked at that infinity of men knew that it was the triumph of Buck's brutal arithmetic. Whether Wayne was right or wrong, wise or foolish, was quite a fair matter for discussion. But it was a matter of history. At the foot of Church Street, opposite Kensington Church, they paused in their glowing good humour.

'Let us send some kind of messenger or herald up to them,' said Buck, turning to Barker and the King.

'Let us send and ask them to cave in without more muddle.'

'What shall we say to them?' said Barker, doubtfully.

'The facts of the case are quite sufficient,' rejoined Buck. 'It is the facts of the case that make an enemy surrender. Let us simply say that our army that is fighting their army, and their army that is fighting our army, amount altogether to about a thousand men. Say that we have four thousand. It is very simple. Of the thousand fighting, they have at the very most, three hundred, so that, with those three hundred, they have now to fight four thousand seven hundred men. Let them do it if it amuses them.'

And the Provost of North Kensington laughed.

The herald who was dispatched up Church Street in all the pomp of the South Kensington blue and gold, with the Three Birds on his tabard, was attended by two trumpeters.

'What will they do when they consent?' asked Barker, for the sake of saying something in the sudden stillness of that immense army.

'I know my Wayne very well,' said Buck, laughing. 'When he submits he will send a red herald flaming with the Lion of Notting Hill. Even defeat will be delightful to him, since it is formal and romantic.'

The King, who had strolled up to the head of the line, broke silence for the first time.

'I shouldn't wonder,' he said, 'if he defied you, and didn't send the herald after all. I don't think you do know your Wayne quite so well as you think.'

'All right, your Majesty,' said Buck, easily; 'if it isn't disrespectful, I'll put my political calculations in a very simple form. I'll lay you ten pounds to a shilling the herald comes with the surrender.'

'All right,' said Auberon. 'I may be wrong, but it's my notion of Adam Wayne that he'll die in his city, and that, till he is dead, it will not be a safe property.'

'The bet's made, your Majesty,' said Buck.

Another long silence ensued, in the course of which Barker alone, amid the motionless army, strolled and stamped in his restless way.

Then Buck suddenly leant forward.

'It's taking your money, your Majesty,' he said. 'I knew it was. There comes the herald from Adam Wayne.'

'It's not,' cried the King, peering forward also. 'You brute, it's a red omnibus.'

'It's not,' said Buck, calmly; and the King did not answer, for down the centre of the spacious and silent Church Street was walking, beyond question, the herald of the Red Lion, with two trumpeters.

Buck had something in him which taught him how to be magnanimous. In his hour of success he felt magnanimous towards Wayne, whom he really admired; magnanimous towards the King, off whom he had scored so publicly; and, above all, magnanimous towards Barker, who was the titular leader of this vast South Kensington army, which his own talent had evoked.

'General Barker,' he said, bowing, 'do you propose now to receive the message from the besieged?'

Barker bowed also, and advanced towards the herald.

'Has your master, Mr. Adam Wayne, received our request for surrender?' he asked.

The herald conveyed a solemn and respectful affirmative.

Barker resumed, coughing slightly, but encouraged.

'What answer does your master send?'

The herald again inclined himself submissively, and answered in a kind of monotone.

'My message is this. Adam Wayne, Lord High Provost of Notting Hill, under the charter of King Auberon and the laws of God and all mankind, free and of a free city, greets James Barker, Lord High Provost of South Kensington, by the same rights free and honourable, leader of the army of the South. With all friendly reverence, and with all constitutional consideration, he desires James Barker to lay down his arms, and the whole army under his command to lay down their arms also.'

Before the words were ended the King had run forward into the open space with shining eyes. The rest of the staff and the forefront of the army were literally struck breathless. When they recovered they began to laugh beyond restraint; the revulsion was too sudden.

'The Lord High Provost of Notting Hill,' continued the herald, 'does not propose, in the event of your surrender, to use his victory for any of those repressive purposes which others have entertained against him. He will leave you your free laws and your free cities, your flags and your governments. He will not destroy the religion of South Kensington, or crush the old customs of Bayswater.'

An irrepressible explosion of laughter went up from the forefront of the great army.

'The King must have had something to do with this humour,' said Buck, slapping his thigh. 'It's too deliciously insolent. Barker, have a glass of wine.'

And in his conviviality he actually sent a soldier across to the restaurant opposite the church and brought out two glasses for a toast.

When the laughter had died down, the herald continued quite monotonously:

'In the event of your surrendering your arms and dispersing under the superintendence of our forces, these local rights of yours shall be carefully observed. In the event of your not doing so, the Lord High Provost of Notting Hill desires to announce that he has just captured the Waterworks Tower, just above you, on Campden Hill, and that within ten minutes from now, that is, on the reception through me of your refusal, he will open the great reservoir and flood the whole valley where you stand in thirty feet of water. God save King Auberon!'

Buck had dropped his glass and sent a great splash of wine over the road.

'But—but——' he said; and then by a last and splendid effort of his great sanity, looked the facts in the face.

'We must surrender,' he said. 'You could do nothing against fifty thousand tons of water coming down a steep hill, ten minutes hence. We must surrender. Our four thousand men might as well be four. *Vicisti Galilaea!* Perkins, you may as well get me another glass of wine.'

In this way the vast army of South Kensington surrendered and the Empire of Notting Hill began. One further fact in this connexion is perhaps worth mentioning—the fact that, after his victory, Adam Wayne caused the great tower on Campden Hill to be plated with gold and inscribed with a great epitaph, saying that it was the monument of Wilfrid Lambert, the heroic defender of the place, and surmounted with a statue, in which his large nose was done something less than justice to.

BOOK V

CHAPTER I

THE EMPIRE OF NOTTING HILL

On the evening of the third of October, twenty years after the great victory of Notting Hill, which gave it the dominion of London, King Auberon, came, as of old, out of Kensington Palace.

He had changed little, save for a streak or two of grey in his hair, for his face had always been old, and his step slow, and, as it were, decrepit.

If he looked old, it was not because of anything physical or mental. It was because he still wore, with a quaint conservatism, the frock-coat and high hat of the days before the great war. 'I have survived the Deluge,' he said. 'I am a pyramid, and must behave as such.'

As he passed up the street the Kensingtonians, in their picturesque blue smocks, saluted him as a King, and then looked after him as a curiosity. It seemed odd to them that men had once worn so elvish an attire.

The King, cultivating the walk attributed to the oldest inhabitant ('Gaffer Auberon' his friends were now confidentially desired to call him), went toddling northward. He paused, with reminiscence in his eye, at the Southern Gate of Notting Hill, one of those nine great gates of bronze and steel, wrought with reliefs of the old battles, by the hand of Chiffy himself.

'Ah!' he said, shaking his head and assuming an unnecessary air of age, and a provincialism of accent, 'Ah! I mind when there warn't none of this here.'

He passed through the Ossington Gate, surmounted

171

by a great lion, wrought in red copper on yellow brass, with the motto, 'Nothing Ill'. The guard in red and gold saluted him with his halberd.

It was about sunset, and the lamps were being lit. Auberon paused to look at them, for they were Chiffy's finest work, and his artistic eye never failed to feast on them. In memory of the Great Battle of the Lamps, each great iron lamp was surmounted by a veiled figure, sword in hand, holding over the flame an iron hood or extinguisher, as if ready to let it fall if the armies of the South and West should again show their flags in the city. Thus no child in Notting Hill could play about the streets without the very lamp-posts reminding him of the salvation of his country in the dreadful year.

'Old Wayne was right in a way,' commented the King. 'The sword does make things beautiful. It has made the whole world romantic by now. And to think people once thought me a buffoon for suggesting a romantic Notting Hill. Deary me, deary me (I think that is the expression). It seems like a previous existence.'

Turning a corner he found himself in Pump Street, opposite the four shops which Adam Wayne had studied twenty years before. He entered idly the shop of Mr. Mead, the grocer. Mr. Mead was somewhat older, like the rest of the world, and his red beard, which he now wore with a moustache, and long and full, was partly blanched and discoloured. He was dressed in a long and richly embroidered robe of blue, brown, and crimson, interwoven with an Eastern complexity of pattern, and covered with obscure symbols and pictures, representing his wares passing from hand to hand and from nation to nation. Round his neck was the chain with the Blue Argosy cut in turquoise, which he wore as Grand Master of the Grocers. The whole shop had the sombre and sumptuous look of its owner. The wares were displayed as prominently as in the old days, but they were now blended and arranged with a sense of tint and grouping, too often neglected by the dim grocers of those forgotten days. The wares were shown plainly, but shown not so much as an old grocer would have shown his stock, but rather as an educated virtuoso would have shown his treasures. The tea was stored in great blue and green vases, inscribed with the nine indispensable sayings of the wise men of China. Other vases of a confused orange and purple, less rigid and dominant, more humble and dreamy, stored symbolically the tea of India. A row of caskets of a simple silvery metal contained tinned meats. Each was wrought with some rude but rhythmic form, as a shell, a horn, a fish, or an apple, to indicate what material had been canned in it.

'Your Majesty,' said Mr. Mead, sweeping an Oriental reverence. 'This is an honour to me, but yet more an honour to the city.'

Auberon took off his hat.

'Mr. Mead,' he said, 'Notting Hill, whether in giving or taking, can deal in nothing but honour. Do you happen to sell liquorice?'

'Liquorice, sire,' said Mr. Mead, 'is not the least important of our benefits out of the dark heart of Arabia.'

And going reverently towards a green and silver canister, made in the form of an Arabian mosque, he proceeded to serve his customer.

'I was just thinking, Mr. Mead,' said the King reflectively, 'I don't know why I should think about it just now, but I was just thinking of twenty years ago. Do you remember the times before the war?'

The grocer, having wrapped up the liquorice sticks in a piece of paper (inscribed with some appropriate sentiment), lifted his large grey eyes dreamily, and looked at the darkening sky outside.

'Oh, yes, your Majesty,' he said. 'I remember these streets before the Lord Provost began to rule us. I can't remember how we felt very well. All the great songs and the fighting change one so; and I don't think we can really estimate all we owe to the Provost; but I can remember his coming into this very shop twenty-two years ago, and I remember the things he said. The singular thing is that as far as I remember I thought the things he said odd at that time. Now it's the things that I said, as far as I can recall them, that seem to me odd—as odd as a madman's antics.'

'Ah!' said the King; and looked at him with an unfathomable quietness.

'I thought nothing of being a grocer then,' he said. 'Isn't that odd enough for anybody? I thought nothing of all the wonderful places that my goods come from, and wonderful ways that they are made. I did not know that I was for all practical purposes a king with slaves spearing fishes near the secret pool, and gathering fruits in the islands under the world. My mind was a blank on the thing. I was as mad as a hatter.'

The King turned also, and stared out into the dark, where the great lamps that commemorated the battle were already flaming.

'And is this the end of poor old Wayne?' he said, half to himself. 'To inflame every one so much that he is lost himself in the blaze. Is this his victory, that he, my incomparable Wayne, is now only one in a

world of Waynes? Has he conquered and become by
conquest commonplace? Must Mr. Mead, the grocer,
talk as high as he? Lord! what a strange world in
which a man cannot remain unique even by taking the
trouble to go mad.'

And he went dreamily out of the shop.

He paused outside the next one almost precisely as
the Provost had done two decades before.

'How uncommonly creepy this shop looks,' he said.
'But yet somehow encouragingly creepy, invitingly
creepy. It looks like something in a jolly old nursery
story in which you are frightened out of your skin,
and yet know that things always end well. The way
those low sharp gables are carved like great black bat's
wings folded down, and the way those queer-coloured
bowls underneath are made to shine like giant's eye-
balls. It looks like a benevolent warlock's hut. It is
apparently a chemist's.'

Almost as he spoke, Mr. Bowles, the chemist, came
to his shop door in a long black velvet gown and hood,
monastic as it were, but yet with a touch of the diabolic.
His hair was still quite black, and his face even paler
than of old. The only spot of colour he carried was
a red star cut in some precious stone of strong tint,
hung on his breast. He belonged to the Society of the
Red Star of Charity, founded on the lamps displayed
by doctors and chemists.

'A fine evening, sir,' said the chemist. 'Why, I can
scarcely be mistaken in supposing it to be your Majesty.
Pray step inside and share a bottle of sal volatile, or
anything that may take your fancy. As it happens
there is an old acquaintance of your Majesty's in my
shop carousing (if I may be permitted the term) upon
that beverage at this moment.'

The King entered the shop, which was an Aladdin's garden of shades and hues, for as the chemist's scheme of colour was more brilliant than the grocer's scheme, so it was arranged with even more delicacy and fancy. Never, if the phrase may be employed, had such a nosegay of medicines been presented to the artistic eye.

But even the solemn rainbow of that evening interior was rivalled or even eclipsed by the figure standing in the centre of the shop. His form, which was a large and stately one, was clad in a brilliant blue velvet, cut in the richest Renaissance fashion, and slashed so as to show gleams and gaps of a wonderful lemon or pale yellow. He had several chains round his neck and his plumes, which were of several tints of bronze and gold, hung down to the great gold hilt of his long sword. He was drinking a dose of sal volatile, and admiring its opal tint. The King advanced with a slight mystification towards the tall figure, whose face was in shadow, then he said:

'By the Great Lord of Luck, Barker!'

The figure removed his plumed cap, showing the same dark head and long, almost equine, face which the King had so often seen rising out of the high collar of Bond Street. Except for a grey patch on each temple, it was totally unchanged.

'Your Majesty,' said Barker, 'this is a meeting nobly retrospective, a meeting that has about it a certain October gold. I drink to old days'; and he finished his sal volatile with simple feeling.

'I am delighted to see you again, Barker,' said the King. 'It is, indeed, long since we met. What with my travels in Asia Minor, and my book having to be written (you have read my *Life of Prince Albert for*

Children, of course), we have scarcely met twice since the great war. That is twenty years ago.'

'I wonder,' said Barker, thoughtfully, 'if I might speak freely to your Majesty.'

'Well,' said Auberon, 'it's rather late in the day to start speaking respectfully. Flap away, my bird of freedom.'

'Well, your Majesty,' replied Barker, lowering his voice, 'I don't think it will be so long to the next war.'

'What do you mean?' asked Auberon.

'We will stand this insolence no longer,' burst out Barker, fiercely. 'We are not slaves because Adam Wayne twenty years ago cheated us with a water-pipe. Notting Hill is Notting Hill; it is not the world. We in South Kensington, we also have memories—aye, and hopes. If they fought for these trumpery shops and a few lamp-posts, shall we not fight for the great High Street and the sacred Natural History Museum?'

'Great Heavens!' said the astounded Auberon. 'Will wonders never cease? Have the two greatest marvels been achieved? Have you turned altruistic, and has Wayne turned selfish? Are you the patriot, and he the tyrant?'

'It is not from Wayne himself altogether that the evil comes,' answered Barker. 'He, indeed, is now mostly wrapped in dreams, and sits with his old sword beside the fire. But Notting Hill is the tyrant, your Majesty. Its Council and its crowds have been so intoxicated by the spreading over the whole city of Wayne's old ways and visions, that they try to meddle with every one, and rule every one, and civilize every one, and tell every one what is good for him. I do not deny the great impulse which his old war, wild as it seemed, gave to the civic life of our time. It came when I was still a young man, and I admit it enlarged my career. But we are not going to see our own cities flouted and thwarted from day to day because of something Wayne did for us all nearly a quarter of a century ago. I am just waiting here for news upon this very matter. It is rumoured that Notting Hill has vetoed the statue of General Wilson they are putting up opposite Chepstow Place. If that is so, it is a black and white shameless breach of the terms on which we surrendered to Turnbull after the battle of the Tower. We were to keep our own customs and self-government. If that is so——'

'It is so,' said a deep voice; and both men turned round.

A burly figure in purple robes, with a silver eagle hung round his neck and moustaches almost as florid as his plumes, stood in the doorway.

'Yes,' he said, acknowledging the King's start, 'I am Provost Buck, and the news is true. These men of the Hill have forgotten that we fought round the Tower as well as they did, and that it is sometimes foolish, as well as base, to despise the conquered.'

'Let us step outside,' said Barker, with a grim composure.

Buck did so, and stood rolling his eyes up and down the lamp-lit street.

'I would like to have a go at smashing all this,' he muttered, 'though I am over sixty. I would like——'

His voice ended in a cry, and he reeled back a step, with his hands to his eyes, as he had done in those streets twenty years before.

'Darkness!' he cried—'darkness again! What does it mean?'

For in truth every lamp in the street had gone out, so that they could not see even each other's outline, except faintly. The voice of the chemist came with startling cheerfulness out of the density.

'Oh, don't you know?' he said. 'Did they never tell you this is the Feast of the Lamps, the anniversary of the great battle that almost lost and just saved Notting Hill? Don't you know, your Majesty, that on this night twenty-one years ago we saw Wilson's green uniforms charging down this street, and driving Wayne and Turnbull back upon the gas-works, fighting with their handful of men like fiends from hell? And that then, in that great hour, Wayne sprang through a window of the gas-works, with one blow of his hand brought darkness on the whole city, and then with a cry like a lion's, that was heard through four streets, flew at Wilson's men, sword in hand, and swept them, bewildered as they were, and ignorant of the map, clear out of the sacred street again? And don't you know that upon that night every year all lights are turned out for half an hour while we sing the Notting Hill anthem in the darkness? Hark! there it begins.'

Through the night came a crash of drums, and then a strong swell of human voices:

'When the world was in the balance, there was night on Notting Hill,
(There was night on Notting Hill): it was nobler than the day;
On the cities where the lights are and the firesides glow,
From the seas and from the deserts came the thing we did not know,
Came the darkness, came the darkness, came the darkness on the foe.
    And the old guard of God turned to bay.
For the old guard of God turns to bay, turns to bay,
And the stars fall down before it ere its banners fall to-day.

For when armies were around us as a howling and a horde,
When falling was the citadel and broken was the sword,
The darkness came upon them like the Dragon of the Lord,
    When the old guard of God turned to bay.'

The voices were just uplifting themselves in a second
verse, when they were stopped by a scurry and a yell.
Barker had bounded into the street with a cry of 'South
Kensington!' and a drawn dagger. In less time than
man could blink, the whole packed street was full of
curses and struggling. Barker was flung back against
the shop-front, but used the second only to draw his
sword as well as his dagger, and calling out, 'This is
not the first time I've come through the thick of you',
flung himself again into the press. It was evident that
he had drawn blood at last, for a more violent outcry
arose, and many other knives and swords were discernible in the faint light. Barker, after having
wounded more than one man, seemed on the point of
being flung back again, when Buck suddenly stepped
out into the street. He had no weapon, for he affected
rather the peaceful magnificence of the great burgher,
than the pugnacious dandyism which had replaced the
old sombre dandyism in Barker. But with a blow of
his clenched fist he broke the pane of the next shop,
which was the old curiosity shop, and, plunging in his
hand, snatched a kind of Japanese scimitar, and calling
out, 'Kensington! Kensington!' rushed to Barker's
assistance.

Barker's sword was broken, but he was laying about
him with his dagger. Just as Buck ran up, a man of
Notting Hill struck Barker down, but Buck struck the
man down on top of him, and Barker sprang up again,
the blood running down his face.

Suddenly all these cries were cloven by a great voice,

that seemed to fall out of heaven. It was terrible to Buck and Barker and the King from its seeming to come out the empty skies; but it was more terrible because it was a familiar voice, and one which at the same time they had not heard for so long.

'Turn up the lights,' said the voice from above them, and for a moment there was no reply, but only a tumult.

'In the name of Notting Hill, and of the great Council of the City, turn up the lights.'

There was again a tumult and a vagueness for a moment, then the whole street and every object in it sprang suddenly out of the darkness, as every lamp sprang into life. And looking up they saw, standing upon a balcony near the roof of one of the highest houses, the figure and the face of Adam Wayne, his red hair blowing behind him, a little streaked with grey.

'What is this, my people?' he said. 'Is it altogether impossible to make a thing good without it immediately insisting on being wicked? The glory of Notting Hill in having achieved its independence, has been enough for me to dream of for many years, as I sat beside the fire. Is it really not enough for you, who have had so many other affairs to excite and distract you? Notting Hill is a nation. Why should it condescend to be a mere Empire? You wish to pull down the statue of General Wilson, which the men of Bayswater have so rightly erected in Westbourne Grove. Fools! Who erected that statue? Did Bayswater erect it? No. Notting Hill erected it. Do you not see that it is the glory of our achievement that we have infected the other cities with the idealism of Notting Hill? It is we who have created not only our own side, but both

sides of this controversy. O too humble fools—why
should you wish to destroy your enemies? You have
done something more to them. You have created your
enemies. You wish to pull down that gigantic silver
hammer, which stands, like an obelisk, in the centre
of the Broadway of Hammersmith. Fools! Before
Notting Hill arose, did any person passing through
Hammersmith Broadway expect to see there a gigantic
silver hammer? You wish to abolish the great bronze
figure of a knight standing upon the artificial bridge
at Knightsbridge. Fools! Who would have thought
of it before Notting Hill arose? I have even heard,
and with deep pain I have heard it, that the evil eye
of our imperial envy has been cast towards the remote
horizon of the west, and that we have objected to the
great black monument of a crowned raven, which
commemorates the skirmish of Ravenscourt Park. Who
created all these things? Were they there before we
came? Cannot you be content with that destiny which
was enough for Athens, which was enough for Nazareth?
the destiny, the humble purpose of creating a new
world. Is Athens angry because Romans and Floren-
tines have adopted her phraseology for expressing their
own patriotism? Is Nazareth angry because as a little
village it has become the type of all little villages out of
which, as the Snobs say, no good can come? Has Athens
asked every one to wear the chlamys? Are all the
followers of the Nazarene compelled to wear turbans?
No! but the soul of Athens went forth and made men
drink hemlock, and the soul of Nazareth went forth
and made men consent to be crucified. So has the
soul of Notting Hill gone forth and made men realize
what it is to live in a city. Just as we inaugurated our
symbols and ceremonies, so they have inaugurated

theirs; and are you so mad as to contend against them? Notting Hill is right; it has always been right. It has moulded itself on its own necessities, its own *sine qua non*, it has accepted its own ultimatum. Because it is a nation it has created itself. And because it is a nation it can destroy itself. Notting Hill shall always be the judge. If it is your will because of this matter of General Wilson's statue to make war upon Bayswater——'

A roar of cheers broke in upon his words, and further speech was impossible. Pale to the lips, the great patriot tried again and again to speak; but even his authority could not keep down the dark and roaring masses in the street below him. He said something further, but it was not audible. He descended at last sadly from the garret in which he lived, and mingled with the crowd at the foot of the houses. Finding General Turnbull, he put his hand on his shoulder with a queer affection and gravity, and said:

'To-morrow, old man, we shall have a new experience, as fresh as the flowers of spring. We shall be defeated. You and I have been through three battles together, and have somehow or other missed this peculiar delight. It is unfortunate that we shall not probably be able to exchange our experiences, because, as it most annoyingly happens, we shall probably both be dead.'

Turnbull looked dimly surprised.

'I don't mind so much about being dead,' he said, 'but why should you say that we shall be defeated?'

'The answer is very simple,' replied Wayne, calmly. 'It is because we ought to be defeated. We have been in the most horrible holes before now; but in all those I was perfectly certain that the stars were on our side, and that we ought to get out. Now, I know that we ought not to get out; and that takes away from me everything with which I won.'

As Wayne spoke he started a little, for both men became aware that a third figure was listening to them —a small figure with wondering eyes.

'Is it really true, my dear Wayne,' said the King, interrupting, 'that you think you will be beaten to-morrow?'

'There can be no doubt about it whatever,' replied Adam Wayne; 'the real reason is the one of which I have just spoken. But as a concession to your materialism, I will add that they have an organized army of a hundred allied cities against our one. That in itself, however, would be unimportant.'

Quin, with his round eyes, seemed strangely insistent. 'You are quite sure,' he said, 'that you must be beaten?'

'I am afraid,' said Turnbull, gloomily, 'that there can be no doubt about it.'

'Then,' cried the King, flinging out his arms, 'give me a halberd! Give me a halberd, somebody! I desire all men to witness that I, Auberon, King of England, do here and now abdicate and implore the Provost of Notting Hill to permit me to enlist in his army. Give me a halberd!'

He seized one from some passing guard, and, shouldering it, stamped solemnly after the shouting columns of halberdiers which were, by this time, parading the streets. He had, however, nothing to do with the wrecking of the statue of General Wilson, which took place before morning.

CHAPTER II

THE LAST BATTLE

THE day was cloudy when Wayne went down to die with all his army in Kensington Gardens; it was cloudy again when that army had been swallowed up by the vast armies of a new world. There had been an almost uncanny interval of sunshine, in which the Provost of Notting Hill, with all the placidity of an onlooker, had gazed across to the hostile armies on the great spaces of verdure opposite; the long strips of green and blue and gold lay across the park in squares and oblongs like a proposition in Euclid wrought in a rich embroidery. But the sunlight was a weak and, as it were, a wet sunlight, and was soon swallowed up. Wayne spoke to the King, with a queer sort of coldness and languor, as to the military operations. It was as he had said the night before, that being deprived of his sense of an impracticable rectitude he was, in effect, being deprived of everything. He was out of date, and at sea in a mere world of compromise and competition, of Empire against Empire, of the tolerably right and the tolerably wrong. When his eye fell on the King, however, who was marching very gravely with a top hat and a halberd, it brightened slightly.

'Well, your Majesty,' he said, 'you at least ought to be proud to-day. If your children are fighting each other, at least those who win are your children. Other kings have distributed justice, you have distributed life. Other kings have ruled a nation, you have created nations. Others have made kingdoms, you have begotten them. Look at your children,

father.' And he stretched his hand out towards the
enemy.

Auberon did not raise his eyes.

'See how splendidly,' cried Wayne, 'the new cities
come on—the new cities from across the river. See
where Battersea advances over there—under the flag
of the Lost Dog; and Putney—don't you see the Man
on the White Boar shining on their standard as the
sun catches it? It is the coming of a new age, your
Majesty. Notting Hill is not a common empire; it is
a thing like Athens, the mother of a mode of life, of
a manner of living, which shall renew the youth of the
world—a thing like Nazareth. When I was young I
remember, in the old dreary days, wiseacres used to
write books about how trains would get faster, and all
the world would be one empire, and tram-cars go to
the moon. And even as a child I used to say to myself,
"Far more likely that we shall go on the crusades
again, or worship the gods of the city." And so it has
been. And I am glad, though this is my last battle.'

Even as he spoke there came a crash of steel from
the left, and he turned his head.

'Wilson!' he cried, with a kind of joy. 'Red Wilson
has charged our left. No one can hold him in; he eats
swords. He is as keen a soldier as Turnbull, but less
patient—less really great. Ha! and Barker is moving.
How Barker has improved; how handsome he looks.
It is not all having plumes; it is also having a soul in
one's daily life. Ha!'

And another crash of steel on the right showed that
Barker had closed with Notting Hill on the other side.

'Turnbull is there!' cried Wayne. 'See him hurl
them back! Barker is checked! Turnbull charges—
wins! But our left is broken. Wilson has smashed

Bowles and Mead, and may turn our flank. Forward, the Provost's Guard!'

And the whole centre moved forward, Wayne's face and hair and sword flaming in the van.

The King ran suddenly forward.

The next instant a great jar that went through it told that it had met the enemy. And right over against them through the wood of their own weapons Auberon saw the Purple Eagle of Buck of North Kensington.

On the left Red Wilson was storming the broken ranks, his little green figure conspicuous even in the tangle of men and weapons, with the flaming red moustaches and the crown of laurel. Bowles slashed at his head and tore away some of the wreath, leaving the rest bloody, and, with a roar like a bull's, Wilson sprang at him, and, after a rattle of fencing, plunged his point into the chemist, who fell, crying 'Notting Hill!' Then the Notting Hillers wavered, and Bayswater swept them back in confusion. Wilson had carried everything before him.

On the right, however, Turnbull had carried the Red Lion banner with a rush against Barker's men, and the banner of the Golden Birds bore up with difficulty against it. Barker's men fell fast. In the centre Wayne and Buck were engaged, stubborn and confused. So far as the fighting went, it was precisely equal. But the fighting was a farce. For behind the three small armies with which Wayne's small army was engaged lay the great sea of the allied armies, which looked on as yet as scornful spectators, but could have broken all four armies by moving a finger.

Suddenly they did move. Some of the front contingents, the pastoral chiefs from Shepherd's Bush, with their spears and fleeces, were seen advancing, and the rude clans from Paddington Green. They were advancing for a very good reason. Buck, of North Kensington, was signalling wildly; he was surrounded, and totally cut off. His regiments were a struggling mass of people, islanded in a red sea of Notting Hill.

The allies had been too careless and confident. They had allowed Barker's force to be broken to pieces by Turnbull, and the moment that was done, the astute old leader of Notting Hill swung his men round and attacked Buck behind and on both sides. At the same moment Wayne cried 'Charge!' and struck him in front like a thunderbolt.

Two-thirds of Buck's men were cut to pieces before their allies could reach them. Then the sea of cities came on with their banners like breakers, and swallowed Notting Hill for ever. The battle was not over, for not one of Wayne's men would surrender, and it lasted till sundown, and long after. But it was decided; the story of Notting Hill was ended.

When Turnbull saw it, he ceased a moment from fighting, and looked round him. The evening sunlight struck his face; it looked like a child's.

'I have had my youth,' he said. Then snatching an axe from a man, he dashed into the thick of the spears of Shepherd's Bush, and died somewhere far in the depths of their reeling ranks. Then the battle roared on; every man of Notting Hill was slain before night.

Wayne was standing by a tree alone after the battle. Several men approached him with axes. One struck at him. His foot seemed partly to slip; but he flung his hand out, and steadied himself against the tree.

Barker sprang after him, sword in hand, and shaking with excitement.

'How large now, my Lord,' he cried, 'is the Empire of Notting Hill?'

Wayne smiled in the gathering dark.

'Always as large as this,' he said, and swept his sword round in a semicircle of silver.

Barker dropped, wounded in the neck; and Wilson sprang over his body like a tiger-cat, rushing at Wayne. At the same moment there came behind the Lord of the Red Lion a cry and a flare of yellow, and a mass of the West Kensington halberdiers ploughed up the slope, knee-deep in grass, bearing the yellow banner of the city before them, and shouting aloud.

At the same second Wilson went down under Wayne's sword, seemingly smashed like a fly. The great sword rose again like a bird, but Wilson seemed to rise with it, and, his sword being broken, sprang at Wayne's throat like a dog. The foremost of the yellow halberdiers had reached the tree and swung his axe above the struggling Wayne. With a curse the King whirled up his own halberd and dashed the blade in the man's face. He reeled, and rolled down the slope, just as the furious Wilson was flung on his back again. And again he was on his feet, and again at Wayne's throat. Then he was flung again, but this time laughing triumphantly. Grasped in his hand was the red and yellow favour that Wayne wore as Provost of Notting Hill. He had torn it from the place where it had been carried for twenty-five years.

With a shout the West Kensington men closed round Wayne, the great yellow banner flapping over his head.

'Where is your favour now, Provost?' cried the West Kensington leader.

And a laugh went up.

Adam struck at the standard-bearer and brought him reeling forward. As the banner stooped, he grasped the yellow folds and tore off a shred. A halberdier struck him on the shoulder, wounding bloodily.

'Here is one colour!' he cried, pushing the yellow into his belt; 'and here!' he cried, pointing to his own blood, 'Here is the other.'

At the same instant the shock of a sudden and heavy halberd laid the King stunned or dead. In the wild visions of vanishing consciousness, he saw again something that belonged to an utterly forgotten time, something that he had seen somewhere long ago in a restaurant. He saw, with his swimming eyes, red and yellow, the colours of Nicaragua.

Quin did not see the end. Wilson, wild with joy, sprang again at Adam Wayne, and the great sword of Notting Hill was whirled above once more. Then men ducked instinctively at the rushing noise of the sword coming down out of the sky, and Wilson of Bayswater was smashed and wiped down upon the floor like a fly. Nothing was left of him but a wreck; but the blade that had broken him was broken. In dying he had snapped the great sword and the spell of it; the sword of Wayne was broken at the hilt. One rush of the enemy carried Wayne by force against the tree. They were too close to use halberd or even sword; they were breast to breast, even nostrils to nostrils. But Buck got his dagger free.

'Kill him!' he cried, in a strange stifled voice. 'Kill him! Good or bad, he is none of us! Do not be blinded by the face! . . . God! have we not been blinded all along!' and he drew his arm back for a stab and seemed to close his eyes.

Wayne did not drop the hand that hung on to the

tree-branch. But a mighty heave went over his breast and his whole huge figure, like an earthquake over great hills. And with that convulsion of effort he rent the branch out of the tree, with tongues of torn wood. And swaying it once only, he let the splintered club fall on Buck, breaking his neck. The planner of the Great Road fell face foremost dead, with his dagger in a grip of steel.

'For you and me, and for all brave men, my brother,' said Wayne, in his strange chant, 'there is good wine poured in the inn at the end of the world.'

The packed men made another lurch or heave towards him; it was almost too dark to fight clearly. He caught hold of the oak again, this time getting his hand into a wide crevice and grasping, as it were, the bowels of the tree. The whole crowd, numbering some thirty men, made a rush to tear him away from it; they hung on with all their weight and numbers, and nothing stirred. A solitude could not have been stiller than that group of straining men. Then there was a faint sound.

'His hand is slipping,' cried two men in exultation.

'You don't know much of him,' said another, grimly (a man of the old war). 'More likely his bone cracks.'

'It is neither—by God, it is neither!' said one of the first two.

'What is it, then?' asked the second.

'The tree is falling,' he replied.

'As the tree falleth, so shall it lie,' said Wayne's voice out of the darkness, and it had the same sweet and yet horrible air that it had had throughout, of coming from a great distance, from before or after the event. Even when he was struggling like an eel or battering like a madman, he spoke like a spectator.

'As the tree falleth, so shall it lie,' he said. 'Men have called that a gloomy text. It is the essence of all exultation. I am doing now what I have done all my life, what is the only happiness, what is the only universality. I am clinging to something. Let it fall, and there let it lie. Fools, you go about and see the kingdoms of the earth, and are liberal, and wise, and cosmopolitan, which is all that the devil can give you —all that he could offer to Christ only to be spurned away. I am doing what the truly wise do. When a child goes out into the garden and takes hold of a tree, saying, "Let this tree be all I have", that moment its roots take hold on hell and its branches on the stars. The joy I have is what the lover knows when a woman is everything. It is what a savage knows when his idol is everything. It is what I know when Notting Hill is everything. I have a city. Let it stand or fall.'

As he spoke, the turf lifted itself like a living thing, and out of it rose slowly, like crested serpents, the roots of the oak. Then the great head of the tree, that seemed a green cloud among grey ones, swept the sky suddenly like a broom, and the whole tree heeled over like a ship, smashing every one in its fall.

CHAPTER III

TWO VOICES

In a place in which there was total darkness for hours, there was also for hours total silence. Then a voice spoke out of the darkness, no one could have told from where, and said aloud:

'So ends the Empire of Notting Hill. As it began in blood, so it ended in blood, and all things are always the same.'

And there was silence again, and then again there was a voice, but it had not the same tone; it seemed that it was not the same voice.

'If all things are always the same, it is because they are always heroic. If all things are always the same, it is because they are always new. To each man one soul only is given; to each soul only is given a little power—the power at some moments to outgrow and swallow up the stars. If age after age that power comes upon men, whatever gives it to them is great. Whatever makes men feel old is mean—an empire or a skinflint shop. Whatever makes men feel young is great—a great war or a love-story. And in the darkest of the books of God there is written a truth that is also a riddle. It is of the new things that men tire—of fashions and proposals and improvements and change. It is the old things that startle and intoxicate. It is the old things that are young. There is no sceptic who does not feel that many have doubted before. There is no rich and fickle man who does not feel that all his novelties are ancient. There is no worshipper of change who does not feel upon his neck the vast weight of the weariness of the universe. But we who do the old things are fed by nature with a perpetual infancy. No man who is in love thinks that any one has been in love before. No woman who has a child thinks that there have been such things as children. No people that fight for their own city are haunted with the burden of the broken empires. Yes, oh, dark voice, the world is always the same, for it is always unexpected.'

A little gust of wind blew through the night, and then the first voice answered:

'But in this world there are some, be they wise or foolish, whom nothing intoxicates. There are some who see all your disturbances like a cloud of flies. They know that while men will laugh at your Notting Hill, and will study and rehearse and sing of Athens and Jerusalem, Athens and Jerusalem were silly suburbs like your Notting Hill. They know that the earth itself is a suburb, and can feel only drearily and respectably amused as they move upon it.'

'They are philosophers or they are fools,' said the other voice. 'They are not men. Men live, as I say, rejoicing from age to age in something fresher than progress—in the fact that with every baby a new sun and a new moon are made. If our ancient humanity were a single man, it might perhaps be that he would break down under the memory of so many loyalties, under the burden of so many diverse heroisms, under the load and terror of all the goodness of men. But it has pleased God so to isolate the individual soul that it can only learn of all other souls by hearsay, and to each one goodness and happiness come with the youth and violence of lightning, as momentary and as pure. And the doom of failure that lies on all human systems does not in real fact affect them any more than the worms of the inevitable grave affect a children's game in a meadow. Notting Hill has fallen; Notting Hill has died. But that is not the tremendous issue. Notting Hill has lived.'

'But if,' answered the other voice, 'if what is achieved by all these efforts be only the common contentment of humanity, why do men so extravagantly toil and die in them? Has nothing been done by Notting Hill that any chance clump of farmers or clan of savages would not have done without it? What might have been done to Notting Hill if the world had been different may be a deep question; but there is a deeper. What could have happened to the world if Notting Hill had never been?'

The other voice replied:

'The same that would have happened to the world and all the starry systems if an apple-tree grew six apples instead of seven; something would have been eternally lost. There has never been anything in the world absolutely like Notting Hill. There will never be anything quite like it to the crack of doom. I cannot believe anything but that God loved it as He must surely love anything that is itself and unreplaceable. But even for that I do not care. If God, with all His thunders, hated it, I loved it.'

And with the voice a tall, strange figure lifted itself out of the *débris* in the half-darkness.

The other voice came after a long pause, and as it were hoarsely.

'But suppose the whole matter were really a hocus-pocus. Suppose that whatever meaning you may choose in your fancy to give to it, the real meaning of the whole was mockery. Suppose it was all folly. Suppose——'

'I have been in it,' answered the voice from the tall and strange figure, 'and I know it was not.'

A smaller figure seemed half to rise in the dark.

'Suppose I am God,' said the voice, 'and suppose I made the world in idleness. Suppose the stars, that you think eternal, are only the idiot fireworks of an everlasting schoolboy. Suppose the sun and the moon, to which you sing alternately, are only the two eyes of one vast and sneering giant, opened alternately in a never-ending wink. Suppose the trees, in my eyes, are as foolish as enormous toad-stools. Suppose Socrates and Charlemagne are to me only beasts, made funnier by walking on their hind legs. Suppose I am God, and having made things, laugh at them.'

'And suppose I am man,' answered the other. 'And suppose that I give the answer that shatters even a laugh. Suppose I do not laugh back at you, do not blaspheme you, do not curse you. But suppose, standing up straight under the sky, with every power of my being, I thank you for the fools' paradise you have made. Suppose I praise you, with a literal pain of ecstasy, for the jest that has brought me so terrible a joy. If we have taken the child's games, and given them the seriousness of a Crusade, if we have drenched your grotesque Dutch garden with the blood of martyrs, we have turned a nursery into a temple. I ask you, in the name of Heaven, who wins?'

The sky close about the crest of the hills and trees was beginning to turn from black to grey, with a random suggestion of the morning. The slight figure seemed to crawl towards the larger one, and the voice was more human.

'But suppose, friend,' it said, 'suppose that, in a bitterer and more real sense, it was all a mockery.

Suppose that there had been, from the beginning of these great wars, one who watched them with a sense that is beyond expression, a sense of detachment, of responsibility, of irony, of agony. Suppose that there were one who knew it was all a joke.'

The tall figure answered:

'He could not know it. For it was not all a joke.'

And a gust of wind blew away some clouds that sealed the skyline, and showed a strip of silver behind his great dark legs. Then the other voice came, having crept nearer still.

'Adam Wayne,' it said, 'there are men who confess only in *articulo mortis*; there are people who blame themselves only when they can no longer help others. I am one of them. Here, upon the field of the bloody end of it all, I come to tell you plainly what you would never understand before. Do you know who I am?'

'I know you, Auberon Quin,' answered the tall figure, 'and I shall be glad to unburden your spirit of anything that lies upon it.'

'Adam Wayne,' said the other voice, 'of what I have to say you cannot in common reason be glad to unburden me. Wayne, it was all a joke. When I made these cities, I cared no more for them than I care for a centaur, or a merman, or a fish with legs, or a pig with feathers, or any other absurdity. When I spoke to you solemnly and encouragingly about the flag of your freedom and the peace of your city, I was playing a vulgar practical joke on an honest gentleman, a vulgar practical joke that has lasted for twenty years. Though no one could believe it of me perhaps, it is the truth that I am a man both timid and tender-hearted. I never dared in the early days of your hope, or the central days of your supremacy, to tell you this;

I never dared to break the colossal calm of your face. God knows why I should do it now, when my farce has ended in tragedy and the ruin of all your people! But I say it now. Wayne, it was done as a joke.'

There was silence, and the freshening breeze blew the sky clearer and clearer, leaving great spaces of the white dawn.

At last Wayne said, very slowly:

'You did it all only as a joke?'

'Yes,' said Quin.

'When you conceived the idea,' went on Wayne, dreamily, 'of an army for Bayswater and a flag for Notting Hill, there was no gleam, no suggestion in your mind that such things might be real and passionate?'

'No,' answered Auberon, turning his round, white face to the morning with a dull and splendid sincerity; 'I had none at all.'

Wayne sprang down from the height above him and held out his hand.

'I will not stop to thank you,' he said, with a curious joy in his voice, 'for the great good for the world you have actually wrought. All that I think of that I have said to you a moment ago, even when I thought that your voice was the voice of a derisive omnipotence, its laughter older than the winds of heaven. But let me say what is immediate and true. You and I, Auberon Quin, have both of us throughout our lives been again and again called mad. And we are mad. We are mad, because we are not two men but one man. We are mad, because we are two lobes of the same brain, and that brain has been cloven in two. And if you ask for the proof of it, it is not hard to find. It is not merely that you, the humorist, have been in these dark days stripped of the joy of gravity. It is not merely that I, the fanatic, have had to grope without humour. It is that though we seem to be opposite in everything, we have been opposite like man and woman aiming at the same moment at the same practical thing. We are the father and the mother of the Charter of the Cities.'

Quin looked down at the *débris* of leaves and timber, the relics of the battle and stampede, now glistening in the glowing daylight, and finally said:

'Yet nothing can alter the antagonism—the fact that I laughed at these things and you adored them.'

Wayne's wild face flamed with something god-like, as he turned it to be struck by the sunrise.

'I know of something that will alter that antagonism, something that is outside us, something that you and I have all our lives perhaps taken too little account of. The equal and eternal human being will alter that antagonism, for the human being sees no real antagonism between laughter and respect, the human being, the common man, whom mere geniuses like you and me can only worship like a god. When dark and dreary days come, you and I are necessary, the pure fanatic, the pure satirist. We have between us remedied a great wrong. We have lifted the modern cities into that poetry which every one who knows mankind knows to be immeasurably more common than the commonplace. But in healthy people there is no war between us. We are but the two lobes of the brain of a ploughman. Laughter and love are everywhere. The cathedrals, built in the ages that loved God, are full of blasphemous grotesques. The mother laughs continually at the child, the lover laughs continually at the lover, the wife at the husband, the friend at the friend. Auberon Quin, we have been too long separated; let us go out together. You have a halberd and I a sword, let us start our wanderings over the world. For we are its two essentials. Come, it is already day.'

In the blank white light Auberon hesitated a moment. Then he made the formal salute with his halberd, and they went away together into the unknown world.

THE MAN WHO WAS THURSDAY

Originally published by
Messrs. J. W. Arrowsmith Ltd. in 1908

TO EDMUND CLERIHEW BENTLEY

A cloud was on the mind of men, and wailing went the weather,
Yea, a sick cloud upon the soul when we were boys together.
Science announced nonentity and art admired decay;
The world was old and ended: but you and I were gay;
Round us in antic order their crippled vices came—
Lust that had lost its laughter, fear that had lost its shame.
Like the white lock of Whistler, that lit our aimless gloom,
Men showed their own white feather as proudly as a plume.
Life was a fly that faded, and death a drone that stung;
The world was very old indeed when you and I were young.
They twisted even decent sin to shapes not to be named;
Men were ashamed of honour; but we were not ashamed.
Weak if we were and foolish, not thus we failed, not thus;
When that black Baal blocked the heavens he had no hymns from us.
Children we were—our forts of sand were even as weak as we,
High as they went we piled them up to break that bitter sea.
Fools as we were in motley, all jangling and absurd,
When all church bells were silent our cap and bells were heard.

Not all unhelped we held the fort, our tiny flags unfurled;
Some giants laboured in that cloud to lift it from the world.
I find again the book we found, I feel the hour that flings
Far out of fish-shaped Paumanok some cry of cleaner things;
And the Green Carnation withered, as in forest fires that pass,
Roared in the wind of all the world ten million leaves of grass;
Or sane and sweet and sudden as a bird sings in the rain—
Truth out of Tusitala spoke and pleasure out of pain.
Yea, cool and clear and sudden as a bird sings in the grey,
Dunedin to Samoa spoke, and darkness unto day.
But we were young; we lived to see God break their bitter charms,
God and the good Republic come riding back in arms:
We have seen the City of Mansoul, even as it rocked, relieved—
Blessed are they who did not see, but being blind, believed.

This is a tale of those old fears, even of those emptied hells,
And none but you shall understand the true thing that it tells—
Of what colossal gods of shame could cow men and yet crash,
Of what huge devils hid the stars, yet fell at a pistol flash.
The doubts that were so plain to chase, so dreadful to withstand—
Oh, who shall understand but you; yea, who shall understand?
The doubts that drove us through the night as we two talked amain,
And day had broken on the streets e'er it broke upon the brain.
Between us, by the peace of God, such truth can now be told;
Yea, there is strength in striking root, and good in growing old.
We have found common things at last, and marriage and a creed,
And I may safely write it now, and you may safely read.

G. K. C.

CHAPTER 1

THE TWO POETS OF SAFFRON PARK

THE suburb of Saffron Park lay on the sunset side of London, as red and ragged as a cloud of sunset. It was built of a bright brick throughout; its skyline was fantastic, and even its ground plan was wild. It had been the outburst of a speculative builder, faintly tinged with art, who called its architecture sometimes Elizabethan and sometimes Queen Anne, apparently under the impression that the two sovereigns were identical. It was described with some justice as an artistic colony, though it never in any definable way produced any art. But although its pretensions to be an intellectual centre were a little vague, its pretensions to be a pleasant place were quite indisputable. The stranger who looked for the first time at the quaint red houses could only think how very oddly shaped the people must be who could fit in to them. Nor when he met the people was he disappointed in this respect. The place was not only pleasant, but perfect, if once he could regard it not as a deception but rather as a dream. Even if the people were not 'artists', the whole was nevertheless artistic. That young man with the long, auburn hair and the impudent face—that young man was not really a poet; but surely he was a poem. That old gentleman with the wild, white beard and the wild, white hat—that venerable humbug was not really a philosopher; but at least he was the cause of philosophy in others. That scientific gentleman with the bald, egg-like head and the bare, bird-like neck had no real right to the airs of science that he assumed. He had not discovered anything new in biology; but what biological creature could he have discovered more singular than himself? Thus, and thus only, the whole place had properly to be regarded; it had to be considered not so much as a workshop for artists, but as a frail but finished work of art. A man who stepped into its social atmosphere felt as if he had stepped into a written comedy.

More especially this attractive unreality fell upon it about nightfall, when the extravagant roofs were dark against the afterglow and the whole insane village seemed as separate as a drifting cloud. This again was more strongly true of the many nights of local festivity, when the little gardens were often illuminated, and the big Chinese lanterns glowed in the dwarfish trees like some fierce and monstrous fruit. And this was strongest of all on one particular evening, still vaguely remembered in the locality, of which the auburn-haired poet was the hero. It was not by any means the only evening of which he was the hero. On many nights those passing by his little back garden might hear his high, didactic voice laying down the law to men and particularly to women. The attitude of women in such cases was indeed one of the paradoxes of the place. Most of the women were of the kind vaguely called emancipated, and professed some protest against male supremacy. Yet these new women would always pay to a man the extravagant compliment which no ordinary woman ever pays to him, that of listening while he is talking. And Mr. Lucian Gregory, the red-haired poet, was really (in some sense) a man worth listening to, even if one only laughed at the end of it. He put the old cant of the lawlessness of art and the art of lawlessness with a certain impudent freshness which gave at least a momentary pleasure. He was helped in some degree by the arresting oddity of his appearance, which he worked, as the phrase goes, for all it was worth. His dark red hair parted in the middle was literally like a woman's, and curved into the slow curls of a virgin in a pre-Raphaelite picture. From within this almost saintly oval, however, his face projected suddenly broad and brutal, the chin carried forward with a look of cockney contempt. This combination at once tickled and terrified the nerves of a neurotic population. He seemed like a walking blasphemy, a blend of the angel and the ape.

This particular evening, if it is remembered for nothing else, will be remembered in that place for its strange sunset. It looked like the end of the world. All the heaven seemed covered with a quite vivid and palpable plumage; you could only say that the sky was full of feathers, and of feathers that almost brushed the face. Across the great part of the dome they were grey, and with the strangest tints of violet and mauve and an unnatural pink or pale green; but towards the west the whole grew past description, transparent and passionate, and the last red-hot plumes of it covered up the sun like something too good to be seen. The whole was so close about the earth, as to express nothing but a violent secrecy. The very empyrean seemed to be a secret. It expressed that splendid smallness which is the soul of local patriotism. The very sky seemed small.

I say that there are some inhabitants who may remember the evening if only by that oppressive sky. There are others who may remember it because it marked the first appearance in the place of the second poet of Saffron Park. For a long time the red-haired revolutionary had reigned without a rival; it was upon the night of the sunset that his solitude suddenly ended. The new poet, who introduced himself by the name of Gabriel Syme, was a very mild-looking mortal, with a fair, pointed beard and faint, yellow hair. But an impression grew that he was less meek than he looked. He signalized his entrance by differing with the established poet, Gregory, upon the whole nature of poetry. He said that he (Syme) was a poet of law, a poet of order; nay, he said he was a poet of respectability. So all the Saffron Parkers looked at him as if he had that moment fallen out of that impossible sky.

In fact, Mr. Lucian Gregory, the anarchic poet, connected the two events.

'It may well be,' he said, in his sudden lyrical manner, 'it may well be on such a night of clouds and cruel colours that there is brought forth upon the earth such a portent as a respectable poet. You say you are a poet of law; I say you are a contradiction in terms. I only wonder there were not comets and earthquakes on the night you appeared in this garden.'

The man with the meek blue eyes and the pale, pointed beard endured these thunders with a certain submissive solemnity. The third party of the group, Gregory's sister Rosamond, who had her brother's braids of red hair, but a kindlier face underneath them, laughed with such mixture of admiration and disapproval as she gave commonly to the family oracle.

Gregory resumed in high oratorical good humour.

'An artist is identical with an anarchist,' he cried. 'You might transpose the words anywhere. An anarchist is an artist. The man who throws a bomb is an artist, because he prefers a great moment to every-thing. He sees how much more valuable is one burst of blazing light, one peal of perfect thunder, than the mere common bodies of a few shapeless policemen. An artist disregards all governments, abolishes all conventions. The poet delights in disorder only. If it were not so, the most poetical thing in the world would be the Underground Railway.'

'So it is,' said Mr. Syme.

'Nonsense!' said Gregory, who was very rational when any one else attempted paradox. 'Why do all the clerks and navvies in the railway trains look so sad and tired, so very sad and tired? I will tell you. It is because they know that the train is going right. It is because they know that whatever place they have taken a ticket for that place they will reach. It is because after they have passed Sloane Square they know that the next station must be Victoria, and nothing but Victoria. Oh, their wild rapture! oh, their eyes like stars and their souls again in Eden, if the next station were unaccountably Baker Street!'

'It is you who are unpoetical,' replied the poet Syme. 'If what you say of clerks is true, they can only be as prosaic as your poetry. The rare, strange thing is to hit the mark; the gross, obvious thing is to miss it. We feel it is epical when man with one wild arrow strikes a distant bird. Is it not also epical when man with one wild engine strikes a distant station? Chaos is dull; because in chaos the train might indeed go anywhere, to Baker Street or to Bagdad. But man is a magician, and his whole magic is in this, that he does say Victoria, and lo! it is Victoria. No, take your books of mere poetry and prose; let me read a time table, with tears of pride. Take your Byron, who commemorates the defeats of man; give me Bradshaw, who commemorates his victories. Give me Bradshaw, I say!'

'Must you go?' inquired Gregory sarcastically.

'I tell you,' went on Syme with passion, 'that every time a train comes in I feel that it has broken past batteries of besiegers, and that man has won a battle against chaos. You say contemptuously that when one has left Sloane Square one must come to Victoria. I say that one might do a thousand things instead, and that whenever I really come there I have the sense of hair-breadth escape. And when I hear the guard shout out the word "Victoria", it is not an unmeaning word. It is to me the cry of a herald announcing conquest. It is to me indeed "Victoria"; it is the victory of Adam.'

Gregory wagged his heavy, red head with a slow and sad smile.

'And even then,' he said, 'we poets always ask the question, "And what is Victoria now that you have got there?" You think Victoria is like the New Jerusalem. We know that the New Jerusalem will only be like Victoria. Yes, the poet will be discontented even in the streets of heaven. The poet is always in revolt.'

'There again,' said Syme irritably, 'what is there poetical about being in revolt? You might as well say that it is poetical to be sea-sick. Being sick is a revolt. Both being sick and being rebellious may be the wholesome thing on certain desperate occasions; but I'm hanged if I can see why they are poetical. Revolt in the abstract is — revolting. It is mere vomiting.'

The girl winced for a flash at the unpleasant word, but Syme was too hot to heed her.

'It is things going right,' he cried, 'that is poetical! Our digestions, for instance, going sacredly and silently right, that is the foundation of all poetry. Yes, the most poetical thing, more poetical than the flowers, more poetical than the stars—the most poetical thing in the world is not being sick.'

'Really,' said Gregory superciliously, 'the examples you choose——'

'I beg your pardon,' said Syme grimly, 'I forgot we had abolished all conventions.'

For the first time a red patch appeared on Gregory's forehead.

"You don't expect me,' he said 'to revolutionize society on this lawn?'

Syme looked straight into his eyes and smiled sweetly.

'No, I don't,' he said; 'but I suppose that if you were serious about your anarchism, that is exactly what you would do.'

Gregory's big bull's eyes blinked suddenly like those of an angry lion, and one could almost fancy that his red mane rose.

'Don't you think, then,' he said in a dangerous voice, 'that I am serious about my anarchism?'

'I beg your pardon?' said Syme.

'Am I not serious about my anarchism?' cried Gregory, with knotted fists.

'My dear fellow!' said Syme, and strolled away.

With surprise, but with a curious pleasure, he found Rosamond Gregory still in his company.

'Mr. Syme,' she said, 'do the people who talk like you and my brother often mean what they say? Do you mean what you say now?'

Syme smiled.

'Do you?' he asked.

'What do you mean?' asked the girl, with grave eyes.

'My dear Miss Gregory,' said Syme gently, 'there are many kinds of sincerity and insincerity. When you say "thank you" for the salt, do you mean what you say? No. When you say "the world is round", do you mean what you say? No. It is true, but you don't mean it. Now, sometimes a man like your brother really finds a thing he does mean. It may be only a half-truth, quarter-truth, tenth-truth; but then he says more than he means—from sheer force of meaning it.'

She was looking at him from under level brows; her face was grave and open, and there had fallen upon it the shadow of that unreasoning responsibility which is at the bottom of the most frivolous woman, the maternal watch which is as old as the world.

'Is he really an anarchist, then?' she asked.

'Only in that sense I speak of,' replied Syme; 'or if you prefer it, in that nonsense.'

She drew her broad brows together and said abruptly:

'He wouldn't really use—bombs or that sort of thing?'

Syme broke into a great laugh, that seemed too large for his slight and somewhat dandified figure.

'Good Lord, no!' he said, 'that has to be done anonymously.'

And at that the corners of her own mouth broke into a smile, and she thought with a simultaneous pleasure of Gregory's absurdity and of his safety.

Syme strolled with her to a seat in the corner of the garden, and continued to pour out his opinions.

For he was a sincere man, and in spite of his superficial airs and graces, at root a humble one. And it is always the humble man who talks too much; the proud man who watches himself too closely. He defended respectability with violence and exaggeration. He grew passionate in his praise of tidiness and propriety. All the time there was a smell of lilac all round him. Once he heard very faintly in some distant street a barrel-organ begin to play, and it seemed to him that his heroic words were moving to a tiny tune from under or beyond the world.

He stared and talked at the girl's red hair and amused face for what seemed to be a few minutes; and then, feeling that the groups in such a place should mix, rose to his feet. To his astonishment, he discovered the whole garden empty. Every one had gone long ago, and he went himself with a rather hurried apology. He left with a sense of champagne in his head, which he could not afterwards explain. In the wild events which were to follow this girl had no part at all; he never saw her again until all his tale was over. And yet, in some indescribable way, she kept recurring like a motive in music through all his mad adventures afterwards, and the glory of her strange hair ran like a red thread through those dark and ill-drawn tapestries of the night. For what followed was so improbable, that it might well have been a dream.

When Syme went out into the starlit street, he found it for the moment empty. Then he realized (in some odd way) that the silence was rather a living silence than a dead one. Directly outside the door stood a street lamp, whose gleam gilded the leaves of the tree that bent out over the fence behind him.

About a foot from the lamp-post stood a figure almost as rigid and motionless as the lamp-post itself. The tall hat and long frock-coat were black; the face, in an abrupt shadow, was almost as dark. Only a fringe of fiery hair against the light, and also something aggressive in the attitude, proclaimed that it was the poet Gregory. He had something of the look of a masked bravo waiting sword in hand for his foe.

He made a sort of doubtful salute, which Syme somewhat more formally returned.

'I was waiting for you,' said Gregory. 'Might I have a moment's conversation?'

'Certainly. About what?' asked Syme in a sort of weak wonder.

Gregory struck out with his stick at the lamp-post, and then at the tree.

'About *this* and *this*,' he cried; 'about order and anarchy. There is your precious order, that lean, iron lamp, ugly and barren; and there is anarchy, rich, living, reproducing itself—there is anarchy, splendid in green and gold.'

'All the same,' replied Syme patiently, 'just at present you only see the tree by the light of the lamp. I wonder when you would ever see the lamp by the light of the tree.' Then after a pause he said, 'But may I ask if you have been standing out here in the dark only to resume our little argument?'

'No,' cried out Gregory, in a voice that rang down the street, 'I did not stand here to resume our argument, but to end it for ever.'

The silence fell again, and Syme, though he understood nothing, listened instinctively for something serious. Gregory began in a smooth voice and with a rather bewildering smile.

'Mr. Syme,' he said, 'this evening you succeeded in doing something rather remarkable. You did something to me that no man born of woman has ever succeeded in doing before.'

'Indeed!'

'Now I remember,' resumed Gregory reflectively, 'one other person succeeded in doing it. The captain of a penny steamer (if I remember correctly) at Southend. You have irritated me.'

'I am very sorry,' replied Syme with gravity.

'I am afraid my fury and your insult are too shocking to be wiped out even with an apology,' said Gregory very calmly. 'No duel could wipe it out. If I struck you dead I could not wipe it out. There is only one way by which that insult can be erased, and that way I choose. I am going, at the possible sacrifice of my life and honour, to *prove* to you that you were wrong in what you said.'

'In what I said?'

'You said I was not serious about being an anarchist.'

'There are degrees of seriousness,' replied Syme. 'I have never doubted that you were perfectly sincere in this sense, that you thought what you said well worth saying, that you thought a paradox might wake men up to a neglected truth.'

Gregory stared at him steadily and painfully.

'And in no other sense,' he asked, 'you think me serious. You think me a *flâneur* who lets fall occasional truths. You do not think that in a deeper, a more deadly sense, I am serious.'

Syme struck his stick violently on the stones of the road.

'Serious!' he cried. 'Good Lord! is this street serious? Are these damned Chinese lanterns serious?

Is the whole caboodle serious? One comes here and talks a pack of bosh, and perhaps some sense as well, but I should think very little of a man who didn't keep something in the background of his life that was more serious than all this talking—something more serious, whether it was religion or only drink.'

'Very well,' said Gregory, his face darkening, 'you shall see something more serious than either drink or religion.'

Syme stood waiting with his usual air of mildness until Gregory again opened his lips.

'You spoke just now of having a religion. Is it really true that you have one?'

'Oh,' said Syme with a beaming smile, 'we are all Catholics now.'

'Then may I ask you to swear by whatever gods or saints your religion involves that you will *not* reveal what I am now going to tell you to any son of Adam, and especially not to the police? Will you swear that! If you will take upon yourself this awful abnegation, if you will consent to burden your soul with a vow that you should never make and a knowledge you should never dream about, I will promise you in return——'

'You will promise me in return?' inquired Syme, as the other paused.

'I will promise you a very entertaining evening.'

Syme suddenly took off his hat.

'Your offer,' he said, 'is far too idiotic to be declined. You say that a poet is always an anarchist. I disagree; but I hope at least that he is always a sportsman. Permit me, here and now, to swear as a Christian, and promise as a good comrade and a fellow-artist, that I will not report anything of this, whatever it is, to the police. And now, in the name of Colney Hatch, what is it?'

'I think,' said Gregory, with placid irrelevancy, 'that we will call a cab.'

He gave two long whistles, and a hansom came rattling down the road. The two got into it in silence. Gregory gave through the trap the address of an obscure public-house on the Chiswick bank of the river. The cab whisked itself away again, and in it these two fantastics quitted their fantastic town.

CHAPTER II

THE SECRET OF GABRIEL SYME

THE cab pulled up before a particularly dreary and greasy beershop, into which Gregory rapidly conducted his companion. They seated themselves in a close and dim sort of bar-parlour, at a stained wooden table with one wooden leg. The room was so small and dark, that very little could be seen of the attendant who was summoned, beyond a vague and dark impression of something bulky and bearded.

'Will you take a little supper?' asked Gregory politely. 'The *pâté de foie gras* is not good here, but I can recommend the game.'

Syme received the remark with stolidity, imagining it to be a joke. Accepting the vein of humour, he said, with a well-bred indifference:

'Oh, bring me some lobster mayonnaise.'

To his indescribable astonishment, the man only said, 'Certainly, sir!' and went away apparently to get it.

'What will you drink?' resumed Gregory, with the same careless yet apologetic air. 'I shall only have a *creme de menthe* myself; I have dined. But the champagne can really be trusted. Do let me start you with a half-bottle of Pommery at least?'

'Thank you!' said the motionless Syme. 'You are very good.'

His further attempts at conversation, somewhat disorganized in themselves, were cut short finally as by a thunderbolt by the actual appearance of the lobster. Syme tasted it, and found it particularly good. Then he suddenly began to eat with great rapidity and appetite.

'Excuse me if I enjoy myself rather obviously!' he said to Gregory, smiling. 'I don't often have the luck to have a dream like this. It is new to me for a nightmare to lead to a lobster. It is commonly the other way.'

'You are not asleep, I assure you,' said Gregory. 'You are, on the contrary, close to the most actual and rousing moment of your existence. Ah, here comes your champagne! I admit that there may be a slight disproportion, let us say, between the inner arrangements of this excellent hotel and its simple and unpretentious exterior. But that is all our modesty. We are the most modest men that ever lived on earth.'

'And who are *we*?' asked Syme, emptying his champagne glass.

'It is quite simple,' replied Gregory. '*We* are the serious anarchists, in whom you do not believe.'

'Oh!' said Syme shortly. 'You do yourselves well in drinks.'

'Yes, we are serious about everything,' answered Gregory.

Then after a pause he added:

'If in a few moments this table begins to turn round a little, don't put it down to your inroads into the champagne. I don't wish you to do yourself an injustice.'

Well, if I am not drunk, I am mad,' replied Syme with perfect calm; 'but I trust I can behave like a gentleman in either condition. May I smoke?'

'Certainly!' said Gregory, producing a cigar-case. 'Try one of mine.'

Syme took the cigar, clipped the end off with a

cigar-cutter out of his waistcoat pocket, put it in his
mouth, lit it slowly, and let out a long cloud of smoke.
It is not a little to his credit that he performed these
rites with so much composure, for almost before he
had begun them the table at which he sat had begun
to revolve, first slowly and then rapidly, as if at an
insane séance.

'You must not mind it,' said Gregory; 'it's a kind
of screw.'

'Quite so,' said Syme placidly, 'a kind of screw!
How simple that is!'

The next moment the smoke of his cigar, which
had been wavering across the room in snaky twists,
went straight up as if from a factory chimney, and the
two, with their chairs and table, shot down through
the floor as if the earth had swallowed them. They
went rattling down a kind of roaring chimney as
rapidly as a lift cut loose, and they came with an
abrupt bump to the bottom. But when Gregory
threw open a pair of doors and let in a red subterranean
light, Syme was still smoking, with one leg thrown
over the other, and had not turned a yellow hair.

Gregory led him down a low, vaulted passage, at
the end of which was the red light. It was an enormous
crimson lantern, nearly as big as a fireplace, fixed over
a small but heavy iron door. In the door there was
a sort of hatchway or grating, and on this Gregory
struck five times. A heavy voice with a foreign accent
asked him who he was. To this he gave the more or
less unexpected reply, "Mr. Joseph Chamberlain".
The heavy hinges began to move; it was obviously
some kind of password.

Inside the doorway the passage gleamed as if it
were lined with a network of steel. On a second

glance, Syme saw that the glittering pattern was really made up of ranks and ranks of rifles and revolvers, closely packed or interlocked.

'I must ask you to forgive me all these formalities,' said Gregory; 'we have to be very strict here.'

'Oh, don't apologize,' said Syme. 'I know your passion for law and order', and he stepped into the passage lined with the steel weapons. With his long, fair hair and rather foppish frock-coat, he looked a singularly frail and fanciful figure as he walked down that shining avenue of death.

They passed through several such passages, and came out at last into a queer steel chamber with curved walls, almost spherical in shape, but presenting, with its tiers of benches, something of the appearance of a scientific lecture-theatre. There were no rifles or pistols in this apartment, but round the walls of it were hung more dubious and dreadful shapes, things that looked like the bulbs of iron plants, or the eggs of iron birds. They were bombs, and the very room itself seemed like the inside of a bomb. Syme knocked his cigar ash off against the wall, and went in.

'And now, my dear Mr. Syme,' said Gregory, throwing himself in an expansive manner on the bench under the largest bomb, 'now we are quite cosy, so let us talk properly. Now no human words can give you any notion of why I brought you here. It was one of those quite arbitrary emotions, like jumping off a cliff or falling in love. Suffice it to say that you were an inexpressibly irritating fellow, and, to do you justice, you are still. I would break twenty oaths of secrecy for the pleasure of taking you down a peg. That way you have of lighting a cigar would make a priest break the seal of confession. Well, you said that you were quite certain I was not a serious anarchist. Does this place strike you as being serious?'

'It does seem to have a moral under all its gaiety,' assented Syme; 'but may I ask you two questions? You need not fear to give me information, because, as you remember, you very wisely extorted from me a promise not to tell the police, a promise I shall certainly keep. So it is in mere curiosity that I make my queries. First of all, what is it really all about? What is it you object to? You want to abolish government?'

'To abolish God!' said Gregory, opening the eyes of a fanatic. 'We do not only want to upset a few despotisms and police regulations; that sort of anarchism does exist, but it is a mere branch of the Nonconformists. We dig deeper and we blow you higher. We wish to deny all those arbitrary distinctions of vice and virtue, honour and treachery, upon which mere rebels base themselves. The silly sentimentalists of the French Revolution talked of the Rights of Man! We hate Rights as we hate Wrongs. We have abolished Right and Wrong.'

'And Right and Left,' said Syme with a simple eagerness, 'I hope you will abolish them too. They are much more troublesome to me.'

'You spoke of a second question,' snapped Gregory.

'With pleasure,' resumed Syme. 'In all your present acts and surroundings there is a scientific attempt at secrecy. I have an aunt who lived over a shop, but this is the first time I have found people living from preference under a public-house. You have a heavy iron door. You cannot pass it without submitting to the humiliation of calling yourself Mr. Chamberlain. You surround yourself with steel instruments which make the place, if I may say so, more impressive than homelike. May I ask why, after taking all this trouble to barricade yourselves in the bowels of the earth, you then parade your whole secret by talking about anarchism to every silly woman in Saffron Park?'

Gregory smiled.

'The answer is simple,' he said. 'I told you I was a serious anarchist, and you did not believe me. Nor do *they* believe me. Unless I took them into this infernal room they would not believe me.'

Syme smoked thoughtfully, and looked at him with interest. Gregory went on.

'The history of the thing might amuse you,' he said. 'When first I became one of the New Anarchists I tried all kinds of respectable disguises. I dressed up as a bishop. I read up all about bishops in our anarchist pamphlets, in *Superstition the Vampire* and *Priests of Prey*. I certainly understood from them that bishops are strange and terrible old men keeping a cruel secret from mankind. I was misinformed. When on my first appearing in episcopal gaiters in a drawing-room I cried out in a voice of thunder, "Down! down! presumptuous human reason!" they found out in some way that I was not a bishop at all. I was nabbed at once. Then I made up as a millionaire; but I defended Capital with so much intelligence that a fool could see that I was quite poor. Then I tried being a major. Now I am a humanitarian myself, but I have, I hope, enough intellectual breadth to understand the position of those who, like Nietzsche, admire violence—the proud, mad war of Nature and all that, you know. I threw myself into the major. I drew my sword and waved it constantly. I called out "Blood!" abstractedly, like a man calling for wine. I often said, "Let the weak perish; it is the Law." Well, well, it seems majors don't do this. I was nabbed again. At last I went in despair to the President of the Central Anarchist Council, who is the greatest man in Europe.'

'What is his name?' asked Syme.

'You would not know it,' answered Gregory. 'That is his greatness. Caesar and Napoleon put all their genius into being heard of, and they *were* heard of. He puts all his genius into not being heard of, and he is not heard of. But you cannot be for five minutes in the room with him without feeling that Caesar and Napoleon would have been children in his hands.'

He was silent and even pale for a moment, and then resumed:

'But whenever he gives advice it is always something as startling as an epigram, and yet as practical as the Bank of England. I said to him, "What disguise will hide me from the world? What can I find more respectable than bishops and majors?" He looked at me with his large but indecipherable face. "You want a safe disguise, do you? You want a dress which will guarantee you harmless; a dress in which no one would ever look for a bomb?" I nodded. He suddenly lifted his lion's voice. "Why, then, dress up as an *anarchist*, you fool!" he roared so that the room shook. "Nobody will ever expect you to do anything dangerous then." And he turned his broad back on me without another word. I took his advice, and have never regretted it. I preached blood and murder to those women day and night, and—by God!—they would let me wheel their perambulators.'

Syme sat watching him with some respect in his large, blue eyes.

'You took me in,' he said. 'It is really a smart dodge.'

Then after a pause he added:

'What do you call this tremendous President of yours?'

'We generally call him Sunday,' replied Gregory with simplicity. 'You see, there are seven members of the Central Anarchist Council, and they are named after days of the week. He is called Sunday, by some of his admirers Bloody Sunday. It is curious you should mention the matter, because the very night you have dropped in (if I may so express it) is the night on which our London branch, which assembles in this room, has to elect its own deputy to fill a vacancy in the Council. The gentleman who has for some time past played, with propriety and general applause, the difficult part of Thursday, has died quite suddenly. Consequently, we have called a meeting this very evening to elect a successor.'

He got to his feet and strolled across the room with a sort of smiling embarrassment.

'I feel somehow as if you were my mother, Syme,' he continued casually. 'I feel that I can confide anything to you, as you have promised to tell nobody. In fact, I will confide to you something that I would not say in so many words to the anarchists who will be coming to the room in about ten minutes. We shall, of course, go through a form of election; but I don't mind telling you that it is practically certain what the result will be.' He looked down for a moment modestly. 'It is almost a settled thing that I am to be Thursday.'

'My dear fellow,' said Syme heartily, 'I congratulate you. A great career!'

Gregory smiled in deprecation, and walked across the room, talking rapidly.

'As a matter of fact, everything is ready for me on this table,' he said, 'and the ceremony will probably be the shortest possible.'

Syme also strolled across the table, and found lying across it a walking-stick, which turned out on examination to be a sword-stick, a large Colt's revolver, a sandwich case, and a formidable flask of brandy. Over the chair, beside the table, was thrown a heavy-looking cape or cloak.

'I have only to get the form of election finished,' continued Gregory with animation, 'then I snatch up this cloak and stick, stuff these other things into my pocket, step out of a door in this cavern, which opens on the river, where there is a steam-tug already waiting for me, and then—then—oh, the wild joy of being Thursday!' And he clasped his hands.

Syme, who had sat down once more with his usual insolent languor, got to his feet with an unusual air of hesitation.

'Why is it,' he asked vaguely, 'that I think you are quite a decent fellow? Why do I positively like you, Gregory?' He paused a moment, and then added with a sort of fresh curiosity, 'Is it because you are such an ass?'

There was a thoughtful silence again, and then he cried out:

'Well, damn it all! This is the funniest situation I have ever been in in my life, and I am going to act accordingly. Gregory, I gave you a promise before I came into this place. That promise I would keep under red-hot pincers. Would you give me, for my own safety, a little promise of the same kind?'

'A promise?' asked Gregory, wondering.

'Yes,' said Syme very seriously, 'a promise. I swore before God that I would not tell your secret to the police. Will you swear by Humanity, or whatever beastly thing you believe in, that you will not tell my secret to the anarchists?'

'Your secret?' asked the staring Gregory. 'Have you got a secret?'

'Yes,' said Syme, 'I have a secret.' Then after a pause, 'Will you swear?'

Gregory glared at him gravely for a few moments, and then said abruptly:

'You must have bewitched me, but I feel a furious curiosity about you. Yes, I will swear not to tell the anarchists anything you tell me. But look sharp, for they will be here in a couple of minutes.'

Syme rose slowly to his feet and thrust his long, white hands into his long, grey trousers pockets. Almost as he did so there came five knocks on the outer grating, proclaiming the arrival of the first of the conspirators.

'Well,' said Syme slowly, 'I don't know how to tell you the truth more shortly than by saying that your expedient of dressing up as an aimless poet is not confined to you or your President. We have known the dodge for some time at Scotland Yard.'

Gregory tried to spring up straight, but he swayed thrice.

'What do you say?' he asked in an inhuman voice.

'Yes,' said Syme simply, 'I am a police detective. But I think I hear your friends coming.'

From the doorway there came a murmur of 'Mr. Joseph Chamberlain'. It was repeated twice and thrice, and then thirty times, and the crowd of Joseph Chamberlains (a solemn thought) could be heard trampling down the corridor.

CHAPTER III

THE MAN WHO WAS THURSDAY

BEFORE one of the fresh faces could appear at the doorway, Gregory's stunned surprise had fallen from him. He was beside the table with a bound, and a noise in his throat like a wild beast. He caught up the Colt's revolver and took aim at Syme. Syme did not flinch, but he put up a pale and polite hand.

'Don't be such a silly man,' he said, with the effeminate dignity of a curate. 'Don't you see it's not necessary? Don't you see that we're both in the same boat? Yes, and jolly sea-sick.'

Gregory could not speak, but he could not fire either, and he looked his question.

'Don't you see we've checkmated each other?' cried Syme. 'I can't tell the police you are an anarchist. You can't tell the anarchists I'm a policeman. I can only watch you, knowing what you are; you can only watch me, knowing what I am. In short, it's a lonely, intellectual duel, my head against yours. I'm a policeman deprived of the help of the police. You, my poor fellow, are an anarchist deprived of the help of that law and organization which is so essential to anarchy. The one solitary difference is in your favour. You are not surrounded by inquisitive policemen; I am surrounded by inquisitive anarchists. I cannot betray you, but I might betray myself. Come, come! wait and see me betray myself. I shall do it so nicely.'

Gregory put the pistol slowly down, still staring at Syme as if he were a sea-monster.

'I don't believe in immortality,' he said at last, 'but if, after all this, you were to break your word, God would make a hell only for you, to howl in for ever.'

'I shall not break my word,' said Syme sternly, 'nor will you break yours. Here are your friends.'

The mass of the anarchists entered the room heavily, with a slouching and somewhat weary gait; but one little man, with a black beard and glasses—a man somewhat of the type of Mr. Tim Healy—detached himself, and bustled forward with some papers in his hand.

'Comrade Gregory,' he said, 'I suppose this man is a delegate?'

Gregory, taken by surprise, looked down and muttered the name of Syme; but Syme replied almost pertly:

'I am glad to see that your gate is well enough guarded to make it hard for any one to be here who is not a delegate.'

The brow of the little man with the black beard was, however, still contracted with something like suspicion.

'What branch do you represent?' he asked sharply.

'I should hardly call it a branch,' said Syme, laughing; 'I should call it at the very least a root.'

'What do you mean?'

'The fact is,' said Syme serenely, 'the truth is I am a Sabbatarian. I have been specially sent here to see that you show a due observance of Sunday.'

The little man dropped one of his papers, and a flicker of fear went over all the faces of the group. Evidently the awful President, whose name was Sunday, did sometimes send down such irregular ambassadors to such branch meetings.

'Well, comrade,' said the man with the papers after a pause, 'I suppose we'd better give you a seat in the meeting?'

'If you ask my advice as a friend,' said Syme with severe benevolence, 'I think you'd better.'

When Gregory heard the dangerous dialogue end, with a sudden safety for his rival, he rose abruptly and paced the floor in painful thought. He was, indeed, in an agony of diplomacy. It was clear that Syme's inspired impudence was likely to bring him out of all merely accidental dilemmas. Little was to be hoped from them. He could not himself betray Syme, partly from honour, but partly also because, if he betrayed him and for some reason failed to destroy him, the Syme who escaped would be a Syme freed from all obligation of secrecy, a Syme who would simply walk to the nearest police station. After all, it was only one night's discussion, and only one detective who would know of it. He would let out as little as possible of their plans that night, and then let Syme go, and chance it.

He strode across to the group of anarchists, which was already distributing itself along the benches.

'I think it is time we began,' he said; 'the steam-tug is waiting on the river already. I move that Comrade Buttons takes the chair.'

This being approved by a show of hands, the little man with the papers slipped into the presidential seat.

'Comrades,' he began, as sharp as a pistol-shot, 'our meeting to-night is important, though it need not be long. This branch has always had the honour of electing Thursdays for the Central European Council. We have elected many and splendid Thursdays. We all lament the sad decease of the heroic worker who occupied the post until last week. As you know, his services to the cause were considerable. He organized the great dynamite coup of Brighton which, under happier circumstances, ought to have killed everybody on the pier. As you also know, his death was as self-denying as his life, for he died through his faith in a hygienic mixture of chalk and water as a substitute for milk, which beverage he regarded as barbaric, and as involving cruelty to the cow. Cruelty, or anything approaching to cruelty, revolted him always. But it is not to acclaim his virtues that we are met, but for a harder task. It is difficult properly to praise his qualities, but it is more difficult to replace them. Upon you, comrades, it devolves this evening to choose out of the company present the man who shall be Thursday. If any comrade suggests a name I will put it to the vote. If no comrade suggests a name, I can only tell myself that that dear dynamiter, who is gone from us, has carried into the unknowable abysses the last secret of his virtue and his innocence.'

There was a stir of almost inaudible applause, such as is sometimes heard in church. Then a large old man, with a long and venerable white beard, perhaps the only real working-man present, rose lumberingly and said:

'I move that Comrade Gregory be elected Thursday,' and sat lumberingly down again.

'Does any one second?' asked the chairman.

A little man with a velvet coat and pointed beard seconded.

'Before I put the matter to the vote,' said the chairman, 'I will call on Comrade Gregory to make a statement.'

Gregory rose amid a great rumble of applause. His face was deadly pale, so that by contrast his queer red hair looked almost scarlet. But he was smiling, and altogether at ease. He had made up his mind, and he saw his best policy quite plain in front of him like a white road. His best chance was to make a softened and ambiguous speech, such as would leave on the detective's mind the impression that the anarchist brotherhood was a very mild affair after all. He believed in his own literary power, his capacity for suggesting fine shades and picking perfect words. He thought that with care he could succeed, in spite of all the people around him, in conveying an impression of the institution, subtly and delicately false. Syme had once thought that anarchists, under all their bravado, were only playing the fool. Could he not now, in the hour of peril, make Syme think so again?

'Comrades,' began Gregory, in a low but penetrating voice, 'it is not necessary for me to tell you what is my policy, for it is your policy also. Our belief has been slandered, it has been disfigured, it has been utterly confused and concealed, but it has never been altered. Those who talk about anarchism and its dangers go everywhere and anywhere to get their information, except to us, except to the fountain head. They learn about anarchists from sixpenny novels; they learn about anarchists from tradesmen's newspapers; they learn about anarchists from *Ally Sloper's Half-Holiday* and the *Sporting Times*. They never learn about anarchists from anarchists. We have no chance of denying the mountainous slanders which are heaped upon our heads from one end of Europe to another. The man who has always heard that we are walking plagues has never heard our reply. I know that he will not hear it to-night, though my passion were to rend the roof. For it is deep, deep under the earth that the persecuted are permitted to assemble, as the Christians assembled in the Catacombs. But, if by some incredible accident, there were here to-night a man who all his life had thus immensely misunderstood us, I would put this question to him: "When those Christians met in those Catacombs, what sort of moral reputation had they in the streets above? What tales were told of their atrocities by one educated Roman to another? Suppose" (I would say to him), "suppose that we are only repeating that still mysterious paradox of history. Suppose we seem as shocking as the Christians because we are really as harmless as the Christians. Suppose we seem as mad as the Christians because we are really as meek." '

The applause that had greeted the opening sentences had been gradually growing fainter, and at the last word it stopped suddenly. In the abrupt silence, the man with the velvet jacket said, in a high, squeaky voice:

'I'm not meek!'

'Comrade Witherspoon tells us,' resumed Gregory, 'that he is not meek. Ah, how little he knows himself! His words are, indeed, extravagant; his appearance is ferocious, and even (to an ordinary taste) unattractive. But only the eye of a friendship as deep and delicate as mine can perceive the deep foundation of solid meekness which lies at the base of him, too deep even for himself to see. I repeat, we are the true early Christians, only that we come too late. We are simple, as they were simple—look at Comrade Witherspoon. We are modest, as they were modest—look at me. We are merciful——'

'No, no!' called out Mr. Witherspoon with the velvet jacket.

'I say we are merciful,' repeated Gregory furiously, 'as the early Christians were merciful. Yet this did not prevent their being accused of eating human flesh. We do not eat human flesh——'

'Shame!' cried Witherspoon. 'Why not?'

'Comrade Witherspoon,' said Gregory, with a feverish gaiety, 'is anxious to know why nobody eats him (laughter). In our society, at any rate, which loves him sincerely, which is founded upon love——'

'No, no!' said Witherspoon, 'down with love.'

'Which is founded upon love,' repeated Gregory, grinding his teeth, 'there will be no difficulty about the aims which we shall pursue as a body, or which I should pursue were I chosen as the representative of that body. Superbly careless of the slanders that represent us as assassins and enemies of human society, we shall pursue, with moral courage and quiet, intellectual pressure, the permanent ideals of brotherhood and simplicity.'

Gregory resumed his seat and passed his hand across his forehead. The silence was sudden and awkward, but the chairman rose like an automaton, and said in a colourless voice:

'Does any one oppose the election of Comrade Gregory?'

The assembly seemed vague and subconsciously disappointed, and Comrade Witherspoon moved restlessly on his seat and muttered in his thick beard. By the sheer rush of routine, however, the motion would have been put and carried. But as the chairman was opening his mouth to put it, Syme sprang to his feet and said in a small and quiet voice:

'Yes, Mr. Chairman, I oppose.'

The most effective fact in oratory is an unexpected change in the voice. Mr. Gabriel Syme evidently understood oratory. Having said these first formal words in a moderated tone and with a brief simplicity, he made his next word ring and volley in the vault as if one of the guns had gone off.

'Comrades!' he cried, in a voice that made every man jump out of his boots, 'have we come here for this? Do we live underground like rats in order to listen to talk like this? This is talk we might listen to while eating buns at a Sunday School treat. Do we line these walls with weapons and bar that door with death lest any one should come and hear Comrade Gregory saying to us, "Be good, and you will be happy", "Honesty is the best policy", and "Virtue is its own reward"? There was not a word in Comrade Gregory's address to which a curate could not have listened with pleasure (hear, hear). But I am not a curate (loud cheers), and I did not listen to it with pleasure (renewed cheers). The man who is fitted to make a good curate is not fitted to make a resolute, forcible, and efficient Thursday (hear, hear).

'Comrade Gregory has told us, in only too apologetic a tone, that we are not the enemies of society. But I say that we are the enemies of society, and so much the worse for society. We are the enemies of society, for society is the enemy of humanity, its oldest and its most pitiless enemy (hear, hear). Comrade Gregory has told us (apologetically again) that we are not murderers. There I agree. We are not murderers, we are executioners (cheers).'

Ever since Syme had risen Gregory had sat staring at him, his face idiotic with astonishment. Now in the pause his lips of clay parted, and he said, with an automatic and lifeless distinctness:

'You damnable hypocrite!'

Syme looked straight into those frightful eyes with his own pale blue ones, and said with dignity:

'Comrade Gregory accuses me of hypocrisy. He knows as well as I do that I am keeping all my engagements and doing nothing but my duty. I do not mince words. I do not pretend to. I say that Comrade Gregory is unfit to be Thursday for all his amiable qualities. He is unfit to be Thursday because of his amiable qualities. We do not want the Supreme Council of Anarchy infected with a maudlin mercy (hear, hear). This is no time for ceremonial politeness, neither is it a time for ceremonial modesty. I set myself against Comrade Gregory as I would set myself against all the Governments of Europe, because the anarchist who has given himself to anarchy has forgotten modesty as much as he has forgotten pride (cheers). I am not a man at all. I am a cause (renewed cheers). I set myself against Comrade Gregory as impersonally and as calmly as I should choose one pistol rather than another out of that rack upon the wall; and I say that rather than have Gregory and his milk-and-water methods on the Supreme Council, I would offer myself for election——'

His sentence was drowned in a deafening cataract of applause. The faces, that had grown fiercer and fiercer with approval as his tirade grew more and more uncompromising, were now distorted with grins of anticipation or cloven with delighted cries. At the moment when he announced himself as ready to stand for the post of Thursday, a roar of excitement and assent broke forth, and became uncontrollable, and at the same moment Gregory sprang to his feet, with foam upon his mouth, and shouted against the shouting.

'Stop, you blasted madmen!' he cried, at the top of a voice that tore his throat. 'Stop, you——'

But louder than Gregory's shouting and louder than the roar of the room came the voice of Syme, still speaking in a peal of pitiless thunder:

'I do not go to the Council to rebut that slander that calls us murderers; I go to earn it (loud and prolonged cheering). To the priest who says these men are the enemies of religion, to the judge who says these men are the enemies of law, to the fat parliamentarian who says these men are the enemies of order and public decency, to all these I will reply, "You are false kings, but you are true prophets. I am come to destroy you, and to fulfil your prophecies."'

The heavy clamour gradually died away, but before it had ceased Witherspoon had jumped to his feet, his hair and beard all on end, and had said:

'I move, as an amendment, that Comrade Syme be appointed to the post.'

'Stop all this, I tell you!' cried Gregory, with frantic face and hands. 'Stop it, it is all——'

The voice of the chairman clove his speech with a cold accent.

'Does any one second this amendment?' he said.

A tall, tired man, with melancholy eyes and an American chin beard, was observed on the back bench to be slowly rising to his feet. Gregory had been screaming for some time past; now there was a change in his accent, more shocking than any scream.

'I end all this!' he said, in a voice as heavy as stone. 'This man cannot be elected. He is a——'

'Yes,' said Syme, quite motionless, 'what is he?'

Gregory's mouth worked twice without sound; then slowly the blood began to crawl back into his dead face.

'He is a man quite inexperienced in our work,' he said, and sat down abruptly.

Before he had done so, the long, lean man with the American beard was again upon his feet, and was repeating in a high American monotone:

'I beg to second the election of Comrade Syme.'

'The amendment will, as usual, be put first,' said Mr. Buttons, the chairman, with mechanical rapidity. 'The question is that Comrade Syme——'

Gregory had again sprung to his feet, panting and passionate.

'Comrades,' he cried out, 'I am not a madman.'

'Oh, oh!' said Mr. Witherspoon.

'I am not a madman,' reiterated Gregory, with a frightful sincerity which for a moment staggered the room, 'but I give you a counsel which you can call mad if you like. No, I will not call it a counsel, for I can give you no reason for it. I will call it a command. Call it a mad command, but act upon it. Strike, but hear me! Kill me, but obey me! Do not elect this man.'

Truth is so terrible, even in fetters, that for a moment Syme's slender and insane victory swayed like a reed. But you could not have guessed it from Syme's bleak blue eyes. He merely began:

'Comrade Gregory commands——'

Then the spell was snapped, and one anarchist called out to Gregory:

'Who are you? You are not Sunday'; and another anarchist added in a heavier tone, 'And you are not Thursday.'

'Comrades,' cried Gregory, in a voice like that of a

martyr who in an ecstasy of pain has passed beyond pain, 'it is nothing to me whether you detest me as a tyrant or detest me as a slave. If you will not take my command, accept my degradation. I kneel to you. I throw myself at your feet. I implore you. Do not elect this man.'

'Comrade Gregory,' said the chairman after a painful pause, 'this is really not quite dignified.'

For the first time in the proceedings there was for a few seconds a real silence. Then Gregory fell back in his seat, a pale wreck of a man, and the chairman repeated, like a piece of clock-work suddenly started again:

'The question is that Comrade Syme be elected to the post of Thursday on the General Council.'

The roar rose like the sea, the hands rose like a forest, and three minutes afterwards Mr. Gabriel Syme, of the Secret Police Service, was elected to the post of Thursday on the General Council of the Anarchists of Europe.

Every one in the room seemed to feel the tug waiting on the river, the sword-stick and the revolver waiting on the table. The instant the election was ended and Syme had received the paper proving his election, they all sprang to their feet, and the fiery groups moved and mixed in the room. Syme found himself, somehow or other, face to face with Gregory, who still regarded him with a stare of stunned hatred. They were silent for many minutes.

'You are a devil!' said Gregory at last.

'And you are a gentleman,' said Syme with gravity.

'It was you that entrapped me,' began Gregory, shaking from head to foot, 'entrapped me into——'

'Talk sense,' said Syme shortly. 'Into what sort of

devils' parliament have you entrapped me, if it comes to that? You made me swear before I made you. Perhaps we are both doing what we think right. But what we think right is so damned different that there can be nothing between us in the way of concession. There is nothing possible between us but honour and death,' and he pulled the great cloak about his shoulders and picked up the flask from the table.

'The boat is quite ready,' said Mr. Buttons, bustling up. 'Be good enough to step this way.'

With a gesture that revealed the shopwalker, he led Syme down a short, iron-bound passage, the still agonized Gregory following feverishly at their heels. At the end of the passage was a door, which Buttons opened sharply, showing a sudden blue and silver picture of the moonlit river, that looked like a scene in a theatre. Close to the opening lay a dark, dwarfish steam-launch, like a baby dragon with one red eye.

Almost in the act of stepping on board, Gabriel Syme turned to the gaping Gregory.

'You have kept your word,' he said gently, with his face in shadow. 'You are a man of honour, and I thank you. You have kept it even down to a small particular. There was one special thing you promised me at the beginning of the affair, and which you have certainly given me by the end of it.'

'What do you mean?' cried the chaotic Gregory. 'What did I promise you?'

'A very entertaining evening,' said Syme, and he made a military salute with the sword-stick as the steamboat slid away.

CHAPTER IV

THE TALE OF A DETECTIVE

GABRIEL SYME was not merely a detective who pretended to be a poet; he was really a poet who had become a detective. Nor was his hatred of anarchy hypocritical. He was one of those who are driven early in life into too conservative an attitude by the bewildering folly of most revolutionists. He had not attained it by any tame tradition. His respectability was spontaneous and sudden, a rebellion against rebellion. He came of a family of cranks, in which all the oldest people had all the newest notions. One of his uncles always walked about without a hat, and another had made an unsuccessful attempt to walk about with a hat and nothing else. His father cultivated art and self-realization; his mother went in for simplicity and hygiene. Hence the child, during his tenderer years, was wholly unacquainted with any drink between the extremes of absinth and cocoa, of both of which he had a healthy dislike. The more his mother preached a more than Puritan abstinence the more did his father expand into a more than pagan latitude; and by the time the former had come to enforcing vegetarianism, the latter had pretty well reached the point of defending cannibalism.

Being surrounded with every conceivable kind of revolt from infancy, Gabriel had to revolt into something, so he revolted into the only thing left—sanity. But there was just enough in him of the blood of these fanatics to make even his protest for common sense a little too fierce to be sensible. His hatred of modern lawlessness had been crowned also by an accident. It happened that he was walking in a side-street at the instant of a dynamite outrage. He had been blind and deaf for a moment, and then seen, the smoke clearing, the broken windows and the bleeding faces. After that he went about as usual—quiet, courteous, rather gentle; but there was a spot on his mind that was not sane. He did not regard anarchists, as most of us do, as a handful of morbid men, combining ignorance with intellectualism. He regarded them as a huge and pitiless peril, like a Chinese invasion.

He poured perpetually into newspapers and their waste-paper baskets a torrent of tales, verses, and violent articles, warning men of this deluge of barbaric denial. But he seemed to be getting no nearer his enemy, and, what was worse, no nearer a living. As he paced the Thames Embankment, bitterly biting a cheap cigar and brooding on the advance of Anarchy, there was no anarchist with a bomb in his pocket so savage or so solitary as he. Indeed, he always felt that Government stood alone and desperate, with its back to the wall. He was too quixotic to have cared for it otherwise.

He walked on the Embankment once under a dark red sunset. The red river reflected the red sky, and they both reflected his anger. The sky, indeed, was so swarthy, and the light on the river relatively so lurid, that the water almost seemed of fiercer flame than the sunset it mirrored. It looked like a stream of literal fire winding under the vast caverns of a subterranean country.

Syme was shabby in those days. He wore an old-fashioned black chimney-pot hat; he was wrapped in a yet more old-fashioned cloak, black and ragged; and the combination gave him the look of the early villains in Dickens and Bulwer Lytton. Also his yellow beard and hair were more unkempt and leonine than when they appeared long afterwards, cut and pointed, on the lawns of Saffron Park. A long, lean, black cigar, bought in Soho for twopence, stood out from between his tightened teeth, and altogether he looked a very satisfactory specimen of the anarchists upon whom he had vowed a holy war. Perhaps this was why a policeman on the Embankment spoke to him, and said, 'Good evening.'

Syme, at a crisis of his morbid fears for humanity, seemed stung by the mere stolidity of the automatic official, a mere bulk of blue in the twilight.

'A good evening is it?' he said sharply. 'You fellows would call the end of the world a good evening. Look at that bloody red sun and that bloody river! I tell you that if that were literally human blood, spilt and shining, you would still be standing here as solid as ever, looking out for some poor harmless tramp whom you could move on. You policemen are cruel to the poor, but I could forgive you even your cruelty if it were not for your calm.'

'If we are calm,' replied the policeman, 'it is the calm of organized resistance.'

'Eh?' said Syme, staring.

'The soldier must be calm in the thick of the battle,' pursued the policeman. 'The composure of an army is the anger of a nation.'

'Good God, the Board Schools!' said Syme. 'Is this undenominational education?'

'No,' said the policeman sadly, 'I never had any of those advantages. The Board Schools came after my time. What education I had was very rough and old-fashioned, I am afraid.'

'Where did you have it?' asked Syme, wondering.

'Oh, at Harrow,' said the policeman.

The class sympathies which, false as they are, are the truest things in so many men, broke out of Syme before he could control them.

'But, good Lord, man,' he said, 'you oughtn't to be a policeman!'

The policeman sighed and shook his head.

'I know,' he said solemnly, 'I know I am not worthy.'

'But why did you join the police?' asked Syme with rude curiosity.

'For much the same reason that you abused the police,' replied the other. 'I found that there was a special opening in the service for those whose fears for humanity were concerned rather with the aberrations of the scientific intellect than with the normal and excusable, though excessive, outbreaks of the human will. I trust I make myself clear.'

'If you mean that you make your opinion clear,' said Syme, 'I suppose you do. But as for making yourself clear, it is the last thing you do. How comes a man like you to be talking philosophy in a blue helmet on the Thames Embankment?'

'You have evidently not heard of the latest development in our police system,' replied the other. 'I am not surprised at it. We are keeping it rather dark from the educated class, because that class contains most of our enemies. But you seem to be exactly in the right frame of mind. I think you might almost join us.'

'Join you in what?' asked Syme.

'I will tell you,' said the policeman slowly. 'This is the situation: the head of one of our departments, one of the most celebrated detectives in Europe, has long been of opinion that a purely intellectual conspiracy would soon threaten the very existence of civilization. He is certain that the scientific and artistic worlds are silently bound in a crusade against the Family and the State. He has, therefore, formed a special corps of policemen, policemen who are also philosophers. It is their business to watch the beginnings of this conspiracy, not merely in a criminal but in a controversial sense. I am a democrat myself, and I am fully aware of the value of the ordinary man in matters of ordinary valour or virtue. But it would obviously be undesirable to employ the common policeman in an investigation which is also a heresy hunt.'

Syme's eyes were bright with a sympathetic curiosity.

'What do you do, then?' he said.

'The work of the philosophical policeman,' replied the man in blue, 'is at once bolder and more subtle than that of the ordinary detective. The ordinary detective goes to pot-houses to arrest thieves; we go to artistic tea-parties to detect pessimists. The ordinary detective discovers from a ledger or a diary that a crime has been committed. We discover from a book of sonnets that a crime will be committed. We have to trace the origin of those dreadful thoughts that drive men on at last to intellectual fanaticism and intellectual crime. We were only just in time to prevent the assassination at Hartlepool, and that was entirely due to the fact that our Mr. Wilks (a smart young fellow) thoroughly understood a triolet.'

'Do you mean,' asked Syme, 'that there is really as much connexion between crime and the modern intellect as all that?'

'You are not sufficiently democratic,' answered the policeman, 'but you were right when you said just now that our ordinary treatment of the poor criminal was a pretty brutal business. I tell you I am sometimes sick of my trade when I see how perpetually it means merely a war upon the ignorant and the desperate. But this new movement of ours is a very different affair. We deny the snobbish English assumption that the uneducated are the dangerous criminals. We remember the Roman Emperors. We remember the great poisoning princes of the Renaissance. We say that the dangerous criminal is the educated criminal. We say that the most dangerous criminal now is the entirely lawless modern philosopher. Compared to him, burglars and bigamists are essentially moral men; my heart goes out to them. They accept the essential ideal of man; they merely seek it wrongly. Thieves respect property. They merely wish the property to become their property that they may more perfectly respect it. But philosophers dislike property as property; they wish to destroy the very idea of personal possession. Bigamists respect marriage, or they would not go through the highly ceremonial and even ritualistic formality of bigamy. But philosophers despise marriage as marriage. Murderers respect human life; they merely wish to attain a greater fullness of human life in themselves by the sacrifice of what seems to them to be lesser lives. But philosophers hate life itself, their own as much as other people's.'

Syme struck his hands together.

'How true that is,' he cried. 'I have felt it from my boyhood, but never could state the verbal antithesis. The common criminal is a bad man, but at least he is, as it were, a conditional good man. He says that if only a certain obstacle be removed—say a wealthy uncle—he is then prepared to accept the universe and to praise God. He is a reformer, but not an anarchist. He wishes to cleanse the edifice, but not to destroy it. But the evil philosopher is not trying to alter things, but to annihilate them. Yes, the modern world has retained all those parts of police work which are really oppressive and ignominious, the harrying of the poor, the spying upon the unfortunate. It has given up its more dignified work, the punishment of powerful traitors in the State and powerful heresiarchs in the Church. The moderns say we must not punish heretics. My only doubt is whether we have a right to punish anybody else.'

'But this is absurd!' cried the policeman, clasping his hands with an excitement uncommon in persons of his figure and costume, 'but it is intolerable! I don't know what you're doing, but you're wasting your life. You must, you shall, join our special army against anarchy. Their armies are on our frontiers. Their bolt is ready to fall. A moment more, and you may lose the glory of working with us, perhaps the glory of dying with the last heroes of the world.'

'It is a chance not to be missed, certainly,' assented Syme, 'but still I do not quite understand. I know as well as anybody that the modern world is full of lawless little men and mad little movements. But, beastly as they are, they generally have the one merit of disagreeing with each other. How can you talk of their leading one army or hurling one bolt. What is this anarchy?'

'Do not confuse it,' replied the constable, 'with those chance dynamite outbreaks from Russia or from Ireland, which are really the outbreaks of oppressed, if mistaken, men. This is a vast philosophic movement, consisting of an outer and an inner ring. You might even call the outer ring the laity and the inner ring the priesthood. I prefer to call the outer ring the innocent section, the inner ring the supremely guilty section. The outer ring—the main mass of their supporters—are merely anarchists; that is, men who believe that rules and formulas have destroyed human happiness. They believe that all the evil results of human crime are the results of the system that has called it crime. They do not believe that the crime creates the punishment. They believe that the punishment has created the crime. They believe that if a man seduced seven women he would naturally walk away as blameless as the flowers of spring. They believe that if a man picked a pocket he would naturally feel exquisitely good. These I call the innocent section.'

'Oh!' said Syme.

'Naturally, therefore, these people talk about "a happy time coming"; "the paradise of the future"; "mankind freed from the bondage of vice and the bondage of virtue", and so on. And so also the men of the inner circle speak—the sacred priesthood. They also speak to applauding crowds of the happiness of the future, and of mankind freed at last. But in their mouths'—and the policeman lowered his voice—'in their mouths these happy phrases have a horrible meaning. They are under no illusions; they are too intellectual to think that man upon this earth can ever be quite free of original sin and the struggle. And they mean death. When they say that mankind shall be free at last, they mean that mankind shall commit suicide. When they talk of a paradise without right or wrong, they mean the grave. They have but two objects, to destroy first humanity and then themselves. That is why they throw bombs instead of firing pistols.

The innocent rank and file are disappointed because the bomb has not killed the king; but the high-priesthood are happy because it has killed somebody.'

'How can I join you?' asked Syme, with a sort of passion.

'I know for a fact that there is a vacancy at the moment,' said the policeman, 'as I have the honour to be somewhat in the confidence of the chief of whom I have spoken. You should really come and see him. Or, rather I should not say see him, nobody ever sees him; but you can talk to him if you like.'

'Telephone?' inquired Syme, with interest.

'No,' said the policeman placidly, 'he has a fancy for always sitting in a pitch-dark room. He says it makes his thoughts brighter. Do come along.'

Somewhat dazed and considerably excited, Syme allowed himself to be led to a side-door in the long row of buildings of Scotland Yard. Almost before he knew what he was doing, he had been passed through the hands of about four intermediate officials, and was suddenly shown into a room, the abrupt blackness of which startled him like a blaze of light. It was not the ordinary darkness, in which forms can be faintly traced; it was like going suddenly stone-blind.

'Are you the new recruit?' asked a heavy voice.

And in some strange way, though there was not the shadow of a shape in the gloom, Syme knew two things: first, that it came from a man of massive stature; and second, that the man had his back to him.

'Are you the new recruit?' said the invisible chief, who seemed to have heard all about it. 'All right. You are engaged.'

Syme, quite swept off his feet, made a feeble fight against this irrevocable phrase.

'I really have no experience,' he began.

'No one has any experience,' said the other, 'of the Battle of Armageddon.'

'But I am really unfit——'

'You are willing, that is enough,' said the unknown.

'Well, really,' said Syme, 'I don't know any profession of which mere willingness is the final test.'

'I do,' said the other—'martyrs. I am condemning you to death. Good day.'

Thus it was that when Gabriel Syme came out again into the crimson light of evening, in his shabby black hat and shabby, lawless cloak, he came out a member of the New Detective Corps for the frustration of the great conspiracy. Acting under the advice of his friend the policeman (who was professionally inclined to neatness), he trimmed his hair and beard, bought a good hat, clad himself in an exquisite summer suit of light blue-grey, with a pale yellow flower in the button-hole, and, in short, became that elegant and rather insupportable person whom Gregory had first encountered in the little garden of Saffron Park. Before he finally left the police premises his friend provided him with a small blue card, on which was written, 'The Last Crusade', and a number, the sign of his official authority. He put this carefully in his upper waistcoat pocket, lit a cigarette, and went forth to track and fight the enemy in all the drawing-rooms of London. Where his adventure ultimately led him we have already seen. At about half-past one on a February night he found himself steaming in a small tug up the silent Thames, armed with sword-stick and revolver, the duly elected Thursday of the Central Council of Anarchists.

When Syme stepped out on to the steam-tug he had a singular sensation of stepping out into something entirely new; not merely into the landscape of a new land, but even into the landscape of a new planet. This was mainly due to the insane yet solid decision of that evening, though partly also to an entire change in the weather and the sky since he entered the little tavern some two hours before. Every trace of the passionate plumage of the cloudy sunset had been swept away, and a naked moon stood in a naked sky. The moon was so strong and full, that (by a paradox often to be noticed) it seemed like a weaker sun. It gave, not the sense of bright moonshine, but rather of a dead daylight.

Over the whole landscape lay a luminous and unnatural discoloration, as of that disastrous twilight which Milton spoke of as shed by the sun in eclipse; so that Syme fell easily into his first thought, that he was actually on some other and emptier planet, which circled round some sadder star. But the more he felt this glittering desolation in the moonlit land, the more his own chivalric folly glowed in the night like a great fire. Even the common things he carried with him— the food and the brandy and the loaded pistol—took on exactly that concrete and material poetry which a child feels when he takes a gun upon a journey or a bun with him to bed. The sword-stick and the brandy-flask, though in themselves only the tools of morbid conspirators, became the expressions of his own more healthy romance. The sword-stick became almost the sword of chivalry, and the brandy the wine of the stirrup-cup. For even the most dehumanized modern fantasies depend on some older and simpler figure; the adventures may be mad, but the adventurer must be sane. The dragon without St. George would not even be grotesque. So this inhuman landscape was only imaginative by the presence of a man really human. To Syme's exaggerative mind the bright, bleak houses and terraces by the Thames looked as empty as the mountains of the moon. But even the moon is only poetical because there is a man in the moon.

The tug was worked by two men, and with much toil went comparatively slowly. The clear moon that had lit up Chiswick had gone down by the time that they passed Battersea, and when they came under the enormous bulk of Westminster day had already begun to break. It broke like the splitting of great bars of lead, showing bars of silver; and these had brightened like white fire when the tug, changing its onward course, turned inward to a large landing-stage rather beyond Charing Cross.

The great stones of the embankment seemed equally dark and gigantic as Syme looked up at them. They were big and black against the huge white dawn. They made him feel that he was landing on the colossal steps of some Egyptian palace; and indeed the thing suited his mood, for he was, in his own mind, mounting to attack the solid thrones of horrible and heathen kings. He leapt out of the boat on to one slimy step, and stood, a dark and slender figure, amid the enormous masonry. The two men in the tug put her off again and turned up stream. They had never spoken a word.

CHAPTER V

THE FEAST OF FEAR

At first the large stone stair seemed to Syme as deserted as a pyramid; but before he reached the top he had realized that there was a man leaning over the parapet of the Embankment and looking out across the river. As a figure he was quite conventional, clad in a silk hat and frock-coat of the more formal type of fashion; he had a red flower in his button-hole. As Syme drew nearer to him step by step, he did not even move a hair; and Syme could come close enough to notice even in the dim, pale morning light that his face was long, pale, and intellectual, and ended in a small triangular tuft of dark beard at the very point of the chin, all else being clean-shaven. This scrap of hair almost seemed a mere oversight; the rest of the face was of the type that is best shaven—clear-cut, ascetic, and in its way noble. Syme drew closer and closer, noting all this, and still the figure did not stir.

At first an instinct had told Syme that this was the man whom he was meant to meet. Then, seeing that the man made no sign, he had concluded that he was not. And now again he had come back to a certainty that the man had something to do with his mad adventure. For the man remained more still than would have been natural if a stranger had come so close. He was as motionless as a wax-work, and got on the nerves somewhat in the same way. Syme looked again and again at the pale, dignified, and delicate face, and the face still looked blankly across the river. Then he took out of his pocket the note from Buttons proving his election, and put it before that sad and beautiful face. Then the man smiled, and his smile was a shock, for it was all on one side, going up in the right cheek and down in the left.

There was nothing, rationally speaking, to scare any one about this. Many people have this nervous trick of a crooked smile, and in many it is even attractive. But in all Syme's circumstances, with the dark dawn and the deadly errand and the loneliness on the great dripping stones, there was something unnerving in it. There was the silent river and the silent man, a man of even classic face. And there was the last nightmare touch that his smile suddenly went wrong.

The spasm of smile was instantaneous, and the man's face dropped at once into its harmonious melancholy. He spoke without further explanation or inquiry, like a man speaking to an old colleague.

'If we walk up towards Leicester Square,' he said, 'we shall just be in time for breakfast. Sunday always insists on an early breakfast. Have you had any sleep?'

'No,' said Syme.

'Nor have I,' answered the man in an ordinary tone. 'I shall try to get to bed after breakfast.'

He spoke with casual civility, but in an utterly dead voice that contradicted the fanaticism of his face. It seemed almost as if all friendly words were to him lifeless conveniences, and that his only life was hate. After a pause the man spoke again.

'Of course, the Secretary of the branch told you everything that can be told. But the one thing that can never be told is the last notion of the President, for his notions grow like a tropical forest. So in case you don't know, I'd better tell you that he is carrying out his notion of concealing ourselves by not concealing ourselves to the most extraordinary lengths just now. Originally, of course, we met in a cell underground, just as your branch does. Then Sunday made us take a private room at an ordinary restaurant. He said that if you didn't seem to be hiding nobody hunted you out. Well, he is the only man on earth, I know; but sometimes I really think that his huge brain is going a little mad in its old age. For now we flaunt ourselves before the public. We have our breakfast on a balcony—on a balcony, if you please—overlooking Leicester Square.'

'And what do the people say?' asked Syme.

'It's quite simple what they say,' answered his guide. 'They say we are a lot of jolly gentlemen who pretend they are anarchists.'

'It seems to me a very clever idea,' said Syme.

'Clever! God blast your impudence! Clever!' cried out the other in a sudden, shrill voice which was as startling and discordant as his crooked smile. 'When you've seen Sunday for a split second you'll leave off calling him clever.'

With this they emerged out of a narrow street, and saw the early sunlight filling Leicester Square. It will never be known, I suppose, why this square itself should look so alien and in some ways so Continental. It will never be known whether it was the foreign look that attracted the foreigners or the foreigners who gave it the foreign look. But on this particular morning the effect seemed singularly bright and clear. Between the open square and the sunlit leaves and the statue and the Saracenic outlines of the Alhambra, it looked the replica of some French or even Spanish public place. And this effect increased in Syme the sensation, which in many shapes he had had through the whole adventure, the eerie sensation of having strayed into a new world. As a fact, he had bought bad cigars round Leicester Square ever since he was a boy. But as he turned that corner, and saw the trees and the Moorish cupolas, he could have sworn that he was turning into an unknown Place de something or other in some foreign town.

At one corner of the square there projected a kind of angle of a prosperous but quiet hotel, the bulk of which belonged to a street behind. In the wall there was one large french window, probably the window of a large coffee-room; and outside this window, almost literally overhanging the square, was a formidably buttressed balcony, big enough to contain a dining-table. In fact, it did contain a dining-table, or more strictly a breakfast-table; and round the breakfast-table, glowing in the sunlight and evident to the street, were a group of noisy and talkative men, all dressed in the insolence of fashion, with white waistcoats and expensive button-holes. Some of their jokes could almost be heard across the square. Then the grave Secretary gave his unnatural smile, and Syme knew that this boisterous breakfast party was the secret conclave of the European Dynamiters.

Then, as Syme continued to stare at them, he saw something that he had not seen before. He had not seen it literally because it was too large to see. At the nearest end of the balcony, blocking up a great part of the perspective, was the back of a great mountain of a man. When Syme had seen him, his first thought was that the weight of him must break down the balcony of stone. His vastness did not lie only in the fact that he was abnormally tall and quite incredibly fat. This man was planned enormously in his original proportions, like a statue carved deliberately as colossal. His head, crowned with white hair, as seen from behind looked bigger than a head ought to be. The ears that stood out from it looked larger than human ears. He was enlarged terribly to scale; and this sense of size was so staggering, that when Syme saw him all the other figures seemed quite suddenly to dwindle and become dwarfish. They were still sitting there as before with their flowers and frock-coats, but now it looked as if the big man was entertaining five children to tea.

As Syme and the guide approached the side-door of the hotel, a waiter came out smiling with every tooth in his head.

'The gentlemen are up there, sare,' he said. 'They do talk and they do laugh at what they talk. They do say they will throw bombs at ze king.'

And the waiter hurried away with a napkin over his arm, much pleased with the singular frivolity of the gentlemen upstairs.

The two men mounted the stairs in silence.

Syme had never thought of asking whether the monstrous man who almost filled and broke the balcony was the great President of whom the others stood in awe. He knew it was so, with an unaccountable but instantaneous certainty. Syme, indeed, was one of those men who are open to all the more nameless psychological influences in a degree a little dangerous to mental health. Utterly devoid of fear in physical dangers, he was a great deal too sensitive to the smell of spiritual evil. Twice already that night little un-meaning things had peeped out at him almost pruriently, and given him a sense of drawing nearer and nearer to the headquarters of hell. And this sense became overpowering as he drew nearer to the great President.

The form it took was a childish and yet hateful fancy. As he walked across the inner room towards the balcony, the large face of Sunday grew larger and larger; and Syme was gripped with a fear that when he was quite close the face would be too big to be possible, and that he would scream aloud. He remembered that as a child he would not look at the mask of Memnon in the British Museum, because it was a face, and so large.

By an effort braver than that of leaping over a cliff, he went to an empty seat at the breakfast-table and sat down. The men greeted him with good-humoured raillery as if they had always known him. He sobered himself a little by looking at their conventional coats and solid, shining coffee-pot; then he looked again at Sunday. His face was very large, but it was still possible to humanity.

In the presence of the President the whole company looked sufficiently commonplace; nothing about them caught the eye at first, except that by the President's caprice they had been dressed up with a festive respectability, which gave the meal the look of a wedding breakfast. One man indeed stood out at even a superficial glance. He at least was the common or garden Dynamiter. He wore, indeed, the high white collar and satin tie that were the uniform of the occasion; but out of this collar there sprang a head quite unmanageable and quite unmistakable, a bewildering bush of brown hair and beard that almost obscured the eyes like those of a Skye terrier. But the eyes did look out of the tangle, and they were the sad eyes of some Russian serf. The effect of this figure was not terrible like that of the President, but it had every diablerie that can come from the utterly grotesque.

If out of that Stiff Tie and Collar there had come abruptly the head of a cat or a dog, it could not have been a more idiotic contrast.

The man's name, it seemed, was Gogol; he was a Pole, and in this circle of days he was called Tuesday. His soul and speech were incurably tragic; he could not force himself to play the prosperous and frivolous part demanded of him by President Sunday. And, indeed, when Syme came in the President, with that daring disregard of public suspicion which was his policy, was actually chaffing Gogol upon his inability to assume conventional graces.

'Our friend Tuesday,' said the President in a deep voice at once of quietude and volume, 'our friend Tuesday doesn't seem to grasp the idea. He dresses up like a gentleman, but he seems to be too great a soul to behave like one. He insists on the ways of the stage conspirator. Now if a gentleman goes about London in a top hat and a frock-coat, no one need know that he is an anarchist. But if a gentleman puts on a top hat and a frock-coat, and then goes about on his hands and knees—well, he may attract attention. That's what Brother Gogol does. He goes about on his hands and knees with such inexhaustible diplomacy, that by this time he finds it quite difficult to walk upright.'

'I am not good at goncealment,' said Gogol sulkily, with a thick foreign accent; 'I am not ashamed of the cause.'

'Yes, you are, my boy, and so is the cause of you,' said the President good-naturedly. 'You hide as much as anybody; but you can't do it, you see, you're such an ass! You try to combine two inconsistent methods. When a householder finds a man under his bed, he will probably pause to note the circumstance. But if he

finds a man under his bed in a top hat, you will agree
with me, my dear Tuesday, that he is not likely even to
forget it. Now when you were found under Admiral
Biffin's bed——'

'I am not good at deception,' said Tuesday gloomily,
flushing.

'Right, my boy, right,' said the President with a
ponderous heartiness, 'you aren't good at anything.'

While this stream of conversation continued, Syme
was looking more steadily at the men around him.
As he did so, he gradually felt all his sense of something
spiritually queer return.

He had thought at first that they were all of common
stature and costume, with the evident exception of the
hairy Gogol. But as he looked at the others, he began
to see in each of them exactly what he had seen in the
man by the river, a demoniac detail somewhere. That
lop-sided laugh, which would suddenly disfigure the
fine face of his original guide, was typical of all these
types. Each man had something about him, perceived
perhaps at the tenth or twentieth glance, which was not
normal, and which seemed hardly human. The only
metaphor he could think of was this, that they all
looked as men of fashion and presence would look,
with the additional twist given in a false and curved
mirror.

Only the individual examples will express this half-
concealed eccentricity. Syme's original cicerone bore
the title of Monday; he was the Secretary of the Council,
and his twisted smile was regarded with more terror
than anything, except the President's horrible, happy
laughter. But now that Syme had more space and light
to observe him, there were other touches. His fine face
was so emaciated, that Syme thought it must be

wasted with some disease; yet somehow the very distress of his dark eyes denied this. It was no physical ill that troubled him. His eyes were alive with intellectual torture, as if pure thought was pain.

He was typical of each of the tribe; each man was subtly and differently wrong. Next to him sat Tuesday, the tousled-headed Gogol, a man more obviously mad. Next was Wednesday, a certain Marquis de St. Eustache, a sufficiently characteristic figure. The first few glances found nothing unusual about him, except that he was the only man at table who wore the fashionable clothes as if they were really his own. He had a black French beard cut square and a black English frock-coat cut even squarer. But Syme, sensitive to such things, felt somehow that the man carried a rich atmosphere with him, a rich atmosphere that suffocated. It reminded one irrationally of drowsy odours and of dying lamps in the darker poems of Byron and Poe. With this went a sense of his being clad, not in lighter colours, but in softer materials; his black seemed richer and warmer than the black shades about him, as if it were compounded of profound colour. His black coat looked as if it were only black by being too dense a purple. His black beard looked as if it were only black by being too deep a blue. And in the gloom and thickness of the beard his dark red mouth showed sensual and scornful. Whatever he was he was not a Frenchman; he might be a Jew; he might be something deeper yet in the dark heart of the East. In the bright-coloured Persian tiles and pictures showing tyrants hunting, you may see just those almond eyes, those blue-black beards, those cruel, crimson lips.

Then came Syme, and next a very old man, Professor

de Worms, who still kept the chair of Friday, though every day it was expected that his death would leave it empty. Save for his intellect, he was in the last dissolution of senile decay. His face was as grey as his long grey beard, his forehead was lifted and fixed finally in a furrow of mild despair. In no other case, not even that of Gogol, did the bridegroom brilliancy of the morning-dress express a more painful contrast. For the red flower in his button-hole showed up against a face that was literally discoloured like lead; the whole hideous effect was as if some drunken dandies had put their clothes upon a corpse. When he rose or sat down, which was with long labour and peril, something worse was expressed than mere weakness, something indefinably connected with the horror of the whole scene. It did not express decrepitude merely, but corruption. Another hateful fancy crossed Syme's quivering mind. He could not help thinking that whenever the man moved a leg or arm might fall off.

Right at the end sat the man called Saturday, the simplest and the most baffling of all. He was a short, square man with a dark, square face clean-shaven, a medical practitioner going by the name of Bull. He had that combination of *savoir-faire* with a sort of well-groomed coarseness which is not uncommon in young doctors. He carried his fine clothes with confidence rather than ease, and he mostly wore a set smile. There was nothing whatever odd about him, except that he wore a pair of dark, almost opaque spectacles. It may have been merely a crescendo of nervous fancy that had gone before, but those black discs were dreadful to Syme; they reminded him of half-remembered ugly tales, of some story about pennies being put on the eyes of the dead. Syme's eye always caught the black glasses and the blind grin. Had the dying Professor worn them, or even the pale Secretary, they would have been appropriate. But on the younger and grosser man they seemed only an enigma. They took away the key of the face. You could not tell what his smile or his gravity meant. Partly from this, and partly because he had a vulgar virility wanting in most of the others, it seemed to Syme that he might be the wickedest of all those wicked men. Syme even had the thought that his eyes might be covered up because they were too frightful to see.

CHAPTER VI

THE EXPOSURE

SUCH were the six men who had sworn to destroy the world. Again and again Syme strove to pull together his common sense in their presence. Sometimes he saw for an instant that these notions were subjective, that he was only looking at ordinary men, one of whom was old, another nervous, another short-sighted. The sense of an unnatural symbolism always settled back on him again. Each figure seemed to be, somehow, on the borderland of things, just as their theory was on the borderland of thought. He knew that each one of these men stood at the extreme end, so to speak, of some wild road of reasoning. He could only fancy, as in some old-world fable, that if a man went westward to the end of the world he would find something—say a tree—that was more or less than a tree, a tree possessed by a spirit; and that if he went east to the end of the world he would find something else that was not wholly itself—a tower, perhaps, of which the very shape was wicked. So these figures seemed to stand up, violent and unaccountable, against an ultimate horizon, visions from the verge. The ends of the earth were closing in.

Talk had been going on steadily as he took in the scene; and not the least of the contrasts of that bewildering breakfast-table was the contrast between the easy and unobtrusive tone of talk and its terrible purport. They were deep in the discussion of an actual and immediate plot. The waiter downstairs had spoken quite correctly when he said that they were talking about bombs and kings. Only three days afterwards the Tsar was to meet the President of the French Republic in Paris, and over their bacon and eggs upon their sunny balcony these beaming gentlemen had decided how both should die. Even the instrument was chosen; the black-bearded Marquis, it appeared, was to carry the bomb.

Ordinarily speaking, the proximity of this positive and objective crime would have sobered Syme, and cured him of all his merely mystical tremors. He would have thought of nothing but the need of saving at least two human bodies from being ripped in pieces with iron and roaring gas. But the truth was that by this time he had begun to feel a third kind of fear, more piercing and practical than either his moral revulsion or his social responsibility. Very simply, he had no fear to spare for the French President or the Tsar; he had begun to fear for himself. Most of the talkers took little heed of him, debating now with their faces closer together, and almost uniformly grave, save when for an instant the smile of the Secretary ran aslant across his face as the jagged lightning runs aslant across the sky. But there was one persistent thing which first troubled Syme and at last terrified him. The President was always looking at him, steadily, and with a great and baffling interest. The enormous man was quite quiet, but his blue eyes stood out of his head. And they were always fixed on Syme.

Syme felt moved to spring up and leap over the balcony. When the President's eyes were on him he felt as he if were made of glass. He had hardly the shred of a doubt that in some silent and extraordinary way Sunday had found out that he was a spy. He looked over the edge of the balcony, and saw a policeman standing abstractedly just beneath, staring at the bright railings and the sunlit trees.

Then there fell upon him the great temptation that was to torment him for many days. In the presence of these powerful and repulsive men, who were the princes of anarchy, he had almost forgotten the frail and fanciful figure of the poet Gregory, the mere æsthete of anarchism. He even thought of him now with an old kindness, as if they had played together when children. But he remembered that he was still tied to Gregory by a great promise. He had promised never to do the very thing that he now felt himself almost in the act of doing. He had promised not to jump over that balcony and speak to that policeman. He took his cold hand off the cold stone balustrade. His soul swayed in a vertigo of moral indecision. He had only to snap the thread of a rash vow made to a villainous society, and all his life could be as open and sunny as the square beneath him. He had, on the other hand, only to keep his antiquated honour, and be delivered inch by inch into the power of this great enemy of mankind, whose very intellect was a torture-chamber. Whenever he looked down into the square he saw the comfortable policeman, a pillar of common sense and common order. Whenever he looked back at the breakfast-table he saw the President still quietly studying him with big, unbearable eyes.

In all the torrent of his thought there were two thoughts that never crossed his mind. First, it never occurred to him to doubt that the President and his Council could crush him if he continued to stand alone. The place might be public, the project might seem impossible. But Sunday was not the man who would carry himself thus easily without having, somehow or somewhere, set open his iron trap. Either by anonymous poison or sudden street accident, by hypnotism or by fire from hell, Sunday could certainly strike him. If he defied the man he was probably dead, either struck stiff there in his chair or long afterwards as by an innocent ailment. If he called in the police promptly, arrested every one, told all, and set against them the whole energy of England, he would probably escape; certainly not otherwise. They were a balconyful of gentlemen overlooking a bright and busy square; but he felt no more safe with them than if they had been a boatful of armed pirates overlooking an empty sea.

There was a second thought that never came to him. It never occurred to him to be spiritually won over to the enemy. Many moderns, inured to a weak worship of intellect and force, might have wavered in their allegiance under this oppression of a great personality. They might have called Sunday the superman. If any such creature be conceivable, he looked, indeed, somewhat like it, with his earth-shaking abstraction, as of a stone statue walking. He might have been called something above man, with his large plans, which were too obvious to be detected, with his large face, which was too frank to be understood. But this was a kind of modern meanness to which Syme could not sink even in his extreme morbidity. Like any man, he was coward enough to fear great force; but he was not quite coward enough to admire it.

The men were eating as they talked, and even in this they were typical. Dr. Bull and the Marquis ate casually and conventionally of the best things on the table—cold pheasant or Strasbourg pie. But the Secretary was a vegetarian, and he spoke earnestly of the projected murder over half a raw tomato and three-quarters of a glass of tepid water. The old Professor had such slops as suggested a sickening second childhood. And even in this President Sunday preserved his curious predominance of mere mass. For he ate like twenty men; he ate incredibly, with a frightful freshness of appetite, so that it was like watching a sausage factory. Yet continually, when he had swallowed a dozen crumpets or drunk a quart of coffee, he would be found with his great head on one side staring at Syme.

'I have often wondered,' said the Marquis, taking a great bite out of a slice of bread and jam, 'whether it wouldn't be better for me to do it with a knife. Most of the best things have been brought off with a knife. And it would be a new emotion to get a knife into a French President and wriggle it round.'

'You are wrong,' said the Secretary, drawing his black brows together. 'The knife was merely the expression of the old personal quarrel with a personal tyrant. Dynamite is not only our best tool, but our best symbol. It is as perfect a symbol of us as is incense of the prayers of the Christians. It expands; it only destroys because it broadens; even so, thought only destroys because it broadens. A man's brain is a bomb,' he cried out, loosening suddenly his strange passion and striking his own skull with violence. 'My brain feels like a bomb, night and day. It must expand! It must expand! A man's brain must expand, if it breaks up the universe.'

'I don't want the universe broken up just yet,' drawled the Marquis. 'I want to do a lot of beastly things before I die. I thought of one yesterday in bed.'

'No, if the only end of the thing is nothing,' said

Dr. Bull with his sphinx-like smile, 'it hardly seems worth doing.'

The old Professor was staring at the ceiling with dull eyes.

'Every man knows in his heart,' he said, 'that nothing is worth doing.'

There was a singular silence, and then the Secretary said:

'We are wandering, however, from the point. The only question is how Wednesday is to strike the blow. I take it we should all agree with the original notion of a bomb. As to the actual arrangements, I should suggest that to-morrow morning he should go first of all to——'

The speech was broken off short under a vast shadow. President Sunday had risen to his feet, seeming to fill the sky above them.

'Before we discuss that,' he said in a small, quiet voice, 'let us go into a private room. I have something very particular to say.'

Syme stood up before any of the others. The instant of choice had come at last, the pistol was at his head. On the pavement below he could hear the policeman idly stir and stamp, for the morning, though bright, was cold.

A barrel-organ in the street suddenly sprang with a jerk into a jovial tune. Syme stood up taut, as if it had been a bugle before the battle. He found himself filled with a supernatural courage that came from nowhere. That jingling music seemed full of the vivacity, the vulgarity, and the irrational valour of the poor, who in all those unclean streets were all clinging to the decencies and the charities of Christendom. His youthful prank of being a policeman had faded from his mind; he did not think of himself as the representative of the corps of gentlemen turned into fancy constables, or of the old eccentric who lived in the dark room. But he did feel himself as the ambassador of all these common and kindly people in the street, who every day marched into battle to the music of the barrel-organ. And this high pride in being human had lifted him unaccountably to an infinite height above the monstrous men around him. For an instant, at least, he looked down upon all their sprawling eccentricities from the starry pinnacle of the commonplace. He felt towards them all that unconscious and elementary superiority that a brave man feels over powerful beasts or a wise man over powerful errors. He knew that he had neither the intellectual nor the physical strength of President Sunday, but in that moment he minded it no more than the fact that he had not the muscles of a tiger or a horn on his nose like a rhinoceros. All was swallowed up in an ultimate certainty that the President was wrong and that the barrel-organ was right. There clanged in his mind that unanswerable and terrible truism in the song of Roland:

'Païens ont tort et Chrétiens ont droit,'

which in the old nasal French has the clang and groan of great iron. This liberation of his spirit from the load of his weakness went with a quite clear decision to embrace death. If the people of the barrel-organ could keep their old-world obligations, so could he. This very pride in keeping his word was that he was keeping it to miscreants. It was his last triumph over these lunatics to go down into their dark room and die for something that they could not even understand.

The barrel-organ seemed to give the marching tune with the energy and the mingled noises of a whole orchestra; and he could hear deep and rolling, under all the trumpets and the pride of life, the drums of the pride of death.

The conspirators were already filing through the open window and into the rooms behind. Syme went last, outwardly calm, but with all his brain and body throbbing with romantic rhythm. The President led them down an irregular side stair, such as might be used by servants, and into a dim, cold, empty room, with a table and benches, like an abandoned board-room. When they were all in, he closed and locked the door.

The first to speak was Gogol, the irreconcilable, who seemed bursting with inarticulate grievance.

'Zso! Zso!' he cried, with an obscure excitement, his heavy Polish accent becoming almost impenetrable. 'You zay you nod 'ide. You zay you show himselves. It is all nuzzinks. Ven you vant talk importance you run yourselves in a dark box!'

The President seemed to take the foreigner's incoherent satire with entire good humour.

'You can't get hold of it yet, Gogol,' he said in a fatherly way. 'When once they have heard us talking nonsense on that balcony they will not care where we go afterwards. If we had come here first, we should have had the whole staff at the keyhole. You don't seem to know anything about mankind.'

'I die for zem,' cried the Pole in thick excitement, 'and I slay zare oppressors. I care not for these games of gonzealment. I would zmite ze tyrant in ze open square.'

'I see, I see,' said the President, nodding kindly

as he seated himself at the top of a long table. 'You die for mankind first, and then you get up and smite their oppressors. So that's all right. And now may I ask you to control your beautiful sentiments, and sit down with the other gentlemen at this table. For the first time this morning something intelligent is going to be said.'

Syme, with the perturbed promptitude he had shown since the original summons, sat down first. Gogol sat down last, grumbling in his brown beard about gombromise. No one except Syme seemed to have any notion of the blow that was about to fall. As for him, he had merely the feeling of a man mounting the scaffold with the intention, at any rate, of making a good speech.

'Comrades,' said the President, suddenly rising, 'we have spun out this farce long enough. I have called you down here to tell you something so simple and shocking that even the waiters upstairs (long inured to our levities) might hear some new seriousness in my voice. Comrades, we were discussing plans and naming places. I propose, before saying anything else, that those plans and places should not be voted by this meeting, but should be left wholly in the control of some one reliable member. I suggest Comrade Saturday, Dr. Bull.'

They all stared at him; then they all started in their seats, for the next words, though not loud, had a living and sensational emphasis. Sunday struck the table.

'Not one word more about the plans and places must be said at this meeting. Not one tiny detail more about what we mean to do must be mentioned in this company.'

Sunday had spent his life in astonishing his followers;

but it seemed as if he had never really astonished them until now. They all moved feverishly in their seats, except Syme. He sat stiff in his, with his hand in his pocket, and on the handle of his loaded revolver. When the attack on him came he would sell his life dear. He would find out at least if the President was mortal.

Sunday went on smoothly:

'You will probably understand that there is only one possible motive for forbidding free speech at this festival of freedom. Strangers overhearing us matters nothing. They assume that we are joking. But what would matter, even unto death, is this, that there should be one actually among us who is not of us, who knows our grave purpose, but does not share it, who——'

The Secretary screamed out suddenly like a woman.

'It can't be!' he cried, leaping. 'There can't——'

The President flapped his large flat hand on the table like the fin of some huge fish.

'Yes,' he said slowly, 'there is a spy in this room. There is a traitor at this table. I will waste no more words. His name——'

Syme half rose from his seat, his finger firm on the trigger.

'His name is Gogol,' said the President. 'He is that hairy humbug over there who pretends to be a Pole.'

Gogol sprang to his feet, a pistol in each hand. With the same flash three men sprang at his throat. Even the Professor made an effort to rise. But Syme saw little of the scene, for he was blinded with a beneficent darkness; he had sunk down into his seat shuddering, in a palsy of passionate relief.

CHAPTER VII

THE UNACCOUNTABLE CONDUCT OF
PROFESSOR DE WORMS

'Sit down!' said Sunday in a voice that he used once
or twice in his life, a voice that made men drop drawn
swords.

The three who had risen fell away from Gogol,
and that equivocal person himself resumed his seat.

'Well, my man,' said the President briskly, addressing
him as one addresses a total stranger, 'will you oblige
me by putting your hand in your upper waistcoat
pocket and showing me what you have there?'

The alleged Pole was a little pale under his tangle
of dark hair, but he put two fingers into the pocket
with apparent coolness and pulled out a blue strip of
card. When Syme saw it lying on the table, he woke
up again to the world outside him. For although the
card lay at the other extreme of the table, and he could
read nothing of the inscription on it, it bore a startling
resemblance to the blue card in his own pocket, the
card which had been given to him when he joined the
anti-anarchist constabulary.

'Pathetic Slav,' said the President, 'tragic child of
Poland, are you prepared in the presence of that card
to deny that you are in this company—shall we say
de trop?'

'Right oh!' said the late Gogol. It made every one
jump to hear a clear, commercial, and somewhat
cockney voice coming out of that forest of foreign
hair. It was irrational, as if a Chinaman had suddenly
spoken with a Scotch accent.

'I gather that you fully understand your position,' said Sunday.

'You bet,' answered the Pole. 'I see it's a fair cop. All I say is, I don't believe any Pole could have imitated my accent like I did his.'

'I concede the point,' said Sunday. 'I believe your own accent to be inimitable, though I shall practise it in my bath. Do you mind leaving your beard with your card?'

'Not a bit,' answered Gogol; and with one finger he ripped off the whole of his shaggy head-covering, emerging with thin red hair and a pale, pert face. 'It was hot,' he added.

'I will do you the justice to say,' said Sunday, not without a sort of brutal admiration, 'that you seem to have kept pretty cool under it. Now listen to me. I like you. The consequence is that it would annoy me for just about two and a half minutes if I heard that you had died in torments. Well, if you ever tell the police or any human soul about us, I shall have that two and a half minutes of discomfort. On your discomfort I will not dwell. Good day. Mind the step.'

The red-haired detective who had masqueraded as Gogol rose to his feet without a word, and walked out of the room with an air of perfect nonchalance. Yet the astonished Syme was able to realize that this ease was suddenly assumed; for there was a slight stumble outside the door, which showed that the departing detective had not minded the step.

'Time is flying,' said the President in his gayest manner, after glancing at his watch, which like everything about him seemed bigger than it ought to be. 'I must be off at once; I have to take the chair at a Humanitarian meeting.'

The Secretary turned to him with working eyebrows.

'Would it not be better,' he said a little sharply, 'to discuss further the details of our project, now that the spy has left us?'

'No, I think not,' said the President with a yawn like an unobtrusive earthquake. 'Leave it as it is. Let Saturday settle it. I must be off. Breakfast here next Sunday.'

But the late loud scenes had whipped up the almost naked nerves of the Secretary. He was one of those men who are conscientious even in crime.

'I must protest, President, that the thing is irregular,' he said. 'It is a fundamental rule of our society that all plans shall be debated in full council. Of course, I fully appreciate your forethought when in the actual presence of a traitor——'

'Secretary,' said the President seriously, 'if you'd take your head home and boil it for a turnip it might be useful. I can't say. But it might.'

The Secretary reared back in a kind of equine anger.

'I really fail to understand——' he began in high offence.

'That's it, that's it,' said the President, nodding a great many times. 'That's where you fail right enough. You fail to understand. Why, you dancing donkey,' he roared, rising, 'you didn't want to be overheard by a spy, did you? How do you know you aren't overheard now?'

And with these words he shouldered his way out of the room, shaking with incomprehensible scorn.

Four of the men left behind gaped after him without any apparent glimmering of his meaning. Syme alone had even a glimmering, and such as it was it froze him to the bone. If the last words of the President meant anything, they meant that he had not after all passed unsuspected. They meant that while Sunday could not denounce him like Gogol, he still could not trust him like the others.

The other four got to their feet grumbling more or less, and betook themselves elsewhere to find lunch, for it was already well past midday. The Professor went last, very slowly and painfully. Syme sat long after the rest had gone, revolving his strange position. He had escaped a thunderbolt, but he was still under a cloud. At last he rose and made his way out of the hotel into Leicester Square. The bright, cold day had grown increasingly colder, and when he came out into the street he was surprised by a few flakes of snow. While he still carried the sword-stick and the rest of Gregory's portable luggage, he had thrown the cloak down and left it somewhere, perhaps on the steam-tug, perhaps on the balcony. Hoping, therefore, that the snow-shower might be slight, he stepped back out of the street for a moment and stood up under the doorway of a small and greasy hairdresser's shop, the front window of which was empty, except for a sickly wax lady in evening-dress.

Snow, however, began to thicken and fall fast; and Syme, having found one glance at the wax lady quite sufficient to depress his spirits, stared out instead into the white and empty street. He was considerably astonished to see, standing quite still outside the shop and staring into the window, a man. His top hat was loaded with snow like the hat of Father Christmas, the white drift was rising round his boots and ankles; but it seemed as if nothing could tear him away from the contemplation of the colourless wax doll in dirty evening-dress. That any human being should stand in such weather looking into such a shop was a matter of sufficient wonder to Syme; but his idle wonder turned suddenly into a personal shock; for he realized that the man standing there was the paralytic old Professor de Worms. It scarcely seemed the place for a person of his years and infirmities.

Syme was ready to believe anything about the perversions of this dehumanized brotherhood; but even he could not believe that the Professor had fallen in love with that particular wax lady. He could only suppose that the man's malady (whatever it was) involved some momentary fits of rigidity or trance. He was not inclined, however, to feel in this case any very compassionate concern. On the contrary, he rather congratulated himself that the Professor's stroke and his elaborate and limping walk would make it easy to escape from him and leave him miles behind. For Syme thirsted first and last to get clear of the whole poisonous atmosphere, if only for an hour. Then he could collect his thoughts, formulate his policy, and decide finally whether he should or should not keep faith with Gregory.

He strolled away through the dancing snow, turned up two or three streets, down through two or three others, and entered a small Soho restaurant for lunch. He partook reflectively of four small and quaint courses, drank half a bottle of red wine, and ended up over black coffee and a black cigar, still thinking. He had taken his seat in the upper room of the restaurant, which was full of the chink of knives and the chatter of foreigners. He remembered that in old days he had imagined that all these harmless and kindly aliens were anarchists. He shuddered, remembering the real thing. But even the shudder had the delightful shame of escape. The wine, the common food, the familiar place, the faces of natural and talkative men, made him almost feel as if the Council of the Seven Days had been a bad dream; and although he knew it was nevertheless an objective reality, it was at least a distant one. Tall houses and populous streets lay between him and his last sight of the shameful seven; he was free in free London, and drinking wine among the free. With a somewhat easier action, he took his hat and stick and strolled down the stair into the shop below.

When he entered that lower room he stood stricken and rooted to the spot. At a small table, close up to the blank window and the white street of snow, sat the old anarchist Professor over a glass of milk, with his lifted livid face and pendent eyelids. For an instant Syme stood as rigid as the stick he leant upon. Then with a gesture as of blind hurry, he brushed past the Professor, dashing open the door and slamming it behind him, and stood outside in the snow.

'Can that old corpse be following me?' he asked himself, biting his yellow moustache. 'I stopped too long up in that room, so that even such leaden feet could catch me up. One comfort is, with a little brisk walking I can put a man like that as far away as Timbuctoo. Or am I too fanciful? Was he really following me? Surely Sunday would not be such a fool as to send a lame man?'

He set off at a smart pace, twisting and whirling his stick, in the direction of Covent Garden. As he crossed the great market the snow increased, growing blinding and bewildering as the afternoon began to

darken. The snow-flakes tormented him like a swarm
of silver bees. Getting into his eyes and beard, they
added their unremitting futility to his already irritated
nerves; and by the time that he had come at a swinging
pace to the beginning of Fleet Street, he lost patience,
and finding a Sunday teashop, turned into it to take
shelter. He ordered another cup of black coffee as
an excuse. Scarcely had he done so, when Professor
de Worms hobbled heavily into the shop, sat down with
difficulty and ordered a glass of milk.

Syme's walking-stick had fallen from his hand
with a great clang, which confessed the concealed
steel. But the Professor did not look round. Syme,
who was commonly a cool character, was literally
gaping as a rustic gapes at a conjuring trick. He had
seen no cab following; he had heard no wheels outside
the shop; to all mortal appearances the man had come
on foot. But the old man could only walk like a snail,
and Syme had walked like the wind. He started up
and snatched his stick, half crazy with the contradiction
in mere arithmetic, and swung out of the swinging
doors, leaving his coffee untasted. An omnibus going
to the Bank went rattling by with an unusual rapidity.
He had a violent run of a hundred yards to reach it;
but he managed to spring, swaying upon the splashboard, and pausing for an instant to pant, he climbed
on to the top. When he had been seated for about
half a minute, he heard behind him a sort of heavy and
asthmatic breathing.

Turning sharply, he saw rising gradually higher
and higher up the omnibus steps a top hat soiled and
dripping with snow, and under the shadow of its
brim the short-sighted face and shaky shoulders of
Professor de Worms. He let himself into a seat with

characteristic care, and wrapped himself up to the chin in the mackintosh rug.

Every movement of the old man's tottering figure and vague hands, every uncertain gesture and panic-stricken pause, seemed to put it beyond question that he was helpless, that he was in the last imbecility of the body. He moved by inches, he let himself down with little gasps of caution. And yet, unless the philosophical entities called time and space have no vestige even of a practical existence, it appeared quite unquestionable that he had run after the omnibus.

Syme sprang erect upon the rocking car, and after staring wildly at the wintry sky, that grew gloomier every moment, he ran down the steps. He had repressed an elemental impulse to leap over the side.

Too bewildered to look back or to reason, he rushed into one of the little courts at the side of Fleet Street as a rabbit rushes into a hole. He had a vague idea, if this incomprehensible old Jack-in-the-box was really pursuing him, that in that labyrinth of little streets he could soon throw him off the scent. He dived in and out of those crooked lanes, which were more like cracks than thoroughfares; and by the time that he had completed about twenty alternate angles and described an unthinkable polygon, he paused to listen for any sound of pursuit. There was none; there could not in any case have been much, for the little streets were thick with the soundless snow. Somewhere behind Red Lion Court, however, he noticed a place where some energetic citizen had cleared away the snow for a space of about twenty yards, leaving the wet, glistening cobble-stones. He thought little of this as he passed it, only plunging into yet another arm of the maze. But when a few

9

hundred yards farther on he stood still again to listen, his heart stood still also, for he heard from that space of rugged stones the clinking crutch and labouring feet of the infernal cripple.

The sky above was loaded with the clouds of snow, leaving London in a darkness and oppression premature for that hour of the evening. On each side of Syme the walls of the alley were blind and featureless; there was no little window or any kind of eye. He felt a new impulse to break out of this hive of houses, to get once more into the open and lamplit street. Yet he rambled and dodged for a long time before he struck the main thoroughfare. When he did so, he struck it much farther up than he had fancied. He came out into what seemed the vast and void of Ludgate Circus, and saw St. Paul's Cathedral sitting in the sky.

At first he was startled to find these great roads so empty, as if a pestilence had swept through the city. Then he told himself that some degree of emptiness was natural; first, because the snow-storm was even dangerously deep, and secondly, because it was Sunday. And at the very word Sunday he bit his lip; the word was henceforth for him like some indecent pun. Under the white fog of snow high up in the heaven the whole atmosphere of the city was turned to a very queer kind of green twilight, as of men under the sea. The sealed and sullen sunset behind the dark dome of St. Paul's had in it smoky and sinister colours—colours of sickly green, dead red or decaying bronze, that were just bright enough to emphasize the solid whiteness of the snow. But right up against these dreary colours rose the black bulk of the cathedral; and upon the top of the cathedral was a random splash and great

stain of snow, still clinging as to an Alpine peak. It
had fallen accidentally, but just so fallen as to half
drape the dome from its very topmost point, and to
pick out in perfect silver the great orb and the cross.
When Syme saw it he suddenly straightened himself,
and made with his sword-stick an involuntary salute.

He knew that that evil figure, his shadow, was
creeping quickly or slowly behind him, and he did
not care. It seemed a symbol of human faith and
valour that while the skies were darkening that high
place of the earth was bright. The devils might
have captured heaven, but they had not yet captured
the cross. He had a new impulse to tear out the
secret of this dancing, jumping, and pursuing paralytic;
and at the entrance of the court as it opened upon the
Circus he turned, stick in hand, to face his pursuer.

Professor de Worms came slowly round the corner
of the irregular alley behind him, his unnatural form
outlined against a lonely gas-lamp, irresistibly recalling
that very imaginative figure in the nursery rhymes,
'the crooked man who went a crooked mile'. He really
looked as if he had been twisted out of shape by the
tortuous streets he had been threading. He came
nearer and nearer, the lamplight shining on his lifted
spectacles, his lifted, patient face. Syme waited for
him as St. George waited for the dragon, as a man waits
for a final explanation or for death. And the old
Professor came right up to him and passed him like
a total stranger, without even a blink of his mournful
eyelids.

There was something in this silent and unexpected
innocence that left Syme in a final fury. The man's
colourless face and manner seemed to assert that the
whole following had been an accident. Syme was

galvanized with an energy that was something between bitterness and a burst of boyish derision. He made a wild gesture as if to knock the old man's hat off, called out something like 'Catch me if you can', and went racing away across the white, open Circus. Concealment was impossible now; and looking back over his shoulder, he could see the black figure of the old gentleman coming after him with long, swinging strides like a man winning a mile race. But the head upon that bounding body was still pale, grave, and professional, like the head of a lecturer upon the body of a harlequin.

This outrageous chase sped across Ludgate Circus, up Ludgate Hill, round St. Paul's Cathedral, along Cheapside, Syme remembering all the nightmares he had ever known. Then Syme broke away towards the river, and ended almost down by the docks. He saw the yellow panes of a low, lighted public-house, flung himself into it and ordered beer. It was a foul tavern, sprinkled with foreign sailors, a place where opium might be smoked or knives drawn.

A moment later Professor de Worms entered the place, sat down carefully, and asked for a glass of milk.

CHAPTER VIII

THE PROFESSOR EXPLAINS

WHEN Gabriel Syme found himself finally established in a chair, and opposite to him, fixed and final also, the lifted eyebrows and leaden eyelids of the Professor, his fears fully returned. This incomprehensible man from the fierce council, after all, had certainly pursued him. If the man had one character as a paralytic and another character as a pursuer, the antithesis might make him more interesting, but scarcely more soothing. It would be a very small comfort that he could not find the Professor out, if by some serious accident the Professor should find him out. He emptied a whole pewter pot of ale before the Professor had touched his milk.

One possibility, however, kept him hopeful and yet helpless. It was just possible that this escapade signified something other than even a slight suspicion of him. Perhaps it was some regular form or sign. Perhaps the foolish scamper was some sort of friendly signal that he ought to have understood. Perhaps it was a ritual. Perhaps the new Thursday was always chased along Cheapside, as the new Lord Mayor is always escorted along it. He was just selecting a tentative inquiry, when the old Professor opposite suddenly and simply cut him short. Before Syme could ask the first diplomatic question, the old anarchist had asked suddenly, without any sort of preparation:

'Are you a policeman?'

Whatever else Syme had expected, he had never

expected anything so brutal and actual as this. Even his great presence of mind could only manage a reply with an air of rather blundering jocularity.

'A policeman?' he said, laughing vaguely. 'Whatever made you think of a policeman in connexion with me?'

'The process was simple enough,' answered the Professor patiently. 'I thought you looked like a policeman. I think so now.'

'Did I take a policeman's hat by mistake out of the restaurant?' asked Syme, smiling wildly. 'Have I by any chance got a number stuck on to me somewhere? Have my boots got that watchful look? Why must I be a policeman? Do, do let me be a postman.'

The old Professor shook his head with a gravity that gave no hope, but Syme ran on with a feverish irony.

'But perhaps I misunderstood the delicacies of your German philosophy. Perhaps policeman is a relative term. In an evolutionary sense, sir, the ape fades so gradually into the policeman, that I myself can never detect the shade. The monkey is only the policeman that may be. Perhaps a maiden lady on Clapham Common is only the policeman that might have been. I don't mind being the policeman that might have been. I don't mind being anything in German thought.'

'Are you in the police service?' said the old man, ignoring all Syme's improvised and desperate raillery. 'Are you a detective?'

Syme's heart turned to stone, but his face never changed.

'Your suggestion is ridiculous,' he began. 'Why on earth——'

The old man struck his palsied hand passionately on the rickety table, nearly breaking it.

'Did you hear me ask a plain question, you paltering spy?' he shrieked in a high, crazy voice. 'Are you, or are you not, a police detective?'

'No!' answered Syme, like a man standing on the hangman's drop.

'You swear it,' said the old man, leaning across to him, his dead face becoming as it were loathsomely alive. 'You swear it! You swear it! If you swear falsely, will you be damned? Will you be sure that the devil dances at your funeral? Will you see that the nightmare sits on your grave? Will there really be no mistake? You are an anarchist, you are a dynamiter! Above all, you are not in any sense a detective? You are not in the British police?'

He leant his angular elbow far across the table, and put up his large loose hand like a flap to his ear.

'I am not in the British police,' said Syme with insane calm.

Professor de Worms fell back in his chair with a curious air of kindly collapse.

'That's a pity,' he said, 'because I am.'

Syme sprang up straight, sending back the bench behind him with a crash.

'Because you are what?' he said thickly. 'You are what?'

'I am a policeman,' said the Professor with his first broad smile, and beaming through his spectacles. 'But as you think policeman only a relative term, of course I have nothing to do with you. I am in the British police force; but as you tell me you are not in the British police force, I can only say that I met you in a dynamiters' club. I suppose I ought to arrest you.' And with these words he laid on the table before Syme an exact facsimile of the blue card which Syme had in his own waistcoat pocket, the symbol of his power from the police.

Syme had for a flash the sensation that the cosmos had turned exactly upside down, that all trees were growing downwards and that all stars were under his feet. Then came slowly the opposite conviction. For the last twenty-four hours the cosmos had really been upside down, but now the capsized universe had come right side up again. This devil from whom he had been fleeing all day was only an elder brother of his own house, who on the other side of the table lay back and laughed at him. He did not for the moment ask any questions of detail; he only knew the happy and silly fact that this shadow, which had pursued him with an intolerable oppression of peril, was only the shadow of a friend trying to catch him up. He knew simultaneously that he was a fool and a free man. For with any recovery from morbidity there must go a certain healthy humiliation. There comes a certain point in such conditions when only three things are possible: first a perpetuation of Satanic pride, secondly tears, and third laughter. Syme's egotism held hard to the first course for a few seconds, and then suddenly adopted the third. Taking his own blue police ticket from his own waistcoat pocket, he tossed it on to the table; then he flung his head back until his spike of yellow beard almost pointed at the ceiling, and shouted with a barbaric laughter.

Even in that close den, perpetually filled with the din of knives, plates, cans, clamorous voices, sudden struggles and stampedes, there was something Homeric in Syme's mirth which made many half-drunken men look round.

'What yer laughing at, guv'nor?' asked one wondering labourer from the docks.

'At myself,' answered Syme, and went off again into the agony of his ecstatic reaction.

'Pull yourself together,' said the Professor, 'or you'll get hysterical. Have some more beer. I'll join you.'

'You haven't drunk your milk,' said Syme.

'My milk!' said the other, in tones of withering and unfathomable contempt, 'my milk! Do you think I'd look at that beastly stuff when I'm out of sight of the bloody anarchists? We're all Christians in this room, though perhaps,' he added, glancing around at the reeling crowd, 'not strict ones. Finish my milk! Great blazes! yes, I'll finish it right enough!' and he knocked the tumbler off the table, making a crash of glass and a splash of silver fluid.

Syme was staring at him with a happy curiosity.

'I understand now,' he cried; 'of course, you're not an old man at all.'

'I can't take my face off here,' replied Professor de Worms. 'It's rather an elaborate make-up. As to whether I'm an old man, that's not for me to say. I was thirty-eight last birthday.'

'Yes, but I mean,' said Syme impatiently, 'there's nothing the matter with you.'

'Yes,' answered the other dispassionately, 'I am subject to colds.'

Syme's laughter at all this had about it a wild weakness of relief. He laughed at the idea of the paralytic Professor being really a young actor dressed up as if for the foot-lights. But he felt that he would have laughed as loudly if a pepper-pot had fallen over.

The false Professor drank and wiped his false beard.

'Did you know,' he asked, 'that that man Gogol was one of us?'

'I? No, I didn't know it,' answered Syme in some surprise. 'But didn't you?'

'I knew no more than the dead,' replied the man who called himself de Worms. 'I thought the President was talking about me, and I rattled in my boots.'

'And I thought he was talking about me,' said Syme, with his rather reckless laughter. 'I had my hand on my revolver all the time.'

'So had I,' said the Professor grimly; 'so had Gogol, evidently.'

Syme struck the table with an exclamation.

'Why, there were three of us there!' he cried. 'Three out of seven is a fighting number. If we had only known that we were three!'

The face of Professor de Worms darkened, and he did not look up.

'We were three,' he said. 'If we had been three hundred we could still have done nothing.'

'Not if we were three hundred against four?' asked Syme, jeering rather boisterously.

'No,' said the Professor with sobriety, 'not if we were three hundred against Sunday.'

And the mere name struck Syme cold and serious; his laughter had died in his heart before it could die on his lips. The face of the unforgettable President sprang into his mind as startling as a coloured photograph, and he remarked this difference between Sunday and all his satellites, that their faces, however fierce and sinister, became gradually blurred by memory like other human faces, whereas Sunday's seemed almost to grow more actual during absence, as if a man's painted portrait should slowly come alive.

They were both silent for a measure of moments, and then Syme's speech came with a rush, like the sudden foaming of champagne.

'Professor,' he cried, 'it is intolerable. Are you afraid of this man?'

The Professor lifted his heavy lids, and gazed at Syme with large, wide-open, blue eyes of an almost ethereal honesty.

'Yes, I am,' he said mildly. 'So are you.'

Syme was dumb for an instant. Then he rose to his feet erect, like an insulted man, and thrust the chair away from him.

'Yes,' he said in a voice indescribable, 'you are right. I am afraid of him. Therefore I swear by God that I will seek out this man whom I fear until I find him, and strike him on the mouth. If heaven were his throne and the earth his footstool, I swear that I would pull him down.'

'How?' asked the staring Professor. 'Why?'

'Because I am afraid of him,' said Syme; 'and no man should leave in the universe anything of which he is afraid.'

De Worms blinked at him with a sort of blind wonder. He made an effort to speak, but Syme went on in a low voice, but with an undercurrent of inhuman exaltation:

'Who would condescend to strike down the mere things that he does not fear? Who would debase himself to be merely brave, like any common prize-fighter? Who would stoop to be fearless—like a tree? Fight the thing that you fear. You remember the old tale of the English clergyman who gave the last rites to the brigand of Sicily, and how on his death-bed the great robber said, "I can give you no money, but I can give you advice for a lifetime: your thumb on the blade, and strike upwards." So I say to you, strike upwards, if you strike at the stars.'

The other looked at the celling, one of the tricks of his pose.

'Sunday is a fixed star,' he said.

'You shall see him a falling star,' said Syme, and put on his hat.

The decision of his gesture drew the Professor vaguely to his feet.

'Have you any idea,' he asked, with a sort of benevolent bewilderment, 'exactly where you are going?'

'Yes,' replied Syme shortly, 'I am going to prevent this bomb being thrown in Paris.'

'Have you any conception how?' inquired the other.

'No,' said Syme with equal decision.

'You remember, of course,' resumed the soi-disant de Worms, pulling his beard and looking out of the window, 'that when we broke up rather hurriedly the whole arrangements for the atrocity were left in the private hands of the Marquis and Dr. Bull. The Marquis is by this time probably crossing the Channel. But where he will go and what he will do it is doubtful whether even the President knows; certainly we don't. The only man who does know is Dr. Bull.'

'Confound it!' cried Syme. 'And we don't know where he is.'

'Yes,' said the other in his curious, absent-minded way, 'I know where he is myself.'

'Will you tell me?' asked Syme with eager eyes.

'I will take you there,' said the Professor, and took down his own hat from a peg.

Syme stood looking at him with a sort of rigid excitement.

'What do you mean?' he asked sharply. 'Will you join me? Will you take the risk?'

'Young man,' said the Professor pleasantly, 'I am amused to observe that you think I am a coward. As to that I will say only one word, and that shall be entirely in the manner of your own philosophical rhetoric. You think that it is possible to pull down the President. I know that it is impossible, and I am going to try it,' and opening the tavern door, which let in a blast of bitter air, they went out together into the dark streets by the docks.

Most of the snow was melted or trampled to mud, but here and there a clot of it still showed grey rather than white in the gloom. The small streets were sloppy and full of pools, which reflected the flaming lamps irregularly, and by accident, like fragments of some other and fallen world. Syme felt almost dazed as he stepped through this growing confusion of lights and shadows; but his companion walked on with a certain briskness towards where, at the end of the street, an inch or two of the lamplit river looked like a bar of flame.

'Where are you going?' Syme inquired.

'Just now,' answered the Professor, 'I am going just round the corner to see whether Dr. Bull has gone to bed. He is hygienic, and retires early.'

'Dr. Bull!' exclaimed Syme. 'Does he live round the corner?'

'No,' answered his friend. 'As a matter of fact he lives some way off, on the other side of the river, but we can tell from here whether he has gone to bed.'

Turning the corner as he spoke, and facing the dim river, flecked with flame, he pointed with his stick to the other bank. On the Surrey side at this point there ran out into the Thames, seeming almost to overhang it, a bulk and cluster of those tall tenements, dotted with lighted windows, and rising like factory chimneys to an almost insane height. Their special poise and position made one block of buildings especially look like a Tower of Babel with a hundred eyes. Syme had never seen any of the sky-scraping buildings in America, so he could only think of the buildings in a dream.

Even as he stared, the highest light in this innumerably lighted turret abruptly went out, as if this black Argus had winked at him with one of his innumerable eyes.

Professor de Worms swung round on his heel, and struck his stick against his boot.

'We are too late,' he said, 'the hygienic Doctor has gone to bed.'

'What do you mean?' asked Syme. 'Does he live over there, then?'

'Yes,' said de Worms, 'behind that particular window which you can't see. Come along and get some dinner. We must call on him to-morrow morning.'

Without further parley, he led the way through several by-ways until they came out into the flare and clamour of the East India Dock Road. The Professor, who seemed to know his way about the neighbourhood, proceeded to a place where the line of lighted shops fell back into a sort of abrupt twilight and quiet, in which an old white inn, all out of repair, stood back some twenty feet from the road.

'You can find good English inns left by accident

everywhere, like fossils,' explained the Professor. 'I once found a decent place in the West End.'

'I suppose,' said Syme, smiling, 'that this is the corresponding decent place in the East End?'

'It is,' said the Professor reverently, and went in.

In that place they dined and slept, both very thoroughly. The beans and bacon, which these unaccountable people cooked well, the astonishing emergence of Burgundy from their cellars, crowned Syme's sense of a new comradeship and comfort. Through all this ordeal his root horror had been isolation, and there are no words to express the abyss between isolation and having one ally. It may be conceded to the mathematicians that four is twice two. But two is not twice one; two is two thousand times one. That is why, in spite of a hundred disadvantages, the world will always return to monogamy.

Syme was able to pour out for the first time the whole of his outrageous tale, from the time when Gregory had taken him to the little tavern by the river. He did it idly and amply, in a luxuriant monologue, as a man speaks with very old friends. On his side, also, the man who had impersonated Professor de Worms was not less communicative. His own story was almost as silly as Syme's.

'That's a good get-up of yours,' said Syme, draining a glass of Mâcon; 'a lot better than old Gogol's. Even at the start I thought he was a bit too hairy.'

'A difference of artistic theory,' replied the Professor pensively. 'Gogol was an idealist. He made up as the abstract or platonic ideal of an anarchist. But I am a realist. I am a portrait painter. But, indeed, to say that I am a portrait painter is an inadequate expression. I am a portrait.'

'I don't understand you,' said Syme.

'I am a portrait,' repeated the Professor. 'I am a portrait of the celebrated Professor de Worms, who is, I believe, in Naples.'

'You mean you are made up like him,' said Syme. 'But doesn't he know that you are taking his nose in vain?'

'He knows it right enough,' replied his friend cheerfully.

'Then why doesn't he denounce you?'

'I have denounced him,' answered the Professor.

'Do explain yourself,' said Syme.

'With pleasure, if you don't mind hearing my story,' replied the eminent foreign philosopher. 'I am by profession an actor, and my name is Wilks. When I was on the stage I mixed with all sorts of Bohemian and blackguard company. Sometimes I touched the edge of the turf, sometimes the riff-raff of the arts, and occasionally the political refugee. In some den of exiled dreamers I was introduced to the great German Nihilist philosopher, Professor de Worms. I did not gather much about him beyond his appearance, which was very disgusting, and which I studied carefully. I understood that he had proved that the destructive principle in the universe was God; hence he insisted on the need for a furious and incessant energy, rending all things in pieces. Energy, he said, was the All. He was lame, shortsighted, and partially paralytic. When I met him I was in a frivolous mood, and I disliked him so much that I resolved to imitate him. If I had been a draughtsman I would have drawn a caricature. I was only an actor, I could only act a caricature. I made myself up into what was meant for a wild exaggeration of the old Professor's dirty old self. When I went into the room full of his supporters I expected to be received with a roar of laughter, or (if they were too far gone) with a roar of indignation at the insult. I cannot describe the surprise I felt when my entrance was received with a respectful silence, followed (when I had first opened my lips) with a murmur of admiration. The curse of the perfect artist had fallen upon me. I had been too subtle, I had been too true. They thought I really was the great Nihilist Professor. I was a healthy-minded young man at the time, and I confess that it was a blow. Before I could fully recover, however, two or three of these admirers ran up to me radiating indignation, and told me that a public insult had been put upon me in the next room. I inquired its nature. It seemed that an impertinent fellow had dressed himself up as a preposterous parody of myself. I had drunk more champagne than was good for me, and in a flash of folly I decided to see the situation through. Consequently it was to meet the glare of the company and my own lifted eyebrows and freezing eyes that the real Professor came into the room.

'I need hardly say there was a collision. The pessimists all round me looked anxiously from one Professor to the other Professor to see which was really the more feeble. But I won. An old man in poor health, like my rival, could not be expected to be so impressively feeble as a young actor in the prime of life. You see, he really had paralysis, and working within this definite limitation, he couldn't be so jolly paralytic as I was. Then he tried to blast my claims intellectually. I countered that by a very simple dodge. Whenever he said something that nobody but he could understand, I replied with something which I could not even understand myself. "I don't fancy," he said, "that you could have worked out the principle that evolution is only negation, since there inheres in it the introduction of lacunae, which are an essential of differentiation." I replied quite scornfully, "You read all that up in Pinckwerts; the notion that involution functioned eugenically was exposed long ago by Glumpe." It is unnecessary for me to say that there never were such people as Pinckwerts and Glumpe. But the people all round (rather to my surprise) seemed to remember them quite well, and the Professor, finding that the learned and mysterious method left him rather at the mercy of an enemy slightly deficient in scruples, fell back upon a more popular form of wit. "I see," he sneered, "you prevail like the false pig in Æsop." "And you fail," I answered, smiling, "like the hedgehog in Montaigne." Need I say that there is no hedgehog in Montaigne? "Your clap-trap comes off," he said; "so would your beard." I had no intelligent answer to this, which was quite true and rather witty. But I laughed heartily, answered, "Like the Pantheist's boots", at random, and turned on my heel with all the honours of victory. The real Professor was thrown out, but not with violence, though one man tried very patiently to pull off his nose. He is now, I believe, received everywhere in Europe as a delightful impostor. His apparent earnestness and anger, you see, make him all the more entertaining.'

'Well,' said Syme, 'I can understand your putting on his dirty old beard for a night's practical joke, but I don't understand your never taking it off again.'

'That is the rest of the story,' said the impersonator. 'When I myself left the company, followed by reverent applause, I went limping down the dark street, hoping that I should soon be far enough away to be able to walk like a human being. To my astonishment, as I was turning the corner, I felt a touch on the shoulder, and turning, found myself under the shadow of an enormous policeman. He told me I was wanted. I struck a sort of paralytic attitude, and cried in a high German accent, "Yes, I am wanted—by the oppressed of the world. You are arresting me on the charge of being the great anarchist, Professor de Worms." The policeman impassively consulted a paper in his hand, "No, sir," he said civilly, "at least, not exactly, sir. I am arresting you on the charge of not being the celebrated anarchist, Professor de Worms." This charge, if it was criminal at all, was certainly the lighter of the two, and I went along with the man, doubtful, but not greatly dismayed. I was shown into a number of rooms, and eventually into the presence of a police officer, who explained that a serious campaign had been opened against the centres of anarchy, and that this, my successful masquerade, might be of considerable value to the public safety. He offered me a good salary and this little blue card. Though our conversation was short, he struck me as a man of very massive common sense and humour, but I cannot tell you much about him personally, because——'

Syme laid down his knife and fork.

'I know, he said, 'because you talked to him in a dark room.'

Professor de Worms nodded and drained his glass.

CHAPTER IX

THE MAN IN SPECTACLES

'Burgundy is a jolly thing,' said the Professor sadly, as he set his glass down.

'You don't look as if it were,' said Syme; 'you drink it as if it were medicine.'

'You must excuse my manner,' said the Professor dismally, 'my position is rather a curious one. Inside I am really bursting with boyish merriment; but I acted the paralytic Professor so well, that now I can't leave off. So that when I am among friends, and have no need at all to disguise myself, I still can't help speaking slow and wrinkling my forehead—just as if it were my forehead. I can be quite happy, you understand, but only in a paralytic sort of way. The most buoyant exclamations leap up in my heart, but they come out of my mouth quite different. You should hear me say, "Buck up, old cock!" It would bring tears to your eyes.'

'It does,' said Syme; 'but I cannot help thinking that apart from all that you are really a bit worried.'

The Professor started a little and looked at him steadily.

'You are a very clever fellow,' he said; 'it is a pleasure to work with you. Yes, I have rather a heavy cloud in my head. There is a great problem to face,' and he sank his bald brow in his two hands.

Then he said in a low voice:

'Can you play the piano?'

'Yes,' said Syme in simple wonder, 'I'm supposed to have a good touch.'

Then, as the other did not speak, he added:

'I trust the great cloud is lifted.'

After a long silence, the Professor said out of the cavernous shadow of his hands:

'It would have done just as well if you could work a typewriter.'

'Thank you,' said Syme, 'you flatter me.'

'Listen to me,' said the other, 'and remember whom we have to see to-morrow. You and I are going to-morrow to attempt something which is very much more dangerous than trying to steal the Crown Jewels out of the Tower. We are trying to steal a secret from a very sharp, very strong, and very wicked man. I believe there is no man, except the President, of course, who is so seriously startling and formidable as that little grinning fellow in goggles. He has not perhaps the white-hot enthusiasm unto death, the mad martyrdom for anarchy, which marks the Secretary. But then that very fanaticism in the Secretary has a human pathos, and is almost a redeeming trait. But the little Doctor has a brutal sanity that is more shocking than the Secretary's disease. Don't you notice his detestable virility and vitality. He bounces like an india-rubber ball. Depend on it, Sunday was not asleep (I wonder if he ever sleeps?) when he locked up all the plans of this outrage in the round, black head of Dr. Bull.'

'And you think,' said Syme, 'that this unique monster will be soothed if I play the piano to him?'

'Don't be an ass,' said his mentor. 'I mentioned the piano because it gives one quick and independent fingers. Syme, if we are to go through this interview and come out sane or alive, we must have some code of signals between us that this brute will not see. I have made a rough alphabetical cipher corresponding to the five fingers—like this, see,' and he rippled with his fingers on the wooden table—'B A D, bad, a word we may frequently require.'

Syme poured himself out another glass of wine, and began to study the scheme. He was abnormally quick with his brains at puzzles, and with his hands at conjuring, and it did not take him long to learn how he might convey simple messages by what would seem to be idle taps upon a table or knee. But wine and companionship had always the effect of inspiring him to a farcical ingenuity, and the Professor soon found himself struggling with the too vast energy of the new language, as it passed through the heated brain of Syme.

'We must have several word-signs,' said Syme seriously—'words that we are likely to want, fine shades of meaning. My favourite word is "coeval". What's yours?'

'Do stop playing the goat,' said the Professor plaintively. 'You don't know how serious this is.'

'"Lush", too,' said Syme, shaking his head sagaciously, 'we must have "lush".—Word applied to grass, don't you know?'

'Do you imagine,' asked the Professor furiously, 'that we are going to talk to Dr. Bull about grass?'

'There are several ways in which the subject could be approached,' said Syme reflectively, 'and the word introduced without appearing forced. We might say, "Dr. Bull, as a revolutionist, you remember that a tyrant once advised us to eat grass; and indeed many of us, looking on the fresh lush grass of summer——'

'Do you understand,' said the other, 'that this is a tragedy?'

'Perfectly,' replied Syme; 'always be comic in a tragedy. What the deuce else can you do? I wish this language of yours had a wider scope. I suppose we could not extend it from the fingers to the toes? That would involve pulling off our boots and socks during the conversation, which however unobtrusively performed——'

'Syme,' said his friend with a stern simplicity, 'go to bed!'

Syme, however, sat up in bed for a considerable time mastering the new code. He was awakened next morning while the east was still sealed with darkness, and found his grey-bearded ally standing like a ghost beside his bed.

Syme sat up in bed blinking; then slowly collected his thoughts, threw off the bed-clothes, and stood up. It seemed to him in some curious way that all the safety and sociability of the night before fell with the bed-clothes off him, and he stood up in an air of cold danger. He still felt an entire trust and loyalty towards his companion; but it was the trust between two men going to the scaffold.

'Well,' said Syme with a forced cheerfulness as he pulled on his trousers, 'I dreamt of that alphabet of yours. Did it take you long to make it up?'

The Professor made no answer, but gazed in front of him with eyes the colour of a wintry sea; so Syme repeated his question.

'I say, did it take you long to invent all this? I'm considered good at these things, and it was a good hour's grind. Did you learn it all on the spot?'

The Professor was silent; his eyes were wide open, and he wore a fixed but very small smile.

'How long did it take you?'

The Professor did not move.

'Confound you, can't you answer?' called out Syme, in a sudden anger that had something like fear underneath. Whether or no the Professor could answer, he did not.

Syme stood staring back at the stiff face like parchment and the blank, blue eyes. His first thought was that the Professor had gone mad, but his second thought was more frightful. After all, what did he know about this queer creature whom he had heedlessly accepted as a friend? What did he know, except that the man had been at the anarchist breakfast and had told him a ridiculous tale? How improbable it was that there should be another friend there beside Gogol! Was this man's silence a sensational way of declaring war? Was this adamantine stare after all only the awful sneer of some threefold traitor, who had turned for the last time? He stood and strained his ears in this heartless silence. He almost fancied he could hear dynamiters come to capture him shifting softly in the corridor outside.

Then his eye strayed downwards, and he burst out laughing. Though the Professor himself stood there as voiceless as a statue, his five dumb fingers were dancing alive upon the dead table. Syme watched the twinkling movements of the talking hand, and read clearly the message:

'I will only talk like this. We must get used to it.'

He rapped out the answer with the impatience of relief:

'All right. Let's get out to breakfast.'

They took their hats and sticks in silence; but as Syme took his sword-stick, he held it hard.

They paused for a few minutes only to stuff down coffee and coarse thick sandwiches at a coffee-stall, and then made their way across the river, which under the grey and growing light looked as desolate as Acheron. They reached the bottom of the huge block of buildings which they had seen from across the river, and began in silence to mount the naked and numberless stone steps, only pausing now and then to make short remarks on the rail of the banisters. At about every other flight they passed a window; each window showed them a pale and tragic dawn lifting itself laboriously over London. From each the innumerable roofs of slate looked like the leaden·surges of a grey, troubled sea after rain. Syme was increasingly conscious that his new adventure had somehow a quality of cold sanity worse than the wild adventures of the past. Last night, for instance, the tall tenements had seemed to him like a tower in a dream. As he now went up the weary and perpetual steps, he was daunted and bewildered by their almost infinite series. But it was not the hot horror of a dream or of anything that might be exaggeration or delusion. Their infinity was more like the empty infinity of arithmetic, something unthinkable, yet necessary to thought. Or it was like the stunning statements of astronomy about the distance of the fixed stars. He was ascending the house of reason, a thing more hideous than unreason itself.

By the time they reached Dr. Bull's landing, a last window showed them a harsh, white dawn edged with banks of a kind of coarse red, more like red clay than red cloud. And when they entered Dr. Bull's bare garret it was full of light.

Syme had been haunted by a half historic memory

in connexion with these empty rooms and that austere daybreak. The moment he saw the garret and Dr. Bull sitting writing at a table, he remembered what the memory was—the French Revolution. There should have been the black outline of a guillotine against that heavy red and white of the morning. Dr. Bull was in his white shirt and black breeches only; his cropped, dark head might well have just come out of its wig; he might have been Marat or a more slipshod Robespierre.

Yet when he was seen properly, the French fancy fell away. The Jacobins were idealists; there was about this man a murderous materialism. His position gave him a somewhat new appearance. The strong, white light of morning coming from one side creating sharp shadows, made him seem both more pale and more angular than he had looked at the breakfast on the balcony. Thus the two black glasses that encased his eyes might really have been black cavities in his skull, making him look like a death's-head. And indeed, if ever Death himself sat writing at a wooden table, it might have been he.

He looked up and smiled brightly enough as the men came in, and rose with the resilient rapidity of which the Professor had spoken. He set chairs for both of them, and going to a peg behind the door, proceeded to put on a coat and waistcoat of rough, dark tweed; he buttoned it up neatly, and came back to sit down at his table.

The quiet good humour of his manner left his two opponents helpless. It was with some momentary difficulty that the Professor broke silence and began, 'I'm sorry to disturb you so early, comrade,' said he, with a careful resumption of the slow de Worms manner. 'You have no doubt made all the arrangements for the Paris affair?' Then he added with infinite slowness, 'We have information which renders intolerable anything in the nature of a moment's delay.'

Dr. Bull smiled again, but continued to gaze on them without speaking. The Professor resumed, a pause before each weary word:

'Please do not think me excessively abrupt; but I advise you to alter those plans, or if it is too late for that, to follow your agent with all the support you can get for him. Comrade Syme and I have had an experience which it would take more time to recount than we can afford, if we are to act on it. I will, however, relate the occurrence in detail, even at the risk of losing time, if you really feel that it is essential to the understanding of the problem we have to discuss.'

He was spinning out his sentences, making them intolerably long and lingering, in the hope of maddening the practical little Doctor into an explosion of impatience which might show his hand. But the little Doctor continued only to stare and smile, and the monologue was uphill work. Syme began to feel a new sickness and despair. The Doctor's smile and silence were not at all like the cataleptic stare and horrible silence which he had confronted in the Professor half an hour before. About the Professor's make-up and all his antics there was always something merely grotesque, like a gollywog. Syme remembered those wild woes of yesterday as one remembers being afraid of Bogy in childhood. But here was daylight; here was a healthy, square-shouldered man in tweeds, not odd save for the accident of his ugly spectacles, not glaring or grinning at all, but smiling steadily and not saying a word. The whole had a sense of unbearable reality.

Under the increasing sunlight the colours of the Doctor's complexion, the pattern of his tweeds, grew and expanded outrageously, as such things grow too important in a realistic novel. But his smile was quite slight, the pose of his head polite; the only uncanny thing was his silence.

'As I say,' resumed the Professor, like a man toiling through heavy sand, 'the incident that has occurred to us and has led us to ask for information about the Marquis, is one which you may think it better to have narrated; but as it came in the way of Comrade Syme rather than me——'

His words he seemed to be dragging out like words in an anthem; but Syme, who was watching, saw his long fingers rattle quickly on the edge of the crazy table. He read the message: 'You must go on. This devil has sucked me dry!'

Syme plunged into the breach with that bravado of improvisation which always came to him when he was alarmed.

'Yes, the thing really happened to me,' he said hastily. 'I had the good fortune to fall into conversation with a detective who took me, thanks to my hat, for a respectable person. Wishing to clinch my reputation for respectability, I took him and made him very drunk at the Savoy. Under this influence he became friendly, and told me in so many words that within a day or two they hope to arrest the Marquis in France. So unless you or I can get on his track——'

The Doctor was still smiling in the most friendly way, and his protected eyes were still impenetrable. The Professor signalled to Syme that he would resume his explanation, and he began again with the same elaborate calm.

'Syme immediately brought this information to me, and we came here together to see what use you would be inclined to make of it. It seems to me unquestionably urgent that——'

All this time Syme had been staring at the Doctor almost as steadily as the Doctor stared at the Professor, but quite without the smile. The nerves of both comrades-in-arms were near snapping under that strain of motionless amiability, when Syme suddenly leant forward and idly tapped the edge of the table. His message to his ally ran, 'I have an intuition.'

The Professor, with scarcely a pause in his monologue, signalled back, 'Then sit on it.'

Syme telegraphed, 'It is quite extraordinary.'

The other answered, 'Extraordinary rot!'

Syme said, 'I am a poet.'

The other retorted, 'You are a dead man.'

Syme had gone quite red up to his yellow hair, and his eyes were burning feverishly. As he said he had an intuition, and it had risen to a sort of light-headed certainty. Resuming his symbolic taps, he signalled to his friend, 'You scarcely realize how poetic my intuition is. It has that sudden quality we sometimes feel in the coming of spring.'

He then studied the answer on his friend's fingers. The answer was, 'Go to hell!'

The Professor then resumed his merely verbal monologue addressed to the Doctor.

'Perhaps I should rather say,' said Syme on his fingers, 'that it resembles that sudden smell of the sea which may be found in the heart of lush woods.'

His companion disdained to reply.

'Or yet again,' tapped Syme, 'it is positive, as is the passionate red hair of a beautiful woman.'

The Professor was continuing his speech, but in the middle of it Syme decided to act. He leant across the table, and said in a voice that could not be neglected:

'Dr. Bull!'

The Doctor's sleek and smiling head did not move, but they could have sworn that under his dark glasses his eyes darted towards Syme.

'Dr. Bull,' said Syme, in a voice peculiarly precise and courteous, 'would you do me a small favour? Would you be so kind as to take off your spectacles?'

The Professor swung round on his seat, and stared at Syme with a sort of frozen fury of astonishment. Syme, like a man who has thrown his life and fortune on the table, leaned forward with a fiery face. The Doctor did not move.

For a few seconds there was a silence in which one could hear a pin drop, split once by the single hoot of a distant steamer on the Thames. Then Dr. Bull rose slowly, still smiling, and took off his spectacles.

Syme sprang to his feet, stepping backwards a little, like a chemical lecturer from a successful explosion. His eyes were like stars, and for an instant he could only point without speaking.

The Professor had also started to his feet, forgetful of his supposed paralysis. He leant on the back of the chair and stared doubtfully at Dr. Bull, as if the Doctor had been turned into a toad before his eyes. And indeed it was almost as great a transformation scene.

The two detectives saw sitting in the chair before them a very boyish-looking young man, with very frank and happy hazel eyes, an open expression, cockney clothes like those of a city clerk, and an unquestionable breath about him of being very good and rather commonplace. The smile was still there, but it might have been the first smile of a baby.

'I knew I was a poet,' cried Syme in a sort of ecstasy. 'I knew my intuition was as infallible as the Pope. It was the spectacles that did it! It was all the spectacles! Given those beastly black eyes, and all the rest of him, his health and his jolly looks, made him a live devil among dead ones.'

'It certainly does make a queer difference,' said the Professor shakily. 'But as regards the project of Dr. Bull——'

'Project be damned!' roared Syme, beside himself. 'Look at him! Look at his face, look at his collar, look at his blessed boots! You don't suppose, do you, that that thing's an anarchist?'

'Syme!' cried the other in an apprehensive agony.

'Why, by God!' said Syme, 'I'll take the risk of that myself! Dr. Bull, I am a police officer. There's my card,' and he flung down the blue card upon the table.

The Professor still feared that all was lost; but he was loyal. He pulled out his own official card and put it beside his friend's. Then the third man burst out laughing, and for the first time that morning they heard his voice.

'I'm awfully glad you chaps have come so early,' he said, with a sort of schoolboy flippancy, 'for we can all start for France together. Yes, I'm in the force right enough,' and he flicked a blue card towards them lightly as a matter of form.

Clapping a brisk bowler on his head and resuming his goblin glasses, the Doctor moved so quickly towards the door, that the others instinctively followed him.

Syme seemed a little distrait, and as he passed under the doorway he suddenly struck his stick on the stone passage so that it rang.

'But Lord God Almighty,' he cried out, 'if this is all right, there were more damned detectives than there were damned dynamiters at the damned Council!'

'We might have fought easily,' said Bull; 'we were four against three.'

The Professor was descending the stairs, but his voice came up from below.

'No,' said the voice, 'we were not four against three—we were not so lucky. We were four against One.'

The others went down the stairs in silence.

The young man called Bull, with an innocent courtesy characteristic of him, insisted on going last until they reached the street; but there his own robust rapidity asserted itself unconsciously, and he walked quickly on ahead towards a railway inquiry office, talking to the others over his shoulder.

'It is jolly to get some pals,' he said. 'I've been half dead with the jumps, being quite alone. I nearly flung my arms round Gogol and embraced him, which would have been imprudent. I hope you won't despise me for having been in a blue funk.'

'All the blue devils in blue hell,' said Syme, 'contributed to my blue funk! But the worst devil was you and your infernal goggles.'

The young man laughed delightedly.

'Wasn't it a rag?' he said. 'Such a simple idea—not my own. I haven't got the brains. You see, I wanted to go into the detective service, especially the anti-dynamite business. But for that purpose they wanted some one to dress up as a dynamiter; and they all swore by blazes that I could never look like a dynamiter. They said my very walk was respectable, and that seen from behind I looked like the British Constitution. They said I looked too healthy and too optimistic, and too reliable and benevolent; they called me all sorts of names at Scotland Yard. They said that if I had been a criminal, I might have made my fortune by looking so like an honest man; but as I had the misfortune to be an honest man, there was not even the remotest chance of my assisting them by ever looking like a criminal. But at last I was brought before some old josser who was high up in the force, and who seemed to have no end of a head on his shoulders. And there the others all talked hopelessly. One asked whether a bushy beard would hide my nice smile; another said that if they blacked my face I might look like a negro anarchist; but this old chap chipped in with a most extraordinary remark. "A pair of smoked spectacles will do it," he said positively. "Look at him now; he looks like an angelic office boy. Put him on a pair of smoked spectacles, and children will scream at the sight of him." And so it was, by George! When once my eyes were covered all the rest, smile and big shoulders and short hair, made me look a perfect little devil. As I say, it was simple enough when it was done, like miracles; but that wasn't the really miraculous part of it. There was one really staggering thing about the business, and my head still turns at it.'

'What was that?' asked Syme.

'I'll tell you,' answered the man in spectacles. 'This big pot in the police who sized me up so that he knew how the goggles would go with my hair and socks—by God, he never saw me at all!'

Syme's eyes suddenly flashed on him.

10

'How was that?' he asked. 'I thought you talked to him.'

'So I did,' said Bull brightly; 'but we talked in a pitch-dark room like a coal-cellar. There, you would never have guessed that.'

'I could not have conceived it,' said Syme gravely.

'It is indeed a new idea,' said the Professor.

Their new ally was in practical matters a whirlwind. At the inquiry office he asked with business-like brevity about the trains for Dover. Having got his information, he bundled the company into a cab, and put them and himself inside a railway carriage before they had properly realized the breathless process. They were already on the Calais boat before conversation flowed freely.

'I had already arranged,' he explained, 'to go to France for my lunch; but I am delighted to have some one to lunch with me. You see, I had to send that beast, the Marquis, over with his bomb, because the President had his eye on me, though God knows how. I'll tell you the story some day. It was perfectly choking. Whenever I tried to slip out of it I saw the President somewhere, smiling out of the bow-window of a club or taking off his hat to me from the top of an omnibus. I tell you, you can say what you like, that fellow sold himself to the devil; he can be in six places at once.'

'So you sent the Marquis off, I understand,' asked the Professor. 'Was it long ago? Shall we be in time to catch him?'

'Yes,' answered the new guide, 'I've timed it all. He'll still be at Calais when we arrive.'

'But when we do catch him at Calais,' said the Professor, 'what are we going to do?'

At this question the countenance of Dr. Bull fell for the first time. He reflected a little, and then said:

'Theoretically, I suppose, we ought to call the police.'

'Not I,' said Syme. 'Theoretically I ought to drown myself first. I promised a poor fellow, who was a real modern pessimist, on my word of honour not to tell the police. I'm no hand at casuistry, but I can't break my word to a modern pessimist. It's like breaking one's word to a child.'

'I'm in the same boat,' said the Professor. 'I tried to tell the police and I couldn't, because of some silly oath I took. You see, when I was an actor I was a sort of all-round beast. Perjury or treason is the only crime I haven't committed. If I did that I shouldn't know the difference between right and wrong.'

'I've been through all that,' said Dr. Bull, 'and I've made up my mind. I gave my promise to the Secretary —you know him, man who smiles upside down. My friends, that man is the most utterly unhappy man that was ever human. It may be his digestion, or his conscience, or his nerves, or his philosophy of the universe, but he's damned, he's in hell! Well, I can't turn on a man like that, and hunt him down. It's like whipping a leper. I may be mad, but that's how I feel; and there's jolly well the end of it.'

'I don't think you're mad,' said Syme. 'I knew you would decide like that when first you——'

'Eh?' said Dr. Bull.

'When first you took off your spectacles.'

Dr. Bull smiled a little, and strolled across the deck to look at the sunlit sea. Then he strolled back again, kicking his heels carelessly, and a companionable silence fell between the three men.

'Well,' said Syme, 'it seems that we have all the same

kind of morality or immorality, so we had better face the fact that comes of it.'

'Yes,' assented the Professor, 'you're quite right; and we must hurry up, for I can see the Grey Nose standing out from France.'

'The fact that comes of it,' said Syme seriously, 'is this, that we three are alone on this planet. Gogol has gone, God knows where; perhaps the President has smashed him like a fly. On the Council we are three men against three, like the Romans who held the bridge. But we are worse off than that, first because they can appeal to their organization and we cannot appeal to ours, and second because——'

'Because one of those other three men,' said the Professor, 'is not a man.'

Syme nodded and was silent for a second or two, then he said:

'My idea is this. We must do something to keep the Marquis in Calais till to-morrow midday. I have turned over twenty schemes in my head. We cannot denounce him as a dynamiter; that is agreed. We cannot get him detained on some trivial charge, for we should have to appear; he knows us, and he would smell a rat. We cannot pretend to keep him on anarchist business; he might swallow much in that way, but not the notion of stopping in Calais while the Tsar went safely through Paris. We might try to kidnap him, and lock him up ourselves; but he is a well-known man here. He has a whole bodyguard of friends; he is very strong and brave, and the event is doubtful. The only thing I can see to do is actually to take advantage of the very things that are in the Marquis's favour. I am going to profit by the fact that he is a highly respected nobleman. I am going to profit by the fact that he has many friends and moves in the best society.'

'What the devil are you talking about?' asked the Professor.

'The Symes are first mentioned in the fourteenth century,' said Syme; 'but there is a tradition that one of them rode behind Bruce at Bannockburn. Since 1350 the tree is quite clear.'

'He's gone off his head,' said the little Doctor, staring.

'Our bearings,' continued Syme calmly, 'are "argent a chevron gules charged with three cross crosslets of the field." The motto varies.'

The Professor seized Syme roughly by the waistcoat.

'We are just inshore,' he said. 'Are you sea-sick or joking in the wrong place?'

'My remarks are almost painfully practical,' answered Syme, in an unhurried manner. 'The house of St. Eustache also is very ancient. The Marquis cannot deny that he is a gentleman. He cannot deny that I am a gentleman. And in order to put the matter of my social position quite beyond a doubt, I propose at the earliest opportunity to knock his hat off. But here we are in the harbour.'

They went on shore under the strong sun in a sort of daze. Syme, who had now taken the lead as Bull had taken it in London, led them along a kind of marine parade until he came to some cafés, embowered in a bulk of greenery and overlooking the sea. As he went before them his step was slightly swaggering, and he swung his stick like a sword. He was making apparently for the extreme end of the line of cafés, but he stopped abruptly. With a sharp gesture he motioned them to silence, but he pointed with one gloved finger to a café table under a bank of flowering foliage at which sat the Marquis de St. Eustache, his teeth shining in his thick, black beard, and his bold, brown face shadowed by a light yellow straw hat and outlined against the violet sea.

CHAPTER X

THE DUEL

SYME sat down at a café table with his companions, his blue eyes sparkling like the bright sea below, and ordered a bottle of Saumur with a pleased impatience. He was for some reason in a condition of curious hilarity. His spirits were already unnaturally high; they rose as the Saumur sank, and in half an hour his talk was a torrent of nonsense. He professed to be making out a plan of the conversation which was going to ensue between himself and the deadly Marquis. He jotted it down wildly with a pencil. It was arranged like a printed catechism, with questions and answers, and was delivered with an extraordinary rapidity of utterance.

'I shall approach. Before taking off his hat, I shall take off my own. I shall say, "The Marquis de Saint Eustache, I believe." He will say, "The celebrated Mr. Syme, I presume." He will say in the most exquisite French, "How are you?" I shall reply in the most exquisite cockney, "Oh, just the Syme——" '

'Oh, shut it,' said the man in spectacles. 'Pull yourself together, and chuck away that bit of paper. What are you really going to do?'

'But it was a lovely catechism,' said Syme pathetically. 'Do let me read it you. It has only forty-three questions and answers, and some of the Marquis's answers are wonderfully witty. I like to be just to my enemy.'

'But what's the good of it all?' asked Dr. Bull in exasperation.

'It leads up to my challenge, don't you see,' said Syme, beaming. 'When the Marquis has given the thirty-ninth reply, which runs——'

'Has it by any chance occurred to you,' asked the Professor, with a ponderous simplicity, 'that the Marquis may not say all the forty-three things you have put down for him? In that case, I understand, your own epigrams may appear somewhat more forced.'

Syme struck the table with a radiant face.

'Why, how true that is,' he said, 'and I never thought of it. Sir, you have an intellect beyond the common. You will make a name.'

'Oh, you're as drunk as an owl!' said the Doctor.

'It only remains,' continued Syme, quite unperturbed, 'to adopt some other method of breaking the ice (if I may so express it) between myself and the man I wish to kill. And since the course of a dialogue cannot be predicted by one of its parties alone (as you have pointed out with such recondite acumen), the only thing to be done, I suppose, is for the one party, as far as possible, to do all the dialogue by himself. And so I will, by George!' And he stood up suddenly, his yellow hair blowing in the slight sea-breeze.

A band was playing in a *café chantant* hidden somewhere among the trees, and a woman had just stopped singing. On Syme's heated head the bray of the brass band seemed like the jar and jingle of that barrel-organ in Leicester Square, to the tune of which he had once stood up to die. He looked across to the little table where the Marquis sat. The man had two companions now, solemn Frenchmen in frock-coats and silk hats, one of them with the red rosette of the Legion of Honour, evidently people of a solid social position. Beside these black, cylindrical costumes, the Marquis, in his loose straw hat and light spring clothes, looked Bohemian and even barbaric; but he looked the Marquis. Indeed, one might say that he looked the king, with his animal elegance, his scornful eyes, and his proud head lifted against the purple sea. But he was no Christian king, at any rate; he was, rather some swarthy despot, half Greek, half Asiatic, who in the days when slavery seemed natural looked down on the Mediterranean, on his galley and his groaning slaves. Just so, Syme thought, would the brown-gold face of such a tyrant have shown against the dark green olives and the burning blue.

'Are you going to address the meeting?' asked the Professor peevishly, seeing that Syme still stood up without moving.

Syme drained his last glass of sparkling wine.

'I am,' he said, pointing across to the Marquis and his companions, 'that meeting. That meeting displeases me. I am going to pull that meeting's great, ugly, mahogany-coloured nose.'

He stepped across swiftly, if not quite steadily. The Marquis, seeing him, arched his black Assyrian eyebrows in surprise, but smiled politely.

'You are Mr. Syme, I think,' he said.

Syme bowed.

'And you are the Marquis de Saint Eustache,' he said gracefully. 'Permit me to pull your nose.'

He leant over to do so, but the Marquis started backwards, upsetting his chair, and the two men in top hats held Syme back by the shoulders.

'This man has insulted me!' said Syme, with gestures of explanation.

'Insulted you?' cried the gentleman with the red rosette, 'when?'

'Oh, just now,' said Syme recklessly. 'He insulted my mother.'

'Insulted your mother!' exclaimed the gentleman incredulously.

'Well, anyhow,' said Syme, conceding a point, 'my aunt.'

'But how can the Marquis have insulted your aunt just now?' said the second gentleman with some legitimate wonder. 'He has been sitting here all the time.'

'Ah, it was what he said!' said Syme darkly.

'I said nothing at all,' said the Marquis, 'except something about the band. I only said that I liked Wagner played well.'

'It was an allusion to my family,' said Syme firmly. 'My aunt played Wagner badly. It was a painful subject. We are always being insulted about it.'

'This seems most extraordinary,' said the gentleman who was *décoré*, looking thoughtfully at the Marquis.

'Oh, I assure you,' said Syme earnestly, 'the whole of your conversation was simply packed with sinister allusions to my aunt's weaknesses.'

'This is nonsense!' said the second gentleman. 'I for one have said nothing for half an hour except that I liked the singing of that girl with black hair.'

'Well, there you are again!' said Syme indignantly. 'My aunt's was red!'

'It seems to me,' said the other, 'that you are simply seeking a pretext to insult the Marquis.'

'By George!' said Syme, facing round and looking at him, 'what a clever chap you are!'

The Marquis started up with eyes flaming like a tiger's.

'Seeking a quarrel with me!' he cried. 'Seeking a fight with me! By God! there was never a man who had to seek long. These gentlemen will perhaps act for me. There are still four hours of daylight. Let us fight this evening.'

Syme bowed with a quite beautiful graciousness.

'Marquis,' he said, 'your action is worthy of your fame and blood. Permit me to consult for a moment with the gentlemen in whose hands I shall place myself.'

In three long strides he rejoined his companions, and they, who had seen his champagne-inspired attack and listened to his idiotic explanations, were quite startled at the look of him. For now that he came back to them he was quite sober, a little pale, and he spoke in a low voice of passionate practicality.

'I have done it,' he said hoarsely. 'I have fixed a fight on the beast. But look here, and listen carefully. There is no time for talk. You are my seconds, and everything must come from you. Now you must insist, and insist absolutely, on the duel coming off after seven to-morrow, so as to give me the chance of preventing him from catching the 7.45 for Paris. If he misses that he misses his crime. He can't refuse to meet you on such a small point of time and place. But this is what he will do. He will choose a field somewhere near a wayside station, where he can pick up the train. He is a very good swordsman, and he will trust to killing me in time to catch it. But I can fence well too, and I think I can keep him in play, at any rate, until the train is lost. Then perhaps he may kill me to console his feelings. You understand? Very well then, let me introduce you to some charming friends of mine,' and leading them quickly across the parade, he presented them to the Marquis's seconds by two very aristocratic names of which they had not previously heard.

Syme was subject to spasms of singular common sense, not otherwise a part of his character. They were (as he said of his impulse about the spectacles) poetic intuitions, and they sometimes rose to the exaltation of prophecy.

He had correctly calculated in this case the policy of his opponent. When the Marquis was informed by his seconds that Syme could only fight in the morning, he must fully have realized that an obstacle had suddenly arisen between him and his bomb-throwing business in the capital. Naturally, he could not explain this objection to his friends, so he chose the course which Syme had predicted. He induced his seconds to settle on a small meadow not far from the railway, and he trusted to the fatality of the first engagement.

When he came down very coolly to the field of honour, no one could have guessed that he had any anxiety about a journey; his hands were in his pockets, his straw hat on the back of his head, his handsome face brazen in the sun. But it might have struck a stranger as odd that there appeared in his train, not only his seconds carrying the sword-case, but two of his servants carrying a portmanteau and a luncheon basket.

Early as was the hour, the sun soaked everything in warmth, and Syme was vaguely surprised to see so many spring flowers burning gold and silver in the tall grass in which the whole company stood almost knee-deep.

With the exception of the Marquis, all the men were in sombre and solemn morning-dress, with hats like black chimney-pots; the little Doctor especially, with the addition of his black spectacles, looked like an undertaker in a farce. Syme could not help feeling a comic contrast between this funereal church parade of apparel and the rich and glistening meadow, growing wild flowers everywhere. But, indeed, this comic contrast between the yellow blossoms and the black hats was but a symbol of the tragic contrast between the yellow blossoms and the black business. On his right was a little wood; far away to his left lay the long curve of the railway line, which he was, so to speak, guarding from the Marquis, whose goal and escape it was. In front of him, behind the black group of his opponents, he could see, like a tinted cloud, a small almond-bush in flower against the faint line of the sea.

The member of the Legion of Honour, whose name it seemed was Colonel Ducroix, approached the Professor and Dr. Bull with great politeness, and suggested that the play should terminate with the first considerable hurt.

Dr. Bull, however, having been carefully coached by Syme upon this point of policy, insisted, with great dignity and in very bad French, that it should continue until one of the combatants was disabled. Syme had made up his mind that he could avoid disabling the Marquis and prevent the Marquis from disabling him for at least twenty minutes. In twenty minutes the Paris train would have gone by.

'To a man of the well-known skill and valour of Monsieur de St. Eustache,' said the Professor solemnly, 'it must be a matter of indifference which method is adopted, and our principal has strong reasons for demanding the longer encounter, reasons the delicacy of which prevent me from being explicit, but for the just and honourable nature of which I can——'

'*Peste!*' broke from the Marquis behind, whose face had suddenly darkened, 'let us stop talking and begin,' and he slashed off the head of a tall flower with his stick.

Syme understood his rude impatience, and instinctively looked over his shoulder to see whether the train was coming in sight. But there was no smoke on the horizon.

Colonel Ducroix knelt down and unlocked the case, taking out a pair of twin swords, which took the sunlight and turned to two streaks of white fire. He offered one to the Marquis, who snatched it without ceremony, and another to Syme, who took it, bent it, and poised it with as much delay as was consistent with dignity. Then the Colonel took out another pair of blades, and taking one himself and giving another to Dr. Bull, proceeded to place the men.

Both combatants had thrown off their coats and waistcoats, and stood sword in hand. The seconds stood on each side of the line of fight with drawn swords also, but still sombre in their dark frock-coats and hats. The principals saluted. The Colonel said quietly, 'Engage!' and the two blades touched and tingled.

When the jar of the joined iron ran up Syme's arm, all the fantastic fears that have been the subject of this story fell from him like dreams from a man waking up in bed. He remembered them clearly and in order as mere delusions of the nerves—how the fear of the Professor had been the fear of the tyrannic accidents of nightmare, and how the fear of the Doctor had been the fear of the airless vacuum of science. The first was the old fear that any miracle might happen, the second the more hopeless modern fear that no miracle can ever happen. But he saw that these fears were fancies, for he found himself in the presence of the great fact of the fear of death, with its coarse and pitiless common sense. He felt like a man who had dreamed all night of falling over precipices, and had woke up on the morning when he was to be hanged. For as soon as he had seen the sunlight run down the channel of his foe's foreshortened blade, and as soon as he had felt the two tongues of steel touch, vibrating like two living things, he knew that his enemy was a terrible fighter, and that probably his last hour had come.

He felt a strange and vivid value in all the earth around him, in the grass under his feet; he felt the love of life in all living things. He could almost fancy that he heard the grass growing; he could almost fancy that even as he stood fresh flowers were springing up and breaking into blossom in the meadow—flowers blood-red and burning gold and blue, fulfilling the whole pageant of the spring. And whenever his eyes strayed for a flash from the calm, staring, hypnotic eyes of the Marquis, they saw the little tuft of almond-tree against the skyline. He had the feeling that if by some miracle he escaped he would be ready to sit for ever before that almond-tree, desiring nothing else in the world.

But while earth and sky and everything had the living beauty of a thing lost, the other half of his head was as clear as glass, and he was parrying his enemy's point with a kind of clockwork skill of which he had hardly supposed himself capable. Once his enemy's point ran along his wrist, leaving a slight streak of blood, but it either was not noticed or was tacitly ignored. Every now and then he *riposted*, and once or twice he could almost fancy that he felt his point go home, but as there was no blood on blade or shirt he supposed he was mistaken. Then came an interruption and a change.

At the risk of losing all, the Marquis, interrupting his quiet stare, flashed one glance over his shoulder at the line of railway on his right. Then he turned on Syme a face transfigured to that of a fiend, and began to fight as if with twenty weapons. The attack came so fast and furious, that the one shining sword seemed a shower of shining arrows. Syme had no chance to look at the railway, but also he had no need. He could guess the reason of the Marquis's sudden madness of battle—the Paris train was in sight.

But the Marquis's morbid energy over-reached itself. Twice Syme, parrying, knocked his opponent's point far out of the fighting circle; and the third time his *riposte* was so rapid, that there was no doubt about the hit this time. Syme's sword actually bent under the weight of the Marquis's body, which it had pierced. Syme was as certain that he had stuck his blade into his enemy as a gardener that he has stuck his spade into the ground. Yet the Marquis sprang back from the stroke without a stagger, and Syme stood staring at his own sword-point like an idiot. There was no blood on it at all.

There was an instant of rigid silence, and then Syme in his turn fell furiously on the other, filled with a flaming curiosity. The Marquis was probably, in a general sense, a better fencer than he, as he had surmised at the beginning, but at the moment the Marquis seemed distraught and at a disadvantage. He fought wildly and even weakly, and he constantly looked away at the railway line, almost as if he feared the train more than the pointed steel. Syme, on the other hand, fought fiercely but still carefully, in an intellectual fury, eager to solve the riddle of his own bloodless sword. For this purpose, he aimed less at the Marquis's body, and more at this throat and head. A minute and a half afterwards he felt his point enter the man's neck below the jaw. It came out clean. Half mad, he thrust again, and made what should have been a bloody scar on the Marquis's cheek. But there was no scar.

For one moment the heaven of Syme again grew black with supernatural terrors. Surely the man had a charmed life. But this new spiritual dread was a more awful thing than had been the mere spiritual topsy-turvydom symbolized by the paralytic who pursued him. The Professor was only a goblin; this man was a devil—perhaps he was the Devil! Anyhow, this was certain, that three times had a human sword been driven into him and made no mark. When Syme had that thought he drew himself up, and all that was good in him sang high up in the air as a high wind sings in the trees. He thought of all the human things in his story—of the Chinese lanterns in Saffron Park, of the girl's red hair in the garden, of the honest, beer-swilling sailors down by the dock, of his loyal companions standing by. Perhaps he had been chosen as a champion of all these fresh and kindly things to cross swords with the enemy of all creation. 'After all,' he said to himself, 'I am more than a devil; I am a man. I can do the one thing which Satan himself cannot do—I can die', and as the word went through his head, he heard a faint and far-off hoot, which would soon be the roar of the Paris train.

He fell to fighting again with a supernatural levity, like a Mohammedan panting for Paradise. As the train came nearer and nearer he fancied he could see people putting up the floral arches in Paris; he joined in the growing noise and the glory of the great Republic whose gate he was guarding against Hell. His thoughts rose higher and higher with the rising roar of the train, which ended, as if proudly, in a long and piercing whistle. The train stopped.

Suddenly, to the astonishment of every one, the Marquis sprang back quite out of sword reach and threw down his sword. The leap was wonderful, and not the less wonderful because Syme had plunged his sword a moment before into the man's thigh.

'Stop!' said the Marquis in a voice that compelled a momentary obedience. 'I want to say something.'

'What is the matter?' asked Colonel Ducroix, staring. 'Has there been foul play?'

'There has been foul play somewhere,' said Dr. Bull, who was a little pale. 'Our principal has wounded the Marquis four times at least, and he is none the worse.'

The Marquis put up his hand with a curious air of ghastly patience.

'Please let me speak,' he said. 'It is rather important. Mr. Syme,' he continued, turning to his opponent, 'we are fighting to-day, if I remember right, because you expressed a wish (which I thought irrational) to pull my nose. Would you oblige me by pulling my nose now as quickly as possible? I have to catch a train.'

'I protest that this is most irregular,' said Dr. Bull indignantly.

'It is certainly somewhat opposed to precedent,' said Colonel Ducroix, looking wistfully at his principal. 'There is, I think, one case on record (Captain Belle-garde and the Baron Zumpt) in which the weapons were changed in the middle of the encounter at the request of one of the combatants. But one can hardly call one's nose a weapon.'

'Will you or will you not pull my nose?' said the Marquis in exasperation. 'Come, come, Mr. Syme! You wanted to do it, do it! You can have no conception of how important it is to me. Don't be so selfish! Pull my nose at once, when I ask you!' and he bent slightly forward with a fascinating smile. The Paris train, panting and groaning, had grated into a little station behind the neighbouring hill.

Syme had the feeling he had more than once had in these adventures—the sense that a horrible and sublime wave lifted to heaven was just toppling over. Walking in a world he half understood, he took two paces forward and seized the Roman nose of this remarkable nobleman. He pulled it hard, and it came off in his hand.

He stood for some seconds with a foolish solemnity, with the pasteboard proboscis still between his fingers, looking at it, while the sun and the clouds and the wooded hills looked down upon this imbecile scene.

The Marquis broke the silence in a loud and cheerful voice.

'If any one has any use for my left eyebrow,' he said, 'he can have it. Colonel Ducroix, do accept my left eyebrow! It's the kind of thing that might come in useful any day,' and he gravely tore off one of his swarthy Assyrian brows, bringing about half his brown forehead with it, and politely offered it to the Colonel, who stood crimson and speechless with rage.

'If I had known,' he spluttered, 'that I was acting for a poltroon who pads himself to fight——'

'Oh, I know, I know!' said the Marquis, recklessly

throwing various parts of himself right and left about the field. 'You are making a mistake; but it can't be explained just now. I tell you the train has come into the station!'

'Yes,' said Dr. Bull fiercely, 'and the train shall go out of the station. It shall go out without you. We know well enough for what devil's work——'

The mysterious Marquis lifted his hands with a desperate gesture. He was a strange scarecrow, standing there in the sun with half his old face peeled off, and half another face glaring and grinning from underneath.

'Will you drive me mad?' he cried. 'The train——'

'You shall not go by the train,' said Syme firmly, and grasped his sword.

The wild figure turned towards Syme, and seemed to be gathering itself for a sublime effort before speaking.

'You great fat, blasted, blear-eyed, blundering, thundering, brainless, God-forsaken, doddering, damned fool!' he said without taking breath. 'You great silly, pink-faced, towheaded turnip! You——'

'You shall not go by this train,' repeated Syme.

'And why the infernal blazes,' roared the other, 'should I want to go by the train?'

'We know all,' said the Professor sternly. 'You are going to Paris to throw a bomb!'

'Going to Jericho to throw a Jabberwock!' cried the other, tearing his hair, which came off easily.

'Have you all got softening of the brain, that you don't realize what I am? Did you really think I wanted to catch that train? Twenty Paris trains might go by for me. Damn Paris trains!'

'Then what did you care about?' began the Professor.

'What did I care about? I didn't care about

catching the train; I cared about whether the train caught me, and now, by God! it has caught me.'

'I regret to inform you,' said Syme with restraint, 'that your remarks convey no impression to my mind. Perhaps if you were to remove the remains of your original forehead and some portion of what was once your chin, your meaning would become clearer. Mental lucidity fulfils itself in many ways. What do you mean by saying that the train has caught you? It may be my literary fancy, but somehow I feel that it ought to mean something.'

'It means everything,' said the other, 'and the end of everything. Sunday has us now in the hollow of his hand.'

'Us!' repeated the Professor, as if stupefied. 'What do you mean by "us"?'

'The police, of course!' said the Marquis, and tore off his scalp and half his face.

The head which emerged was the blond, well brushed, smooth-haired head which is common in the English constabulary, but the face was terribly pale.

'I am Inspector Ratcliffe,' he said, with a sort of haste that verged on harshness. 'My name is pretty well known to the police, and I can see well enough that you belong to them. But if there is any doubt about my position, I have a card——' and he began to pull a blue card from his pocket.

The Professor gave a tired gesture.

'Oh, don't show it us,' he said wearily; 'we've got enough of them to equip a paper-chase.'

The little man named Bull had, like many men who seem to be of a mere vivacious vulgarity, sudden movements of good taste. Here he certainly saved the situation. In the midst of this staggering transformation scene he stepped forward with all the gravity and responsibility of a second, and addressed the two seconds of the Marquis.

'Gentlemen,' he said, 'we all owe you a serious apology; but I assure you that you have not been made the victims of such a low joke as you imagine, or indeed of anything undignified in a man of honour. You have not wasted your time; you have helped to save the world. We are not buffoons, but very desperate men at war with a vast conspiracy. A secret society of anarchists is hunting us like hares; not such unfortunate madmen as may here or there throw a bomb through starvation or German philosophy, but a rich and powerful and fanatical church, a church of eastern pessimism, which holds it holy to destroy mankind like vermin. How hard they hunt us you can gather from the fact that we are driven to such disguises as those for which I apologize, and to such pranks as this one by which you suffer.'

The younger second of the Marquis, a short man with a black moustache, bowed politely, and said:

'Of course, I accept the apology; but you will in your turn forgive me if I decline to follow you further into your difficulties, and permit myself to say good morning! The sight of an acquaintance and distinguished fellow-townsman coming to pieces in the open air is unusual, and, upon the whole, sufficient for one day. Colonel Ducroix, I would in no way influence your actions, but if you feel with me that our present society is a little abnormal, I am now going to walk back to the town.'

Colonel Ducroix moved mechanically, but then tugged abruptly at his white moustache and broke out:

'No, by George! I won't! If these gentlemen are

really in a mess with a lot of low wreckers like that, I'll
see them through it. I have fought for France, and it
is hard if I can't fight for civilization.'

Dr. Bull took off his hat and waved it, cheering as
at a public meeting.

'Don't make too much noise,' said Inspector Ratcliffe,
'Sunday may hear you.'

'Sunday!' cried Bull, and dropped his hat.

'Yes,' retorted Ratcliffe, 'he may be with them.'

'With whom?' asked Syme.

'With the people out of that train,' said the other.

'What you say seems utterly wild,' began Syme.
'Why, as a matter of fact—— But, my God,' he cried
out suddenly, like a man who sees an explosion a long
way off, 'by God! If this is true the whole bally lot of
us on the Anarchist Council were against anarchy!
Every born man was a detective except the President
and his personal Secretary. What can it mean?'

'Mean!' said the new policeman with incredible
violence. 'It means that we are struck dead! Don't
you know Sunday? Don't you know that his jokes are
always so big and simple that one has never thought
of them? Can you think of anything more like Sunday
than this, that he should put all his powerful enemies
on the Supreme Council, and then take care that it
was not supreme? I tell you he has bought every trust,
he has captured every cable, he has control of every
railway line—especially of *that* railway line!' and he
pointed a shaking finger towards the small wayside
station. 'The whole movement was controlled by him;
half the world was ready to rise for him. But there
were just five people, perhaps, who would have resisted
him . . . and the old devil put them on the Supreme
Council, to waste their time in watching each other.

Idiots that we are, he planned the whole of our idiocies! Sunday knew that the Professor would chase Syme through London, and that Syme would fight me in France. And he was combining great masses of capital, and seizing great lines of telegraphy, while we five idiots were running after each other like a lot of confounded babies playing blind man's buff.'

'Well?' asked Syme with a sort of steadiness.

'Well,' replied the other with sudden serenity, 'he has found us playing blind man's buff to-day in a field of great rustic beauty and extreme solitude. He has probably captured the world; it only remains to him to capture this field and all the fools in it. And since you really want to know what was my objection to the arrival of that train, I will tell you. My objection was that Sunday or his Secretary has just this moment got out of it.'

Syme uttered an involuntary cry, and they all turned their eyes towards the far-off station. It was quite true that a considerable bulk of people seemed to be moving in their direction. But they were too distant to be distinguished in any way.

'It was a habit of the late Marquis de St. Eustache,' said the new policeman, producing a leather case, 'always to carry a pair of opera-glasses. Either the President or the Secretary is coming after us with that mob. They have caught us in a nice quiet place where we are under no temptations to break our oaths by calling the police. Dr. Bull, I have a suspicion that you will see better through these than through your own highly decorative spectacles.'

He handed the field-glasses to the Doctor, who immediately took off his spectacles and put the apparatus to his eyes.

'It cannot be as bad as you say,' said the Professor, somewhat shaken. 'There are a good number of them certainly, but they may easily be ordinary tourists.'

'Do ordinary tourists,' asked Bull, with the field-glasses to his eyes, 'wear black masks half-way down the face?'

Syme almost tore the glasses out of his hand, and looked through them. Most men in the advancing mob really looked ordinary enough; but it was quite true that two or three of the leaders in front wore black half-masks almost down to their mouths. This disguise is very complete, especially at such a distance, and Syme found it impossible to conclude anything from the clean-shaven jaws and chins of the men talking in the front. But presently as they talked they all smiled, and one of them smiled on one side.

CHAPTER XI

THE CRIMINALS CHASE THE POLICE

SYME put the field-glasses from his eyes with an almost ghastly relief.

'The President is not with them, anyhow,' he said and wiped his forehead.

'But surely they are right away on the horizon,' said the bewildered Colonel, blinking and but half recovered from Bull's hasty though polite explanation. 'Could you possibly know your President among all those people?'

'Could I know a white elephant among all those people!' answered Syme somewhat irritably. 'As you very truly say, they are on the horizon; but if he were walking with them . . . by God! I believe this ground would shake.'

After an instant's pause the new man called Ratcliffe said with gloomy decision:

'Of course the President isn't with them. I wish to Gemini he were. Much more likely the President is riding in triumph through Paris, or sitting on the ruins of St. Paul's Cathedral.'

'This is absurd!' said Syme. 'Something may have happened in our absence; but he cannot have carried the world with a rush like that. It is quite true,' he added, frowning dubiously at the distant fields that lay towards the little station, 'it is certainly true that there seems to be a crowd coming this way; but they are not all the army that you make out.'

'Oh, they,' said the new detective contemptuously; 'no, they are not a very valuable force. But let me tell you frankly that they are precisely calculated to our value—we are not much, my boy, in Sunday's universe. He has got hold of all the cables and telegraphs himself. But to kill the Supreme Council he regards as a trivial matter, like a post card; it may be left to his private Secretary,' and he spat on the grass.

Then he turned to the others and said somewhat austerely:

'There is a great deal to be said for death; but if any one has any preference for the other alternative, I strongly advise him to walk after me.'

With these words, he turned his broad back and strode with silent energy towards the wood. The others gave one glance over their shoulders, and saw that the dark cloud of men had detached itself from the station and was moving with a mysterious discipline across the plain. They saw already, even with the naked eye, black blots on the foremost faces, which marked the masks they wore. They turned and followed their leader, who had already struck the wood, and disappeared among the twinkling trees.

The sun on the grass was dry and hot. So in plunging into the wood they had a cool shock of shadow, as of divers who plunge into a dim pool. The inside of the wood was full of shattered sunlight and shaken shadows. They made a sort of shuddering veil, almost recalling the dizziness of a cinematograph. Even the solid figures walking with him Syme could hardly see for the patterns of sun and shade that danced upon them. Now a man's head was lit as with a light of Rembrandt, leaving all else obliterated; now again he had strong and staring white hands with the face of a negro. The ex-Marquis had pulled the old straw hat over his eyes, and the black shade of the brim cut his face so squarely in two that it seemed to be wearing one of the black half-masks of their pursuers. The fancy tinted Syme's overwhelming sense of wonder. Was he wearing a mask? Was any one wearing a mask? Was any one anything? This wood of witchery, in which men's faces turned black and white by turns, in which their figures first swelled into sunlight and then faded into formless night, this mere chaos of chiaroscuro (after the clear daylight outside), seemed to Syme a perfect symbol of the world in which he had been moving for three days, this word where men took off their beards and their spectacles and their noses, and turned into other people. That tragic self-confidence which he had felt when he believed that the Marquis was a devil had strangely disappeared now that he knew that the Marquis was a friend. He felt almost inclined to ask after all these bewilderments what was a friend and what an enemy. Was there anything that was apart from what it seemed? The Marquis had taken off his nose and turned out to be a detective. Might he not just as well take off his head and turn out to be a hob-goblin? Was not everything, after all, like this be-wildering woodland, this dance of dark and light? Everything only a glimpse, the glimpse always unfore-seen, and always forgotten. For Gabriel Syme had found in the heart of that sun-splashed wood what many modern painters had found there. He had found the thing which the modern people call Impressionism, which is another name for that final scepticism which can find no floor to the universe.

As a man in an evil dream strains himself to scream and wake, Syme strove with a sudden effort to fling off this last and worst of his fancies. With two im-patient strides he overtook the man in the Marquis's

straw hat, the man whom he had come to address as
Ratcliffe. In a voice exaggeratively loud and cheerful,
he broke the bottomless silence and made conversation.

'May I ask,' he said, 'where on earth we are all
going to?'

So genuine had been the doubts of his soul, that he
was quite glad to hear his companion speak in an easy,
human voice.

'We must get down through the town of Lancy to
the sea,' he said. 'I think that part of the country is
least likely to be with them.'

'What can you mean by all this?' cried Syme.
'They can't be running the real world in that way.
Surely not many working men are anarchists, and
surely if they were, mere mobs could not beat modern
armies and police.'

'Mere mobs!' repeated his new friend with a snort
of scorn. 'So you talk about mobs and the working
classes as if they were the question. You've got that
eternal idiotic idea that if anarchy came it would come
from the poor. Why should it? The poor have been
rebels, but they have never been anarchists; they have
more interest than any one else in there being some
decent government. The poor man really has a stake
in the country. The rich man hasn't; he can go away
to New Guinea in a yacht. The poor have sometimes
objected to being governed badly; the rich have always
objected to being governed at all. Aristocrats were
always anarchists, as you can see from the barons'
wars.'

'As a lecture on English history for the little ones,'
said Syme, 'this is all very nice; but I have not yet
grasped its application.'

'Its application is,' said his informant, 'that most of

old Sunday's right-hand men are South African and American millionaires. That is why he has got hold of all the communications; and that is why the last four champions of the anti-anarchist police force are running through a wood like rabbits.'

'Millionaires I can understand,' said Syme thoughtfully, 'they are nearly all mad. But getting hold of a few wicked old gentlemen with hobbies is one thing; getting hold of great Christian nations is another. I would bet the nose off my face (forgive the allusion) that Sunday would stand perfectly helpless before the task of converting any ordinary healthy person anywhere.'

'Well,' said the other, 'it rather depends what sort of person you mean.'

'Well, for instance,' said Syme, 'we could never convert that person,' and he pointed straight in front of him.

They had come to an open space of sunlight, which seemed to express to Syme the final return of his own good sense; and in the middle of this forest clearing was a figure that might well stand for that common sense in an almost awful actuality. Burnt by the sun and stained with perspiration, and grave with the bottomless gravity of small necessary toils, a heavy French peasant was cutting wood with a hatchet. His cart stood a few yards off, already half full of timber; and the horse that cropped the grass was, like his master, valorous but not desperate; like his master, he was even prosperous, but yet was almost sad. The man was a Norman, taller than the average of the French and very angular; and his swarthy figure stood dark against a square of sunlight, almost like some allegoric figure of labour frescoed on a ground of gold.

'Mr. Syme is saying,' called out Ratcliffe to the French Colonel, 'that this man, at least, will never be an anarchist.'

'Mr. Syme is right enough there,' answered Colonel Ducroix, laughing, 'if only for the reason that he has plenty of property to defend. But I forgot that in your country you are not used to peasants being wealthy.'

'He looks poor,' said Dr. Bull doubtfully.

'Quite so,' said the Colonel; 'that is why he is rich.'

'I have an idea,' called out Dr. Bull suddenly; 'how much would he take to give us a lift in his cart? Those dogs are all on foot, and we could soon leave them behind.'

'Oh, give him anything!' said Syme eagerly. 'I have piles of money on me.'

'That will never do,' said the Colonel; 'he will never have any respect for you unless you drive a bargain.'

'Oh, if he haggles!' began Bull impatiently.

'He haggles because he is a free man,' said the other. 'You do not understand; he would not see the meaning of generosity. He is not being tipped.'

And even while they seemed to hear the heavy feet of their strange pursuers behind them, they had to stand and stamp while the French Colonel talked to the French wood-cutter with all the leisurely badinage and bickering of market-day. At the end of the four minutes, however, they saw that the Colonel was right, for the wood-cutter entered into their plans, not with the vague servility of a tout too-well paid, but with the seriousness of a solicitor who had been paid the proper fee. He told them that the best thing they could do was to make their way down to the little inn on the hills above Lancy, where the innkeeper, an old soldier

who had become *dévot* in his latter years, would be
certain to sympathize with them, and even to take risks
in their support. The whole company, therefore,
piled themselves on top of the stacks of wood, and went
rocking in the rude cart down the other and steeper
side of the woodland. Heavy and ramshackle as was
the vehicle, it was driven quickly enough, and they
soon had the exhilarating impression of distancing
altogether those, whoever they were, who were hunting
them. For, after all, the riddle as to where the
anarchists had got all these followers was still unsolved.
One man's presence had sufficed for them; they had
fled at the first sight of the deformed smile of the
Secretary. Syme every now and then looked back
over his shoulder at the army on their track.

As the wood grew first thinner and then smaller with
distance, he could see the sunlit slopes beyond it and
above it; and across these was still moving the square
black mob like one monstrous beetle. In the very
strong sunlight and with his own very strong eyes,
which were almost telescopic, Syme could see this mass
of men quite plainly. He could see them as separate
human figures; but he was increasingly surprised by
the way in which they moved as one man. They seemed
to be dressed in dark clothes and plain hats, like any
common crowd out of the streets; but they did not spread
and sprawl and trail by various lines to the attack, as
would be natural in an ordinary mob. They moved
with a sort of dreadful and wicked woodenness, like
a staring army of automatons.

Syme pointed this out to Ratcliffe.

'Yes,' replied the policeman, 'that's discipline.
That's Sunday. He is perhaps five hundred miles
off, but the fear of him is on all of them, like the

finger of God. Yes, they are walking regularly; and you bet your boots that they are talking regularly, yes, and thinking regularly. But the one important thing for us is that they are disappearing regularly.'

Syme nodded. It was true that the black patch of the pursuing men was growing smaller and smaller as the peasant belaboured his horse.

The level of the sunlit landscape, though flat as a whole, fell away on the farther side of the wood in billows of heavy slope towards the sea, in a way not unlike the lower slopes of the Sussex downs. The only difference was that in Sussex the road would have been broken and angular like a little brook, but here the white French road fell sheer in front of them like a waterfall. Down this direct descent the cart clattered at a considerable angle, and in a few minutes, the road growing yet steeper, they saw below them the little harbour of Lancy and a great blue arc of the sea. The travelling cloud of their enemies had wholly disappeared from the horizon.

The horse and cart took a sharp turn round a clump of elms, and the horse's nose nearly struck the face of an old gentleman who was sitting on the benches outside the little café of 'Le Soleil d'Or'. The peasant grunted an apology, and got down from his seat. The others also descended one by one, and spoke to the old gentleman with fragmentary phrases of courtesy, for it was quite evident from his expansive manner that he was the owner of the little tavern.

He was a white-haired, apple-faced old boy, with sleepy eyes and a grey moustache; stout, sedentary, and very innocent, of a type that may often be found in France, but is still commoner in Catholic Germany. Everything about him, his pipe, his pot of beer, his flowers, and his beehive, suggested an ancestral peace; only when his visitors looked up as they entered the inn-parlour, they saw the sword upon the wall.

The Colonel, who greeted the innkeeper as an old friend, passed rapidly into the inn-parlour, and sat down ordering some ritual refreshment. The military decision of his action interested Syme, who sat next to him, and he took the opportunity when the old innkeeper had gone out of satisfying his curiosity.

'May I ask you, Colonel,' he said in a low voice, 'why we have come here?'

Colonel Ducroix smiled behind his bristly white moustache.

'For two reasons, sir,' he said; 'and I will give first, not the most important, but the most utilitarian. We came here because this is the only place within twenty miles in which we can get horses.'

'Horses!' repeated Syme, looking up quickly.

'Yes,' replied the other; 'if you people are really to distance your enemies it is horses or nothing for you, unless of course you have bicycles and motor-cars in your pocket.'

'And where do you advise us to make for?' asked Syme doubtfully.

'Beyond question,' replied the Colonel, 'you had better make all haste to the police station beyond the town. My friend, whom I seconded under somewhat deceptive circumstances, seems to me to exaggerate very much the possibilities of a general rising; but even he would hardly maintain, I suppose, that you were not safe with the gendarmes.'

Syme nodded gravely; then he said abruptly:

'And your other reason for coming here?'

'My other reason for coming here,' said Ducroix

soberly, 'is that it is just as well to see a good man or two when one is possibly near to death.'

Syme looked up at the wall, and saw a crudely painted and pathetic religious picture. Then he said:

'You are right,' and then almost immediately afterwards; 'has any one seen about the horses?'

'Yes,' answered Ducroix, 'you may be quite certain that I gave orders the moment I came in. Those enemies of yours gave no impression of hurry, but they were really moving wonderfully fast, like a well-trained army. I had no idea that the anarchists had so much discipline. You have not a moment to waste.'

Almost as he spoke, the old innkeeper with the blue eyes and white hair came ambling into the room, and announced that six horses were saddled outside.

By Ducroix's advice the five others equipped themselves with some portable form of food and wine, and keeping their duelling swords as the only weapons available, they clattered away down the steep, white road. The two servants, who had carried the Marquis's luggage when he was a marquis, were left behind to drink at the café by common consent, and not at all against their own inclination.

By this time the afternoon sun was slanting westward, and by its rays Syme could see the sturdy figure of the old innkeeper growing smaller and smaller, but still standing and looking after them quite silently, the sunshine in his silver hair. Syme had a fixed, superstitious fancy, left in his mind by the chance phrase of the Colonel, that this was indeed, perhaps, the last honest stranger whom he should ever see upon the earth.

He was still looking at this dwindling figure, which stood as a mere grey blot touched with a white flame against the great green wall of the steep down behind him. And as he stared, over the top of the down behind the innkeeper, there appeared an army of black-clad and marching men. They seemed to hang above the good man and his house like a black cloud of locusts. The horses had been saddled none too soon.

CHAPTER XII

THE EARTH IN ANARCHY

Urging the horses to a gallop, without respect to the rather rugged descent of the road, the horsemen soon regained their advantage over the men on the march, and at last the bulk of the first buildings of Lancy cut off the sight of their pursuers. Nevertheless, the ride had been a long one, and by the time they reached the real town the west was warming with the colour and quality of sunset. The Colonel suggested that, before making finally for the police station, they should make the effort, in passing, to attach to themselves one more individual who might be useful.

'Four out of the five rich men in this town,' he said, 'are common swindlers. I suppose the proportion is pretty equal all over the world. The fifth is a friend of mine, and a very fine fellow; and what is even more important from our point of view, he owns a motorcar.'

'I am afraid,' said the Professor in his mirthful way, looking back along the white road on which the black, crawling patch might appear at any moment, 'I am afraid we have hardly time for afternoon calls.'

'Doctor Renard's house is only three minutes off,' said the Colonel.

'Our danger,' said Dr. Bull, 'is not two minutes off.'

'Yes,' said Syme, 'if we ride on fast we must leave them behind, for they are on foot.'

'He has a motor-car,' said the Colonel.

'But we may not get it,' said Bull.

'Yes, he is quite on your side.'

'But he might be out.'

'Hold your tongue,' said Syme suddenly. 'What is that noise?'

For a second they all sat as still as equestrian statues, and for a second—for two or three or four seconds—heaven and earth seemed equally still. Then all their ears, in an agony of attention, heard along the road that indescribable thrill and throb that means only one thing—horses!

The Colonel's face had an instantaneous change as if lightning had struck it, and yet left it scatheless.

'They have done us,' he said, with brief military irony. 'Prepare to receive cavalry!'

'Where can they have got the horses?' asked Syme, as he mechanically urged his steed to a canter.

The Colonel was silent for a little, then he said in a strained voice:

'I was speaking with strict accuracy when I said that the "Soleil d'Or" was the only place where one can get horses within twenty miles.'

'No!' said Syme violently, 'I don't believe he'd do it. Not with all that white hair.'

'He may have been forced,' said the Colonel gently. 'They must be at least a hundred strong, for which reason we are all going to see my friend Renard, who has a motor-car.'

With these words he swung his horse suddenly round a street corner, and went down the street with such thundering speed, that the others, though already well at the gallop, had difficulty in following the flying tail of his horse.

Dr. Renard inhabited a high and comfortable house at the top of a steep street, so that when the riders alighted at his door they could once more see the solid green ridge of the hill, with the white road across it, standing up above all the roofs of the town. They breathed again to see that the road as yet was clear, and they rang the bell.

Dr. Renard was a beaming, brown-bearded man, a good example of that silent but very busy professional class which France has preserved even more perfectly than England. When the matter was explained to him he pooh-poohed the panic of the ex-Marquis altogether; he said, with the solid French scepticism, that there was no conceivable probability of a general anarchist rising. 'Anarchy,' he said, shrugging his shoulders, 'it is childishness!'

'*Et ça*,' cried out the Colonel suddenly, pointing over the other's shoulder, 'and that is childishness, isn't it?'

They all looked round, and saw a curve of black cavalry come sweeping over the top of the hill with all the energy of Attila. Swiftly as they rode, however, the whole rank still kept well together, and they could see the black vizards of the first line as level as a line of uniforms. But although the main black square was the same, though travelling faster, there was now one sensational difference which they could see clearly upon the slope of the hill, as if upon a slanted map. The bulk of the riders were in one block; but one rider flew far ahead of the column, and with frantic movements of hand and heel urged his horse faster and faster, so that one might have fancied that he was not the pursuer but the pursued. But even at that great distance they could see something so fanatical, so unquestionable in his figure, that they knew it was the Secretary himself.

'I am sorry to cut short a cultured discussion,' said the Colonel, 'but can you lend me your motor-car now, in two minutes?'

'I have a suspicion that you are all mad,' said Dr. Renard, smiling sociably; 'but God forbid that madness should in any way interrupt friendship. Let us go round to the garage.'

Dr. Renard was a mild man with monstrous wealth; his rooms were like the Musée de Cluny, and he had three motor-cars. These, however, he seemed to use very sparingly, having the simple tastes of the French middle class, and when his impatient friends came to examine them, it took them some time to assure themselves that one of them even could be made to work. This with some difficulty they brought round into the street before the Doctor's house. When they came out of the dim garage they were startled to find that twilight had already fallen with the abruptness of night in the tropics. Either they had been longer in the place than they imagined, or some unusual canopy of cloud had gathered over the town. They looked down the steep streets, and seemed to see a slight mist coming up from the sea.

'It is now or never,' said Dr. Bull. 'I hear horses.'

'No,' corrected the Professor, 'a horse.'

And as they listened, it was evident that the noise, rapidly coming nearer on the rattling stones, was not the noise of the whole cavalcade but that of the one horseman, who had left it far behind—the insane Secretary.

Syme's family, like most of those who end in the simple life, had once owned a motor-car, and he knew all about them. He had leapt at once into the chauffeur's seat, and with flushed face was wrenching and tugging at the disused machinery. He bent his strength upon one handle, and then said quite quietly:

'I am afraid it's no go.'

As he spoke, there swept round the corner a man rigid on his rushing horse, with the rush and rigidity of an arrow. He had a smile that thrust out his chin as if it were dislocated. He swept alongside of the stationary car, into which its company had crowded, and laid his hand on the front. It was the Secretary, and his mouth went quite straight in the solemnity of triumph.

Syme was leaning hard upon the steering-wheel, and there was no sound but the rumble of the other pursuers riding into the town. Then there came quite suddenly a scream of scraping iron, and the car leapt forward. It plucked the Secretary clean out of his saddle, as a knife is whipped out of its sheath, trailed him kicking terribly for twenty yards, and left him flung flat upon the road far in front of his frightened horse. As the car took the corner of the street with a splendid curve, they could just see the other anarchists filling the street and raising their fallen leader.

'I can't understand why it has grown so dark,' said the Professor at last in a low voice.

'Going to be a storm, I think,' said Dr. Bull. 'I say, it's a pity we haven't got a light on this car, if only to see by.'

'We have,' said the Colonel, and from the floor of the car he fished up a heavy, old-fashioned, carved iron lantern with a light inside it. It was obviously an antique, and it would seem as if its original use had been in some way semi-religious, for there was a rude moulding of a cross upon one of its sides.

'Where on earth did you get that?' asked the Professor.

'I got it where I got the car,' answered the Colonel, chuckling, 'from my best friend. While our friend here was fighting with the steering-wheel, I ran up the front steps of the house and spoke to Renard, who was standing in his own porch, you will remember. "I suppose," I said, "there's no time to get a lamp." He looked up, blinking amiably at the beautiful arched ceiling of his own front hall. From this was suspended, by chains of exquisite ironwork, this lantern, one of the hundred treasures of his treasure-house. By sheer force he tore the lamp out of his own ceiling, shattering the painted panels, and bringing down two blue vases with his violence. Then he handed me the iron lantern, and I put it in the car. Was I not right when I said that Dr. Renard was worth knowing?'

'You were,' said Syme seriously, and hung the heavy lantern over the front. There was a certain allegory of their whole position in the contrast between the modern automobile and its strange, ecclesiastical lamp.

Hitherto they had passed through the quietest part of the town, meeting at most one or two pedestrians, who could give them no hint of the peace or the hostility of the place. Now, however, the windows in the houses began one by one to be lit up, giving a greater sense of habitation and humanity. Dr. Bull turned to the new detective who had led their flight, and permitted himself one of his natural and friendly smiles.

'These lights make one feel more cheerful.'

Inspector Ratcliffe drew his brows together.

'There is only one set of lights that make me more cheerful,' he said, 'and they are those lights of the police station which I can see beyond the town. Please God we may be there in ten minutes.'

Then all Bull's boiling good sense and optimism broke suddenly out of him.

'Oh, this is all raving nonsense!' he cried. 'If you really think that ordinary people in ordinary houses are anarchists, you must be madder than an anarchist yourself. If we turned and fought these fellows, the whole town would fight for us.'

'No,' said the other with an immovable simplicity, 'the whole town would fight for them. We shall see.'

While they were speaking the Professor had leant forward with sudden excitement.

'What is that noise?' he said.

'Oh, the horses behind us, I suppose,' said the Colonel. 'I thought we had got clear of them.'

'The horses behind us! No,' said the Professor, 'it is not horses, and it is not behind us.'

Almost as he spoke, across the end of the street before them two shining and rattling shapes shot past. They were gone almost in a flash, but every one could see that they were motor-cars, and the Professor stood up with a pale face and swore that they were the other two motor-cars from Dr. Renard's garage.

'I tell you they were his,' he repeated, with wild eyes, 'and they were full of men in masks!'

'Absurd!' said the Colonel angrily. 'Dr. Renard would never give them his cars.'

'He may have been forced,' said Ratcliffe quietly. 'The whole town is on their side.'

'You still believe that?' asked the Colonel incredulously.

'You will all believe it soon,' said the other with a hopeless calm.

There was a puzzled pause for some little time, and then the Colonel began again abruptly:

'No, I can't believe it. The thing is nonsense. The plain people of a peaceable French town——'

He was cut short by a bang and a blaze of light, which seemed close to his eyes. As the car sped on it left a floating patch of white smoke behind it, and Syme had heard a shot shriek past his ear.

'My God!' said the Colonel, 'some one has shot at us.'

'It need not interrupt conversation,' said the gloomy Ratcliffe. 'Pray resume your remarks, Colonel. You were talking, I think, about the plain people of a peaceable French town.'

The staring Colonel was long past minding satire. He rolled his eyes all round the street.

'It is extraordinary,' he said, 'most extraordinary.'

'A fastidious person, said Syme, 'might even call it unpleasant. However, I suppose those lights out in the field beyond this street are the Gendarmerie. We shall soon get there.'

'No,' said Inspector Ratcliffe, 'we shall never get there.'

He had been standing up and looking keenly ahead of him. Now he sat down and smoothed his sleek hair with a weary gesture.

'What do you mean?' asked Bull sharply.

'I mean that we shall never get there,' said the pessimist placidly. 'They have two rows of armed men across the road already; I can see them from here. The town is in arms, as I said it was. I can only wallow in the exquisite comfort of my own exactitude.'

And Ratcliffe sat down comfortably in the car and lit a cigarette, but the others rose excitedly and stared down the road. Syme had slowed down the car as their plans became doubtful, and he brought it finally to a standstill just at the corner of a side-street that ran down very steeply to the sea.

The town was mostly in shadow, but the sun had not sunk; wherever its level light could break through, it painted everything a burning gold. Up this side-street the last sunset light shone as sharp and narrow as the shaft of artificial light at the theatre. It struck the car of the five friends, and lit it like a burning chariot. But the rest of the street, especially the two ends of it, was in the deepest twilight, and for some seconds they could see nothing. Then Syme, whose eyes were the keenest, broke into a little bitter whistle, and said:

'It is quite true. There is a crowd or an army or some such thing across the end of that street.'

'Well, if there is,' said Bull impatiently, 'it must be something else—a sham fight or the mayor's birthday or something. I cannot and will not believe that plain, jolly people in a place like this walk about with dynamite in their pockets. Get on a bit, Syme, and let us look at them.'

The car crawled about a hundred yards farther, and then they were all startled by Dr. Bull breaking into a high crow of laughter.

'Why, you silly mugs!' he cried, 'what did I tell you. That crowd's as law-abiding as a cow, and if it weren't, it's on our side.'

'How do you know?' asked the Professor, staring.

'You blind bat,' cried Bull, 'don't you see who is leading them?'

They peered again, and then the Colonel, with a catch in his voice, cried out:

'Why, it's Renard!'

There was, indeed, a rank of dim figures running across the road, and they could not be clearly seen; but far enough in front to catch the accident of the evening light was stalking up and down the unmistakable Dr. Renard, in a white hat, stroking his long brown beard, and holding a revolver in his left hand.

'What a fool I've been!' exclaimed the Colonel. 'Of course, the dear old boy has turned out to help us.'

Dr. Bull was bubbling over with laughter, swinging the sword in his hand as carelessly as a cane. He jumped out of the car and ran across the intervening space, calling out:

'Dr. Renard! Dr. Renard!'

An instant after Syme thought his own eyes had gone mad in his head. For the philanthropic Dr. Renard had deliberately raised his revolver and fired twice at Bull, so that the shots rang down the road.

Almost at the same second as the puff of white cloud went up from this atrocious explosion a long puff of white cloud went up also from the cigarette of the cynical Ratcliffe. Like all the rest he turned a little pale, but he smiled. Dr. Bull, at whom the bullets had been fired, just missing his scalp, stood quite still in the middle of the road without a sign of fear, and then turned very slowly and crawled back to the car, and climbed in with two holes through his hat.

'Well,' said the cigarette-smoker slowly, 'what do you think now?'

'I think,' said Dr. Bull with precision, 'that I am lying in bed at No. 217 Peabody Buildings, and that

I shall soon wake up with a jump; or, if that's not
it, I think that I am sitting in a small cushioned cell
in Hanwell, and that the doctor can't make much of my
case. But if you want to know what I don't think,
I'll tell you. I don't think what you think. I don't
think, and I never shall think, that the mass of ordinary
men are a pack of dirty modern thinkers. No, sir,
I'm a democrat, and I still don't believe that Sunday
could convert one average navvy or counter-jumper.
No, I may be mad, but humanity isn't.'

Syme turned his bright blue eyes on Bull with an
earnestness which he did not commonly make clear.

'You are a very fine fellow,' he said. 'You can
believe in a sanity which is not merely your sanity.
And you're right enough about humanity, about
peasants and people like that jolly old innkeeper.
But you're not right about Renard. I suspected
him from the first. He's rationalistic, and, what's
worse, he's rich. When duty and religion are really
destroyed, it will be by the rich.'

'They are really destroyed now,' said the man
with a cigarette, and rose with his hands in his pockets.
'The devils are coming on!'

The men in the motor-car looked anxiously in the
direction of his dreamy gaze, and they saw that the
whole regiment at the end of the road was advancing
upon them, Dr. Renard marching furiously in front,
his beard flying in the breeze.

The Colonel sprang out of the car with an intolerant
exclamation.

'Gentlemen,' he cried, 'the thing is incredible.
It must be a practical joke. If you knew Renard as
I do—it's like calling Queen Victoria a dynamiter.
If you had got the man's character into your head——'

'Dr. Bull,' said Syme sardonically, 'has at least got it into his hat.'

'I tell you it can't be!' cried the Colonel, stamping. 'Renard shall explain it. He shall explain it to me,' and he strode forward.

'Don't be in such a hurry,' drawled the smoker. 'He will very soon explain it to all of us.'

But the impatient Colonel was already out of earshot, advancing towards the advancing enemy. The excited Dr. Renard lifted his pistol again, but perceiving his opponent, hesitated, and the Colonel came face to face with him with frantic gestures of remonstrance.

'It is no good,' said Syme. 'He will never get anything out of that old heathen. I vote we drive bang through the thick of them, bang as the bullets went through Bull's hat. We may be all killed, but we must kill a tidy number of them.'

'I won't 'ave it,' said Dr. Bull, growing more vulgar in the sincerity of his virtue. 'The poor chaps may be making a mistake. Give the Colonel a chance.'

'Shall we go back, then?' asked the Professor.

'No,' said Ratcliffe in a cold voice, 'the street behind us is held too. In fact, I seem to see there another friend of yours, Syme.'

Syme spun round smartly, and stared backwards at the track which they had travelled. He saw an irregular body of horsemen gathering and galloping towards them in the gloom. He saw above the foremost saddle the silver gleam of a sword, and then as it grew nearer the silver gleam of an old man's hair. The next moment, with shattering violence, he had swung the motor round and sent it dashing down the steep side-street to the sea, like a man that desired only to die.

'What the devil is up?' cried the Professor, seizing his arm.

'The morning star has fallen!' said Syme, as his own car went down the darkness like a falling star.

The others did not understand his words, but when they looked back at the street above they saw the hostile cavalry coming round the corner and down the slopes after them; and foremost of all rode the good innkeeper, flushed with the fiery innocence of the evening light.

'The world is insane!' said the Professor, and buried his face in his hands.

'No,' said Dr. Bull in adamantine humility, 'it is I.'

'What are we going to do?' asked the Professor.

'At this moment,' said Syme, with a scientific detachment, 'I think we are going to smash into a lamp-post.'

The next instant the automobile had come with a catastrophic jar against an iron object. The instant after that four men had crawled out from under a chaos of metal, and a tall lean lamp-post that had stood up straight on the edge of the marine parade stood out, bent and twisted, like the branch of a broken tree.

'Well, we smashed something,' said the Professor, with a faint smile. 'That's some comfort.'

'You're becoming an anarchist,' said Syme, dusting his clothes with his instinct of daintiness.

'Every one is,' said Ratcliffe.

As they spoke, the white-haired horseman and his followers came thundering from above, and almost at the same moment a dark string of men ran shouting along the sea-front. Syme snatched a sword, and took it in his teeth; he stuck two others under his arm-pits, took a fourth in his left hand and the lantern in his right, and leapt off the high parade on to the beach below.

The others leapt after him, with a common acceptance of such decisive action, leaving the *débris* and the gathering mob above them.

'We have one more chance,' said Syme, taking the steel out of his mouth. 'Whatever all this pandemonium means, I suppose the police station will help us. We can't get there, for they hold the way. But there's a pier or breakwater runs out into the sea just here, which we could defend longer than anything else, like Horatius and his bridge. We must defend it till the Gendarmerie turn out. Keep after me.'

They followed him as he went crunching down the beach, and in a second or two their boots broke not on the sea gravel, but on broad, flat stones. They marched down a long, low jetty, running out in one arm into the dim, boiling sea, and when they came to the end of it they felt that they had come to the end of their story. They turned and faced the town.

That town was transfigured with uproar. All along the high parade from which they had just descended was a dark and roaring stream of humanity, with tossing arms and fiery faces, groping and glaring towards them. The long dark line was dotted with torches and lanterns; but even where no flame lit up a furious face, they could see in the farthest figure, in the most shadowy gesture, an organized hate. It was clear that they were the accursed of all men, and they knew not why.

Two or three men, looking little and black like monkeys, leapt over the edge as they had done and dropped on to the beach. These came ploughing down the deep sand, shouting horribly, and strove to wade into the sea at random. The example was followed, and the whole black mass of men began to run and drip over the edge like black treacle.

Foremost among the men on the beach Syme saw the peasant who had driven their cart. He splashed into the surf on a huge cart-horse, and shook his axe at them.

'The peasant!' cried Syme. 'They have not risen since the Middle Ages.'

'Even if the police do come now,' said the Professor mournfully, 'they can do nothing with this mob.'

'Nonsense!' said Bull desperately; 'there must be some people left in the town who are human.'

'No,' said the hopeless Inspector, 'the human being will soon be extinct. We are the last of mankind.'

'It may be,' said the Professor absently. Then he added in his dreamy voice, 'What is all that at the end of the *Dunciad*?

> 'Nor public flame, nor private, dares to shine;
> Nor human light is left, nor glimpse divine!
> Lo! thy dread Empire, Chaos, is restored;
> Light dies before thine uncreating word:
> Thy hand, great Anarch, lets the curtain fall;
> And universal darkness buries all.'

'Stop!' cried Bull suddenly, 'the gendarmes are out.'

The low lights of the police station were indeed blotted and broken with hurrying figures, and they heard through the darkness the clash and jingle of a disciplined cavalry.

'They are charging the mob!' cried Bull in ecstasy or alarm.

'No,' said Syme, 'they are formed along the parade.'

'They have unslung their carbines,' cried Bull, dancing with excitement.

'Yes,' said Ratcliffe, 'and they are going to fire on us.'

As he spoke there came a long crackle of musketry, and bullets seemed to hop like hailstones on the stones in front of them.

'The gendarmes have joined them!' cried the Professor, and struck his forehead.

'I am in the padded cell,' said Bull solidly.

There was a long silence, and then Ratcliffe said, looking out over the swollen sea, all a sort of grey purple:

'What does it matter who is mad or who is sane? We shall all be dead soon.'

Syme turned to him and said:

'You are quite hopeless, then?'

Mr. Ratcliffe kept a stony silence; then at last he said quietly:

'No; oddly enough I am not quite hopeless. There is one insane little hope that I cannot get out of my mind. The power of this whole planet is against us, yet I cannot help wondering whether this one silly little hope is hopeless yet.'

'In what or whom is your hope?' asked Syme with curiosity.

'In a man I never saw,' said the other, looking at the leaden sea.

'I know what you mean,' said Syme in a low voice, 'the man in the dark room. But Sunday must have killed him by now.'

'Perhaps,' said the other steadily; 'but if so, he was the only man whom Sunday found it hard to kill.'

'I heard what you said,' said the Professor, with his back turned. 'I am also holding hard on to the thing I never saw.'

All of a sudden, Syme who was standing as if blind with introspective thought, swung round and cried out, like a man waking from sleep:

'Where is the Colonel? I thought he was with us!'

'The Colonel! Yes,' cried Bull, 'where on earth is the Colonel?'

'He went to speak to Renard,' said the Professor.

'We cannot leave him among all those beasts,' cried Syme. 'Let us die like gentlemen if——'

'Do not pity the Colonel,' said Ratcliffe, with a pale sneer. 'He is extremely comfortable. He is——'

'No! no! no!' cried Syme in a kind of frenzy, 'not the Colonel too! I will never believe it!'

'Will you believe your eyes?' asked the other, and pointed to the beach.

Many of their pursuers had waded into the water shaking their fists, but the sea was rough, and they could not reach the pier. Two or three figures, however, stood on the beginning of the stone footway, and seemed to be cautiously advancing down it. The glare of a chance lantern lit up the faces of the two foremost. One face wore a black half-mask, and under it the mouth was twisting about in such a madness of nerves that the black tuft of beard wriggled round and round like a restless, living thing. The other was the red face and white moustache of Colonel Ducroix. They were in earnest consultation.

'Yes, he is gone too,' said the Professor, and sat

down on a stone. 'Everything's gone. I'm gone! I can't trust my own bodily machinery. I feel as if my own hand might fly up and strike me.'

'When my hand flies up,' said Syme, 'it will strike somebody else', and he strode along the pier towards the Colonel, the sword in one hand and the lantern in the other.

As if to destroy the last hope or doubt, the Colonel, who saw him coming, pointed his revolver at him and fired. The shot missed Syme, but struck his sword, breaking it short at the hilt. Syme rushed on, and swung the iron lantern above his head.

'Judas before Herod!' he said, and struck the Colonel down upon the stones. Then he turned to the Secretary, whose frightful mouth was almost foaming now, and held the lamp high with so rigid and arresting a gesture, that the man was, as it were, frozen for a moment, and forced to hear.

'Do you see this lantern?' cried Syme in a terrible voice. 'Do you see the cross carved on it, and the flame inside? You did not make it. You did not light it. Better men than you, men who could believe and obey, twisted the entrails of iron and preserved the legend of fire. There is not a street you walk on, there is not a thread you wear, that was not made as this lantern was, by denying your philosophy of dirt and rats. You can make nothing. You can only destroy. You will destroy mankind; you will destroy the world. Let that suffice you. Yet this one old Christian lantern you shall not destroy. It shall go where your empire of apes will never have the wit to find it.'

He struck the Secretary once with the lantern so that he staggered; and then, whirling it twice round his head, sent it flying far out to sea, where it flared like a roaring rocket and fell.

'Swords!' shouted Syme, turning his flaming face to the three behind him. 'Let us charge these logs, for our time has come to die.'

His three companions came after him sword in hand. Syme's sword was broken, but he rent a bludgeon from the fist of a fisherman, flinging him down. In a moment they would have flung themselves upon the face of the mob and perished, when an interruption came. The Secretary, ever since Syme's speech, had stood with his hand to his stricken head as if dazed; now he suddenly pulled off his black mask.

The pale face thus peeled in the lamplight revealed not so much rage as astonishment. He put up his hand with an anxious authority.

'There is some mistake,' he said. 'Mr. Syme, I hardly think you understand your position. I arrest you in the name of the law.'

'Of the law?' said Syme, and dropped his stick.

'Certainly!' said the Secretary. 'I am a detective from Scotland Yard,' and he took a small blue card from his pocket.

'And what do you suppose we are?' asked the Professor, and threw up his arms.

'You,' said the Secretary stiffly, 'are, as I know for a fact, members of the Supreme Anarchist Council. Disguised as one of you, I——'

Dr. Bull tossed his sword into the sea.

'There never was any Supreme Anarchist Council,' he said. 'We were all a lot of silly policemen looking at each other. And all these nice people who have been peppering us with shot thought we were the dynamiters. I knew I couldn't be wrong about the mob,' he said, beaming over the enormous multitude, which stretched away to the distance on both sides. 'Vulgar people are never mad. I'm vulgar myself, and I know. I am now going on shore to stand a drink to everybody here.'

CHAPTER XIII

THE PURSUIT OF THE PRESIDENT

NEXT morning five bewildered but hilarious people took the boat for Dover. The poor old Colonel might have had some cause to complain, having first been forced to fight for two factions that didn't exist, and then knocked down with an iron lantern. But he was a magnanimous old gentleman, and being much relieved that neither party had anything to do with dynamite, he saw them off on the pier with great geniality.

The five reconciled detectives had a hundred details to explain to each other. The Secretary had to tell Syme how they had come to wear masks originally in order to approach the supposed enemy as fellow-conspirators; Syme had to explain how they had fled with such swiftness through a civilized country. But above all these matters of detail which could be explained, rose the central mountain of the matter that they could not explain. What did it all mean? If they were all harmless officers, what was Sunday? If he had not seized the world, what on earth had he been up to? Inspector Ratcliffe was still gloomy about this.

'I can't make head or tail of old Sunday's little game any more than you can,' he said. 'But whatever else Sunday is, he isn't a blameless citizen. Damn it! do you remember his face?'

'I grant you,' answered Syme, 'that I have never been able to forget it.'

'Well,' said the Secretary, 'I suppose we can find

out soon, for to-morrow we have our next general meeting. You will excuse me,' he said, with a rather ghastly smile, 'for being well acquainted with my secretarial duties.'

'I suppose you are right,' said the Professor reflectively. 'I suppose we might find it out from him; but I confess that I should feel a bit afraid of asking Sunday who he really is.'

'Why?' asked the Secretary, 'for fear of bombs?'

'No,' said the Professor, 'for fear he might tell me.'

'Let us have some drinks,' said Dr. Bull, after a silence.

Throughout their whole journey by boat and train they were highly convivial, but they instinctively kept together. Dr. Bull, who had always been the optimist of the party, endeavoured to persuade the other four that the whole company could take the same hansom cab from Victoria; but this was overruled, and they went in a four-wheeler, with Dr. Bull on the box, singing. They finished their journey at an hotel in Piccadilly Circus, so as to be close to the early breakfast next morning in Leicester Square. Yet even then the adventures of the day were not entirely over. Dr. Bull, discontented with the general proposal to go to bed, had strolled out of the hotel at about eleven to see and taste some of the beauties of London. Twenty minutes afterwards, however, he came back and made quite a clamour in the hall. Syme, who tried at first to soothe him, was forced at last to listen to his communication with quite new attention.

'I tell you I've seen him!' said Dr. Bull, with thick emphasis.

'Whom?' asked Syme quickly. 'Not the President?'

'Not so bad as that,' said Dr. Bull, with unnecessary laughter, 'not so bad as that. I've got him here.'

'Got whom here?' asked Syme impatiently.

'Hairy man,' said the other lucidly, 'man that used to be hairy man—Gogol. Here he is,' and he pulled forward by a reluctant elbow the identical young man who five days before had marched out of the Council, with thin red hair and a pale face, the first of all the sham anarchists who had been exposed.

'Why do you worry with me?' he cried. 'You have expelled me as a spy.'

'We are all spies!' whispered Syme.

'We're all spies!' shouted Dr. Bull. 'Come and have a drink.'

Next morning the battalion of the reunited six marched stolidly towards the hotel in Leicester Square.

'This is more cheerful,' said Dr. Bull; 'we are six men going to ask one man what he means.'

'I think it is a bit queerer than that,' said Syme. 'I think it is six men going to ask one man what they mean.'

They turned in silence into the Square, and though the hotel was in the opposite corner, they saw at once the little balcony and a figure that looked too big for it. He was sitting alone with bent head, poring over a newspaper. But all his councillors, who had come to vote him down, crossed that Square as if they were watched out of heaven by a hundred eyes.

They had disputed much upon their policy, about whether they should leave the unmasked Gogol without and begin diplomatically, or whether they should bring him in and blow up the gunpowder at once. The influence of Syme and Bull prevailed for the latter course, though the Secretary to the last asked them why they attacked Sunday so rashly.

'My reason is quite simple,' said Syme. 'I attack him rashly because I am afraid of him.'

They followed Syme up the dark stair in silence, and they all came out simultaneously into the broad sunlight of the morning and the broad sunlight of Sunday's smile.

'Delightful!' he said. 'So pleased to see you all. What an exquisite day it is. Is the Tsar dead?'

The Secretary, who happened to be the foremost, drew himself together for a dignified outburst.

'No, sir,' he said sternly, 'there has been no massacre. I bring you news of no such disgusting spectacles.'

'Disgusting spectacles?' repeated the President, with a bright, inquiring smile. 'You mean Dr. Bull's spectacles?'

The Secretary choked for a moment, and the President went on with a sort of smooth appeal:

'Of course, we all have our opinions and even our eyes, but really to call them disgusting before the man himself——'

Dr. Bull tore off his spectacles and broke them on the table.

'My spectacles are blackguardly,' he said, 'but I'm not. Look at my face.'

'I dare say it's the sort of face that grows on one,' said the President, 'in fact, it grows on you; and who am I to quarrel with the wild fruits upon the Tree of Life? I dare say it will grow on me some day.'

'We have no time for tomfoolery,' said the Secretary, breaking in savagely. 'We have come to know what all this means. Who are you? What are you? Why did you get us all here? Do you know who and what we are? Are you a half-witted man playing the conspirator, or are you a clever man playing the fool? Answer me, I tell you.'

'Candidates,' murmured Sunday, 'are only required to answer eight out of the seventeen questions on the paper. As far as I can make out, you want me to tell you what I am, and what you are, and what this table is, and what this Council is, and what this world is for all I know. Well, I will go so far as to rend the veil of one mystery. If you want to know what you are, you are a set of highly well-intentioned young jackasses.'

'And you,' said Syme, leaning forward, 'what are you?'

'I? What am I?' roared the President, and he rose slowly to an incredible height, like some enormous wave about to arch above them and break. 'You want to know what I am, do you? Bull, you are a man of science. Grub in the roots of those trees and find out the truth about them. Syme, you are a poet. Stare at those morning clouds. But I tell you this, that you will have found out the truth of the last tree and the topmost cloud before the truth about me. You will understand the sea, and I shall be still a riddle; you shall know what the stars are, and not know what I am. Since the beginning of the world all men have hunted me like a wolf—kings and sages, and poets and law-givers, all the churches, and all the philosophies. But I have never been caught yet, and the skies will fall in the time I turn to bay. I have given them a good run for their money, and I will now.'

Before one of them could move, the monstrous man had swung himself like some huge ourang-outang over the balustrade of the balcony. Yet before he dropped he pulled himself up again as on a horizontal bar, and thrusting his great chin over the edge of the balcony, said solemnly:

'There's one thing I'll tell you though about who I am. I am the man in the dark room, who made you all policemen.'

With that he fell from the balcony, bouncing on the stones below like a great ball of india-rubber, and went bounding off towards the corner of the Alhambra, where he hailed a hansom cab and sprang inside it. The six detectives had been standing thunderstruck and livid in the light of his last assertion; but when he disappeared into the cab, Syme's practical senses returned to him, and leaping over the balcony so recklessly as almost to break his legs, he called another cab.

He and Bull sprang into the cab together, the Professor and the Inspector into another, while the Secretary and the late Gogol scrambled into a third just in time to pursue the flying Syme, who was pursuing the flying President. Sunday led them a wild chase towards the north-west, his cabman, evidently under the influence of more than common inducements, urging the horse at breakneck speed. But Syme was in no mood for delicacies, and he stood up in his own cab shouting, 'Stop thief!' until crowds ran along beside his cab, and policemen began to stop and ask questions. All this had its influence upon the President's cabman, who began to look dubious, and to slow down to a trot. He opened the trap to talk reasonably to his fare, and in so doing let the long whip droop over the front of the cab. Sunday leant forward, seized it, and jerked it violently out of the man's hand. Then standing up in front of the cab himself, he lashed the horse and roared aloud, so that they went down the streets like a flying storm. Through street after street and square after square went whirling this preposterous vehicle, in which the fare was urging the horse and the driver trying desperately to stop it. The other three cabs came after it (if the phrase be permissible of a cab) like panting hounds. Shops and streets shot by like rattling arrows.

At the highest ecstasy of speed, Sunday turned round on the splashboard where he stood, and sticking his great grinning head out of the cab, with white hair whistling in the wind, he made a horrible face at his pursuers, like some colossal urchin. Then raising his right hand swiftly, he flung a ball of paper in Syme's face and vanished. Syme caught the thing while instinctively warding it off, and discovered that it consisted of two crumpled papers. One was addressed to himself, and the other to Dr. Bull, with a very long, and it is to be feared partly ironical, string of letters after his name. Dr. Bull's address was, at any rate, considerably longer than his communication, for the communication consisted entirely of the words:

'What about Martin Tupper *now*?'

'What does the old maniac mean?' asked Bull, staring at the words. 'What does yours say, Syme?'

Syme's message was, at any rate, longer, and ran as follows:

'No one would regret anything in the nature of an interference by the Archdeacon more than I. I trust it will not come to that. But, for the last time, where are your goloshes? The thing is too bad, especially after what uncle said.'

The President's cabman seemed to be regaining some control over his horse, and the pursuers gained a little as they swept round into the Edgware Road. And here there occurred what seemed to the allies a providential stoppage. Traffic of every kind was swerving to right or left or stopping, for down the long road was coming the unmistakable roar announcing the fire-engine, which in a few seconds went by like a brazen thunder-bolt. But quick as it went by, Sunday had bounded out of his cab, sprung at the fire-engine, caught it, slung himself on to it, and was seen as he disappeared in the noisy distance talking to the astonished fireman with explanatory gestures.

'After him!' howled Syme. 'He can't go astray now. There's no mistaking a fire-engine.'

The three cabmen, who had been stunned for a moment, whipped up their horses and slightly decreased the distance between themselves and their disappearing prey. The President acknowledged this proximity by coming to the back of the car, bowing repeatedly, kissing his hand, and finally flinging a neatly folded note into the bosom of Inspector Ratcliffe. When that gentleman opened it, not without impatience, he found it contained the words:

'Fly at once. The truth about your trouser-stretchers is known.—A Friend.'

The fire-engine had struck still farther to the north, into a region that they did not recognize; and as it ran by a line of high railings shadowed with trees, the six friends were startled, but somewhat relieved, to see the President leap from the fire-engine, though whether through another whim or the increasing protest of his entertainers they could not see. Before the three cabs, however, could reach up to the spot, he had gone up the high railings like a huge grey cat, tossed himself over, and vanished in a darkness of leaves.

Syme, with a furious gesture, stopped his cab, jumped out, and sprang also to the escalade. When he had one leg over the fence and his friends were following, he turned a face on them which shone quite pale in the shadow.

'What place can this be?' he asked. 'Can it be the old devil's house? I've heard he has a house in North London.'

'All the better,' said the Secretary grimly, planting a foot in a foothold, 'we shall find him at home.'

'No, but it isn't that,' said Syme, knitting his brows. 'I hear the most horrible noises, like devils laughing and sneezing and blowing their devilish noses!'

'His dogs barking, of course,' said the Secretary.

'Why not say his black-beetles barking!' said Syme furiously, 'snails barking! geraniums barking! Did you ever hear a dog bark like that?'

He held up his hand, and there came out of the thicket a long growling roar that seemed to get under the skin and freeze the flesh—a low thrilling roar that made a throbbing in the air all about them.

'The dogs of Sunday would be no ordinary dogs,' said Gogol, and shuddered.

Syme had jumped down on the other side, but he still stood listening impatiently.

'Well, listen to that,' he said, 'is that a dog—anybody's dog?'

There broke upon their ears a hoarse screaming as of things protesting and clamouring in sudden pain; and then, far off like an echo, what sounded like a long nasal trumpet.

'Well, his house ought to be hell!' said the Secretary; 'and if it is hell, I'm going in!' and he sprang over the tall railings almost with one swing.

The others followed. They broke through a tangle of plants and shrubs, and came out on an open path. Nothing was in sight, but Dr. Bull suddenly struck his hands together.

'Why, you asses,' he cried, 'it's the Zoo!'

As they were looking round wildly for any trace of their wild quarry, a keeper in uniform came running along the path with a man in plain clothes.

'Has it come this way?' gasped the keeper.

'Has what?' asked Syme.

'The elephant!' cried the keeper. 'An elephant has gone mad and run away!'

'He has run away with an old gentleman,' said the other stranger breathlessly, 'a poor old gentleman with white hair!'

'What sort of old gentleman?' asked Syme, with great curiosity.

'A very large and fat old gentleman in light grey clothes,' said the keeper eagerly.

'Well,' said Syme, 'if he's that particular kind of old gentleman, if you're quite sure that he's a large and fat old gentleman in grey clothes, you may take my word for it that the elephant has not run away with him. He has run away with the elephant. The elephant is not made by God that could run away with him if he did not consent to the elopement. And, by thunder, there he is!'

There was no doubt about it this time. Clean across the space of grass, about two hundred yards away, with a crowd screaming and scampering vainly at his heels, went a huge grey elephant at an awful stride, with his trunk thrown out as rigid as a ship's bowsprit, and trumpeting like the trumpet of doom. On the back of the bellowing and plunging animal sat President Sunday with all the placidity of a sultan, but goading the animal to a furious speed with some sharp object in his hand.

'Stop him!' screamed the populace. 'He'll be out of the gate!'

'Stop a landslide!' said the keeper. 'He is out of the gate!'

And even as he spoke, a final crash and roar of terror announced that the great grey elephant had broken out of the gates of the Zoological Gardens, and was careering down Albany Street like a new and swift sort of omnibus.

'Great Lord!' cried Bull, 'I never knew an elephant could go so fast. Well, it must be hansom cabs again if we are to keep him in sight.'

As they raced along to the gate out of which the elephant had vanished, Syme felt a glaring panorama of the strange animals in the cages which they passed. Afterwards he thought it queer that he should have seen them so clearly. He remembered especially seeing pelicans, with their preposterous, pendent throats. He wondered why the pelican was the symbol of charity, except it was that it wanted a good deal of charity to admire a pelican. He remembered a hornbill, which was simply a huge yellow beak with a small bird tied on behind it. The whole gave him a sensation, the vividness of which he could not explain, that Nature was always making quite mysterious jokes. Sunday had told them that they would understand him when they had understood the stars. He wondered whether even the archangels understood the hornbill.

The six unhappy detectives flung themselves into cabs and followed the elephant, sharing the terror which he spread through the long stretch of the streets. This time Sunday did not turn round, but offered them the solid stretch of his unconscious back, which maddened them, if possible, more than his previous mockeries. Just before they came to Baker Street, however, he was seen to throw something far up into the air, as a boy does a ball meaning to catch it again. But at their rate of racing it fell far behind, just by the cab containing Gogol; and in faint hope of a clue or for some impulse unexplainable, he stopped his cab so as to pick it up. It was addressed to himself, and was quite a bulky parcel. On examination, however, its bulk was found to consist of thirty-three pieces of paper of no value wrapped one round the other. When the last covering was torn away it reduced itself to a small slip of paper, on which was written:

'The word, I fancy, should be "pink".'

The man once known as Gogol said nothing, but the movements of his hands and feet were like those of a man urging a horse to renewed efforts.

Through street after street, through district after district, went the prodigy of the flying elephant, calling crowds to every window, and driving the traffic left and right. And still through all this insane publicity the three cabs toiled after it, until they came to be regarded as part of a procession, and perhaps the advertisement of a circus. They went at such a rate that distances were shortened beyond belief, and Syme saw the Albert Hall in Kensington when he thought that he was still in Paddington. The animal's pace was even more fast and free through the empty, aristocratic streets of South Kensington, and he finally headed towards that part of the skyline where the enormous Wheel of Earl's Court stood up in the sky. The wheel grew larger and larger, till it filled heaven like the wheel of stars.

The beast outstripped the cabs. They lost him round several corners, and when they came to one of the gates of the Earl's Court Exhibition they found themselves finally blocked. In front of them was an enormous crowd; in the midst of it was an enormous elephant, heaving and shuddering as such shapeless creatures do. But the President had disappeared.

'Where has he gone to?' asked Syme, slipping to the ground.

'Gentleman rushed into the Exhibition, sir!' said an official in a dazed manner. Then he added in an injured voice: 'Funny gentleman, sir. Asked me to hold his horse, and gave me this.'

He held out with distaste a piece of folded paper, addressed: 'To the Secretary of the Central Anarchist Council.'

The Secretary, raging, rent it open, and found written inside it:

> 'When the herring runs a mile,
> Let the Secretary smile;
> When the herring tries to *fly*
> Let the Secretary die.
>   Rustic Proverb'

'Why the eternal crikey,' began the Secretary, 'did you let the man in? Do people commonly come to your Exhibition riding on mad elephants? Do——'

'Look!' shouted Syme suddenly. 'Look over there!'

'Look at what?' asked the Secretary savagely.

'Look at the captive balloon!' said Syme, and pointed in a frenzy.

'Why the blazes should I look at a captive balloon?' demanded the Secretary. 'What is there queer about a captive balloon?'

'Nothing,' said Syme, 'except that it isn't captive!'

They all turned their eyes to where the balloon swung and swelled above the Exhibition on a string, like a child's balloon. A second afterwards the string came in two just under the car, and the balloon, broken loose, floated away with the freedom of a soap bubble.

'Ten thousand devils!' shrieked the Secretary. 'He's got into it!' and he shook his fists at the sky.

The balloon, borne by some chance wind, came right above them, and they could see the great white head of the President peering over the side and looking benevolently down on them.

'God bless my soul!' said the Professor with the elderly manner that he could never disconnect from his bleached beard and parchment face. 'God bless my soul! I seemed to fancy that something fell on the top of my hat!'

He put up a trembling hand and took from that shelf a piece of twisted paper, which he opened absently, only to find it inscribed with a true lover's knot and the words;

'Your beauty has not left me indifferent.—From LITTLE SNOWDROP.'

There was a short silence, and then Syme said, biting his beard:

'I'm not beaten yet. The blasted thing must come down somewhere. Let's follow it!'

CHAPTER XIV

THE SIX PHILOSOPHERS

ACROSS green fields, and breaking through blooming hedges, toiled six draggled detectives, about five miles out of London. The optimist of the party had at first proposed that they should follow the balloon across South England in hansom cabs. But he was ultimately convinced of the persistent refusal of the balloon to follow the roads, and the still more persistent refusal of the cabmen to follow the balloon. Consequently the tireless though exasperated travellers broke through black thickets and ploughed through ploughed fields till each was turned into a figure too outrageous to be mistaken for a tramp. Those green hills of Surrey saw the final collapse and tragedy of the admirable light grey suit in which Syme had set out from Saffron Park. His silk hat was broken over his nose by a swinging bough, his coat-tails were torn to the shoulder by arresting thorns, the clay of England was splashed up to his collar; but he still carried his yellow beard forward with a silent and furious determination, and his eyes were still fixed on that floating ball of gas, which in the full flush of sunset seemed coloured like a sunset cloud.

'After all,' he said, 'it is very beautiful!'

'It is singularly and strangely beautiful!' said the Professor. 'I wish the beastly gas-bag would burst!'

'No,' said Dr. Bull, 'I hope it won't. It might hurt the old boy.'

'Hurt him!' said the vindictive Professor, 'hurt him!

Not as much as I'd hurt him if I could get up with him. Little Snowdrop!'

'I don't want him hurt, somehow,' said Dr. Bull.

'What!' cried the Secretary bitterly. 'Do you believe all that tale about his being our man in the dark room? Sunday would say he was anybody.'

'I don't know whether I believe it or not,' said Dr. Bull. 'But it isn't that that I mean. I can't wish old Sunday's balloon to burst because——'

'Well,' said Syme impatiently, 'because?'

'Well, because he's so jolly like a balloon himself,' said Dr. Bull desperately. 'I don't understand a word of all that idea of his being the same man who gave us all our blue cards. It seems to make everything nonsense. But I don't care who knows it, I always had a sympathy for old Sunday himself, wicked as he was. Just as if he was a great bouncing baby. How can I explain what my queer sympathy was? It didn't prevent my fighting him like hell! Shall I make it clear if I say that I liked him because he was so fat?'

'You will not,' said the Secretary.

'I've got it now,' cried Bull, 'it was because he was so fat and so light. Just like a balloon. We always think of fat people as heavy, but he could have danced against a sylph. I see now what I mean. Moderate strength is shown in violence, supreme strength is shown in levity. It was like the old speculations—what would happen if an elephant could leap up in the sky like a grasshopper?'

'Our elephant,' said Syme, looking upwards, 'has leapt into the sky like a grasshopper.'

'And somehow,' concluded Bull, 'that's why I can't help liking old Sunday. No, it's not an admiration of force, or any silly thing like that. There is a kind of gaiety in the thing, as if he were bursting with some good news. Haven't you sometimes felt it on a spring day? You know Nature plays tricks, but somehow that day proves they are good-natured tricks. I never read the Bible myself, but that part they laugh at is literal truth, "Why leap ye, ye high hills?" The hills do leap—at least, they try to. . . . Why do I like Sunday? . . . how can I tell you? . . . because he's such a Bounder.'

There was a long silence, and then the Secretary said in a curious, strained voice:

'You do not know Sunday at all. Perhaps it is because you are better than I, and do not know hell. I was a fierce fellow, and a trifle morbid from the first. The man who sits in darkness, and who chose us all, chose me because I had all the crazy look of a conspirator—because my smile went crooked, and my eyes were gloomy, even when I smiled. But there must have been something in me that answered to the nerves in all these anarchic men. For when I first saw Sunday he expressed to me, not your airy vitality, but something both gross and sad in the Nature of Things. I found him smoking in a twilight room, a room with brown blind down, infinitely more depressing than the genial darkness in which our master lives. He sat there on a bench, a huge heap of a man, dark and out of shape. He listened to all my words without speaking or even stirring. I poured out my most passionate appeals, and asked my most eloquent questions. Then, after a long silence, the Thing began to shake, and I thought it was shaken by some secret malady. It shook like a loathsome and living jelly. It reminded me of everything I had ever read about the base bodies that are the origin of life—the deep sea lumps and protoplasm. It seemed like the final form of matter, the most shapeless and the most shameful. I could only tell myself, from its shudderings, that it was something at least that such a monster could be miserable. And then it broke upon me that the bestial mountain was shaking with a lonely laughter, and the laughter was at me. Do you ask me to forgive him that? It is no small thing to be laughed at by something at once lower and stronger than oneself.'

'Surely you fellows are exaggerating wildly,' cut in the clear voice of Inspector Ratcliffe. 'President Sunday is a terrible fellow for one's intellect, but he is not such a Barnum's freak physically as you make out. He received me in an ordinary office, in a grey check coat, in broad daylight. He talked to me in an ordinary way. But I'll tell you what is a trifle creepy about Sunday. His room is neat, his clothes are neat, everything seems in order; but he's absent-minded. Sometimes his great bright eyes go quite blind. For hours he forgets that you are there. Now absent-mindedness is just a bit too awful in a bad man. We think of a wicked man as vigilant. We can't think of a wicked man who is honestly and sincerely dreamy, because we daren't think of a wicked man alone with himself. An absent-minded man means a good-natured man. It means a man who, if he happens to see you, will apologize. But how will you bear an absent-minded man who, if he happens to see you, will kill you? That is what tries the nerves, abstraction combined with cruelty. Men have felt it sometimes when they went through wild forests, and felt that the animals there were at once innocent and pitiless. They might ignore or slay. How would you like to pass ten mortal hours in a parlour with an absent-minded tiger?'

'And what do you think of Sunday, Gogol?' asked Syme.

'I don't think of Sunday on principle,' said Gogol simply, 'any more than I stare at the sun at noonday.'

'Well, that is a point of view,' said Syme thoughtfully. 'What do you say, Professor?'

The Professor was walking with bent head and trailing stick, and he did not answer at all.

'Wake up, Professor!' said Syme genially. 'Tell us what you think of Sunday.'

The Professor spoke at last very slowly.

'I think something,' he said, 'that I cannot say clearly. Or, rather, I think something that I cannot even think clearly. But it is something like this. My early life, as you know, was a bit too large and loose. Well, when I saw Sunday's face I thought it was too large—everybody does, but I also thought it was too loose. The face was so big, that one couldn't focus it or make it a face at all. The eye was so far away from the nose, that it wasn't an eye. The mouth was so much by itself, that one had to think of it by itself. The whole thing is too hard to explain.'

He paused for a little, still trailing his stick, and then went on:

'But put it this way. Walking up a road at night, I have seen a lamp and a lighted window and a cloud make together a most complete and unmistakable face. If any one in heaven has that face I shall know him again. Yet when I walked a little farther I found that there was no face, that the window was ten yards away, the lamp ten hundred yards, the cloud beyond the world. Well, Sunday's face escaped me; it ran away to right and left, as such chance pictures run away. And so his face has made me, somehow, doubt whether there are any faces. I don't know whether your face, Bull, is a face or a combination in perspective. Perhaps one black disk of your beastly glasses is quite close and another fifty miles away. Oh, the doubts of a materialist are not worth a dump. Sunday has taught me the last and the worst doubts, the doubts of a spiritualist. I am a Buddhist, I suppose; and Buddhism is not a creed, it is a doubt. My poor dear Bull, I do not believe that you really have a face. I have not faith enough to believe in matter.'

Syme's eyes were still fixed upon the errant orb, which, reddened in the evening light, looked like some rosier and more innocent world.

'Have you noticed an odd thing,' he said, 'about all your descriptions? Each man of you finds Sunday quite different, yet each man of you can only find one thing to compare him to—the universe itself. Bull finds him like the earth in spring, Gogol like the sun at noonday. The Secretary is reminded of the shapeless protoplasm, and the Inspector of the carelessness of virgin forests. The Professor says he is like a changing landscape. This is queer, but it is queerer still that I also have had my odd notion about the President, and I also find that I think of Sunday as I think of the whole world.'

'Get on a little faster, Syme,' said Bull; 'never mind the balloon.'

'When I first saw Sunday,' said Syme slowly, 'I only saw his back; and when I saw his back, I knew he was the worst man in the world. His neck and shoulders were brutal, like those of some apish god. His head had a stoop that was hardly human, like the stoop of an ox. In fact, I had at once the revolting fancy that this was not a man at all, but a beast dressed up in men's clothes.'

'Get on,' said Dr. Bull.

'And then the queer thing happened. I had seen his back from the street, as he sat in the balcony. Then I entered the hotel, and coming round the other side of him, saw his face in the sunlight. His face frightened me, as it did every one; but not because it was brutal, not because it was evil. On the contrary, it frightened me because it was so beautiful, because it was so good.'

'Syme,' exclaimed the Secretary, 'are you ill?'

'It was like the face of some ancient archangel, judging justly after heroic wars. There was laughter in the eyes, and in the mouth honour and sorrow. There was the same white hair, the same great, grey-clad shoulders that I had seen from behind. But when I saw him from behind I was certain he was an animal, and when I saw him in front I knew he was a god.'

'Pan,' said the Professor dreamily, 'was a god and an animal.'

'Then, and again and always,' went on Syme like a man talking to himself, 'that has been for me the mystery of Sunday, and it is also the mystery of the world. When I see the horrible back, I am sure the noble face is but a mask. When I see the face but for an instant, I know the back is only a jest. Bad is so bad, that we cannot but think good an accident; good is so good, that we feel certain that evil could be explained. But the whole came to a kind of crest yesterday when I raced Sunday for the cab, and was just behind him all the way.'

'Had you time for thinking then?' asked Ratcliffe.

'Time,' replied Syme, 'for one outrageous thought.

I was suddenly possessed with the idea that the blind, blank back of his head really was his face—an awful, eyeless face staring at me! And I fancied that the figure running in front of me was really a figure running backwards, and dancing as he ran.'

'Horrible!' said Dr. Bull, and shuddered.

'Horrible is not the word,' said Syme. 'It was exactly the worst instant of my life. And yet ten minutes afterwards, when he put his head out of the cab and made a grimace like a gargoyle, I knew that he was only like a father playing hide-and-seek with his children.'

'It is a long game,' said the Secretary, and frowned at his broken boots.

'Listen to me,' cried Syme with extraordinary emphasis. 'Shall I tell you the secret of the whole world? It is that we have only known the back of the world. We see everything from behind, and it looks brutal. That is not a tree, but the back of a tree. That is not a cloud, but the back of a cloud. Cannot you see that everything is stooping and hiding a face? If we could only get round in front——'

'Look!' cried out Bull clamorously, 'the balloon is coming down!'

There was no need to cry out to Syme, who had never taken his eyes off it. He saw the great luminous globe suddenly stagger in the sky, right itself, and then sink slowly behind the trees like a setting sun.

The man called Gogol, who had hardly spoken through all their weary travels, suddenly threw up his hands like a lost spirit.

'He is dead!' he cried. 'And now I know he was my friend—my friend in the dark!'

'Dead!' snorted the Secretary. 'You will not find

him dead easily. If he has been tipped out of the car, we shall find him rolling as a colt rolls in a field, kicking his legs for fun.'

'Clashing his hoofs,' said the Professor. 'The colts do, and so did Pan.'

'Pan again!' said Dr. Bull irritably. 'You seem to think Pan is everything.'

'So he is,' said the Professor, 'in Greek. He means everything.'

'Don't forget,' said the Secretary, looking down, 'that he also means Panic.'

Syme had stood without hearing any of the exclamations.

'It fell over there,' he said shortly. 'Let us follow it!'

Then he added with an indescribable gesture:

'Oh, if he has cheated us all by getting killed! It would be like one of his larks.'

He strode off towards the distant trees with a new energy, his rags and ribbons fluttering in the wind. The others followed him in a more footsore and dubious manner. And almost at the same moment all six men realized that they were not alone in the little field.

Across the square of turf a tall man was advancing towards them, leaning on a strange long staff like a sceptre. He was clad in a fine but old-fashioned suit with knee-breeches; its colour was that shade between blue, violet, and grey which can be seen in certain shadows of the woodland. His hair was whitish grey, and at the first glance, taken along with his knee-breeches, looked as if it was powdered. His advance was very quiet; but for the silver frost upon his head, he might have been one of the shadows of the wood.

'Gentlemen,' he said, 'my master has a carriage waiting for you in the road just by.'

'Who is your master?' asked Syme, standing quite still.

'I was told you knew his name,' said the man respectfully.

There was a silence, and then the Secretary said:

'Where is this carriage?'

'It has been waiting only a few moments,' said the stranger. 'My master has only just come home.'

Syme looked left and right upon the patch of green field in which he found himself. The hedges were ordinary hedges, the trees seemed ordinary trees; yet he felt like a man entrapped in fairy-land.

He looked the mysterious ambassador up and down, but he could discover nothing except that the man's coat was the exact colour of the purple shadows, and that the man's face was the exact colour of the red and brown and golden sky.

'Show us the place,' Syme said briefly, and without a word the man in the violet coat turned his back and walked towards a gap in the hedge, which let in suddenly the light of a white road.

As the six wanderers broke out upon this thorough-fare, they saw the white road blocked by what looked like a long row of carriages, such a row of carriages as might close the approach to some house in Park Lane. Along the side of these carriages stood a rank of splendid servants, all dressed in the grey-blue uniform, and all having a certain quality of stateliness and freedom which would not commonly belong to the servants of a gentleman, but rather to the officials and ambassadors of a great king. There were no less than six carriages waiting, one for each of the tattered and miserable band. All the attendants (as if in court-dress) wore swords, and as each man crawled into his carriage they drew them, and saluted with a sudden blaze of steel.

'What can it all mean?' asked Bull of Syme as they separated. 'Is this another joke of Sunday's?'

'I don't know,' said Syme as he sank wearily back in the cushions of his carriage; 'but if it is, it's one of the jokes you talk about. It's a good-natured one.'

The six adventurers had passed through many adventures, but not one had carried them so utterly off their feet as this last adventure of comfort. They had all become inured to things going roughly; but things suddenly going smoothly swamped them. They could not even feebly imagine what the carriages were; it was enough for them to know that they were carriages, and carriages with cushions. They could not conceive who the old man was who had led them; but it was quite enough that he had certainly led them to the carriages.

Syme drove through a drifting darkness of trees in utter abandonment. It was typical of him that while he had carried his bearded chin forward fiercely so long as anything could be done, when the whole business was taken out of his hands he fell back on the cushions in a frank collapse.

Very gradually and very vaguely he realized into what rich roads the carriage was carrying him. He saw that they passed the stone gates of what might have been a park, that they began gradually to climb a hill which, while wooded on both sides, was somewhat more orderly than a forest. Then there began to grow upon him, as upon a man slowly waking from a healthy sleep, a pleasure in everything. He felt that the hedges were what hedges should be, living walls; that a hedge is like a human army, disciplined, but all the more alive. He saw high elms behind the hedges, and vaguely thought how happy boys would be climbing there. Then his carriage took a turn of the path, and he saw suddenly and quietly, like a long, low, sunset cloud, a long, low house, mellow in the mild light of sunset. All the six friends compared notes afterwards and quarrelled; but they all agreed that in some unaccountable way the place reminded them of their boyhood. It was either this elm-top or that crooked path, it was either this scrap of orchard or that shape of a window; but each man of them declared that he could remember this place before he could remember his mother.

When the carriages eventually rolled up to a large, low, cavernous gateway, another man in the same uniform, but wearing a silver star on the grey breast of his coat, came out to meet them. This impressive person said to the bewildered Syme:

'Refreshments are provided for you in your room.'

Syme, under the influence of the same mesmeric sleep of amazement, went up the large oaken stairs after the respectful attendant. He entered a splendid suite of apartments that seemed to be designed specially for him. He walked up to a long mirror with the ordinary instinct of his class, to pull his tie straight or to smooth his hair; and there he saw the frightful figure that he was—blood running down his face from where the bough had struck him, his hair standing out like yellow rags of rank grass, his clothes torn into long, wavering tatters. At once the whole enigma sprang up, simply as the question of how he had got there, and how he was to get out again. Exactly at the same moment a man in blue, who had been appointed as his valet, said very solemnly:

'I have put out your clothes, sir.'

'Clothes!' said Syme sardonically. 'I have no clothes except these', and he lifted two long strips of his frock-coat in fascinating festoons, and made a movement as if to twirl like a ballet girl.

'My master asks me to say,' said the attendant, 'that there is a fancy dress ball to-night, and that he desires you to put on the costume that I have laid out. Meanwhile, sir, there is a bottle of Burgundy and some cold pheasant, which he hopes you will not refuse, as it is some hours before supper.'

'Cold pheasant is a good thing,' said Syme reflectively, 'and Burgundy is a spanking good thing. But really I do not want either of them so much as I want to know what the devil all this means, and what sort of costume you have got laid out for me. Where is it?'

The servant lifted off a kind of ottoman a long peacock-blue drapery, rather of the nature of a domino, on the front of which was emblazoned a large golden sun, and which was splashed here and there with flaming stars and crescents.

'You're to be dressed as Thursday, sir,' said the valet somewhat affably.

'Dressed as Thursday!' said Syme in meditation. 'It doesn't sound a warm costume.'

'Oh, yes, sir,' said the other eagerly, 'the Thursday costume is quite warm, sir. It fastens up to the chin.'

'Well, I don't understand anything,' said Syme, sighing. 'I have been used so long to uncomfortable adventures that comfortable adventures knock me out. Still, I may be allowed to ask why I should be particularly like Thursday in a green frock spotted all over with the sun and moon. Those orbs, I think, shine on other days. I once saw the moon on Tuesday, I remember.'

'Beg pardon, sir,' said the valet, 'Bible also provided for you', and with a respectful and rigid finger he pointed out a passage in the first chapter of Genesis. Syme read it wondering. It was that in which the fourth day of the week is associated with the creation of the sun and moon. Here, however, they reckoned from a Christian Sunday.

'This is getting wilder and wilder,' said Syme as, he sat down in a chair. 'Who are these people who provide cold pheasant and Burgundy, and green clothes and Bibles? Do they provide everything?'

'Yes, sir, everything,' said the attendant gravely. 'Shall I help you on with your costume?'

'Oh, hitch the bally thing on!' said Syme impatiently.

But though he affected to despise the mummery, he felt a curious freedom and naturalness in his movements as the blue and gold garment fell about him; and when he found that he had to wear a sword, it stirred a a boyish dream. As he passed out of the room he flung the folds across his shoulder with a gesture, his sword stood out at an angle, and he had all the swagger of a troubadour. For these disguises did not disguise, but reveal.

CHAPTER XV

THE ACCUSER

As Syme strode along the corridor he saw the Secretary standing at the top of a great flight of stairs. The man had never looked so noble. He was draped in a long robe of starless black, down the centre of which fell a band or broad stripe of pure white, like a single shaft of light. The whole looked like some very severe ecclesiastical vestment. There was no need for Syme to search his memory or the Bible in order to remember that the first day of creation marked the mere creation of light out of darkness. The vestment itself would alone have suggested the symbol; and Syme felt also how perfectly this pattern of pure white and black expressed the soul of the pale and austere Secretary, with his inhuman veracity and his cold frenzy, which made him so easily make war on the anarchists, and yet so easily pass for one of them. Syme was scarcely surprised to notice that, amid all the ease and hospitality of their new surroundings, this man's eyes were still stern. No smell of ale or orchards could make the Secretary cease to ask a reasonable question.

If Syme had been able to see himself, he would have realized that he, too, seemed to be for the first time himself and no one else. For if the Secretary stood for that philosopher who loves the original and formless light, Syme was a type of the poet who seeks always to make the light in special shapes, to split it up into sun and star. The philosopher may sometimes love the infinite; the poet always loves the finite. For him the great moment is not the creation of light, but the creation of the sun and moon.

As they descended the broad stairs together they overtook Ratcliffe, who was clad in spring green like a huntsman, and the pattern upon whose garment was a green tangle of trees. For he stood for that third day on which the earth and green things were made, and his square, sensible face, with its not unfriendly cynicism, seemed appropriate enough to it.

They were led out of another broad and low gateway into a very large old English garden, full of torches and bonfires, by the broken light of which a vast carnival of people were dancing in motley dress. Syme seemed to see every shape in Nature imitated in some crazy costume. There was a man dressed as a windmill with enormous sails, a man dressed as an elephant, a man dressed as a balloon; the two last, together, seemed to keep the thread of their farcical adventures. Syme even saw, with a queer thrill, one dancer dressed like an enormous hornbill, with a beak twice as big as himself—the queer bird which had fixed itself on his fancy like a living question while he was rushing down the long road at the Zoological Gardens. There were a thousand other such objects, however. There was a dancing lamp-post, a dancing apple-tree, a dancing ship. One would have thought that the untamable tune of some mad musician had set all the common objects of field and street dancing an eternal jig. And long afterwards, when Syme was middle-aged and at rest, he could never see one of those particular objects—a lamp-post, or an apple-tree, or a windmill—without thinking that it was a strayed reveller from that revel of masquerade.

On one side of this lawn, alive with dancers, was a

sort of green bank, like the terrace in such old-fashioned gardens.

Along this, in a kind of crescent, stood seven great chairs, the thrones of the seven days. Gogol and Dr. Bull were already in their seats; the Professor was just mounting to his. Gogol, or Tuesday, had his simplicity well symbolized by a dress designed upon the division of the waters, a dress that separated upon his forehead and fell to his feet, grey and silver, like a sheet of rain. The Professor, whose day was that on which the birds and fishes—the ruder forms of life—were created, had a dress of dim purple, over which sprawled goggle-eyed fishes and outrageous tropical birds, the union in him of unfathomable fancy and of doubt. Dr. Bull, the last day of Creation, wore a coat covered with heraldic animals in red and gold, and on his crest a man rampant. He lay back in his chair with a broad smile, the picture of an optimist in his element.

One by one the wanderers ascended the bank and sat in their strange seats. As each of them sat down a roar of enthusiasm rose from the carnival, such as that with which crowds receive kings. Cups were clashed and torches shaken, and feathered hats flung in the air. The men for whom these thrones were reserved were men crowned with some extraordinary laurels. But the central chair was empty.

Syme was on the left hand of it and the Secretary on the right. The Secretary looked across the empty throne at Syme, and said, compressing his lips:

'We do not know yet that he is not dead in a field.'

Almost as Syme heard the words, he saw on the sea of human faces in front of him a frightful and beautiful alteration, as if heaven had opened behind his head. But Sunday had only passed silently along the front like a shadow, and had sat in the central seat. He was draped plainly, in a pure and terrible white, and his hair was like a silver flame on his forehead.

For a long time—it seemed for hours—that huge masquerade of mankind swayed and stamped in front of them to marching and exultant music. Every couple dancing seemed a separate romance; it might be a fairy dancing with a pillar-box, or a peasant girl dancing with the moon; but in each case it was, somehow, as absurd as Alice in Wonderland, yet as grave and kind as a love-story. At last, however, the thick crowd began to thin itself. Couples strolled away into the garden-walks, or began to drift towards that end of the building where stood smoking, in huge pots like fish-kettles, some hot and scented mixtures of old ale or wine. Above all these, upon a sort of black framework on the roof of the house, roared in its iron basket a gigantic bonfire, which lit up the land for miles. It flung the homely effect of firelight over the face of vast forests of grey or brown, and it seemed to fill with warmth even the emptiness of upper night. Yet this also, after a time, was allowed to grow fainter; the dim groups gathered more and more round the great cauldrons, or passed, laughing and clattering, into the inner passages of that ancient house. Soon there were only some ten loiterers in the garden; soon only four. Finally the last stray merry-maker ran into the house whooping to his companions. The fire faded, and the slow, strong stars came out. And the seven strange men were left alone, like seven stone statues on their chairs of stone. Not one of them had spoken a word.

They seemed in no haste to do so, but heard in silence the hum of insects and the distant song of one bird. Then Sunday spoke, but so dreamily that he might have been continuing a conversation rather than beginning one.

'We will eat and drink later,' he said. 'Let us remain together a little, we who have loved each other so sadly, and have fought so long. I seem to remember only centuries of heroic war, in which you were always heroes—epic on epic, iliad on iliad, and you always brothers in arms. Whether it was but recently (for time is nothing), or at the beginning of the world, I sent you out to war. I sat in the darkness, where there is not any created thing, and to you I was only a voice commanding valour and an unnatural virtue. You heard the voice in the dark, and you never heard it again. The sun in heaven denied it, the earth and sky denied it, all human wisdom denied it. And when I met you in the daylight I denied it myself.'

Syme stirred sharply in his seat, but otherwise there was silence, and the incomprehensible went on.

'But you were men. You did not forget your secret honour, though the whole cosmos turned an engine of torture to tear it out of you. I knew how near you were to hell. I know how you, Thursday, crossed swords with King Satan, and how you, Wednesday, named me in the hour without hope.'

There was complete silence in the starlit garden, and then the black-browed Secretary, implacable, turned in his chair towards Sunday, and said in a harsh voice:

'Who and what are you?'

'I am the Sabbath,' said the other without moving. 'I am the peace of God.'

The Secretary started up, and stood crushing his costly robe in his hand.

'I know what you mean,' he cried, 'and it is exactly

that that I cannot forgive you. I know you are contentment, optimism, what do they call the thing?—an
ultimate reconciliation. Well, I am not reconciled.
If you were the man in the dark room, why were you
also Sunday, an offence to the sunlight? If you were
from the first our father and our friend, why were you
also our greatest enemy? We wept, we fled in terror;
the iron entered into our souls—and you are the peace
of God! Oh, I can forgive God His anger, though it
destroyed nations; but I cannot forgive Him His peace.'

Sunday answered not a word, but very slowly he
turned his face of stone upon Syme as if asking a
question.

'No,' said Syme, 'I do not feel fierce like that. I am
grateful to you, not only for wine and hospitality here,
but for many a fine scamper and free fight. But I
should like to know. My soul and heart are as happy
and quiet here as this old garden, but my reason is
still crying out. I should like to know.'

Sunday looked at Ratcliffe, whose clear voice said:

'It seems so *silly* that you should have been on both
sides and fought yourself.'

Bull said:

'I understand nothing, but I am happy. In fact, I am
going to sleep.'

'I am not happy,' said the Professor with his head in
his hands, 'because I do not understand. You let me
stray a little too near to hell.'

And then Gogol said, with the absolute simplicity
of a child:

'I wish I knew why I was hurt so much.'

Still Sunday said nothing, but only sat with his mighty
chin upon his hand, and gazed at the distance. Then
at last he said:

'I have heard your complaints, in order. And here I think, comes another to complain, and we will hear him also.'

The falling fire in the great cresset threw a last long gleam, like a bar of burning gold, across the dim grass. Against this fiery band were outlined in utter black the advancing legs of a black-clad figure. He seemed to have a fine close suit with knee-breeches such as that which was worn by the servants of the house, only that it was not blue, but of this absolute sable. He had, like the servants, a kind of sword by his side. It was only when he had come quite close to the crescent of the seven and flung up his face to look at them, that Syme saw, with thunder-struck clearness, that the face was the broad, almost ape-like face of his old friend Gregory, with its rank red hair and its insulting smile.

'Gregory!' gasped Syme, half-rising from his seat. 'Why, this is the real anarchist!'

'Yes,' said Gregory, with a great and dangerous restraint, 'I am the real anarchist.'

' "Now there was a day," ' murmured Bull, who seemed really to have fallen asleep, ' "when the sons of God came to present themselves before the Lord, and Satan came also among them." '

'You are right,' said Gregory, and gazed all round. 'I am a destroyer. I would destroy the world if I could.'

A sense of a pathos far under the earth stirred up in Syme, and he spoke brokenly and without sequence.

'Oh, most unhappy man,' he cried, 'try to be happy! You have red hair like your sister.'

'My red hair, like red flames, shall burn up the world,' said Gregory. 'I thought I hated everything more than common men can hate anything; but I find that I do not hate everything so much as I hate you!'

'I never hated you,' said Syme very sadly.

Then out of this unintelligible creature the last thunders broke.

'You!' he cried. 'You never hated because you never lived. I know what you are all of you, from first to last—you are the people in power! You are the police—the great fat, smiling men in blue and buttons! You are the Law, and you have never been broken. But is there a free soul alive that does not long to break you, only because you have never been broken? We in revolt talk all kind of nonsense doubtless about this crime or that crime of the Government. It is all folly! The only crime of the Government is that it governs. The unpardonable sin of the supreme power is that it is supreme. I do not curse you for being cruel. I do not curse you (though I might) for being kind. I curse you for being safe! You sit in your chairs of stone, and have never come down from them. You are the seven angels of heaven, and you have had no troubles. Oh, I could forgive you everything, you that rule all mankind, if I could feel for once that you had suffered for one hour a real agony such as I——'

Syme sprang to his feet, shaking from head to foot.

'I see everything,' he cried, 'everything that there is. Why does each thing on the earth war against each other thing? Why does each small thing in the world have to fight against the world itself? Why does a fly have to fight the whole universe? Why does a dandelion have to fight the whole universe? For the same reason that I had to be alone in the dreadful Council of the Days. So that each thing that obeys law may have the glory and isolation of the anarchist. So that each man fighting for order may be as brave and good a man as the dynamiter. So that the real lie of Satan may be flung back in the face of this blasphemer, so that by tears and torture we may earn the right to say to this man, "You lie!" No agonies can be too great to buy the right to say to this accuser, "We also have suffered."

'It is not true that we have never been broken. We have been broken upon the wheel. It is not true that we have never descended from these thrones. We have descended into hell. We were complaining of unforgettable miseries even at the very moment when this man entered insolently to accuse us of happiness. I repel the slander; we have not been happy. I can answer for every one of the great guards of Law whom he has accused. At least——'

He had turned his eyes so as to see suddenly the great face of Sunday, which wore a strange smile.

'Have you,' he cried in a dreadful voice, 'have you ever suffered?'

As he gazed, the great face grew to an awful size, grew larger than the colossal mask of Memnon, which had made him scream as a child. It grew larger and larger, filling the whole sky; then everything went black. Only in the blackness before it entirely destroyed his brain he seemed to hear a distant voice saying a commonplace text that he had heard somewhere, 'Can ye drink of the cup that I drink of?'

.   .   .   .   .

When men in books awake from a vision, they commonly find themselves in some place in which they might have fallen asleep; they yawn in a chair, or lift themselves with bruised limbs from a field. Syme's experience was something much more psychologically strange if there was indeed anything unreal, in the earthly sense, about the things he had gone through. For while he could always remember afterwards that he had swooned before the face of Sunday, he could not remember having ever come to at all. He could only remember that gradually and naturally he knew that he was and had been walking along a country lane with an easy and conversational companion. That companion had been a part of his recent drama; it was the red-haired poet Gregory. They were walking like old friends, and were in the middle of a conversation about some triviality. But Syme could only feel an unnatural buoyancy in his body and a crystal simplicity in his mind that seemed to be superior to everything that he said or did. He felt he was in possession of some impossible good news, which made every other thing a triviality, but an adorable triviality.

Dawn was breaking over everything in colours at once clear and timid; as if Nature made a first attempt at yellow and a first attempt at rose. A breeze blew so clean and sweet, that one could not think that it blew from the sky; it blew rather through some hole in the sky. Syme felt a simple surprise when he saw rising all round him on both sides of the road the red, irregular buildings of Saffron Park. He had no idea that he had walked so near London. He walked by instinct along one white road, on which early birds hopped and sang, and found himself outside a fenced garden. There he saw the sister of Gregory, the girl with the gold-red hair, cutting lilac before breakfast, with the great unconscious gravity of a girl.

THE FLYING INN

Originally published by Messrs. Methuen in 1914

TO
HUGH RIVIÈRE

CHAPTER I

A SERMON ON INNS

THE sea was a pale elfin green and the afternoon had already felt the fairy touch of evening, as a young woman with dark hair, dressed in a crinkly copper-coloured sort of dress of the artistic order, was walking rather listlessly along the parade of Pebbleswick-on-Sea, trailing a parasol and looking out upon the sea's horizon. She had a reason for looking instinctively out at the sea-line: a reason that many young women have had in the history of the world. But there was no sail in sight.

On the beach below the parade were a succession of small crowds surrounding the usual orators of the seaside; whether niggers or Socialists, whether clowns or clergymen. Here would stand a man doing something or other with paper boxes; and the holiday-makers would watch him for hours in the hope of some time knowing what it was he was doing with them. Next to him would be a man in a top-hat with a very big Bible and a very small wife, who stood silently beside him, while he fought with his clenched fist against the heresy of Milnian Sublapsarianism, so wide-spread in fashionable watering-places. It was not easy to follow him, he was so very much excited, but every now and then the words 'our Sublapsarian friends' would recur with a kind of wailing sneer. Next was a young man talking of nobody knew what (least of all himself), but apparently relying for public favour mainly on having a ring of carrots round his hat. He had more money lying in front of him than the others. Next were niggers. Next was a children's service conducted by a man with a long neck who beat time with a little wooden spade. Farther along there was an atheist in a towering rage, who pointed every now and then at the children's service; and spoke of Nature's fairest things being corrupted with the secrets of the Spanish Inquisition—by the man with the little spade, of course. The atheist (who wore a red rosette) was very withering to his own audience as well. 'Hypocrites!' he would say; and then they would throw him money. 'Dupes and dastards!' and then they would throw him more money. But between the atheist and the children's service was a little owlish old man in a red fez, weakly waving a green gamp umbrella. His face was brown and wrinkled like a walnut, his nose was of the sort we associate with Judaea, his beard was the sort of black wedge we associate rather with Persia. The young woman had never seen him before; he was a new exhibit in the now familiar museum of cranks and quacks. The young woman was one of those people in whom a real sense of humour is always at issue with a certain temperamental tendency to boredom or melancholia; and she lingered a moment, and leaned on the rail to listen.

It was fully four minutes before she could understand a word the man was saying: he spoke English with so extraordinary an accent that she supposed at first that he was talking in his own Oriental tongue. All the noises of that articulation were odd; the most marked was an extreme prolongation of the short 'u' into 'oo' as in 'poo-oot' for 'put'. Gradually the girl got used to the dialect; and began to understand the words; though some time elapsed even then before she could form any conjecture of their subject-matter. Eventually it appeared to her that he had some fad

about English civilization having been founded by the
Turks; or perhaps by the Saracens after their victory in
the Crusades. He also seemed to think that Englishmen would soon return to this way of thinking; and
seemed to be urging the spread of teetotalism as an evidence of it. The girl was the only person listening to him.

'Loo-ook,' he said, wagging a curled brown finger,
'loo-ook at you own inns' (which he pronounced as
'ince'). 'Your inns of which you write in your boo-ooks!
Those inns were not poo-oot up in the beginning to
sell ze alcoholic Christian drink. They were put up
to sell ze non-alcoholic Islamic drink. You can see
this in the names of your inns. They are Eastern
names, Asiatic names. You have a famous public-
house to which your omnibuses go on the pilgrimage.
It is called "The Elephant and Castle". That is not
an English name. It is an Asiatic name. You will
say there are Castles in England, and I will agree with
you. There is the Windsor Castle. But where,' he
cried sternly, shaking his green umbrella at the girl in
an angry oratorical triumph, 'where is the Windsor
Elephant? They have searched all Windsor Park.
No elephant!'

The girl with the dark hair smiled; and began to
think that this man was better than any of the others.
In accordance with the strange system of concurrent
religious endowment which prevails at watering-places,
she dropped a two-shilling piece into the round copper
tray beside him. With honourable and disinterested
eagerness, the old gentleman in the red fez took no
notice of this, but went on warmly, if obscurely, with
his argument.

'Then you have a place of drink in this town which
you call "The Bool".'

'We generally call it "The Bull",' said the interested young lady, with a very melodious voice.

'You have a place of drink which you call "The Bool",' he reiterated in a sort of abstract fury, 'and surely you see that this is all vary ridiculous!'

'No, no,' said the girl softly, and in deprecation.

'Why should there be a Bull,' he cried, prolonging the word in his own way. 'Why should there be a Bull in connexion with a festive locality? Who thinks about a Bull in gardens of delight? What need is there of a Bull when we watch the tulip-tinted maidens dance or pour the sparkling sherbet? You yourselves, my friends'—and he looked around radiantly, as if addressing an enormous mob—'you yourselves have a proverb, "It is not calculated to promote prosperity to have a Bull in a china-shop." Equally, my friends, it would not be calculated to promote prosperity to have a Bull in a wine-shop. All this is clear.'

He stuck his umbrella upright in the sand and struck one finger against another, like a man getting to business at last.

'It iss as clear as the sun at noon,' he said solemnly. 'It is as clear as the sun at noon that this word "Bull", which is devoid of restful and pleasurable associations, is but the corruption of another word, which possesses restful and pleasurable associations. The word is not Bull; it is the Bul-Bul!' His voice rose suddenly like a trumpet and he spread abroad his hands like the fans of a tropic palm-tree.

After this great effect he was a little more subdued and leaned gravely on his umbrella. 'You will find the same trace of Asiatic nomenclature in the names of all your English inns,' he went on. 'Nay, you will find it, I am almost certain, in all your terms in any

way connected with your revelries and your reposes.
Why, my good friends, the very name of that insidious
spirit by which you make strong your drinks is an
Arabic word: alcohol. It is obvious, is it not, that this
is the Arabic article 'Al' as in Alhambra, as in Algebra;
and we need not pause here to pursue its many appearances in connexion with your festive institutions, as
in your Alsop's beer, your Ally Sloper, and your partly
joyous institution of the Albert Memorial. Above all,
in your greatest feasting day, in your Christmas Day,
which you so erroneously suppose to be connected with
your religion. What do you say, then? Do you say
the names of the Christian nations? Do you say, 'I will
have a little France. I will have a little Ireland. I will
have a little Scotland. I will have a little Spain?"
No-o.' And the noise of the negative seemed to waggle
as does the bleating of a sheep. 'You say, "I will have
a little Turkey"; which is your name for the country
of the servants of the Prophet!'

And once more he stretched out his arms sublimely
to the east and west and appealed to earth and heaven.
The young lady, looking at the sea-green horizon with
a smile, clapped her grey gloved hands softly together
as if at a peroration. But the little old man with the
fez was far from exhausted yet.

'In reply to this you will object——' he began.

'Oh, no, no,' breathed the young lady, in a sort of
dreamy rapture. 'I don't object. I don't object the
littlest bit!'

'In reply to this you will object,' proceeded her
preceptor, 'that some inns are actually named after
the symbols of your national superstitions. You will
hasten to point out to me that the Golden Cross is
situated opposite Charing Cross; and you will expatiate

at length on King's Cross, Gerrard's Cross, and the
many crosses that are to be found in or near London.
But you must not forget'—and here he wagged his
green umbrella roguishly at the girl, as if he was going
to poke her with it—'none of you, my friends, must
forget, what a large number of Crescents there are in
London! Denmark Crescent, Mornington Crescent,
St. Mark's Crescent, St. George's Crescent, Grosvenor
Crescent, Regent's Park Crescent! Nay, Royal Crescent! And why should we forget Pelham Crescent?
Why indeed? Everywhere, I say, homage paid to the
holy symbol of the religion of the Prophet! Compare
with this network and pattern of crescents, this city almost consisting of crescents, the meagre array of crosses,
which remain to attest the ephemeral superstition to
which you were, for one weak moment, inclined.'

The crowds on the beach were rapidly thinning as
tea-time drew near. The west grew clearer and clearer
with the evening, till the sunshine seemed to have got
behind the pale sea and to be shining through, as
through a wall of thin, green glass. The very trans-
parency of sky and sea might have to this girl, for
whom the sea was the romance and the tragedy, the
hint of a sort of radiant hopelessness. The flood made
of a million emeralds was ebbing as slowly as the sun
was sinking; but the river of human nonsense flowed
on for ever.

'I will not for one moment maintain,' said the old
gentleman, 'that there are no difficulties in my case;
or that all the examples are as obviously true as those
that I have just demonstrated. No-o. It is obvious,
let us say, that "The Saracen's Head" is a corruption
of the historic truth "The Saracen is Ahead". I am
far from saying it is equally obvious that "The Green

Dragon" was originally "The Agreeing Dragoman";
though I hope to prove in my book that it is so. I will
only say here that it is su-urely more probable that one
poo-ooting himself forward to attract the wayfarer in
the desert, would compare himself to a friendly and
persuadable guide or courier, rather than to a voracious
monster. Sometimes the true origin is very hard to
trace; as in the inn that commemorates our great
Moslem warrior, Amir Ali Ben Bhoze, whom you have
so quaintly abbreviated into Admiral Benbow. Sometimes it is even more difficult for the seeker after truth.
There is a place of drink near to here called "The
Old Ship"——'

The eyes of the girl remained on the ring of the
horizon as rigid as the ring itself; but her whole face
had coloured and altered. The sands were almost
emptied by now: the atheist was as non-existent as his
God; and those who had hoped to know what was being
done to the paper boxes had gone away to their tea
without knowing it. But the young woman still leaned
on the railing. Her face was suddenly alive; and it
looked as if her body could not move.

'It should be admitted,' bleated the old man with
the green umbrella, 'that there is no literally self-
evident trace of the Asiatic nomenclature in the old
words "The Old Ship". But even here the see-eeker
after truth can poot himself in touch with facts. I
questioned the proprietor of "The Old Ship", who is,
according to such notes as I have kept, a Mr. Pumph.'

The girl's lip trembled.

'Poor old Hump!' she said. 'Why, I'd forgotten
about him. He must be very nearly as worried as I
am! I hope this man won't be silly about this! I'd
rather it weren't about this!'

'And Mr. Pumph to-old me the inn was named by a vary intimate friend of his, an Irishman who had been a Captain in the Britannic Royal Navy, but had resigned his po-ost in anger at the treatment of Ireland. Though quitting the service, he retained joost enough of the superstition of your Western sailors to wish his friend's inn to be named after his old ship. But as the name of the ship was *The United Kingdom*——'

His female pupil, if she could not exactly be said to be sitting at his feet, was undoubtedly leaning out very eagerly above his head. Amid the solitude of the sands she called out, in a loud and clear voice, 'Can you tell me the Captain's name?'

The old gentleman jumped, blinked and stared like a startled owl. Having been talking for hours as if he had an audience of thousands, he seemed suddenly very much embarrassed to find that he had even an audience of one. By this time they seemed to be almost the only human creatures along the shore; almost the only living creatures, except the seagulls. The sun, in dropping finally, seemed to have broken as a blood orange might break; and lines of blood-red light were spilt along the split, low, level skies. This abrupt and belated brilliancy took all the colour out of the man's red cap and green umbrella; but his dark figure, distinct against the sea and the sunset, remained the same, save that it was more agitated than before.

'The name,' he said, 'the Captain's name. I—I understood it was Dalroy. But what I wish to indicate, what I wish to expound, is that here again the seeker after truth can find the connexion of his ideas. It was explained to me by Mr. Pumph that he was re-arranging the place of festivity, in no inconsiderable proportion because of the anticipated return of the

Captain in question, who had, as it appeared, taken service in some not very large navy, but had left it and was coming home. Now mark, all of you, my friends,' he said to the seagulls, 'that even here the chain of logic holds.'

He said it to the seagulls because the young lady, after staring at him with starry eyes for a moment and leaning heavily on the railing, had turned her back and disappeared rapidly into the twilight. After her hasty steps had fallen silent there was no other noise than the faint but powerful purring of the now distant sea, the occasional shriek of a sea-bird, and the continuous sound of a soliloquy.

'Mark, all of you,' continued the man, flourishing his green umbrella so furiously that it almost flew open like a green flag unfurled, and then striking it deep in the sand, in the sand in which his fighting fathers had so often struck their tents. 'Mark, all of you, this marvellous fact! That when, being for a time astonished—embarrassed—brought up, as you would say, short—by the absence of any absolute evidence of Eastern influence in the phrase "The Old Ship", I inquired from what country the Captain was returning, Mr. Pumph said to me in solemnity, "From Turkey". From Turkey! From the nearest country of the Religion! I know men say it is not our country. What does it matter where we come from, if we carry a message from Paradise? With a great galloping of horses we carry it, and have no time to stop in places. But what we bring is the only creed that has regarded what you will call in your great words the virginity of a man's reason, that has put no man higher than a prophet, and has respected the solitude of God.'

And again he spread his arms out, as if addressing a mass meeting of millions, all alone on the dark seashore.

CHAPTER II

THE END OF OLIVE ISLAND

THE great sea-dragon of the changing colours that
wriggles round the world like a chameleon was pale
green as it washed on Pebbleswick, but strong blue
where it broke on the Ionian Isles. One of the innumerable islets, hardly more than a flat white rock
in the azure expanse, was celebrated as the Isle of
Olives; not because it was rich in such vegetation,
but because, by some freak of soil or climate, two or
three olives grew there to an unparalleled height.
Even in the full heat of the South it is very unusual
for an olive-tree to grow up any taller than a small
pear-tree; but the three olives that stood up, signals
on this sterile place, might well be mistaken, except
for the shape, for moderate-sized pines or larches of
the North. It was also connected with some ancient
Greek legend about Pallas, the patroness of the olive;
for all that sea was alive with the first fairyland of
Hellas; and from the platform of marble under the
olive-tree could be seen the grey outline of Ithaca.

On the island and under the trees was a table set in
the open air and covered with papers and inkstands.
At the table were sitting four men, two in uniforms,
and two in plain black clothes. Aides-de-camp,
equerries, and such persons stood in a group in the
background; and behind them a string of two or three
silent battleships lay along the sea. For peace was
being given to Europe.

There had just come to an end the long agony of one
of the many unsuccessful efforts to break the strength

of Turkey and save the small Christian tribes. There had been many other such meetings in the later phases of the matter as, one after another, the smaller nations gave up the struggle, or the greater nations came in to coerce them. But the interested parties had now dwindled to these four. For the Powers of Europe, being entirely agreed on the necessity for peace on a Turkish basis, were content to leave the last negotiations to England and Germany, who could be trusted to enforce it; there was a representative of the Sultan, of course; and there was a representative of the only enemy of the Sultan who had not hitherto come to terms.

For one tiny power had alone carried on the war month after month and with a tenacity and temporary success that was a new nine days' marvel every morning. An obscure and scarcely recognized prince, calling himself the 'King of Ithaca', had filled the Eastern Mediterranean with exploits that were not unworthy of the audacious parallel that the name of his island suggested. Poets could not help asking if it were Odysseus come again; patriotic Greeks, even if they themselves had been forced to lay down their arms, could not help feeling curious as to what Greek race or name was boasted by the new heroic royal house. It was therefore with some amusement that the world at last discovered that the descendant of Ulysses was a cheeky Irish adventurer named Patrick Dalroy; who had once been in the English Navy, had got into a quarrel through his Fenian sympathies and resigned his commission. Since then he had seen many adventures in many uniforms; and always got himself or some one else into hot water with an extraordinary mixture of cynicism and quixotry. In his fantastic little kingdom,

of course, he had been his own General, his own
Admiral, his own Foreign Secretary, and his own
Ambassador; but he was always careful to follow the
wishes of his people in the essentials of peace and war;
and it was at their direction that he had come to lay
down his sword at last. Besides his professional skill,
he was chiefly famous for his enormous bodily strength
and stature. It is the custom in newspapers nowadays
to say that mere barbaric muscular power is valueless
in modern military actions; but this view may be as
much exaggerated as its opposite. In such wars as
these of the Near East, where whole populations are
slightly armed and personal assault is common, a
leader who can defend his head often has a real advantage; and it is not true, even in a general way, that
strength is of no use. This was admitted by Lord
Ivywood, the English Minister, who was pointing out
in detail to King Patrick the hopeless superiority of
the light pattern of Turkish field gun; and the King of
Ithaca, remarking that he was quite convinced, said
he would take it with him, and ran away with it under
his arm. It would be conceded by the greatest of the
Turkish warriors, the terrifying Oman Pasha, equally
famous for his courage in war and his cruelty in peace;
but who carried on his brow a scar from Patrick's
sword, taken after three hours' mortal combat—and
taken without spite or shame, be it said, for the Turk
is always at his best in that game. Nor would the
quality be doubted by Mr. Hart, a financial friend of
the German Minister, whom Patrick Dalroy, after
asking him which of his front windows he would prefer
to be thrown into, threw into his bedroom window on
the first floor with so considerate an exactitude that
he alighted on the bed where he was in a position to

receive any medical attention. But, when all is said, one muscular Irish gentleman on an island cannot fight all Europe for ever, and he came, with a kind of gloomy good humour, to offer the terms now dictated to him by his adopted country. He could not even knock all the diplomatists down (for which he possessed both the power and the inclination), for he realized, with the juster part of his mind, that they were only obeying orders, as he was. So he sat heavily and sleepily at the little table; in the green and white uniform of the navy of Ithaca (invented by himself); a big bull of a man, monstrously young for his size, with a bull neck and two blue bull's eyes for eyes, and red hair rising so steadily off his scalp that it looked as if his head had caught fire: as some said it had.

The most dominant person present was the great Oman Pasha himself, with his strong face starved by the asceticism of war, his hair and moustache seeming rather blasted with lightning than blanched with age; a red fez on his head, and between the red fez and the moustache a scar at which the King of Ithaca did not look. His eyes had an awful lack of expression.

Lord Ivywood, the English Minister, was probably the handsomest man in England; save that he was almost colourless both in hair and complexion. Against that blue marble sea he might almost have been one of its old marble statues that are faultless in line but show nothing but shades of grey or white. It seemed a mere matter of the luck of lighting whether his hair looked dull silver or pale brown; and his splendid mask never changed in colour or expression. He was one of the last of the old Parliamentary orators; and yet he was probably a comparatively young man: he could make anything he had to mention blossom into verbal beauty:

yet his face remained dead while his lips were alive.
He had little old-fashioned ways, as out of older
Parliaments; for instance, he would always stand up,
as in a senate, to speak to those three other men, alone
on a rock in the ocean.

In all this he perhaps appeared more personal in
contrast to the man sitting next to him, who never
spoke at all but whose face seemed to speak for him.
This man was Dr. Gluck, the German Minister, whose
face had nothing German about it; neither the German
vision nor the German sleep. His face was as vivid
as a highly coloured photograph and altered like a
cinema; but his scarlet lips never moved in speech.
His almond eyes seemed to shine with all the shifting
fires of the opal; his small curled black moustache
seemed sometimes almost to twist itself afresh, like
a live black snake: but there came from him no sound.
He put a paper in front of Lord Ivywood. Lord
Ivywood took a pair of eyeglasses to read it, and
looked ten years older by the act.

It was merely a statement of agenda; of the few last
things to be settled at this last conference. The first
item ran:

'The Ithacan Ambassador asks that the girls taken
to harems after the capture of Pylos be restored to
their families. This cannot be granted.' Lord Ivywood
rose. The mere beauty of his voice startled every one
who had not heard it before.

'Your Excellencies and gentlemen,' he said, 'a statesman to whose policy I by no means assent, but to whose
historic status I could not conceivably aspire, has
familiarized you with a phrase about peace with
honour. But when we have to celebrate a peace
be.ween such historic soldiers as Oman Pasha and His

Majesty the King of Ithaca, I think we may say that
it is peace with glory.'

He paused for half an instant; yet even the silence
of sea and rock seemed full of multitudinous applause,
so perfectly had the words been spoken.

'I think there is but one thought among us, whatever
our many just objections through these long and
harassing months of negotiation—I think there is but
one thought now. That the peace may be as full as
the war—that the peace may be as fearless as the war.'

Once more he paused an instant; and felt a phantom
clapping, as it were, not from the hands but the heads
of men. He went on:

'If we are to leave off fighting, we may surely leave
off haggling. A statute of limitations or, if you will, an
amnesty, is surely proper when so sublime a peace
seals so sublime a struggle. And if there be anything
in which an old diplomatist may advise you, I would
most strongly say this: that there should be no new
disturbance of whatever amicable or domestic ties have
been formed during this disturbed time. I will admit
I am sufficiently old-fashioned to think any interference
with the interior life of the family a precedent of no
little peril. Nor will I be so illiberal as not to extend
to the ancient customs of Islam what I would extend
to the ancient customs of Christianity. A suggestion
had been brought before us that we should enter into
a renewed war or recrimination as to whether certain
women have left their homes with or without their
consent. I can conceive no controversy more perilous
to begin or more impossible to conclude. I will venture
to say that I express all your thoughts when I say
that, whatever wrongs may have been wrought on
either side, the homes, the marriages, the family

arrangements of this great Ottoman Empire shall remain as they are to-day.'

No one moved except Patrick Dalroy, who put his hand on his sword-hilt for a moment and looked at them all with bursting eyes; then his hand fell and he laughed out loud and sudden.

Lord Ivywood took no notice, but picked up the agenda paper again, and again fitted on the glasses that made him look older. He read the second item— needless to say, not aloud. The German Minister with the far from German face had written this note for him:

'Booth Coote and the Bernsteins insist there must be Chinese for the marble. Greeks cannot be trusted in the quarries just now.'

'But while,' continued Lord Ivywood, 'we desire these fundamental institutions, such as the Moslem family, to remain as they are even at this moment, we do not assent to social stagnation. Nor do we say for one moment that the great tradition of Islam is capable alone of sustaining the necessities of the Near East. But I would seriously ask your Excellencies, why should we be so vain as to suppose that the only cure for the Near East is of necessity the Near West? If new ideas are needed, if new blood is needed, would it not be more natural to appeal to those most living, those most laborious, civilizations which form the vast reserve of the Orient. Asia in Europe, if my friend Oman Pasha, will allow me the criticism, has hitherto been Asia in arms. May we not yet see Asia in Europe and yet Asia in peace? These at least are the reasons which lead me to consent to a scheme of colonization.'

Patrick Dalroy sprang erect, pulling himself out of his seat by clutching at an olive-branch above his head. He steadied himself by putting one hand on the trunk of the tree; and simply stared at them all. There fell on him the huge helplessness of mere physical power. He could throw them into the sea; but what good would that do? More men on the wrong side would be accredited to the diplomatic campaign; and the only man on the right side would be discredited for anything. He shook the branching olive-tree above him in his fury. But he did not for one moment disturb Lord Ivywood, who had just read the third item on his private agenda ('Oman Pasha insists on the destruction of the vineyards'), and was by this time engaged in a peroration which afterwards became famous and may be found in many rhetorical text-books and primers. He was well into the middle of it before Dalroy's rage and wonder allowed him to follow the words.

'. . . do we indeed owe nothing,' the diplomatist was saying, 'to that gesture of high refusal in which, so many centuries ago, the great Arabian mystic put the wine-cup from his lips? Do we owe nothing to the long vigil of a valiant race, the long fast by which they have testified against the venomous beauty of the vine? Ours is an age when men come more and more to see that the creeds hold treasures for each other, that each religion has a secret for its neighbour, that faith unto faith uttereth speech and church unto church showeth knowledge. If it be true, and I claim again the indulgence of Oman Pasha when I say I think it is true, that we of the West have brought some light to Islam in the matter of the preciousness of peace and of civil order, may we not say that Islam, in answer, shall give us peace in a thousand homes, and encourage us to cut down that curse that has done so much to thwart and madden the virtues of Western Christendom? Already in my own country the orgies that made horrible the nights of the noblest families are no more. Already the legislature takes more and more sweeping action to deliver the populace from the bondage of the all-destroying drug. Surely the Prophet of Mecca is reaping his harvest; the cession of the disputed vineyards to the greatest of his champions is of all acts the most appropriate to this day; to this happy day that may yet deliver the East from the curse of war and the West from the curse of wine. The gallant prince who meets us here at last, to offer an olive-branch even more glorious than his sword, may well have our sympathy if he himself views the cession with some sentimental regret; but I have little doubt that he also will live to rejoice in it at last. And I would remind you that it is not the vine alone that has been the sign of the glory of the South. There is another sacred tree unstained by loose and violent memories, guiltless of the blood of Pentheus or of Orpheus and the broken lyre. We shall pass from this place in a little while as all things pass and perish:

> 'Far called, our navies melt away,
>   On dune and headland sinks the fire,
> And all our pomp of yesterday
>   Is one with Nineveh and Tyre.'

But so long as sun can shine and soil can nourish, happier men and women after us shall look on this lonely islet and it shall tell its own story: for they shall see these three holy olive-trees lifted in everlasting benediction, over the humble spot out of which came the peace of the world.'

The other two men were staring at Patrick Dalroy; his hand had tightened on the tree, and a giant billow of effort went over his broad breast. A small stone jerked itself out of the ground at the foot of the tree, as if it were a grasshopper jumping: and then the coiled roots of the olive-tree rose very slowly out of the earth like the limbs of a dragon lifting itself from sleep.

'I offer an olive-branch,' said the King of Ithaca, totteringly leaning out the loose tree so that its vast shadow, much larger than itself, fell across the whole council. 'An olive-branch,' he gasped, 'more glorious than my sword. Also heavier.'

Then he made another effort and tossed it into the sea below. The German who was no German had put his arm up in apprehension when the shadow fell across him. Now he got up and edged away from the table, seeing that the wild Irishman was tearing up the second tree. This one came out more easily; and before he flung it after the first, he stood with it a moment, looking like a man juggling with a tower.

Lord Ivywood showed more firmness; but he rose in tremendous remonstrance. Only the Turkish Pasha still sat with blank eyes, immovable. Dalroy rent out the last tree and hurled it, leaving the island bare.

'There!' said Dalroy, when the third and last olive had splashed in the tide. 'Now I will go. I have seen something to-day that is worse than death: and the name of it is Peace.'

Oman Pasha rose and held out his hand.

'You are right,' he said in French, 'and I hope we meet again in the only life that is a good life. Where are you going now?'

'I am going,' said Dalroy dreamily, 'to "The Old Ship".'

'Do you mean,' asked the Turk, 'that you are going back to the warships of the English King?'

'No,' answered the other. 'I am going back to

"The Old Ship" that is behind apple-trees by Pebbles-wick; where the Ule flows among the trees. I fear I shall never see you there.'

After an instant's hesitation he wrung the red hand of the great tyrant and walked to his boat without a glance at the diplomatists.

CHAPTER III

THE SIGN OF 'THE OLD SHIP'

Upon few of the children of men has the surname of Pump fallen, and of these few have been maddened into naming a child Humphrey in addition to it. To such extremity, however, had the parents of the inn-keeper at 'The Old Ship' proceeded; that their son might come at last to be called 'Hump' by his dearest friends and 'Pumph' by an aged Turk with a green umbrella. All this, or all he knew of it, he endured with a sour smile; for he was of a stoical temper.

Mr. Humphrey Pump stood outside his inn, which was almost on the sea-shore, screened only by one line of apple-trees, dwarfed, twisted, and salted by the sea air; but in front of it was a highly banked bowling green; and beside it the land sank abruptly; so that one very steep, sweeping road vanished into the depth and mystery of taller trees. Mr. Pump was standing imme-diately under his inn sign: which stood erect in the turf; a wooden pole painted white and suspending a square wooden board, also painted white, but further decorated with a highly grotesque blue ship, such as a child might draw, but into which Mr. Pump's patriotism had insinuated a disproportionately large red St. George's cross.

Mr. Humphrey Pump was a man of middle size, with very broad shoulders, wearing a sort of shooting suit with gaiters. Indeed, he was engaged at the moment in cleaning and reloading a double-barrelled gun, a short but powerful weapon which he had invented, or at least improved, himself: and which, though eccentric enough as compared with latest scientific arms, was neither clumsy nor necessarily out of date. For Pump was one of those handy men who seem to have a hundred hands, like Briareus: he made nearly everything for himself, and everything in his house was slightly different from the same thing in any one else's house. He was also as cunning as Pan or a poacher in everything affecting every bird or fish, every leaf or berry in the woods. His mind was a rich soil of subconscious memories and traditions; and he had a curious kind of gossip so allusive as to almost amount to reticence; for he always took it for granted that every one knew his county and its tales as intimately as he did; so he would mention the most mysterious and amazing things without relaxing a muscle of his face, which seemed to be made of knotted wood. His dark brown hair ended in two rudimentary side-whiskers, giving him a slightly horsy look, but in the old-fashioned sportsman's style. His smile was rather wry and crabbed, but his brown eyes were kindly and soft. He was very English.

As a rule his movements, though quick, were cool; but on this occasion he put down the gun on the table outside the inn in a rather hurried manner and came forward dusting his hands in an unusual degree of animation and even deference. Beyond the goblin-green apple-trees and against the sea had appeared the tall, slight figure of a girl in a dress about the colour of copper and a large shady hat. Under the hat her face was grave and beautiful, though rather swarthy. She shook hands with Mr. Pump; then he very ceremoniously put a chair for her and called her 'Lady Joan'.

'I thought I would like a look at the old place,' she

said. 'We have had some happy times here when we were boys and girls. I suppose you hardly see any of your old friends now.'

'Very little,' answered Pump, rubbing his short whisker reflectively. 'Lord Ivywood's become quite a Methody parson, you know, since he took the Place; he's pulling down beershops right and left. And Mr. Charles was sent to Australia for lying down flat at the funeral. Pretty stiff, I call it; but the old lady was a terror.'

'Do you ever hear,' asked Lady Joan Brett carelessly, 'of that Irishman, Captain Dalroy?'

'Yes, more often than from the rest,' answered the innkeeper. 'He seems to have done wonders in this Greek business. Ah! He was a sad loss to the Navy!'

'They insulted his country,' said the girl, looking at the sea with a heightened colour. 'After all, Ireland was his country; and he had a right to resent its being spoken of like that.'

'And when they found he'd painted him green,' went on Mr. Pump.

'Painted him what?' asked Lady Joan.

'Painted Captain Dawson green,' continued Mr. Pump in colourless tones. 'Captain Dawson said green was the colour of Irish traitors, so Dalroy painted him green. It was a great temptation, no doubt, with this fence being painted at the same time and the pail of stuff there: but of course it had a very prejudicial effect on his professional career.'

'What an extraordinary story!' said the staring Lady Joan, breaking into a rather joyless laugh. 'It must go down among your county legends. I never heard that version before. Why, it might be the origin of "The Green Man", over there by the town.'

'Oh, no,' said Pump simply. 'That's been there since before Waterloo times. Poor old Noyle had it until they put him away. You remember old Noyle, Lady Joan? Still alive, I hear, and still writing love-letters to Queen Victoria. Only of course they aren't posted now.'

'Have you heard from your Irish friend lately?' asked the girl, keeping a steady eye on the skyline.

'Yes, I had a letter last week,' answered the inn-keeper. 'It seems not impossible that he may return to England. He's been acting for one of these Greek places, and the negotiations seem to be concluded. It's a queer thing that his lordship himself was the English Minister in charge of them.'

'You mean Lord Ivywood,' said Lady Joan rather coldly. 'Yes, he has a great career before him evidently.'

'I wish he hadn't got his knife into us so much,' chuckled Pump. 'I don't believe there'll be an inn left in England. But the Ivywoods were always cranky. It's only fair to him to remember his grand-father.'

'I think it's very ungallant on your part,' said Lady Joan, with a mournful smile, 'to ask a lady to remember his grandfather.'

'You know what I mean, Lady Joan,' said he, most good-humouredly. 'And I never was hard on the case myself; we all have our little ways. I shouldn't like it done to my pig; but I don't see why a man shouldn't have his own pig in his own pew with him if he likes it. It wasn't a free seat. It was the family pew.'

Lady Joan broke out laughing again. 'What horrible things you do seem to have heard of,' she said. 'Well, I must be going, Mr. Hump—I mean Mr. Pump—

I used to call you Hump. . . . Oh, Hump, do you think any of us will ever be happy again?'

'I suppose it rests with Providence,' he said, looking at the sea.

'Oh, do say Providence again!' cried the girl. 'It's as good as *Masterman Ready*.'

With which inconsequent words she betook herself again to the path by the apple-trees and walked back by the sea-front to Pebbleswick.

The inn of 'The Old Ship' lay a little beyond the old fishing village of Pebbleswick; and that again was separated by an empty half-mile or so from the new watering-place of Pebbleswick-on-Sea. But the dark-haired lady walked steadily along the sea-front, on a sort of parade which had been stretched out to east and west in the insane optimism of watering-places, and as she approached the more crowded part looked more and more carefully at the groups on the beach. Most of them were much the same as she had seen more than a month before. The seekers after truth (as the man in the fez would say) who assembled daily to find out what the man was doing with the paper boxes, had not found out yet; neither had they wearied of their intellectual pilgrimage. Pennies were still thrown to the thundering atheist in acknowledgment of his incessant abuse; and this was all the more mysterious because the crowd was obviously indifferent, and the atheist was obviously sincere. The man with the long neck who led Low Church hymns with a little wooden spade had indeed disappeared, for children's services of this kind are generally a moving feast; but the man whose only claim consisted of carrots round his hat was still there; and seemed to have even more money than before. But Lady Joan could see no sign of the little old man in the fez. She could only suppose that he had failed entirely; and, being in a bitter mood, she told herself bitterly that he had sunk out of sight precisely because there was in his rubbish a touch of unearthly and insane clear-headedness of which all these vulgar idiots were incapable. She did not confess to herself consciously that what had made both the man in the fez and the man at the inn interesting was the subject of which they had spoken.

As she walked on rather wearily along the parade she caught sight of a girl in black with faint fair hair and a tremulous intelligent face which she was sure she had seen before. Pulling together all her aristo-cratic training for the remembering of middle-class people, she managed to remember that this was a Miss Browning who had done typewriting work for her a year or two before; and immediately went forward to greet her, partly out of genuine good-nature and partly as a relief from her own rather dreary thoughts. Her tone was so seriously frank and friendly that the lady in black summoned the social courage to say:

'I've so often wanted to introduce you to my sister, who's much cleverer than I am, though she does live at home; which I suppose is very old-fashioned. She knows all sorts of intellectual people. She is talking to one of them, now; this Prophet of the Moon that every one's talking about. Do let me introduce you.'

Lady Joan Brett had met many prophets of the moon and of other things. But she had the spon-taneous courtesy which redeems the vices of her class, and she followed Miss Browning to a seat on the parade. She greeted Miss Browning's sister with glowing politeness; and this may really be counted to her credit; for she had great difficulty in looking at Miss Browning's sister at all. For on the seat beside her, still in a red fez but in a brilliantly new black frock-coat and every appearance of prosperity, sat the old gentleman who had lectured on the sands about the inns of England.

'He lectured at our Ethical Society,' whispered Miss Browning, 'on the word "alcohol". Just on the word "alcohol". He was perfectly thrilling. All about Arabia and Algebra, you know, and how everything comes from the East. You really would be interested.'

'I am interested,' said Lady Joan.

'Poot it to yourselfs,' the man in the fez was saying to Miss Browning's sister, 'joost what zort of meaning the names of your ince can have if they do not commemorate the unlimitable influence of Islam. There is a vary populous inn in London, one of the most distinguished, one of the most of the centre, and it is called "The Horseshoe". Now, my friends, why should any one commemorate a horseshoe? It iss but an appendage to a creature more interesting than itself. I have already demonstrated to you that the very fact that you have in your town a place of drink called "The Bool"——'

'I should like to ask——' began Lady Joan suddenly.

'A place of drink called "The Bool",' went on the man in the fez deaf to all distractions, 'and I have urged that the Bool is a disturbing thought, while the Bul-bul is a reassuring thought. But even you, my friends, would not name a place after the ring in the Bool's nose and not after the Bool. Why then name an equivalent place after the shoo, the mere shoo, upon a horse's hoof, and not after the noble horse? Surely it is clear, surely it is evident, that the term "horseshoe" is a cryptic term, an esoteric term, a term made during the days when the ancient Moslem faith of this English country was oppressed by the passing superstition of the Galilaeans. That bent shape, that duplex curving shape, which you call "Horseshoe", is it not clearly the Crescent?'—and he cast his arms wide as he had done on the sands—'the Crescent of the Prophet of the only God?'

'I should like to ask,' began Lady Joan again, 'how you would explain the name of the inn called "The Green Man", just behind that row of houses.'

'Exactly! exactly!' cried the Prophet of the Moon, in almost insane excitement. 'The seeker after truth could not at all probably find a more perfect example of these principles. My friends, how could there be a green man? You are acquainted with green grass, with green leaves, with green cheese, with green chartreuse. I ask if any of you, however wide her social circle, has ever been acquainted with a green man. Surely, surely, it is evident, my friends, that this is an imperfect version, an abbreviated version, of the original words. What can be clearer than that the original expression, the reasonable expression, the highly historical expression, was "the green-turban'd man", in allusion to the well-known uniform of the descendants of the Prophet? "Turban'd" surely is just the sort of word, exactly the sort of foreign and unfamiliar word, that might easily be slurred over and ultimately suppressed.'

'There is a legend in these parts,' said Lady Joan steadily, 'that a great hero, hearing the colour that was sacred to his holy island insulted, really poured it over his enemy for a reply.'

'A legend! A fable!' cried the man in the fez, with another radiant and rational expansion of the hands. 'Is it not evident that no such thing can have really happened?'

'Oh, yes—it really happened,' said the young lady softly. 'There is not much to comfort one in this world; but there are some things. Oh, it really happened.'

And taking a graceful farewell of the group, she resumed her rather listless walk along the parade.

CHAPTER IV

THE INN FINDS WINGS

Mr. Humphrey Pump stood in front of his inn once more; the cleaned and loaded gun lay on the table, and the white sign of the Ship still swung in the slight sea-breeze over his head; but his leatherish features were knotted over a new problem. He held two letters in his hand, letters of a very different sort, but letters that pointed to the same difficult problem. The first ran:

'Dear Hump,

'I am so bothered that I simply must call you by the old name again. You understand I've got to keep in with my people: Lord Ivywood is a sort of cousin of mine, and for that and some other reasons, my poor old mother would just die if I offended him. You know her heart is weak; you know everything there is to know in this county. Well, I only write to warn you that something is going to be done against your dear old inn. I don't know what this country's coming to. Only a month or two ago I saw a shabby old pantaloon on the beach with a green gamp, talking the craziest stuff you ever heard in your life. Three weeks ago I heard he was lecturing at Ethical Societies—whatever they are—for a handsome salary. Well, when I was last at Ivywood—I must go because Mamma likes it—there was the living lunatic again, in evening-dress, and talked about by people who really *know*. I mean who know better.

'Lord Ivywood is entirely under his influence and thinks him the greatest prophet the world has ever seen. And Lord Ivywood is not a fool; one can't help admiring him. Mamma, I think, wants me to do more than admire him. I am telling you everything, Hump, because I think perhaps this is the last honest letter I shall ever write in the world. And I warn you seriously that Lord Ivywood is *sincere*, which is perfectly terrible. He will be the biggest English statesman, and he does really mean to ruin— the old ships. If ever you see me here again taking part in such work, I hope you may forgive me.

'Somebody we mentioned, whom I shall never see again, I leave to your friendship. It is the second best thing I can give, and I am not sure it may not be better than the first would have been. Good-bye.

'J. B.'

This letter seemed to distress Mr. Pump rather than puzzle him. The second letter seemed to puzzle him more than it distressed him. It ran as follows:

'SIR,

'The Committee of the Imperial Commission of Liquor Control is directed to draw your attention to the fact that you have disregarded the Committee's communication under sections 5A of the Act for the Regulation of Places of Public Entertainment; and that you are now under section 47C of the Act amending the Act for the Regulation of Places of Public Entertainment aforesaid. The charges on which prosecution will be founded are as follows:

'(1) Violation of sub-section 23*f* of the Act, which enacts that no pictorial signs shall be exhibited before premises of less than the rateable value of £400 per annum.

'(2) Violation of sub-section 113*d* of the Act, which enacts that no liquor containing alcohol shall be sold in any inn, hotel, tavern, or public-house, except when demanded under a medical certificate from one of the doctors licensed by the State Medical Council, or in the specially excepted cases of Claridge's Hotel and the Criterion Bar, where urgency has already been proved.

'As you have failed to acknowledge previous communications on this subject, this is to warn you that legal steps will be taken immediately.

'We are yours truly,

'IVYWOOD, *President.*

'J. LEVESON, *Secretary.*

Mr. Humphrey Pump sat down at the table outside this inn and whistled in a way which, combined with his little whiskers, made him for the moment seem literally like an ostler. Then the very real wit and learning he had returned slowly into his face, and with his warm brown eyes he considered the cold grey sea. There was not much to be got out of the sea. Humphrey Pump might drown himself in the sea; which would be better for Humphrey Pump than being finally separated from 'The Old Ship'. England might be sunk under the sea; which would be better for England than never again having such places as 'The Old Ship'. But these were not serious remedies nor rationally attainable; and Pump could only feel that the sea had simply warped him as it had warped his apple-trees. The sea was a dreary business altogether. There was only one figure walking on the sands. It was only when the figure drew nearer and nearer and grew to more than human size, that he sprang to his feet with a cry. Also the level light of morning lit the man's hair, and it was red.

The late King of Ithaca came casually and slowly up the slope of the beach that led to 'The Old Ship'. He had landed in a boat from a battleship that could still be seen near the horizon, and he still wore the astounding uniform of sea-green and silver which he had himself invented as that of a navy that had never existed very much, and which now did not exist at all. He had a straight naval sword at his side; for the terms of his capitulation had never required him to surrender it; and inside the uniform and beside the sword there was what there always had been, a big and rather bewildered man with rough red hair, whose misfortune was that he had good brains, but that his bodily strength and bodily passions were a little too strong for his brains.

He had flung his crashing weight on the chair outside the inn before the innkeeper could find words to express his astounded pleasure in seeing him. His first words were, 'Have you got any rum?'

Then, as if feeling that his attitude needed explanation, he added, 'I suppose I shall never be a sailor again after to-night. So I must have some rum.'

Humphrey Pump had a talent for friendship and understood his old friend. He went into the inn without a word; and came back idly pushing or rolling with an alternate foot (as if he were playing football with two footballs at once) two objects that rolled very easily. One was a big keg or barrel of rum and the other a great solid drum of a cheese. Among his

thousand other technical tricks he had a way of tapping
a cask without a tap, or anything that could impair
its revolutionary or revolving qualities. He was
feeling for the instrument with which he solved such
questions in his pocket, when his Irish friend suddenly
sat bolt upright, as one startled out of sleep, and spoke
with his strongest and most unusual brogue.

'Oh, thank you, Hump, a thousand times; and I
don't think I really want anything to drink at arl.
Now I know I can have it I don't seem to want it at
arl. But hwhat I do want'—and he suddenly dashed
his big fist on the little table so that one of its legs
leapt and nearly snapped—'hwhat I do want is some
sort of account of what's happening in this England
of yours that shan't be just obviously rubbish.'

'Ah,' said Pump, fingering the two letters thoughtfully. 'And what do you mean by rubbish?'

'I carl it rubbish,' cried Patrick Dalroy, 'when
ye put the Koran into the Bible and not the Apocrypha;
and I carl it rubbish when a mad person's allowed
to propose to put a crescent on St. Paul's Cathedral.
I know the Turks are our allies now; but they often
were before, and I never heard that Palmerston or
Colin Campbell had any truck with such trash.'

'Lord Ivywood is very enthusiastic, I know,' said
Pump, with a restrained amusement. 'He was saying
only the other day at the Flower Show here that the
time had come for a full unity between Christianity
and Islam.'

'Something called Chrislam perhaps,' said the
Irishman, with a moody eye. He was gazing across
the grey and purple woodlands that stretched below
them at the back of the inn; and into which the steep
white road swept downwards and disappeared. The

steep road looked like the beginning of an adventure; and he was an adventurer.

'But you exaggerate, you know,' went on Pump, polishing his gun, 'about the crescent on St. Paul's. It wasn't exactly that. What Dr. Moole suggested, I think, was some sort of double emblem, you know combining cross and crescent——'

'And called the Croscent,' muttered Dalroy.

'And you can't call Dr. Moole a parson either,' went on Mr. Humphrey Pump, polishing industriously. 'Why, they say he's a sort of atheist, or what they call an agnostic, like Squire Brunton who used to bite elm-trees by Marley. The grand folks have these fashions, Captain, but they've never lasted long that I know of.'

'I think it's serious this time,' said his friend, shaking his big red head. 'This is the last inn on this coast, and will soon be the last inn in England. Do you remember "The Saracen's Head", Plumlea, along the shore there?'

'I know,' assented the innkeeper. 'My aunt was there when he hanged his mother; but it's a charming place.'

'I passed there just now; and it has been destroyed,' said Dalroy.

'Destroyed by fire?' asked Pump, pausing in his gun-scrubbing.

'No,' said Dalroy, 'destroyed by lemonade. They've taken away its licence, or whatever you call it. I made a song about it, which I'll sing to you now.' And with an astounding air of suddenly revived spirits he roared in a voice like thunder the following verses, to a simple but spirited tune of his own invention:

'"The Saracen's Head" looks down the lane,
Where we shall never drink wine again,
For the wicked old women who feel well-bred
Have turned to a tea-shop "The Saracen's Head".

"The Saracen's Head" out of Araby came,
King Richard riding in arms like flame,
And where he established his folk to be fed
He set up a spear—and the Saracen's Head.

But "The Saracen's Head" outlived the Kings,
It thought and it thought of most horrible things,
Of Health and of Soap and of Standard Bread,
And of Saracen drinks at "The Saracen's Head".'

'Hullo!' cried Pump, with another low whistle. 'Why, here comes his lordship. And I suppose that young man in the goggles is a Committee or something.'

'Let him come,' said Dalroy, and continued in a yet more earthquake bellow:

'So "The Saracen's Head" fulfils its name,
They drink no wine—a ridiculous game—
And I shall wonder until I'm dead,
How it ever came into the Saracen's Head.'

As the last echo of this lyrical roar rolled away among the apple-trees, and down the steep white road into the woods, Captain Dalroy leaned back in his chair and nodded good-humouredly to Lord Ivywood, who was standing on the lawn with his usual cold air, but with slightly compressed lips. Behind him was a dark young man with double eyeglasses, and a number of printed papers in his hand; presumably J. Leveson, Secretary. In the road outside stood a group of three which struck Pump as strangely incongruous, like a group in a three-act farce. The first was a police inspector in uniform; the second was a workman in a leather apron, more or less like a carpenter, and the third was an old man in a scarlet Turkish fez, but otherwise dressed in very fashionable English clothes in which he did not seem very comfortable. He was explaining something about the inn to the policeman and the carpenter, who appeared to be restraining their amusement.

'Fine song that, my lord,' said Dalroy, with cheerful egotism. 'I'll sing you another.' And he cleared his throat.

'Mr. Pump,' said Lord Ivywood, in his bell-like and beautiful voice, 'I thought I would come in person, if only to make it clear that every indulgence has been shown you. The mere date of this inn brings it within the statute of 1909; it was erected when my great-grandfather was Lord of the Manor here, though I believe it then bore a different name, and——'

'Ah, my lord,' broke in Pump, with a sigh, 'I'd rather deal with your great-grandfather, I would, though he married a hundred negresses instead of one, than see a gentleman of your family taking away a poor man's livelihood.'

'The Act is specially designed in the interests of the relief of poverty,' proceeded Lord Ivywood in an unruffled manner, 'and its final advantages will accrue to all citizens alike.' He turned for an instant to the dark Secretary, saying, 'You have that second report'; and receiving a folded paper in answer.

'It is here fully explained,' said Lord Ivywood, putting on his elderly eyeglasses, 'that the purpose of the Act is largely to protect the savings of the more humble and necessitous classes. I find in paragraph three, "We strongly advise that the deleterious element

of alcohol be made illegal, save in such few places
as the Government may specially exempt for Parliamentary or other public reasons, and that the provocative and demoralizing display of inn signs be strictly
forbidden except in the case thus specially exempted;
the absence of such temptations will, in our opinion,
do much to improve the precarious financial conditions
of the working class." That disposes, I think, of any
such suggestion as Mr. Pump's that our inevitable
acts of social reform are in any sense oppressive. To
Mr. Pump's prejudice it may appear for the moment
to bear hardly upon him; but' (and here Lord Ivywood's voice took one of its moving oratorical turns)
'what better proof could we desire of the insidiousness
of the sleepy poison we denounce, what better evidence
could we offer of the civic corruption that we seek
to cure, than the very fact that good and worthy men
of established repute in the country can, by living in
such places as these, become so stagnant and sodden
and unsocial, whether through the fumes of wine or
through meditations as maudlin about the past, that
they consider the case solely as their own case, and
laugh at the long agony of the poor?'

Captain Dalroy had been studying Ivywood with a
very bright blue eye; and he spoke now much more
quietly than he generally did.

'Excuse me one moment, my lord,' he said. 'But
there was one point in your important explanation
which I am not sure I have got right. Do I understand
you to say that, though sign-boards are to be abolished,
yet where, if anywhere, they are retained, the right
to sell fermented liquor will be retained also? In
other words, though an Englishman may at last find
only one inn and sign in England, yet if the place has

an inn sign, it will also have your gracious permission to be really an inn?'

Lord Ivywood had an admirable command of temper, which had helped him much in his career as a statesman. He did not waste time in wrangling about the Captain's *locus standi* in the matter; he replied quite simply:

'Yes. Your statement of facts is correct.'

'Wherever I find an inn sign permitted by the police, I may go in and ask for a glass of beer—also permitted by the police.'

'If you find any such, yes,' answered Ivywood, quite temperately. 'But we hope soon to have removed them altogether.'

Captain Patrick Dalroy rose enormously from his seat, with a sort of stretch and yawn.

'Well, Hump,' he said to his friend, 'the best thing, it seems to me, is to take the important things with us.'

With two sight-staggering kicks he sent the keg of rum and the round cheese flying over the fence, in such a direction that they bounded on the descending road and rolled more and more rapidly down towards the dark woods into which the path disappeared. Then he gripped the pole of the inn sign, shook it twice, and plucked it out of the turf like a tuft of grass.

It had all happened before any one could move, but as he strode out into the road the policeman ran forward. Dalroy smote him flat across face and chest with the wooden sign-board, so as to send him flying into the ditch on the other side of the road. Then turning on the man in the fez, he poked him with the end of the pole so sharply in his new white waistcoat and watch-chain as to cause him to sit down suddenly in the road, looking very serious and thoughtful.

The dark Secretary made a movement of rescue, but Humphrey Pump, with a cry, caught up his gun from the table and pointed it at him; which so alarmed J. Leveson, Secretary, as to cause him almost to double up with his emotions. The next moment Pump, with his gun under his arm, was scampering down the hill after the Captain, who was scampering after the barrel and the cheese.

Before the policeman had struggled out of the ditch, they had all disappeared into the darkness of the forest. Lord Ivywood, who had remained firm through the scene, without a sign of fear or impatience (or, I will add, amusement), held up his hand and stopped the policeman in his pursuit.

'We should only make ourselves and the law ridiculous,' he said, 'by pursuing those ludicrous rowdies now. They can't escape or do any real harm in the state of modern communications. What is far more important, gentlemen, is to destroy their stores and their base. Under the Act of 1911 we have a right to confiscate and destroy any property in an inn where the law has been violated.'

And he stood for hours on the lawn, watching the smashing of bottles and the breaking up of casks, and feeding on fanatical pleasure: the pleasure which his strange, cold, courageous nature could not get from food or wine or woman.

CHAPTER V

THE ASTONISHMENT OF THE AGENT

LORD IVYWOOD shared the mental weakness of most men who have fed on books; he ignored, not the value but the very existence of other forms of information. Thus Humphrey Pump was perfectly aware that Lord Ivywood considered him an ignorant man who carried a volume of *Pickwick* and could not be got to read any other book. But Lord Ivywood was quite unaware that Humphrey never looked at him without thinking that he could be most successfully hidden in a wood of small beeches, as his grey-brown hair and sallow ashen face exactly reproduced the three predominant tints of such a sylvan twilight. Mr. Pump, I fear, had sometimes partaken of partridge or pheasant, in his early youth, under circumstances in which Lord Ivywood was not only unconscious of the hospitality he was dispensing, but would have sworn that it was physically impossible for any one to elude the vigilance of his efficient system of gamekeeping. But it is very unwise in one who counts himself superior to physical things to talk about physical impossibility.

Lord Ivywood was in error, therefore, when he said that the fugitives could not possibly escape in modern England. You can do a great many things in modern England if you have noticed some things in fact which others know by pictures or current speech: if you know, for instance, that most roadside hedges are taller and denser than they look, and that even the largest man lying just behind them takes up far less room than you would suppose; if you know that

many natural sounds are much more like each other
than the enlightened ear can believe, as in the case
of wind in leaves and of the sea; if you know that it
is easier to walk in socks than in boots if you know
how to take hold of the ground; if you know that
the proportion of dogs who will bite a man under any
circumstances is rather less than the proportion of
men who will murder you in a railway carriage; if
you know that you need not be drowned even in a
river, unless the tide is very strong, and unless you
practise putting yourself into the special attitudes
of a suicide; if you know that country stations have
objectless extra waiting-rooms that nobody ever goes
into; and if you know that country folk will forget
you if you speak to them, but talk about you all day
if you don't.

By the exercise of these and other arts and sciences
Humphrey Pump was able to guide his friend across
country, mostly in the character of trespasser and
occasionally in that of something like housebreaker,
and eventually, with sign, keg, cheese and all, to step
out of a black pine-wood on to a white road in a part
of the country where they would not be sought for the
present.

Opposite them was a cornfield and on their right,
in the shades of the pine-trees, a cottage, a very tumble-
down cottage that seemed to have collapsed under
its own thatch. The red-haired Irishman's face wore
a curious smile. He stuck the inn sign erect in the
road and went and hammered on the door.

It was opened tremulously by an old man with a
face so wrinkled that the wrinkles seemed more distinctly graven than the features themselves, which
seemed lost in the labyrinth of them. He might have

crawled out of the hole in a gnarled tree and he might have been a thousand years old.

He did not seem to notice the sign-board, which stood rather to the left of the door; and what life remained in his eyes seemed to awake in wonder at Dalroy's stature and strange uniform and the sword at his side. 'I beg your pardon,' said the Captain courteously. 'I fear my uniform startles you. It is Lord Ivywood's livery. All his servants are to dress like this. In fact, I understand the tenants also and even yourself perhaps . . . excuse my sword. Lord Ivywood is very particular that every man should have a sword. You know his beautiful eloquent way of putting his views. "How can we profess," he was saying to me yesterday while I was brushing his trousers, "how can we profess that all men are brothers while we refuse to them the symbol of manhood; or with what assurance can we claim it as a movement of modern emancipation to deny the citizen that which has in all ages marked the difference between the free man and the slave? Nor need we anticipate any such barbaric abuses as my honourable friend who is cleaning the knives had prophesied, for this gift is a sublime act of confidence in your universal passion for the severe splendours of Peace; and he that has the right to strike is he who has learnt to spare." '

Talking all this nonsense with extreme rapidity and vast oratorical flourishes of the hand, Captain Dalroy proceeded to trundle both the big cheese and the cask of rum into the house of the astonished cottager: Mr. Pump following with a grim placidity and his gun under his arm.

'Lord Ivywood,' said Dalroy, setting the rum cask

with a bump on the plain deal table, 'wishes to take wine with you. Or, more strictly speaking, rum. Don't you run away, my friend, with any of these stories about Lord Ivywood being opposed to drink. Three-bottle Ivywood, we call him in the kitchen. But it must be rum: nothing but rum for the Ivywoods. "Wine may be a mocker," he was saying the other day (and I particularly noted the phrasing, which seemed to be very happy even for his lordship; he was standing at the top of the steps, and I stopped cleaning them to make a note of it), "wine may be a mocker; strong drink may be raging, but nowhere in the sacred pages will you find one word of censure of the sweeter spirit sacred to them that go down to the sea in ships, no tongue of priest and prophet was ever lifted to break the sacred silence of Holy Writ about rum." He then explained to me,' went on Dalroy, signing to Pump to tap the cask according to his own technical secret, 'that the great tip for avoiding any bad results that a cask or two of rum might have on young and inexperienced people was to eat cheese with it, particularly this kind of cheese that I have here. I've forgotten its name.'

'Cheddar,' said Pump quite gravely.

'But mind you!' continued the Captain almost ferociously, shaking his big finger in warning at the aged man. 'Mind you, no *bread* with the cheese. All the devastating ruin wrought by cheese in the once happy homes of this country, has been due to the reckless and insane experiment of eating bread with it. You'll get no bread from me, my friend. Indeed, Lord Ivywood has given directions that the allusion to this ignorant and depraved habit shall be eliminated from the Lord's Prayer. Have a drink.'

He had already poured out a little of the spirit into two thick tumblers and a broken teacup, which he had induced the aged man to produce; and now solemnly pledged him.

'Thank ye kindly, sir,' said the old man, using his cracked voice for the first time. Then he drank; and his old face changed as if it were an old lantern in which the flame began to rise.

'Ar,' he said. 'My son be a sailor.'

'I wish him a happy voyage,' said the Captain. 'And I'll sing you a song about the first sailor there ever was in the world; and who (as Lord Ivywood acutely observes) lived before the time of rum.'

He sat down on a wooden chair and lifted his loud voice once more, beating on the table with the broken teacup.

'Old Noah he had an ostrich farm and fowls on the largest scale,
He ate his egg with a ladle in an egg-cup big as a pail,
And the soup he took was Elephant Soup and the fish he took was Whale,
But they all were small to the cellar he took when he set out to sail,
And Noah he often said to his wife when he sat down to dine,
"I don't care where the water goes if it doesn't get into the wine."

The cataract of the cliff of heaven fell blinding off the brink
As if it would wash the stars away as suds go down a sink,
The seven heavens came roaring down for the throats of hell to drink,
And Noah he cocked his eye and said, "It looks like rain I think,
The water has drowned the Matterhorn as deep as a Mendip mine,
But I don't care where the water goes if it doesn't get into the wine."

But Noah he sinned, and we have sinned; on tipsy feet we trod,
Till a great big black teetotaller was sent to us for a rod,

And you can't get wine at a P.S.A., or chapel, or Eisteddfod
For the Curse of Water has come again because of the wrath of
    God,
And water is on the Bishop's board and the Higher Thinker's
    shrine,
But I don't care where the water goes if it doesn't get into the
    wine.'

'Lord Ivywood's favourite song,' concluded Mr. Patrick Dalroy, drinking. 'Sing us a song yourself.'

Rather to the surprise of the two humorists, the old gentleman actually began in a quavering voice to chant:

> 'King George that lives in London Town,
> I hope they will defend his crown,
> And Bonyparte be quite put down,
>   On Christmas Day in the morning.
>
> Old Squire is gone to the Meet to-day,
> All in his——'

It is perhaps fortunate for the rapidity of this narrative that the old gentleman's favourite song, which consists of forty-seven verses, was interrupted by a curious incident. The door of the cottage opened, and a sheepish-looking man in corduroys stood silently in the room for a few seconds and then said, without preface or further explanation:

'Four ale.'

'I beg your pardon?' inquired the polite Captain.

'Four ale,' said the man, with solidity; then catching sight of Humphrey seemed to find a few more words in his vocabulary.

'Morning, Mr. Pump. Didn't know as how you'd moved "The Old Ship".'

Mr. Pump, with a twist of a smile, pointed to the old man whose song had been interrupted.

'Mr. Marne's seeing after it now, Mr. Gowl,' said Pump, with the strict etiquette of the country-side. 'But he's got nothing but this rum in stock as yet.'

'Better'nowt,' said the laconic Mr. Gowl; and put down some money in front of the aged Marne, who eyed it wonderingly. As he was turning with a farewell and wiping his mouth with the back of his hand, the door once more moved, letting in white sunlight and a man with a red neckerchief.

'Morning, Mr. Marne. Morning, Mr. Pump. Morning, Mr. Gowl,' said the man in the red neckerchief.

'Morning, Mr. Coote,' said the other three, one after another.

'Have some rum, Mr. Coote?' asked Humphrey Pump genially. 'That's all Mr. Marne's got just now.'

Mr. Coote also had a little rum; and also laid a little money under the rather vague gaze of the venerable cottager. Mr. Coote was just proceeding to explain that these were bad times, but if you saw a sign you were all right still; a lawyer up at Grunton Abbot had told him so; when the company was increased and greatly excited by the arrival of a boisterous and popular tinker, who ordered glasses all round and said he had his donkey and cart outside. A prolonged, rich, and confused conversation about his donkey and cart then ensued, in which the most varied views were taken of their merits; and it gradually began to dawn on Dalroy that the tinker was trying to sell them.

An idea suited to the romantic opportunism of his present absurd career suddenly swept over his mind, and he rushed out to look at the cart and donkey. The next moment he was back again, asking the tinker what his price was, and almost in the same breath offering a much bigger price than the tinker would have dreamed of asking. This was considered, however, as a lunacy specially allowed to gentlemen; the tinker had some more rum on the strength of the payment, and then Dalroy, offering his excuses, sealed up the cask and took it and the cheese to be stowed in the bottom of the cart. The money, however, he still left lying in shining silver and copper before the silver beard of old Marne.

No one acquainted with the quaint and often wordless *camaraderie* of the English poor will require to be told that they all went out and stared at him as he loaded the cart and saw to the harness of the donkey —all except the old cottager, who sat as if hypnotized by the sight of the money. While they were standing there they saw, coming down the white hot road where it curled over the hill, a figure that gave them no pleasure, even when it was a mere marching black spot in the distance. It was a Mr. Bullrose, the agent of Lord Ivywood's estates.

Mr. Bullrose was a short square man with a broad square head with ridges of close black curls on it, with a heavy, frog-like face, and starting, suspicious eyes; a man with a good silk hat but a square business jacket. Mr. Bullrose was not a nice man. The agent on that sort of estate hardly ever is a nice man. The landlord often is; and even Lord Ivywood had an arctic magnanimity of his own, which made most people want, if possible, to see him personally. But Mr. Bullrose was petty. Every really practical tyrant must be petty.

He evidently failed to understand the commotion in front of Mr. Marne's partly collapsed cottage, but he felt there must be something wrong about it. He wanted to get rid of the cottage altogether, and had not, of course, the faintest intention of giving the cottager any compensation for it. He hoped the old man would die; but in any case he could easily clear him out if it became suddenly necessary, for he could not possibly pay the rent for this week. The rent was not very much; but it was immeasurably too much for the old man, who had no conceivable way of borrowing or earning it. That is where the chivalry of our aristocratic land system comes in.

'Good-bye, my friends,' the enormous man in the fantastic uniform was saying. 'All roads lead to Rum, as Lord Ivywood said at the Church Congress, and we hope to be back soon, establishing the first-class hotel here, of which prospectuses will soon be sent out.'

The heavy, frog-like face of Mr. Bullrose the agent grew uglier with astonishment; and the eyes stood out more like a snail's than a frog's. The indefensible allusion to Lord Ivywood would in any case have caused a choleric intervention, if it had not been swallowed up in the earthquake suggestion of an un-licensed hotel on the estate. This again would have effected the explosion, if that and everything else had not been struck still and rigid by the sight of a solid wooden sign-post already erected outside old Marne's miserable cottage.

'I've got him now,' muttered Mr. Bullrose. 'He can't possibly pay; and out he shall go.' And he walked swiftly towards the door of the cottage, almost at the same moment that Dalroy went to the donkey's head, as if to lead it off along the road.

'Look here, my man,' burst out Bullrose the instant

he was inside the cottage. 'You've cooked yourself this time. His lordship has been a great deal too indulgent with you; but this is going to be the end of it. The insolence of what you've done outside, especially when you know his lordship's wishes in such things, has just put the lid on.' He stopped a moment and sneered. 'So unless you happen to have the exact rent down to a farthing or two about you, out you go. We're sick of your sort.'

In a very awkward and fumbling manner the old man pushed a heap of coins across the table. Mr. Bullrose sat down suddenly on the wooden chair with his silk hat on, and began counting them furiously. He counted them once; he counted them twice; and he counted them again. Then he stared at them more steadily than the cottager had done.

'Where did you get this money?' he asked in a thick, gross voice. 'Did you steal it?'

'I ain't very spry for stealin',' said the old man in quavering comedy.

Bullrose looked at him and then at the money; and remembered with fury that Ivywood was a just though cold magistrate on the bench.

'Well, anyhow,' he cried, in a hot, heady way. 'We've got enough against you to turn you out of this. Haven't you broken the law, my man, to say nothing of the regulations for tenants, in sticking up that fancy sign of yours outside the cottage? Eh?'

The tenant was silent.

'Eh?' reiterated the agent.

'Ar,' replied the tenant.

'Have you or have you not a sign-board outside this house?' shouted Bullrose, hammering the table.

The tenant looked at him for a long time with a

patient and venerable face, and then said, 'Mubbe, yes. Mubbe, no.'

'I'll mubbe you,' cried Mr. Bullrose, springing up and sticking his silk hat on the back of his head. 'I don't know whether you people are too drunk to see anything, but I saw the thing with my own eyes out in the road. Come out, and deny it if you dare!'

'Ar,' said Mr. Marne dubiously.

He tottered after the agent, who flung open the door with a business-like fury, and stood outside on the threshold. He stood there quite a long time. And he did not speak. Deep in the hardened mud of his materialist mind there had stirred two things that were its ancient enemies: the old fairy tale in which everything can be believed; the new scepticism in which nothing can be believed—not even one's own eyes. There was no sign, nor sign of a sign, in the landscape.

On the withered face of the old man Marne there was a faint renewal of that laughter that has slept since the Middle Ages.

CHAPTER VI

THE HOLE IN HEAVEN

THAT delicate ruby light which is one of the rarest but one of the most exquisite of evening effects warmed the land, sky, and seas as if the whole world were washed in wine: and dyed almost scarlet the strong red head of Patrick Dalroy as he stood on the waste of furze and bracken, where he and his friends had halted. One of his friends was re-examining a short gun, rather like a double-barrelled carbine, the other was eating thistles.

Dalroy himself was idle and ruminant, with his hands in his pockets and his eye on the horizon. Landwards the hills, plains, and woods lay bathed in the rose-red light; but it changed somewhat to purple, to cloud and something like storm over the distant violet strip of sea. It was towards the sea that he was staring.

Suddenly he woke up; and seemed almost to rub his eyes, or at any rate to rub his red eyebrow.

'Why, we're on the road back to Pebbleswick!' he said. 'That's the damned little tin chapel by the beach.'

'I know,' answered his friend and guide. 'We've done the old hare trick; doubled, you know. Nine times out of ten it's the best. Parson Whitelady used to do it when they were after him for dog-stealing. I've pretty much followed his trail; you can't do better than stick to the best examples. They tell you in London that Dick Turpin rode to York. Well, I know he didn't; for my old grandfather up at Cobble's

End knew the Turpins intimately—threw one of them into the river on a Christmas Day: but I think I can guess what he did do and how the tale got about. If Dick was wise, he went flying up the old North Road, shouting "York! York!" or what not, before people recognized him: then if he did the thing properly, he might half an hour afterwards walk down the Strand with a pipe in his mouth. They say old Boney said, "Go where you aren't expected", and I suppose as a soldier he was right. But for a gentleman dodging the police like yourself, it isn't exactly the right way of putting it. I should say, "Go where you ought to be expected"—and you'll generally find your fellow-creatures don't do what they ought about expecting any more than about anything else.'

'Well, this bit between here and the sea,' said the Captain, in a brown study; 'I know it so well—so well that—that I rather wish I'd never seen it again. Do you know,' he asked, suddenly pointing to a patch and pit of sand that showed white in the dusky heath a hundred yards away, 'do you know what makes that spot so famous in history?'

'Yes,' answered Mr. Pump; 'that's where old Mother Grouch shot the Methodist.'

'You are in error,' said the Captain. 'Such an incident as you describe would in no case call for special comment or regret. No, that spot is famous, because a very badly brought-up girl once lost a ribbon off a plait of black hair and somebody helped her to find it."

'Has the other person been well brought up?' asked Pump, with a faint smile.

'No,' said Dalroy, staring at the sea. 'He has

been brought down.' Then, rousing himself again, he made a gesture towards a farther part of the heath. 'Do you know the remarkable history of that old wall, the one beyond the last gorge over there?'

'No,' replied the other, 'unless you mean Dead Man's Circus; and that happened farther along.'

'I do not mean Dead Man's Circus,' said the Captain. 'The remarkable history of that wall is that somebody's shadow once fell on it: and that shadow was more desirable than the substance of all other living things. It is *this*,' he cried, almost violently resuming his flippant tone, 'it is this circumstance, Hump, and not the trivial and everyday incident of a dead man going to a circus to which you have presumed to compare it, it is *this* historical event which Lord Ivywood is about to commemorate by rebuilding the wall with solid gold and Greek marbles stolen by the Turks from the grave of Socrates, enclosing a column of solid gold four hundred feet high and surmounted by a colossal equestrian statue of a bankrupt Irishman riding backwards on a donkey.'

He lifted one of his long legs over the animal, as if about to pose for the group; then swung back on both feet again and again looked at the purple limit of the sea.

'Do you know, Hump,' he said, 'I think modern people have somehow got their minds all wrong about human life. They seem to expect what Nature has never promised; and then try to ruin all that Nature has really given. At all those atheist chapels of Ivywood's they're always talking of Peace, Perfect Peace, and Utter Trust, and Universal Joy and souls that beat as one. But they don't look any more cheerful than any one else: and the next thing they do is to start smashing a thousand good jokes and good stories and good songs and good friendships by pulling down "The Old Ship".' He gave a glance at the loose sign-post lying on the heath beside him, almost as if to reassure himself that it was not stolen. 'Now, it seems to me,' he went on, 'that this is asking for too much and getting too little. I don't know whether God means a man to have happiness in that All in All and Utterly Utter sense of happiness. But God does mean man to have a little Fun; and I mean to go on having it. If I mustn't satisfy my heart, I can gratify my humour. The cynical fellows who think themselves so damned clever have a sort of saying, "Be good and you will be happy; but you will not have a jolly time." The cynical fellows are quite wrong, as they generally are. They have got hold of the exact opposite of the truth. God knows I don't set up to be good; but even a rascal sometimes has to fight the world in the same way as a saint. I think I have fought the world; *et militavi non sine*— what's the Latin for having a lark? I can't pretend to Peace and Joy, and all the rest of it, particularly in this original briar-patch. I haven't been happy, Hump; but I have had a jolly time.'

The sunset stillness settled down again, save for the cropping of the donkey in the undergrowth; and Pump said nothing sympathetically; and it was Dalroy once more who took up his parable.

'So I think there's too much of this playing on our emotions, Hump; as this place is certainly playing the cat and banjo with mine. Damn it all, there are other things to do with the rest of one's life! I don't like all this fuss about feeling things—it only makes people miserable. In my present frame of mind I'm in favour of doing things. All of which, Hump,' he said, with a sudden lift of the voice that always went in him with a rushing irrational return of merely animal spirits, 'all of which I have put into a Song Against Songs, that I will now sing you.'

'I shouldn't sing it here,' said Humphrey Pump, picking up his gun and putting it under his arm. 'You look large in this open place; and you sound large. But I'll take you to the Hole in Heaven you've been talking about so much, and hide you as I used to hide you from that tutor—I couldn't catch his name—man who could only get drunk on Greek wine at Squire Wimpole's.'

'Hump!' cried the Captain. 'I abdicate the throne of Ithaca. You are far wiser than Ulysses. Here I have had my heart torn with temptations to ten thousand things between suicide and abduction, and all by the mere sight of that hole in the heath, where we used to have picnics. And all that time I'd forgotten we used to call it the Hole in Heaven. And, by God, what a good name—in both senses!'

'I thought you'd have remembered it, Captain,' said the innkeeper, 'from the joke young Mr. Matthews made.'

'In the heat of some savage hand-to-hand struggle in Albania,' said Mr. Dalroy sadly, passing his palm across his brow, 'I must have forgotten for one fatal instant the joke young Mr. Matthews made.'

'It wasn't very good,' said Mr. Pump simply. 'Ah, his aunt was the one for things like that. She went too far with old Gudgeon, though.'

With these words he jumped and seemed to be swallowed up by the earth. But they had merely strolled the few yards needed to bring them to the

edge of the sand-pit on the heath of which they had
been speaking. And it is one of the truths concealed
by Heaven from Lord Ivywood, and revealed by
Heaven to Mr. Pump, that a hiding-place can be
covered when you are close to it; and yet be open
and visible from some spot of vantage far off. From
the side by which he approached it, the sudden hollow
of sand, a kind of collapsed chamber in the heath,
seemed covered with a natural curve of fern and furze,
and he flashed out of sight like a fairy.

'It's all right,' he called out from under a floor
or roof of leaves. 'You'll remember it all when you
get here. This is the place to sing your song, Captain.
Lord bless me, Captain, don't I remember your
singing that Irish song you made up at college—
bellowing it like a bull of Bashan—all about hearts
and sleeves, or some such things—and her ladyship
and the tutor never heard a breath, because that bank
of sand breaks everything? It's worth knowing all
this, you know. It's a pity it's not part of a young
gentleman's education. Now you shall sing me the
song in favour of having no feelings, or whatever you
call it.'

Dalroy was staring about him at the cavern of his
old picnics, so forgotten and so startlingly familiar.
He seemed to have lost all thought of singing anything
and simply to be groping in the dark house of his own
boyhood. There was a slight trickle from a natural
spring, in sandstone just under the ferns, and he
remembered they used to try to boil the water in a
kettle. He remembered a quarrel about who had
upset the kettle which, in the morbidity of first love,
had given him for days the tortures of the damned.
When the energetic Pump broke once more through

the rather thorny roof, on an impulse to accumulate their other eccentric possessions, Patrick remembered about a thorn in a finger, that made his heart stop with something that was pain and perfect music. When Pump returned with the rum-keg and the cheese, and rolled them with a kick down the shelving sandy side of the hole, he remembered, with almost wrathful laughter, that in the old days he had rolled down that slope himself, and thought it rather a fine thing to do. He felt then as if he were rolling down a smooth side of the Matterhorn. He observed now that the height was rather less than that of the second story of one of the stunted cottages he had noted on his return. He suddenly understood he had grown bigger; bigger in a bodily sense. He had doubts about any other.

'The Hole in Heaven!' he said. 'What a good name! What a good poet I was in those days! The Hole in Heaven! But does it let one in, or let one out?'

In the last level shafts of the fallen sun the fantastic shadow of the long-eared quadruped, whom Pump had now tethered to a new and nearer pasture, fell across the last sunlit scrap of sand. Dalroy looked at the long, exaggerated shadow of the ass: and laughed that short explosive laugh he had uttered when the doors of the harems had been closed after the Turkish war. He was normally a man much too loquacious; but he never explained those laughs.

Humphrey Pump plunged down again into the sunken nest, and began to broach the cask of rum in his own secret style, saying:

'We can get something else somehow to-morrow. For to-night we can eat cheese and drink rum, especially as there's water on tap, so to speak. And now, Captain, sing us the song against songs.'

Patrick Dalroy drank a little rum out of a small medicine-glass which the generally unaccountable Mr. Pump unaccountably produced from his waistcoat pocket; but Patrick's colour had risen, his brow was almost as red as his hair; and he was evidently reluctant.

'I don't see why I should sing all the songs,' he said. 'Why the divil don't you sing a song yourself? And now I come to think of it,' he cried, with an accumulating brogue not, perhaps, wholly unaffected by the rum, which he had not in fact drunk for years, —'and now I come to think of it, what about that song of yours? All me youth's coming back in this blest and cursèd place; and I remember that song of yours, that never existed nor ever will. Don't ye remember now, Humphrey Pump, that night when I sang ye no less than seventeen songs of me own composition?'

'I remember it very well,' answered the Englishman with restraint.

'And don't ye remember,' went on the exhilarated Irishman, with solemnity, 'that unless ye could produce a poetic lyric of your own, written and sung by your-self, I threatened to——'

'To sing again,' said the impenetrable Pump. 'Yes, I know.'

He calmly proceeded to take out of his pockets, which were, alas! more like those of a poacher than an innkeeper, a folded and faded piece of paper.

'I wrote it when you asked me,' he said simply. 'I have never tried to sing it. But I'll sing it myself, when you've sung your song against anybody's singing at all.'

'All right!' cried the somewhat excited Captain. 'To hear a song from you—why, I'll sing anything. This is the Song against Songs, Hump.'

And again he let his voice out in a bellow against the evening silence.

'The song of the sorrow of Melisande is a weary song and a dreary song,

The glory of Mariana's grange had got into great decay,

The song of the Raven Never More has never been called a cheery song,

And the brightest things in Baudelaire are anything else but gay.

> But who will write us a riding song
> Or a hunting song or a drinking song,
> Fit for them that arose and rode
> When day and the wine were red?
> But bring me a quart of claret out,
> And I will write you a clinking song,
> A song of war and a song of wine
> And a song to wake the dead.

The song of the fury of Fragolette is a florid song and a torrid song,

The song of the sorrow of Tara is sung to a harp unstrung,

The song of the cheerful Shropshire Lad I consider a perfectly horrid song,

And the song of the happy Futurist is a song that can't be sung.

> But who will write us a riding song
> Or a fighting song or a drinking song,
> Fit for the fathers of you and me,
> That knew how to think and thrive?
> But the song of Beauty and Art and Love
> Is simply an utterly stinking song,
> To double you up and drag you down
> And damn your soul alive.'

'Take some more rum,' concluded the Irish officer affably; 'and let's hear your song at last.'

With gravity inseparable from the deep conventionality of country people, Mr. Pump unfolded the paper on which he had recorded the only antagonistic emotion that was strong enough in him to screw his infinite English tolerance to the pitch of song. He read out the title very carefully and in full.

'Song against Grocers, by Humphrey Pump, sole Proprietor of "The Old Ship", Pebbleswick. Good Accommodation for Man and Beast. Celebrated as the House at which both Queen Charlotte and Jonathan Wilde put up on different occasions; and where the chimpanzee man was mistaken for Bonaparte. This song is written against Grocers:

> 'God made the wicked Grocer
> For a mystery and a sign,
> That men might shun the awful shops
> And go to inns to dine;
> Where the bacon's on the rafter
> And the wine is in the wood,
> And God that made good laughter
> Has seen that they are good.
>
> The evil-hearted Grocer
> Would call his mother "Ma'am",
> And bow at her and bob at her
> Her aged soul to damn,
> And rub his horrid hands and ask
> What article was next,
> Though *mortis in articulo*
> Should be her proper text.
>
> His props are not his children,
> But pert lads underpaid,
> Who call out "Cash!" and bang about
> To work his wicked trade;
> He keeps a lady in a cage
> Most cruelly all day,
> And makes her count and calls her "Miss"
> Until she fades away.

The righteous minds of innkeepers
Induce them now and then
To crack a bottle with a friend,
Or treat unmoneyed men;
But who hath seen the Grocer
Treat housemaids to his teas
Or crack a bottle of fish-sauce
Or stand a man a cheese?

He sells us sands of Araby
As sugar for cash down;
He sweeps his shop and sells the dust
The purest salt in town,
He crams with cans of poisoned meat
Poor subjects of the King,
And when they die by thousands
Why, he laughs like anything.

The wicked Grocer groces
In spirits and in wine,
Not frankly and in fellowship
As men in inns do dine;
But packed with soap and sardines
And carried off by grooms,
For to be snatched by Duchesses
And drunk in dressing-rooms.

The hell-instructed Grocer
Has a temple made of tin,
And the ruin of good innkeepers
Is loudly urged therein;
But now the sands are running out
From sugar of a sort,
The Grocer trembles; for his time,
Just like his weight, is short.'

Captain Dalroy was getting considerably heated with his nautical liquor, and his appreciation of Pump's song was not merely noisy but active. He leapt to his feet and waved his glass. 'Ye ought to be Poet

Laureate, Hump—ye're right, ye're right; we'll stand all this no longer!'

He dashed wildly up the sand slope and pointed with the sign-post towards the darkening shore, where the low shed of corrugated iron stood almost isolated.

'There's your tin temple!' he said. 'Let's burn it!'

They were some way along the coast from the large watering-place of Pebbleswick, and between the gathering twilight and the rolling country it could not be clearly seen. Nothing was now in sight but the corrugated iron hall by the beach and three half-built red-brick villas.

Dalroy appeared to regard the hall and the empty houses with great malevolence.

'Look at it!' he said. 'Babylon!'

He brandished the inn sign in the air like a banner, and began to stride towards the place, showering curses.

'In forty days,' he cried, 'shall Pebbleswick be destroyed. Dogs shall lap the blood of J. Leveson, Secretary, and Unicorns——'

'Come back, Pat!' cried Humphrey. 'You've had too much rum.'

'Lions shall howl in its high places!' vociferated the Captain.

'Donkeys will howl anyhow,' said Pump. 'But I suppose the other donkey must follow.'

And loading and untethering the quadruped, he began to lead him along.

CHAPTER VII

THE SOCIETY OF SIMPLE SOULS

UNDER a sunset, at once softer and more sombre, under which the leaden sea took on a Lenten purple, a tint appropriate to tragedy, Lady Joan Brett was once more drifting moodily along the sea-front. The evening had been rainy and lowering; the watering-place season was nearly over; and she was almost alone on the shore; but she had fallen into the habit of restlessly pacing the place, and it seemed to satisfy some subconscious hunger in her rather mixed psychology. Through all her brooding her animal senses always remained abnormally active: she could *smell* the sea when it had ebbed almost to the horizon and in the same way she heard, through every whisper of waves or wind, the swish or flutter of another woman's skirt behind her. There is, she felt, something unmistakable about the movements of a lady who is generally very dignified and rather slow, and who happens to be in a hurry.

She turned to look at the lady who was thus hastening to overtake her; lifted her eyebrows a little and held out her hand. The interruption was known to her as Lady Enid Wimpole, cousin of Lord Ivywood; a tall and graceful lady who unbalanced her own elegance by a fashionable costume that was at once funereal and fantastic; her fair hair was pale but plentiful; her face was not only handsome and fastidious in the aquiline style, but when considered seriously was sensitive, modest, and even pathetic, but her wan blue eyes seemed slightly prominent, with that expression of cold eagerness that is seen in the eyes of ladies who ask questions at public meetings.

Joan Brett was herself, as she had said, a connexion of the Ivywood family; but Lady Enid was Ivywood's first cousin, and for all practical purposes his sister. For she kept house for him and his mother, who was now so incredibly old that she only survived to satisfy conventional opinion in the character of a speechless and useless chaperon. And Ivywood was not the sort who would be likely to call out any activity in an old lady exercising that office. Nor, for that matter, was Lady Enid Wimpole; there seemed to shine on her face the same kind of inhuman absent-minded common sense that shone on her cousin's.

'Oh, I'm so glad I've caught you up,' she said to Joan. 'Lady Ivywood wants you *so* much to come to us for the week-end or so, while Philip is still there. He always admired your sonnet on Cyprus so much, and he wants to talk to you about this policy of his in Turkey. Of course he's awfully busy; but I shall be seeing him to-night after the meeting.'

'No living creature,' said Lady Joan, with a smile, 'ever saw him except before or after a meeting.'

'Are you a Simple Soul?' asked Lady Enid carelessly.

'Am I a simple soul?' asked Joan, drawing her black brows together. 'Merciful Heaven—no! What can you mean?'

'Their meeting's on to-night at the small Universal Hall, and Philip's taking the chair,' explained the other lady. 'He's very annoyed that he has to leave early to get up to the House; but Mr. Leveson can take the chair for the last bit. They've got Misysra Ammon.'

'Got Mrs. who?' asked Joan, in honest doubt.

'You make game of everything,' said Lady Enid, in

cheerless amiability. 'It's the man every one's talking about—*you* know as well as I do. It's really his influence that has *made* the Simple Souls.'

'Oh!' said Lady Joan Brett.

Then, after a long silence, she added, 'Who are the Simple Souls? I should be interested in them, if I could meet any.' And she turned her dark brooding face on the darkening purple sea.

'Do you mean to say, my dear,' asked Lady Enid Wimpole, 'that you haven't met any of them yet?'

'No,' said Joan, looking at the last dark line of sea. 'I never met but one simple soul in my life.'

'But you must come to the meeting!' cried Lady Enid, with frosty and sparkling gaiety. 'You must come at once! Philip is certain to be eloquent on a subject like this. And of course Misysra Ammon is *always* so wonderful.'

Without any very distinct idea of where she was going or why she was going there, Joan allowed herself to be piloted to a low iron or tin shed, beyond the last straggling hotels; out of the echoing shell of which she could prematurely hear a voice that she thought she recognized. When she came in Lord Ivywood was on his feet, in exquisite evening-dress, but with a light overcoat thrown over the seat behind him. Beside him, in less tasteful but more obvious evening-dress, was the little old man she had heard on the beach.

No one else was on the platform; but just under it, rather to Joan's surprise, sat Miss Browning, her old typewriting friend in her old black dress, industriously taking down Lord Ivywood's words in shorthand. A yard or two off, even more to her surprise, sat Miss Browning's more domestic sister, also taking down the same words in shorthand.

'That is Misysra Ammon,' whispered Lady Enid earnestly, pointing a delicate finger at the little old man beside the chairman.

'Where's the umbrella?' said Joan. 'He can't *really* do it without the umbrella.'

' . . . at least evident,' Lord Ivywood was saying, 'that one of those ancestral impossibilities is no longer impossible. The East and the West are one. The East is no longer East nor the West West; for a small isthmus has been broken; and the Atlantic and Pacific are a single sea. No man assuredly has done more of this mighty work of unity than the brilliant and distinguished philosopher to whom you will have the pleasure of listening to-night; and I profoundly wish that affairs more practical, for I will not call them more important, did not prevent my remaining to enjoy his eloquence as I have so often enjoyed it before. Mr. Leveson has kindly consented to take my place; and I can do no more than express my deep sympathy with the aims and ideals which will be developed before you to-night. I have long been increasingly convinced that underneath a certain mask of stiffness which the Mohammedan religion has worn through certain centuries, as a somewhat similar mask has been worn by the religion of the Jews, Islam has in it the potentialities of being the most progressive of all religions; so that a century or two to come we may see the cause of peace, of science, and of reform everywhere supported by Islam as it is everywhere supported by Israel. Not in vain, I think, is the symbol of that faith the Crescent, the growing thing. While other creeds carry emblems implying more or less of finality, for this great creed of hope its very imperfection is its pride; and men shall walk fearlessly in new and wonderful paths, following the increasing curve which contains and holds up before them the eternal promise of the orb.'

It was characteristic of Lord Ivywood that, though he was really in a hurry, he sat down slowly and gravely amid the outburst of applause. The quiet resumption of the speaker's seat, like the applause itself, was an artistic part of the peroration. When the last clap or stamp had subsided, he sprang up alertly, his light great-coat over his arm, shook hands with the lecturer, bowed to the audience, and slid quickly out of the hall. Mr. Leveson, the swarthy young man with the drooping double eyeglass, came rather bashfully to the front, took the empty seat on the platform, and in a few words presented the eminent Turkish mystic, Misysra Ammon, sometimes called the Prophet of the Moon.

Lady Joan found the Prophet's English accent somewhat improved by good society; but he still elongated the letter 'u' in the same bleating manner; and his remarks had exactly the same rabidly wrongheaded ingenuity as his lecture upon English inns. It appeared that he was speaking on the Higher Polygamy; but he began with a sort of general defence of the Moslem civilization, especially against the charges of sterility and worldly ineffectiveness.

'It iss joost in the practical tings,' he was saying, 'it iss joost in the practical tings, if you could come to consider them in a manner quite equal that our methods are better than your methods. My ancestors invented the curved swords; because one cuts better with a curved sword. Your ancestors possessed the straight swords, out of some romantic fancy of being what you call straight. Or I will take a more plain example, of which I have myself experience. When I first had the honour of meeting Lord Ivywood, I was unused to your various ceremonies; and had a little difficulty, joost a little difficulty, in entering Mr. Claridge's hotel, where his lordship had invited me. A servant of the hotel was standing joost beside me on the doorstep. I stoo-ooped down to take off my boo-oots; and he asked me what I was doing. I said to him, "My friend, I am taking off my boo-oots." '

A smothered sound came from Lady Joan Brett; but the lecturer did not notice it, and went on with a beautiful simplicity:

'I told him that in my country, when showing respect for any spot, we do not take off our hats; we take off our boo-oots. And because I would keep on my hat and take off my boo-oots, he suggested to me that I had been afflicted by Allah in the head. Now was not that foony?'

'Very,' said Lady Joan inside her handkerchief, for she was choking with laughter. Something like a faint smile passed over the earnest faces of the two or three most intelligent of the Simple Souls; but for the most part the Souls seemed very simple indeed, helpless-looking people, with limp hair and gowns like green curtains; and their dry faces were as dry as ever.

'But I explained to him, I explained to him for a long time, for a carefully occupied time, that it was more practical, more business-like, more altogether for utility, to take off the boo-oots than to remove the hat. "Let us," I said to him, "consider what many complaints are made against the footwear, what few complaints against the headwear. You complain if in your drawing-rooms is the marching about of muddy boo-oots. Are any of your drawing-rooms marked thus with the marching about of muddy hats?

How very many of your husbands kick you with the boo-oot? Yet how few of your husbands on any occasion butt you with the hat?"'

He looked round with radiant seriousness, which made Lady Joan almost as speechless for sympathy as she was for amusement. With all that was most sound in her too complicated soul, she realized the presence of a man really convinced.

'The man on the doorstep, he would not listen to me,' went on Misysra Ammon pathetically. 'He said there would be a crowd if I stood on the doorstep, holding in my hand my boo-oots. Well, I do not know why, in your country, you always send the young males to be the first of your crowds. They certainly were making a number of noises, the young males.'

Lady Joan Brett stood up suddenly and displayed enormous interest in the rest of the audience in the back parts of the hall. She felt that if she looked for one moment more at the serious face with the Jewish nose and the Persian beard, she would publicly disgrace herself; or, what was quite as bad (for she was the generous sort of aristocrat), publicly insult the lecturer. She had a feeling that the sight of all the Simple Souls in bulk might have a soothing effect. It had. It had what might have been mistaken for a depressing effect. Lady Joan resumed her seat with a controlled countenance.

'Now why,' asked the Eastern philosopher, 'do I tell so simple a story of your London streets—a thing happening any day? The little mistake had no prejudicial effect. Lord Ivywood came out, at the end. He made no attempt to explain the true view of so important matters to Mr. Claridge's servant; though Mr. Claridge's servant remained on the doorstep.

But he commanded Mr. Claridge's servant to restore to me one of my boo-oots, which had fallen down the front steps while I was explaining this harmlessness of the hat in the home. So all was for me very well. But why do I tell such little tales?'

He spread out his hands again in his fan-like Eastern style. Then he clapped them together, so suddenly that Joan jumped and looked instinctively for the entrance of five hundred negro slaves laden with jewels. But it was only his emphatic gesture of eloquence. He went on, with an excited thickening of the accent:

'Because, my friends, this is the best example I could give of the wrong and slanderous character of the charge that we fail in our domesticities; that we fail especially in our treatment of the womankind. I appeal to any lady, to any Christian lady. Is not the boo-oot more devastating, more dreaded in the home than the hat? The boot jumps, he bound, he run about, he break things, he leave on the carpet the earths of the garden. The hat, he remain quiet on his hat-peg. Look at him on his hat-peg; how quiet and good he remain! Why not let him remain quiet also on his head?'

Lady Joan applauded warmly, as did several other ladies; and the sage went on, encouraged:

'Can you not therefore trust, dear ladies, this great religion to understand you concerning other things, as it understands you regarding boo-oots? What is the common objection our worthy enemies make against our polygamy? That it is disdainful of the woman-hood. But how can this be so, my friends, when it allows the womanhood to be present in so large num-bers? When in your House of Commons you put a hundred English members and joost one little Welsh member, you do not say, "The Welshman is on top; he is our Sultan; may he live for ever!" If your jury contained eleven great large ladies and one leetle man, you would not say, "This is unfair to the great large ladies." Why should you shrink, then, ladies, from this great polygamical experiment, which Lord Ivywood himself——'

Joan's dark eyes were still fixed on the wrinkled, patient face of the lecturer; but every word of the rest of the lecture was lost to her. Under her glowing Spanish tint she had turned pale with extraordinary emotions; but she did not stir a hair.

The door of the hall stood open; and occasional sounds came even from that deserted end of the town. Two men seemed to be passing along the distant parade; one of them was singing. It was common enough for workmen to sing going home at night; and the voice, though a loud one, would have been too far off for Joan to hear the words. Only Joan happened to know the words. She could almost see them before her, written in a round, swaggering hand on the pink page of an old school-girl album at home. She knew the words; and the voice.

'I come from Castlepatrick, and me heart is on me sleeve,
And any sword or pistol boy can hit ut with me leave,
It shines there for an epaulette, as golden as a flame,
As naked as me ancestors, as noble as me name.
For I come from Castlepatrick, and me heart is on me sleeve,
But a lady stole it from me on St. Gallowglass's Eve.'

Startlingly and with strong pain, there rose up before Joan's eyes a patch of broken heath, with a very deep hollow of white sand, blinding in the sun. No words, no name; only the place.

THE SOCIETY OF SIMPLE SOULS

'The folk that live in Liverpool, their heart is in their boots;
They go to hell like lambs, they do, because the hooter hoots.
Where men may not be dancin', though the wheels may dance
    all day;
And men may not be smokin'; but only chimneys may.
But I come from Castlepatrick, and me heart is on me sleeve,
But a lady stole it from me on St. Poleander's Eve.

The folk that live in black Belfast, their heart is in their mouth,
They see us making murders in the meadows of the South;
They think a plough's a rack, they do, and cattle-calls are creeds,
And they think we're burnin' witches when we're only burnin'
    weeds;
But I come from Castlepatrick, and me heart is on me sleeve;
But a lady stole it from me on St. Barnabas's Eve.'

The voice had stopped suddenly; but the last lines
were so much more distinct that it was certain the
singer had come nearer, and was not marching away.

It was only after all this, and through a sort of cloud,
that Lady Joan heard the indomitable Oriental
bringing his whole eloquent address to a conclusion.

'. . . And if you do not refu-use the sun that returns
and rises in the East with every morning, you will not
refu-use either this great social experiment, this great
polygamical method which also arose out of the East,
and always returns. For this is that Higher Polygamy
which always comes like the sun itself, out of the Orient,
but it is only at its noontide splendour when the sun
is high in heaven.'

She was but vaguely conscious of Mr. Leveson, the
man with the dark face and the eyeglasses, acknowledging the entrancing lecture in suitable terms, and
calling on any of the Simple Souls who might have
questions to ask, to ask them. It was only when the
Simple Souls had displayed their simplicity with the

usual parade of well-bred reluctance and fussy self-effacement, that any one addressed the chair. And it was only after somebody had been addressing the chair for some time that Joan gradually awoke to the fact that the address was somewhat unusual.

CHAPTER VIII

VOX POPULI VOX DEI

'I AM sure,' Mr. Leveson the Secretary had said, with a somewhat constrained smile, 'that after the eloquent and epoch-making speech to which we have listened there will be some questions asked; and we hope we have a debate afterwards. I am sure somebody will ask a question.' Then he looked interrogatively at one weary-looking gentleman in the fourth row and said, 'Mr. Hinch?'

Mr. Hinch shook his head with a pallid passion of refusal wonderful to watch, and said, 'I couldn't! I really couldn't!'

'We should be very pleased,' said Mr. Leveson, 'if any lady would ask a question.'

In the silence that followed it was somehow psychologically borne in on the whole audience that one particular great large lady (as the lecturer would say) sitting at the end of the second row was expected to ask a question. Her own wax-work immobility was witness both to the expectation and its disappointment.

'Are there any other questions?' asked Mr. Leveson— as if there had been any yet. He seemed to speak with a slight air of relief.

There was a sort of stir at the back of the hall and half-way down one side of it. Choked whispers could be heard of 'Now then, Garge!' 'Go it, Garge! Is there any questions! Gor!'

Mr. Leveson looked up with an alertness somewhat akin to alarm. He realized for the first time that a few quite common men, in coarse, unclean clothes, had somehow strolled in through the open door. They were not true rustics, but semi-rustic labourers that linger about the limits of the large watering-places. There was no 'Mr.' among them. There was a general tendency to call everybody George.

Mr. Leveson saw the situation and yielded to it. He modelled himself on Lord Ivywood and did much what he would have done in all cases, but with a timidity Lord Ivywood would not have shown. And the same social training that made him ashamed to be with such men, made him ashamed to own his shame. The same modern spirit that taught him to loathe such rags, also taught him to lie about his loathing.

'I am sure we should be very glad,' he said nervously, 'if any friends from outside care to join in our inquiry. Of course, we're all Democrats,' and he looked round at the grand ladies with a ghastly smile, 'and believe in the Voice of the People, and so on. If our friend at the back of the hall will put his questions briefly, we need not insist, I think, on his putting it in writing.'

There were renewed hoarse encouragements to George (that rightly christened champion), and he wavered forward on legs tied in the middle with string. He did not appear to have had any seat since his arrival, and made his remarks standing half-way down what we may call the central aisle.

'Well, I want to ask the proprietor——' he began.

'Questions,' said Mr. Leveson, swiftly seizing a chance for that obstruction of debate which is the main business of a modern chairman, 'must be asked of the chair, if they are points of order. If they concern the .ddress, they should be asked of the lecturer.'

'Well, I ask the lecturer,' said the patient Garge, 'whether it ain't right that when you 'ave the thing outside you should 'ave the thing inside?' (Hoarse applause at the back.)

Mr. Leveson was evidently puzzled and already suspicious that something was quite wrong. But the enthusiasm of the Prophet of the Moon sprang up instantly at any sort of question, and swept the chairman along with it.

'But it iss the essence of our who-ole message,' he cried, spreading out his arms to embrace the world, 'that the outer manifestation should be one with the inner manifestation. My friendss, it iss this very tru-uth our friend has stated, that iss responsible for our apparent lack of symbolism in Islam! We appear to neglect the symbol because we insist on the satisfactory symbol. My friend in the middle will walk round all our mosques and say loudly, "Where is the statue of Allah?" But can my friend in the middle really execute a complete and generally approved statue of Allah?'

Misysra Ammon sat down greatly satisfied with his answer; but it was doubted by many whether he had conveyed the satisfaction to his friend in the middle. That seeker after truth wiped his mouth with the back of his hand with an unsatisfied air and said:

'No offence, sir. But ain't it the Law, sir, that if you 'ave that outside we're all right? I came in 'ere as natural as could be. But Gorlumme, I never see a place like this afore." (Hoarse laughter behind.)

'No apology is needed, my friend,' cried the Eastern sage eagerly; 'I can conceive you are not perhaps du-uly conversant with such schools of truth. But the Law is All. The Law is Allah. The inmost u-unity of——'

'Well, ain't it the Law?' repeated the dogged George; and every time he mentioned the law the poor men who are its chief victims applauded loudly. 'I'm not one to make a fuss. I never was one to make a fuss. I'm a law-abidin' man, I am.' (More applause.) 'Ain't it the Law that if so be such is your sign and such is your profession, you ought to serve us?'

'I fear I not quite follow,' cried the eager Turk. 'I ought?'

'To serve us,' shouted a throng of thick voices from the back of the hall, which was already much more crowded than before.

'Serve you!' cried Misysra, leaping up like a spring released. 'The Holy Prophet came from heaven to serve you! The virtue and valour of a thousand years, my friends, has had no hunger but to serve you! We are of all faiths the most the faith of service. Our highest prophet is no more than the servant of God, as I am, as you all are. Even for our symbol we choose a satellite; and honour the Moon because it only serves the Earth, and does not pretend to be the Sun.'

'I'm sure,' cried Mr. Leveson, jumping up with a tactful grin, 'that the lecturer has answered this last point in a most eloquent and effective way; and the motor-cars are waiting for some of the ladies who have come from some distance, and—and I really think the proceedings——'

All the artistic ladies were already getting on their wraps with faces varying from bewilderment to blank terror. Only Lady Joan lingered, trembling with un-explained excitement. The hitherto speechless Hinch had slid up to the chairman's seat and whispered to him:

'You must get all the ladies away. I can't imagine what's up; but something's up.'

'Well?' repeated the patient George. 'So be it's the Law, where is it?'

'Ladies and gentlemen,' said Mr. Leveson in his most ingratiating manner, 'I think we have had a most delightful evening, and——'

'No, we ain't,' cried a new and nastier voice from a corner of the room. 'Where is it?'

'That's what we got a right to know,' said the law-abiding George. 'Where is it?'

'Where is what?' cried the nearly demented Secretary in the chair. 'What do you want?'

The law-abiding Mr. George made a half-turn and a gesture towards the man in the corner and said:

'What's yours, Jim?'

'I'll have a drop of Scotch,' said the man in the corner.

Lady Enid Wimpole, who had lingered a little in loyalty to Joan, the only other lady still left, caught both her wrists, and cried in a thrilling whisper:

'Oh, we must go to the car, dear! They're using the most awful language!'

.   .   .   .   .

Away on the wettest edge of the sands by the sea the print of two wheels and four hoofs were being slowly washed away by a slowly rising tide; which was, indeed, the only motive of the man Humphrey Pump, leading the donkey-cart, in leading it almost ankle-deep in water.

'I hope you're sober again now,' he said with some seriousness to his companion, a huge man walking heavily and even humbly with a straight sword swinging to and fro at his hip; 'for honestly it was a mug's game to go and stick up the old sign before that tin place. I haven't often spoken to you like this, Captain, but I don't believe any other man in the county could get you out of the hole as I can. But to go down there and frighten the ladies—why, there's been nothing so silly here since Bishop's Folly. You could hear the ladies screaming before we left.'

'I heard worse than that long before we left,' said the large man, without lifting his head. 'I heard one of them laugh. . . . Christ, do you think I shouldn't hear her laugh?'

There was a silence. 'I didn't mean to speak sharp,' said Humphrey Pump, with that incorruptible kindliness which was the root of his Englishry, and may yet save the soul of the English, 'but it's the truth, I was pretty well bothered about how to get out of this business. You're braver than I am, you see, and I own I was frightened about both of us. If I hadn't known my way to the lost tunnel, I should be fairly frightened still.'

'Known your way to what?' asked the Captain, lifting his red head for the first time.

'Oh, you know all about No Nose Ivywood's lost tunnel,' said Pump carelessly. 'Why, we all used to look for it when we were boys. Only I happened to find it.'

'Have mercy on an exile,' said Dalroy humbly. 'I don't know which hurt him most, the things he forgets or the things he remembers.'

Mr. Pump was silent for a little while and then said, more seriously than usual, 'Well, the people from London say you must put up placards and statues and subscriptions and epitaphs and the Lord knows what, to the people who've found some new trick and made it come off. But only a man that knows his own land for forty miles round, knows what a lot of people, and clever people too, there were who found new tricks,

and had to hide them because they didn't come off.
There was Dr. Boone, up by Gill-in-Hugby, who held
out against Dr. Collison and the vaccination. His
treatment saved sixty patients who had got smallpox;
and Dr. Collison's killed ninety-two patients who hadn't
got anything. But Boone had to keep it dark; naturally,
because all his lady patients grew moustaches. It was
the result of the treatment. But it wasn't a result he
wishes to dwell on. Then there was old Dean Arthur,
who discovered balloons, if ever a man did. He discovered them long before they were discovered. But
people were suspicious about such things just then—
there was a revival of the witch business in spite of all
the parsons—and he had to sign a paper saying where
he'd got the notion. Well, it stands to reason, you
wouldn't like to sign a paper saying you'd got it from
the village idiot when you were both blowing soap-
bubbles: and that's all he could have signed; for he was
an honest gentleman, the poor old Dean. Then there
was Jack Arlingham and the diving-bell—but you
remember all about that. Well, it was just the same
with the man that made this tunnel—one of the mad
Ivywoods. There's many a man, Captain, that has a
statue in the great London squares for helping to make
the railway trains. There's many a man has his name
in Westminster Abbey for doing something in discovering steamboats. Poor old Ivywood discovered both at
once; and had to be put under control. He had a
notion that a railway train might be made to rush
right into the sea and turn into a steamboat; and it
seemed all right, according as he worked it out. But
his family were so ashamed of the thing that they
didn't like the tunnel even mentioned. I don't think
anybody knows where it is but me and Bunchy

Robinson. We shall be there in a minute or two. They've thrown the rocks about at this end; and let the thick plantation grow at the other; but I've got a race-horse through before now, to save it from Colonel Chepstow's little games; and I think I can manage this donkey. Honestly, I think it's the only place we'll be safe in after what we've left behind us at Pebbleswick. But it's the best place in the world, there's no doubt, for lying low and starting afresh. Here we are. You think you can't get behind that rock, but you can. In fact, you have.'

Dalroy found himself, with some bewilderment, round the corner of a rock, and in a long bore or barrel of blackness that ended in a very dim spot of green. Hearing the hoofs of the ass and the feet of his friend behind him, he turned his head, but could see nothing but the pitch blackness of a closed coal cellar. He turned again to the dim green speck, and marching forward was glad to see it grow larger and brighter, like a big emerald, till he came out on a throng of trees, mostly thin, but growing so thickly and so close to the cavernous entrance of the tunnel that it was quite clear the place was meant to be choked up by forests and forgotten. The light that came glimmering through the trees was so broken and tremulous that it was hard to tell whether it was daybreak or moonrise.

'I know there's water here,' said Pump. 'They couldn't keep it out of the stone-work when they made the tunnel; and old Ivywood hit the hydraulic engineer with a spirit-level. With the bit of covert here and the sea behind us we ought to be able to get food of one kind or another, when the cheese has given out; and donkeys can eat anything. By the way,' he added, with some embarrassment, 'you don't mind my saying, Captain, but I think we'd better keep that rum for rare occasions. It's the best rum in England, and may be the last, if these mad games are going on. It'll do us good to feel it's there, so we can have it when we want it. The cask's still nearly full.'

Dalroy put out his hand and shook the other's. 'Hump,' he said seriously, 'you're right. It's a sacred trust for Humanity; and we'll only drink it ourselves to celebrate great victories. In token of which I will take a glass now, to celebrate our glorious victory over Leveson and his tin tabernacle.'

He drained one glass and then sat down on the cask, as if to put temptation behind him. His blue ruminant bull's eyes seemed to plunge deeper and deeper into the emerald twilight of the trees in front of him; and it was long before he spoke again.

At last he observed, 'I think you said, Hump, that a friend of yours—a gentleman named Bunchy Robinson, I think—was also a *habitué* here'.

'Yes; he knew the way,' answered Pump, leading the donkey to the most suitable patch of pasturage.

'May we, do you think, have the pleasure of a visit from Mr. Robinson?' inquired the Captain.

'Not unless they're jolly careless up in Blackstone Jail,' replied Pump. And he moved the cheese well into the arch of the tunnel. Dalroy still sat with his square chin on his hand, staring at the mystery of the little wood.

'You seem absent-minded, Captain,' remarked Humphrey.

'The deepest thoughts are all commonplaces,' said Dalroy. 'That is why I believe in Democracy; which is more than you do, you foul blood-stained old British

Tory. And the deepest commonplace of all is that *vanitas vanitatum*; which is not pessimism but is really the opposite of pessimism. It is man's futility that makes us feel he must be a god. And I think of this tunnel; and how the poor old lunatic walked about on this grass, watching it being built, the soul in him on fire with the future. And he saw the whole world changed and the seas thronged with his new shipping; and now'—and Dalroy's voice changed and broke—'now there is good pasture for the donkey and it is very quiet here.'

'Yes,' said Pump; in some way that conveyed his knowledge that the Captain was thinking of other things also. The Captain went on dreamily:

'And I think about another Lord Ivywood recorded in history who also had a great vision. For it is a great vision, after all; and though the man is a prig, he is brave. He also wants to drive a tunnel—between East and West—to make the British Empire more Indian; to effect what he calls the orientation of England and I call the ruin of Christendom. And I am wondering just now, whether the clear intellect and courageous will of a madman will be strong enough to burst and drive that tunnel, as everything seems to show at this moment that it will. Or whether there be indeed enough life and growth in your England to leave it at last as this is left, buried in English forests and wasted by an English sea.'

The silence fell between them again, and again there was only the slight sound the animal made in eating. As Dalroy had said, it was very quiet there.

But it was not quiet in Pebbleswick that night; when the Riot Act was read; and all the people who had seen the sign-board outside fought all the people who hadn't seen the sign-board outside; or when babies and scientists next morning, seeking for shells and other common objects of the sea-shore, found that their study included fragments of the outer clothing of J. Leveson, and scraps of corrugated iron.

CHAPTER IX

THE HIGHER CRITICISM AND MR. HIBBS

PEBBLESWICK boasted an enterprising evening paper of its own, called the *Pebbleswick Globe*, and it was the great vaunt of the editor's life that he had got out an edition announcing the mystery of the vanishing signboard almost simultaneously with its vanishing. In the rows that followed sandwich-men found no little protection from the blows indiscriminately given them behind and before, in the large wooden boards they carried inscribed:

THE VANISHING PUB

PEEBLESWICK'S FAIRY TALE

SPECIAL

And the paper contained a categorical and mainly correct account of what had happened, or what seemed to have happened, to the eyes of the amazed Garge and his crowd of sympathizers. 'George Burn, carpenter, of this town, with Samuel Gripes, drayman in the service of Messrs. Jay and Gubbins, brewers, together with a number of other well-known residents, passed by the new building erected on the West Beach for various forms of entertainment and popularly called the small Universal Hall. Seeing outside it one of the old inn signs now so rare, they drew the quite proper inference that the place retained the licence to sell alcoholic liquors, which so many other places in this neighbourhood have recently lost. The persons inside, however, appear to have denied all knowledge of the fact, and when the party (after some regrettable scenes in which no life was lost) came out on the beach again, it was found that the inn sign had been destroyed or stolen. All parties were quite sober; and had indeed obtained no opportunity to be anything else. The mystery is undergoing inquiry.'

But this comparatively realistic record was local and spontaneous; and owed not a little to the accidental honesty of the editor. Moreover, evening papers are often more honest than morning papers, because they are written by ill-paid and hard-worked underlings in a great hurry; and there is no time for more timid people to correct them. By the time the morning papers came out next day a faint but perceptible change had passed over the story of the vanishing sign-board. In the daily paper which had the largest circulation and the most influence in that part of the world, the problem was committed to a gentleman known by what seemed to the non-journalistic world the singular name of Hibbs However. It had been affixed to him in jest in connexion with the almost complicated caution with which all his public criticisms were qualified at every turn; so that everything came to depend upon the conjunctions; upon 'but' and 'yet' and 'though' and similar words. As his salary grew larger (for editors and proprietors like that sort of thing) and his old friends fewer (for the most generous of friends cannot but feel faintly acid at a success which has in it nothing of the infectious flavour of glory) he grew more and more to value himself as a diplomatist; a man who always said the right thing. But he was not without his intellectual Nemesis; for at last he became so very diplomatic as to be darkly and densely unintelligible. People who knew him had no difficulty in believing that what he had said was the right thing, the tactful thing, the thing that should save the situation; but they had great difficulty in discovering what it was. In his early days he had had a great talent for one of the worst tricks of modern journalism; the trick of dismissing the important part of a question as if it could wait, and appearing to get to business on the unimportant part of it. Thus, he would say, 'Whatever we may think of the rights and wrongs of the vivisection of pauper children, we shall all agree that it should only be done, in any event, by fully qualified practitioners.' But in the later and darker days of his diplomacy, he seemed rather to dismiss the important part of a subject, and get to grips with some totally different subject, following some timid and elusive train of associations of his own. In his late bad manner, as they say of painters, he was just as likely to say, 'Whatever we may think of the rights and wrongs of the vivisection of pauper children, no progressive mind can doubt that the influence of the Vatican is on the decline.' His nickname had stuck to him in honour of a paragraph he was alleged to have written when the American President was wounded by a bullet fired by a lunatic in New Orleans, and which was said to have run: 'The President passed a good night and his condition is greatly improved. The assassin is not, however, a German, as was at first supposed.' Men stared at that mysterious remark till they wanted to go mad and to shoot somebody themselves.

Hibbs However was a long, lank man with straight yellowish hair and a manner that was externally soft and mild but secretly supercilious. He had been when at Cambridge a friend of Leveson, and they had both prided themselves on being moderate politicians. But if you have had your hat smashed over your nose by one who has very recently described himself as a 'law-abidin' man', and if you have had to run for your life with one coat-tail, and encouraged to further bodily activity by having irregular pieces of a corrugated iron roof thrown after you by men more energetic than yourself, you will find you emerge with emotions which are not solely those of a moderate politician. Hibbs However had already composed a leaderette on the Pebbleswick incident, which rather pointed to the truth of the story, so far as his articles ever pointed to anything. His motives for veering vaguely in this direction were, as usual, complex. He knew the millionaire who owned the paper had a hobby of Spiritualism; and something might always come out of not suppressing a marvellous story. He knew that two at least of the preposterous artisans or small tradesmen who had attested the tale were staunch supporters of The Party. He knew that Lord Ivywood must be mildly and not effectually checked; for Lord Ivywood was of The Other Party. And there could be no milder or less effectual way of checking him than allowing the paper to lend at least a temporary credit to a well-supported story that came from outside; and certainly had not been (like so many stories) created in the office. Amid all these considerations had Hibbs However steered his way to a more or less confirmatory article, when the sudden apparition of J. Leveson, Secretary, in the sub-editor's room, with a burst collar and broken eyeglasses, led Mr. Hibbs into a long private conversation with him and a comparative reversal of his plans. But of course he did not write a new article; he was not of that divine order who make all things new. He chopped and changed his original article in such a way that it was something quite beyond the most bewildering article he had written in the past; and is still prized by those highly cultured persons who collect the worst literature of the world.

It began, indeed, with the comparatively familiar formula, 'Whether we take the more lax or the more advanced of the old disputed problem of the morality or immorality of the wooden sign-board as such, we shall all agree that the scenes enacted at Pebbleswick were very discreditable, to most, though not all, concerned.' After that, tact degenerated into a riot of irrelevance. It was a wonderful article. The reader could get from it a faint glimpse of Mr. Hibbs's opinion on almost every other subject except the subject of the article. The first half of the next sentence made it quite clear that Mr. Hibbs (had he been present) would not have lent his active assistance to the Massacre of St. Bartholomew or the Massacres of September. But the second half of the sentence suggested with equal clearness that, since these two acts were no longer, as it were, in contemplation, and all attempts to prevent them would probably arrive a little late, he felt the warmest friendship for the French nation. He merely insisted that his friendship should never be mentioned except in the French language. It must be called an 'entente' in the language taught to tourists by waiters. It must on no account be called an 'understanding', in a language understanded of the people. From the first half of the sentence following it might safely be inferred that Mr. Hibbs had read Milton, or at least the passage about sons of Belial; from the second half that he knew nothing about bad wine, let alone good. The next sentence began with the corruption of the Roman Empire and contrived

to end with Dr. Clifford. Then there was a weak plea
for Eugenics; and a warm plea against Conscription,
which was not True Eugenics. That was all; and it
was headed, 'The Riot at Pebbleswick'.

Yet some injustice would be done to Hibbs However,
if we concealed the fact that this chaotic leader was
followed by quite a considerable mass of public corre-
spondence. The people who write to newspapers are,
it may be supposed, a small eccentric body, like most
of those that sway a modern State. But at least, unlike
the lawyers, or the financiers, or the members of
Parliament, or the men of science, they are people of
all kinds scattered all over the country, of all classes,
counties, ages, sects, sexes, and stages of insanity.
The letters that followed Hibbs's article are still worth
looking up in the dusty old files of his paper.

A dear old lady in the densest part of the Midlands
wrote to suggest that there might really have been an
old ship wrecked on the shore during the proceedings.
'Mr. Leveson may have omitted to notice it; or, at
that late hour of the evening, it may have been mistaken
for a sign-board, especially by a person of defective
sight. My own sight has been failing for some time;
but I am still a diligent reader of your paper.' If
Mr. Hibbs's diplomacy had left one nerve in his soul
undrugged, he would have laughed, or burst into tears,
or got drunk, or gone into a monastery over a letter
like that. As it was, he measured it with a pencil, and
decided that it was just too long to get into the column.

Then there was a letter from a theorist; and a theorist
of the worst sort. There is no great harm in the
theorist who makes up a new theory to fit a new event.
But the theorist who starts with a false theory and then
sees everything as making it come true is the most

dangerous enemy of human reason. The letter began like a bullet let loose by the trigger. 'Is not the whole question met by Ex. iv. 3? I enclose several pamphlets in which I have proved the point quite plainly; and which none of the Bishops or the so-called Free Church Ministers have attempted to answer. The connexion between the rod or pole, and the snake, so clearly indicated in Scripture, is neglected by the well-paid prostitutors of religion for their own ends. Moses distinctly testifies to a rod or pole turning into a snake. We all know that those following after strong drink are given over to believe a lie; and profess that they behold a snake. It is therefore perfectly natural that these unhappy men should have professed to see a pole. They may have seen it before or after the well-known change which . . .' The letter went on for nine closely written pages; and this time Mr. Hibbs may be excused for thinking it a little long.

Then there was the scientific correspondent, who said —Might it not be due to the acoustic qualities of the hall? He had never believed in the corrugated iron hall. The very word 'hall' itself (he added playfully) was often so sharpened and shortened by the abrupt echoes of those repeated metallic curves, that it had every appearance of being the word 'hell'; and had caused many theological entanglements, and some police prosecutions. In the light of these facts, he wished to draw the editor's attention to some very curious details about this supposed presence or absence of an inn sign. It would be noted that many of the witnesses, and especially the most respectable of them, constantly refer to something that is supposed to be outside. The word 'outside' occurs at least five times in the depositions of the complaining persons. Surely by all scientific analogy we may infer that the unusual phrase 'inn sign' is an acoustic error for 'inside'. The word 'inside' would so naturally occur in any discussion either about the building or the individual, when the debate was of a hygienic character. This letter was signed 'Medical Student': and the less intelligent parts of it were selected for publication in the paper.

Then there was a really humorous man, who wrote and said there was nothing at all inexplicable or unusual about the case. He himself (he said) had often seen a sign-board outside a pub when he went into it; and had been quite unable to see it when he came out. This letter (the only one that had any quality of literature) was sternly set aside by Mr. Hibbs.

Then came a cultured gentleman with a light touch, who merely made a suggestion. Had any one read H. G. Wells's story about the kink in space? He contrived indescribably to suggest that no one had even heard of it except himself; or perhaps of Mr. Wells either. The story indicated that men's feet might be in one part of the world and their eyes in another. He offered the suggestion for what it was worth. The particular pile of letters on which Hibbs However threw it, showed only too clearly what it was worth.

Then there was a man, of course, who called it all a plot of frenzied foreigners against Britain's shore. But as he did not make it quite clear whether the chief wickedness of these aliens had lain in sticking the sign up or in pulling it down, his remarks (the remainder of which referred exclusively to the conversational mis-conduct of an Italian ice-cream man, whose side of the case seemed insufficiently represented) carried the less weight.

And then, last but the reverse of least, there plunged

16

in all the people who think they can solve a problem they cannot understand by abolishing everything that has contributed to it. We all know these people. If a barber has cut his customer's throat because the girl has changed her partner for a dance or donkey-ride on Hampstead Heath, there are always people to protest against the mere institutions that led up to it. This would not have happened if barbers were abolished, or if cutlery were abolished, or if the objection felt by girls to imperfectly grown beards were abolished, or if the girls were abolished, or if heaths and open spaces were abolished, or if dancing were abolished, or if donkeys were abolished. But donkeys, I fear, will never be abolished.

There were plenty of such donkeys in the common land of this particular controversy. Some made it an argument against democracy, because poor Garge was a carpenter. Some made it an argument against Alien Immigration, because Misysra Ammon was a Turk. Some proposed that ladies should no longer be admitted to any lectures anywhere; because they had constituted a slight temporary difficulty at this one, without the faintest fault of their own. Some urged that all holiday resorts should be abolished; some urged that all holidays should be abolished. Some vaguely denounced the seaside; some, still more vaguely, proposed to remove the sea. All said that if this or that, stones or seaweed, or strange visitors, or bad weather, or bathing-machines were swept away with a strong hand, this which had happened would not have happened. They only had one slight weakness, all of them; that they did not seem to have the faintest notion of what *had* happened. And in this they were not inexcusable. Nobody did know what had happened: nobody knows it to this day, of course; or it would be unnecessary to write this story. No one can suppose this story is written from any motive save that of telling the plain, humdrum truth.

That queer, confused cunning which was the only definable quality possessed by Hibbs However had certainly scored a victory so far; for the tone of the weekly papers followed him; with more intelligence and less trepidation: but they followed him. It seemed more and more clear that some kind of light and sceptical explanation was to be given of the whole business; and that the whole business was to be dropped.

The story of the sign-board and the ethical chapel of corrugated iron was discussed and somewhat disparaged in all the more serious and especially in the religious weeklies; though the Low Church papers seemed to reserve their distaste chiefly for the sign-board; and the High Church papers chiefly for the chapel. All agreed that the combination was incongruous; and most treated it as fabulous. The only intellectual organs which seemed to think it might have happened were the Spiritualist papers; and their interpretation had not that solidity which would have satisfied Mr. Garge.

It was not until almost a year after that it was felt in philosophical circles that the last word had been said on the matter. An estimate of the incident and of its bearing on natural and supernatural history occurred in Professor Widge's celebrated *Historicity of the Petro-Piscatorial Phenomena*; which so profoundly affected modern thought when it came out in parts in the *Hibbert Journal*. Every one remembers Professor Widge's main contention; that the modern critic must apply to the thaumaturgics of the Lake of Tiberias the same principle of criticism which Dr. Bunk and others have so successfully applied to the thaumaturgics of the Cana narrative: 'Authorities as final as Pink and Toscher,' wrote the Professor, 'have now shown with an emphasis that no emancipated mind is entitled to question, that the Aqua-Vinic thaumaturgy at Cana is wholly inconsistent with the psychology of the "master of the feast" as modern research has analysed it; and, indeed, with the whole Judæo-Aramaic psychology at that stage of its development; as well as being painfully incongruous with the elevated ideas of the ethical teacher in question. But as we rise to higher levels of moral achievement it will probably be found necessary to apply the Canaic principle to other and later events in the narrative. This principle has, of course, been mainly expounded by Huscher in the sense that the whole episode is unhistorical; while the alternative theory, that the wine was non-alcoholic and was naturally infused into the water, can claim on its side the impressive name of Minns. It is clear that if we apply the same alternative to the so-called Miraculous Draught of Fishes we must either hold with Gilp that the fishes were stuffed representations of fishes artificially placed in the lake (see the Rev. Y. Wyse's *Christo-Vegetarianism as a World-System*, where this position is forcibly set forth) or we must, on the Huscherian hypothesis, deprive the Piscatorial narrative of all claim to historicity whatever.

'The difficulty felt by the most daring critics (even Pooke) in adopting this entirely destructive attitude, is the alleged improbability of so detailed a narrative being found on so slight a phrase as the anti-historical critics refer it to. It is urged by Pooke, with characteristic relentless reasoning, that according to Huscher's theory a metaphorical but at least noticeable remark, such as, "I will make you fishers of men", was expanded into a realistic chronicle of events; which contains no mention, even in the passages evidently interpolated, of any men actually found in the nets when they were hauled up out of the sea; or, more properly, lagoon.

'It must appear presumptuous or even bad taste for any one in the modern world to differ on any subject from Pooke; but I would venture to suggest that the very academic splendour and unique standing of the venerable professor (whose ninety-seventh birthday was so beautifully celebrated in Chicago last year) may have forbidden him all but intuitive knowledge of how errors arise among the vulgar. I crave pardon for mentioning a modern case known to myself (not indeed by personal presence, but by careful study of all the reports) which presents a curious parallel to such ancient expansions of a text into an incident, in accordance with Huscher's law.

'It occurred at Pebbleswick, in the south of England. The town had long been in a state of dangerous religious excitement. The great religious genius who has since so much altered our whole attitude to the religions of the world, Misysra Ammon, had been lecturing on the sands to thousands of enthusiastic hearers. Their meetings were often interrupted, both by children's services run on the most ruthless lines of orthodoxy; and by the League of the Red Rosette, the formidable atheist and anarchist organization. As if this were not enough to swell the whirlpool of fanaticism, the old popular controversy between the

Milnian and the Complete Sublapsarians broke out again on the fated beach. It is natural to conjecture that, in the thickening atmosphere of theology in Pebbleswick, some controversialist quoted the text, "An evil and adulterous generation *seek for a sign*. But no sign shall be given it save the sign of the prophet Jonas".

'A mind like that of Pooke will find it hard to credit, but it seems certain that the effect of this text on the ignorant peasantry of southern England was actually to make them go about looking for a sign, in the sense of those old tavern signs now so happily disappearing. The "sign of the prophet Jonas" they somehow translated in their stunted minds into a sign-board of the ship out of which Jonah was thrown. They went about literally looking for "The Sign of the Ship": and there are some cases of their suffering Smail's Hallucination and actually seeing it. The whole incident is a curious parallel to the Gospel narrative, and a triumphant vindication of Huscher's law.'

Lord Ivywood paid a public compliment to Professor Widge, saying that he had rolled back from his country what might have been an ocean of superstitions. But indeed poor Hibbs had struck the first and stunning blow, that scattered the brains of all men.

CHAPTER X

THE CHARACTER OF QUOODLE

THERE lay about in Lord Ivywood's numerous gardens, terraces, outhouses, stable-yards, and similar places, a dog who came to be called by the name of Quoodle. Lord Ivywood did not call him Quoodle. Lord Ivywood was almost physically incapable of articulating such sounds. Lord Ivywood did not care for dogs. He cared for the Cause of Dogs, of course; and he cared still more for his own intellectual self-respect and consistency. He would never have permitted a dog in his house to be physically ill-treated; nor, for that matter, a rat; nor, for that matter, even a man. But if Quoodle was not physically ill-treated, he was at least socially neglected: and Quoodle did not like it. For dogs care for companionship more than for kindness itself.

Lord Ivywood would probably have sold the dog: but he consulted experts (as he did on everything he didn't understand and many things that he did), and the impression he gathered from them was that the dog, technically considered, would fetch very little; mostly, it seemed, because of the mixture of qualities that it possessed. It was a sort of mongrel bull-terrier; but with rather too much of the bull-dog; and this fact seemed to weaken its price as much as it strengthened its jaw. His lordship also gained a hazy impression that the dog might have been valuable as a watch-dog if it had not been able to follow game like a pointer; and that even in the latter walk of life it would always be discredited by an unfortunate talent for swimming as well as a retriever. But Lord Ivywood's impressions may very well have been slightly confused; as he was probably thinking about the Black Stone of Mecca, or some such subject at the moment. The victim of this entanglement of virtues, therefore, still lay about in the sunlight of Ivywood; exhibiting no general result of that entanglement except the most appalling ugliness.

Now Lady Joan Brett did appreciate dogs. It was the whole of her type and a great deal of her tragedy that all that was natural in her was still alive under all that was artificial; and she could smell hawthorn or the sea as far off as a dog can smell his dinner. Like most aristocrats, she would carry cynicism almost to the suburbs of the city of Satan; she was quite as irreligious as Lord Ivywood, or rather more. She could be quite equally frigid or supercilious when she felt inclined; and in the great social talent of being tired, she could beat him any day of the week. But the difference remained in spite of her sophistries and ambitions; that her elemental communications were not cut, and his were. For her the sunrise was still the rising of a sun, and not the turning on of a light by a convenient cosmic servant. For her the spring was really the Season in the country, and not merely the Season in town. For her cocks and hens were natural appendages to an English house; and not (as Lord Ivywood had proved to her from an encyclopaedia) animals of Indian origin, recently imported by Alexander the Great. And so for her a dog was a dog, and not one of the higher animals, nor one of the lower animals, nor something that had the sacredness of life, nor something that ought to be muzzled, nor something that ought not to be vivisected. She knew that in every practical sense proper provision would be made for the dog; as, indeed, provision was made for the yellow dogs in Constantinople by Abdul Hamid; whose life Lord Ivywood was writing for the *Progressive Potentates* series. Nor was she in the least sentimental about the dog or anxious to turn him into a pet. It simply came natural to her in passing to rub all his hair the wrong way and call him something which she instantly forgot.

The man who was mowing the garden lawn looked up for a moment; for he had never seen the dog behave in exactly that way before. Quoodle arose, shook himself, and trotted on in front of the lady, leading her up an iron side staircase, of which, as it happened, she had never made use before. It was then, most probably, that she first took any special notice of him; and her pleasure, like that which she took in the sublime prophet from Turkey, was of a humorous character. For the complex quadruped had retained the bow legs of the bull-dog; and seen from behind, reminded her ridiculously of a swaggering little Major waddling down to his club.

The dog and the iron stairway between them led her into a series of long rooms, one opening into the other. They formed part of what she had known in earlier days as the disused wing of Ivywood House; which had been neglected or shut up, probably because it bore some defacements from the fancies of the mad ancestor, the memory of whom the present Lord Ivywood did not think helpful to his own political career. But it seemed to Joan that there were indications of a recent attempt to rehabilitate the place. There was a pail of whitewash in one of the empty rooms; a step-ladder in another, here and there a curtain-rod, and at last, in the fourth room, a curtain. It hung all alone in the old wood-work; but it was a very gorgeous curtain, being a kind of orange-gold relieved with wavy bars of crimson, which somehow seemed to suggest the very spirit and presence of serpents; though they had neither eyes nor mouths among them.

In the next of the endless series of rooms she came upon a kind of ottoman, striped with green and silver, standing alone on the bare floor. She sat down on it from a mixed motive of fatigue and of impudence; for she dimly remembered a story which she had always thought one of the funniest in the world: about a lady only partly initiated in Theosophy who had been in the habit of resting on a similar object, only to discover afterwards that it was a Mahatma, covered with his Eastern garment and prostrate and rigid in ecstasy. She had no hopes of sitting on a Mahatma herself; but the very thought of it made her laugh; because it would make Lord Ivywood look such a fool. She was not sure whether she liked or disliked Lord Ivywood; but she felt quite certain that it would gratify her to make him look a fool. The moment she had sat down on the ottoman, the dog, who had been trotting beside her, sat down also, and on the edge of her skirt.

After a minute or two she rose (and the dog rose), and she looked yet farther down that long perspective of large rooms, in which men like Philip Ivywood forget that they are only men. The next was more ornate and the next yet more so; it was plain that the scheme of decoration that was in progress had been started at the other end. She could now see that the long lane ended in rooms that from afar off looked like the end of a kaleidoscope, rooms like nests made only from humming-birds or palaces built of fixed fireworks. Out of this furnace of fragmentary colours, she saw Ivywood advancing towards her, with his black suit and his white face accented by the contrast. His lips were moving; for he was talking to himself, as many orators do. He did not seem to see her; and she had to strangle a subconscious and utterly senseless cry, 'He is blind!'

The next moment he was welcoming her intrusion with the well-bred surprise and rather worldly simplicity suitable to such a case: and Joan fancied she understood why his face had seemed a little bleaker and blinder than usual. It was by contrast. He was carrying clutched to his forefinger, as his ancestors might have carried a falcon clutched to the wrist, a small bright-coloured, semi-tropical bird the expression of whose head, neck, and eye was the very opposite of his own. Joan thought she had never seen a living creature with a head so lively and insulting. Its provocative eye and pointed crest seemed to be offering to fight fifty game-cocks. It was no wonder (she told herself) that by the side of this gaudy guttersnipe with feathers Ivywood's faint-coloured hair and frigid face looked like the hair and face of a corpse walking.

'You'll never know what this is,' said Ivywood, in his most charming manner. 'You've heard of him a hundred times and never had a notion of what he was. This is the bul-bul.'

'I never knew,' replied Joan. 'I am afraid I never cared. I always thought it was something like a nightingale.'

'Ah, yes,' answered Ivywood, 'but this is the real bul-bul peculiar to the East: *Pycnonotus Haemorrhus*. You are thinking of *Daulias Golzii*.'

'I suppose I am,' replied Lady Joan, with a faint smile. 'It is an obsession. When shall I not be thinking of Daulias Galsworthy? Was it Galsworthy?' Then feeling quite touched by the soft austerity of her companion's face, she caressed the gaudy and pugnacious bird with one finger and said, 'It's a dear little thing.'

The quadruped ultimately called Quoodle did not approve of all this at all. Like most dogs, he liked to be with human beings when they were silent; and he extended a magnificent toleration to them as long as they were talking to each other. But conversational attention paid to any other animal at all remote from a mongrel bull-terrier, wounded Mr. Quoodle in his most sensitive and gentlemanly feelings. He emitted a faint growl. Joan, with all the instincts that were in her, bent down and pulled his hair about once more, and felt the instant necessity of diverting the general admiration from *Pycnonotus Haemorrhus*. She turned it to the decoration at the end of the refurnished wing; for they had already come to the last of the long suite of rooms; which ended in some unfinished but exquisite panelling in white and coloured woods, inlaid in the Oriental manner. At one corner the whole corridor ended by curving into a round turret chamber overlooking the landscape; and which Joan, who had known the house in childhood, was sure was an innovation. On the other hand, a black gap still left in the lower left-hand corner of the Oriental woodwork suddenly reminded her of something she had forgotten.

'Surely,' she said (after much mere aesthetic ecstasy), 'there used to be a staircase there, leading to the old kitchen garden, or the old chapel or something.'

Ivywood nodded gravely. 'Yes,' he said, 'it did lead to the ruins of a medieval chapel, as you say. The truth is it led to several things that I cannot altogether consider a credit to the family in these days. All that scandal and joking about the unsuccessful tunnel (your mother may have told you of it), well, it did us no good in the country, I'm afraid; so as it's a mere scrap of land bordering on the sea, I've fenced it off and let it grow wild. But I'm boarding up the end of the room here for quite another reason. I want you to come and see it.'

He led her into the round corner turret in which the new architecture ended; and Joan, with her thirst for the beautiful, could not stifle a certain thrill of beatitude at the prospect. Five open windows of a light and exquisite Saracenic outline looked over the bronze and copper and purple of the autumn parks and forests to the peacock colours of the sea. There was neither house nor living thing in sight; and familiar as she had been with that coast she knew she was looking out from a new angle of vision on a new landscape of Ivywood.

'You can write sonnets?' said Ivywood, with something more like emotion in his voice than she had ever heard in it. 'What comes first into your mind with these open windows?'

'I know what you mean,' said Joan, after a silence. ' "The same that oft——" '

'Yes,' he said. 'That is how I felt . . . "of perilous seas in fairy lands forlorn".'

There was another silence and the dog sniffed round and round the circular turret chamber.

'I want it to be like that,' said Ivywood, in a low and singularly moved intonation. 'I want this to be the end of the house. I want this to be the end of the world. Don't you feel that is the real beauty of all this Eastern art; that it is coloured like the edges of things; like the little clouds of morning and the islands of the blest? Do you know,' and he lowered his voice yet more, 'it has the power over me of making me feel as if I were myself absent and distant; some Oriental traveller who was lost and for whom men were looking. When I see that greenish lemon-yellow enamel there let into the white, I feel that I am standing thousands of leagues from where I stand.'

'You are right,' said Joan, looking at him with some wonder. 'I have felt like that myself.'

'This art,' went on Ivywood as in a dream, 'does indeed take the wings of the morning and abide in the uttermost parts of the sea. They say it contains no form of life; but surely we can read its alphabet as easily as the red hieroglyphics of sunrise and sunset, which are on the fringes of the robe of God.'

'I never heard you talk like that before,' said the lady; and again stroked the vivid violet feathers of the small Eastern bird.

Mr. Quoodle could stand it no longer. He had evidently formed a very low opinion of the turret chamber and of Oriental art generally; but seeing Joan's attention once more transferred to his rival, he trotted out into the longer rooms; and finding the gap in the woodwork which was soon to be boarded up, but which still opened on an old dark staircase, he went galumphing down the stairs.

Lord Ivywood gently placed the bird on the girl's own finger; and went to one of the open windows, leaning out a little.

'Look here,' he said, 'doesn't this express what we both feel? Isn't this the sort of fairy-tale house that ought to hang on the last wall of the world?'

And he motioned her to the window-sill, just outside which hung the bird's empty cage, beautifully wrought in brass or some of the yellow metals.

'Why, that is the best of all!' cried Lady Joan. 'It makes one feel as if it really were the Arabian Nights. As if this were the tower of the gigantic Genii with turrets up to the moon; and this were an enchanted Prince caged in a golden palace suspended by the evening star.'

Something stirred in her dim but teeming sub-consciousness; something like a chill or change, like that by which we half know that weather has altered, or distant and unnoticed music suddenly ceased.

'Where is the dog?' she asked suddenly.

Ivywood turned with a mild grey eye.

'Was there a dog here?' he asked.

'Yes,' said Lady Joan Brett; and gave him back the bird, which he restored carefully to its cage.

.   .   .   .   .

The dog after whom she inquired had in truth trundled down a dark winding staircase and turned into the daylight into a part of the garden he had never seen before; nor, indeed, had anybody else for some time past. It was altogether tangled and over-grown with weeds; and the only trace of human handi-work, the wreck of an old Gothic chapel, stood waist

high in numberless nettles and soiled with crawling
fungoids. Most of these merely discoloured the grey
crumbling stone with shades of bronze or brown;
but some of them, particularly on the side farthest
from the house, were of orange or purple tints almost
bright enough for Lord Ivywood's Oriental decoration. Some fanciful eyes that fell on the place afterwards found something like an allegory in those
graven and broken saints or archangels feeding such
fiery and ephemeral parasites as those toad-stools
like blood or gold. But Mr. Quoodle had never set
himself up as an allegorist; and he merely trotted
deeper and deeper into the grey-green English jungle.
He grumbled very much at the thistles and nettles;
much as a City man will grumble at the jostling of a
crowd. But he continued to press forward, with his
nose near the ground, as if he had already smelt
something that interested him. And indeed he had
smelt something in which a dog, except on special
occasions, is much more interested than he is in dogs.
Breaking through a last barrier of high and hoary
purple thistles he came out on a semicircle of somewhat
clearer ground, dotted with slender trees, and having,
by way of a back scene, the brown brick arch of an
old tunnel. The tunnel was boarded up with a very
irregular fence or mask of motley wooden laths; and
looking somehow rather like a pantomime cottage.
In front of this a sturdy man in a very shabby shooting
clothes was standing attending to a battered old
frying-pan which he held over a rather irregular
flame which, small as it was, smelt strongly of burning
rum. In the frying-pan, and also on the top of a cask
or barrel that served for a table hard by, were a number
of the grey, brown, and even orange fungi which were

plastered over the stone angels and dragon of the fallen chapel.

'Hullo, old man,' said the person in the shooting jacket, with tranquillity and without looking up from his cooking. 'Come to pay us a visit? Come along, then.' He flashed one glance at the dog and returned to the frying-pan. 'If your tail were two inches shorter, you'd be worth a hundred pounds. Had any breakfast?'

The dog trotted across to him and began nosing and sniffing round his dilapidated leather gaiters. The man did not interrupt his cookery, on which his eyes were fixed and both his hands were busy; but he crooked his knee and foot so as to caress the quadruped in a nerve under the angle of the jaw, the stimulation of which (as some men of science have held) is for a dog what a good cigar is for a man. At the same moment a huge voice like an ogre's came from within the masked tunnel, calling out, 'And who are ye talking to?'

A very crooked kind of window in the upper part of the pantomime cottage burst open and an enormous head, with erect, startling and almost scarlet hair and blue eyes as big as a bull frog's, was thrust out above the scene.

'Hump,' cried the ogre. 'Me moral counsels have been thrown away. In the last week I've sung you fourteen and a half songs of me own composition; instead of which you go about stealing dogs. You're following in the path of Parson What's-his-name in every way, I'm afraid.'

'No,' said the man with the frying-pan, impartially. 'Parson Whitelady struck a very good path for doubling on Pebbleswick, that I was glad to follow. But I think he was quite silly to steal dogs. He was young and brought up pious. I know too much about dogs to steal one.'

'Well,' asked the large red-haired man, 'and how do you get a dog like that?'

'I let him steal me,' said the person stirring the pan. And indeed the dog was sitting erect and even arrogant at his feet, as if he was a watch-dog at a high salary, and had been there before the building of the tunnel.

CHAPTER XI

VEGETARIANISM IN THE DRAWING-ROOM

THE company that assembled to listen to the Prophet of the Moon on the next occasion of his delivering any formal address, was much more select than the comparatively mixed and middle-class society of the Simple Souls. Miss Browning and her sister, Mrs. Mackintosh, were indeed present; for Lord Ivywood had practically engaged them both as private secretaries; and kept them pretty busy too. There was also Mr. Leveson, because Lord Ivywood believed in his organizing power; and also Mr. Hibbs, because Mr. Leveson believed in his political judgment, whenever he could discover what it was. Mr. Leveson had straight dark hair; and looked nervous. Mr. Hibbs had straight fair hair; and also looked nervous. But the rest of the company were more of Ivywood's own world; or the world of high finance with which it mixes both here and on the Continent. Lord Ivywood welcomed with something approaching to warmth a distinguished foreign diplomatist; who was, indeed, none other than that silent German representative who had sat beside him in that last conference on the Island of the Olives. Dr. Gluck was no longer in his quiet black suit, but wore an ornate diplomatic uniform with a sword, and Prussian, Austrian, or Turkish Orders; for he was going on from Ivywood to a function at Court. But his curl of red lips, his screw of black moustache, and his unanswering almond eyes had no more changed than the face of a wax figure in a barber's shop window.

The Prophet had also effected an improvement in his dress. When he had orated on the sands his costume, except for the fez, was the shabby but respectable costume of any rather unsuccessful English clerk. But now that he had come among aristocrats who petted their souls as they did their senses, there must be no such incongruity. He must be a proper fresh-picked Oriental tulip or lotus. So he wore long flowing robes of white, relieved here and there by flame-coloured threads of tracery, and round his head was a turban of a kind of pale golden-green. He had to look as if he had come flying across Europe on the magic carpet; or fallen a moment before from his paradise in the moon.

The ladies of Lord Ivywood's world were much as we have already found them. Lady Enid Wimpole still overwhelmed her earnest and timid face with a tremendous costume, that was more like a procession than a dress. It looked rather like the funeral procession of Aubrey Beardsley. Lady Joan Brett still looked like a very beautiful Spaniard with no illusions left about her castle in Spain. The large and resolute lady who had refused to ask any questions at Misysra's earlier lecture, and who was known as Lady Crump, the distinguished Feminist, still had the air of being so full and bursting with questions fatal to Man as to have passed the speaking and reached the speechless stage of hostility. Throughout the proceedings she contributed nothing but bursting silence and a malevolent eye. And old Lady Ivywood, under the oldest and finest lace and the oldest and finest manners, had a look like death on her, which can often be seen in the parents of pure intellectuals. She had that face of a lost mother that is more pathetic than the face of a lost child.

'And what are you going to delight us with to-day?' Lady Enid was asking of the Prophet.

'My lecture,' answered Misysra gravely, 'is on the Pig.'

It was part of a simplicity really respectable in him that he never saw any incongruity in the arbitrary and isolated texts or symbols out of which he spun his thousand insane theories. Lady Enid endured the impact of this singular subject for debate without losing that expression of wistful sweetness, which she wore on principle when talking to such people.

'The Pig, he is a large subject,' continued the Prophet, making curves in the air, as if embracing some particularly prize specimen. 'He include many subjects. It is to me very strange that the Christians should so laugh and be surprised because we hold ourselves to be defiled by pork; we and also another of the Peoples of the Book. But surely you Christians yourselves consider the pig as a manner of pollution; since it is your most usual expression of your despising, of your very great dislike. You say "swine", my dear lady; you do not say animals far more unpopular, such as the alligator.'

'I see,' said the lady; 'how wonderful!'

'If you are annoyed,' went on the encouraged and excited gentleman—'if you are annoyed with any one, with a—what you say?—a lady's maid, you do not say to her "Horse". You do not say to her "Camel".'

'Ah, no,' said Lady Enid earnestly.

' "Pig of a lady's maid," you say in your colloquial English,' continued the Prophet triumphantly. 'And yet this great and awful Pig, this monster whose very name, when whispered, you think will wither all your enemies, you allow, my dear lady, to approach yet closer to you. You incorporate this great Pig in the substance of your own person.'

Lady Enid Wimpole was looking a little dazed at last, at this description of her habits; and Joan gave Lord Ivywood a hint that the lecturer had better be transferred to his legitimate sphere of lecturing. Ivywood led the way into a larger room that was full of ranked chairs, with a sort of lectern at the other end; and flanked on all four sides with tables laden with all kinds of refreshments. It was typical of the strange, half-fictitious enthusiasm and curiosity of that world, that one long table was set out entirely with vegetarian foods, especially of an Eastern sort (like a table spread in the desert for a rather fastidious Indian hermit); but that tables covered with game patties, lobster, and champagne were equally provided; and very much more frequented. Even Mr. Hibbs, who would honestly have thought entering a public-house more disgraceful than entering a brothel, could not connect any conception of disgrace with Lord Ivywood's champagne.

For the purpose of the lecture was not wholly devoted to the great and awful Pig; and the purpose of the meeting even less. Lord Ivywood, the white furnace of whose mind was always full of new fancies hardening into ambitions, wanted to have a debate on the diet of East and West; and felt that Misysra might very appropriately open with an account of the Eastern veto on pork or other coarse forms of flesh food. He reserved it to himself to speak second.

The Prophet began indeed with some of his dizziest flights. He informed the company that they, the English, had always gone in hidden terror and loathing of the pig, as a sacred symbol of evil. He proved it by the common English custom of drawing a pig with one's eyes shut. Lady Joan smiled; and yet she asked herself (in a doubt that had been darkening round her about many modern things lately) whether it was really much more fanciful than many things the scientists told her: as, the traces of Marriage by Capture which they found in that ornamental and even frivolous being, the Best Man.

He said that the dawn of greater enlightenment is shown in the use of the word 'gammon', which still expresses disgust at 'the porcine image' but no longer fear of it, but rather a rational disdain and disbelief. 'Rowley,' said the Prophet solemnly. And then, after a long pause, 'Powley. *Gammon* and spinach.' Lady Joan smiled again: but again asked herself if it was much more far-fetched than a history book she had read, which proved the unpopularity of Catholicism in Tudor times from the word 'hocus-pocus'.

He got into a most amazing labyrinth of philology between the red primeval sins of the first pages of Genesis and the common English word 'ham'. But again Joan wondered whether it was much wilder than the other things she had heard said about Primitive Man, by people who had never seen him.

He suggested that the Irish were set to keep pigs because they were a low and defiled caste, and the serfs of the pig-scorning Saxon. And Joan thought it was about as sensible as what the dear old Archdeacon had said about Ireland years ago; which had caused an Irishman of her acquaintance to play 'The Shan Van Voght' and then smash the piano.

Joan Brett had been thoughtful for the last few days. It was partly due to the scene in the turret, where she had struck a sensitive and artistic side of Philip Ivywood she had never seen before; and partly to disturbing news of her mother's health, which, though not menacing, made her feel hypothetically how isolated she was in the world. On all previous occasions she had merely enjoyed the mad lecturer now at the reading-desk. To-day she felt a strange desire to analyse him: and imagine how a man could be so connected and so convinced and yet so wildly wide of the mark. As she listened carefully, looking at the hands in her lap, she began to think she understood.

The lecturer did really try to prove that the 'porcine image' had never been used in English history or literature except in contempt. And the lecturer really did know a very great deal about English history and literature: much more than she did: much more than the aristocrats round her did. But she noted that in every case what he knew was a fragmentary fact. In every case what he did not know was the truth behind the fact. What he did not know was the atmosphere. What he did not know was the tradition. She found herself ticking off the cases like counts in an indictment.

Misysra Ammon knew, what next to none of the English present knew, that Richard III was called a 'boar' by an eighteenth-century poet and a 'hog' by a fifteenth-century poet. What he did not know was the habit of sport and of heraldry. He did not know (what Joan knew instantly, though she had never thought of it before in her life) that beasts courageous and hard to kill are noble beasts, by the law of chivalry. Therefore the boar was a noble beast; and a common crest for great captains. Misysra tried to show that

Richard had only been called a pig after he was cold pork at Bosworth.

Misysra Ammon knew, what next to none of the English present knew, that there never was such a person as Lord Bacon. The phrase is a falsification of what should be Lord Verulam or Lord St. Albans. What he did not know was exactly what Joan did know (though it had never crossed her mind till that moment), that when all is said and done, a title is a sort of joke, while a surname is a serious thing. Bacon was a gentleman, and his name was Bacon; whatever titles he took. But Misysra seriously tried to prove that 'Bacon' was a term of abuse applied to him during his unpopularity or after his fall.

Misysra Ammon knew, what next to none of the English present knew, that the poet Shelley had a friend called Hogg, who treated him on one occasion with grave treachery. He instantly tried to prove that the man was only called 'Hogg' because he had treated Shelley with grave treachery. And he actually adduced the fact that another poet, practically contemporary, was called 'Hogg' as completing the connexion with Shelley. What he did not know was just what Joan had always known without knowing it; the kind of people concerned; the traditions of aristocrats like the Shelleys or of Borderers like the Ettrick Shepherd.

The lecturer concluded with a passage of impenetrable darkness about pig-iron and pigs of lead, which Joan did not even venture to understand. She could only say that if it did not mean that some day our diet might become so refined that we ate lead and iron, she could form no fancy of what it did mean.

'Can Philip Ivywood believe this kind of thing?'

she asked herself; and even as she did so Philip Ivywood rose.

He had, as Pitt and Gladstone had, an impromptu classicism of diction, his words wheeling and deploying into their proper places like a well-disciplined army in its swiftest advance. And it was not long before Joan perceived that the last phase of the lecture, obscure and monstrous as it seemed, gave Ivywood exactly the opening he wanted. Indeed, she felt no doubt that he had arranged for it beforehand.

'It is within my memory,' said Lord Ivywood, 'though it need in no case have encumbered yours, that when it was my duty to precede the admired lecturer whom I now feel it a privilege even to follow, I submitted a suggestion which, however simple, would appear to many paradoxical. I affirmed or implied the view that the religion of Mahomet was, in a peculiar sense, a religion of progress. This is so contrary, not only to historical convention but to common platitude, that I shall find no ground either of surprise or censure if it takes a perceptible time before it sinks into the mind of the English public. But I think, ladies and gentlemen, that this period is notably abbreviated by the remarkable exposition which we have heard to-day. For this question of the attitude of Islam towards food affords as excellent an example of its special mode of progressive purification as the more popular example of its attitude towards drink. For it illustrates that principle which I have ventured to call the principle of the Crescent: the principle of perpetual growth towards an implied and infinite perception.

'The great religion of Islam does not itself forbid the eating of flesh foods. But in accordance with that principle of growth which is its life, it has pointed the way to a perfection not yet perhaps fully attainable by our nature; it has taken a plain and strong example of the dangers of meat-eating; and hung up the repellent carcass as a warning and a sign. In the gradual emergence of mankind from a gross and sanguinary mode of sustenance, the Semite has led the way. He has laid, as it were, a symbolic embargo upon the beast typical, the beast of beasts. With the instinct of the true mystic, he selected for exemption from such cannibal feasts the creature which appeals to both sides of the higher vegetarian ethic. The pig is at once the creature whose helplessness most moves our pity, and whose ugliness most repels our taste.

'It would be foolish to affirm that no difficulty arises out of the different stages of moral evolution in which the different races find themselves. Thus it is constantly said, and such things are not said without some excuse in document or incident, that followers of the Prophet have specialized in the arts of war, and have come into a contact, not invariably friendly, with those Hindus of India who have specialized in the arts of peace. In the same way the Hindus, it must be confessed, have been almost as much in advance of Islam in the question of meat, as Islam is in advance of Christianity in the matter of drink. It must be remembered again and again, ladies and gentlemen, that every allegation we have of any difference between Hindu and Moslems comes through a Christian channel; and is therefore tainted evidence. But in this matter even, can we not see the perils of disregarding such plain danger-signals as the veto on pork? Did not an Empire nearly slip out of our hands, because our hands were greased

with cow-fat? And did not the well of Cawnpore
brim with blood instead of water, because we would
not listen to the instinct of the Oriental about the
shedding of sacred blood?

'But if it be proposed, with whatever graduation,
to approach that repudiation of flesh food which
Buddhism mainly and Islam partly recommends, it
will always be asked by those who hate the very
vision of Progress: "Where do you draw the line?
May I eat oysters? May I eat eggs? May I drink
milk?" You may. You may eat or drink anything
essential to your stage of evolution, so long as you
are evolving towards a clearer and cleaner ideal of
bodily life. If,' he said gravely, 'I may employ a
phrase of flippancy, I would say that you may eat
six dozen oysters to-day; but I should strongly advise
five dozen oysters to-morrow. For how else has all
progress in public or private manners been achieved?
Would not the primitive cannibals be surprised at
the strange distinction we draw between men and
beasts? All historians pay high honour to the Hugue-
nots, and the great Huguenot Prince, Henri Quatre.
None need deny that his aspiration that every Frenchman should have a chicken in his pot was, for his
period, a high aspiration. It is no disrespect to him
that we, mounting to higher levels, and looking down
longer perspectives, consider the chicken. And this
august march of discovery passes figures higher than
that of Henry of Navarre. I shall always give a high
place, as Islam has always given a high place, to
that figure, mythical or no, which we find presiding
over the foundations of Christianity. I cannot doubt
that the fable, incredible and revolting otherwise,
which records the rush of swine into the sea, was an

allegory of his early realization that a spirit, evil indeed, does reside in all animals in so far as they tempt us to devour them. I cannot doubt that the Prodigal leaving his sins among the swine is another illustration of the great thesis of the Prophet of the Moon. But here also progress and relativity are relentless in their advance; and not a few of us may have risen to-day to the point of regretting that the joyful sounds around the return of the Prodigal should be marred by the moaning of a calf. For the rest, he who asks us whither we go, knows not the meaning of Progress. If we come at last to live on light, as men said of the chameleon, if some cosmic magic closed to us now, as radium was but recently closed, allows us to transmute the very metals into flesh without breaking into the bloody house of life, we shall know these things when we achieve them. It is enough for us now if we have reached a spiritual station, in which at least the living head we lop has not eyes to reproach us; and the herbs we gather cannot cry against our cruelty like the mandrake.'

Lord Ivywood resumed his seat, his colourless lips still moving. By some previous arrangement probably, Mr. Leveson rose to move a motion about Vegetarianism. Mr. Leveson was of opinion that the Jewish and Moslem veto on pork had been the origin of Vegetarianism. He thought it was a great step; and showed how progressive the creed could be. He thought the persecution of the Hindus by Moslems had probably been much exaggerated; he thought our experience in the Indian Mutiny showed we considered the feeling of Easterns too little in such matters. He thought Vegetarianism in some ways an advance on orthodox Christianity. He thought we must be

ready for yet further advances; and he sat down.
And as he had said precisely, clause by clause, everything that Lord Ivywood had said, it is needless to
say that that nobleman afterwards congratulated him
on the boldness and originality of his brilliant speech.

At a similar sort of preconcerted signal, Hibbs
However rose rather vaguely to his feet to second the
motion. He rather prided himself on being a man of
few words, in the vocal sense. He was no orator, as
Brutus was. It was only with pen in hand, in an
office lined with works of reference, that he could
feel that sense of confused responsibility that was the
one pleasure of his life. But on this occasion he was
brighter than usual; partly because he liked being
in a lord's house; partly because he had never tasted
champagne before, and he felt it agreed with him;
partly because he saw in the subject of Progress an
infinite opportunity of splitting hairs.

'Whatever,' said Hibbs, with a solemn cough,
'whatever we may think of the old belief that Moslems
have differed from Buddhism in a regrettable way,
there can be no doubt the responsibility lay with
the Christian Churches. Had the Free Churches
put their foot down and met Messrs. Opalstein's
demand, we should have heard nothing of these old
differences between one belief and another.' As
was, it reminded him of Napoleon. He gave his own
opinion for what it was worth; but he was not afraid
to say at any cost, even there and in that company,
that this business of Asiatic vegetation had occupied
less of the time of the Wesleyan Conference than it
should have done. He would be the last to say, of
course, that any one was in any sense to blame. They
all knew Dr. Coon's qualifications. They all knew

as well as he did that a more strenuous social worker than Charles Chadder had never rallied the forces of Progress. But that which was not really an indiscretion might be represented as an indiscretion; and perhaps we had had enough of that just lately. It was all very well to talk about coffee, but it should be remembered, with no disrespect to those in Canada to whom we owe so much, that all that happened before 1891. No one had less desire to offend our Ritualist friends than he had, but he had no hesitation in saying that the question was a question that could be asked; and though no doubt, from one point of view, the goats——

Lady Joan moved sharply in her chair, as if gripped by sudden pain. And indeed she had suddenly felt the chronic and recurrent pain of her life. She was brave about bodily pain, as are most women, even luxurious women: but the torment that from time to time returned and tore her was one to which many philosophical names have been given: but no name so philosophical as Boredom.

She felt she could not stand a minute more of Mr. Hibbs. She felt she would die if she heard about the goats—from one or any point of view. She slipped from her chair and somehow slid round the corner, in pretence of seeking one of the tables of refreshment in the new wing. She was soon among the new Oriental apartments, now almost completed; but she took no refreshments, though attenuated tables could still be found here and there. She threw herself on an ottoman and stared towards the empty elfin turret chamber in which Ivywood had made her understand that he also could thirst for beauty and desire to be at peace. He certainly had a poetry of his own, after all; a poetry that never touched earth; the poetry of Shelley rather than Shakespeare. His phrase about the fairy turret was true: it did look like the end of the world. It did seem to teach her that there is always some serene limit at last.

She started and half rose on her elbow with a small laugh. A dog of ludicrous but familiar appearance came shuffling towards her and she lifted herself in the act of lifting him. She also lifted her head; and saw something that seemed to her, in a sense more Christian and catastrophic, very like the end of the world.

CHAPTER XII

VEGETARIANISM IN THE FOREST

HUMPHREY PUMP'S cooking a fungus in an old frying-pan (which he had found on the beach) was extremely typical of him. He was, indeed, without any pretence of book-learning, a certain kind of scientific man that science has really been unfortunate in losing. He was the old-fashioned English naturalist, like Gilbert White or even Izaak Walton, who learnt things not academically like an American Professor, but actually, like an American Indian. And every truth a man has found out as a man of science is always subtly different from any truth he has found out as a man; because a man's family, friends, habits, and social type have always got well under way before he has thoroughly learnt the theory of anything. For instance, any eminent botanist at a *soirée* of the Royal Society could tell you, of course, that other edible fungi exist as well as mushrooms and truffles. But long before he was a botanist, still less an eminent botanist, he had begun, so to speak, on a basis of mushrooms and truffles. He felt, in a vague way, that these were really edible: that mushrooms were a moderate luxury, proper to the middle classes; while truffles were a much more expensive luxury, more suitable to the Smart Set. But the old English naturalists, of whom Izaak Walton was perhaps the first and Humphrey Pump perhaps the last, had in many cases really begun at the other end; and found by experience (often most disastrous experience) that some fungi are wholesome and some are not; but the wholesome ones are, on the whole, the majority. So a man like Pump was no more afraid of a fungus as such than he was of an animal as such. He no more started with the supposition that a grey or purple growth on a stone must be a poisonous growth than he started with the supposition that the dog who came to him out of the wood must be a mad dog. Most of them he knew; those he did not know he treated with rational caution, but to him, as a whole race, these weird-hued and one-legged goblins of the forests were creatures friendly to man.

'You see,' he said to his friend the Captain, 'eating vegetables isn't half bad, so long as you know what vegetables there are and eat all of them that you can. But there are two ways where it goes wrong among the gentry. First, they've never had to eat a carrot or a potato because it was all there was in the house; so they've never learnt how to be really hungry for carrots, as that donkey might be. They only know the vegetables that are meant to help the meat. They know you take duck and peas; and when they turn vegetarian they can only think of peas without the duck. They know you take lobster in a salad; and when they turn vegetarian they can only think of the salad without the lobster. But the other reason is worse. There's plenty of good people even round here, and still more in the north, who get meat very seldom. But then, when they do get it, they gobble it up like good 'uns. But the trouble with the gentry is different. The trouble is, the same sort of gentry that don't want to eat meat don't really want to eat anything. The man called a vegetarian who goes to Ivywood House is generally like a cow trying to live on a blade of grass a day. You and I, Captain, have pretty well been vegetarians for some time, so as not to break into the cheese; and we haven't found it so difficult, because we eat as much as we can.'

'It's not so difficult as being teetotallers,' answered Dalroy, 'so as not to break into the cask. But I'll never deny that I feel the better for that, too, on the whole. But only because I could leave off being one whenever I chose. And, now I come to think of it,' he cried, with one of his odd returns of animal energy, 'if I'm to be a vegetarian why shouldn't I drink? Why shouldn't I have a purely vegetarian drink? Why shouldn't I take vegetables in their highest form, so to speak? The modest vegetarians ought obviously to stick to wine or beer, plain vegetarian drinks, instead of filling their goblets with the blood of bulls and elephants, as all conventional meat-eaters do, I suppose. What is the matter?'

'Nothing,' answered Pump. 'I was looking out for somebody who generally turns up about this time. But I think I'm fast.'

'I should never have thought so from the look of you,' answered the Captain; 'but what I'm saying is that the drinking of decent fermented liquor is just simply the triumph of vegetarianism. Why, it's an inspiring idea! I could write a sort of song about it. As, for instance:

> 'You will find me drinking rum,
>   Like a sailor in a slum,
> You will find me drinking beer like a Bavarian.
>   You will find me drinking gin
>   In the lowest kind of inn,
> Because I am a rigid Vegetarian.'

'Why, it's a vista of verbal felicity and spiritual edification! It has I don't know how many hundred

aspects! Let's see; how could the second verse go?
Something like:

> 'So I cleared the inn of wine,
>   And I tried to climb the sign,
> And I tried to hail the constable as "Marion".
>   But he said I couldn't speak,
>   And he bowled me to the Beak
> Because I was a Happy Vegetarian.'

'I really think something instructive to the human
race may come out of all this. . . . Hullo! Is that
what you were looking for?'

The quadruped Quoodle came in out of the woods
a whole minute later than the usual time and took
his seat beside Humphrey's left foot with a preoccupied
air.

'Good old boy!' said the Captain. 'You seem to
have taken quite a fancy to us. I doubt, Hump,
if he's properly looked after up at the house. I particularly don't want to talk against Ivywood, Hump.
I don't want his soul to be able in all eternity to accuse
my soul of a mean detraction. I want to be fair to
him, because I hate him like hell, and he has taken
from me all for which I lived. But I don't think,
with all this in my mind, I don't think I say anything
beyond what he would own himself (for his brain is
clear) when I say that he could never understand an
animal. And so he could never understand the animal
side of a man. He doesn't know to this day, Hump,
that your sight and hearing are sixty times quicker
than his. He doesn't know that I have a better
circulation. That explains the extraordinary people
he picks up and acts with: he never looks at them
as you and I look at that dog. There was a fellow

calling himself Gluck who was (mainly by Ivywood's influence, I believe) his colleague on the Turkish conferences, being supposed to represent Germany. My dear Hump, he was a man a great gentleman like Ivywood ought not to have touched with a barge-pole. It's not the race he was—if it was one race—it's the Sort he was. A coarse, common, Levantine nark and eavesdropper—but you mustn't lose your temper, Hump. I implore you, Hump, to control this tendency to lose your temper, when talking at any length about such people. Have recourse, Hump, to that consoling system of versification which I have already explained to you.

> 'Oh, I knew a Doctor Gluck,
>   And his nose it had a hook,
> And his attitudes were anything but Aryan;
>   So I gave him all the pork
>   That I had, upon a fork;
> Because I am myself a Vegetarian.'

'If you are,' said Humphrey Pump, 'you'd better come and eat some vegetables. The White Hat can be eaten cold—or raw, for that matter. But Blood-spots wants some cooking.'

'You are right, Hump,' said Dalroy, seating himself with every appearance of speechless greed. 'I will be silent. As the poet says:

> 'I am silent in the Club,
>   I am silent in the pub,
> I am silent on a bally peak in Darien;
>   For I stuff away for life
>   Shoving peas in with a knife,
> Because I am at heart a Vegetarian.'

He fell to his food with great gusto, dispatched a good deal of it in a very short time, threw a glance of gloomy envy at the cask; and then sprang to his feet again. He caught up the inn sign from where it leant against the pantomime cottage, and planted it like a pike in the ground beside him. Then he began to sing again, in an even louder voice than before.

> 'O Lord Ivywood may lop,
>   And is also free to top,
> And his privilege is sylvan and riparian.
>   But——'

'Do you know,' said Hump, also finishing his lunch, 'that I'm rather tired of that particular tune.'

'Tired, is it?' said the indignant Irishman. 'Then I'll sing you a longer song, to an even worse tune, about more and more vegetarians; and you shall see me dance as well; and I will dance till you burst into tears and offer me the half of your kingdom; and I shall ask for Mr. Leveson's head on the frying-pan. For this, let me tell you, is a song of Oriental origin, celebrating the caprices of an ancient Babylonian Sultan and should be performed in palaces of ivory with palm-trees and a bul-bul accompaniment.'

And he began to bellow another and older lyric of his own on vegetarianism.

> 'Nebuchadnezzar the King of the Jews
> Suffered from new and original views,
> He crawled on his hands and knees, it's said,
> With grass in his mouth and a crown on his head.
>
>   With a wowtyiddly, etc.
>
> Those in traditional paths that trod
> Thought the thing was a curse from God,
> But a Pioneer men always abuse
> Like Nebuchadnezzar the King of the Jews.'

Dalroy, as he sang this, actually began to dance about like a ballet girl, an enormous and ridiculous figure in the sunlight; waving the wooden sign round his head. Quoodle opened his eyes and pricked up his ears and seemed much interested in these extra-ordinary evolutions. Suddenly, with one of those startling changes that will transfigure the most seden-tary dogs, Quoodle decided that the dance was a game, and began to bark and bound round the performer, sometimes leaping so far into the air as almost to threaten the man's throat. But though the sailor naturally knew less about dogs than the countryman, he knew enough about them (as about many other things) not to be afraid; and the voice he sang with might have drowned the baying of a pack.

'Black Lord Foulon the Frenchman slew,
Thought it a Futurist thing to do.
He offered them grass instead of bread.
So they stuffed him with grass when they cut off his
    head.
            With a wowtyiddly, etc.

For the pride of his soul he perished then—
But of course it is always of Pride that men
A Man in Advance of his Age accuse,
Like Nebuchadnezzar the King of the Jews.

Simeon Scudder of Styx, in Maine,
Thought of the thing and was at it again.
He gave good grass and water in pails
To a thousand Irishmen hammering rails.
            With a wowtyiddly, etc.

Appetites differ; and tied to a stake
He was tarred and feathered for Conscience' Sake.
But stoning the prophets is ancient news,
Like Nebuchadnezzar the King of the Jews.'

In an abandon unusual even for him, he had danced his way down through the thistles into the jungle of weeds risen round the sunken chapel. And the dog, now fully convinced that it was not only a game, but an expedition, perhaps a hunting expedition, ran barking in front of him, along the path that his own dog's paws had already burst through the tangle. Before Patrick Dalroy well knew what he was doing, or even remembered that he still carried the ridiculous sign-board in his hand, he found himself outside the open porch of a sort of narrow tower at the angle of a building which, to the best of his recollection, he had never seen before. Quoodle instantly ran up four or five steps in the dark staircase inside, and then, lifting up his ears again, looked back for his companion.

There is perhaps such a thing as asking too much of a man. If there is, it was asking too much of Patrick Dalroy to ask him not to accept so eccentric an invitation. Hurriedly plunging his unwieldly wooden ensign upright in the thick of thistles and grass, he bent his gigantic neck and shoulders to enter the porch, and proceeded to climb the stair. It was quite dark, and it was only after at least two twists of the stone spiral that he saw light ahead of him; and then it was a sort of rent in the wall that seemed to him as ragged as the mouth of a Cornish cave. It was also so low that he had some difficulty in squeezing his bulk through it; but the dog had jumped through with an air of familiarity, and once more looked back to see him follow.

If he had found himself inside any ordinary domestic interior he would have instantly repented his escapade and gone back. But he found himself in surroundings which he had never seen before or even, in one sense, believed possible.

His first feeling was that he was walking in the most sealed and secret suite of apartments in the castle of a dream. All the chambers had that air of perpetually opening inwards, which is the soul of the *Arabian Nights*. And the ornament was of the same tradition: gorgeous and flamboyant yet featureless and stiff. A purple mansion seemed to be built inside a green mansion and a golden mansion inside that. And the quaintly cut doorways or fretted lattices all had wavy lines like a dancing sea; and for some reason (sea-sickness for all he knew) this gave him a feeling as if the place was beautiful, but faintly evil: as if it were bored and twisted for the fallen palace of the Worm.

But, he had also another sensation, which he could not analyse; but it reminded him of being a fly on the ceiling or the wall. Was it the Hanging Gardens of Babylon coming back to his imagination; or the Castle East of the Sun and West of the Moon? Then he remembered that in some boyish illness he had stared at a rather Moorish sort of wall-paper, which was like rows and rows of brightly coloured corridors empty and going on for ever. And he remembered that a fly was walking along one of the parallel lines: and it seemed to his childish fancy that the corridors were all dead in front of the fly, but all came to life as he passed.

'By George!' he cried. 'I wonder whether that's the real truth about East and West! That the gorgeous East offers everything needed for adventures except the man to enjoy them. It would explain the tradition of the Crusades uncommonly well. Perhaps that's what God meant by Europe and Asia. We dress the characters and they paint the scenery. Well, anyhow, three of the least Asiatic things in the world are lost in this endless Asiatic palace—a good dog, a straight sword, and an Irishman.'

But as he went down this telescope of tropical colours he really felt something of that hard fatalistic freedom of the heroes (or should we say villains?) in the *Arabian Nights*. He was prepared for any impossibility. He would hardly have been surprised if from under the lid of one of the porcelain pots standing in a corner had come a serpentine string of blue or yellow smoke, as if some wizard's oil were within. He would hardly have been surprised if from under the curtains or closed doors had crawled out a snaky track of blood, or if a dumb negro dressed in white had come out with a bow-string having done his work. He would not have been surprised if he had walked suddenly into the still chamber of some Sultan asleep, whom to wake was a death in torments. And yet he was very much more surprised by what he did see; and when he saw it, he was certain at last that he was only wandering in the labyrinth of his own brain. For what he saw was what was really in the core of all his dreams.

What he saw indeed was more appropriate to that inmost Eastern chamber than anything he had imagined. On a divan of blood-red and orange cushions lay a startlingly beautiful woman, with a skin almost swarthy enough for an Arab's; and who might well have been the Princess proper to such an Arabian tale. But in truth it was not her appropriateness to the scene, but rather her inappropriateness, that made his heart bound. It was not her strangeness but her familiarity that made his big feet suddenly stop.

The dog ran on yet more rapidly; and the princess on the sofa welcomed him warmly, lifting him on his short hind legs. Then she looked up; and seemed turned to stone.

'Bismillah,' said the Oriental traveller affably, 'may your shadow never grow less—or more, as the ladies would say. The Commander of the Faithful has deputed his least competent slave to bring you back a dog. Owing to temporary delay in collecting the fifteen largest diamonds in the moon, he has been compelled to send the animal without any collar. Those responsible for the delay will instantly be beaten to death with the tails of dragons——'

The frightful shock, which had not yet left the lady's face, brought him back to responsible speech.

'In short,' he said, 'in the name of the Prophet, dog. I say, Joan, I wish this wasn't a dream.'

'It isn't,' said the girl, speaking for the first time, 'and I don't know yet whether I wish it was.'

'Well,' argued the dreamer rationally, 'what are you, any time, if you're not a dream—or a vision? And what are all these rooms, if they aren't a dream—or rather a nightmare?'

'This is the new wing of Ivywood House,' said the lady addressed as Joan, speaking with great difficulty. 'Lord Ivywood has fitted them up in the Eastern style; he is inside conducting a most interesting debate in defence of Eastern Vegetarianism. I only came out because the room was rather hot.'

'Vegetarian!' cried Dalroy, with abrupt and rather unreasonable exasperation. 'That table seems to fall a bit short of Vegetarianism.' And he pointed to one of the long, narrow tables, laid somewhere in almost all the central rooms, and loaded with elaborate cold meats and expensive wines.

'He must be liberal-minded,' cried Joan, who seemed

to be on the verge of something; possibly temper. 'He can't expect people suddenly to begin being Vegetarians when they've never been before.'

'It has been done,' said Dalroy tranquilly, walking across to look at the table. 'I say, your ascetical friends seem to have made a pretty good hole in the champagne. You may not believe it, Joan, but I haven't touched what you call alcohol for a month.'

With which words he filled with champagne a large tumbler intended for claret-cup, and swallowed it at a draught.

Lady Joan Brett stood up straight but trembling.

'Now that's really wrong, Pat,' she cried. 'Oh, don't be silly—you know I don't care about the alcohol or all that. But you're in the man's house; uninvited; and he doesn't know. That wasn't like you.'

'He shall know all right,' said the large man quietly. 'I know the exact price of a tumbler of that champagne.'

And he scribbled some words in pencil on the back of a bill of fare on the table; and then carefully laid three shillings on top of it.

'And there you do Philip the worst wrong of all,' cried Lady Joan, flaming white. 'You know as well as I do, anyhow, that he would not take your money.'

Patrick Dalroy stood looking at her for some seconds with an expression on his broad and usually open face which she found utterly puzzling.

'Curiously enough,' he observed at last, and with absolutely even temper, 'curiously enough, it is you who are doing Philip Ivywood a wrong. I think him quite capable of breaking England or creation. But I do honestly think he would never break his word. And what is more, I think the more arbitrary and literal his word had been, the more he would keep it. You

will never understand a man like that till you understand that he can have devotion to a definition; even
a new definition. He can really feel about an amendment to an Act of Parliament, inserted at the last
moment, as you feel about England or your mother.'

'Oh, don't philosophize,' cried Joan suddenly. 'Can't
you see this has been a shock?'

'I only want you to see the point,' he replied. 'Lord
Ivywood clearly told me, with his own careful lips,
that I might go in and pay for fermented liquor in any
place displaying a public sign outside. And he won't
go back on that definition, or on any definition. If he
finds me here, he may quite possibly put me in prison
on some other charge, as a thief or a vagabond, or
what not. But he will not grudge the champagne.
And he will accept the three shillings. And I shall
honour him for his glorious consistency.'

'I don't understand,' said Joan, 'one word of what
you are talking about. Which way did you come? How
can I get you away? You don't seem to grasp that
you're in Ivywood House.'

'You see, there's a new name outside the gate,'
observed Patrick conversationally; and led the lady
to the end of the corridor by which he had entered,
and into its ultimate turret chamber.

Following his indications, Lady Joan peered a little
over the edge of the window, where hung the brilliant
purple bird in its brilliant golden cage. Almost
immediately below, outside the entrance to the half-
closed stairway, stood a wooden tavern sign, as solid
and still as if it had been there for centuries.

'All back at the sign of "The Old Ship", you see,'
said the Captain. 'Can I offer you anything in a
ladylike way?'

There was a vast impudence in the slight hospitable movement of his hand that disturbed Lady Joan's features with an emotion other than any that she desired to show.

'Well!' cried Patrick, with a wild geniality, 'I've made you laugh again, my dear.'

He caught her to him in a whirlwind; and then vanished from the fairy turret like a blast, leaving her standing with her hand up to her wild black hair.

CHAPTER XIII

THE BATTLE OF THE TUNNEL

WHAT Joan Brett really felt as she went back from the second *tête-à-tête* she had experienced in the turret, it is doubtless if any one will ever know. But she was full of the pungent feminine instinct to 'drive at practice': and what she did clearly realize was the pencil writing Dalroy had left on the back of Lord Ivywood's menu. Heaven alone knew what it was: and (as it pleased her profane temper to tell herself) she was not satisfied with Heaven alone knowing. She went swiftly back with swishing skirts to the table where it had been left. But her skirts fell more softly and her feet trailed slower and more in her usual manner as she came near the table. For standing at it was Lord Ivywood, reading the card with tranquil, lowered eyelids, that set off perfectly the long and perfect oval of his face. He put down the card with a quite natural action; and, seeing Joan, smiled at her in his most sympathetic way.

'So you've come out too,' he said. 'So have I: it's really too hot for anything. Dr. Gluck is making an uncommonly good speech, but I couldn't stop even for that. Don't you think my Eastern decorations are rather a success after all? A sort of Vegetarianism in design, isn't it?'

He led her up and down the corridors, pointing out lemon-coloured crescents or crimson pomegranates in the scheme of ornament, with such utter detachment that they twice passed the open mouth of the hall of debate; and Joan could distinctly hear the voice of the diplomatic Gluck saying:

'Indeed, we owe our knowledge of the pollution of the pork primarily to the Jewth and not the Mothlemth. I do not thare that prejudithe against the Jewth, which ith too common in my family and all the arithtocratic military Prutthian familieth. I think we Prutthian arithocrats owe everything to the Jewth. The Jewth have given to our old Teutonic rugged virtueth, jutht that touch of refinement, jutht that intellectual thuperiority which——'

And then the voice would die away behind, as Lord Ivywood lectured luxuriantly, and very well, on the peacock tail in decoration, or some more extravagant Eastern version of the Greek Key. But the third time they turned, they heard the noise of subdued applause and the breaking up the meeting; and people came pouring forth.

With stillness and swiftness Ivywood pitched on the people he wanted and held them. He buttonholed Leveson and was evidently asking him to do something which neither of the two liked doing.

'If your lordship insists,' she heard Leveson whispering. 'Of course I will go myself. But there is a great deal to be done here with your lordship's immediate matters. And if there were any one else——'

If Philip, Lord Ivywood, had ever looked at a human being in his life, he would have seen that J. Leveson, Secretary, was suffering from a very ancient human malady; excusable in all men, and rather more excusable in one who has had his top-hat smashed over his eyes and has run for his life. As it was, he saw nothing, but merely said: 'Oh, well, get some one else. What about your friend Hibbs?'

Leveson ran across to Hibbs, who was drinking another glass of champagne at one of the innumerable buffets.

'Hibbs,' said Leveson rather nervously. 'Will you do Lord Ivywood a favour? He says you have so much tact. It seems possible that a man may be hanging about the grounds just below that turret there. He is a man it would certainly be Lord Ivywood's public duty to put into the hands of the police, if he is there. But then, again, he is quite capable of not being there at all—I mean of having sent his message from somewhere else and in some other way. Naturally, Lord Ivywood doesn't want to alarm the ladies, and perhaps turn the laugh against himself, by getting up a sort of police raid about nothing. He wants some sensible, tactful friend of his to go down and look round the place—it's a sort of disused garden—and report if there's any one about. I'd go myself, but I'm wanted here.'

Hibbs nodded, and filled another glass.

'But there's a further difficulty,' went on Leveson. 'He's a clever brute, it seems, "a remarkable and a dangerous man," were his lordship's words: and it looks as if he'd spotted a very good hiding-place; a disused tunnel leading to the sands, just beyond the disused garden and chapel. It's a smart choice, you see, for he can bolt into the woods if any one comes from the shore, or on to the shore if any one comes from the woods. But it would take a good time even to get the police here: and it would take ten times longer to get 'em round to the sea end of the tunnel, especially as the sea comes up to the cliffs once or twice between here and Pebbleswick. So we mustn't frighten him away, or he'll get a start. If you meet any one down there, talk to him quite naturally, and come back with the news. We won't send for the police till you come. Talk as if you were just wandering, like himself.

His lordship wishes your presence to appear quite
accidental.

'Wishes my presence to appear quite accidental,'
repeated Hibbs gravely.

When the feverish Leveson had flashed off, satisfied,
Hibbs took a glass or two more of wine; feeling that
he was going on a great diplomatic mission to please
a lord. Then he went through the opening, picked his
way down the stair, and somehow found his way out
into the neglected garden and shrubbery.

It was already evening, and an early moon was
brightening over the sunken chapel, with its dragon-
coloured scales of fungus. The night breeze was very
fresh, and had a marked effect on Mr. Hibbs. He
found himself taking a meaningless pleasure in the
scene; especially in one fungus that was white with
brown spots. He laughed shortly, to think that it
should be white with brown spots. Then he said, with
carefully accurate articulation: 'His lordship wishes my
presence to appear quite accidental.' Then he tried
to remember something else that Leveson had said.

He began to wade through the waves of weed and
thorn past the chapel, but he found the soil much more
uneven and obstructive than he had supposed.

He slipped, and sought to save himself by throwing
one arm round a broken stone angel at a corner of the
heap of Gothic fragments; but it was loose and rocked
in its socket.

Mr. Hibbs presented for a moment the appearance
of waltzing with the angel in the moonlight, in a very
amorous and irreverent manner. Then the statue
rolled over one way and he rolled over the other; and
lay on his face in the grass, making inaudible remarks.
He might have lain there for some time, or at least

found some difficulty in rising, but for another circumstance. The dog Quoodle, with characteristic officiousness, had followed him down the dark stairs and out of the doorway, and finding him in this unusual posture, began to bark as if the house were on fire.

This brought a heavy human footstep from the more hidden part of the copse; and in a minute or two the large man with the red hair was looking down at him in undisguised wonder. Hibbs said, in a muffled voice which came obscurely from under his hidden face:

'Wish my presence to appear quite accidental.'

'It does,' said the Captain. 'Can I help you up? Are you hurt?'

He gently set the prostrate gentleman on his feet; and looked genuinely concerned. The fall had somewhat sobered Lord Ivywood's representative; and he really had a red graze on the left cheek, that looked more ugly than it was.

'I am so sorry,' said Patrick Dalroy cordially. 'Come and sit down in our camp. My friend Pump will be back presently, and he's a capital doctor.'

His friend Pump may or may not have been a capital doctor, but the Captain himself was certainly a most inefficient one. So small was his talent for diagnosing the nature of a disease at sight, that having given Mr. Hibbs a seat on a fallen tree by the tunnel, he proceeded to give him (in mere automatic hospitality) a glass of rum.

Mr. Hibbs' eyes awoke again when he had sipped it; but they awoke to a new world.

'Wharever may be our individual 'pinions,' he said; and looked into space with an expression of humorous sagacity.

He then put his hand hazily in his pocket, as if to

find some letter he had to deliver. He found nothing but his old journalistic note-book, which he often carried when there was a chance of interviewing any-body. The feel of it under his fingers changed the whole attitude of his mind. He took it out and said:

'And wha' would you say of Vegetarianism, Colonel Pump?'

'I think it palls,' replied the recipient of this complex title, staring.

'Sha'we say,' asked Hibbs brightly, turning a leaf in his note-book, 'sha'we say long been strong veg'tarian by conviction?'

'No; I have only once been convicted,' answered Dalroy, with restraint. 'And I hope to lead a better life when I come out.'

'Hopes lead better life,' murmured Hibbs, writing eagerly with the wrong end of his pencil. 'And wha' would you shay was the best vegable food for really strong veg'tarian by conviction?'

'Thistles,' said the Captain wearily. 'But I don't know much about it, you know.'

'Lord Ivywoo' strong veg'tarian by conviction,' said Mr. Hibbs, shaking his head with unction. 'Lord Ivywoo' says tact. Talk to him naturally. And so I do. That's what I do. Talk to him naturally.'

Humphrey Pump came through the clearer part of the wood leading the donkey, which had just partaken of the diet recommended to a vegetarian by conviction. The dog sprang up and ran to them. Pump was, perhaps, the most naturally polite man in the world, and said nothing. But his eyes had accepted with one snap of surprise the other fact, also not unconnected with diet, which had escaped Dalroy's notice when he administered rum as a restorative.

'Lord Ivywoo' says,' murmured the journalistic diplomatist, 'Lord Ivywoo' says, "Talk as if you were just wandering." That's it. That's tact. That's what I've got to do—talk as if I was just wandering. Long way round to other end tunnel: sea and cliffs. Don' s'pose they can swim.' He seized his note-book again and looked in vain for his pencil. 'Good subjec' cosspondence. Can Policem'n Swim?'

'Policemen?' said Dalroy, in a dead silence. The dog looked up; and the innkeeper did not.

'Get to Ivywood one thing,' reasoned the diplomatist. 'Get policemen beach other end other thing. No good do one thing no' do other thing, no goo' do other thing no' do other thing. Wish my presence appear quite accidental. Haw!'

'I'll harness the donkey,' said Pump.

'Will he go through that door?' asked Dalroy, with a gesture towards the entrance of the rough boarding with which they had faced the tunnel, 'or shall I smash it all at once?'

'He'll go through all right,' answered Pump. 'I saw to that when I made it. And I think I'll get him to the safe end of the tunnel before I load him up. The best thing you can do is to pull up one of those saplings to bar the door with. That'll delay them a minute or two; though I think we've got warning in pretty easy time.'

He led his donkey to the cart and carefully harnessed the donkey; like all men cunning in the old healthy sense, he knew that the last chance of leisure ought to be leisurely, in order that it may be lucid. Then he led the whole equipment through the temporary wooden door of the tunnel, the inquisitive Quoodle, of course, following at his heels.

'Excuse me if I take a tree,' said Dalroy politely to his guest, like a man reaching across another man for a match. And with that he rent up a young tree by its roots, as he had done in the Island of the Olives; and carried it on his shoulder, like the club of Hercules.

.   .   .   .   .

Up in Ivywood House, Lord Ivywood had telephoned twice to Pebbleswick. It was a delay he seldom suffered; and though he never expressed impatience in unnecessary words, he expressed it in unnecessary walking. He would not yet send for the police without news from his ambassador, but he thought a pre-liminary conversation with some police authorities he knew well might advance matters. Seeing Leveson rather shrunk in a corner, he wheeled round in his walk and said abruptly:

'You must go and see what has happened to Hibbs. If you have any other duties here, I authorize you to neglect them. Otherwise I can only say——'

At this moment the telephone rang, and the impatient nobleman rushed for his delayed call with the rapidity he seldom showed. There was simply nothing for Leveson to do except to do as he was told, or be sacked. He walked swiftly towards the staircase, and only stopped once at the table where Hibbs had stood, and gulped down two goblets of the same wine. But let no man attribute to Mr. Leveson the loose and luxurious social motives of Mr. Hibbs. Mr. Leveson did not drink for pleasure; in fact, he hardly knew what he was drinking. His motive was something far more simple and sincere; a sentiment forcibly described in legal phraseology as going in bodily fear.

He was partly nerved, but by no means reconciled

to his adventure, when he crept carefully down the stairs and peered about the thicket for any sign of his diplomatic friend. He could find neither sight nor sound to guide him, except a sort of distant singing, which greatly increased in volume of sound as he pursued it. The first words he heard seemed to run something like:

> 'No more the milk of cows
> Shall pollute my private house
> Than the milk of the wild mares of the Barbarian;
> I will stick to port and sherry
> For they are so very, very,
> So very, very, very Vegetarian.'

Leveson did not know the huge and horrible voice in which these words were shouted. But he had a most strange and sickening suspicion that he did know the voice, however altered, the quavering and rather refined voice, that joined in the chorus and sang:

> 'Because they are so vegy,
> So vegy, vegy, very Veretarian.'

Terror lit up his wits; and he made a wild guess at what had happened. With a gasp of relief he realized that he had now good excuse for returning to the house with the warning. He ran there like a hare, still hearing the great voice from the woods like the roaring of a lion in his rear.

He found Lord Ivywood in consultation with Dr. Gluck; and also with Mr. Bullrose the agent, whose frog-like eyes hardly seemed to have recovered yet from the fairy tale of the flying sign-board in the English lane; but who, to do him justice, was more plucky and practical than most of Lord Ivywood's present advisers.

'I'm afraid Mr. Hibbs has inadvertently,' stammered

Leveson. 'I'm afraid he has. . . . I'm afraid the man is making his escape, my lord. You had better send for the police.'

Ivywood turned to the agent. 'You go and see what's happening,' he said simply. 'I will come myself when I've rung them up. And get some of the servants up with sticks and things. Fortunately the ladies have gone to bed. Hullo! Is that the Police Station?'

Bullrose went down into the shrubbery, and had, for many reasons, less difficulty in crossing it than the hilarious Hibbs. The moon had increased to an almost unnatural brilliancy, so that the whole scene was like a rather silver daylight. And in this clear medium he beheld a very tall man with erect red hair and a colossal cylinder of cheese carried under one arm, while he employed the other to wag a big forefinger at a dog with whom he was conversing.

It was the agent's duty and desire to hold the man, whom he recognized from the sign-board mystery, in play and conversation, and prevent his final escape. But there are some people who really cannot be courteous, even when they want to be, and Mr. Bullrose was one of them.

'Lord Ivywood,' he said abruptly, 'wants to know what you want.'

'Do not, however, fall into the common error, Quoodle,' Dalroy was saying to the dog, whose unfathomable eyes were fixed on his face, 'of supposing that the phrase "good dog" is used in its absolute sense. A dog is good or bad relatively to a limited scheme of duties created by human civilization——'

'What are you doing here?' asked Mr. Bullrose.

'A dog, my dear Quoodle,' continued the Captain, 'cannot be either so good or bad as a man. Nay, I

should go further. I would almost say a dog cannot
be so stupid as a man. He cannot be utterly wanting
as a dog—as some men are as men.'

'Answer me, you there!' roared the agent.

'It is all the more pathetic,' continued the Captain,
to whose monologue Quoodle seemed to listen with
magnetized attention, 'it is all the more pathetic
because this mental insufficiency is sometimes found
in the good; though there are, I should imagine, at
least an equal number of opposite examples. The
person standing a few feet off us, for example, is both
stupid *and* wicked. But be very careful, Quoodle, to
remember that any disadvantage under which we
place him should be based on his *moral* and not his
mental defects. Should I say to you at any time, "Go
for him, Quoodle," or "Hold him, Quoodle," be
certain in your own mind, please, that it is solely because
he is *wicked* and not because he is *stupid*, that I am
entitled to do so. The fact that he is *stupid* would not
justify me in saying, "Hold him, Quoodle," with the
realistic intonation I now employ——'

'Curse you, call him off!' cried Mr. Bullrose, retreating. For Quoodle was coming towards him with the
bull-dog part of his pedigree very prominently displayed, like a pennon. 'Should Mr. Bullrose find it
expedient to climb a tree, or even a sign-post,' proceeded
Dalroy (for indeed the agent had already clasped the
pole of 'The Old Ship', which was stouter than the
slender trees standing just around it), 'you will keep an
eye on him, Quoodle, and, I doubt not, constantly
remind him that it is his *wickedness*, and not, as he might
hastily be inclined to suppose, his *stupidity*, that has
placed him on so conspicuous an elevation.'

'Some of you'll wish yourself dead for this,' said the

agent; who was by this time clinging to the wooden sign like a monkey on a stick, while Quoodle watched him from below with an unsated interest. 'Some of you'll see something. Here comes his lordship and the police, I reckon.'

'Good morning, my lord,' said Dalroy, as Ivywood, paler than ever in the strong moonshine, came through the thicket towards them. It seemed to be his fate that his faultless and hueless face should always be contrasted with richer colours; and even now it was thrown up by the gorgeous diplomatic uniform of Dr. Gluck, who walked just behind him.

'I am glad to see you, my lord,' said Dalroy, in a stately manner; 'it is always so awkward doing business with an agent. Especially for the agent.'

'Captain Dalroy,' said Lord Ivywood, with a more serious dignity, 'I am sorry we meet again like this, and such things are not of my seeking. It is only right to tell you that the police will be here in a moment.'

'Quite time too!' said Dalroy, shaking his head. 'I never saw anything so disgraceful in my life. Of course, I am sorry it's a friend of yours; and I hope the police will keep Ivywood House out of the papers. But I won't be a party to one law for the rich and another for the poor; and it would be a great shame if a man in that state got off altogether merely because he had got the stuff at your house.'

'I do not understand you,' said Ivywood. 'What are you talking of?'

'Why, of him,' replied the Captain, with a genial gesture towards a fallen tree-trunk that lay a yard or two from the tunnel wall, 'the poor chap the police are coming for.'

Lord Ivywood looked at the forest log by the tunnel,

which he had not glanced at before; and in his pale eyes, perhaps for the first time, stood a simple astonishment.

Above the log appeared two duplicate objects, which, after a prolonged stare, he identified as the soles of a pair of patent-leather shoes, offered to his gaze, as if demanding his opinion in the matter of resoling. They were all that was visible of Mr. Hibbs, who had fallen backwards off his woodland seat and seemed contented with his new situation.

His lordship put up the pince-nez that made him look ten years older, and said with a sharp, steely accent, 'What is all this?'

The only effect of his voice upon the faithful Hibbs was to cause him to feebly wave his legs in the air, in recognition of a feudal superior. He clearly considered it hopeless to attempt to get up; so Dalroy, striding across to him, lugged him up by his shirt collar and exhibited him, limp and wild-eyed, to the company.

'You won't want many policemen to take him to the station,' said the Captain. 'I'm sorry, Lord Ivywood, I'm afraid it's no use your asking me to overlook it again. We can't afford it,' and he shook his head implacably. 'We've always kept a respectable house, Mr. Pump and I. "The Old Ship" has a reputation all over the country—in quite a lot of different parts, in fact. People in the oddest places have found it a quiet family house. Nothing gadabout in "The Old Ship". And if you think you can send all your staggering revellers——'

'Captain Dalroy,' said Ivywood simply, 'you seem to be under a misapprehension which I think it would be hardly honourable to leave undisturbed. Whatever these extraordinary events may mean, and whatever be fitting in the case of this gentleman, when I spoke of the police coming, I meant they were coming for you and your confederate.'

'For me!' cried the Captain, with a stupendous air of surprise. 'Why, I have never done anything naughty in my life.'

'You have been selling alcohol contrary to Clause V of the Act of——'

'But I've got a sign,' cried Dalroy excitedly; 'you told me yourself it was all right if I'd got a sign. Oh, do look at our new sign! The Sign of the Agile Agent.'

Mr. Bullrose had remained silent, feeling his position none of the most dignified and hoping his employer would go away. But Lord Ivywood looked up at him; and thought he had wandered into a planet of monsters.

As he slowly recovered himself Patrick Dalroy said briskly, 'All quite correct and conventional, you see. You can't run us in for not having a sign: we've rather an extra life-like one. And you can't run us in as rogues and vagabonds either. Visible means of subsistence,' and he slapped the huge cheese under his arm with his great flat hand, so that it reverberated like a drum. 'Quite visible. Perceptible,' he added, holding it out suddenly almost under Lord Ivywood's nose—'perceptible to the naked eye through your lordship's eyeglasses.'

He turned abruptly, burst open the pantomime door behind him, and bowled the big cheese down the tunnel with a noise like thunder, which ended in a cry of acceptation in the distant voice of Mr. Humphrey Pump. It was the last of their belongings left at this end of the tunnel; and Dalroy turned again, a man totally transfigured.

'And now, Ivywood,' he said, 'what can I be charged with? Well, I have a suggestion to make. I will surrender to the police quite quietly when they come, if you will do me one favour. Let me choose my crime.'

'I don't understand you,' answered the other coolly; 'what crime? What favour?'

Captain Dalroy unsheathed the straight sword that still hung on his now shabby uniform. The slender blade sparkled splendidly in the moonlight as he pointed it straight at Dr. Gluck.

'Take away his sword from the little pawnbroker,' he said. 'It's about the length of mine; or we'll change if you like. Give me ten minutes on that strip of turf. And then it may be, Ivywood, that I shall be removed from your public path in a way a little worthier of enemies who have once been friends; than if you tripped me up with Bow Street runners, of whose help every ancestor you have would have been ashamed. Or, on the other hand, it may be—that when the police come, there will be something to arrest me for.'

There was a long silence; and the elf of irresponsibility peeped out again for an instant in Dalroy's mind.

'Mr. Bullrose will see fair play for you, from a throne above the lists,' he said. 'I have already put my honour in the hands of Mr. Hibbs.'

'I must decline Captain Dalroy's invitation,' said Ivywood at last, in a curious tone. 'Not so much because——'

Before he could proceed, Leveson came racing across the copse, halloaing, 'The police are here!'

Dalroy, who loved leaving everything to the last instant, tore up the sign, with Bullrose literally hanging to it, shook him off like a ripe fruit; and then plunged into the tunnel, the clamorous Quoodle at his heels. Before even Ivywood (the promptest of his party) could reach the spot, he had clashed to the wood door and bolted it across with his wooden staple. He had not had time even to sheath his sword.

'Break down this door,' said Ivywood calmly. 'I noticed they haven't finished loading their cart.'

Under his directions, and vastly against their will, Bullrose and Leveson lifted the tree-trunk vacated by Hibbs, and swinging it thrice as a battering-ran, burst in the door. Lord Ivywood instantly sprang into the entrance.

A voice called out to him quietly from the other end of the tunnel. There was something touching and yet terrible about a voice so human coming out of that inhuman darkness. If Philip Ivywood had been really a poet, and not rather its opposite, an aesthete, he would have known that all the past and people of England were uttering their oracle out of the cavern. As it was, he only heard a publican wanted by the police. Yet even he paused, and indeed seemed spellbound.

'My lord, I would like a word. I learned my catechism; and never was with the Radicals. I want you to look at what you've done to me. You've stolen a house that was mine, as that one's yours. You've made me a dirty tramp, that was a man respected in church and market. Now you send me where I might have cells or the cat. If I might make so bold, what do you suppose I think of you? Do you think because you go up to London and settle it with lords in Parliament, and bring back a lot of papers and long words, that makes any difference to the man you do it to? By what I can see, you're just a bad and cruel master, like those God punished in the old days; like Squire Varney the weasels killed in Holy Wood. Well, parson always said we might shoot at robbers. And I want to tell your lordship,' he ended respectfully, 'that I have a gun.'

Ivywood instantly stepped into the darkness; and spoke in a voice shaken with some emotion, the nature of which was never certainly known.

'The police are here,' he said. 'But I'll arrest you myself.'

A shot shrieked and rattled through the thousand echoes of the tunnel: Lord Ivywood's legs doubled and twisted under him; and he collapsed on the earth with a bullet above his knee.

Almost at the same instant a shout and a bark announced that the cart had started as a complete equipage. It was even more than complete, for the instant it moved Mr. Quoodle had sprung into it; and as it was driven off, sat erect in it, looking solemn.

CHAPTER XIV

THE CREATURE THAT MAN FORGETS

DESPITE the natural hubbub round the wound of Lord Ivywood and the difficulties of the police in finding their way to the shore, the fugitives of The Flying Inn must almost certainly have been captured, but for a curious accident; which also flowed, as it happened, from the great Ivywood debate on Vegetarianism.

The comparatively late hour at which Lord Ivywood had made his discovery had been largely due to a very long speech which Joan had not heard, and which was delivered immediately before the few concluding observations she had heard from Dr. Gluck. The speech was made by an eccentric, of course. Most of those who attended, and nearly all of those who talked, were eccentric in one way or another. But he was an eccentric of great wealth and good family, an M.P., a J.P., a relation of Lady Enid, a man well known in art and letters—in short, a personality who could not be prevented from being anything he chose, from a revolutionist to a bore.

Dorian Wimpole had first become famous outside his own class under the fanciful title of the Poet of the Birds. A volume of verse, expanding the several notes or cries of separate song-birds into fantastic soliloquies of these feathered philosophers, had really contained a great deal of ingenuity and elegance. Unfortunately he was one of those who always tend to take their own fancies seriously; and in whose otherwise legitimate extravagance there is too little of the juice of jest. Hence, in his later works, when he explained 'The fable of the Angel' by trying to prove that the fowls of the air were creatures higher than man or the anthropoids, his manner was felt to be too austere. And when he moved an amendment to Lord Ivywood's scheme for the model village called Peaceways, urging that its houses should all follow the more hygienic architecture of nests hung in trees, many regretted that he had lost his light touch. But when he went beyond birds and filled his poems with conjectural psychology about all the Zoological Gardens, his meaning became obscure; and Lady Susan had even described it as his bad period. It was all the more uncomfortable reading because he poured forth the imaginary hymns, love-songs, and war-songs of the lower animals, without a word of previous explanation. Thus if some one seeking for an ordinary drawing-room song came on lines that were headed 'A Desert Love Song', and which began:

> 'Her head is high against the stars,
> Her hump is heaved in pride',

the compliment to the lady would at first seem startling; until the reader realized that all the characters in the idyll were camels. Or if he began a simple poem entitled 'The March of Democracy' and found in the first lines:

> 'Comrades, marching evermore,
> Fix your teeth in floor and door',

he might be doubtful about such a policy for the masses; until he discovered that it was supposed to be addressed by an eloquent and aspiring rat to the social solidarity of his race. Lord Ivywood had nearly quarrelled with his poetic relative over the uproarious realism of the

18

verses called 'A Drinking Song'; until it was carefully explained to him that the drink was water, and that the festive company consisted of bisons. His visions of the perfect husband, as it exists in the feelings of the young female walrus, is thoughtful and suggestive; but would doubtless receive many emendations from any one who had experienced those feelings. And in his sonnet called 'Motherhood' he has made the young scorpion consistent and convincing, yet somehow not wholly lovable. In justice to him, however, it should be remembered that he attacked the most difficult cases on principle; declaring that there was no earthly creature that a poet should forget.

He was of the blond type of his cousin, with flowing fair hair and moustache, and a bright blue absent-minded eye; he was very well dressed in the carefully careless manner, with a brown velvet jacket; and the image on his ring of one of those beasts men worshipped in Egypt.

His speech was graceful and well worded and enormously long; and it was all about an oyster. He passionately protested against the suggestion of some humanitarians, who were vegetarians in other respects, but maintained that organisms so simple might fairly be counted as exceptions. Man, he said, even at his miserable best, was always trying to excommunicate some one citizen of the cosmos, to forget some one creature that he should remember. Now, it seemed that creature was the oyster. He gave a long account of the tragedy of the oyster, a really imaginative and picturesque account: full of fantastic fishes; and coral crags crawling and climbing; and bearded creatures streaking the sea-shore; and the green darkness in the cellars of the sea.

'What a horrid irony it is,' he cried, 'that this is the only one of the lower creatures whom we call a Native! We speak of him, and of him alone, as if he were a native of the country. Whereas, indeed, he is an exile in the universe. What can be conceived more pitiful than the eternal frenzy of the impotent amphibian? What is more terrible than the tear of an oyster? Nature herself has sealed it with the hard seal of eternity. The creature man forgets bears against him a testimony that cannot be forgotten. For the tears of widows and of captives are wiped away at last like the tears of children. They vanish like the mists of morning or the small pools after a flood. But the tear of the oyster is a pearl.'

The Poet of the Birds was so excited with his own speech that, after the meeting, he walked out with a wild eye to the motor-car, which had been long awaiting him, the chauffeur giving some faint signs of relief.

'Towards home, for the present,' said the poet, and stared at the moon with an inspired face.

He was very fond of motoring, finding it fed him with inspirations; and he had been doing it from an early hour that morning, having enjoyed a slightly lessened sleep. He had scarcely spoken to anybody until he spoke to the cultured crowd at Ivywood. He did not wish to speak to any one for many hours yet. His ideas were racing. He had thrown on a fur coat over his velvet jacket; but he let it fly open, having long forgotten the coldness in the splendour of the moonstruck night. He realized only two things: the swiftness of his car and the swiftness of his thoughts. He felt, as it were, a fury of omniscience: he seemed flying with every bird that sped or spun above the woods, with every squirrel that had leapt and tumbled

within them, with every tree that had swung under and
sustained the blast.

Yet in a few moments he leaned forward and tapped
the glass frontage of the car; and the chauffeur, suddenly squaring his shoulders, jarringly stopped the
wheels. Dorian Wimpole had just seen something
in the clear moonlight by the roadside, which appealed
both to this and to the other side of his tradition;
something that appealed to Wimpole as well as to
Dorian.

Two shabby-looking men, one in tattered gaiters
and the other in what looked like the remains of
fancy dress, with the addition of hair of so wild a red
that it looked like a wig, were halted under the hedge,
apparently loading a donkey-cart. At least two
rounded, rudely cylindrical objects, looking more or
less like tubs, stood out in the road beside the wheels;
along with a sort of loose wooden post that lay along
the road beside them. As a matter of fact, the man in
the old gaiters had just been feeding and watering the
donkey, and was now adjusting its harness more easily.
But Dorian Wimpole naturally did not expect that
sort of thing from that sort of man. There swelled up
in him the sense that his omnipotence went beyond
the poetical; that he was a gentleman, a magistrate, an
M.P. and J.P., and so on. This callousness or ignorance
about animals should not go on while he was a J.P.;
especially since Ivywood's last Act. He simply strode
across to the stationary cart and said:

'You are overloading that animal; and it is forfeited.
And you must come with me to the police-station.'

Humphrey Pump, who was very considerate to
animals, and had always tried to be considerate to
gentlemen, in spite of having put a bullet into one of

their legs, was simply too astonished and distressed to make any answer at all. He moved a step or two backwards and stared with brown, blinking eyes at the poet, the donkey, the cask, the cheese, and the sign-board lying in the road.

But Captain Dalroy, with the quicker recovery of his national temperament, swept the poet and magis-trate a vast fantastic bow and said with agreeable impudence, 'Interested in donkeys, no doubt?'

'I am interested in all things men forget,' answered the poet, with a fine touch of pride, 'but mostly in those like this, that are most easily forgotten.'

Somehow, from those two first sentences, Pump realized that these two eccentric aristocrats had un-consciously recognized each other. The fact that it was unconscious seemed, somehow, to exclude him all the more. He stirred a little the moonlit dust of the road with his rather dilapidated boots, and even-tually strolled across to speak to the chauffeur.

'Is the next police-station far from here?' he asked.

The chauffeur answered with one syllable of which the nearest literal rendering is 'D'no'. Other spellings have been attempted; but the sentiment expressed is that of agnosticism.

But something of special brutality of abbreviation made the shrewd, and therefore sensitive, Mr. Pump look at the man's face. And he saw it was not only the moonlight that made it white.

With that dumb delicacy that was so English in him, Pump looked at the man again; and saw he was leaning heavily on the car with one arm; and saw that the arm was shaking. He understood his countryman enough to know that whatever he said he must say in a careless manner.

'I hope it's nearer to your place. You must be a bit done up.'

'Oh, hell!' said the driver, and spat on the road.

Pump was sympathetically silent, and Mr. Wimpole's chauffeur broke out incoherently, as if in another place:

'Blarsted beauties o' dibrike and no breakfast. Blarsted lunch Hivywood and no lunch. Blarsted black everlastin' hours artside while 'e 'as 'is cike an' champine. And then it's a dornkey!'

'You don't mean to say,' said Pump, in a very serious voice, 'that you've had no food to-day?'

'Ow no!' replied the cockney, with the irony of the death-bed. 'Ow, of course not.'

Pump strolled back into the road again, picked up the cheese in his left hand, and landed it on the seat beside the driver. Then his right hand went to one of his large, loose equivocal pockets, and the blade of a big jack-knife caught and recaught the steady splendours of the moon.

The driver stared for several instants at the cheese, with the knife shaking in his hand. Then he began to hack it; and in that white witchlike light the happiness of his face was almost horrible.

Pump was wise in all such things; and knew that just a little food will sometimes prevent sheer intoxication, so a little stimulant will sometimes prevent sudden and dangerous indigestion. It was practically impossible to make the man stop eating cheese. It was far better to give him a very little of the rum; especially as it was very good rum, and better than anything he could find in any of the public-houses that were still permitted. He walked across the road again and picked up the small cask; which he put on the other side of the cheese and from which he filled, in his own manner, the little cup he carried in his pocket.

But at the sight of this the cockney's eyes lit at once with terror and desire.

'But yer cawn't do it,' he whispered hoarsely, 'it's the pleece. It's gile for that, with no doctor's letter nor sign-board nor nothing.'

Mr. Humphrey Pump made yet another march back into the road. When he got there he hesitated for the first time; but it was quite clear from the attitude of the two insane aristocrats who were arguing and posturing in the road that they would notice nothing except each other. He picked the loose post off the road and brought it to the car, humorously propping it erect in the aperture between keg and cheese.

The little glass of rum was wavering in the poor chauffeur's hand exactly as the big knife had done. But when he looked up and actually saw the wooden sign above him, he seemed, not so much to pluck up his courage, but rather to drag up some forgotten courage from the foundations of some unfathomable sea. It was indeed the forgotten courage of the people.

He looked once at the bleak black pine-woods around him and took the mouthful of golden liquid at a gulp, as if it were a fairy potion. He sat silent; and then very slowly a sort of stony glitter began to come into his eyes. The brown and vigilant eyes of Humphrey Pump were studying him with some anxiety or even fear. He did look rather like a man enchanted or turned to stone. But he spoke very suddenly.

'The blighter!' he said. 'I'll give 'im 'ell! I'll give 'im bleeding 'ell. I'll give 'im somethink wot 'e don't expect.'

'What do you mean?' asked the innkeeper.

'Why,' answered the chauffeur, with abrupt composure, 'I'll give 'im a little dornkey.'

Mr. Pump looked troubled. 'Do you think,' he observed, affecting to speak lightly, 'that he's fit to be trusted even with a little donkey?'

'Ow, yes,' said the man. 'He's very amiable with dornkeys. And dornkeys we is to be amiable with 'im.'

Pump still looked at him doubtfully; appearing or affecting not to follow his meaning. Then he looked equally anxiously across at the other two men: but they were still talking. Different as they were in every other way, they were of the sort who forget everything, class, quarrel, time, place, and physical facts in front of them, in the lust of lucid explanation and equal argument.

Thus, when the Captain began by lightly alluding to the fact that after all it was his donkey, since he had bought it from a tinker for a just price, the policestation practically vanished from Wimpole's mind— and I fear the donkey-cart also. Nothing remained but the necessity of dissipating the superstition of personal property.

'I own nothing,' said the poet, waving his hands outwards—'I own nothing save in the sense that I own everything. All depends whether wealth or power be used for or against the higher purposes of the cosmos.'

'Indeed,' replied Dalroy, 'and how does your motorcar serve the higher purposes of the cosmos?'

'It helps me,' said Mr. Wimpole, with honourable simplicity, 'to produce my poems.'

'And if it could be used for some higher purpose (if such a thing could be), if some new purpose had come into his cosmos's head by accident,' inquired the other, 'I suppose it would cease to be your property?'

'Certainly,' replied the dignified Dorian. 'I should

not complain. Nor have you any title to complain when the donkey ceases to be yours when you depress it in the cosmic scale.'

'What makes you think,' asked Dalroy, 'that I wanted to depress it?'

'It is my firm belief,' replied Dorian Wimpole sternly, 'that you wanted to ride on it' (for indeed the Captain had once repeated his playful gesture of putting his large leg across). 'Is not that so?'

'No,' answered the Captain innocently. 'I never ride on a donkey. I'm afraid of it.'

'Afraid of a donkey!' cried Wimpole incredulously.

'Afraid of an historical comparison,' said Dalroy.

There was a short pause; and Wimpole said coolly enough, 'Oh, well; we've outlived those comparisons.'

'Easily,' answered the Irish Captain. 'It is wonderful how easily one outlives some one else's crucifixion.'

'In this case,' said the other grimly, 'I think it is the donkey's crucifixion.'

'Why, you must have drawn that old Roman caricature of the crucified donkey,' said Patrick Dalroy, with an air of some wonder. 'How well you have worn! Why, you look quite young! Well, of course, if this donkey is crucified, he must be uncrucified. But are you quite sure,' he added, very gravely, 'that you know how to uncrucify a donkey? I assure you it's one of the rarest of human arts. All a matter of knack. It's like the doctor's with the rare diseases, you know; the necessity so seldom arises. Granted that, by the higher purposes of the cosmos, I am unfit to look after this donkey, I must still feel a faint shiver of responsibility in passing him on to you. Will you understand this donkey? He is a delicate-minded donkey. He is a complex donkey. How can I be certain that, on so

short an acquaintance, you will understand every
shade of his little likes and dislikes?'

The dog Quoodle, who had been sitting as still as
the sphinx under the shadow of the pine-trees, waddled
out for an instant into the middle of the road and
then returned. He ran out when a slight noise as of
rotatory grinding was heard; and ran back when it had
ceased. But Dorian Wimpole was much too keen on
his philosophical discovery to notice either dog or wheel.

'I shall not sit on its back, anyhow,' he said proudly,
'but if that were all it would be a small matter. It is
enough for you that you have left it in the hands of the
only person who could really understand it; one who
searches the skies and seas so as not to neglect the
smallest creature.'

'That is a very curious creature,' said the Captain
anxiously. 'He has all sorts of odd antipathies. He
can't stand a motor-car, for instance, especially one
that throbs like that while it's standing still. He doesn't
mind a fur coat so much; but if you wear a brown velvet
jacket under it, he bites you. And you must keep him
out of the way of a certain kind of people. I don't
suppose you've met them; but they always think that
anybody with less than two hundred a year is drunk
and very cruel, and that anybody with more than two
thousand a year is conducting the day of Judgment.
If you will keep our dear donkey from the society of
such persons—— Hullo! Hullo! Hullo!'

He turned in genuine disturbance, and dashed after
the dog, who had dashed after the motor-car and
jumped inside. The Captain jumped in after the dog,
to pull him out again. But before he could do so he
found the car was flying along too fast for any such
leap. He looked up and saw the sign of 'The Old Ship'

erect in the front like a rigid banner; and Pump, with his cask and cheese, sitting stolidly beside the driver.

The thing was more of an earthquake and transformation to him even than to any of the others; but he rose waveringly to his feet and shouted out to Wimpole:

'You've left it in the right hands. I've never been cruel to a motor.'

In the moonlight of the magic pine-wood far behind, Dorian and the donkey were left looking at each other.

To the mystical mind, when it is a mind at all (which is by no means always the case), there are no two things more impressive and symbolical than a poet and a donkey. And the donkey was a very genuine donkey. And the poet was a very genuine poet; however lawfully he might be mistaken for the other animal at times. The interest of the donkey in the poet will never be known. The interest of the poet in the donkey was perfectly genuine; and survived even that appalling private interview in the owlish secrecy of the woods.

But I think even the poet would have been enlightened if he had seen the white, set, frantic face of the man on the driver's seat of his vanishing motor. If he had seen it he might have remembered the name, or perhaps even begun to understand the nature, of a certain animal which is neither the donkey nor the oyster; but the creature whom man has always found it easier to forget, since the hour he forgot God in a garden.

CHAPTER XV

THE SONGS OF THE CAR CLUB

MORE than once as the car flew through blank and silver fairylands of fir-wood and pine-wood, Dalroy put his head out of the side window and remonstrated with the chauffeur without effect. He was reduced at last to asking him where he was going.

'I'm goin' 'ome,' said the driver, in an undecipherable voice. 'I'm a-goin' 'ome to my mar.'

'And where does she live?' asked Dalroy, with something more like diffidence than he had ever shown before in his life.

'Wiles,' said the man, 'but I ain't seen 'er since I was born. But she'll do.'

'You must realize,' said Dalroy, with difficulty, 'that you may be arrested—it's the man's own car; and he's left behind with nothing to eat, so to speak.'

' 'E's got 'is dornkey,' grunted the man. 'Let the stinker eat 'is dornkey, with thistle sauce. 'E would if 'e was as 'ollow as I was.'

Humphrey Pump opened the glass window that separated him from the rear part of the car, and turned to speak to his friend over his square elbow and shoulder.

'I'm afraid,' he said, 'he won't stop for anything just yet. He's as mad as Moody's aunt, as they say.'

'Do they say it?' asked the Captain, with a sort of anxiety. 'They never said it in Ithaca.'

'Honestly, I think you'd better leave him alone,' answered Pump, with his sagacious face. 'He'd just run us into a Scotch Express, like Dandy Mutton did, when they said he was driving carelessly. We can send the car back to Ivywood, somehow, later on. And really, I don't think it'll do the gentleman any harm to spend a night with a donkey. The donkey might teach him something, I tell you.'

'It's true he denied the Principle of Private Property,' said Dalroy reflectively. 'But I fancy he was thinking of a plain house fixed on the ground. A house on wheels, such as this, he might perhaps think a more permanent possession. But I never understand it'; and again he passed a weary palm across his open forehead. 'Have you ever noticed, Hump, what is really odd about those people?'

The car shot on amid the comfortable silence of Pump; and then the Irishman said again:

'That poet in the pussy-cat clothes wasn't half bad. Lord Ivywood isn't cruel; but he's inhuman. But that man wasn't inhuman. He was ignorant: like most cultured fellows. But what's odd about them is that they try to be simple and never clear away a single thing that's complicated. If they have to choose between beef and pickles, they always abolish the beef. If they have to choose between a meadow and a motor, they forbid the meadow. Shall I tell you the secret? These men only surrender the things that bind them to other men. Go and dine with a temperance millionaire, and you won't find he's abolished the hors-d'œuvres or the five courses or even the coffee. What he's abolished is the port and sherry; because poor men like that as well as rich. Go a step farther, and you won't find he's abolished the fine silver forks and spoons; but he's abolished the meat: because poor men like meat—when they can get it. Go a step farther; and you won't find he goes without gardens or gorgeous rooms, which poor men can't enjoy at all. But you will find he boasts of early rising; because sleep is a thing poor men can still enjoy. About the only thing they can still enjoy. Nobody ever heard of a modern philanthropist giving up petrol or typewriting or troops of servants. No, no! What he gives up must be some simple and universal thing. He will give up beef or beer or sleep—because these pleasures remind him that he is only a man.

Humphrey Pump nodded, but still answered nothing; and the voice of the sprawling Dalroy took one of its upward turns of a sort of soaring flippancy; which commonly embodied itself in remembering some song he had composed.

'Such,' he said, 'was the case of the late Mr. Mandragon, so long popular in English aristocratic society as a bluff and simple democrat from the West, until he was unfortunately sandbagged by six men whose wives he had had shot by private detectives, on his incautiously landing on American soil.

'Mr. Mandragon the Millionaire he wouldn't have wine or wife,
He couldn't endure complexity; he lived the simple life;
He ordered his lunch by megaphone in manly simple tones,
And used all his motors for canvassing voters, and twenty tele-
    phones;
        Besides a dandy little machine,
        Cunning and neat as ever was seen,
        With a hundred pulleys and cranks between,
        Made of iron and kept quite clean,
To hoist him out of his healthful bed on every day of his life,
And wash him, and brush him, and shave him, and dress him to
    live the Simple Life.

Mr. Mandragon was most refined, and quietly, neatly dressed,
Say all the American newspapers that know refinement best;
Quiet and neat the hair and hat, and the coat quiet and neat,
A trouser worn upon either leg, while boots adorn the feet;

And not, as any one might expect,
A Tiger Skin, all striped and specked,
And a Peacock Hat with the tail erect,
A scarlet tunic with sunflowers decked,
—That might have had a more marked effect,
And pleased the pride of a weaker man that yearned for wine or wife,
But fame and the flagon for Mr. Mandragon obscured the Simple Life.

Mr. Mandragon the Millionaire, I am happy to say, is dead,
He enjoyed a quiet funeral in a crematorium shed,
And he lies there fluffy and soft and grey, and certainly quite refined,
When he might have rotted to flowers and fruit with Adam and all mankind.
Or been eaten by bears that fancy blood,
Or burnt on a big tall tower of wood,
In a towering flame as a heathen should,
Or even sat with us here at food,
Merrily taking twopenny rum and cheese with a pocket-knife;
But these were luxuries lost for him that lived for the Simple Life.'

Mr. Pump had made many attempts to arrest this song; but they were as vain as all attempts to arrest the car. The angry chauffeur seemed, indeed, rather inspired to further energy by the violent vocal noises behind; and Pump again found it best to fall back on conversation.

'Well, Captain,' he said amicably, 'I can't quite agree with you about those things. Of course you can trust foreigners too much, as poor Thompson did; but then you can go too far the other way. Aunt Sarah lost a thousand pounds that way. I told her again and again he wasn't a nigger, but she wouldn't believe me. And of course that was just the kind of thing to offend an ambassador, if he *was* an Austrian. It seems to me, Captain, you aren't quite fair to these foreign chaps. Take these Americans now. There were many Americans went by Pebbleswick, you may suppose. But in all the lot there was never a bad lot; never a nasty American, nor a stupid American—nor, well, never an American that I didn't rather like.'

'I know,' said Dalroy; 'you mean there was never an American who did not appreciate "The Old Ship".'

'I suppose I do mean that,' answered the innkeeper, 'and somehow I feel "The Old Ship" might appreciate the American too.'

'You English are an extraordinary lot,' said the Irishman, with a sudden and sombre quietude. 'I sometimes feel you may pull through after all.'

After another silence he said, 'You're always right, Hump, and one oughtn't to think of Yankees like that. The rich are the scum of the earth in every country. And a vast proportion of the real Americans are among the most courteous, intelligent, self-respecting people in the world. Some attribute this to the fact that a vast proportion of the real Americans are Irishmen.'

Pump was still silent; and the Captain resumed in a moment.

'All the same,' he said, 'it's very hard for a man, especially a man of a small country like me, to understand how it must feel to be an American; especially in the matter of nationality. I shouldn't like to have to write the American National Anthem; but fortunately there is no great probability of the commission being given. The shameful secret of my inability to write an American patriotic song is one that will die with me.'

'Well, what about an English one?' said Pump sturdily. 'You might do worse, Captain.'

'English, you bloody tyrant!' said Patrick indignantly. 'I could no more fancy a song by an Englishman than you could one by that dog.'

Mr. Humphrey Pump gravely took the paper from his pocket, on which he had previously inscribed the sin and desolation of grocers; and felt in another of his innumerable pockets for a pencil.

'Hallo,' cried Dalroy, 'are you going to have a shy at the Ballad of Quoodle?'

Quoodle lifted his ears at his name. Mr. Pump smiled a slight and embarrassed smile. He was secretly proud of Dalroy's admiration for his previous literary attempt, and he had some natural knack for verse as a game, as he had for all games; and his reading, though desultory, had not been merely rustic or low.

'On condition,' he said deprecatingly, 'that you write a song for the English.'

'Oh, very well,' said Patrick, with a huge sigh that really indicated the very opposite of reluctance. 'We must do something till the thing stops, I suppose, and this seems a blameless parlour game. "Songs of the Car Club." Sounds quite aristocratic.'

And he began to make marks with a pencil on the fly-leaf of a little book he had in his pocket—Wilson's *Noctes Ambrosianae*. Every now and then, however, he looked up and delayed his own composition by watching Pump and the dog; whose proceedings amused him very much. For the owner of 'The Old Ship' sat sucking his pencil and looking at Mr. Quoodle with eyes of fathomless attention. Every now and then he slightly scratched his brown hair with the pencil, and wrote down a word. And the dog Quoodle, with that curious canine power of either understanding, or most brazenly pretending to understanding, what is going on, sat erect with his head at an angle, as if he were sitting for his portrait.

Hence it happened that though Pump's poem was a little long, as are often the poems of inexperienced poets, and though Dalroy's poem was very short (being much hurried towards the end) the long poem was finished some time before the short one.

Therefore it was that there was first produced for the world the song more familiarly known as 'No Noses'; or more correctly called 'The Song of Quoodle'. Part of it ran eventually thus:

> 'They haven't got no noses,
> The fallen sons of Eve;
> Even the smell of roses
> Is not what they supposes;
> But more than mind discloses
> And more than men believe.
>
> They haven't got no noses,
> They cannot even tell
> When door and darkness closes
> The park a Jew encloses,
> Where even the Law of Moses
> Will let you steal a smell.
>
> The brilliant smell of water,
> The brave smell of a stone,
> The smell of dew and thunder,
> The old bones buried under,
> Are things in which they blunder
> And err, if left alone.
>
> The wind from winter forests,
> The scent of scentless flowers.
> The breath of brides' adorning,
> The smell of snare and warning,
> The smell of Sunday morning,
> God gave to us for ours.

．　．　．　．　．　：

And Quoodle here discloses
All things that Quoodle can,
They haven't got no noses,
They haven't got no noses,
And goodness only knowes
The Noselessness of Man.'

This poem also shows traces of haste in its termination; and the present editor (who has no aim save truth) is bound to confess that parts of it were supplied in the criticisms of the Captain; and even enriched (in later and livelier circumstances) by the Poet of the Birds himself. At the actual moment the chief features of this realistic song about dogs was a crashing chorus of 'Bow-wow, wow,' begun by Mr. Patrick Dalroy, but immediately imitated (much more successfully) by Mr. Quoodle. In the face of all this Dalroy suffered some real difficulty in fulfilling the bargain by reading out his much shorter poem about what he imagined an Englishman might feel. Indeed, there was something very rough and vague in his very voice as he read it out; as of one who had not found the key to his problem. The present compiler (who has no aim save truth) must confess that the verses ran as follows:

'St. George he was for England,
And before he killed the dragon
He drank a pint of English ale
Out of an English flagon.
For though he fast right readily
In hair-shirt or in mail,
It isn't safe to give him cakes
Unless you give him ale.

St. George he was for England,
And right gallantly set free
The lady left for dragon's meat
And tied up to a tree;

But since he stood for England
And knew what England means,
Unless you give him bacon
You mustn't give him beans.

St. George he is for England,
And shall wear the shield he wore
When we go out in armour
With the battle-cross before.
But though he is jolly company
And very pleased to dine,
It isn't safe to give him nuts
Unless you give him wine.'

'Very philosophical song that,' said Dalroy, shaking his head solemnly, 'full of deep thought. I really think that is about the truth of the matter, in the case of the Englishman. Your enemies say you're stupid; and you boast of being illogical—which is about the only thing you do that really *is* stupid. As if anybody ever made an Empire or anything else by saying that two and two make five! Or as if any one was ever the stronger for *not* understanding anything—if it were only tip-cat or chemistry. But this *is* true about you, Hump. You English are supremely an artistic people; and therefore you go by associations, as I said in my song. You won't have one thing without the other thing that goes with it. And as you can't imagine a village without a squire and parson, or a college without port and old oak, you get the reputation of a conservative people. But it's because you're sensitive, Hump, not because you're stupid, that you won't part with things. It's lies, lies and flattery, they tell you, Hump, when they tell you you're fond of compromise. I tell ye, Hump, every real revolution is a compromise. D'ye think Wolfe Tone or Charles Stewart Parnell never compromised? But it's just because you're afraid of a compromise that you won't have a revolution. If you really overhauled "The Old Ship"—or Oxford—you'd have to make up your mind what to take and what to leave. And it would break your heart, Humphrey Pump.'

He stared in front of him with a red and ruminant face and at length added, somewhat more gloomily:

'This aesthetic way ye have, Hump, has only two little disadvantages, which I will now explain to you. The first is exactly what has sent us flying in this contraption. When the beautiful, smooth, harmonious thing you've made is worked by a new type, in a new spirit, then I tell you it would be better for you a thousand times to be living under the thousand paper constitutions of Condorcet and Sieyes. When the English oligarchy is run by an Englishman who hasn't got an English mind—then you have Lord Ivywood and all this nightmare, of which God could only guess the end.'

The car had beaten some roods of dust behind it, and he ended still more darkly:

'And the other disadvantage, my amiable aesthete, is this. If ever, in blundering about the planet, you come on an island in the Atlantic—Atlantic, let us say—which won't accept *all* your pretty picture—to which you can't give everything—*then*, you will probably decide to give nothing. You will say in your hearts: "Perhaps they will starve soon"; and you will become, for that island, the deafest and the most evil of all the princes of the earth.'

It was already daybreak; and Pump, who knew the English boundaries almost by intuition, could tell even through the twilight that the tail of the little town they were leaving behind was of a new sort, the sort to be seen in the western border. The chauffeur's phrase about his mother might merely have been a music-hall joke: but certainly he had driven darkly in that direction.

White morning lay about the grey stony streets like spilt milk. A few proletarian early risers, wearier at morning than most men at night, seemed merely of opinion that it was no use crying over it. The two or three last houses, which looked almost too tired to stand upright, seemed to have moved the Captain into another sleepy exposition.

'There are two kinds of idealists, as everybody knows—or must have thought of. There are those who idealize the real and those who (precious seldom) realize the ideal. Artistic and poetical people like the English generally idealize the real. This I have expressed in a song, which——'

'No, really,' protested the innkeeper, 'really now, Captain——'

'This I have expressed in a song,' repeated Dalroy in an adamantine manner, 'which I will now sing with every circumstance of leisure, loudness or any other——'

He stopped because the flying universe seemed to stop. Charging hedgerows came to a halt, as if challenged by the bugle. The racing forests stood rigid. The last few tottering houses stood suddenly at attention. For a noise like a pistol-shot from the car itself had stopped all that race, as a pistol-shot might start any other.

The driver clambered out very slowly, and stood about in various tragic attitudes round the car. He opened an unsuspected number of doors and windows in the car, and touched things and twisted things and felt things.

'I must back as best I can to that there garrige, sir,' he said, in a heavy and husky tone they had not heard from him before.

Then he looked round on the long woods and the last houses; and seemed to gnaw his lip, like a great general who has made a great mistake. His brow seemed as black as ever; yet his voice, when he spoke again, had fallen many further degrees towards its dull and daily tone.

'Yer see, this is a bit bad,' he said. 'It'll be a beastly job even at the best plices, if I'm gettin' back at all.'

'Getting back,' repeated Dalroy, opening the blue eyes of a bull. 'Back where?'

'Well, yer see,' said the chauffeur reasonably, 'I was bloody keen to show 'im it was me drove the car and not 'im. By a bit o' bad luck I done damage to 'is car. Well—if *you* can stick in 'is car——'

Captain Patrick Dalroy sprang out of the car so rapidly that he almost reeled and slipped upon the road. The dog sprang out after him, barking furiously.

'Hump,' said Patrick quietly, 'I've found out everything about you. I know what always bothered me about the Englishman.'

Then, after an instant's silence, he said: 'That Frenchman was right who said (I forget how he put it) that you march to Trafalgar Square to rid yourself of your temper; not to rid yourself of your tyrant. Our friend was quite ready to rebel, rushing away. To rebel sitting still was too much for him. Do you read *Punch*? I am sure you do. Pump and *Punch* must

be almost the only survivors of the Victorian Age.
Do you remember an old joke in an excellent picture,
representing two ragged Irishmen with guns, waiting
behind a stone wall to shoot a landlord? One of the
Irishmen says the landlord is late; and adds, "I hope
no accident's happened to the poor gintleman."
Well, it's all perfectly true; I knew that Irishman
intimately, but I want to tell you a secret about him.
He was an Englishman.'

The chauffeur had backed with breathless care to
the entrance of the garage; which was next door to
a milkman's, or merely separated from it by a black
and lean lane, looking no larger than the crack of a
door. It must, however, have been larger than it
looked; because Captain Dalroy disappeared down it.

He seemed to have beckoned the driver after him:
at any rate that functionary instantly followed. The
functionary came out again in an almost guilty haste,
touching his cap and stuffing loose papers into his
pocket. Then the functionary returned yet again
from what he called the 'garrige', carrying larger and
looser things over his arm.

All this did Mr. Humphrey Pump observe, not
without interest. The place, remote as it was, was
evidently a rendezvous for motorists. Otherwise a
very tall motorist, throttled and masked in the most
impenetrable degree, would hardly have strolled up
to speak to him. Still less would the tall motorist
have handed him a similar horrid disguise of wraps
and goggles, in a bundle over his arm. Least of all
would any motorist, however tall, have said to him
from behind the cap and goggles, 'Put on these things,
Hump, and then we'll go into the milk-shop. I'm
waiting for the car. Which car, my seeker after

truth? Why, the car I'm going to buy for you to drive.'

The remorseful chauffeur, after many adventures, did actually find his way back to the little moonlit wood where he had left his master and the donkey. But his master and the donkey had vanished.

CHAPTER XVI

THE SEVEN MOODS OF DORIAN

THAT timeless clock of all lunatics which was so bright in the sky that night may really have had some elfin luck about it, like a silver penny. Not only had it initiated Mr. Hibbs into the mysteries of Dionysus and Mr. Bullrose into the arboreal habits of his ancestors, but one night of it made a very considerable and rather valuable change in Mr. Dorian Wimpole, the Poet of the Birds. He was a man neither foolish nor evil, any more than Shelley; only a man made sterile by living in a world of indirectness and insincerity; with words rather than with things. He had not had the smallest intention of starving his chauffeur; he did not realize that there was worse spiritual murder in merely forgetting him. But as hour after hour passed over him, alone with the donkey and the moon, he went through a raging and shifting series of frames of mind, such as his cultured friends would have described as moods.

The First Mood, I regret to say, was one of black and grinding hatred. He had no notion of the chauffeur's grievance; and could only suppose he had been bribed or intimidated by the daemonic donkey-torturers. But Mr. Wimpole was much more capable at that moment of torturing a chauffeur than Mr. Pump had ever been of torturing a donkey: for no sane man can hate an animal. He kicked the stones in the road, sending them flying into the forest; and wished that each one of them was a chauffeur. The bracken by the roadside he tore up by the roots, as representing the hair of the chauffeur; to which it bore no resemblance. He hit with his fist such trees, as (I suppose) seemed in form and expression most reminiscent of the chauffeur; but desisted from this; finding that in this apparently one-sided contest the tree had rather the best of it. But the whole wood and the whole world had become a kind of omnipresent and pantheistic chauffeur, and he hit at him everywhere.

The thoughful reader will realize that Mr. Wimpole had already taken a considerable upward stride in what he would have called the cosmic scale. The next best thing to really loving a fellow-creature is really hating him: especially when he is a poorer man, separated from you otherwise by mere social stiffness. The desire to murder him is at least an acknowledgment that he is alive. Many a man has owed the first white gleams of the dawn of Democracy in his soul to a desire to find a stick and beat the butler. And we have it on the unimpeachable local authority of Mr. Humphrey Pump that Squire Merriman chased his librarian through three villages with a horse-pistol: and was a Radical ever after.

His rage also did him good merely as a relief; and he soon passed into a second and more positive mood of meditation.

'The damnable monkeys go on like this,' he muttered, 'and then they call a donkey one of the lower animals. Ride on a donkey, would he? I'd like to see the donkey riding on him for a bit. Good old man.'

The patient ass turned mild eyes on him when he patted it, and Dorian Wimpole discovered, with a sort of subconscious surprise, that he really was fond of the donkey. Deeper still in his subliminal self he knew that he had never been fond of an animal before. His poems about fantastic creatures had been quite sincere; and quite cold. When he said he loved a shark, he meant he saw no reason for hating a shark; which was right enough. There is no reason for hating a shark, however much reason there may be for avoiding one. There is no harm in a Craken if you keep it in a tank—or in a sonnet.

But he also realized that his love of creatures had been turned clean round and was working from the other end. The donkey was a companion, and not a monstrosity. It was dear because it was near, not because it was distant. The oyster had attracted him because it was utterly unlike a man; unless it be counted a touch of masculine vanity to grow a beard. The fancy is no idler than that he had himself used, in suggesting a sort of feminine vanity in the permanence of a pearl. But in that maddening vigil among the mystic pines he found himself more and more drawn towards the donkey, because it was more like a man than anything else around him; because it had eyes to see, and ears to hear—the latter even unduly developed.

'He that hath ears to hear, let him hear,' he said, scratching those grey, hairy flappers with affection. 'Haven't you lifted your ears towards heaven? And will you be the first to hear the Last Trumpet?'

The ass rubbed his nose against him with what seemed almost like a human caress. And Dorian caught himself wondering how a caress from an oyster could be managed. Everything else around him was beautiful but inhuman. Only in the first glory of anger could he really trace in a tall pine-tree the features of an ex-taxi-cabman from Kennington.

Trees and ferns had no living ears that they could wag nor mild eyes that they could move. He patted the donkey again.

But the donkey had reconciled him to the landscape; and in his third mood he began to realize how beautiful it was. On a second study, he was not sure it was so inhuman. Rather he felt that its beauty at least was half human; that the aureole of the sinking moon behind the woods was chiefly lovely because it was like the tender-coloured aureole of an early saint; and that the young trees were after all noble because they held up their heads like virgins. Cloudily there crowded into his mind ideas with which it was imperfectly familiar, especially an idea which he had heard called 'The Image of God'. It seemed to him more and more that all these things, from the donkey to the very docks and ferns by the roadside, were dignified and sanctified by their partial resemblance to something else. It was as if they were baby drawings; the wild, crude sketches of Nature in her first sketch-books of stone.

He had flung himself on a pile of pine-needles to enjoy the gathering darkness of the pine-woods as the moon sank behind them. There is nothing more deep and wonderful than really impenetrable pine-woods, where the nearer trees show against the more shadowy; a tracery of silver upon grey and of grey upon black.

It was, by this time, in pure pleasure and idleness that he picked up a pine-needle to philosophize about it.

'Think of sitting on needles!' he said. 'Yet I suppose this is the sort of needle that Eve, in the old legend, used in Eden. Aye, and the old legend was right too!

Think of sitting on all the needles in London! Think
of sitting on all the needles in Sheffield! Think of sitting
on any needles, except on all the needles of Paradise!
Oh, yes, the old legend was right enough. The very
needles of God are softer than the carpets of men.'

He took a pleasure in watching the weird little
forest animals creeping out from under the green
curtains of the wood. He reminded himself that in
the old legend they had been as tame as the ass, as
well as being comic. He thought of Adam naming
the animals; and said to a beetle, 'I should call *you*
Budger.'

The slugs gave him great entertainment, and so
did the worms. He felt a new and realistic interest
in them which he had not known before; it was,
indeed, the interest that a man feels in a mouse in
a dungeon; the interest of any man tied by the leg
and forced to see the fascination of small things.
Creatures of the wormy kind especially crept out at
very long intervals; yet he found himself waiting
patiently for hours for the pleasure of their acquaintance. One of them rather specially arrested his eye,
because it was a little longer than most worms and
seemed to be turning its head in the direction of the
donkey's left fore-leg. Also, it had a head to turn,
which most worms have not.

Dorian Wimpole did not know much about exact
Natural History; except what he had once got up
very thoroughly from an encyclopaedia for purposes
of a sympathetic *vilanelle*. But as this information
was entirely concerned with the conjectural causes
of laughter in the Hyena, it was not directly helpful in
this case. But though he did not know much Natural
History, he knew some. He knew enough to know

that a worm ought not to have a head; and especially
not a squared and flattened head, shaped like a spade
or a chisel. He knew enough to know that a creeping
thing with a head of that pattern survives in the
English country-sides, though it is not common. In
short, he knew enough to step across the road and
set a sharp and savage boot-heel on the neck and
spine of the creature, breaking it into three black
bits that writhed once more before they stiffened.

Then he gave out a great explosive sigh. The
donkey, whose leg had been in such danger, looked
at the dead adder with eyes that had never lost their
moony mildness. Even Dorian himself looked at it
for a long time, and with feelings he could neither
arrest nor understand; before he remembered that
he had been comparing the little wood to Eden.

'And even in Eden,' he said at last; and then the
words of Fitzgerald failed upon his lips.

And while he was warring with such words and
thoughts, something happened about him and behind
him, something he had written about a hundred times
and read about a thousand; something he had never
seen in his life. It flung faintly across the broad
foliage a wan and pearly light far more mysterious
than the lost moonshine. It seemed to enter through
all the doors and windows of the woodland, pale and
silent but confident, like men that keep a tryst; soon
its white robes had threads of gold and scarlet: and
the name of it was morning.

For some time past, loud and in vain, all the birds
had been singing to the Poet of the Birds. But when
that minstrel actually saw broad daylight breaking
over wood and road, the effect on him was somewhat
curious. He stood staring at it in gaping astonishment,

until it had fulfilled the fullness of its shining fate; and the pine-cones and the curling ferns and the live donkey and the dead viper were almost as distinct as they could be at noon, or in a Pre-Raphaelite picture. And then the Fourth Mood fell upon him like a bolt from the blue, and he strode across and took the donkey's bridle, as if to lead it along.

'Damn it all,' he cried, in a voice as cheerful as the cock-crow that rang recently from the remote village, 'it's not everybody who's killed a snake.' Then he added reflectively, 'I bet Dr. Gluck never did. Come along, donkey; let's have some adventures.'

The finding and fighting of positive evil is the beginning of all fun—and even of all farce. All the wild woodland looked jolly now the snake was killed. It was one of the fallacies of his literary clique to refer all natural emotions to literary names: but it might not untruly be said that he had passed out of the mood of Maeterlinck into the mood of Whitman, and out of the mood of Whitman into the mood of Stevenson. He had not been a hypocrite when he asked for gilded birds of Asia or purple polypi out of the Southern Seas: he was not a hypocrite now, when he asked for mere comic adventures along a common English road. It was his misfortune and not his fault if his first adventure was his last; and was much too comic to laugh at.

Already the wan morning had warmed into a pale blue and was spotted with those little plump pink clouds which must surely have been the origin of the story that pigs might fly. The insects of the grass chattered so cheerfully that every green tongue seemed to be talking. The skyline on every side was broken only by objects that encouraged such swashbucklering comedy. There was a windmill that Chaucer's Miller might have inhabited, or Cervantes' champion charged. There was an old leaden church spire that might have been climbed by Robert Clive. Away towards Pebbleswick and the sea, there were the two broken stumps of wood which Humphrey Pump declares to this day to have been the stands for an unsuccessful children's swing; but which tourists always accept as the remains of the antique gallows. In the gaiety of such surroundings, it is small wonder if Dorian and the donkey stepped briskly along the road. The donkey reminded him of Sancho Panza.

He did not wake out of this boisterous reverie of the white road and the wind till a motor-horn had first hooted and then howled, till the ground had shaken with the shock of a stoppage, and till a human hand fell heavily and tightly on his shoulder. He looked up and saw the complete costume of a police inspector. He did not worry about the face. And there fell on him the Fifth, or Unexpected Mood, which is called by the vulgar Astonishment.

In despair he looked at the motor-car itself that had anchored so abruptly under the opposite hedge. The man at the steering-wheel was so erect and unresponsive that Dorian felt sure he was feasting his eyes on yet another policeman. But on the seat behind was a very different figure, a figure that baffled him all the more because he felt certain he had seen it somewhere. The figure was long and slim, with sloping shoulders: and the costume, which was untidy, yet contrived to give the impression that it was tidy on other occasions. The individual had bright yellow hair, one lock of which stuck straight up and was exalted, like the little horn in his favourite

19

scriptures. Another tuft of it, in a bright but blinding
manner, fell across and obscured the left optic, as in
literal fulfilment of the parable of a beam in the eye.
The eyes, with or without beams in them, looked a
little bewildered; and the individual was always
nervously resettling his necktie. For the individual
went by the name of Hibbs, and had only recently
recovered from experiences wholly new to him.

'What on earth do you want?' asked Wimpole of
the policeman.

His innocent and startled face, and perhaps other
things about his appearance, evidently caused the
inspector to waver.

'Well, it's about this 'ere donkey, sir,' he said.

'Do you think I stole it?' cried the indignant aristocrat. 'Well, of all the mad worlds! A pack of thieves
steal my limousine, I save their damned donkey's
life at the risk of my own—and *I'm* run in for stealing.'

The clothes of the indignant aristocrat probably
spoke louder than his tongue; the officer dropped his
hand, and after consulting some papers in his hand,
walked across to consult with the unkempt gentleman
in the car.

'That seems to be a similar cart and donkey,'
Dorian heard him saying. 'But the clothes don't seem
to fit your description of the men you saw.'

Now Mr. Hibbs had extremely vague and wild
recollections of the men he saw. He could not even
tell what he had done and what he had merely dreamed.
If he had spoken sincerely, he would have described
a sort of green nightmare of forests, in which he found
himself in the power of an ogre about twelve feet high,
with scarlet flames for hair and dressed rather like
Robin Hood. But a long course of what is known

as 'keeping the party together' had made it as unnatural to him to tell any one (even himself) what
he really thought about anything, as it would have
been to spit—or to sing. He had at present only
three motives and strong resolves: (1) not to admit
that he had been drunk; (2) not to let any one escape
whom Lord Ivywood might possibly want to question;
and (3) not to lose his reputation for sagacity and
tact.

'This party has a brown velvet suit, you see, and
a furred overcoat,' the inspector continued. 'And
in the notes I have from you, you say the man wore
a uniform.'

'When we say uniform,' said Mr. Hibbs, frowning
intellectually—'when we say *uniform*, of course—we
must distinguish. Some of our friends who don't quite
see eye to eye with us, you know,' and he smiled with
tender leniency, 'some of our friends wouldn't like it
called a *uniform*, perhaps. But . . . of course . . . well,
it wasn't a police uniform, for instance. Ha ha!'

'I should hope not,' said the official shortly.

'So . . . in a way . . . however,' said Hibbs,
clutching his verbal talisman at last, 'it might be
brown velvet in the dark.'

The inspector replied to this helpful suggestion
with some wonder. 'But it was a moon like limelight,'
he protested.

'Yars, yars,' cried Hibbs, in a high tone that can
only be described as a hasty drawl. 'Yars—discolours
everything, of course. The flowers and things——'

'But look here,' said the inspector, 'you said the
principal man's hair was red.'

'A blond type! A blond type!' said Hibbs, waving
his hand with a solemn lightness; 'reddish, yellowish

brownish sort of hair, you know.' Then he shook his head and said with the heaviest solemnity the word was capable of carrying, 'Teutonic. Purely Teutonic.'

The inspector began to feel some wonder that, even in the confusion following on Lord Ivywood's fall, he had been put under the guidance of this particular guide. The truth was that Leveson, once more masking his own fears under his usual parade of hurry, had found Hibbs at a table by an open window, with wild hair and sleepy eyes, picking himself up with some sort of medicine. Finding him already fairly clear-headed in a dreary way, he had not scrupled to use the remains of his bewilderment to dispatch him with the police in the first pursuit. Even the mind of a semi-recovered drunkard he thought could be trusted to recognize any one so unmistakable as the Captain.

But though the diplomatist's debauch was barely over, his strange, soft fear and cunning were awake. He felt fairly certain the man in the fur coat had something to do with the mystery: as men with fur coats do not commonly wander about with donkeys. He was afraid of offending Lord Ivywood, and at the same time afraid of exposing himself to a policeman.

'You have large discretion,' he said gravely. 'Very right you should have large discretion in the interests of the public. I think you would be quite authorized, for the present, in preventing the man's escape.'

'And the other man?' inquired the officer, with knitted brow. 'Do you suppose he has escaped?'

'The *other* man,' repeated Hibbs However, regarding the distant windmill through half-closed lids, as if this were a new fine shade introduced into an already delicate question.

'Well, hang it all,' said the police officer, 'you must know whether there were two men or one.'

Gradually it dawned, in a grey dawn of horror, over the brain of Hibbs that this was what he specially couldn't know. He had always heard, and read in comic papers, that a drunken man 'sees double' and beholds two lamp-posts, one of which is (as the Higher Critic would have said) purely subjective. For all he knew (being a mere novice) inebriation might produce the impression of the two men of his dream-like adventure, when in truth there had only been one.

'Two men, you know—one man,' he said, with a sort of moody carelessness. 'Well, we can go into their numbers later: they can't have a very large following.' Here he shook his head very firmly. 'Quite impossible. And as the late Lord Goschen used to say, "You can prove anything by statistics".'

And here came an interruption from the other side of the road.

'And how long am I to wait here for you and your Goschens, you silly goat?' were the intemperate wood-notes issuing from the Poet of the Birds. 'I'm shot if I'll stand this! Come along, donkey, and let's pray for a better adventure next time. These are very inferior specimens of your own race.'

And seizing the bridle of the ass again, he strode past them swiftly, and almost as if urging the animal to a gallop.

Unfortunately this disdainful dash for liberty was precisely what was wanting to weigh down the rocking intelligence of the inspector on the wrong side. If Wimpole had stood still a minute or two longer, the official, who was no fool, might have ended in disbelieving Hibbs's story altogether. As it was, there was a scuffle, not without blows on both sides; and eventually the Honourable Dorian Wimpole, donkey and all, was marched off to the village: in which there was a police-station; in which there was a temporary cell; in which the Sixth Mood was experienced.

His complaints, however, were at once so clamorous and so convincing, and his coat was so unquestionably covered with fur, that after some questioning and cross purposes they agreed to take him in the afternoon to Ivywood House, where there was a magistrate incapacitated by a shot, only recently extracted from his leg.

They found Lord Ivywood lying on a purple ottoman in the midst of his Chinese puzzle of Oriental apartments. He continued to look away as they entered, as if expecting, with Roman calm, the entrance of a recognized enemy. But Lady Enid Wimpole, who was attending to the wants of the invalid, gave a sharp cry of astonishment; and the next moment the three cousins were looking at each other. One could almost have guessed they were cousins, all being (as Mr. Hibbs subtly put it) a blond type. But two of the blond type expressed amazement; and one blond type merely rage.

'I am sorry, Dorian,' said Ivywood, when he had heard the whole story. 'These fanatics are capable of anything, I fear, and you very rightly resent their stealing your car——'

'You are wrong, Philip,' answered the poet emphatically. 'I do not even faintly resent their stealing my car. What I do resent is the continued existence on God's earth of this Fool' (pointing to the serious Hibbs) 'and of that Fool' (pointing to the inspector), 'and—yes, by thunder, of *that* Fool too' (and he pointed straight at Lord Ivywood). 'And I tell you frankly, Philip, if there really are, as you say, two men who are bent on smashing your schemes and making your life a hell—I am very happy to put my car at their disposal. And now I'm off.'

'You'll stop to dinner?' inquired Ivywood, with frigid forgiveness.

'No, thanks,' said the disappearing bard; 'I'm going up to town.'

The Seventh Mood of Dorian Wimpole had a grand finale at the Café Royal: and consisted largely of oysters.

CHAPTER XVII

THE POET IN PARLIAMENT

DURING the singular entrance and exit of Dorian Wimpole, M.P., J.P., etc., Lady Joan was looking out of the magic casements of that turret room which was now literally, and not only poetically, the last limit of Ivywood House. The old broken hole and black staircase up which the lost dog Quoodle used to come and go, had long ago been sealed up and cemented with a wall of exquisite Eastern workmanship. All through the patterns Lord Ivywood had preserved and repeated the principle that no animal shape must appear. But, like all lucid dogmatists, he perceived all the liberties his dogma allowed him. And he had irradiated this remote end of Ivywood with sun and moon and solar and starry systems, with the Milky Way for a dado and a few comets for comic relief. The thing was well done of its kind (as were all the things that Philip Ivywood got done for him); and if all the windows of the turret were closed with their peacock curtains, a poet with anything like a Hibbsian appreciation of the family champagne might almost fancy he was looking out across the sea on a night crowded with stars. And (what was yet more important) even Misysra (that exact thinker) could not call the moon a live animal without falling into Idolatry.

But Joan, looking out of real windows on a real sky and sea, thought no more about the astronomical wall-paper than about any other wall-paper. She was asking herself in sullen emotionalism, and for the

thousandth time, a question she had never been able
to decide. It was the final choice between an ambition
and a memory. And there was this heavy weight in
the scale: that the ambition would probably materialize;
and the memory probably wouldn't. It has been the
same weight in the same scale a million times, since
Satan became the prince of this world. But the
evening stars were strengthening over the old sea-shore:
and they also wanted weighing like diamonds.

As once before, at the same stage of brooding, she
heard behind her the swish of Lady Enid's skirts, that
never came so fast save for serious cause.

'Joan! Please do come! Nobody but you, I do
believe, could move him.' Joan looked at Lady Enid
and realized that the lady was close on crying. She
turned a trifle pale and asked quietly for the question.
'Philip says he's going to London now, with that
leg and all,' cried Enid, 'and he won't let us say a
word.'

'But how did it all happen?' asked Joan.

Lady Enid Wimpole was quite incapable of explaining how it all happened, so the task must for the
moment devolve on the author. The simple fact was
that Ivywood, in the course of turning over magazines
on his sofa, happened to look at a paper from the
Midlands.

'The Turkish news,' said Mr. Leveson, rather
nervously, 'is on the other side of the page.'

But Lord Ivywood continued to look at the side of
that paper that did not contain the Turkish news, with
the same dignity of lowered eyelids and unconscious
brow with which he had looked at the Captain's
message when Joan found him by the turret.

On the page covered merely with casual provincial

happenings was a paragraph, 'Echo of Pebbleswick Mystery. Reported Reappearance of the Vanishing Inn.' Underneath was printed in smaller letters:

'An almost incredible report from Wyddington announces that the mysterious "Sign of the Old Ship" has once more been seen in this country; though it has long been relegated by scientific investigators to the limbo of old rustic superstitions. According to the local version, Mr. Simmons, a dairyman of Wyddington, was serving in his shop, when two motorists entered, one of them asking for a glass of milk. They were in the most impenetrable motoring panoply, with darkened goggles and waterproof collars turned up, so that nothing can be recalled of them personally, except that one was a person of unusual stature. In a few moments this latter individual went out of the shop again and returned with a miserable specimen out of the street, one of the tattered loafers that linger about our most prosperous towns, tramping the streets all night and even begging in defiance of the police. The filth and disease of the creature were so squalid that Mr. Simmons at first refused to serve him with the glass of milk which the taller motorist wished to provide for him. At length, however, Mr. Simmons consented; and was immediately astonished by an incident against which he certainly had a more assured right to protest.

'The taller motorist, saying to the loafer, "But, man, you're blue in the face"; made a species of sign to the smaller motorist, who thereupon appears to have pierced a sort of cylindrical trunk or chest, that seemed to be his only luggage: and drawn from it a few drops of a yellow liquid, which he deliberately dropped into the ragged creature's milk. It was afterwards discovered to be rum; and the protests of Mr. Simmons may be imagined. The tall motorist, however, warmly defended his action, having apparently some wild idea that he was doing an act of kindness. "Why, I found the man nearly fainting," he said. "If you'd picked him off a raft, he couldn't be more collapsed with cold and sickness. And if you'd picked him off a raft you'd have given him rum —yes, by St. Patrick, if you were a bloody pirate and made him walk the plank afterwards." Mr. Simmons replied with dignity that he did not know how it was with rafts: and could not permit such language in his shop. He added that he would lay himself open to a police prosecution if he permitted the consumption of alcohol in his shop; since he did not display a sign. The motorist then made the amazing reply, "But you *do* display a sign, you jolly old man. Did you think I couldn't find my way to the sign of 'The Old Ship', you sly-boots?" Mr. Simmons was now fully convinced of the intoxication of his visitors; and refusing a glass of rum rather boisterously offered him, went outside his shop to look round for a policeman. To his surprise he found the officer engaged in dispersing a considerable crowd, which was staring up at some object behind him. On looking round (he states in his deposition) he "saw what was undoubtedly one of the low tavern signs at one time common in England". He was wholly unable to explain its presence outside his premises, and as it undoubtedly legalized the motorist's action, the police declined to move in the matter.

'*Later*.—The two motorists have apparently left the town unmolested, in a small second-hand two-seater. There is no clue to their destination, except it be indicated by a single incident. It appears that when they were waiting for the second glass of milk, one of them drew attention to a milk-can of a shape seemingly unfamiliar to him; which was, of course, the Mountain Milk now so much recommended by doctors. The taller motorist (who seemed in every way strangely ignorant of modern science and social life) asked his companion where it came from: receiving, of course, the reply that it is manufactured in the model village of Peaceways, under the personal superintendence of its distinguished and philanthropic inventor, Dr. Meadows. Upon this the taller person, who appeared highly irresponsible, actually bought the whole can; observing, as he tucked it under his arm, that it would help him to remember the address.

'*Later.*—Our readers will be glad to hear that the legend of "The Old Ship" sign has once more yielded to the wholesome scepticism of science. Our representative reached Wyddington after the practical jokers, or whatever they were, had left; but he searched the whole frontage of Mr. Simmon's shop; and we are in a position to assure the public that there is no trace of the alleged sign.'

Lord Ivywood laid down the newspaper and looked at the rich and serpentine embroideries on the wall with the expression that a great general might have if he saw a chance of really ruining his enemy, if he would also ruin all his previous plan of campaign. His pallid and classic profile was as immovable as a cameo: but any one who had known him at all would have known that his brain was going like a motor-car that has broken the speed limit long ago.

Then he turned his head and said, 'Please tell Hicks to bring round the long blue car in half an hour; it can be fitted up for a sofa. And ask the gardener to cut a pole of about 4ft. 9in., and put a cross-piece for a crutch. I'm going up to London to-night.'

Mr. Leveson's lower jaw literally fell with astonishment.

'The doctor said three weeks,' he said. 'If I may ask, where are you going?'

'St. Stephen's, Westminster,' answered Ivywood.

'Surely,' said Mr. Leveson, 'I could take a message.'

'You could take a message,' assented Ivywood. 'I'm afraid they would not allow you to make a speech.'

It was a moment or two afterwards that Enid Wimpole had come into the room; and striven in vain to shake his decision. Then it was that Joan had been brought out of the turret and saw Philip standing sustained upon a crutch of garden timber; and admired him as she had never admired him before. While he was being helped downstairs; while he was being propped in the car with such limited comfort as was possible, she did really feel in him something worthy of his ancient roots, worthy of such hills and of such a sea. For she felt God's wind from nowhere which is called the Will; and is man's only excuse upon this earth. In the small hoot of the starting motor she could hear a hundred trumpets, such as might have called her ancestors and his to the glories of the Third Crusade.

Such imaginary military honours were not, at least in the strategic sense, undeserved. Lord Ivywood really had seen the whole map of the situation in front of him and swiftly formed a plan to meet it, in a manner not unworthy of Napoleon. The realities of the situation unrolled themselves before him; and his mind was marking them one by one as with a pencil.

First, he knew that Dalroy would probably go to the model village. It was just the sort of place he would go to. He knew Dalroy was almost constitutionally incapable of not kicking up some kind of row in a place of that kind.

Second, he knew that if he missed Dalroy at this address, it was very likely to be his last address: he and Mr. Pump were quite clever enough to leave no more hints behind.

Third, he guessed, by careful consideration of map and clock, that they could not get to so remote a region in so cheap a car under something like two days; nor do anything very conclusive in less than three. Thus, he had just time to turn round in.

Fourth, he realized that ever since that day when Dalroy swung round the sign-board and smote the policeman into the ditch, Dalroy had swung round the Ivywood Act on Lord Ivywood. He (Lord Ivywood) had thought, and might well have thought rightly, that by restricting the old sign-posts to a few places so select that they can afford to be eccentric, and forbidding such artistic symbols to all other places, he could sweep fermented liquor for all practical purposes out of the land. The arrangement was exactly that at which all such legislation is consciously or unconsciously aiming. A sign-board could be a favour granted by the governing class to itself. If a gentleman wished to claim the liberties of a Bohemian, the path would be open. If a Bohemian wished to claim the liberties of a gentleman, the path would be shut. So gradually, Lord Ivywood had thought, the old signs which alone can sell alcohol will dwindle down to mere curiosities, like rare Tokay or the mead that may still be found in the New Forest. The calculation was by no means unstatesmanlike. But like many other statesmanlike calculations, it did not take into account the idea of dead wood walking about. So long as his flying foes might set up their sign anywhere, it mattered little whether the result was enjoyment or disappointment for the populace. In either case it must mean constant scandal or riot. If there was one thing worse than the appearance of 'The Old Ship', it was its disappearance.

He realized that his own law was letting them loose every time: for the local authorities hesitated to act on the spot in defiance of a symbol now so exclusive and therefore impressive. He realized that the law must be altered. Must be altered at once; must be altered, if possible, before the fugitives broke away from the model village of Peaceways.

He realized that it was Thursday. This was the day on which any private member of Parliament could introduce any private Bill of the kind called 'non-contentious' and pass it without a division, so long as no particular member made any particular fuss. He realized that it was improbable that any particular member would make any particular fuss about Lord Ivywood's own improvement on Lord Ivywood's own Act.

Finally, he realized that the whole case could be met by so slight an improvement as this. Change the words of the Act (which he knew by heart as happier men might know a song), 'If such sign be present liquids containing alcohol can be sold on the premises', to these other words, 'Liquids containing alcohol can be sold, if previously preserved for three days on the premises'; it was mate in a few moves. Parliament could never reject or even examine so slight an emendation. And the revolution of 'The Old Ship' and the late King of Ithaca would be crushed for ever.

It does undoubtedly show, as we have said, something Napoleonic in the man's mind that the whole of this excellent and even successful plan was complete long before he saw the great glowing clock on the towers of Westminster; and knew he was in time.

It was unfortunate, perhaps, that about the same time, or not long after, another gentleman of the same rank, and indirectly of the same family, having left the restaurant in Regent Street and the tangle of Piccadilly, had drifted serenely down Whitehall, and had seen the same great golden goblin's eye on the tall tower of St. Stephen.

The Poet of the Birds, like most aesthetes, had known as little of the real town as he had of the real country. But he remembered a good place for supper; and as he passed certain great cold clubs built of stone and looking like Assyrian sarcophagi, he remembered that he belonged to many of them. And so when he saw afar off, sitting above the river, what has been very erroneously described as the best club in London, he suddenly remembered that he belonged to that too. He could not at the moment recall what constituency in South England it was that he sat for; but he knew he could walk into the place if he wanted to. He might not so have expressed the matter, but he knew that in an oligarchy things go by respect for persons and not for claims; by visiting-cards and not by voting-cards. He had not been near the place for years, being permanently paired against a famous Patriot who had accepted an important Government appointment in a private madhouse. Even in his silliest days he had never pretended to feel any respect for modern politics; and made all haste to put his 'leaders' and the mad Patriot's 'leaders' on the well-selected lists of the creatures whom man forgets. He had made one really eloquent speech in the House (on the subject of gorillas), and then found he was speaking against his party. It was an indescribable sort of place, anyhow. Even Lord Ivywood did not go to it except to do some business that could be done nowhere else; as was the case that night.

Ivywood was what is called a peer by courtesy; his place was in the Commons and for the time being on the Opposition side. But, though he visited the House but seldom, he knew far too much about it to go into the Chamber itself. He limped into the smoking-room (though he did not smoke), procured a needless cigarette and a much-needed sheet of note-paper; and composed a curt but careful note to the one member of the Government who he knew must be in the House. Having sent it up to him, he waited.

Outside, Mr. Dorian Wimpole also waited, leaning on the parapet of Westminster Bridge and looking down the river. He was becoming one with the oysters in a more solemn and solid sense than he had hitherto conceived possible, and also with a strictly vegetarian beverage which bears the noble and starry name of Nuits. He felt at peace with all things, even in a manner with politics. It was one of those magic hours of evening when the red and golden lights of men are already lit along the river, and look like the lights of goblins, but daylight still lingers in a cold and delicate green. He felt about the river something of that smiling and glorious sadness which two Englishmen have expressed under the figure of the white wood of

an old ship fading like a phantom; Turner in painting
and Henry Newbolt in poetry. He had come back to
earth like a man fallen from the moon; he was at
bottom not only a poet but a patriot; and a patriot is
always a little sad. Yet his melancholy was mixed
up with that immutable yet meaningless faith which
few Englishmen, even in modern times, fail to feel at
the unexpected sight either of Westminster or of that
height on which stands the temple of St. Paul.

> 'While flows the sacred river,
> While stands the sacred hill,'

he murmured in some schoolboy echo of the ballad of
Lake Regillus.

> 'While flows the sacred river,
> While stands the sacred hill,
> The proud old pantaloons and nincompoops
> Who yawn at the very length of their own lies
> in that accursed sanhedrim where
> people put each other's hats on in a poisonous room
> with no more windows than hell,
> Shall have such honour still.'

Relieved by this rendering of Macaulay in the style
known among his cultured friends as *vers libre*, or
poesy set free from the shackles of formal metre, he
strolled towards the members' entrance and went in.

Lacking Lord Ivywood's experience, he strolled into
the Commons Chamber itself and sat down on a green
bench, under the impression that the House was not
sitting. He was, however, gradually able to distinguish
some six or eight drowsy human forms from the seats
on which they sat; and to hear a senile voice with an
Essex accent, saying all on one note and without

beginning or end, in a manner which it is quite impossible to punctuate:

'. . . no wish at all that this proposal should be regarded except in the right way and have tried to put it in the right way and cannot think the honourable member was altogether adding to his reputation in putting it in what those who think with me must of course consider the wrong way and I for one am free to say that if in his desire to settle this great question he takes this hasty course and this revolutionary course about slate pencils he may not be able to prevent the extremists behind him from applying it to lead pencils and while I should be the last to increase the heat and the excitement and the personalities of this debate if I could possibly help it I must confess that in my opinion the honourable gentleman has himself encouraged that heat and personality in a manner that he now doubtless regrets I have no desire to use abusive terms indeed you Mr. Speaker would not allow me of course to use abusive terms but I must tell the honourable member face to face that the perambulators with which he has twitted me cannot be germane to this discussion I should be the last person . . .'

Dorian Wimpole had softly risen to go, when he was arrested by the sight of some one sliding into the House and handing a note to the solitary young man with heavy eyelids who was at that moment governing all England from the Treasury Bench. Seeing him go out, Dorian had a sickening sweetness of hope (as he might have said in his earlier poems) that something intelligible might happen after all, and followed him out almost with alacrity.

The solitary and sleepy governor of Great Britain went down into the lower crypts of its temple of freedom and turned into an apartment where Wimpole was astonished to see his cousin Ivywood sitting at a little table with a large crutch leaning beside him, as serene as Long John Silver. The young man with the heavy eyelids sat down opposite him and they had a conversation, which Wimpole, of course, did not hear. He withdrew into an adjoining room, where he managed to procure coffee and a liqueur; an excellent liqueur which he had forgotten and of which he had more than one glass.

But he had so posted himself that Ivywood could not come out without passing him; and he waited for what might happen with exquisite patience. The only thing that seemed to him queer was that every now and then a bell rang in several rooms at once. And whenever the bell rang, Lord Ivywood nodded, as if he were part of the electrical machinery. And whenever Lord Ivywood nodded the young man turned and sped upstairs like a mountaineer, returning in a short time to resume the conversation. On the third occasion the poet began to observe that many others from the other rooms could be heard running upstairs at the sound of this bell and returning with the slightly less rapid step which expresses relief after a duty done. Yet he did not know that this duty was Representative Government; and that it is thus that the cry of Cumberland or Cornwall can come to the ears of an English king.

Suddenly the sleepy young man sprang erect, uninspired by any bell, and strode out once more. The poet could not help hearing him say as he left the table, jotting down something with a pencil, 'Alcohol can be sold if previously preserved for three days on the premises. I think we can do it, but you can't come on for half an hour.'

Saying this, he darted upstairs again; and when Dorian saw Ivywood come out laboriously afterwards on his large country crutch, he had exactly the same revulsion in his favour that Joan had had. Jumping up from his table, which was in one of the private dining-rooms, he touched the other on the elbow and said:

'I want to apologize to you, Philip, for my rudeness this afternoon. Honestly, I am sorry. Pine-woods and prison-cells try a man's temper; but I had no rag of excuse for not seeing that neither of them were your fault. I'd no notion you were coming up to town to-night; with your leg and all. You mustn't knock yourself up like this. Do sit down a minute.'

It seemed to him that the bleak face of Philip softened a little; how far he really softened will never be known until such men as he are understood by their fellows. It is certain that he carefully unhooked himself from his crutch and sat down opposite his cousin. Whereupon his cousin struck the table so that it rang like a dinner-bell and called out 'Waiter!' as if he were in a crowded restaurant. Then, before Lord Ivywood could protest, he said:

'It's awfully jolly that we've met. I suppose you've come up to make a speech. I *should* like to hear it. We haven't always agreed; but, by God, if there's anything good left in literature it's your speeches reported in a newspaper. That thing of yours that ended "death and the last shutting of the iron doors of defeat"—why, you must go back to Strafford's last speech for such English. Do let me hear your speech! I've got a seat upstairs, you know.'

'If you wish it,' said Ivywood hurriedly, 'but I shan't make much of a speech to-night.' And he looked at the wall behind Wimpole's head with thunderous wrinkles thickening on his brow. It was essential to his brilliant and rapid scheme, of course, that the Commons should make no comment at all on his little alteration in the law.

An attendant hovered near in response to the demand for a waiter; and was much impressed by the presence and condition of Lord Ivywood. But as that exalted cripple resolutely refused anything in the way of liquor, his cousin was so kind as to have a little more himself, and resumed his remarks.

'It's about this public-house affair of yours, I suppose. I'd like to hear you speak on that. P'raps I'll speak myself. I've been thinking about it a good deal all day, and a good deal of last night too. Now here's what I should say to the House if I were you. "To begin with, can you abolish the public-house? Are you *important* enough now to abolish the public-house? Whether it's right or wrong, can you in the long run prevent haymakers having ale any more than you can prevent me having this glass of Chartreuse?"'

The attendant, hearing the word, once more drew near; but heard no further order; or, rather, the orders he heard were such as he was less able to cope with.

'Remember the curate!' said Dorian abstractedly shaking his head at the functionary, 'remember the sensible little High Church curate, who when asked for a Temperance Sermon preached on the text "Suffer us not to be overwhelmed in the water-floods." Indeed, indeed, Philip, you are in deeper waters than you know. *You* will abolish ale! *You* will make Kent forget hoppoles and Devonshire forget cider! The fate of the Inn is to be settled in that hot little room upstairs! Take care its fate and yours are not settled in the Inn. Take care Englishmen don't sit in judgment on you as they do on many another corpse at an inquest—at a common public-house! Take care that the one tavern that is really neglected and shut up and passed like a house of pestilence, is not the tavern in which I drink to-night; and that merely because it is the worst tavern on the king's highway. Take care this place where we sit does not get a name like any pub where sailors are hocussed or girls debauched. That is what I shall say to them,' said he, rising cheerfully, 'that's what I shall say. See you to it,' he cried, with sudden passion and apparently to the waiter, 'see you to it if the sign that is destroyed is not the sign of "The Old Ship" but the sign of the Mace and Bauble, and, in the words of a highly historical brewer, if we see a dog bark at your going.'

Lord Ivywood was observing him with a deathly quietude; another idea had come into his fertile mind. He knew his cousin, though excited, was not in the least intoxicated; he knew he was quite capable of making a speech and even a good one. He knew that any speech, good or bad, would wreck his whole plan and send the wild inn flying again. But the orator had resumed his seat and drained his glass, passing a hand across his brow. And he remembered that a man who keeps a vigil in a wood all night and drinks wine on the following evening is liable to an accident that is not drunkenness, but something much healthier.

'I suppose your speech will come on pretty soon,' said Dorian, looking at the table. 'You'll let me know when it does, of course. Really and truly, I don't want to miss it. And I've forgotten all the ways here, and feel pretty tired. You'll let me know?'

'Yes,' said Lord Ivywood.

Stillness fell along all the rooms until Lord Ivywood broke it by saying:

'Debate is a most necessary thing: but there are times when it rather impedes than assists parliamentary government.'

He received no reply. Dorian still sat as if looking at the table; but his eyelids had lightly fallen; he was asleep. Almost at the same moment the Member of the Government, who was nearly asleep, appeared at the entrance of the long room and made some sort of weary signal.

Philip Ivywood raised himself on his crutch and stood for a moment looking at the sleeping man. Then he and his crutch trailed out of the long room, leaving the sleeping man behind. Nor was that the only thing that he left behind. He also left behind an unlighted cigarette and his honour and all the England of his fathers—everything that could really distinguish that high house beside the river from any tavern for the hocussing of sailors. He went upstairs and did his business in twenty minutes in the only speech he had ever delivered without any trace of eloquence. And from that hour forth he was the naked fanatic; and could feed on nothing but the future.

CHAPTER XVIII

THE REPUBLIC OF PEACEWAYS

In a hamlet round about Windermere, let us say, or somewhere in Wordsworth's country, there could be found a cottage, in which could be found a cottager. So far all is as it should be: and the visitor would first be conscious of a hearty and even noisy elderly man, with an apple face and a short white beard. This person would then loudly proffer to the visitor the opportunity of seeing his father—a somewhat more elderly man, with a somewhat longer white beard, but still 'up and about'. And these two together would then initiate the neophyte into the joys of the society of a grandfather, who was more than a hundred years old, and still very proud of the fact.

The miracle, it seemed, had been worked entirely on milk. The subject of this diet the oldest of the three men continued to discuss in enormous detail. For the rest, it might be said that his pleasures were purely arithmetical. Some men count their years with dismay; and he counted his with a juvenile vanity. Some men collect stamps or coins; and he collected days. Newspaper men interviewed him about the historic times through which he had lived, without eliciting anything whatever; except that he had apparently taken to an exclusive milk diet at about the age when most of us leave it off. Asked if he was alive in 1815, he said that was the very year he found it wasn't *any* milk, but must be Mountain Milk, like Dr. Meadows says. Nor would his calculating creed of life have allowed him to understand you, if you had said that in a meadowland oversea that lies before the city of Brussels, boys of his old school in that year gained the love of the gods and died young.

It was the philanthropic Dr. Meadows, of course, who discovered this deathless tribe; and erected on it the whole of his great dietic philosophy, to say nothing of the houses and dairies of Peaceways. He attracted many pupils and backers among the wealthy and influential; young men who were, so to speak, training for extreme old age; infant old men; embryo nonagenarians. It would be an exaggeration to say that they watched joyfully for the first white hair as Fascination Fledgeby watched for his first whisker: but it is quite true to say that they seemed to have scorned the beauty of woman and the feasting of friends and, above all, the old idea of death with glory: in comparison with this vision of the sports of second childhood.

Peaceways was in its essential plan much like what we call a Garden City; a ring of buildings where the workpeople did their work, with a pretty ornamental town in the centre, where they lived in the open country outside. This was no doubt much healthier than the factory system in the great towns and may have partly accounted for the serene expression of Dr. Meadows and his friends, if any part of the credit can be spared from the splendours of Mountain Milk. The place lay far from the common highways of England; and its inhabitants were enabled to enjoy their quiet skies and level woods almost undisturbed, and fully absorb whatever may be valuable in the Meadows method and view; until one day a small and very dirty motor drove into the middle of their town. It stopped beside one of those triangular islets of grass that are common at forked roads; and two men in goggles, one tall and the other short, got out and stood on the central space of grass, as if they were buffoons about to do tricks. As, indeed, they were.

Before entering the town they had stopped by a splendid mountain stream quickening and thickening rapidly into a river; unhelmed and otherwise eased themselves, eaten a little bread bought at Wyddington and drank the water of the widening current which opened on the valley of Peaceways.

'I'm beginning quite to like water,' said the taller of the two knights. 'I used to think it a most dangerous drink. In theory, of course, it ought only to be given to people who are fainting. It's really good for them, much better than brandy. Besides, think of wasting good brandy on people who are fainting. But I don't go so far as I did. I shouldn't insist on a doctor's prescription before I allowed people water. That was the too severe morality of youth: that was my innocence and goodness. I thought that if I fell once, water-drinking might become a habit. But I do see the good side of water now. How good it is when you're really thirsty; how it glitters and gurgles! How alive it is! After all, it's the best of drinks, after the other. As it says in the song:

> 'Feast on wine or fast on water,
> And your honour shall stand sure,
> God Almighty's son and daughter,
> He the valiant, she the pure;
> If an angel out of heaven
> Brings you other things to drink,
> Thank him for his kind intentions,
> Go and pour them down the sink.
>
> Tea is like the East he grows in,
> A great yellow Mandarin
> With urbanity of manner
> And unconsciousness of sin;

All the women, like a harem,
At his pig-tail troop along;
And, like all the East he grows in,
He is poison when he's strong.

Tea, although an Oriental,
Is a gentleman at least;
Cocoa is a cad and coward,
Cocoa is a vulgar beast,
Cocoa is a dull, disloyal,
Lying, crawling cad and clown,
And may very well be grateful
To the fool that takes him down.

As for all the windy waters,
They were rained like tempests down
When good drink had been dishonoured
By the tipplers of the town;
When red wine had brought red ruin
And the death-dance of our times,
Heaven sent us Soda Water
As a torment for our crimes.'

'Upon my soul, this water tastes quite nice. I wonder
what vintage, now?' and he smacked his lips with
solemnity. 'It tastes just like the year 1881 tasted.'

'You can fancy anything in the tasting way,' returned his shorter companion. 'Mr. Jack, who was
always up to his tricks, did serve plain water in those
little glasses they drink liqueurs out of, and every one
swore it was a delicious liqueur, and wanted to know
where they could get it—all except old Admiral
Guffin, who said it tasted too strong of olives. But
water's much the best for our game certainly.'

Patrick nodded; and then said:

'I doubt if I could do it, if it weren't for the comfort
of looking at that,' and he kicked the rum-keg, 'and
feeling we shall have a good swig at it some day. It

feels like a fairy tale, carrying that about—as if rum were a pirates' treasure, as if it were molten gold. Besides, we can have such fun with it with other people —what was that joke I thought of this morning? Oh, I remember! Where's that milk-can of mine?'

For the next twenty minutes he was industriously occupied with his milk-can and the cask; Pump watching him with an interest amounting to anxiety. Lifting his head, however, at the end of that time, he knotted his red brows and said, 'What's that?'

'What's what?' asked the other traveller.

'That,' said Captain Patrick Dalroy, and pointed to a figure approaching on the road parallel to the river. 'I mean, what's it for?'

The figure had a longish beard and very long hair falling far below its shoulders. It had a serious and steadfast expression. It was dressed in what the inexperienced Mr. Pump at first took to be its night-gown, but afterwards learned to be its complete goats'-hair tunic, unmixed even with a thread of the destructive and deadly wool of the sheep. It had no boots on its feet. It walked very swiftly to a particular turn of the stream and then turned very sharply (since it had accomplished its constitutional) and walked back towards the perfect town of Peaceways.

'I suppose it's somebody from that milk place,' said Humphrey Pump indulgently. 'They seem to be pretty mad.'

'I don't mind that so much,' said Dalroy; 'I'm mad myself sometimes. But a madman has only one merit and last link with God. A madman is always logical. Now what is the logical connexion between living on milk and wearing your hair long? Most of us lived on milk when we had no hair at all. How do they connect it up? Are there any heads even for a synopsis? Is it, say, "milk—water—shaving-water—shaving— hair?" Is it "milk—kindness—unkindness—convicts —hair?" What is the logical connexion between having too much hair and having far too few boots? What *can* it be? Is it "hair—hair-trunk—leather-trunk—leather-boots?" Is it "hair—beard—oysters— seaside—paddling—no boots?" Man is liable to err— especially when every mistake he makes is called a movement—but why should all the lunacies live together?'

'Because all the lunatics should live together,' said Humphrey, 'and if you'd seen what happened up at Crampton, with the farming-out idea, you'd know. It's all very well, Captain; but if people can prevent a guest of great importance being buried up to the neck in farm manure, they will. They will, really.' He coughed almost apologetically. He was about to attempt a resumption of the conversation, when he saw his companion slap the milk-can and keg back into the car; and get into it himself. 'You drive,' he said, 'drive me where those things live; you know, Hump.'

They did not, however, arrive in the civic centre of such things without yet another delay. They left the river and followed the man with the long hair and the goats'-hair frock; and he stopped, as it happened, at a house on the outskirts of the village. The adventurers stopped also, out of curiosity; and were at first relieved to see the man almost instantly reappear, having transacted his business with a quickness that seemed incredible. A second glance showed them it was not the man, but another man dressed exactly like him. A few minutes more of inquisitive delay showed them many of the milky and goatish sect going in and out of this particular place, each clad in his innocent uniform.

'This must be the temple and chapel,' muttered Patrick; 'it must be here they sacrifice a glass of milk to a cow, or whatever it is they do. Well, the joke is pretty obvious; but we must wait for a lull in the crowding of the congregation.'

When the last long-haired phantom had faded up the road, Dalroy sprang from the car and drove the sign-board deep into the earth with savage violence and then very quietly knocked at the door.

The apparent owner of the place, of whom the two last of the long-haired and bare-footed idealists were taking a rather hurried farewell, was a man curiously ill-fitted for the part he seemed cast for in the only possible plot.

Both Pump and Dalroy thought they had never seen a man look so sullen. His face was of the rubicund sort that does not suggest jollity, but merely a stagnant indigestion in the head. His moustache hung heavy and dark, his brows yet heavier and darker. Dalroy had seen something of the sort on the faces of defeated peoples disgracefully forced into submission; but he could not make head or tail of it in connexion with the priggish perfections of Peaceways. It was all the odder because he was manifestly prosperous: his clothes were smartly cut in something of the sporting manner: and the inside of his house was at least four times grander than the outside.

But what mystified them most was this: that he did not so much exhibit the natural curiosity of a gentleman whose private house is entered by strangers, but rather an embarrassed and restless expectation. During Dalroy's eager apologies and courteous inquiries about

the direction and accommodations of Peaceways, the
man's eye (which was of the boiled gooseberry order)
perpetually wandered from them to the cupboard and
then again to the window; and at last he got up and
went to look out into the road.

'Oh, yes, sir; very healthy place Peaceways,' he
said, peering through the lattice. 'Very . . . dash
it, what they mean? . . . Very healthy place. Of
course they have their little ways.'

'Only drink pure milk, don't they?' asked Dalroy.

The householder looked at him with a rather wild
eye and grunted.

'Yes; so they say.' And he went again to the
window.

'I've bought some of it,' said Patrick, patting his pet
milk-can, which he carried under his arm, as if unable
to be separated from Dr. Meadows's discovery. 'Have
a glass of milk, sir?'

The man's boiled eye began to bulge in anger—or
some other emotion.

'What you want?' he muttered; 'are you 'tecs or
what?'

'Agents and distributors of the Meadows' Mountain
Milk,' said the Captain, with simple pride. 'Taste it?'

The dazed householder took a glass of the blameless
liquid and sipped it: and the change on his face was
extraordinary.

'Well, I'm jiggered!' he said, with a broad and rather
coarse grin. 'That's a queer dodge. You're in the
joke, I see.' Then he went again restlessly to the
window, and added:

'But if we're all friends, why the blazes don't the
others come in? I've never known trade so slow
before.'

'Who are the others?' asked Mr. Pump.

'Oh, the usual Peaceways people,' said the other. 'They generally come here before work. Dr. Meadows don't work them for very long hours, that wouldn't be healthy or whatever he calls it: but he's particular about their being punctual. I've seen 'em running with all their pure-minded togs on, when the hooter gave the last call.'

Then he abruptly opened the front door and called out impatiently but not loudly:

'Come along in, if you're coming. You'll give the show away if you play the fool out there.'

Patrick looked out also and the view of the road outside was certainly rather singular. He was used to crowds, large and small, collecting outside houses which he had honoured with the sign of 'The Old Ship'; but they generally stared up at it in unaffected wonder and amusement. But outside this open door, some twenty or thirty persons in what Pump had called their night-gowns were moving to and fro like somnambulists, apparently blind to the presence of the sign; looking at the other side of the road, looking at the horizon, looking at the clouds of morning; and only occasionally stopping to whisper to each other. But when the owner of the house called to one of these ostentatiously abstracted beings and asked him hoarsely what the devil was the matter, it was natural for the milk-fed one to turn his feeble eye towards the sign. The gooseberry eyes followed his; and the face to which they belonged was a study in apoplectic astonishment.

'What the hell have you done to my house?' he demanded. 'Of course they can't come in if this thing's here.'

20

'I'll take it down, if you like,' said Dalroy, stepping out and picking it up like a flower from the front garden (to the amazement of the men in the road, who thought they had strayed into a nursery fairy tale), 'but I wish, in return, you'd give me some idea of what the blazes all this means.'

'Wait till I've served these men,' replied his host.

The goat-garbed persons went very sheepishly (or goatishly) into the now signless building; and were rapidly served with raw spirits, which Mr. Pump suspected to be of no very superior quality. When the last goat was gone, Captain Dalroy said:

'I mean that all this seems to me topsy-turvy. I understood that as the law stands now, if there's a sign they are allowed to drink and if there isn't they aren't.'

'The law!' said the man, in a voice thick with scorn. 'Do you think these poor brutes are afraid of the law as they are of the Doctor?'

'Why should they be afraid of the Doctor?' asked Dalroy innocently. 'I always heard that Peaceways was a self-governing republic.'

'Self-governing be damned!' was the illiberal reply. 'Don't he own all the houses and could turn 'em out in a snow-storm? Don't he pay all the wages and could starve 'em stiff in a month? The law!' And he snorted.

A moment after he squared his elbows on the table and began to explain more fully:

'I was a brewer about here and had the biggest brewery in these parts. There were only two houses which didn't belong to me, and the magistrates took away their licences after a time. Ten years ago you could see Hugby's Ales written beside every sign in the county. Then came these cursed Radicals and our leader Lord Ivywood must go over to their side about it; and let this Doctor buy all the land under some new law that there shan't be any pubs at all. And so my business is ruined so that he can sell his milk. Luckily I'd done pretty well before and had some compensation, of course; and I still do a fair trade on the Q.T., as you see. But of course that don't amount to half the old one, for they're afraid of old Meadows finding out. Snuffling old blighter!'

And the gentleman with the good clothes spat on the carpet.

'I am a Radical myself,' said the Irishman rather coldly; 'for all information on the Conservative party I must refer you to my friend, Mr. Pump, who is, of course, in the inmost secrets of his leaders. But it seems to me very rum sort of Radicalism to eat and drink at the orders of a master who is a madman, merely because he's also a millionaire. O Liberty, what very complicated and even unsatisfactory social developments are committed in thy name! Why don't they kick the old ass round the town a bit! No boots? Is that why they're allowed no boots? Oh, roll him downhill in a milk-can: he can't object to that.'

'I don't know,' said Pump, in his ruminant way, 'Master Christian's aunt did; but ladies are more particular, of course.'

'Look here!' cried Dalroy, in some excitement. 'If I stick up that sign outside, and stay here to help, will you defy them? You'd be strictly within the law, and any private coercion I can promise you they shall repent. Plant the sign and sell the stuff openly like a man; and you may stand in English history like a deliverer.'

Mr. Hugby of Hugby's Ales only looked gloomily at the table. His was not the sort of drinking nor the

sort of drink-selling on which the revolutionary sentiment flourishes.

'Well,' said the Captain, 'will you come with me and
say, "Hear, hear!" and "How true!"—"What match-
less eloquence!" if I make a speech in the market-place?
Come along. There's room in our car.'

'Well, I'll come with you, if you like,' replied Mr.
Hugby heavily. 'It's true if yours is allowed we might
get our trade back too.' And putting on a silk hat he
followed the Captain and the innkeeper out to their
little car. The model village was not an appropriate
background for Mr. Hugby's silk hat. Indeed, the
hat seemed somehow to bring out by contrast all that
was fantastic in the place.

It was a superb morning, some hours after sunrise.
The edges of the sky touching the ring of dim woods
and distant hills were still jewelled with the tiny transparent clouds of daybreak, delicate red and green or
yellow. But above the vault of heaven rose through
turquoise into a torrid and solid blue in which the
other clouds, the colossal cumuli, tumbled about like
a celestial pillow-fight. The bulk of the houses were
as white as the clouds, so that it looked (to use another
simile) as if some of the whitewashed cottages were
flying and falling about the sky. But most of the white
houses were picked out here and there with bright
colours, here an ornament in orange or there a stripe
of lemon-yellow, as if by the brush of a baby giant.
The houses had no thatching (thatching is not hygienic)
but were mostly covered with a sort of peacock-green
tiles bought cheap at a Pre-Raphaelite Bazaar: or less
frequently by some still more esoteric sort of terra-
cotta bricks. The houses were not English nor homelike nor suited to the landscape; for the houses had not

been built by free men for themselves, but at the fancy of a whimsical lord. But considered as a sort of elfin city in a pantomime, it was a really picturesque background for pantomimic proceedings.

I fear Mr. Dalroy's proceedings from the first rather deserved that name. To begin with he left the sign, the cask, and the keg all wrapped and concealed in the car, but removed all the wraps of his own disguise, and stood on the central patch of grass in that green uniform that looked all the more insolent for being as ragged as the grass. Even that was less ragged than his red hair, which no red jungle of the East could imitate. Then he took out, almost tenderly, the large milk-can: and deposited it, almost reverently, on the island of turf. Then he stood beside it, like Napoleon beside a gun, with an expression of tremendous seriousness and even severity. Then he drew his sword, and with that flashing weapon as with a flail lashed and thrashed the echoing metal can till the din was deafening, and Mr. Hugby hastily got out of the car and withdrew to a slight distance, stopping his ears. Mr. Pump sat solidly at the steering-wheel, well knowing it might be necessary to start in some haste.

'Gather, gather, gather, Peaceways!' shouted Patrick, still banging on the can and lamenting the difficulties of adapting 'Macgregor's Gathering' to the name and occasion. 'We're landless, *landless*, Landless, Peace-ways!'

Two or three of the goat-clad, recognizing Mr. Hugby with a guilty look, drew near with great caution; and the Captain shouted at them as if they were an army covering Salisbury Plain.

'Citizens,' he roared, saying anything that came into his head, 'try the only original unadulterated Mountain Milk for which alone Mohammed came to the

mountain. The original milk of the land flowing with
milk and honey; the high quality of which could alone
have popularized so unappetizing a combination. Try
our milk! None others are genuine! Who can do
without milk? Even whales can't do without milk.
If any lady or gentleman keeps a favourite whale at
home, now's their chance! The early whale catches
the milk. Just look at our milk! If you say you can't
look at the milk, because it's in the can—well, look at
the can! You must look at the can! You simply must!
When Duty whispers low, "Thou Must!" ' he bellowed
at the top of his voice in a highly impromptu peroration
—'when Duty whispers low, "Thou Must!" the Youth
replies, "I can!" ' And with the word 'Can' he hit the
can with a shocking and shattering noise, like a peal of
demoniac bells of steel.

This introductory speech is open to criticism from
those who regard it as intended for the study rather
than the stage. The present chronicler (who has no
aim save the truth) is bound to record that for its own
unscrupulous purpose it was extremely successful: a
great mass of the citizens of Peaceways having been
attracted by the noise of one man shouting like a crowd.
There are crowds who do not care to revolt; but there
are no crowds who do not like some one else to do
it for them; a fact which the safest oligarchs may be
wise to learn.

But Dalroy's ultimate triumph (I regret to say)
consisted in actually handing to a few of the foremost
of his audience some samples of his blameless beverage.
The fact was certainly striking. Some were paralysed
with surprise. Some were abruptly broken double
with laughter. Many chuckled. Some cheered. All
looked radiantly towards the eccentric orator.

And yet the radiance died quietly and suddenly from their faces. And only because one little old man had joined the group; a little old man in white linen with a white, pointed beard and a white powder-puff of hair like thistledown; a man whom almost every man present could have killed with the left arm.

CHAPTER XIX

THE HOSPITALITY OF THE CAPTAIN

DR. MOSES MEADOWS, whether that was his name or an Anglicized version of it, had certainly come in the first instance from a little town in Germany, and his first two books were written in German. His first two books were his best: for he began with a genuine enthusiasm for physical science, and this was adulterated with nothing worse than a hatred of what he thought was superstition, and what many of us think is the soul of the State. The first enthusiasm was most notable in the first book, which was concerned to show that the, in the female, out upsprouting of the whiskers was from the therewith increasing arrested mentality derived. In his second book he came more to grips with delusions; and for some time he was held to have proved (to every one who agreed with him already) that the Time Ghost had been walking particularly rapidly lately; and that the Christus Mythus was by the alcoholic mind's trouble explained. Then, unfortunately, he came across the institution called Death, and began to argue with it. Not seeing any rational explanation of this custom of dying, so prevalent among his fellow-citizens, he concluded that it was merely traditional (which he thought meant 'effete'), and began to think of nothing but ways of evading or delaying it. This had a rather narrowing effect on him; and he lost much of that acrid ardour which had humanized the atheism of his youth, when he would almost have committed suicide for the pleasure of taunting God with not being there. His later idealism grew more and more materialist; and consisted of his changing hypotheses and discoveries about the healthiest foods. There is no need to detain the reader over what has been called his Oil Period; his Seaweed Period has been authoritatively expounded in Professor Nym's valuable little work; and on the events of his Glue Period it is perhaps not very generous to dwell. It was during his prolonged stay in England that he chanced on the instance of the longevity of milk consumers; and built on it a theory which was, at the beginning at least, sincere. Unfortunately it was also successful: wealth flowed into the inventor and proprietor of Mountain Milk; and he began to feel a fourth and last enthusiasm, which also can come late in life and have a narrowing effect on the mind.

In the altercation which naturally followed on his discovery of the antics of Mr. Patrick Dalroy, he was very dignified but naturally not very tolerant; for he was quite unused to anything happening in spite of him, or anything important even happening without him, in the land that lay around. At first he hinted severely that the Captain had stolen the milk-can from the milk-producing premises, and sent several workmen to count the cans in each shed; but Dalroy soon put him right about that.

'I bought it in a shop at Wyddington,' he said. 'And since then I have used no other. You'll hardly believe me,' he said, with some truth, 'but when I went into that shop I was quite a little man. I had one glass of your Mountain Milk; and look at me now.'

'You have no right to sell the milk here,' said Dr. Meadows, with the faintest trace of a German accent. 'You are not in my employment. I am not responsible for your methods. You are not a representative of the business.'

'I'm an Advertisement,' said the Captain. 'We advertise you all over England. You see that lean, skimpy little man over there,' pointing to the indignant Mr. Pump. 'He's Before Taking Meadows' Mountain Milk. I'm After,' added Mr. Dalroy, with satisfaction.

'You shall laugh at the magistrate,' said the other, with a thickening accent.

'I shall,' agreed Patrick. 'Well, I'll make a clean breast of it, sir. The truth is, it isn't your milk at all. It has quite a different taste. These gentlemen will tell you so.'

A smothered giggle sent all the blood to the eminent capitalist's face.

'Then either you have stolen my can and are a thief,' he said, stamping, 'or you have introduced inferior substances into my discovery and are an adulterer—er——'

'Try adulteratist,' said Dalroy kindly. 'Prince Albert always said "adulteratarian." Dear old Albert! It seems like yesterday! But it is, of course, to-day. And it's as true as daylight that this stuff tastes different. I can't tell you what the taste is' (subdued guffaws from the outskirts of the crowd). 'It's something between the taste of your first sugar-stick and the fag-end of your father's cigar. It's as innocent as heaven and as hot as hell. It tastes like a paradox. It tastes like a prehistoric inconsistency—I trust I make myself clear. The men who taste it most are the simplest men that God has made, and it always reminds them of the salt; because it is made out of sugar. Have some!'

And with a gesture of staggering hospitality, he shot

out his long arm with the little glass at the end of it. The despotic curiosity of the Prussian overcame even his despotic dignity. He took a sip of the liquid; and his eyes stood out from his face.

'You've been mixing something with the milk,' were the first words that came to him.

'Yes,' answered Dalroy, 'and so have you, unless you're a swindler. Why is your milk advertised as different from every one else's milk, if you haven't made the difference? Why does a glass of your milk cost threepence; and a glass of ordinary milk a penny, if you haven't put twopennorth of something into it? Now, look here, Dr. Meadows. The Public Analyst who would judge this happens to be an honest man. I have a list of the twenty-one and a half honest men still employed in such posts. I make you a fair offer. He shall decide what it is I add to the milk, if you let him decide what it is you add to the milk. You must add something to the milk: or what can all these wheels and pumps and pulleys be for? Will you tell me, here and now, what you add to the milk which makes it so exceedingly Mountain?'

There was a long silence, full of the same sense of submerged mirth in the mob. But the philanthropist had fallen into a naked frenzy in the sunlight; and shaking his fists aloft in a way unknown to all the English around him, he cried out:

'Ach! but I know what you add! I know what you add! It is the Alcohol! And you have no sign, and you shall laugh at a magistrate.'

Dalroy, with a bow, retired to the car, removed a number of wrappings and produced the prodigious wooden sign-post of 'The Old Ship', with its blue three-decker and red St. George's cross conspicuously displayed. This he planted on his narrow territory of turf and looked round serenely.

'In this old oak-panelled inn of mine,' he said, 'I will laugh at a million magistrates. Not that there's anything unhygienic about this inn. No low ceilings or stuffiness here. Windows open everywhere, except in the floor. And as I hear some are saying there ought always to be food sold with fermented liquor, why, my dear Dr. Meadows, I've got a cheese here that will make another man of you. At least, we'll hope so. We can but try.'

But Dr. Meadows was long past being merely angry. The exhibition of the sign had put him into a serious difficulty. Like most sceptics, like even the most genuine sceptics such as Bradlaugh, he was as legal as he was sceptical. He had a profound fear, which also had in it something better than fear, of being ultimately found in the wrong in a police-court or a public inquiry. And he also suffered the tragedy of all such men living in modern England; that he must always be certain to respect the law, while never being certain of what it was. He could only remember generally that Lord Ivywood, when introducing or defending the great Ivywood Act on this matter, had dwelt very strongly on the unique and significant nature of the sign. And he could not be certain that if he disregarded it altogether, he might not eventually be cast in heavy damages—or even go to prison, in spite of his success in business. Of course he knew quite well that he had a thousand answers to such nonsense: that a patch of grass in the road couldn't be an inn; that the sign wasn't even produced when the Captain began to hand round the rum. But he also knew quite well that in the black peril we call

British law, that is not the point. He had heard points quite as obvious urged to a judge, and urged in vain. At the bottom of his mind he found this fact. Rich as he was, Lord Ivywood had made him—and on which side would Lord Ivywood be?

'Captain,' said Humphrey Pump, speaking for the first time, 'we'd better be getting away. I feel it in my bones.'

'Inhospitable innkeeper!' cried the Captain indignantly. 'And after I have gone out of the way to license your premises! Why, this is the dawn of peace in the great city of Peaceways. I don't despair of Dr. Meadows tossing off another bumper before we've done. For the moment, Brother Hugby will engage.'

As he spoke, he served out milk and rum at random; and still the Doctor had too much terror of our legal technicalities to make a final interference. But when Mr. Hugby of Hugby's Ales heard his name called, he first of all jumped so as almost to dislodge the silk hat: then he stood quite still. Then he accepted a glass of the new Mountain Milk: and then his very face became full of speech, before he had spoken a word.

'There's a motor coming along the road from the far hills,' said Humphrey quietly. 'It'll be across the last bridge down-stream in ten minutes and come up on this side.'

'Well,' said the Captain impatiently, 'I suppose you've seen a motor before.'

'Not in this valley all this morning,' answered Pump.

'Mr. Chairman,' said Mr. Hugby, feeling a dim disposition to say 'Mr. Vice', in memory of old commercial banquets. 'I'm sure we're all law-abiding

people here; and wish to remain friends, especially
with our good friend the Doctor: may he never want a
friend or a bottle—that is, in short, anything he wants.
As we go up the hill of prosperity and so on. But as
our friend here with the sign-board seems to be within
his rights, well, I think, the time's come when we can
look at these things more broadly, so to speak. Now
I know it's quite true those dirty little pubs do a lot
of harm to a property, and you get a lot of ignorant
people there who are just like pigs; and I don't say
our friend the Doctor hasn't done good by clearing
'em away. But a big, well-managed business with
plenty of capital behind it is quite another thing.
Well, friends, you all know that I was originally in the
Trade; though I have, of course, left off selling under
the new regulations.' Here the goats looked rather
guiltily at their cloven hooves. 'But I've got my little
bit and I wouldn't mind putting it into this "Old Ship"
here, if our friend would allow it to be run on business
lines. And especially if he'd enlarge the premises a
bit. Ha ha! And if our good friend the Doctor——'

'You rascal fellow!' spluttered Meadows, 'your goot
friend the Doctor will make you dance before a
magistrate.'

'Now, don't be unbusiness-like,' reasoned the brewer.
'It won't hurt your sales. It's quite a different public,
don't you see? Do talk like a business man.'

'I am not a business man,' said the scientist, with a
fiery eye. 'I am a servant of humanity.'

'Then,' said Dalroy, 'why do you never do what
your master tells you?'

'The motor has passed the river,' said Humphrey
Pump.

'You would undo all my works,' cried the Doctor

with sincere passion. 'When I have built this town myself, when I have made it sober and healthful myself, when I am awake and about before any one in the town myself, watching over its interests—you would ruin all to sell your barbaric and fundamentally beastly beer. And then you call me a goot friend. I am not a goot friend!'

'That I can't say,' growled Hugby. 'But if it comes to that—aren't you trying to sell——'

A motor-car drove up with a white explosion of dust; and about six very dusty people got out of it. Even through the densest disguise of the swift motorist, Pump perceived in many of them the peculiar style and bodily carriage of the police. The most evident exception was a long and more slender figure, which, on removing its cap and goggles, disclosed the dark and drooping features of J. Leveson, Secretary. He walked across to the little old millionaire, who instantly recognized him and shook hands. They confabulated for some little time, turning over some official documents. Dr. Meadows cleared his throat and said to the whole crowd:

'I am very glad to be able to announce to you all that this extraordinary outrage has been too late attempted. Lord Ivywood, with the promptitude he so invariably shows, has immediately communicated to places of importance such as this a most just and right alteration of the law, which exactly meets the present case.'

'We shall sleep in jail to-night,' said Humphrey Pump. 'I knew it in my bones.'

'It is enough to say,' proceeded the millionaire, 'that by the law as it now stands any innkeeper, even if he display a sign, is subject to imprisonment if he sells alcohol on premises where it has not been previously kept for three days.'

'I thought it would be something like that,' muttered Pump. 'Shall we give up, Captain, or shall we try a bolt for it?'

Even the impudence of Dalroy appeared for the instant dazed and stilled. He was staring forlornly up into the abyss of sky above him; as if, like Shelley, he could get inspiration from the last and purest clouds and the perfect hues of the ends of heaven.

At last he said in a soft and meditative voice, the single syllable:

'Sells!'

Pump looked at him sharply, with a remarkable expression growing on his grim face. But the Doctor was far too rapidly rejoicing in his triumph to understand the Captain's meaning.

'Sells alcohol are the exact words,' he insisted, brandishing the blue oblong of the new Act of Parliament.

'So far as I am concerned they are inexact words,' said Captain Dalroy, with polite indifference. 'I have not been selling alcohol; I have been giving it away. Has anybody here paid me money? Has anybody here seen anybody else pay me money? I'm a philanthropist just like Dr. Meadows. I'm his living image.'

Mr. Leveson and Dr. Meadows looked across at each other, and on the face of the first was consternation and of the second a full return of all his terrors of the complicated law.

'I shall remain here for several weeks,' continued the Captain, leaning elegantly on the can, 'and shall give away gratis such supplies of this excellent drink as may be demanded by the citizens. It appears that there is no such supply at present in this district; and I feel sure that no person present can object to so strictly legal and highly charitable an arrangement.'

In this he was apparently in error; for several persons present seemed to object to it. But curiously enough it was not the withered and fanatical face of the philanthropist Meadows, nor the dark and equine face of the official Leveson, which stood out most vividly as a picture of protest. The face most strangely unsympathetic with this form of charity was that of the ex-proprietor of Hugby's Ales. His gooseberry eyes were almost dropping from his head and his words sprang from his lips before he could stop them.

'And you blooming well think you can come here like a big buffoon, you beast, and take away all my trade——'

Old Meadows turned on him with the swiftness of an adder.

'And what is your trade, Mr. Hugby?' he asked.

The brewer bubbled with a sort of bursting anger. The goats all looked at the ground as is, according to a Roman poet, the habit of the lower animals. Man (in the character of Mr. Patrick Dalroy), taking advantage of a free but fine translation of the Latin passage, 'looked aloft and with uplifted eyes, beheld his own hereditary skies'.

'Well, all I can say is,' roared Mr. Hugby, 'if the police come all this way and can't lock up a dirty loafer whose coat's all in rags, there's an end of me paying these fat infernal taxes and——'

'Yes,' said Dalroy, in a voice that fell like an axe, 'there is an end of you, please God. It's brewers like you that have made the inns stink with poison, till even good men asked for no inns at all. And you are worse than the teetotallers, for you perverted what they never knew. And as for you, eminent man of science, great philanthropist, idealist and destroyer of inns, let me give one cold fact for your information. You are not respected. You are obeyed. Why should I or any one respect you particularly? You say you built this town and get up at daybreak to watch this town. You built it for money and you watch it for more money. Why should I respect you because you are fastidious about food, that your poor old digestion may outlive the hearts of better men? Why should you be the god of this valley, whose god is your belly, merely because you do not even love your god, but only fear him? Go home to your prayers, old man; for all men shall die. Read the Bible, if you like, as they do in your German home; and I suppose you once read it to pick texts, as you now read it to pick holes. I don't read it myself, I'm afraid, but I remember some words in old Mulligan's translation; and I leave them with you. "Unless God"'—and he made a movement with his arm, so natural and yet so vast that for an instant the town really looked like a toy of bright-coloured cardboard at the feet of the giant—'"unless God build the city, their labour is but lost that build it; unless God keep the city, the watchman watcheth in vain. It is lost labour that you rise up early in the morning and eat the bread of carefulness; for He giveth His beloved sleep." Try and understand what that means; and never mind whether it's Elohistic. And now, Hump, we'll away and away. I'm tired of the green tiles over there. Come, fill up my cup,' and he banged down the cask in the car. 'Come, fill up my can?' and he banged down the can.

'Come, saddle my horses and call out my men.
And tremble, gay goats, in the midst of your glee;
For you've no' seen the last of my milk-can and me.'

This song was joyously borne away with Mr. Dalroy in the disappearing car; and the motorists were miles beyond pursuit from Peaceways before they thought of halting again. But they were still beside the bank of that noble and enlarging river; and in a place of deep fern and fairy-ribboned birches with the glooming and gleaming water behind them, Patrick asked his friend to stop the car.

'By the way,' said Humphrey suddenly, 'there was one thing I didn't understand. Why was he so afraid of the Public Analyst? What poison and chemicals does he put in the milk?'

'H_2O,' answered the Captain, 'I take it without milk myself.'

And he bent over as if to drink of the stream, as he had done at daybreak.

CHAPTER XX

THE TURK AND THE FUTURISTS

MR. ADRIAN CROOKE was a successful chemist whose shop was in the neighbourhood of Victoria; but his face expressed more than is generally required in a successful chemist. It was a curious face, prematurely old and like parchment, but acute and decisive, with real headwork in every line of it. Nor was his conversation, when he did converse, out of keeping with this: he had lived in many countries, and had a rich store of anecdote about the more quaint and sometimes the more sinister side of his work, visions of the vapour of Eastern drugs or guesses at the ingredients of Renaissance poisons. He himself, it need hardly be said, was a most respectable and reliable apothecary, or he would not have had the custom of families, especially among the upper classes; but he enjoyed as a hobby the study of the dark days and lands where his science had lain sometimes on the borders of magic and sometimes upon the borders of murder. Hence it often happened that persons who in their serious senses were well aware of his harmless and useful habits, would leave his shop on some murky and foggy night, with their heads so full of wild tales of the eating of hemp or the poisoning of roses, they could hardly help fancying that the shop, with its glowing moon of crimson or saffron, like bowls of blood and sulphur, was really a house of the Black Art.

It was doubtless for such conversational pleasure in part that Hibbs However entered the shop; as well as for a small glass of the same restorative medicine which he had been taking when Leveson found him by the open window. But this did not prevent Hibbs from expressing considerable surprise and some embarrassment when Leveson entered the same chemist's and asked for the same chemical. Indeed Leveson looked harassed and weary enough to want it.

'You've been out of town, haven't you?' said Leveson. 'No luck. They got away again on some quibble. The police wouldn't make the arrest; and even old Meadows thought it might be illegal. I'm sick of it. Where are you going?'

'I thought,' said Mr. Hibbs, 'of dropping in at this Post-Futurist exhibition. I believe Lord Ivywood will be there; he is showing it to the Prophet. I don't pretend to know much about art; but I hear it's very fine.'

There was a long silence and Mr. Leveson said, 'People are always prejudiced against new ideas.'

Then there was another long silence, and Mr. Hibbs said, 'After all, they said the same of Whistler.'

Refreshed by this ritual, Mr. Leveson became conscious of the existence of Crooke and said to him cheerfully, 'That's so in your department, too, isn't it? I suppose the greatest pioneers in chemistry were unpopular in their own time.'

'Look at the Borgias,' said Mr. Crooke. 'They got themselves quite disliked.'

'You're very flippant, you know,' said Leveson, in a fatigued way. 'Well, so long. Are you coming, Hibbs?'

And the two gentlemen, who were both attired in high hats and afternoon-caller's coats, betook themselves down the street. It was a fine sunny day, the twin of the day before that had shone so brightly on

the white town of Peaceways; and their walk was a
pleasant one, along a handsome street with high
houses and small trees that overlooked the river all
the way. For the pictures were exhibited in a small
but famous gallery, a rather rococo building of which
the entrance steps almost descended upon the Thames.
The building was girt on both sides and behind with
gaudy flower-beds, and on the top of the steps in front
of the Byzantine doorway stood their old friend Misysra
Ammon smiling broadly and in an unusually sumptuous
costume. But even the sight of that fragrant Eastern
flower did not seem to revive altogether the spirits of
the drooping Secretary.

'You have coome,' said the beaming Prophet, 'to
see the decoration? It is approo-ooved. I haf approo-
ooved it.'

'We came to see the Post-Futurist pictures,' began
Hibbs: but Leveson was silent.

'There are no pictures,' said the Turk simply. 'If
there had been I could not haf approo-ooved. For
those of our Religion pictures are not goo-ood; they
are Idols, my friendss. Loo-ook in there,' and he
turned and darted a solemn forefinger just under his
nose towards the gates of the gallery. 'Loo-ook in
there, and you will find no Idols. No Idols at all. I
have most carefully loo-ooked into every one of the
frames. Every one I have approo-ooved. No trace
of ze Man form. No trace of ze Animal form. All
decoration as goo-ood as the goo-oodest of carpets: it
harms not. Lord Ivywood smile of happiness; for I
tell him Islam indeed progresses. Ze old Moslems
allow to draw the picture of the vegetable. Here I
hunt even for the vegetable. And there is no vegetable.'

Hibbs, whose trade was tact, naturally did not think

it wise that the eminent Misysra should go on lecturing from a tall flight of steps to the whole street and river; so he had slipped past with a general proposal to go in and see. The Prophet and the Secretary followed; and all entered the outer hall where Lord Ivywood stood with the white face of a statue. He was the only statue the New Moslems were allowed to worship.

On a sofa, like a purple island in the middle of the sea of floor, sat Enid Wimpole, talking eagerly to her cousin Dorian; being, in fact, fighting her best to prevent the family quarrel which threatened to follow hard on the incident at Westminster. In the deeper perspective of the rooms Lady Joan Brett was floating about. And if her attitudes before the Post-Futurist pictures could not be called humble, or even inquiring, it is but just to that school to say that she seemed to be quite as bored with the floor that she walked on and the parasol she held. Bit by bit other figures or groups of that world drifted through the Exhibition of the Post-Futurists. It is a very small world: but it is just big enough and just small enough to govern a country— that is, a country with no religion. And it has all the vanity of a mob; and all the reticence of a secret society.

Leveson instantly went up to Lord Ivywood, pulled papers from his pocket, and was plainly telling him of the escape from Peaceways. Ivywood's face hardly changed; he was, or felt, above some things; and one of them was blaming a servant before the servant's social superiors. But no one could say he looked less like cold marble than before.

'I made all possible inquiries about their subsequent route,' the Secretary was heard saying, 'and the most serious feature is that they seem to have taken the road for London.'

'Quite so,' replied the statue. 'They will be easier to capture here.'

Lady Enid, by a series of assurances (most of which were, I regret to say, lies) had succeeded in preventing the scandal of her cousin Dorian actually cutting her cousin Philip. But she knew very little of the masculine temper if she really thought she had prevented the profound intellectual revolt of the poet against the politician. Ever since he heard Mr. Hibbs say, 'Yars! Yars!' and order his arrest by a common policeman, the feelings of Dorian Wimpole had flowed for some four days and night in a direction highly contrary to the ideals of Mr. Hibbs; and the sudden appearance of that blameless diplomatist quickened the mental current to a cataract. But as he could not insult Hibbs, whom socially he did not even know; and could not insult Ivywood, with whom he had just had a formal reconciliation, it was absolutely necessary that he should insult something else instead. All watchers for the Dawn will be deeply distressed to know that the Post-Futurist School of Painting received the full effects of this perverted wrath. In vain did Mr. Leveson affirm from time to time, 'People are always prejudiced against new ideas.' Vainly did Mr. Hibbs say, at the proper intervals, 'After all, they said the same of Whistler.' Not by such decent formalities was the frenzy of Dorian to be appeased.

'That little Turk has more sense than you have,' he said; 'he passes it as a good wall-paper. I should say it was a bad wall-paper; the sort of wall-paper that gives a sick man fever when he hasn't got it. But to call it pictures—you might as well call it seats for the Lord Mayor's Show. A seat isn't a seat if you can't see the Lord Mayor's Show. A picture isn't a

picture if you can't see any picture. You can sit down
at home more comfortably than you can at a procession. And you can walk about at home more comfortably than you can at a picture gallery. There's
only one thing to be said for a street show or a picture
show—and that is whether there is anything to be
shown. Now then! Show me something!'

'Well,' said Lord Ivywood good-humouredly, motion-
ing towards the wall in front of him, 'let me show you
the "Portrait of an Old Lady".'

'Well,' said Dorian stolidly, 'which is it?'

Mr. Hibbs made a hasty gesture of identification,
but was so unfortunate as to point to the picture of
'Rain in the Apennines' instead of the 'Portrait of an
Old Lady', and his intervention increased the irritation
of Dorian Wimpole. Most probably, as Mr. Hibbs
afterwards explained, it was because a vivacious
movement of the elbow of Mr. Wimpole interfered
with the exact pointing of the forefinger of Mr. Hibbs.
In any case, Mr. Hibbs was sharply and horridly
fixed by embarrassment: so that he had to go away to
the refreshment bar, and eat three lobster-patties and
even a glass of that champagne that had once been
his ruin. But he stopped at one glass; and returned
with a full diplomatic responsibility.

He returned to find that Dorian Wimpole had forgotten all the facts of time, place, and personal pride,
in an argument with Lord Ivywood, exactly as he had
forgotten such facts in an argument with Patrick
Dalroy, in a dark wood with a donkey-cart. And
Philip Ivywood was interested also: his cold eyes even
shone; for though his pleasure was almost purely
intellectual, it was utterly sincere.

'And I do trust the untried; I do follow the

inexperienced,' he was saying quietly, with his fine inflexions of voice. 'You say this is changing the very nature of Art. I want to change the very nature of Art. Everything lives by turning into something else. Exaggeration is growth.'

'But exaggeration of what?' demanded Dorian. 'I cannot see a trace of exaggeration in these pictures; because I cannot find a hint of what it is they want to exaggerate. You can't exaggerate the feathers of a cow or the legs of a whale. You can draw a cow with feathers or a whale with legs for a joke—though I hardly think such jokes are in your line. But don't you see, my good Philip, that even then the joke depends upon its looking like a cow and not only like a thing with feathers. Even then the joke depends upon the whale as well as the legs. You can combine up to a certain point; you can distort up to a certain point: after that you lose the identity: and with that you lose everything. A Centaur is so much of a man with so much of a horse. The Centaur must not be hastily identified with the Horsy Man. And the Mermaid must be maidenly; even if there is something fishy about her social conduct.'

'No,' said Lord Ivywood, in the same quiet way, 'I understand what you mean; and I don't agree. I should like the Centaur to turn into something else, that is neither man nor horse.'

'But not something that has nothing of either?' asked the poet.

'Yes,' answered Ivywood, with the same queer quiet gleam in his colourless eyes, 'something that has nothing of either.'

'But what's the good?' argued Dorian. 'A thing that has changed entirely has not changed at all. It has no bridge of crisis. It can remember no change. If you wake up to-morrow and you simply *are* Mrs. Dope, an old woman who lets lodgings at Broadstairs—well, I don't doubt Mrs. Dope is a saner and happier person than you are. But in what way have *you* progressed? What part of *you* is better? Don't you see this prime fact of identity is the limit set on all living things?'

'No!' said Philip, with suppressed but sudden violence. 'I deny that any limit is set upon living things?'

'Why, then I understand,' said Dorian, 'why, though you make such good speeches, you have never written any poetry.'

Lady Joan, who was looking with tedium at a rich pattern of purple and green in which Misysra attempted to interest her (imploring her to disregard the mere title, which idolatrously stated it as 'First Communion in the Snow'), abruptly turned her full face to Dorian. It was a face to which few men could feel indifferent, especially when thus suddenly shown them.

'Why can't he write poetry?' she asked. 'Do you mean he would resent the limits of metre and rhyme and so on?'

The poet reflected for a moment and then said, 'Well, partly; but I mean more than that too. As one can be candid in the family, I may say that what every one says about him is that he has no humour. But that's not my complaint at all. I think my complaint is that he has no pathos. That is, he does not feel human limitations. That is, he will not write poetry.'

Lord Ivywood was looking with his cold, unconscious profile into a little black and yellow picture called 'Enthusiasm'; but Joan Brett leaned across to him with swarthy eagerness and cried quite provocatively:

'Dorian says you've no pathos. Have you any pathos? He says it's a sense of human limitations.'

Ivywood did not remove his gaze from the picture of 'Enthusiasm', but simply said, 'No; I have no sense of human limitations.' Then he put up his elderly eye-glass to examine the picture better. Then he dropped it again and confronted Joan with a face paler than usual.

'Joan,' he said, 'I would walk where no man has walked; and find something beyond tears and laughter. My road shall be my road indeed; for I will make it like the Romans. And my adventures shall not be in the hedges and the gutters; but in the borders of the ever-advancing brain. I will think what was unthinkable until I thought it; I will love what never lived until I loved it—I will be as lonely as the first man.'

'They say,' she said, after a silence, 'that the first man fell.'

'You mean the priests?' he answered. 'Yes; but even they admit that he discovered good and evil. So are these artists trying to discover some distinction that is still dark to us.'

'Oh,' said Joan, looking at him with a real and unusual interest, 'then you don't *see* anything in the pictures yourself?'

'I see the breaking of the barriers,' he answered; 'beyond that I see nothing.'

She looked at the floor for a little time and traced patterns with her parasol, like one who has really received food for thought. Then she said suddenly:

'But perhaps the breaking of barriers might be the breaking of everything.'

The clear and colourless eyes looked at her quite steadily.

'Perhaps,' said Lord Ivywood.

Dorian Wimpole made a sudden movement a few yards off, where he was looking at a picture, and said, 'Hullo! what's this?' Mr. Hibbs was literally gaping in the direction of the entrance.

Framed in that fine Byzantine archway stood a great big bony man in threadbare but careful clothes, with a harsh, high-featured, intelligent face, to which a dark beard under the chin gave something of the Puritanic cast. Somehow his whole personality seemed to be pulled together and explained when he spoke with a North Country accent.

'Weel, lards,' he said genially, 't'hoose be main great on t'pictures. But I coom for suthin' in a moog. Haw haw!'

Leveson and Hibbs looked at each other. Then Leveson rushed from the room. Lord Ivywood did not move a finger; but Mr. Wimpole, with a sort of poetic curiosity, drew nearer to the stranger, and studied him.

'It's perfectly awful,' cried Enid Wimpole, in a loud whisper. 'The man must be drunk.'

'Na, lass,' said the man, with gallantry. 'A've not been droonk, nobbut at Hurley Fair, these years and all; a'm a decent lad and workin' ma way back t'Wharfedale. No harm in a moog of ale, lass.'

'Are you quite sure,' asked Dorian Wimpole, with a singular sort of delicate curiosity—'are you quite *sure* you're not drunk?'

'A'm not droonk,' said the man jovially.

'Even if these were licensed premises,' began Dorian, in the same diplomatic manner.

'There's t'sign on t'hoose,' said the stranger.

The black, bewildered look on the face of Joan Brett suddenly altered. She took four steps towards the doorway; and then went back and sat on the purple ottoman. But Dorian seemed fascinated with his inquiry into the alleged decency of the lad who was working his way to Wharfedale.

'Even if these were licensed premises,' he repeated, 'drink could be refused you if you were drunk. Now, are you *really* sure you're not drunk? Would you know if it was raining, say?'

'Aye,' said the man, with great conviction.

'Would you know any common object of your country-side,' inquired Dorian scientifically, 'a woman —let us say an old woman.'

'Aye,' said the man, with good humour.

'What on earth are you doing with the creature?' whispered Enid feverishly.

'I am trying,' answered the poet, 'to prevent a very sensible man from smashing a very silly shop. I beg your pardon, sir. As I was saying, would you know these things in a picture, now? Do you know what a landscape is and what a portrait is? Forgive my asking; you see, we are responsible while we keep the place going.'

There soared up into the sky like a cloud of rooks the eager vanity of the North.

'We collier lads are none so badly educated, lad,' he said. 'In the town a' was born in there was a gallery of pictures as fine as Lunnon. Aye, and a' knew 'em too.'

'Thank you,' said Wimpole, pointing suddenly at the wall. 'Would you be so kind, for instance, as to look at those two pictures. One represents an old woman and the other rain in the hills. It's a mere formality. You shall have your drink when you've said which is which.'

The northerner bowed his huge body before the two frames and peered into them patiently. The long stillness that followed seemed to be something of a strain on Joan, who rose in a restless manner, first went to look out of a window and then went out of the front doors.

At length the art-critic lifted a large, puzzled, but still philosophical face.

'Soomhow or other,' he said, 'a'mon be droonk after all.'

'You have testified,' cried Dorian, with animation. 'You have all but saved civilization. And, by God, you shall have your drink.'

And he brought from the refreshment table a huge bumper of the Hibbsian champagne; and declined payment by the rapid method of running out of the gallery on to the steps outside.

Joan was already standing there. Out the little side window she had seen the incredible thing she expected to see: which explained the ludicrous scene inside. She saw the red and blue wooden flag of Mr. Pump standing up in the flower-beds in the sun, as serenely as if it were a tall and tropical flower. And yet, in the brief interval between the window and the door it had vanished, as if to remind her it was a flying dream. But two men were in a little motor outside, which was in the very act of starting. They were in motoring disguise; but she knew who they were. All that was deep in her, all that was sceptical, all that was stoical, all that was noble, made her stand as still as one of the pillars of the porch. But a dog, bearing the name of Quoodle, sprang up in the moving car, and barked with joy at the mere sight of her. And though she had borne all else, something in that bestial innocence of an animal, suddenly blinded her with tears.

It could not, however, blind her to the extraordinary fact that followed. Mr. Dorian Wimpole, attired in anything but motoring costume, dressed in that compromise between fashion and art which seems proper to the visiting of picture galleries, did not by any means stand as still as one of the pillars of the porch. He rushed down the steps, ran after the car and actually sprang into it, without disarranging his Whistlerian silk hat.

'Good afternoon,' he said to Dalroy pleasantly. 'You owe me a motor-ride, you know.'

CHAPTER XXI

THE ROAD TO ROUNDABOUT

PATRICK DALROY looked at the invader with a heavy and yet humorous expression, and merely said, 'I didn't steal your car; really I didn't.'

'Oh, no,' answered Dorian, 'I've heard all about it since; and as you're rather the persecuted party, so to speak, it wouldn't be fair not to tell you that I don't agree much with Ivywood about all this. I disagree with him. Or rather, to speak medically, he disagrees with me. He has; ever since I woke up after an oyster supper, and found myself in the House of Commons with policemen calling out, "Who Goes Home?"'

'Indeed,' inquired Dalroy, drawing his red bushy eyebrows together. 'Do the officials in Parliament say, "Who Goes Home?"'

'Yes,' answered Wimpole indifferently. 'It's a part of some old custom in the days when Members of Parliament might be attacked in the street.'

'Well,' inquired Patrick, in a rational tone, 'why aren't they attacked in the street?'

There was a silence. 'It is a holy mystery,' said the Captain at last. 'But "Who Goes Home?"—that is uncommonly good.'

The Captain had received the poet into the car with all possible expressions of affability and satisfaction, but the poet, who was keen-sighted enough about people of his own sort, could not help thinking that the Captain was a little absent-minded. As they flew thundering through the mazes of South London (for Pump had crossed Westminster Bridge and was making for the Surrey hills), the big blue eye of the big red-haired man rolled perpetually up and down the streets; and after longer and longer silences he found expression for his thoughts.

'Doesn't it strike you that there are a very large number of chemists in London nowadays?'

'Are there?' asked Wimpole carelessly. 'Well, there certainly are two very close to each other just over there.'

'Yes, and both the same name,' replied Dalroy— 'Crooke. And I saw the same Mr. Crooke chemical-izing round the corner. He seems to be a highly omnipresent deity.'

'A large business, I suppose,' observed Dorian Wimpole.

'Too large for its profits, I should say,' said Dalroy. 'What can people want with two chemists of the same sort within a few yards of each other? Do they put one leg into one shop and one into the other, and have their corns done in both at once? Or do they take an acid in one shop and an alkali in the next, and wait for the fizz? Or do they take the poison in the first shop and an emetic in the second shop? It seems like carrying delicacy too far. It almost amounts to living a double life.'

'But perhaps,' said Dorian, 'he is an uproariously popular chemist, this Mr. Crooke. Perhaps there's a rush on some speciality of his.'

'It seems to me,' said the Captain, 'that there are certain limitations to such popularity in the case of a chemist. If a man sells very good tobacco, people may smoke more and more of it from sheer self-indulgence. But I never heard of anybody exceeding in cod-liver oil. Even castor oil, I should say, is regarded with respect rather than true affection.'

After a few minutes of silence he said, 'Is it safe to stop here for an instant, Pump?'

'I think so,' replied Humphrey, 'if you'll promise me not to have any adventures in the shop.'

The motor-car stopped before yet a fourth arsenal of Mr. Crooke and his pharmacy; and Dalroy went in. Before Pump and his companion could exchange a word, the Captain came out again, with a curious expression on his countenance, especially round the mouth.

'Mr. Wimpole,' said Dalroy, 'will you give us the pleasure of dining with us this evening? Many would consider it an unceremonious invitation to an unconventional meal; and it may be necessary to eat it under a hedge or even up a tree. But you are a man of taste; and one does not apologize for Hump's rum or Hump's cheese to persons of taste. We will eat and drink of our best to-night. It is a banquet. I am not very certain whether you and I are friends or enemies; but at least there shall be peace to-night.'

'Friends, I hope,' said the poet, smiling. 'But why peace especially to-night?'

'Because there will be war to-morrow,' answered Patrick Dalroy, 'whichever side of it you may be on. I have just made a singular discovery.'

And he relapsed into his silence as they flew out of the fringe of London into the woods and hills beyond Croydon. Dalroy remained in the same mood of brooding. Dorian was brushed by the butterfly wing of that fleeting slumber that will come on a man hurried through the air after long lounging in hot drawing-rooms; even the dog Quoodle was asleep at the bottom of the car. As for Humphrey Pump, he very seldom talked when he had anything else to do.

Thus it happened that long landscapes and perspectives were shot past them like suddenly shifted slides, and long stretches of time elapsed before any of them spoke again. The sky was changing from the pale golds and greens of evening to the burning blue of a strong summer night, a night of strong stars. The walls of woodland that flew past them like long assagais were mostly, at first, of the fenced and park-like sort; endless oblong blocks of blank pine-wood shut in by boxes of thin grey wood. But soon fences began to sink and pine-woods to straggle and roads to split and even to sprawl. Half an hour later Dalroy had begun to realize something romantic and even faintly reminiscent in the roll of the country; and Humphrey Pump had long known he was on the marches of his native land.

So far as the difference could be defined by a detail, it seemed to consist not so much in the road rising as in the road perpetually winding. It was more like a path; and even where it was abrupt or aimless, it seemed the more alive. They appeared to be ascending a big dim hill that was built of a crowd of little hills with rounded tops; it was like a cluster of domes. Among these domes the road climbed and curled in multitudinous curves and angles. It was almost impossible to believe that it could turn itself and round on itself so often without tying itself in a knot and choking.

'I say,' said Dalroy, breaking the silence suddenly, 'this car will get giddy and fall down.'

'Perhaps,' said Dorian, beaming at him; 'my car, as you may have noticed, was much steadier.'

Patrick laughed, but not without a shade of confusion.

'I hope you got back your car all right,' he said.

'This is really nothing for speed; but it is an uncommonly good little climber. And it seems to have some climbing to do just now. And even more wandering.'

'The roads certainly seem to be very irregular,' said Dorian reflectively.

'Well,' cried Patrick, with a queer kind of impatience, 'you're English, and I'm not. You ought to know why the road winds about like this. Why, the Saints deliver us,' he cried, 'it's one of the wrongs of Ireland that she can't understand England. England won't understand herself. England won't tell us why these roads go wriggling about. Englishmen won't tell us! You won't tell us!'

'Don't be too sure,' said Dorian, with a quiet irony.

Dalroy, with an irony far from quiet, emitted a loud yell of victory.

'Right,' he shouted. 'More Songs of the Car Club! We're all poets here, I hope. Each shall write something about why the road jerks about so much. So much as this, for example,' he added, as the whole vehicle nearly rolled over in a ditch.

For indeed Pump appeared to be attacking such inclines as are more suitable for a goat than a small motor-car. This may have been exaggerated in the emotions of his companions, who had both, for different reasons, seen much of mere flat country lately. The sensation was like a combination of trying to get into the middle of the maze at Hampton Court, and climbing the spiral staircase to the Belfry at Bruges.

'This is the right way to roundabout,' said Dalroy cheerfully. 'Charming place. Salubrious spot. You can't miss it. First to the left and right and straight on round the corner and back again. That'll do for

my poem. Get on, you slackers; why aren't you writing
your poems?'

'I'll try one if you like,' said Dorian, treating his
flattered egotism lightly. 'But it's too dark to write;
and getting darker.'

Indeed they had come under a shadow between them
and the stars like the brim of a giant's hat; only through
the holes and rents in which the summer stars could
now look down on them. The hill like a cluster of
domes, though smooth and even bare in its lower con-
tours, was topped with a tangle of spreading trees that
sat above them like a bird brooding over its nest. The
wood was larger and vaguer than the clump that is
the crown of the hill at Chanctonbury; but was rather
like it and held much the same high and romantic
position. The next moment they were in the wood
itself, and winding in and out among the trees by a
ribbon of paths. The emerald twilight between the
stems, combined with the dragon-like contortions of
the great grey roots of the beeches, had a suggestion
of monsters and the deep sea; especially as a long litter
of crimson and copper-coloured fungi, which might
well have been the more gorgeous types of anemone or
jelly-fish, reddened the ground like a sunset dropped
from the sky. And yet, contradictorily enough, they
had also a strong sense of being high up; and even
near to heaven; and the brilliant summer stars that
stared through the chinks of the leafy roof, might
almost have been white starry blossoms on the trees
of the wood.

But though they had entered the wood as if it were
a house; their strongest sensation still was the rotatory;
it seemed as if that high green-house went round and
round like a revolving lighthouse or the whizzygig

temple in the old pantomimes. The stars seemed to circle over their heads; and Dorian felt almost certain he had seen the same beech-tree twice.

At length they came to a central place where the hill rose in a sort of cone in the thick of its trees, lifting its trees with it. Here Pump stopped the car; and clambering up the slope came to the crawling colossal roots of a very large but very low beech-tree. It spread out to the four quarters of heaven more in the manner of an octopus than a tree; and within its low crown branches there was a kind of hollow, like a cup, into which Mr. Humphrey Pump, of 'The Old Ship', Pebbleswick, suddenly and entirely disappeared.

When he appeared it was with a kind of rope ladder, which he politely hung over the side for his companions to ascend by; but the Captain preferred to swing himself on to one of the octopine branches with a whirl of large wild legs worthy of a chimpanzee. When they were established there, each propped in a hollow against a branch, almost as comfortably as in an arm-chair, Humphrey himself descended once more and began to take out their simple stores. The dog was still asleep in the car.

'An old haunt of yours, Hump, I suppose,' said the Captain. 'You seem quite at home.'

'I am at home,' answered Pump, with gravity. 'At the sign of "The Old Ship".' And he stuck the old blue and red sign-board erect among the toadstools, as if inviting the passer-by to climb the tree for a drink.

The tree just topped the mound or clump of trees, and from it they could see the whole champaign of the country they had passed; with the silver roads roaming about in it like rivers. They were so exalted they could almost fancy the stars would burn them.

'Those roads remind me of the songs you've all promised,' said Dalroy at last. 'Let's have some supper, Hump, and then recite.'

Humphrey had hung one of the motor lanterns on to a branch above him, and proceeded, by the light of it, to tap the keg of rum and hand round the cheese.

'What an extraordinary thing!' exclaimed Dorian Wimpole suddenly. 'Why, I'm quite comfortable! Such a thing has never happened before, I should imagine. And how holy this cheese tastes!'

'It has gone on a pilgrimage,' answered Dalroy, 'or rather a crusade. It's a heroic, a fighting cheese. "Cheese of all Cheeses, Cheese of all the world," as my compatriot, Mr. Yeats, says to the Something-or-other of Battle. It's almost impossible that this cheese can have come out of such a coward as a cow. I suppose,' he added, wistfully, 'I suppose it wouldn't do to explain that in this case Hump had milked the bull. That would be classed by scientists among Irish legends—those that have the Celtic glamour and all that. No, I think this cheese must have come from that Dun Cow of Dunsmore Heath, who had horns bigger than elephant's tusks; and who was so ferocious that one of the greatest of the old heroes of chivalry was required to do battle with it. The rum's good, too. I've earned this glass of rum—earned it by Christian humility. For nearly a month I've lowered myself to the beasts of the field, and gone about on all fours like a teetotaller. Hump, circulate the bottle —I mean the cask—and let us have some of this poetry you're so keen about. Each poem must have the same title, you know; it's a rattling good title. It's called "An Inquiry into the causes geological, historical, agricultural, psychological, psychical, moral, spiritual, and theological of the alleged cases of double, treble, quadruple, and other curvature in the English Road, conducted by a specially appointed secret commission in a hole in a tree by admittedly judicious and academic authorities specially appointed by themselves to report to the Dog Quoodle, having power to add to their number and also to take away the number they first thought of; God save the King.'' Having delivered this formula with blinding rapidity, he added rather breathlessly, 'That's the note to strike. The lyric note.'

For all his rather formless hilarity, Dalroy still impressed the poet as being more *distrait* than the others, as if his mind were labouring with some bigger thing in the background. He was in a sort of creative trance; and Humphrey Pump, who knew him like his own soul, knew well that it was not mere literary creation. Rather it was a kind of creation which many modern moralists would call destruction. For Patrick Dalroy was, not a little to his misfortune, what is called a man of action; as Captain Dawson realized, when he found his entire person a bright pea-green. Fond as he was of jokes and rhymes, nothing he could write, or even sing, ever satisfied him like something he could do.

Thus it happened that his contribution to the metrical inquiry into the crooked roads was avowedly hasty and flippant; while Dorian, who was of the opposite temper, the temper that receives impressions instead of pushing out to make them, found his artist's love of beauty fulfilled as it had never been before in that noble nest; and was far more serious and human than usual. Patrick's verses ran:

'Some say that Guy of Warwick,
The man that killed the Cow
And brake the mighty Boar alive
Beyond the Bridge at Slough;
Went up against a Loathly Worm
That wasted all the Downs,
And so the roads they twist and squirm
(If I may be allowed the term)
From the writhing of the stricken Worm
That died in seven towns.
    I see no scientific proof
    That this idea is sound,
    And I should say they wound about
    To find the town of Roundabout,
    The merry town of Roundabout,
    That makes the world go round.

Some say that Robin Goodfellow,
Whose lantern lights the meads
(To steal a phrase Sir Walter Scott
In heaven no longer needs),
Such dance around the trysting-place
The moonstruck lover leads;
Which superstition I should scout
There is more faith in honest doubt
(As Tennyson has pointed out)
Than in those nasty creeds.
    But peace and righteousness (St. John)
    In Roundabout can kiss,
    And since that's all that's found about
    The pleasant town of Roundabout,
    The roads they simply bound about
    To find out where it is.

Some say that when Sir Lancelot
Went forth to find the Grail,
Grey Merlin wrinkled up the roads
For hope that he should fail;
All roads led back to Lyonesse
And Camelot in the Vale,

I cannot yield assent to this
Extravagant hypothesis,
The plain, shrewd Briton will dismiss
Such rumours (*Daily Mail*).
       But in the streets of Roundabout
       Are no such factions found,
       Or theories to expound about,
       Or roll upon the ground about,
       In the happy town of Roundabout,
       That makes the world go round.'

Patrick Dalroy relieved his feelings by finishing with a shout, draining a stiff glass of his sailor's wine, turning restlessly on his elbow and looking across the landscape towards London.

Dorian Wimpole had been drinking golden rum and strong starlight and the fragrance of forests; and though his verses too were burlesque, he read them more emotionally than was his wont:

'Before the Roman came to Rye or out to Severn strode,
The rolling English drunkard made the rolling English road.
A reeling road, a rolling road, that rambles round the shire,
And after him the parson ran, the sexton and the squire;
A merry road, a mazy road, and such as we did tread
The night we went to Birmingham by way of Beachy Head.

I knew no harm of Bonaparte and plenty of the Squire,
And for to fight the Frenchman I did not much desire;
But I did bash their baggonets because they came arrayed
To straighten out the crooked road an English drunkard made,
Where you and I went down the lane with ale-mugs in our hands,
The night we went to Glastonbury by way of Goodwin Sands.

His sins they were forgiven him; or why do flowers run
Behind him; and the hedges all strengthening in the sun?
The wild thing went from left to right and knew not which was
    which,
But the wild rose was above him when they found him in the
    ditch.

God pardon us, nor harden us; we did not see so clear
The night we went to Bannockburn by way of Brighton Pier.

My friends, we will not go again nor ape an ancient rage,
Or stretch the folly of our youth to be the shame of age,
But walk with clearer eyes and ears this path that wandereth,
And see undrugged in evening light the decent inn of death;
For there is good news yet to hear and fine things to be seen,
Before we go to Paradise by way of Kensal Green.'

'Have you written one, Hump?' asked Dalroy. Humphrey, who had been scribbling hard under the lamp, looked up with a dismal face.

'Yes,' he said. 'But I write under a great disadvantage. You see, I know why the road curves about.' And he read very rapidly all on one note:

'The road turned first towards the left
Where Pinker's quarry made the cleft;
The path turned next towards the right,
Because the mastiff used to bite,
Then left, because of Slippery Height,
And then again towards the right—
We could not take the left because
It would have been against the laws:
Squire closed it in King William's day
Because it was a Right of Way.
Still right; to dodge the ridge of chalk
Where Parson's Ghost it used to walk,
Till some one Parson used to know
Met him blind drunk in Callao.
Then left, a long way round, to skirt
The good land, where old Doggy Burt
Was owner of the "Crown and Cup",
And would not give his freehold up;
Right, missing the old river-bed,
They tried to make him take instead
Right, since they say Sir Gregory
Went mad and let the Gipsies be,
And so they have their camp secure:
And though not honest, they are poor;

And that is something; then along
And first to right—no, I am wrong!
Second to right of course; the first
Is what the holy sisters cursed,
And none defy their awful oaths
Since the policeman lost his clothes
Because of fairies; right again
What used to be High Toby Lane,
Left by the double larch and right
Until the milestone is in sight,
Because the road is firm and good
From past the milestone to the wood.
And I was told by Dr. Lowe,
Whom Mr. Wimpole's aunt would know,
Who lives at Oxford writing books,
And ain't so silly as he looks,
The Romans did that little bit
And we've done all the rest of it,
By which we hardly seem to score.
Left and then forward as before
To where they nearly hanged Miss Browne,
Who told them not to cut her down,
But loose the rope or let her swing
Because it was a waste of string;
Left once again by Hunker's Cleft
And right beyond the elm, and left
By Pills's, right by Nineteen Nicks
And left——'

'No! No! No! Hump! Hump! Hump!' cried Dalroy, in a sort of terror. 'Don't be exhaustive! Don't be a scientist, Hump, and lay waste fairyland! How long does it go on? Is there a lot more of it?'

'Yes,' said Pump, in a stony manner. 'There is a lot more of it.'

'And it's all true?' inquired Dorian Wimpole, with interest.

'Yes,' replied Pump, with a smile, 'it's all true.'

'My complaint exactly,' said the Captain. 'What

you want is legends. What you want is lies, especially at this time of night, and on rum like this, and on our first and our last holiday. What do you think about rum?' he asked Wimpole.

'About this particular rum, in this particular tree, at this particular moment,' answered Wimpole, 'I think it is the nectar of the younger gods. If you ask me in a general, synthetic sense what I think of rum—well, I think it's rather rum.'

'You find it a trifle sweet, I suppose,' said Dalroy, with some bitterness. 'Sybarite! By the way,' he said abruptly, 'what a silly word that word "Hedonist" is! The really self-indulgent people generally like sour things and not sweet, bitter things like caviare and curries or what-not. It's the saints who like the sweets. Anyhow, I've known at least five women who were practically saints; and they all preferred sweet champagne. Look here, Wimpole. Shall I tell you the ancient oral legend about the origin of rum? I told you what you wanted was legends. Be careful to preserve this one, and hand it on to your children; for unfortunately my parents carelessly neglected the duty of handing it on to me. After the words "A Farmer had three sons . . ." all that I owe to tradition ceases. But when the three boys last met in the village market-place, they were all sucking sugar-sticks. Nevertheless, they were all discontented; and on that day parted for ever. One remained on his father's farm, hungering for his inheritance. One went up to London to seek his fortune, as fortunes are found to-day in that town forgotten by God. The third ran away to sea. And the first two flung away their sugar-sticks in shame; and he on the farm was always drinking smaller and sourer beer for the love of money. And he that was in town was always drinking richer and richer wines, that men might see that he was rich. But he who ran away to sea actually ran on board with the sugar-stick in his mouth. And St. Peter or St. Andrew, or whoever is the patron of men in boats, touched it and turned it into a fountain for the comfort of men upon the sea. That is the sailor's theory of the origin of the rum. Inquiry addressed to any busy captain with a new crew in the act of shipping an unprecedented cargo, will elicit a sympathetic agreement.'

'Your rum at least,' said Dorian good-humouredly, 'may well produce a fairy tale. But, indeed, I think all this would have been a fairy tale without it.'

Patrick raised himself from his arboreal throne; and leaned against his branch with a curious and sincere sense of being rebuked.

'Yours was a good poem,' he said, with seeming irrelevance, 'and mine was a bad one. Mine was bad, partly because I'm not a poet as you are; but almost as much because I was trying to make up another song at the same time. And it went to another tune, you see.'

He looked out over the rolling roads and said almost to himself:

'In the city set upon slime and loam
They cry in their parliament "Who goes home?"
And there comes no answer in arch or dome.
For none in the city of graves goes home.
Yet these shall perish and understand,
For God has pity on this great land.
Men that are men again; who goes home?
Tocsin and trumpeter! Who goes home?
For there's blood on the field and blood on the foam
And blood on the body when Man goes home.
And a voice valedictory. . . . Who is for Victory?
Who is for Liberty? Who goes home?'

Softly and idly as he had said this second rhyme, there were circumstances about his attitude that must have troubled or interested any one who did not know him well.

'May I ask,' asked Dorian, laughing, 'why it is necessary to draw your sword at this stage of the affair?'

'Because we have left the place called Roundabout,' answered Patrick, 'and we have come to a place called Rightabout.'

And he lifted his sword towards London; and the grey glint upon it came from a low grey light in the east.

CHAPTER XXII

THE CHEMISTRY OF MR. CROOKE

WHEN the celebrated Hibbs next visited the shop of Crooke, that mystic and criminologist chemist, he found the premises were impressively and even amazingly enlarged with decorations in the Eastern style. Indeed, it would not have been too much to say that Mr. Crooke's shop occupied the whole of one side of a showy street in the West End; the other side being a blank façade of public buildings. It would be no exaggeration to say that Mr. Crooke was the only shopkeeper for some distance round. Mr. Crooke still served in his shop, however; and politely hastened to serve his customer with the medicine that was customary. Unfortunately, for some reason or other, history was, in connexion with this shop, only too prone to repeat itself. And after a vague but soothing conversation with the chemist (on the subject of vitriol and its effects on human happiness) Mr. Hibbs experienced the acute annoyance of once more beholding his most intimate friend, Mr. Joseph Leveson, enter the same fashionable emporium. But, indeed, Leveson's own annoyance was much too acute for him to notice any on the part of Hibbs.

'Well,' he said, stopping dead in the middle of the shop. 'Here is a fine confounded kettle of fish!'

It is one of the tragedies of the diplomatic that they are not allowed to admit either knowledge or ignorance. So Hibbs looked gloomily wise; and said, pursing his lips, 'You mean the *general* situation.'

'I mean the situation about this everlasting business

of the inn signs,' said Leveson impatiently. 'Lord Ivywood went up specially, when his leg was really bad, to get it settled in the House in a small non-contentious Bill, providing that the sign shouldn't be enough if the liquor hadn't been on the spot three days.'

'Oh, but,' said Hibbs, sinking his voice to soft solemnity, as being one of the initiate. 'A thing like *that* can be managed, don't you know.'

'Of course it can,' said the other, still with the same slightly irritable air. 'It was. But it doesn't seem to occur to you, any more than it did to his lordship, that there is rather a weak point after all in this business of passing Acts quietly before they're unpopular. Has it ever occurred to you that if a law is really kept too quiet to be opposed, it may also be kept too quiet to be obeyed? It's not so easy to hush it up from a big politician without running the risk of hushing it up even from a common policeman.'

'But surely that can't happen, by the nature of things?'

'Can't it, by God!' said J. Leveson, appealing to a less pantheistic authority.

He unfolded a number of papers from his pocket, chiefly cheap local newspapers, but some of them letters and telegrams.

'Listen to this!' he said. ' "A curious incident occurred in the village of Poltwell in Surrey yesterday morning. The baker's shop of Mr. Whiteman was suddenly besieged by a knot of the looser types of the locality, who appear to have demanded beer instead of bread; basing their claim on some ornamental object erected outside the shop; which object they asserted to be a sign-board within ·the meaning of the Act." '

There, you see, they haven't even heard of the new Act! What do you think of this, from the *Clapton Conservator*? "The contempt of Socialists for the law was well illustrated yesterday; when a crowd, collected round some wooden ensign of Socialism, set up before Mr. Dugdale's Drapery Stores, refused to disperse, though told that their action was contrary to the law. Eventually the malcontents joined the procession following the wooden emblem." And what do you say to this? "*Stop Press News.* A chemist in Pimlico has been invaded by a huge crowd, demanding beer; and asserting the provision of it to be among his duties. The chemist is, of course, well acquainted with his immunities in the matter, especially under the new Act; but the old notion of the importance of the sign seems still to possess the populace and even, to a certain extent, paralyse the police." What do you say to that? Isn't it as plain as Monday morning that this Flying Inn has flown a day in front of us, as all such lies do?' There was a diplomatic silence.

'Well,' asked the still angry Leveson of the still dubious Hibbs, 'what do you make of all that?'

One ill-acquainted with that relativity essential to all modern minds might possibly have fancied that Mr. Hibbs could not make much of it. However that may be, his explanations, or incapacity for explanations, were soon tested with a fairly positive test. For Lord Ivywood actually walked into the shop of Mr. Crooke.

'Good day, gentlemen,' he said, looking at them with an expression which they both thought baffling and even a little disconcerting. 'Good morning, Mr. Crooke. I have a celebrated visitor for you.' And he introduced the smiling Misysra. The Prophet had fallen back on a comparatively quiet costume this

morning; a mere matter of purple and orange or what-
not; but his aged face was now perennially festive.

'The Cause progresses,' he said. 'Everywhere the
Cause progresses. You hear his lordship's beautiful
speech?'

'I have heard many,' said Hibbs gracefully, 'that
can be so described.'

'The Prophet means what I was saying about the
Ballot Paper Amendment Act,' said Ivywood casually.
'It seems to me the alphabet of statesmanship to
recognize now that the great Oriental British Empire
has become one corporate whole with the Occidental
one. Look at our universities, with their Mohammedan
students; soon they may be a majority. Now are we,'
he went on, still more quietly, 'are we to rule this
country under the forms of representative government?
I do not pretend to believe in democracy, as you know;
but I think it would be extremely unsettling and
incalculable to destroy representative government. If
we are to give Moslem Britain representative government, we must not make the mistake we made about
the Hindus and military organization—which led to
the Mutiny. We must not ask them to make a cross
on their ballot papers; for though it seems a small thing,
it may offend them. So I brought in a little Bill to
make it optional between the old-fashioned cross and
an upward curved mark that might stand for a crescent
—and as it's rather easier to make, I believe it will be
generally adopted.'

'And so,' said the radiant old Turk, 'the little, light,
easily made, curly mark is substituted for the hard,
difficult, double-made, cutting-both-ways mark. It is
the more good for hygi-e-ene. For you must know,
and indeed our good and wise chemist will tell you,

that the Saracenic and the Arabian and the Turkish physicians were the first of all physicians; and taught all medicals to the barbarians of the Frankish territories. And many of the moost modern, the moost fashionable remedies are thus of the Oriental origin.'

'Yes, that is quite true,' said Crooke, in his rather cryptic and unsympathetic way. 'The powder called Arenine, lately popularized by Mr. Boze, now Lord Helvellyn, who tried it first on birds, is made of plain desert sand. And what you see in prescriptions as *Cannabis Indiensis* is what our lively neighbours of Asia describe more energetically as bhang.'

'And so-o—in the sa-ame way,' said Misysra, making soothing passes with his brown hand like a mesmerist —'in the sa-ame way the making of the crescent is hy . . . gienic; the making of the cross is non-hy . . . gienic. The crescent was a little wave, as a leaf, as a little curling feather,' and he waved his hand with real artistic enthusiasm towards the capering curves of the new Turkish decoration which Ivywood made fashionable in many of the fashionable shops. 'But when you make the cross you must make the one line *so-o*,' and he swept the horizon with the brown hand, 'and then you go back and make the other line so-o'; and he made an upward gesture, suggestive of one constrained to lift a pine-tree. 'And then you become very ill.'

'As a matter of fact, Mr. Crooke,' said Ivywood, in his polite manner, 'I brought the Prophet here to consult you, as the best authority, on the very point you have just mentioned—the use of hashish, or the hemp-plant. I have it on my conscience to decide whether these Oriental stimulants or sedatives shall come under the general veto we are attempting to impose on the vulgar intoxicants. Of course, one has heard of the horrible and voluptuous visions, and a kind of insanity attributed to the Assassins and the Old Man of the Mountain. But, on the one hand, we must clearly discount much for the illimitable pro-Christian bias with which the history of these Eastern tribes is told in this country. Would you say the effect of hashish was extremely bad?' And he turned first to the Prophet.

'You will see mosques,' said that seer, with candour, 'many mosques—more mosques—taller and taller mosques till they reach the moon, and you hear a dreadful voice in the very high mosque calling the muezzin; and you will think it is Allah. Then you will see wives—many, many wives—more wives than you yet have. Then you will be rolled over and over in a great pink and purple sea—which is still wives. Then you will go to sleep. I have only done it once,' he concluded mildly.

'And what do you think about hashish, Mr. Crooke?' asked Ivywood thoughtfully.

'I think it's hemp at both ends,' said the chemist.

'I fear,' said Lord Ivywood, 'I don't quite understand you.'

'A hempen drink, a murder, and a hempen rope. That's my experience in India,' said Mr. Crooke.

'It is true,' said Ivywood, yet more reflectively, 'that the thing is not Moslem in any sense in its origin. There is that against the Assassins always. And of course,' he added, with a simplicity that had something noble about it, 'their connexion with St. Louis discredits them rather.'

After a space of silence, he said suddenly, looking at Crooke:

'So it isn't the sort of thing you chiefly sell?'

'No, my lord; it isn't what I chiefly sell,' said the chemist. He also looked steadily; and the wrinkles of his young-old face were like hieroglyphics.

'The Cause progress! Everywhere it progress!' cried Misysra, spreading his arms and relieving a momentary tension of which he was totally unaware. 'The hygienic curve of the crescent will soon superimpose himself for your plus sign. You already use him for the short syllables in your dactyl; which is doubtless of Oriental origin. You see the new game?'

He said this so suddenly that every one turned round, to see him produce from his purple clothing a brightly coloured and highly polished apparatus from one of the grand toyshops; which on examination seemed to consist of a kind of blue slate in a red and yellow frame; a number of divisions being already marked on the slate, about seventeen slate pencils with covers of different colours, and a vast number of printed instructions, stating that it was but recently introduced from the remote East, and was called Naughts and Crescents.

Strangely enough, Lord Ivywood, with all his enthusiasm, seemed almost annoyed at the emergence of this Asiatic discovery; more especially as he really wanted to look at Mr. Crooke as hard as Mr. Crooke was looking at him.

Hibbs coughed considerately and said, 'Of course all our things came from the East, and——' and he paused, being suddenly unable to remember anything but curry; to which he was very rightly attached. He then remembered Christianity, and mentioned that too. 'Everything from the East good, of course,' he ended, with an air of light omniscience.

Those who in later ages and other fashions failed to understand how Misysra had ever got a mental hold on men like Lord Ivywood, left out two elements in the man which are very attractive, especially to other men. One was that there was *no* subject on which the little Turk could not instantly produce a theory. The other was that though the theories were crowded, they were consistent. He was never known to accept an illogical compliment.

'You are in error,' he said solemnly to Hibbs, 'because you say all things from the East are good. There is the east wind. I do not like him. He is not good. And I think very much that all the warmth and all the wealthiness and the colours and the poems and the religiousness, that the East was meant to give you have been much poisoned by this accident, this east wind. When you see the green flag of the Prophet, you do not think of a green field in summer, you think it blown by the east wind. When you read of the moon-faced houris, you think not of our moons like oranges, but of your moons like snowballs——'

Here a new voice contributed to the conversation. Its contribution, though imperfectly understood, appeared to be:

'Nar! Why sh'd I wite for a little Jew in 'is dressin'-gown? Little Jews in their dressin'-gowns 'as their drinks, as we as our drinks. Bitter, miss.'

The speaker, who appeared to be a powerful person of the plastering occupation, looked round for the unmarried female he had ceremonially addressed; and seemed honestly abashed that she was not present.

Ivywood looked at the man with that expression of one turned to stone which his physique made so effective in him. But J. Leveson, Secretary, could summon no such powers of self-petrification. Upon his soul the slaughter red of that unhallowed eve arose when first 'The Ship' and he were foes; when he discovered that the poor are human beings, and therefore are polite and brutal within a comparatively short space of time. He saw that two other men were standing behind the plastering person, one of them apparently urging him to counsels of moderation: which was an ominous sign. And then he lifted his eyes and saw something worse than any omen.

All the glass frontage of the shop was a cloud of crowding faces. They could not be clearly seen, since night was closing in on the street; and the dazzling fires of ruby and amethyst which the lighted shop gave to its great globes of liquid, rather veiled than revealed them. But the foremost actually flattened and whitened their noses on the glass: and the most distant were nearer than Mr. Leveson wanted them. Also he saw a shape erect outside the shop; the shape of an upright staff and a square board. He could not see what was on the board. He did not need to see.

Those who saw Lord Ivywood at such moments understood why he stood out so strongly in the history of his time, in spite of his frozen face and his fanciful dogmas. He had all the negative nobility that is possible to man. Unlike Nelson and most of the great heroes, he knew not fear. Thus he was never conquered by a surprise; but was cold and collected when other men had lost their heads, even if they had not lost their nerve.

'I will not conceal from you, gentlemen,' said Lord Ivywood, 'that I have been expecting this. I will not even conceal from you that I have been occupying

Mr. Crooke's time until it occurred. So far from excluding the crowd, I suggest it would be an excellent thing if Mr. Crooke could accommodate them all in this shop. I want to tell as soon as possible as large a crowd as possible that the law is altered and this folly about the Flying Inn has ceased. Come in, all of you! Come in and listen!'

'Thank yer,' said a man connected in some way with motor-buses, who lurched in behind the plasterer.

'Thanky, sir,' said a bright little clock-mender from Croydon, who immediately followed him.

'Thanks,' said a rather bewildered clerk from Camberwell, who came next in the rather bewildered procession.

'Thank you,' said Mr. Dorian Wimpole, who entered, carrying a large round cheese.

'Thank you,' said Captain Dalroy, who entered carrying a large cask of rum.

'Thank you very much,' said Mr. Humphrey Pump, who entered the shop carrying the sign of 'The Old Ship'.

I fear it must be recorded that the crowd which followed them dispensed with all expressions of gratitude. But though the crowd filled the shop so that there was no standing room to spare, Leveson still lifted his gloomy eyes and beheld his gloomy omen. For though there were very many more people standing in the shop, there seemed to be no less people looking in at the window.

'Gentlemen,' said Ivywood, 'all jokes come to an end. This one has gone so far as to be serious; and it might have become impossible to correct public opinion, and expound to law-abiding citizens the true state of the law, had I not been able to meet so representative an assembly in so central a place. It is not

pertinent to my purpose to indicate what I think of
the jest which Captain Dalroy and his friends have
been playing upon you for the last few weeks. But I
think Captain Dalroy will himself concede that I am
not jesting.'

'With all my heart,' said Dalroy, in a manner that
was unusually serious and even sad. Then he added,
with a sigh, 'And as you truly say, my jest has come
to an end.'

'That wooden sign,' said Ivywood, pointing at the
queer blue ship, 'can be cut up for firewood. It shall
lead decent citizens a devil's dance no more. Understand it once and for all, before you learn it from
policemen or prison warders. You are under a new
law. That sign is the sign of nothing. You can no
more buy and sell alcohol by having that outside your
house than if it were a lamp-post.'

'D'you meanter say, guv'ner,' said the plasterer,
with a dawn of intelligence on his large face which
was almost awful to watch, 'that I ain't to 'ave a glass
of bitter?'

'Try a glass of rum,' said Patrick.

'Captain Dalroy,' said Lord Ivywood, 'if you give
one drop from that cask to that man, you are breakng
the law and you shall sleep in jail.'

'Are you quite sure?' asked Dalroy, with a strange
sort of anxiety. 'I might escape.'

'I am quite sure,' said Ivywood. 'I have posted the
police with full powers for the purpose, as you will find.
I mean that this business shall end here to-night.'

'If I find that pleeceman what told me I could 'ave
a drink just now, I'll knock 'is 'elmet into a fancy
necktie, I will,' said the plasterer 'Why ain't people
allowed to know the law?'

'They ain't got no right to alter the law in the dark like that,' said the clock-mender. 'Damn the new law!'

'What is the new law?' asked the clerk.

'The words inserted by the recent Act,' said Lord Ivywood, with the cold courtesy of the conqueror, 'are to the effect that alcohol cannot be sold, even under a lawful sign, unless alcoholic liquors have been kept for three days on the premises. Captain Dalroy, that cask of yours has not, I think, been three days on these premises. I command you to seal it up and take it away.'

'Surely,' said Patrick, with an innocent air, 'the best remedy would be to wait till it *has* been three days on the premises. We might all get to know each other better.' And he looked round at the ever-increasing multitude with hazy benevolence.

'You shall do nothing of the kind,' said his lordship, with sudden fierceness.

'Well,' answered Patrick wearily, 'now I come to think of it, perhaps I won't. I'll have one drink here and go home to bed like a good little boy.'

'And the constables shall arrest you!' thundered Ivywood.

'Why, nothing seems to suit you,' said the surprised Dalroy. 'Thank you, however, for explaining the new law so clearly—"unless alcoholic liquors have been three days on the premises"—I shall remember it now. You always explain such things so clearly. You only made one legal slip. The constables will not arrest me.'

'And why not?' demanded the nobleman, white with passion.

'Because,' cried Patrick Dalroy, and his voice lifted itself like a lonely trumpet before the charge—'because

I shall not have broken the law. Because alcoholic liquors *have* been three days on these premises. Three months, more likely. Because this is a common grog-shop, Philip Ivywood. Because that man behind the counter lives by selling spirits to all the cowards and hypocrites who are rich enough to bribe a bad doctor.'

And he pointed suddenly at the small medicine-glass on the counter by Hibbs and Leveson.

'What is that man drinking?' he demanded.

Hibbs put out his hand hastily for his glass, but the indignant clock-mender had snatched it first and drained it at a gulp.

'Scotch,' he said, and dashed the glass to atoms on the floor. 'Right you are too,' roared the plasterer, seizing a big medicine-bottle in each hand. 'We're goin' to 'ave a little of the fun now, we are. What's in that big red bowl up there—I reckon it's port. Fetch it down, Bill.'

Ivywood turned to Crooke and said, scarcely moving his lips of marble:

'This is a lie.'

'It is the truth,' answered Crooke, looking back at him with equal steadiness. 'Do you think you made the world, that you should make it over again so easily?'

'The world was made badly,' said Philip, with a terrible note in his voice, 'and I *will* make it over again.'

Almost as he spoke the glass front of the shop fell inward, shattered; and there was wreckage among the moonlike coloured bowls; almost as if spheres of celestial crystal cracked at his blasphemy. Through the broken windows came the roar of that confused tongue that is more terrible than the elements; the cry that the

deaf kings have heard at last; the terrible voice of
mankind. All the way down the long, fashionable
street, lined with the Crooke plate-glass, that glass was
crashing amid the cries of a crowd. Rivers of gold and
purple wines sprawled about the pavement.

'Out in the open!' shouted Dalroy, rushing out of
the shop, sign-board in hand, the dog Quoodle barking
furiously at his heels; while Dorian with the cheese and
Humphrey with the keg followed as rapidly as they
could. 'Good night, my lord.

> 'Perhaps our meeting next may fall
> At Tamworth, in your castle hall.'

'Come along, friends, and form up. Don't waste time
destroying property. We're all to start now.'

'Where are we all going to?' asked the plasterer.

'We're all going into Parliament,' answered the
Captain, as he went to the head of the crowd.

The marching crowd turned two or three corners,
and at the end of the next long street, Dorian Wimpole,
who was towards the tail of the procession, saw again
the grey cyclops tower of St. Stephen's, with its one
great golden eye, as he had seen it against that pale
green sunset that was at once quiet and volcanic, on
the night he was betrayed by sleep and by a friend.
Almost as far off, at the head of the procession, he
could see the sign with the ship and the cross going
before them like an ensign; and hear a great voice
singing:

> 'Men that are men again, Who goes home?
> Tocsin and trumpeter; Who goes home?
> The voice valedictory—who is for Victory?
> Who is for Liberty? Who goes home?'

CHAPTER XXIII

THE MARCH ON IVYWOOD

THAT storm-spirit or eagle of liberty which is the sudden soul in a crowd, had descended upon London after a foreign tour of some centuries in which it had commonly alighted upon other capitals. It is always impossible to define the instant and the turn of mood which makes the whole difference between danger being worse than endurance and endurance being worse than danger. The actual outbreak generally has a symbolic or artistic, or what some would call whimsical, cause. Somebody fires off a pistol, or appears in an unpopular uniform, or refers in a loud voice to a scandal that is never mentioned in the newspapers; somebody takes off his hat, or somebody doesn't take off his hat; and a city is sacked before midnight. When the ever-swelling army of revolt smashed a whole street full of the shops of Mr. Crooke the chemist, and then went on to Parliament, the Tower of London and the road to the sea, the sociologists hiding in their coal-cellars could think (in that clarifying darkness) of many material and spiritual explanations of such a storm in human souls; but of none that explained it quite enough. Doubtless there was a great deal of sheer drunkenness when the urns and goblets of Æsculapius were reclaimed as belonging to Bacchus: and many who went roaring down that road were merely stored with rich wines and liqueurs, which are more comfortably and quietly digested at a City banquet or a West End restaurant. But many of these had been blind drunk twenty times without a thought of rebellion; you could not stretch the material explanation to cover a corner of the case. Much more general was a savage sense of the meanness of Crooke's wealthy patrons, in keeping a door open for themselves which they had wantonly shut on less happy people. But no explanation can explain it; and no man can say when it will come.

Dorian Wimpole was at the tail of the procession which grew more and more crowded every moment. For one space of the march he even had the misfortune to lose it altogether; owing to the startling activity which the rotund cheese, when it escaped from his hands showed, in descending a somewhat steep road towards the river. But in recent days he had gained a pleasure in practical events which was like a second youth. He managed to find a stray taxi-cab; and had little difficulty in picking up again the trail of the extraordinary cortège. Inquiries addressed to a policeman with a black eye outside the House of Commons informed him sufficiently of the rebels' line of retreat or advance, or whatever it was; and in a very short time he beheld the unmistakable legion once more. It was unmistakable, because in front of it there walked a red-headed giant, apparently carrying with him a wooden portion of some public building; and also because so big a crowd had never followed any man in England for a long time past. But except for such things the unmistakable crowd might well have been mistaken for another one. Its aspect had been altered almost as much as if it had grown horns or tusks; for many of the company walked with outlandish weapons like iron teeth or horns, bills and pole-axes, and spears with strangely shaped heads. What was stranger still, whole rows and rows of them had rifles, and even marched with a certain discipline; and yet again others seemed to have snatched up household or workshop tools, meat-axes and pick-axes, hammers, and even carving knives. Such things need be none the less deadly because they are domestic. They have figured in millions of private murders before they appeared in any public war.

Dorian was so fortunate as to meet the flame-haired Captain almost face to face, and easily fell into step with him at the head of the march. Humphrey Pump walked on the other side, with the celebrated cask suspended round his neck by something resembling braces, as if it were a drum. Mr. Wimpole had himself taken the opportunity of his brief estrangement to carry the cheese somewhat more easily in a very large loose waterproof knapsack on his shoulders. The effect in both cases was to suggest dreadful deformities in two persons who happened to be exceptionally cleanly built. The Captain, who seemed to be in tearing and towering spirits, gained great pleasure from this. But Dorian had his sources of amusement too.

'What have you been doing with yourselves since you lost my judicious guidance?' he asked, laughing, 'and why are parts of you a dull review and parts of you a fancy dress ball? What have you been up to?'

'We've been shopping,' said Mr. Patrick Dalroy, with some pride. 'We are country cousins. I know all about shopping; let us see, what are the phrases about it? Look at those rifles now! We got them quite at a bargain. We went to all the best gunsmiths in London, and we didn't pay much. In fact, we didn't pay anything. That's what is called a bargain, isn't it? Surely I've seen in those things they send to ladies something about "giving them away". Then we went to a remnant sale. At least, it was a remnant sale when we left. And we bought that piece of stuff we've tied round the sign. Surely it must be what ladies called chiffon?'

Dorian lifted his eyes and perceived that a very coarse strip of red rag, possibly collected from a dust-bin, had been tied round the wooden sign-post by way of a red flag of revolution.

'Not what ladies call chiffon?' inquired the Captain, with anxiety. 'Well, anyhow it is what *chiffoniers* call it. But as I'm going to call on a lady shortly, I'll try to remember the distinction.'

'Is your shopping over, may I ask?' asked Mr. Wimpole.

'All but one thing,' answered the other. 'I must find a music shop—you know what I mean. Place where they sell pianos and things of that sort.'

'Look here,' said Dorian, 'this cheese is pretty heavy as it is. Have I got to carry a piano too?'

'You misunderstand me,' said the Captain calmly; and as he had never thought of music shops until his eye had caught one an instant before, he darted into the doorway. Returning almost immediately with a long parcel under his arm, he resumed the conversation.

'Did you go anywhere else?' asked Dorian, 'except to shops?'

'Anywhere else!' cried Patrick indignantly. 'Haven't you got any country cousins? Of course we went to all the right places. We went to the Houses of Parliament. But Parliament isn't sitting: so there are no eggs of the quality suitable for elections. We went to the Tower of London—you can't tire country cousins like us. We took away some curiosities of steel and iron. We even took away the halberds from the Beef-eaters. We pointed out that for the purpose of eating beef (their only avowed public object) knives and forks had always been found more convenient. To tell the truth, they seemed rather relieved to be relieved of them.'

'And may I ask,' said the other, with a smile, 'where you are off to now?'

'Another beauty spot!' cried the Captain boisterously; 'no tiring the country cousin! I am going to show my young friends from the provinces what is perhaps the finest old country house in England. We are going to Ivywood, not far from that big watering-place they call Pebbleswick.'

'I see,' said Dorian; and for the first time looked back with intelligent trouble on his face on the marching ranks behind him.

'Captain Dalroy,' said Dorian Wimpole in a slightly altered tone, 'there is one thing that puzzles me. Ivywood talked about having set the police to catch us; and though this is a pretty big crowd, I simply cannot believe that the police, as I knew them in my youth, could not catch us. But where are the police? You seem to have marched through half London with much (if you'll excuse me) of the appearance of carrying murderous weapons. Lord Ivywood threatened that the police would stop us. Well, why didn't they stop us?'

'Your subject,' said Patrick cheerfully, 'divides itself into three heads.'

'I hope not,' said Dorian.

'There really are three reasons why the police should not be prominent in this business; as their worst enemy cannot say that they were.'

He began ticking off the three on his own huge fingers; and seemed to be quite serious about it.

'First,' he said, 'you have been a long time away from town. Probably you do not know a policeman when you see him. They do not wear helmets, as our line regiments did after the Prussians had won. They wear fezes, because the Turks have won. Shortly, I have little doubt, they will wear pigtails, because the Chinese have won. It is a very interesting branch of moral science. It is called Efficiency.'

'Second,' explained the Captain, 'you have perhaps omitted to notice that a very considerable number of those wearing such fezes are walking just behind us. Oh, yes, it's quite true. Don't you remember that the whole French Revolution really began because a sort of City Militia refused to fire on their own fathers and wives; and even showed some slight traces of a taste for firing on the other side? You'll see lots of them behind; and you can tell them by their revolver belts and their walking in step; but don't look back on them too much; it makes them nervous.'

'And the third reason?' asked Dorian.

'For the real reason,' answered Patrick. 'I am not fighting a hopeless fight. People who have fought in real fights don't, as a rule. But I noticed something singular about the very point you mention. Why are there no more police? Why are there no more soldiers? I will tell you. There really are very few policemen or soldiers left in England to-day.'

'Surely that,' said Wimpole, 'is an unusual complaint.'

'But very clear,' said the Captain gravely, 'to any one who has ever seen sailors or soldiers. I will tell you the truth. Our rulers have come to count on the bare bodily cowardice of a mass of Englishmen as a sheep-dog counts on the cowardice of a flock of sheep. Now, look here, Mr. Wimpole. Wouldn't a shepherd be wise to limit the number of his dogs if he could make his sheep pay by it? At the end you might find millions of sheep managed by a solitary dog. But that is because they are sheep. Suppose the sheep were turned by a miracle into wolves. There are very few dogs they could not tear in pieces. But, what is my practical point, there are really very few dogs to tear.'

'You don't mean,' said Dorian, 'that the British Army is practically disbanded?'

'There are the sentinels outside Whitehall,' replied Patrick, in a low voice. 'But indeed your question puts me in a difficulty. No; the army is not entirely disbanded, of course. But the *British* army—— Did you ever hear, Wimpole, of the great destiny of the Empire?'

'I seem to have heard the phrase,' replied his companion.

'It is in four acts,' said Dalroy. 'Victory over barbarians. Employment of barbarians. Alliance with barbarians. Conquest by barbarians. That is the great destiny of Empire.'

'I think I begin to see what you mean,' returned Dorian Wimpole. 'Of course Ivywood and the authorities do seem very prone to rely on the Sepoy troops.'

'And other troops as well,' said Patrick. 'I think you will be surprised when you see them.'

He tramped on for a little in silence and then said, with some air of abruptness, which yet did not seem to be entirely a changing of the subject:

'Do you know the man who lives now on the estate next to Ivywood?'

'No,' replied Dorian, 'I am told he keeps himself very much to himself.'

'And his estate too,' said Patrick rather gloomily. 'If you would climb his garden-wall, Wimpole, I think you would find an answer to a good many of your questions. Oh, yes, the right honourable gentlemen are making full provision for public order and national defence—in a way.'

He fell into an almost sullen silence again; and several villages had been passed before he spoke again.

They tramped through the darkness: and dawn surprised them somewhere in the wilder and more wooded parts where the roads began to rise and roam. Dalroy gave an exclamation of pleasure and pointed ahead, drawing the attention of Dorian to the distance. Against the silver and scarlet bars of the daybreak could be seen afar a dark purple dome, with a crown of dark green leaves; the place they had called Round-about.

Dalroy's spirits seemed to revive at the sight, with the customary accompaniment of the threat of vocalism.

'Been making any poems lately?' he asked of Wimpole.

'Nothing particular,' replied the poet.

'Then,' said the Captain, portentously clearing his throat, 'you shall listen to one of mine, whether you like it or not—nay, the more you dislike it the longer and longer it will be. I begin to understand why soldiers want to sing when on the march; and also why they put up with such rotten songs.

> 'The Druids waved their golden knives
> And danced around the Oak
> When they had sacrificed a man;
> But though the learned search and scan,
> No single modern person can
> Entirely see the joke.

But though they cut the throats of men
They cut not down the tree,
And from the blood the saplings sprang
Of oak-woods yet to be,
    But Ivywood, Lord Ivywood,
    He rots the tree as ivy would,
    He clings and crawls as ivy would
    About the sacred tree.

King Charles he fled from Worcester fight
And hid him in an Oak;
In convent schools no man of tact
Would trace and praise his every act,
Or argue that he was in fact
A strict and sainted bloke,
But not by him the sacred woods
Have lost their fancies free,
And though he was extremely big
He did not break the tree.
    But Ivywood, Lord Ivywood,
    He breaks the tree as ivy would,
    And eats the woods as ivy would
    Between us and the sea.

Great Collingwood walked down the glade
And flung the acorns free,
That oaks might still be in the grove
As oaken as the beams above,
When the great Lover sailors love
Was kissed by Death at sea.
But though for him the oak-trees fell
To build the oaken ships
The woodman worshipped what he smote
And honoured even the chips.
    But Ivywood, Lord Ivywood,
    He hates the tree as ivy would,
    As the dragon of the ivy would
    That has us in his grips.'

They were ascending a sloping road, walled in on
both sides by solemn woods, which somehow seemed

as watchful as owls awake. Though daybreak was
going over them with banners, scrolls of scarlet and
gold, and with a wind like trumpets of triumph, the
dark woods screened their secret like dark cool cellars;
nor was the strong sunlight seen in them, save in
one or two brilliant scars, that looked like splintered
emeralds.

'I should not wonder,' said Dorian, 'if the ivy does
not find the tree knows a thing or two also.'

'The tree does,' assented the Captain. 'The trouble
was that until a little while ago the tree did not know
that it knew.'

There was a silence; and as they went up the incline
grew steeper and steeper and the tall trees seemed
more and more to be guarding something from sight
as with the grey shields of giants.

'Do you remember this road, Hump?' asked Dalroy
of the innkeeper.

'Yes,' answered Humphrey Pump, and said no
more; but few have ever heard such fullness in an
affirmative.

They marched on in silence, and about two hours
afterwards, towards eleven o'clock, Dalroy called a
halt in the forest, and said that everybody had better
have a few hours' sleep. The impenetrable quality in
the woods and the comparative softness of the carpet
of beech-mast, made the spot as appropriate as the
time was inappropriate. And if some one thinks that
common people, casually picked up in the street, could
not follow a random leader on such a journey or sleep
at his command in such a spot, given the state of the
soul, then some one knows no history.

'I'm afraid,' said Dalroy, 'you'll have to have your
supper for breakfast. I know an excellent place for

having breakfast; but it's too exposed for sleep. And sleep you must have; so we won't unpack the stores just now. We'll lie down like Babes in the Wood, and any bird of an industrious disposition is free to start covering me with leaves. Really, there are things coming before which you will want sleep.'

When they resumed the march it was nearly the middle of the afternoon; and the meal which Dalroy insisted buoyantly on describing as breakfast was taken about that mysterious hour when ladies die without tea. The steep road had consistently grown steeper and steeper; and at last Dalroy said to Dorian Wimpole:

'Don't drop that cheese again just here, or it will roll right away down into the woods. I know it will. No scientific calculations of grades and angles are necessary: because I have seen it do so myself. In fact, I have run after it.'

Wimpole realized they were mounting to the sharp edge of a ridge; and in a few moments he knew by the oddness in the shape of the trees what it had been that the trees were hiding.

They had been walking along a swelling woodland path beside the sea. On a particular high plateau, projecting above the shore stood some dwarfed and crippled apple-trees, of whose apples no man alive would have eaten, so sour and salt they must be. All the rest of the plateau was bald and featureless, but Dalroy looked at every inch of it, as if at an inhabited place.

'This is where we'll have breakfast,' he said, pointing to the naked grassy waste. 'It's the best inn in England.' Then as if introducing Humphrey: 'The Parish Pump.'

Some of his audience began to laugh; but somehow suddenly ceased doing so, as Dalroy strode forward and planted the sign of 'The Old Ship' on the desolate sea-shore.

'And now,' he said, 'you have charge of the stores we brought, Hump, and we will picnic. As it said in a song I once sang:

> 'The Saracen's Head out of Araby came,
> King Richard riding in arms like flame,
> And where he established his folk to be fed
> He set up his spear, and the Saracen's Head.'

It was nearly dusk before the mob, much swelled by the many discontented on the Ivywood estates, reached the gates of Ivywood House. Strategically, and for the purposes of a night surprise, this might have done credit to the Captain's military capacity. But the use to which he put it actually was what some might call eccentric. When he had disposed his forces, with swift injunctions of silence for the first few minutes, he turned to Pump and said:

'And now, before we do anything else, I'm going to make a noise.'

And he produced from under brown paper what appeared to be a musical instrument.

'A summons to parley?' inquired Dorian, with interest; 'a trumpet of defiance or something of that kind?'

'No,' said Patrick, 'a serenade.'

CHAPTER XXIV

THE ENIGMAS OF LADY JOAN

On an evening when the sky was clear and only its fringes embroidered with the purple arabesques of the sunset, Joan Brett was walking on the upper lawn of the terraced garden at Ivywood, where the peacocks trail themselves about. She was not unlike one of the peacocks herself in beauty, and some might have said in inutility; she had the proud head and the sweeping train; nor was she, in these days, devoid of the occasional disposition to scream. For indeed, for some time past she had felt her existence closing round her with an incomprehensible quietude; and that is harder for the patience than an incomprehensible noise. Whenever she looked at the old yew hedges of the garden they seemed to be higher than when she saw them last; as if those living walls could still grow to shut her in. Whenever from the turret windows she had a sight of the sea, it seemed to be farther away. Indeed, the whole closing of the end of the turret wing with the new wall of Eastern woodwork seemed to symbolize all her shapeless sensations. In her childhood the wing had ended with a broken-down door and a disused staircase. They led to an uncultivated copse and an abandoned railway tunnel, to which neither she nor any one else ever wanted to go. Still she knew what they led to. Now it seemed that this scrap of land had been sold and added to the adjoining estate; and about the adjoining estate nobody seemed to know anything in particular. The sense of things closing in increased upon her. All sorts of silly little

details magnified the sensation. She could discover
nothing about this new landlord next door, so to speak,
since he was, it seemed, an elderly man who preferred
to live in the greatest privacy. Miss Browning, Lord
Ivywood's secretary, could give her no further information than that he was a gentleman from the
Mediterranean coast; which singular form of words
seemed to have been put into her mouth. As a
Mediterranean gentleman might mean anything from
an American gentleman living in Venice to a black
African on the edge of the Atlas, the description did
not illuminate; and probably was not intended to do
so. She occasionally saw his liveried servants going
about; and their liveries were not like English liveries.
She was also, in her somewhat morbid state, annoyed
by the fact that the uniforms of the old Pebbleswick
militia had been changed, under the influence of the
Turkish prestige in the recent war. They wore fezes
like the French Zouaves; they were certainly much
more practical than the heavy helmets they used to
wear. It was a small matter; but it annoyed Lady
Joan, who was, like so many clever women, at once
subtle and conservative. It made her feel as if the
whole world was being altered outside; and she was
not allowed to know about it.

But she had deeper spiritual troubles also, while,
under the pathetic entreaties of old Lady Ivywood and
her own sick mother, she stayed on week after week
at Ivywood House. If the matter be stated cynically
(as she herself was quite capable of stating it) she was
engaged in the feminine occupation of trying to like
a man. But the cynicism would have been false; as
cynicism nearly always is; for during the most crucial
days of that period, she had really liked the man.

She had liked him when he was brought in with
Pump's bullet in his leg; and was still the strongest
and calmest man in the room. She had liked him
when the hurt took a dangerous turn; and when he
bore pain to admiration. She had liked him when he
showed no malice against the angry Dorian; she had
liked him with something like enthusiasm on the night
he rose rigid on his rude crutch, and crushing all
remonstrance, made his rash and swift rush to London.
But, despite the queer closing-in sensations of which
we have spoken, she never liked him better than that
evening when he lifted himself laboriously on his
crutch up the terraces of the old garden and came to
speak to her as she stood among the peacocks. He
even tried to pat a peacock in a hazy way, as if it were
a dog. He told her that these beautiful birds were,
of course, imported from the East—by the semi-
Eastern empire of Macedonia. But, all the same, Joan
had a dim suspicion that he had never noticed before
that there were any peacocks at Ivywood. His greatest
fault was a pride in the faultlessness of his mental and
moral strength; but, if he had only known, something
faintly comic in the unconscious side of him did him
more good with the woman than all the rest.

'They were said to be the birds of Juno,' he said;
'but I have little doubt that Juno, like so much else of
the Homeric mythology, has also an Asiatic origin.'

'I always thought,' said Joan, 'that Juno was rather
too stately for the seraglio.'

'You ought to know,' replied Ivywood, with a
courteous gesture, 'for I never saw any one who looked
so like Juno as you do. But indeed there is a great
deal of misunderstanding about the Arabian or Indian
view of women. It is, somehow, too simple and solid

for our paradoxical Christendom to comprehend. Even the vulgar joke against the Turks, that they like their brides fat, has in it a sort of distorted shadow of what I mean. They do not look so much at the individual, as at Womanhood and the power of Nature.'

'I sometimes think,' said Joan, 'that these fascinating theories are a little strained. Your friend Misysra told me the other day that women had the highest freedom in Turkey; as they were allowed to wear trousers.'

Ivywood smiled his rare and dry smile. 'The Prophet has something of a simplicity often found with genius,' he answered. 'I will not deny that some of the arguments he has employed have seemed to me crude and even fanciful. But he is right at the root. There is a kind of freedom that consists in never rebelling against Nature; and I think they understand it in the Orient better than we do in the West. You see, Joan, it is all very well to talk about love in our narrow personal, romantic way; but there is something higher than the love of a lover or the love of love.'

'What is that?' asked Joan, looking down.

'The love of Fate,' said Lord Ivywood, with something like spiritual passion in his eyes. 'Doesn't Nietzsche say somewhere that the delight in destiny is the mark of the hero? We are mistaken if we think that the heroes and saints of Islam say "Kismet" with bowed heads and in sorrow. They say "Kismet" with a shout of joy. That which is fitting—that is what they really mean. In the Arabian tales, the most perfect prince is wedded to the most perfect princess—because it is fitting. The spiritual giants, the Genii, achieve it—that is, the purposes of Nature. In the selfish, sentimental European novels, the loveliest princess on earth might have run away with her middle-aged drawing-master. These things are not in the Path. The Turk rides out to wed the fairest queen of the earth; he conquers empires to do it; and he is not ashamed of his laurels.'

The crumpled violet clouds around the edge of the silver evening looked to Lady Joan more and more like vivid violet embroideries hemming some silver curtain in the closed corridor at Ivywood. The peacocks looked more lustrous and beautiful than they ever had before; but for the first time she really felt they came out of the land of the Arabian Nights.

'Joan,' said Philip Ivywood, very softly in the twilight, 'I am not ashamed of my laurels. I see no meaning in what these Christians call humility. I will be the greatest man in the world if I can; and I think I can. Therefore something that is higher than love itself, Fate and what is fitting, make it right that I should wed the most beautiful woman in the world. And she stands among the peacocks; and is more beautiful and more proud than they.'

Joan's troubled eyes were on the violet horizon and her troubled lips could utter nothing but something like 'don't'.

'Joan,' said Philip again, 'I have told you you are the woman one of the great heroes could have desired. Let me now tell you something I could have told no one to whom I had not thus spoken of love and betrothal. When I was twenty years old, in a town in Germany, pursuing my education, I did what the West calls falling in love. She was a fisher-girl from the coast; for this town was near the sea. My story might have ended there. I could not have entered diplomacy with such a wife; but I should not have minded then. But a little while after I wandered

into the edges of Flanders, and found myself standing
above some of the last great reaches of the Rhine. And
things came over me, but for which I might be crying
stinking fish to this day. I thought how many holy
or lovely nooks that river had left behind, and gone on.
It might anywhere in Switzerland have spent its weak
youth in a spurt over a high crag; or anywhere in the
Rhinelands, lost itself in a marsh covered with flowers.
But it went on to the perfect sea, which is the fulfilment
of a river.'

Again Joan could not speak; and again it was Philip
who went on:

'Here is yet another thing that could not be said,
till the hand of the prince had been offered to the
princess. It may be that in the East they carry too
far this matter of infant marriages. But look round
on the mad young marriages that go to pieces everywhere, and ask yourself whether you don't wish they
had been infant marriages! People talk in the newspapers of the heartlessness of royal weddings. But
you and I do not believe the newspapers, I suppose.
We know there is no King in England; nor has been
since his head fell before Whitehall. You know that
you and I and the families are the Kings of England:
and our marriages are royal marriages. Let the
suburbs call them heartless. Let us say they need
the brave heart that is the only badge of aristocracy.
Joan,' he said very gently, 'perhaps you have been
near a crag in Switzerland, or a marsh covered with
flowers. Perhaps you have known—a fisher-girl.
But there is something greater and simpler than all
that; something you find in the great epics of the
East—the beautiful woman, and the great man, and
Fate.'

'My lord,' said Joan, using the formal phrase by an unfathomable instinct, 'will you allow me a little more time to think of this? And let there be no notion of disloyalty, if my decision is one way or the other?'

'Why, of course,' said Ivywood, bowing over his crutch; and he limped off, picking his way among the peacocks.

For days afterwards Joan tried to build the foundations of her earthly destiny. She was still quite young; but she felt as if she had lived thousands of years, worrying over the same question. She told herself again and again, and truly, that many a better woman than she had taken a second-best which was not so first-class a second best. But there was something complicated in the very atmosphere. She like listening to Philip Ivywood at his best, as any one likes listening to a man who can really play the violin. But the great trouble always is that at certain awful moments you cannot be certain whether it is the violin or the man.

Moreover, there was a curious tone and spirit in the Ivywood household, especially after the wound and convalescence of Ivywood, about which she could say nothing except that it annoyed her somehow. There was something in it glorious—but also languorous. By an impulse by no means uncommon among intelligent fashionable people, she felt a desire to talk to a sensible woman of the middle or lower classes; and almost threw herself on the bosom of Miss Browning for sympathy.

But Miss Browning, with her curling reddish hair and white, very clever face, struck the same indescribable note. Lord Ivywood was assumed as a first principle; as if he were Father Time, or the Clerk of

the Weather. He was called 'He'. The fifth time
he was called 'He', Joan could not understand why
she seemed to smell the plants in the hot conservatory.

'You see,' said Miss Browning, 'we mustn't interfere
with his career; that is the important thing. And,
really, I think the quieter we keep about everything
the better. I am sure he is maturing very big plans.
You heard what the Prophet said the other night?'

'The last thing the Prophet said to me,' said the
darker lady in a dogged manner, 'was that when we
English see the English youth, we cry out, 'He is
crescent!'' But when we see the English aged man
we cry out, "He is cross!"'

A lady with so clever a face could not but laugh
faintly; but she continued on a determined theme.
'The Prophet said, you know, that all real love had
in it an element of fate. And I am sure that is his
view, too. People cluster round a centre as little stars
do round a star; because a star is a magnet. You are
never wrong when destiny blows behind you like a
great big wind; and I think many things have been
judged unfairly that way. It's all very well to talk
about the infant marriages in India——'

'Miss Browning,' said Joan, 'are you interested in
the infant marriages in India?'

'Well——' said Miss Browning.

'Is your sister interested in them. I'll run and ask
her,' cried Joan, plunging across the room to where
Mrs. Mackintosh was sitting at a table scribbling
secretarial notes.

'Well,' said Mrs. Mackintosh, turning up a rich-
haired, resolute head, more handsome than her
sister's. 'I believe the Indian way is the best. When
people are left to themselves in early youth, any of

them might marry anything. We might have married a nigger or fish-wife or—a criminal.'

'Now, Mrs. Mackintosh,' said Joan, with black-browed severity, 'you well know you would never have married a fish-wife. Where is Enid?' she ended suddenly.

'Lady Enid,' said Miss Browning, 'is looking out music in the music-room, I think.'

Joan walked swiftly through several long salons, and found her fair-haired and pallid relative actually at the piano.

'Enid,' cried Joan, 'you know I've always been fond of you. For God's sake tell me what is the matter with this house? I admire Philip as everybody does. But what is the matter with the house? Why do all these rooms and gardens seem to be shutting me in and in and in? Why does everything look more and more the same? Why does everybody say the same thing? Oh, I don't often talk metaphysics; but there is a purpose in this. That's the only way of putting it; there is a purpose. And I don't know what it is.'

Lady Enid Wimpole played a preliminary bar or two on the piano. Then she said:

'Nor do I, Joan. I don't indeed. I know exactly what you mean. But it's just because there is a purpose that I have faith in him and trust him.' She began softly to play a ballad tune of the Rhineland; and perhaps the music suggested her next remark. 'Suppose you were looking at some of the last reaches of the Rhine, where it flows——'

'Enid!' cried Joan, 'if you say "into the North Sea", I shall scream. Scream—do you hear—? louder than all the peacocks together.'

'Well,' expostulated Lady Enid, looking up rather

wildly. 'The Rhine *does* flow into the North Sea, doesn't it?'

'I dare say,' said Joan recklessly; 'but the Rhine might have flowed into the Round Pond, before you would have known or cared, until——'

'Until what?' asked Enid; and the music suddenly ceased.

'Until something happened that I cannot understand,' said Joan, moving away.

'*You* are something I cannot understand,' said Enid Wimpole. 'But I will play something else if this annoys you." And she fingered the music again with an eye to choice.

Joan walked back again through the corridor of the music-room, and restlessly resumed her seat in the room with the two lady secretaries.

'Well,' asked the red-haired and good-humoured Mrs. Mackintosh, without looking up from her work of scribbling, 'have you discovered anything?'

For some moments Joan appeared to be in a blacker state of brooding than usual; then she said, in a candid and friendly tone, which somehow contrasted with her knit and swarthy brows:

'No, really. At least, I think I've only found out two things; and they are only things about myself. I've discovered that I do like heroism, but I don't like hero worship.'

'Surely,' said Miss Browning, in the Girton manner, 'the one always flows from the other.'

'I hope not,' said Joan.

'But what else can you do with the hero?' asked Mrs. Mackintosh, still without looking up from her writing, 'except worship him?'

'You might crucify him,' said Joan, with a sudden

return of savage restlessness, as she rose from her chair. 'Things seem to happen then.'

'Aren't you tired?' said the unmarried Browning who had the clever face.

'Yes,' said Joan, 'and the worst sort of tiredness; when you don't even know what you're tired of. To tell the honest truth, I think I'm tired of this house.'

'It's very old, of course, and parts of it are still dismal,' said Miss Browning, 'but he has enormously improved it. The decoration, with the moon and stars, down in the wing with the turret is really——'

Away in the distant music-room, Lady Enid, having found the music she preferred, was fingering its prelude on the piano. At the first few notes, Joan Brett stood up like a tigress.

'Thanks,' she said, with a hoarse softness, 'that's it, of course! and that's just what we all are! She's found the right tune now.'

'What tune is it?' asked the wondering secretary.

'The tune of harp, sacbut, psaltery, dulcimer, and all kinds of music,' said Joan softly and fiercely, 'when we shall bow down and worship the Golden Image that Nebuchadnezzar the King has set up. Girls! Women! Do you know what this place is? Do you know why it is all doors within doors and lattice behind lattice; and everything is curtained and cushioned; and why the flowers that are so fragrant here are not the flowers of our hills?'

From the distant and slowly darkening music-room Enid Wimpole's song came thin and clear:

'Less than the dust beneath thy chariot wheel,
Less than the rust that never stained thy sword——'

'Do you know what we are?' demanded Joan Brett again. 'We are a harem.'

'Why, what can you mean?' cried the younger girl in great agitation. 'Why, Lord Ivywood has never——'

'I know he has never. I am not sure,' said Joan, 'even whether he would ever. I shall never understand that man, nor will anybody else. But I tell you that is the spirit. That is what we *are*, and this room stinks of polygamy as certainly as it smells of lilies.'

'Why, Joan,' cried Lady Enid, entering the room like a well-bred ghost, 'what on earth is the matter with you? You all look as white as sheets.'

Joan took no heed of her, but went on with her own obstinate argument.

'And besides,' she said, 'if there's one thing we do know about him, it is that he believes on principle in doing things slowly. He calls it evolution and relativity, and the expanding of an idea into larger ideas. How do we know he isn't doing that slowly; getting us accustomed to living like this, so that it may be the less shock when he goes farther—steeping us in the atmosphere before he actually introduces'— and she shuddered—'the institution? Is it any more calmly outrageous a scheme than any other of Ivywood's schemes; than a Sepoy Commander-in-Chief or Misysra preaching in Westminster Abbey, or the destruction of all the inns in England? I will not wait and expand. I will not be evolved. I will not develop into something that is not me. My feet shall be outside these walls, if I walk the roads for it afterwards; or I will scream as I would scream trapped in any den by the docks.'

She swept down the rooms towards the turret, with

a sudden passion for solitude; but as she passed the astronomical wood-carving that had closed up the end of the old wing, Enid saw her strike it with her clenched hand.

It was in the turret that she had a strange experience. She was again, later on, using its isolation to worry out the best way of having it out with Philip, when he should return from his visit to London. For to tell old Lady Ivywood what was on her mind, would be about as kind and useful as describing Chinese tortures to a baby. The evening was very quiet, of the pale grey sort, and all that side of Ivywood was always the most undisturbed. She was the more surprised when her dreaming took note of a sort of stirring in the grey-purple dusk of the bushes; of whisperings; and of many footsteps. Then the silence settled down again; and then it was startlingly broken by a big voice singing in the dark distance. It was accompanied by faint sounds that might have been the fingering of some lute or viol:

'Lady, the light is dying in the skies,
Lady, and let us die when honour dies;
Your dear, dropped glove was like a gauntlet flung
  When you and I were young,
For something more than splendour stood; and ease was not the
  only good,
About the woods in Ivywood, when you and I were young.

Lady, the stars are falling pale and small,
Lady, we will not live if life be all,
Forgetting those good stars in heaven hung,
  When all the world was young;
For more than gold was in a ring, and love was not a little thing,
Between the trees in Ivywood, when all the world was young.'

The singing ceased; and the bustle in the bushes could hardly be called more than a whisper. But sounds of the same sort and somewhat louder seemed wafted round corners from other sides of the house; and the whole night seemed full of something that was alive, but was more than a single man.

She heard a cry behind her; and Enid rushed into the room as white as one of the lilies.

'What awful thing is happening?' she cried. 'The courtyard is full of men shouting; and there are torches everywhere and——'

Joan heard a tramp of men marching, and heard afar off another song, sung on a more derisive note, something like:

> 'But Ivywood, Lord Ivywood,
> He rots the tree as ivy would.'

'I think,' said Joan thoughtfully, 'it is the end of the world.'

'But where are the police?' wailed her cousin. 'They don't seem to be anywhere about since they wore those fezes. We shall be murdered or——'

Three thundering and measured blows shook the decorative wood panelling at the end of the wing; as if admittance were demanded with the club of a giant. Enid remembered that she had thought Joan's little blow energetic, and shuddered. Both the girls stared at the stars and moons and suns blazoned on that sacred wall that leapt and shuddered under the strokes of doom.

Then the sun fell from heaven, and the moon and stars dropped down, and were scattered about the Persian carpet; and by the opening of the end of the world, Patrick Dalroy came in, carrying a mandolin.

CHAPTER XXV

THE FINDING OF THE SUPERMAN

'I've brought you a little dog,' said Mr. Dalroy, introducing the rampant Quoodle. 'I had him brought down here in a large hamper labelled "Explosives", a title which appears to have been well selected.'

He had bowed to Lady Enid on entering and taken Joan's hand with the least suggestion that he wanted to do something else with it. But he resolutely resumed his conversation, which was on the subject of dogs.

'People who bring back dogs,' he said, 'are always under a cloud of suspicion. Sometimes it is hideously hinted that the citizen who brings the dog back with him is identical with the citizen who took the dog away with him. In my case, of course, such conduct is inconceivable. But the returners of dogs, that prosperous and increasing class, are also accused,' he went on, looking straight at Joan with blank blue eyes, 'of coming back for a Reward. There is more truth in this charge.'

Then, with a change of manner more extraordinary than any revolution, even the revolution that was roaring round the house, he took her hand again and kissed it; saying with a confounding seriousness:

'I know at least that you will pray for my soul.'

'You had better pray for mine, if I have one,' answered Joan; 'but why now?'

'Because,' said Patrick, 'you will hear from outside, you may even see from that turret window, something which in brute fact has never been seen in

England since poor Monmouth's army went down.
In spirit and in truth it has not happened since
Saladin and Cœur de Lion crashed together. I only
add one thing, and that you know already. I have
lived loving you and I shall die loving you. It is the
only dimension of the universe in which I have not
wandered and gone astray. I leave the dog to guard
you'; and he disappeared down the old broken staircase.

Lady Enid was much mystified that no popular
pursuit assailed this stair or invaded the house. But
Lady Joan knew better. She had gone, on the suggestion she most cared about, into the turret room and
looked out of its many windows on the abandoned
copse and tunnel, which were now fenced off with
high walls, the boundary of the mysterious property
next door. Across that high barrier she could not
even see the tunnel, and barely the tops of the tallest
trees which hid its entrance from sight. But in an
instant she knew that Dalroy was not hurling his
forces on Ivywood at all, but on the house and estate
beyond it.

And then followed a sight that was not an experience
but rather a revolving vision. She could never describe
it afterwards, nor could any of those involved in so
violent and mystical a wheel. She had seen a huge
wall of a breaker wash all over the parade at Pebbleswick; and wondered that so huge a hammer could
be made merely of water. She had never had a
notion of what it is like when it is made of men.

The palisade put up by the new landlord in front of
the old tangled ground by the tunnel she had long
regarded as something as settled and ordinary as one
of the walls of the drawing-room. It swung and split

and sprang into a thousand pieces under the mere blow of human bodies bursting with rage; and the great wave crested the obstacle more clearly than she had ever seen any great wave crest the parade. Only, when the fence was broken, she saw behind it something that robbed her of reason; so that she seemed to be living in all ages and all lands at once. She never could describe the vision afterwards; but she always denied it was a dream. She said it was worse; it was something more real than reality. It was a line of real soldiers, which is always a magnificent sight. But they might have been the soldiers of Hannibal or of Attila, they might have been dug up from the cemeteries of Sidon and Babylon, for all Joan had to do with them. There, encamped in English meadows, with a hawthorn-tree in front of them and three beeches behind, was something that had never been in camp nearer than some leagues south of Paris, since that Carolus called the Hammer broke it backwards at Tours.

There flew the green standard of that great faith and strong civilization which has so often almost entered the great cities of the West; which long encircled Vienna, which was barely barred from Paris; but which had never before been seen in arms on the soil of England. At one end of the line stood Philip Ivywood, in a uniform of his own special creation, a compromise between the Sepoy and Turkish uniform. The compromise worked more and more wildly in Joan's mind. If any impression remained, it was merely that England had conquered India: and Turkey had conquered England. Then she saw that Ivywood, for all his uniform, was not the commander of these forces. For an old man with a great scar on his face, which was not a European face, set himself in front of the battle, as if it had been a battle in the old epics, and crossed swords with Patrick Dalroy. He had come to return the scar upon his forehead; and he returned it with many wounds, though at last it was he who sank under the sword-thrust. He fell on his face; and Dalroy looked at him with something that is much more great than pity. Blood was flowing from Patrick's wrist and forehead, but he made a salute with his sword. As he was doing so, the corpse, as it appeared, laboriously lifted a face with feeble eye-lids. And seeming to understand the quarters of the sky by instinct, Oman Pasha dragged himself a foot or so to the left; and fell with his face towards Mecca.

And after that the turret turned round and round about Joan, and she knew not whether the things she saw were history or prophecy. Something in that last fact of being crushed by the weapons of brown men and yellow, secretly entrenched in English meadows, had made the English what they had not been for centuries. The hawthorn-tree was twisted and broken as it was at the Battle of Ashdown when Alfred led his first charge against the Danes. The beech-trees were splashed up to their lowest branches with the mingling of brave heathen and brave Christian blood. She knew no more than that when a column of the Christian rebels, led by Humphrey of the Sign of the Ship, burst through the choked and forgotten tunnel and took the Turkish regiment in the rear, it was the end.

That violent and revolving vision became something beyond the human voice or human ear. She could not intelligently hear even the shots and shouts

round the last magnificent rally of the Turks. It was
natural, therefore, that she should not hear the words
Lord Ivywood addressed to his next-door neighbour,
a Turkish officer; or rather to himself. But his words
were:

'I have gone where God has never dared to go. I
am above the silly Supermen as they are above mere
men. Where I walk in the heavens, no man has
walked before me; and I am alone in the garden. All
this passing about me is like the lonely plucking of
garden flowers. I will have this blossom; I will have
that . . .'

The sentence ended so suddenly that the officer
looked at him, as if expecting him to speak. But he
did not speak.

. . . . . .

But Patrick and Joan wandering together in a world
made warm and fresh again, as it can be for few in a
world that calls courage frenzy and love superstition,
feeling every branching tree as a friend with arms open
for the man, or every sweeping slope as a great train
trailing behind the woman, did one day climb up to
the little white cottage that was now the home of the
Superman.

He sat playing, with a pale reposeful face, with
scraps of stick and weed put before him on a wooden
table. He did not notice them, nor anything else
around him; scarcely even Enid Wimpole, who
attended to all his wants.

'He is perfectly happy,' she said quietly.

Joan, with the glow on her dark face, could not
prevent herself from replying, 'And we are so
happy.'

'Yes,' said Enid, 'but his happiness will last.' And she wept.

'I understand,' said Joan, and kissed her cousin; not without tears of her own. But they were of pity, which is the opposite of fear.

PRINTED BY
JARROLD AND SONS LTD.
NORWICH

Originally published by
Messrs. John Lane The Bodley Head Ltd. in 1904